TALTOS

TALTOS

LIVES OF THE
MAYFAIR WITCHES

Anne Rice

ALFRED A. KNOPF

NEW YORK

1994

THIS IS A BORZOI BOOK
PUBLISHED BY ALFRED A. KNOPF

Library of Congress Cataloging-in-Publication Data
Rice, Anne.
Taltos : lives of the Mayfair witches / Anne Rice. — 1st ed.
p. cm.
Sequel to: Lasher.
ISBN 0-679-42573-X
1. Witchcraft—Louisiana—New Orleans—Fiction.   2. New Orleans
(La.)—Fiction.   I. Title.
PS3568.I265T35   1994
813'.54—dc20   93-35693
CIP

Manufactured in the United States of America
First Edition

THE GARDEN OF LOVE

I went to the Garden of Love,
And saw what I never had seen:
A Chapel was built in the midst,
Where I used to play on the green.

And the gates of this Chapel were shut,
And Thou shalt not. writ over the door;
So I turn'd to the Garden of Love,
That so many sweet flowers bore.

And I saw it was filled with graves,
And tomb-stones where flowers should be:
And Priests in black gowns, were walking their rounds,
And binding with briars, my joys & desires.

From *Songs of Experience*,
William Blake

TALTOS

One

I T HAD snowed all day. As the darkness fell, very close and quickly, he stood at the window looking down on the tiny figures in Central Park. A perfect circle of light fell on the snow beneath each lamp. Skaters moved on the frozen lake, though he could not make them out in detail. And cars pushed sluggishly over the dark roads.

To his right and his left, the skyscrapers of midtown crowded near him. But nothing came between him and the park, except, that is, for a jungle of lower buildings, rooftops with gardens, and great black hulking pieces of equipment, and sometimes even pointed roofs.

He loved this view; it always surprised him when others found it so unusual, when a workman coming to fix an office machine would volunteer that he'd never seen New York like this before. Sad that there was no marble tower for everyone; that there was no series of towers, to which all the people could go, to look out at varying heights.

Make a note: Build a series of towers which have no function except to be parks in the sky for the people. Use all the beautiful marbles which you so love. Maybe he would do that this year. Very likely, he would do it. And the libraries. He wanted to establish more of these, and that would mean some travel. But he would do all this, yes, and soon. After all, the parks were almost completed now, and the little schools had been opened in seven cities. The carousels had been opened in twenty different places. Granted, the animals were synthetic, but each was a meticulous and indestructible reproduction of a famous European handcarved masterpiece. People loved the carousels. But it was a time for a spate of new plans. The winter had caught him dreaming . . .

In the last century, he had put into material form a hundred such ideas. And this year's little triumphs had their comforting charm. He had made an antique carousel within this building, all of the original old horses, lions, and such that had provided molds for his replicas. The museum of classic automobiles now filled one level of the basement. The public flocked to see the Model T's, the Stutz Bearcats, the MG-TD's with their wire wheels.

And of course there were the doll museums—in large, well-lighted rooms on two floors above the lobby—the company showcase, filled with the dolls he'd collected from all parts of the world. And the private museum, open only now and then, including the dolls which he himself had personally cherished.

Now and then he slipped downstairs to watch the people, to walk through the crowds, never unnoticed, but at least unknown.

A creature seven feet in height can't avoid the eyes of people. That had been true forever. But a rather amusing thing had happened in the last two hundred years. Human beings had gotten taller! And now, miracle of miracles, even at his height, he did not stand out so very much. People gave him a second glance, of course, but they weren't frightened of him anymore.

Indeed, occasionally a human male came into the building who was in fact taller than he was. Of course the staff would alert him. They thought it one of his little quirks that he wanted such people reported to him. They found it amusing. He didn't mind. He liked to see people smile and laugh.

"Mr. Ash, there's a tall one down here. Camera five."

He'd turn to the bank of small glowing screens, and quickly catch sight of the individual. Only human. He usually knew for certain right away. Once in a great while, he wasn't sure of it. And he went down in the silent, speeding elevator, and walked near the person long enough to ascertain from a score of details that this was only a man.

Other dreams: small play buildings for children, made exquisitely out of space-age plastics with rich and intricate detail. He saw small cathedrals, castles, palaces—perfect replicas of the larger architectural treasures—produced with lightning speed, and "cost effective," as the board would put it. There would be numerous sizes, from dwellings for dolls to houses which children could enter themselves. And carousel horses for sale, made of wood resin, which almost anyone could afford. Hundreds could be given to schools, hospitals, other such institutions. Then there was the ongoing obsession—truly beautiful dolls for poor children, dolls that would not break, and could be cleaned with ease—but that he had been working on, more or less, since the new century dawned.

For the last five years he had produced cheaper and cheaper dolls, dolls superior to those before them, dolls of new chemical materials, dolls that were durable and lovable; yet still they cost too much for poor children. This year he would try something entirely different . . . He had plans on the drawing board, a couple of promising prototypes. Perhaps . . .

He felt a consoling warmth steal through him as he thought of these many projects, for they would take him hundreds of years. Long ago, in ancient times as they called them, he had dreamed of monuments. Great circles of stone for all to see, a dance of giants in the high grass of the plain. Even modest towers had obsessed him for decades, and once the lettering of beautiful books had taken all his joy for centuries.

But in these playthings of the modern world, these dolls, these tiny images of people, not children really, for dolls never really did look like children, he had found a strange and challenging obsession.

Monuments were for those who traveled to see them. The dolls and toys he refined and manufactured reached every country on the globe. Indeed, machines had made all sorts of new and beautiful objects available for people of all nations—the rich, the impoverished, those in need of comfort, or sustenance and shelter, those kept in sanitariums and asylums which they could never leave.

His company had been his redemption; even his wildest and most daring ideas had been put into successful production. Indeed, he did not understand why other toy companies made so few innovations, why cookie-cutter dolls with vapid faces lined the shelves of emporiums, why the ease of manufacture had not produced a wilderness of originality and invention. Unlike his joyless colleagues, with each of his triumphs he had taken greater risks.

It didn't make him happy to drive others out of the market. No, competition was still something he could only grasp intellectually. His secret belief was that the number of potential buyers in today's world was unlimited. There was room for anyone marketing anything of worth. And within these walls, within this soaring and dangerous tower of steel and glass, he enjoyed his triumphs in a state of pure bliss which he could share with no one else.

No one else. Only the dolls could share it. The dolls who stood on the glass shelves against the walls of colored marble, the dolls who stood on pedestals in the corners, the dolls who clustered together on his broad wooden desk. His Bru, his princess, his French beauty, a century old; she was his most enduring witness. Not a day passed that he didn't go down to the second floor of the building and visit the

Bru—a bisque darling of impeccable standards, three feet tall, her mohair curls intact, her painted face a masterpiece, her torso and wooden legs as perfect now as they were when the French company had manufactured her for the Paris market over one hundred years ago.

That had been her allure, that she was a thing for hundreds of children to enjoy; a pinnacle had been reached in her, of craft and mass production. Even her factory clothes of silk represented that special achievement. Not for one, but for many.

There had been years when, wandering the world, he had carried her with him, taking her out of the suitcase at times just to look into her glass eyes, just to tell her his thoughts, his feelings, his dreams. In the night, in squalid lonely rooms, he had seen the light glint in her ever-watchful eyes. And now she was housed in glass, and thousands saw her yearly, and all the other antique Bru dolls now clustered around her. Sometimes he wanted to sneak her upstairs, put her on a bedroom shelf. Who would care? Who would dare say anything? Wealth surrounds one with a blessed silence, he thought. People think before they speak. They feel they have to. He could talk to the doll again if he wanted to. In the museum, he was silent when they met, the glass of the case separating them. Patiently she waited to be reclaimed, the humble inspiration for his empire.

Of course this company of his, this enterprise of his, as it was so often called by papers and magazines, was predicated on the development of an industrial and mechanical matrix which had existed now for only three hundred years. What if war were to destroy it? But dolls and toys gave him such sweet happiness that he imagined he would never hereafter be without them. Even if war reduced the world to rubble, he would make little figures of wood or clay and paint them himself.

Sometimes he saw himself this way, alone in the ruins. He saw New York as it might have appeared in a science-fiction movie, dead and silent and filled with overturned columns and broken pediments and shattered glass. He saw himself sitting on a broken stone stairway, making a doll from sticks and tying it together with bits of cloth which he took quietly and respectfully from a dead woman's silk dress.

But who would have imagined that such things would have caught his fancy? That wandering a century ago through a wintry street in Paris, he would turn and gaze into a shop window, into the glass eyes of his Bru, and fall passionately in love?

Of course, his breed had always been known for its capacity to play, to cherish, to enjoy. Perhaps it was not at all surprising. Though studying a breed, when you were one of the only surviving specimens of it, was a tricky situation, especially for one who could not love medical philosophy or terminology, whose memory was good but far from preternatural, whose sense of the past was often deliberately relinquished to a "childlike" immersion in the present, and a general fear of thinking in terms of millennia or eons or whatever people wanted to call the great spans of time which he himself had witnessed, lived through, struggled to endure, and finally cheerfully forgotten in this great enterprise suited to his few and special talents.

Nevertheless, he did study his own breed, making and recording meticulous notes on himself. And he was not good at predicting the future, or so he felt.

A low hum came to his ears. He knew it was the coils beneath the marble floor, gently heating the room around him. He fancied he could feel the heat, coming up through his shoes. It was never chilly or smotheringly hot in his tower. The coils took care of him. If only such comfort could belong to the entire world outside. If only all could know abundant food, warmth. His company sent millions in aid to those who lived in deserts and jungles across the seas, but he was never really sure who received what, who benefited.

In the first days of motion pictures, and later television, he had thought war would end. Hunger would end. People could not bear to see it on the screen before them. How foolish a thought. There seemed to be more war and more hunger now than ever. On every continent, tribe fought tribe. Millions starved. So much to be done. Why make such careful choices? Why not do everything?

The snow had begun again, with flakes so tiny he could barely see them. They appeared to melt when they hit the dark streets below. But those streets were some sixty floors down. He couldn't be certain. Half-melted snow was piled in the gutters and on the nearby roofs. In a little while, things would be freshly white again, perhaps, and in this sealed and warm room, one could imagine the entire city dead and ruined, as if by pestilence which did not crumble buildings but killed the warm-blooded beings which lived within them, like termites in wooden walls.

The sky was black. That was the one thing he did not like about snow. You lost the sky when you had it. And he did so love the skies over New York City, the full panoramic skies which the people in the streets never really saw.

"Towers, build them towers," he said. "Make a big museum high up in the sky with terraces around it. Bring them up in glass elevators, heavenward to see . . ."

Towers for pleasure among all these towers that men had built for commerce and gain.

A thought took him suddenly, an old thought, really, that often came to him and prodded him to meditate and perhaps even to surmise. The first writings in all the world had been commercial lists of goods bought and sold. This was what was in the cuneiform tablets found at Jericho, inventories . . . The same had been true at Mycenea.

No one had thought it important then to write down his or her ideas or thoughts. Buildings had been wholly different. The grandest were houses of worship—temples or great mud-brick ziggurats, faced in limestone, which men had climbed to sacrifice to the gods. The circle of sarsens on the Salisbury Plain.

Now, seven thousand years later, the greatest buildings were commercial buildings. They were inscribed with the names of banks or great corporations, or immense private companies such as his own. From his window he could see these names burning in bright, coarse block letters, through the snowy sky, through the dark that wasn't really dark.

As for temples and places of worship, they were relics or almost nought. Somewhere down there he could pick out the steeples of St. Patrick's if he tried. But it was a shrine now to the past more than a vibrant center of communal religious spirit, and it looked quaint, reaching to the skies amid the tall, indifferent glass buildings around it. It was majestic only from the streets.

The scribes of Jericho would have understood this shift, he thought. On the other hand, perhaps they would not. He barely understood it himself, yet the implications seemed mammoth and more wonderful than human beings knew. This commerce, this endless multiplicity of beautiful and useful things, could save the world, ultimately, if only . . . Planned obsolescence, mass destruction of last year's goods, the rush to antiquate or render irrelevent others' designs, it was the result of a tragic lack of vision. Only the most limited implications of the marketplace theory were to blame for it. The real revolution came not in the cycle of make and destroy, but in a great inventive and endless expansion. Old dichotomies had to fall. In his darling Bru, and her factory-assembled parts, in the pocket calculators carried by millions on the streets, in the light beautiful stroke of rolling-ball pens, in five-dollar Bibles, and in toys, beautiful toys sold on drugstore shelves for pennies—there lay salvation.

It seemed he could get his mind around it, he could penetrate it, make tight, easily explainable theories, if only—

"Mr. Ash." It was a soft voice that interrupted him. Nothing more was required. He'd trained them all. Don't make a sound with the door. Speak quietly. I'll hear you.

And this voice came from Remmick, who was gentle by nature, an Englishman (with a little Celtic blood, though Remmick didn't know it), a manservant who had been indispensable in this last decade, though the time would soon come when, for security's sake, Remmick must be sent away.

"Mr. Ash, the young woman's here."

"Thank you, Remmick," he said in a voice that was even softer than that of his servant. In the dark window glass, if he let himself, he could see Remmick's reflection—a comely man, with small, very brilliant blue eyes. They were too close together, these eyes. But the face was not unattractive, and it wore always a look of such quiet and non-dramatic devotion that he had grown to love it, to love Remmick himself.

There were lots of dolls in the world with eyes too close together—in particular, the French dolls made years ago by Jumeau, and Schmitt and Sons, and Huret, and Petit and Demontier—with moon faces, and glittering glass eyes crowding their little procelain noses, with mouths so tiny they seemed at first glance to be tiny buds, or bee stings. Everybody loved these dolls. The bee-sting queens.

When you loved dolls and studied them, you started to love all kinds of people too, because you saw the virtue in their expressions, how carefully they had been sculpted, the parts contrived to create the triumph of this or that remarkable face. Sometimes he walked through Manhattan, deliberately seeing every face as made, no nose, no ear, no wrinkle accidental.

"She's having some tea, sir. She was terribly cold when she arrived."

"We didn't send a car for her, Remmick?"

"Yes, sir, but she's cold nevertheless. It's very cold outside, sir."

"But it's warm in the museum, surely. You took her there, didn't you?"

"Sir, she came up directly. She is so excited, you understand."

He turned, throwing one bright gleam of a smile (or so he hoped it was) on Remmick and then waving him away with the smallest gesture that the man could see. He walked to the doors of the adjoining office, across the floor of Carrara marble, and looked beyond that room, to yet another, also paved, as were all his rooms, in shining marble, where the young woman sat alone at the desk. He could see her profile. He could see that she was anxious. He could see that she wanted the tea, but then she didn't. She didn't know what to do with her hands.

"Sir, your hair. Will you allow me?" Remmick touched his arm.

"Must we?"

"Yes, sir, we really ought to." Remmick had his soft little brush out, the kind that men used because they could not be seen using the same kind of brush as women, and reaching up, Remmick brought it quickly and firmly through his hair, hair that ought to be trimmed and cut, Remmick had said, hair that fell sloppily and defiantly over his collar.

Remmick stood back, rocking on the balls of his feet.

"Now you look splendid, Mr. Ash," he said with raised eyebrows. "Even if it is a bit long."

He made a soft chuckle.

"You're afraid I'll frighten her, aren't you?" he asked, teasingly, affectionately. "Surely you don't really care what she thinks."

"Sir, I care that you look your best always, for your own benefit."

"Of course you do," he said quietly. "I love you for it."

He walked towards the young woman, and as he drew closer, he made a polite and decent amount of noise. Slowly she turned her head; she looked up; she saw him, and there came the inevitable shock.

He extended his arms as he approached.

She rose, beaming, and she clasped his hands. Warm, firm grip. She looked at his hands, at the fingers, and at the palms.

"I surprise you, Miss Paget?" he asked, offering her his most gracious smile. "My hair has been groomed for your approval. Do I look so very bad?"

"Mr. Ash, you look fabulous," she said quickly. She had a crisp California-style voice. "I didn't expect that . . . I didn't expect that you would be so tall. Of course, everyone said you were . . ."

"And do I look like a kindly man, Miss Paget? They say this of me too." He spoke slowly. Often Americans could not understand his "British accent."

"Oh, yes, Mr. Ash," she said. "Very kindly. And your hair is so nice and long. I love your hair, Mr. Ash."

This was really very gratifying, very amusing. He hoped that Remmick was listening. But wealth makes people withhold judgment on what you have done, it makes them search for the good in your choices, your style. It brings out not the obsequious but the more thoughtful side of humans. At least sometimes . . .

She was plainly telling the truth. Her eyes feasted on him and he loved it. He gave her hands a tender squeeze and then he let them go.

As he moved around the desk, she took her seat again, eyes still locked upon him. Her own face was narrow and deeply lined for one so young. Her eyes were bluish violet. She was beautiful in her own way—ashen-haired, disheveled yet graceful, in exquisitely crushed old clothes.

Yes, don't throw them away, save them from the thrift-shop rack, reinvent them with nothing more than a few stitches and an iron; the destiny of manufactured things lies in durability and changing contexts, crushed silk beneath fluorescent light, elegant tatters with buttons of plastic in colors never achieved within geological strata, with stockings of such strong nylon they could have been made into braided rope of incalculable strength if only people didn't rip them off and toss them into wastebaskets. So many things to do, ways to see . . . If he had the contents of every wastebasket in Manhattan, he could make another billion just from what he would find there.

"I admire your work, Miss Paget," he said. "It's a pleasure to meet you at last." He gestured to the top of the desk. It was littered with large color photographs of her dolls.

Was it possible she hadn't noticed these? She seemed overcome with pleasure, her cheeks reddening. Perhaps she was even a little infatuated with his style and manner, he wasn't sure. He did tend to infatuate people, sometimes without trying to do it.

"Mr. Ash," she said. "This is one of the most important days of my life." She said it as if trying to realize it, and then she became silently flustered, perhaps because she thought she had said too much in saying what really mattered.

He let his smile brighten, and dipped his head slightly, as he often did—a trait people remarked on—so that he appeared to be looking up at her for a moment, though he was much taller than she.

"I want your dolls, Miss Paget," he said. "All of them. I'm very pleased with what you've done. You've worked so well in all the new materials. Your dolls aren't like anyone else's. That's what I want."

She was smiling in spite of herself. It was always a thrilling moment, this, for them and for him. He loved making her happy!

"Have my lawyers presented everything? Are you quite sure of the terms?"

"Yes, Mr. Ash. I understand everything. I accept your offer, completely. This is my dream."

She said the last word with gentle emphasis. And this time she did not falter or blush.

"Miss Paget, you need someone to bargain for you!" he scolded. "But if I've ever cheated anyone, I don't remember it, and I would honestly like to be reminded so that I could correct what I've done."

"I'm yours, Mr. Ash," she said. Her eyes had brightened, but they were not filling with tears. "The terms are generous. The materials are dazzling. The methods . . ." She gave a little shake of her head. "Well, I don't really understand the mass-production methods, but I know your dolls. I've been hanging around in the stores, just looking at everything marketed by Ashlar. I know this is simply going to be great."

Like so many, she had made her dolls in her kitchen, then in a garage workroom, firing the clay in a kiln she could barely afford. She had haunted flea markets for her fabrics. She had taken her inspiration from figures in motion pictures and in novels. Her works had been "one of a kind" and "limited edition," the sort of thing they liked in the exclusive doll shops and galleries. She had won awards, both large and small.

But her molds could be used now for something utterly different— half a million beautiful renditions of one doll, and another and another, out of a vinyl so skillfully worked that it would look as lovely as porcelain, with eyes painted as brilliantly as if they were real glass.

"But what about the names, Miss Paget? Why won't you choose the dolls' names?"

"The dolls have never had names for me, Mr. Ash," she said. "And the names you chose are fine."

"You know you'll be rich soon, Miss Paget."

"So they tell me," she said. She seemed suddenly vulnerable, indeed fragile.

"But you have to keep your appointments with us, you have to approve each step. It won't take so much time, really . . ."

"I'm going to love it. Mr. Ash, I want to make—"

"I want to see anything that you make, immediately. You'll call us."

"Yes."

"But don't be sure you will enjoy the process here. As you have observed, manufacture is not the same thing as crafting or creating. Well, it is. But seldom do people see it that way. Artists don't always see mass production as an ally."

He did not have to explain his old reasoning, that he did not care for the one-of-a-kinds and the limited editions, that he cared only for dolls that could belong to everyone. And he would take these molds of hers, and he would produce dolls from them year after year, varying them only when there seemed a reason to do it.

Everyone knew this about him now—that he had no interest in elitist values or ideas.

"Any questions about our contracts, Miss Paget? Don't hesitate to put these questions directly to me."

"Mr. Ash, I've signed your contracts!" She gave another little riff of laughter, distinctly careless and young.

"I'm so glad, Miss Paget," he said. "Prepare to be famous." He brought up his hands and folded them on the desk. Naturally, she was looking at them; she was wondering at their immense size.

"Mr. Ash, I know you're busy. Our appointment's for fifteen minutes."

He nodded as if to say, This is not important, go on.

"Let me ask you. Why do you like my dolls? I mean, really, Mr. Ash. I mean—"

He thought for a moment. "Of course there's a stock answer," he said, "which is wholly true. That your dolls are original, as you've said. But what I like, Miss Paget, is that your dolls are all smiling broadly. Their eyes are crinkled; their faces are in motion. They have shining teeth. You can almost hear them laugh."

"That was the risk, Mr. Ash." Suddenly she herself laughed, and looked for one second as happy as her creations.

"I know, Miss Paget. Are you perhaps going to make me some very sad children now?"

"I don't know if I can."

"Make what you want. I'm behind you. Don't make sad children. Too many other artists do that well."

He started to rise, slowly, the signal of dismissal, and he wasn't surprised when she rushed to her feet.

"Thank you, Mr. Ash," she said again, reaching for his hand—his huge, long-fingered hand. "I can't tell you how much . . ."

"You don't have to."

He let her take his hand. Sometimes people didn't want to touch him a second time. Sometimes they knew he wasn't a human. Never repelled by his face, it seemed, they were often repelled by his big feet and hands. Or, deep in their subconscious, they realized his neck was just a little too long, his ears too narrow. Humans are skilled at recognizing their own kind, tribe, clan, family. A great part of the human brain is organized around merely recognizing and remembering types of faces.

But she was not repelled, merely young and overwhelmed, and anxious over simple transitions.

"And by the way, Mr. Ash, if you don't mind my saying it, the white streaks in your hair are very becoming. I hope you don't ever color them out. White hair is always becoming on a young man."

"Now, what made you say that, Miss Paget?"

She flushed once more, but then gave in to laughter. "I don't know," she admitted. "It's just that the hair is so white, and you're so young. I didn't expect you to be so young. That's what is so surprising—" She broke off, unsure; he had best release her before she tumbled too quickly into her own imagined failures.

"Thank you, Miss Paget," he said. "You've been very kind. I've enjoyed talking with you." Reassurance, blunt and memorable. "I hope to see you again very soon. I hope you'll be happy."

Remmick had come to spirit the young woman away. She said something else hastily, thanks, avowals of inspiration and determination to please the whole world. Words to that sweet effect. He gave her one final sober smile as she went out and the bronze doors were shut behind her.

When she got home, of course, she would drag out her magazines. She would do addition on her fingers, maybe even with a calculator. She would realize he couldn't be young, not by anyone's count. She'd conclude he was past forty, and carefully fighting fifty. That was safe enough.

But how must he deal with this in the long run, for the long run was always his problem? Here was a life he loved, but he would have to make adjustments. Oh, he couldn't think of something so awful just now. What if the white hair really began to flourish? That would help, wouldn't it? But what did it really mean, the white hair? What did it reveal? He was too content to think of it. Too content to court cold fear.

Once again he turned to the windows, and to the falling snow. He could see Central Park as clearly from this office as from the others. He put his hand on the glass. Very cold.

The skating lake was deserted now. The snow had covered the park, and the roof just below him; and he noticed another curious sight which always made him give a little laugh.

It was the swimming pool on top of the Parker Meridien Hotel. Snow fell steadily on the transparent glass roof while, beneath it, a man was swimming back and forth in the brightly illuminated green water, and this was some fifty floors perhaps above the street.

"Now that is wealth and that is power," he mused quietly to himself. "To swim in the sky in a storm." Build swimming pools in the sky, another worthy project.

"Mr. Ash," said Remmick.

"Yes, my dear boy," he said absently, watching the long strokes of the swimmer, seeing clearly now that it was an elderly and very thin man. Such a figure would have been the victim of starvation in times past. But this was a physically fit individual—he could see it—a businessman, perhaps, snared by economic circumstances in the bitter winter of New York, swimming back and forth in deliciously heated and safely sanitized water.

"Phone call for you, sir."

"I don't think so, Remmick. I'm tired. It's the snow. It makes me want to curl up in bed and go to sleep. I want to go to bed now, Remmick. I want some hot chocolate and then to sleep and sleep."

"Mr. Ash, the man said you would want to speak to him, that I was to tell you . . ."

"They all say that, Remmick," he answered.

"Samuel, sir. He said to tell you that name."

"Samuel!"

He turned from the window, and looked at the manservant, at his placid face. There was no judgment or opinion in his expression. Only devotion and quiet acceptance.

"He said to come to you directly, Mr. Ash, that it was the custom when he called. I took the chance that he—"

"You did right. You can leave me alone for a little while now."

He took his chair at the desk.

As the doors closed, he picked up the receiver, and pressed the tiny red button.

"Samuel!" he whispered.

"Ashlar," came the answer, clear as if his friend were truly at his ear. "You've kept me waiting fifteen minutes. How important you've become."

"Samuel, where are you? Are you in New York?"

"Certainly not," came the reply. "I'm in Donnelaith, Ash. I'm at the Inn."

"Phones in the glen." It was a low murmur. The voice was coming all the way from Scotland . . . from the glen.

"Yes, old friend, phones in the glen, and other things as well. A Taltos came here, Ash. I saw him. A full Taltos."

"Wait a minute. It sounded as if you said—"

"I did say this. Don't get too excited about it, Ash. He's dead. He was an infant, blundering. It's a long story. There's a gypsy involved in it, a very clever gypsy named Yuri, from the Talamasca. The gypsy would be dead right now if it weren't for me."

"Are you sure the Taltos is dead?"

"The gypsy told me. Ash, the Talamasca is in a dark time. Something tragic has happened with the Order. They'll kill this gypsy soon, perhaps, but he's determined to go back to the Motherhouse. You must come as soon as you can."

"Samuel, I'll meet you in Edinburgh tomorrow."

"No, London. Go directly to London. I promised the gypsy. But come quickly, Ash. If his brothers in London catch sight of him, he'll be dead."

"Samuel, this can't be a correct story. The Talamasca wouldn't do such things to anyone, let alone its own people. Are you sure this gypsy is saying true things?"

"Ash, it has to do with this Taltos. Can you leave now?"

"Yes."

"You won't fail me?"

"No."

"Then there's one more thing I must tell you right now. You'll see it in the papers in London as soon as you land. They've been digging here in Donnelaith, in the ruins of the cathedral."

"I know this, Samuel. You and I have talked about this before."

"Ash, they dug up the grave of St. Ashlar. They found the name engraved in the stone. You'll see it in the papers, Ashlar. Scholars are here from Edinburgh. Ash, there are witches involved in this tale. But the gypsy will tell you. People are watching me. I have to go."

"Samuel, people are always watching you, wait—"

"Your hair, Ash. I saw you in a magazine. Are those white streaks in your hair? Never mind."

"Yes, my hair *is* turning white. But it's happening slowly. I haven't aged otherwise. There are no real shocks for you, except the hair."

"You'll live till the end of the world, Ash, and be the one to make it crumble."

"No!"

"Claridge's in London. We are leaving now ourselves. That's a hotel where a man can make a big oak fire in the grate, and sleep in a big old cozy bedroom full of chintz and hunter-green velvet. I'll be waiting for you there. And Ash. Pay the hotel, will you? I've been out here in the glen for two years."

Samuel rang off.

"Maddening," he whispered. He laid down the phone.

For long moments he looked at the bronze doors.

He didn't blink or focus when the doors opened. He scarcely saw the blurred figure who came into the room. He was not thinking, he was merely repeating the words *Taltos* and *Talamasca* inside his head.

When he did look up, he saw only Remmick pouring chocolate from a small, heavy silver pitcher into a pretty china cup. The steam rose in Remmick's patient and slightly weary face. Gray hair, now that was gray hair, an entire head of it. I do not have so much gray hair.

Indeed, he had only the two streaks flowing back from his temples, and a bit of white in his sideburns, as they were called. And yes, just a tiny touch of white in the dark hair of his chest. Fearfully he looked down at his wrist. There were white hairs there, mingled with the dark hair that had covered his arms now for so many years.

Taltos! Talamasca. The world will crumble . . .

"Was it the right thing, sir, the phone call?" asked Remmick, in that wonderful, near-inaudible British murmur that his employer loved. Lots of people would have called it a mumble. And we are going now to England, we are going back among all the agreeable, gentle people . . . England, the land of the bitter cold, seen from the coast of the lost land, a mystery of winter forests and snow-capped mountains.

"Yes, indeed, it was the right thing, Remmick. Always come to me directly when it's Samuel. I have to go to London, right now."

"Then I have to hurry, sir. La Guardia's been closed all day. It's going to be very difficult—"

"Hurry, then, please, don't say anything further."

He sipped the chocolate. Nothing tasted richer to him, sweeter, or better, except perhaps unadulterated fresh milk.

"Another Taltos," he whispered loud. He set down the cup. "Dark time in the Talamasca." This he wasn't sure he believed.

Remmick was gone. The doors had closed, the beautiful bronze gleaming as if it were hot. There was a trail of light across the marble floor from the light embedded in the ceiling, rather like the moon on the sea.

"Another Taltos, and it was male."

There were so many thoughts racing through his head, such a clatter of emotion! For a moment he thought he'd give way to tears. But no. It was anger that he felt, anger that once again he had been teased by this bit of news, that his heart was beating, that he was flying over the sea to learn more about another Taltos, who was already dead—a male.

And the Talamasca—so they had come into a dark time, had they? Well, wasn't it inevitable? And what must he do about it? Must he be drawn into all this once more? Centuries ago, he had knocked on their doors. But who among them knew this now?

Their scholars he knew by face and name, only because he feared them enough to keep track of them. Over the years, they had never stopped coming to the glen . . . Someone knew something, but nothing ever really changed.

Why did he feel he owed them some protective intervention now? Because they had once opened their doors, they had listened, they had begged him to remain, they hadn't laughed at his tales, they'd promised to keep his secret. And like him, the Talamasca was old. Old as the trees in the great forests.

How long ago had it been? Before the London house, long before, when the old palazzo in Rome had been lighted still with candles. No records, they had promised. No records, in exchange for all he had told . . . which was to remain impersonal, anonymous, a source of legend and fact, of bits and pieces of knowledge from ages past. Exhausted, he had slept beneath that roof; they had comforted him. But in the final analysis they were ordinary men, possessed of an extraordinary interest perhaps, but ordinary, short-lived, awestruck by him, scholars, alchemists, collectors.

Whatever the case, it was no good to have them in a dark time, to use Samuel's words, not with all they knew and kept within their archives. Not good. And for some strange reason his heart went out to this gypsy in the glen. And his curiosity burned as fierce as ever regarding the Taltos, the witches.

Dear God, the very thought of witches.

When Remmick came back, he had the fur-lined coat over his arm.

"Cold enough for this, sir," he said, as he put it over the boss's shoulders. "And you looked chilled, sir, already."

"It's nothing," he replied. "Don't come down with me. There's something you must do. Send money to Claridge's in London. It's for a man named Samuel. The management will have no trouble identifying Samuel. He is a dwarf and he is a hunchback and he has very red hair, and a very wrinkled face. You must arrange everything so that this little man has exactly what he wants. Oh, and there is someone with him. A gypsy. I have no idea what this means."

"Yes, sir. The surname, sir?"

"I don't know what it is, Remmick," he answered, rising to go, and pulling the fur-lined cape closer under his neck. "I've known Samuel for so long."

He was in the elevator before he realized that this last statement was absurd. He said too many things of late that were absurd. The other day Remmick had said how much he loved the marble in all these rooms, and he had answered, "Yes, I loved marble from the first time I ever saw it," and that had sounded absurd.

The wind howled in the elevator shaft as the cab descended at astonishing speed. It was a sound heard only in winter, and a sound which frightened Remmick, though he himself rather liked it, or thought it amusing at the very least.

When he reached the underground garage the car was waiting, giving off a great flood of noise and white smoke. His suitcases were being loaded. There stood his night pilot, Jacob, and the nameless copilot, and the pale, straw-colored young driver who was always on duty at this hour, the one who rarely ever spoke.

"You're sure you want to make this trip, tonight, sir?" asked Jacob.

"Is nobody flying?" he asked. He stopped, eyebrows raised, hand on the door. Warm air came from the inside of the car.

"No, sir, there are people flying."

"Then we're going to fly, Jacob. If you're frightened, you don't have to come."

"Where you go, I go, sir."

"Thank you, Jacob. You once assured me that we fly safely above the weather now, and with far greater security than a commercial jet."

"Yes, I did do that, sir, didn't I?"

He sat back on the black leather seat and stretched out his long legs, planting his feet on the seat opposite, which no man of normal height could have done in this long stretch limousine. The driver was comfortably shut away behind glass, and the others followed in the car behind him. His bodyguards were in the car ahead.

The big limousine rushed up the ramp, taking the curbs with perilous but exciting speed, and then out the gaping mouth of the garage into the enchanting white storm. Thank God the beggars had been rescued from the streets. But he had forgotten to ask about the beggars. Surely some of them had been brought into his lobby and given warm drink and cots upon which to sleep.

They crossed Fifth Avenue and sped towards the river. The storm was a soundless torrent of lovely tiny flakes. They melted as they struck the dark windows and the wet sidewalks. They came down through the dark faceless buildings as if into a deep mountain pass.

Taltos.

For a moment the joy went out of his world—the joy of his accomplishments, and his dreams. In his mind's eye he saw the pretty young woman, the dollmaker from California, in her crushed violet silk dress. He saw her in his mind dead on a bed, with blood all around her, making her dress dark.

Of course it wouldn't happen. He never let it happen anymore, hadn't in so long he could scarce remember what it was like to wrap his arms around a soft female body, scarce remember the taste of the milk from a mother's breast.

But he thought of the bed, and the blood, and the girl dead and cold, and her eyelids turning blue, as well as the flesh beneath her fingernails, and finally even her face. He pictured this because if he didn't, he would picture too many other things. The sting of this kept him chastened; kept him within bounds.

"Oh, what does it matter? Male. And dead."

Only now did he realize that he would see Samuel! He and Samuel would be together. Now that was something that flooded him with happiness, or would if he let it. And he had become a master of letting the floods of happiness come when they would.

He hadn't seen Samuel in five years, or was it more? He had to think. Of course they had talked on the phone. As the wires and phones themselves improved, they had talked often. But he hadn't actually seen Samuel.

In those days there had only been a little white in his hair. God, was it growing so fast? But of course Samuel had seen the few white hairs and remarked on it. And Ash had said, "It will go away."

For one moment the veil lifted, the great protective shield which so often saved him from unendurable pain.

He saw the glen, the smoke rising; he heard the awful ring and clatter of swords, saw the figures rushing towards the forest. Smoke rising from the brochs and from the wheelhouses . . . Impossible that it could have happened!

The weapons changed; the rules changed. But massacres were otherwise the same. He had lived on this continent now some seventy-five years, returning to it always within a month or two of leaving, for many reasons, and no small part of it was that he did not want to be near the flames, the smoke, the agony and terrible ruin of war.

The memory of the glen wasn't leaving him. Other memories were connected—of green fields, wildflowers, hundreds upon hundreds of tiny blue wildflowers. On the river he rode in a small wooden craft, and the soldiers stood on the high battlements; ah, what these creatures did, piling one rock upon another to make great mountains of their own! But what were his own monuments, the great sarsens which hundreds dragged across the plain to make the circle?

The cave, he saw that too again, as if a dozen vivid photographs were shuffled suddenly before him, and one moment he was running down the cliff, slipping, nearly falling, and at another Samuel stood there, saying,

"Let's leave here, Ash. Why do you come here? What is there to see or to learn?"

He saw the Taltos with the white hair.

"The wise ones, the good ones, the knowing ones," they had called them. They had not said "old." It would never have been a word they would have used in those times, when the springs of the island were warm, and the fruit fell from the trees. Even when they'd come to the glen, they had never said the word "old," but everyone knew they had lived the longest. Those with the white hair knew the longest stories . . .

"Go up now and listen to the story."

On the island, you could pick which of the white-haired ones you wanted, because they themselves would not choose, and you sat there listening to the chosen one sing, or talk, or say the verses, telling the deepest things that he could remember. There had been a white-haired woman who sang in a high, sweet voice, her eyes always fixed on the sea. And he had loved to listen to her.

And how long, he thought, how many decades would it be before his own hair was completely white?

Why, it might be very soon, for all he knew. Time itself had meant nothing then. And the white-haired females were so few, because the birthing made them wither young. No one talked about that either, but everybody knew it.

The white-haired males had been vigorous, amorous, prodigious eaters, and ready makers of predictions. But the white-haired woman had been frail. That is what birth had done to her.

Awful to remember these things, so suddenly, so clearly. Was there perhaps another magic secret to the white hair? That it made you remember from the beginning? No, it wasn't that, it was only that in all the years of never knowing how long, he had imagined that he would greet death with both arms, and now he did not feel that way.

His car had crossed the river, and was speeding towards the airport. It was big and heavy and hugged the slippery asphalt. It held steady against the beating wind.

On the memories tumbled. He'd been old when the horsemen had ridden down upon the plain. He'd been old when he saw the Romans on the battlements of the Antonine Wall, when he'd looked down from Columba's door on the high cliffs of Iona.

Wars. Why did they never go out of his memory, but wait there in all their full glory, right along with the sweet recollections of those he'd loved, of the dancing in the glen, of the music? The riders coming down upon the grassland, a dark mass spreading out as if it were ink upon a peaceful painting, and then the low roar just reaching their ears, and the sight of the smoke rising in endless clouds from their horses.

He awoke with a start.

The little phone was ringing for him. He grasped it hard and pulled it from its black hook.

"Mr. Ash?"

"Yes, Remmick?"

"I thought you'd like to know, sir. At Claridge's, they are familiar with your friend Samuel. They have arranged his usual suite for him, second floor, corner, with the fireplace. They are waiting for you. And, Mr. Ash, they don't know his surname either. Seems he doesn't use it."

"Thank you, Remmick. Say a little prayer. The weather's very volatile and dangerous, I think."

He hung up before Remmick could begin the conventional warnings. Should never have said such a thing, he thought.

But that was really amazing—their knowing Samuel at Claridge's. Imagine their having gotten used to Samuel. The last time Ash had seen Samuel, Samuel's red hair had been matted and shaggy, and his face so deeply wrinkled that his eyes were no longer fully visible, but flashed now and then in random light, like broken amber in the soft, mottled flesh. In those days Samuel had dressed in rags and carried his pistol in his belt, rather like a little pirate, and people had veered out of his path on the street.

"They're all afraid of me, I can't remain here. Look at them, they're more afraid in these times than long ago."

And now they were used to him in Claridge's! Was he having his suits made for him on Savile Row? Did his dirty leather shoes not have holes? Had he forsaken his gun?

The car stopped, and he had to force the door open, his driver rushing to help him, as the snow swept against him in the wind.

Nevertheless, the snow was so pretty, and so clean before it struck the ground. He stood up, feeling a stiffness in his limbs for a moment, and then he put his hand up to keep the soft, moist flakes from striking his eyes.

"It's not so bad, really, sir," said Jacob. "We can get out of here in less than an hour. You should board immediately, sir, if you please."

"Yes, thank you, Jacob," he said. He stopped. The snow was falling all over his dark coat. He could feel it melting in his hair. Nevertheless, he reached into his pocket, felt for the small toy, the rocking horse, yes, it was there.

"This is for your son, Jacob," he said. "I promised him."

"Mr. Ash, for you to remember something like that on a night like this."

"Nonsense, Jacob. I'll bet your son remembers."

It was embarrassingly insignificant, this little toy of wood; he wished now that it were something infinitely better. He would make a note—something better for Jacob's son.

Taking big steps, he walked too fast for the driver to follow. He was too tall for the umbrella anyway. It was just a gesture, the man rushing beside him, umbrella in hand, for him to take it if he wanted it, which he never did.

He boarded the warm, close, and always frightening jet plane.

"I have your music, Mr. Ash."

He knew this young woman, but he couldn't remember her name. She was one of the best of the night secretaries. She'd been with him on the last trip to Brazil. He had meant to remember her. Shameful not to have her name on the very tip of his tongue.

"Evie, isn't it?" he asked, smiling, begging forgiveness with a little bit of a frown.

"No, sir, Leslie," she said, forgiving him instantly.

If she'd been a doll, she would have been bisque, no doubt of it, face underpainted with a soft rose blush to cheeks and lips, eyes deliberately small, but dark and deeply focused. Timidly she waited.

As he took his seat, the great leather chair made especially for him, longer than the others, she put the engraved program in his hand.

There were the usual selections—Beethoven, Brahms, Shostakovich. Ah, here was the composition he had requested—the Verdi Requiem. But he couldn't listen to it now. If he slipped himself into those dark chords and dark voices, the memories would close in.

He put his head back, ignoring the winter spectacle outside the little window. "Sleep, you fool," he said without moving his lips.

But he knew he wouldn't. He would think about Samuel and the things Samuel had said, over and over, until they saw one another again. He would remember the smell of the Talamasca house, and how much the scholars had looked like clerics, and a human hand with a quill pen, writing in great curled letters. "Anonymous. Legends of the lost land. Of Stonehenge."

"Just want to be quiet, sir?" asked the young Leslie.

"No, Shostakovich, the Fifth Symphony. It will make me cry, but you must ignore me. I'm hungry. I want cheese and milk."

"Yes, sir, everything's ready." She began to speak the names of the cheeses, those fancy triple creams that they ordered for him from

France and Italy and God only knows where else. He nodded, accepting, waiting for the rush of the music, the divinely piercing quality of this engulfing electronic system, which would make him forget the snow outside, and the fact that they would soon be over the great ocean, pushing steadily towards England, towards the plain, towards Donnelaith, and towards heartbreak.

Two

AFTER the first day, Rowan didn't talk. She spent her time out under the oak, in a white wicker chair, her feet propped on a pillow, or sometimes merely resting on the grass. She stared at the sky, eyes moving as if there were a procession of clouds above, and not the clear spring blue, and the bits of white fleece that blew silently across it.

She looked at the wall, or the flowers, or the yew trees. She never looked down at the ground.

Perhaps she'd forgotten that the double grave was right beneath her feet. The grass was growing over it, quick and wild, as it always does in spring in Louisiana. There had been rain aplenty to help it, and sometimes the glory of the sun and rain at the same time.

She ate her meals—approximately a fourth to one-half of what they gave her. Or so Michael said. She didn't look hungry. But she was pale, still, and her hands, when she did move them, would shake.

All the family came to see her. Groups came across the lawn, standing back as if they might hurt her. They said their hellos, they asked about her health. They told her she looked beautiful. That was true. Then they gave up and they went away.

Mona watched all this.

At night Rowan slept, Michael said, as if she were exhausted, as if she'd been hard at work. She bathed alone, though this scared him. But she always locked the bathroom door, and if he tried to stay inside with her, she merely sat there on the chair, looking off, doing nothing. He had to leave before she'd get up. Then he'd hear the lock turn.

She listened when people spoke, at least in the beginning. And now and then when Michael pleaded with her to speak, she clasped his hand warmly as if comforting him, or pleading with him to be patient. This was sad to watch.

Michael was the only one she touched, or acknowledged, though often this little gesture was made without a change in her remote expression or even a movement of her gray eyes.

Her hair was growing full again. It was even a little yellow from her sitting in the sun. When she'd been in the coma, it had been the color of driftwood, the kind you can see on the muddy riverbanks. Now it looked alive, though if memory served Mona correctly, hair was dead, wasn't it? Already dead by the time you brushed it, curled it, did stuff to it.

Every morning Rowan rose of her own accord. She would walk slowly down the stairs, holding the railing to the left, and leaning on her cane with the right hand, placing it firmly on each tread. She didn't seem to care if Michael helped her. If Mona took her arm, it didn't matter.

Now and then Rowan stopped at her dresser before she went down, and put on a bit of lipstick.

Mona always noticed. Sometimes Mona was waiting for Rowan in the hallway, and she saw Rowan do this. Very significant.

Michael always remarked on it too. Rowan wore nightgowns and negligees, depending upon the weather. Aunt Bea kept buying them and Michael would wash them, because Rowan only wore new clothes after they had been washed, or so he had remembered, and he laid them out for her on the bed.

No, this was no catatonic stupor, Mona figured. And the doctors had confirmed it, though they could not say what was wrong with her. The one time one of them, an idiot Michael had said, stuck a pin in her hand, Rowan quietly withdrew the hand and covered it with her other one. And Michael went into a rage. But Rowan didn't look at the guy or say a word.

"I wish I'd been here for that," said Mona.

Of course Mona had known he was telling the truth. Let the doctors speculate and stick pins in people. Maybe when they went back to the hospital, they stuck pins in a doll of Rowan—voodoo accupuncture. Mona wouldn't have been surprised.

WHAT *did* Rowan feel? What did she remember? Nobody was sure anymore. They had only Michael's word that she had awakened from the coma fully aware, that she had spoken with him for hours after, that she knew everything that had happened, that in the coma she had heard and understood. Something terrible on the day of her awakening, *another one.* And the two buried together beneath the oak.

"I never should have let her do it," Michael had said to Mona a hundred times. "The smell that came out of that hole, the sight of what was left . . . I should have taken care of things."

And what had the other one looked like, and who had carried it down, and tell me all the things that Rowan said—Mona had asked him these questions too often.

"I washed the mud from her hands," Michael had told Aaron and Mona. "She kept looking at it. I guess a doctor doesn't want her hands to be soiled. Think about it, how often a surgeon washes her hands. She asked me how I was, she wanted . . ." And there he had choked up, both times that he told this story. "She wanted to take my pulse. She was worried about *me.*"

Wish to God I had seen it, what they buried! Wish to God she had spoken to me!

It was the strangest thing—to be rich now, the designee at thirteen, to have a driver and a car (vulgate translation: flashy black stretch limo with disc, tape player, color TV, and lots of room for ice and Diet Coke), and money in her purse all the time, like twenty-dollar bills, no less, and heaps of new clothes, and people patching up the old house on St. Charles and Amelia, catching her on the fly with swatches of "raw silk" or handpainted "wall coverings."

And to want *this,* to want to know, to want to be part of, to want to understand the secrets of this woman and this man, this house that would one day come to her. A ghost is dead beneath the tree. A legend lies under the spring rains. And in its arm, *another one.* It was like turning away from the sure, bright glitter of gold, to take dark trinkets of inestimable power from a small hiding place. Ah, this is magic. Not even her own mother's death had so distracted Mona.

Mona talked to Rowan. A lot.

She came on the property with her own key, the heiress and all that. And because Michael said she could. And Michael, no longer looking at her with lust in the eye, had practically adopted her.

She went back to the rear garden, crossed the lawn, skirting the grave if she remembered, and sometimes she didn't, and then she sat at the wicker table and said, "Rowan, good morning." And then talked and talked.

She told Rowan all about the development of Mayfair Medical, that they had chosen a site, that they had agreed upon a great geothermal system for the heating and cooling, that plans were being drawn. "Your dream is coming into being," she told Rowan. "The Mayfair family knows this city as well as anybody. We don't need feasibility studies and things like that. We're making the hospital happen as you wanted it."

No response from Rowan. Did she even care anymore about the great medical complex that would revolutionize the relationship between patients and their attending families, in which teams of caretakers would assist even the anonymous patients?

"I found your notes," said Mona. "I mean, they weren't locked up. They didn't look private."

No answer. The giant black limbs of the oak moved just a little. The banana leaves fluttered against the brick wall.

"I myself have stood outside Touro Infirmary, asking people what they wanted in an ideal hospital, you know, talking to people for hours."

Nothing.

"My Aunt Evelyn is in Touro," Mona said quietly. "She's had a stroke. They ought to bring her home, but I don't think she knows the difference." Mona would cry if she talked about Ancient Evelyn. She'd cry if she talked about Yuri. She didn't. She didn't say that Yuri had not written or called for three weeks now. She didn't say that she, Mona, was in love, and with a dark, charming, British-mannered man of mystery who was more than twice her age.

She'd explained all that several days ago to Rowan—the way that Yuri had come from London to help Aaron Lightner. She'd explained that Yuri had been a gypsy and he understood things that Mona understood. She even described how they'd met together in her bedroom the night before Yuri went away. "I worry all the time about him," she had said.

Rowan had never looked at her.

What could she say now? That last night, she had some terrible dream about Yuri that she couldn't remember.

"Of course, he's a grown man," she said. "I mean he's past thirty and all, and he knows how to take care of himself, but the thought that somebody in the Talamasca might hurt him." Oh, stop this!

Maybe this was all wrong. It was too easy to dump all these words on a person who couldn't or wouldn't answer.

But Mona could swear there was a vague acknowledgment in Rowan that Mona was there. Maybe it was only that Rowan didn't look annoyed, or sealed off.

Mona didn't sense displeasure.

Her eyes swept Rowan's face. Rowan's expression was so serious. Had to be a mind in there, just had to be. Why, she looked twenty million times better than she had looked in the coma. And look, she'd buttoned her negligee. Michael swore he didn't do those things for her. She'd buttoned three buttons. Yesterday it had only been one.

But Mona knew that despair can fill up a mind so completely that trying to read its thoughts is like trying to read through thick smoke. Was it despair that had settled on Rowan?

Mary Jane Mayfair had come this last weekend, the mad country girl from Fontevrault. Wanderer, buccaneer, seer, and genius, to hear her tell it, and part old lady and part fun-loving girl, at the ripe old age of nineteen and a half. A fearsome, powerful witch, so she described herself.

"Rowan's just fine," Mary Jane had declared after staring and squinting at Rowan, and then pushing her own cowboy hat off her head so it laid against the back of her neck. "Yep, just brace yourself. She's taking her time, but this lady here knows what's happening."

"Who *is* this nut case?" Mona had demanded, though she'd felt a wild compassion for the child actually, never mind that she was six years older than Mona. This was a noble savage decked out in a Wal-Mart denim skirt no longer than the middle of her thighs, and a cheap white blouse that was much too tight across her egregious breasts, and even missing a crucial button. Severely deprived, and playing it off beautifully.

Of course, Mona had known who Mary Jane was. Mary Jane Mayfair actually lived in the ruins of Fontevrault Plantation, in the Bayou Country. This was the legendary land of poachers who killed beautiful white-necked herons just for their meat, alligators that could overturn your boat and eat your child, and crazy Mayfairs who'd never made it to New Orleans and the wooden steps of the famous New Orleans Fontevrault outpost, otherwise known as the house on St. Charles and Amelia.

Mona was actually dying to see this place, Fontevrault, that stood still with its six columns up and six columns down, even though the first floor was flooded with three feet of water. Seeing the legendary Mary Jane was the next best thing, the cousin only recently returned from "away" who tethered her pirogue to the newel post, and paddled across a stagnant pool of treacherous slime to get to the pickup truck she drove into town for her groceries.

Everybody was talking about Mary Jane Mayfair. And because Mona was thirteen, and the heiress now, and the only legacy-connected person who would talk to people or acknowledge their presence, everybody thought Mona would find it especially interesting to speak about a teenaged hick cousin who was "brilliant" and "psychic" and wandered about the way Mona did, on her own.

Nineteen and a half. Until Mona laid eyes on this brilliant bit of work, she had not considered someone of that age a true teenager.

Mary Jane was just about the most interesting discovery they had made since they'd started rounding up everyone for genetic testing of the entire Mayfair family. It was bound to happen, finding a throwback like Mary Jane. Mona wondered what else might crawl out of the swamps soon.

But imagine a flooded plantation house of Greek Revival grandeur, gradually sinking into the duckweed, with globs of plaster falling off "with a splash" into the murky waters. Imagine fish swimming through the stairway balusters.

"What if that house falls on her?" Bea had asked. "The house is *in* the water. She can't stay there. This girl must be brought here to New Orleans."

"Swamp water, Bea," Celia had said. "Swamp water, remember. It's not a lake or the Gulf Stream. And besides, if this child does not have sense to get out of there and take the old woman to safety—"

The old woman.

Mona had all of this fresh in her memory this last weekend when Mary Jane had walked into the backyard and plunged into the little crowd that surrounded the silent Rowan as if it were a picnic.

"I knew about y'all," Mary Jane had declared. She'd addressed her words to Michael too, who stood by Rowan's chair as if posing for an elegant family portrait. And how Michael's eyes had locked onto her.

"I come over here sometimes and look at you," said Mary Jane. "Yeah, I do. I came the day of the wedding. You know, when you married her?" She pointed to Michael, then to Rowan. "I stood over there, 'cross the street, and looked at your party?"

Her sentences kept going up on the end, though they weren't questions, as though she was always asking for a nod or a word of agreement.

"You should have come inside," Michael had said kindly, hanging on every syllable the girl spouted. The trouble with Michael was that he did have a weakness for pubescent pulchritude. His tryst with Mona had been no freak of nature or twist of witchcraft. And Mary Jane Mayfair was as succulent a little swamp hen as Mona had ever beheld. Even wore her bright yellow hair in braids over the top of her head, and filthy white patent leather shoes with straps, like a little kid. The fact that her skin was dark, sort of olive and possibly tanned, made the girl look something like a human palomino.

"What did the tests say on you?" Mona had asked. "That's what you're doing here, isn't it? They tested you?"

"I don't know," said the genius, the mighty powerful swamp witch.

"They're so mixed up over there, wonder they got anything right. First they called me Florence Mayfair and then Ducky Mayfair, finally I says, 'Look, I'm Mary Jane Mayfair, looky there, right there, on that form you got in front of you.'"

"Well, that's not very good," Celia had muttered.

"But they said I was fine and go home and they'd tell me if anything was wrong with me. Look, I figure I've probably got witch genes coming out the kazoo, I expect to blow the top off the graph, you know? And, boy, I have never seen so many Mayfairs as I saw in that building."

"We own the building," said Mona.

"And every one of them I could recognize on sight, every single person. I never made a mistake. There was one infidel in there, one outcast, you know, or no, it was a half-breed type, that's what it was, ever notice that there are all these Mayfair types? I mean there are a whole bunch that have no chins and have kind of pretty noses that dip down just a little right here and eyes that tilt at the outside. And then there's a bunch that look like you," she said to Michael, "yeah, just like you, real Irish with bushy brows and curly hair and big crazy Irish eyes."

"But, honey," Michael had protested in vain, "I'm not a Mayfair."

"—and the ones with the red hair like her, only she's just about the most pretty one I've seen. You must be Mona. You have the gleam and glow of somebody who's just come into tons of money."

"Mary Jane, darling," said Celia, unable to follow up with an intelligent bit of advice or a meaningless little question.

"Well, what does it feel like to be so rich?" Mary Jane asked, big, quivering eyes fastened still to Mona. "I mean really deep in here." She pounded her cheap little gaping blouse with a knotted fist, squinting up her eyes again, and bending forward so that the well between her breasts was plainly visible even to someone as short as Mona. "Never mind, I know I'm not supposed to ask that sort of question. I came over here to see her, you know, because Paige and Beatrice told me to do it."

"Why did they do that?" asked Mona.

"Hush up, dear," said Beatrice. "Mary Jane is a Mayfair's Mayfair. Darling Mary Jane, you ought to bring your grandmother up here immediately. I'm serious, child. We want you to come. We have an entire list of addresses, both temporary and permanent."

"I know what she means," Celia had said. She'd been sitting beside Rowan, and was the only one bold enough to wipe Rowan's face now and then with a white handkerchief. "I mean about the Mayfairs with no chins. She means Polly. Polly has an implant. She wasn't born with that chin."

"Well, if she has an implant," declared Beatrice, "then Polly has a visible chin, doesn't she?"

"Yeah, but she's got the slanty eyes and the tipped nose," said Mary Jane.

"Exactly," said Celia.

"You all afraid of the extra genes?" Mary Jane had thrown her voice out like a lasso, catching everybody's attention. "You, Mona, you afraid?"

"I don't know," said Mona, who was in fact not afraid.

"Of course, it's nothing that's even remotely likely to happen!" Bea said. "The genes. It's purely theoretical, of course. Do we have to talk about this?" Beatrice threw a meaningful look at Rowan.

Rowan had stared, as she always did, at the wall, maybe at the sunshine on the bricks, who could possibly know?

Mary Jane had plunged ahead. "I don't think anything that wild will ever happen to this family again. I think the moment for that kind of witchcraft is past, and another eon of new witchcraft—"

"Darling, we really don't take this entire witchcraft thing too seriously," said Bea.

"You know the family history?" Celia had asked gravely.

"Know it? I know things about it you don't know. I know things my granny told me, that she heard from Old Tobias, I know things that are written on the walls in that house, still. When I was a little child, I sat on Ancient Evelyn's knee. Ancient Evelyn told me all kinds of things that I remember. Just one afternoon, that's all it took."

"But the file on our family, the file by the Talamasca . . ." Celia had pressed. "They did give it to you at the clinic?"

"Oh, yeah, Bea and Paige brought that stuff to me," said Mary Jane. "Look here." She pointed to the Band-Aid on her arm that was just like the Band-Aid on her knee. "This is where they stuck me! Took enough blood to sacrifice to the devil. I understand the entire situation. Some of us have a whole string of extra genes. You breed two close kins with the double dose of double helix, and wham, you've got a Taltos. Maybe! Maybe! After all, think about it, how many cousins have married and married, and it never happened, did it, till . . . Look, we shouldn't talk about it in front of her, you're right."

Michael had given a weary little smile of gratitude.

Mary Jane again squinted at Rowan. Mary Jane blew a big bubble with her gum, sucked it in, and popped it.

Mona laughed. "Now that's some trick," she said. "I could never do that."

"Oh, well, that might be a blessing," said Bea.

"But you did read the file," Celia had pressed. "It's very important that you know everything."

"Oh, yeah, I read every word of it," Mary Jane had confessed, "even the ones I had to look up." She slapped her slender, tanned little thigh and shrieked with laughter. "Y'all talking about giving me things. Help me get some education, that's about the only thing I could really use. You know, the worst thing that ever happened to me was my mama taking me out of school. 'Course, I didn't want to go to school then. I had much more fun in the public library, but—"

"I think you're right about the extra genes," Mona said. And right about needing the education.

Many, many of the family had the extra chromosomes which could make monsters, but none had ever been born to the clan, no matter what the coupling, until this terrible time.

And what of the ghost this monster had been for so long, a phantom to drive young women mad, to keep First Street under a cloud of thorns and gloom? There was something poetic about the strange bodies lying right here, beneath the oak, under the very grass where Mary Jane stood in her short denim skirt with her flesh-colored Band-Aid on her little knee, and her hands on her little hips, and her little filthy white patent leather buckle shoe rolled to one side and smeared with fresh mud—with her little dirty sock half down in her heel.

Maybe Bayou witches are just plain dumb, Mona thought. They can stand over the graves of monsters and never know it. Of course, none of the other witches in this family knew it either. Only the woman who won't talk, and Michael, the big hunk of Celtic muscle and charm standing beside Rowan.

"You and I are second cousins," Mary Jane had said to Mona, renewing her approach. "Isn't that something? You weren't born when I came to Ancient Evelyn's house and ate her homemade ice cream."

"I don't recall Ancient Evelyn ever making homemade ice cream."

"Darlin', she made the best homemade ice cream that I ever tasted. My mama brought me into New Orleans to—"

"You've got the wrong person," said Mona. Maybe this girl was an impostor. Maybe she wasn't even a Mayfair. No, no such luck on that. And there was something about her eyes that reminded Mona a little of Ancient Evelyn.

"No, I got the right person," Mary Jane had insisted. "But we didn't really come on account of the ice cream. Let me see your hands. Your hands are normal."

"So what?"

"Mona, be nice, dear," said Beatrice. "Your cousin is just sort of outspoken."

"Well, see these hands?" said Mary Jane. "I had a sixth finger when I was little, on both hands? Not a real finger? You know? I mean just a little one. And that's why my mother brought me to see Ancient Evelyn, because Ancient Evelyn has just such a finger herself."

"Don't you think I know that?" asked Mona. "I grew up with Ancient Evelyn."

"I know you did. I know all about you. Just cool off, honey. I'm not trying to be rude, it's just I am a Mayfair, same as you, and I'll pit my genes against your genes anytime."

"Who told you all about me?" Mona asked.

"Mona," said Michael softly.

"How come I never met you before?" said Mona. "I'm a Fontevrault Mayfair. Your second cousin, as you just said. And how come you talk like you're from Mississippi when you say you lived all that time in California?"

"Oh, listen, there's a story to it," said Mary Jane. "I've done my time in Mississippi, believe you me, couldn't have been any worse on Parchman Farm." It had been impossible to crack the kid's patience. She had shrugged. "You got any iced tea?"

" 'Course we do, dear, I'm so sorry." Off Beatrice had gone to get it. Celia had shaken her head with shame. Even Mona had felt negligent, and Michael had quickly apologized.

"No, I'll git it myself, tell me where it is," Mary Jane had cried.

But Bea had disappeared already, conveniently enough. Mary Jane popped her gum again, and then again in a whole side-mouth series of little pops.

"Awesome," said Mona.

"Like I said, there's a story to it all. I could tell you some terrible things about my time in Florida. Yeah, I been there, and in Alabama for a while, too. I had to sort of work my way back down here."

"No lie," said Mona.

"Mona, don't be sarcastic."

"I seen you before," Mary Jane had said, going on as if nothing at all had happened. "I remember you when you and Gifford Mayfair came out to L.A. to go to Hawaii. That's the first time I was ever in an airport. You were sleeping right there by the table, stretched out on two chairs, under Gifford's coat, and Gifford Mayfair bought us the best meal???"

Don't describe it, Mona had thought. But Mona did have some hazy memory of that trip, and waking up with a crick in her neck in the Los Angeles airport, known by the snappy name of LAX, and Gifford saying to Alicia that they had to bring "Mary Jane" back home someday.

Only thing, Mona had no memory of any other little girl there. So this was Mary Jane. And now she was back home. Gifford must be working miracles from heaven.

Bea had returned with the iced tea. "Here it is, precious, lots of lemon and sugar, the way you like it, isn't that right? Yes, darling."

"I don't remember seeing you at Michael and Rowan's wedding," said Mona.

"That's 'cause I never came in," said Mary Jane, who took the iced tea from Bea as soon as it entered the nearest orbit, and drank half of it, slurping it and wiping it off her chin with the back of her hand. Chipped nail polish, but what a gorgeous shade of crape myrtle purple.

"I told you to come," said Bea. "I called you. I left a message for you three times at the drugstore."

"I know you did, Aunt Beatrice, ain't nobody who could say that you didn't do your level best to get us to that wedding. But, Aunt Beatrice, I didn't have shoes! I didn't have a dress? I didn't have a hat? See these shoes? I found these shoes. These are the first shoes that are not tennis shoes that I have worn in a decade! Besides, I could see perfect from across the street. And hear the music. That was fine music you had at your wedding, Michael Curry. Are you sure you aren't a Mayfair? You look like a Mayfair to me; I could make let's say seven different points about your appearance that's Mayfair."

"Thank you, sweetheart. I'm not a Mayfair."

"Oh, you are in your heart," said Celia.

"Well, of course," said Michael, never taking his eyes off the girl even once, no matter who spoke to him. And what do men see when they look at bundles of charm like this?

"You know when we were little," Mary Jane had gone on, "we didn't have anything out there, we just had an oil lamp and a cooler with some ice in it and a lot of mosquito netting hung all over the porch and Granny would light the lamp every evening and . . ."

"You didn't have electricity?" Michael had asked. "How long ago was this? How long ago could it have been?"

"Michael, you've never been in the Bayou Country," said Celia. And Bea gave a knowing nod.

"Michael Curry, we were squatters, that's what we were," said Mary Jane. "We were just hiding out in Fontevrault. Aunt Beatrice could tell you. Sheriff would come to throw us out periodically. We'd pack and he'd take us into Napoleonville and then we would go back and he'd give up on us, and we'd be in peace for a while, till some goody-two-shoes passed by in a boat, some game warden, somebody like that, and called in on us. We had bees, you know, on the porch for honey? We could fish right off the back steps? We had fruit trees all around the landing then, before the wisteria got them like a giant boa constrictor, you know, and blackberries? Why, I'd just pick all I wanted right there where the road forks. We had everything. Besides, now I *have* electricity! I hooked it up myself from the highway, and I did the same thing with the cable TV."

"You really did that?" asked Mona.

"Honey, that's against the law," said Bea.

"I certainly did. My life's far too interesting for me to ever tell lies about it. Besides, I've got more courage than imagination, that's always been the case." She drank the iced tea with another noisy slurp, spilling more of it. "God, that's good. That's so sweet. That's artificial sweetener, isn't it?"

"I'm afraid so," said Bea, staring at her in mingled horror and embarrassment. And to think she had said "sugar." And Bea did hate people who ate and drank sloppily.

"Now, just think of it," said Mary Jane, wiping the back of her hand across her mouth and then wiping her hand on her denim skirt. "I'm tasting something now that is fifty times sweeter than anything anybody ever tasted on earth until this very time. That's why I've bought stock in artificial sweetener."

"You've bought what?" asked Mona.

"Oh, yeah. I have my own broker, honey, discount broker but that's the best kind, since I do the picking most of the time anyway. He's in Baton Rouge. I've got twenty-five thousand dollars sunk in the stock market. And when I make it rich, I'm draining and raising Fontevrault. I'm bringing it all back, every peg and board! You wait and see. You're looking at a future member of the Fortune Five Hundred."

Maybe there was something to this dingbat, Mona had thought. "How did you get twenty-five thousand dollars?"

"You could be killed, fiddling with electricity," declared Celia.

"Earned every penny of it on the way home, and that took a year, and don't ask me how I did it. I had a couple of things going for me, I did. But that's a story, now, really."

"You could be electrocuted," said Celia. "Hooking up your own wires."

"Darling, you are not in the witness box," said Bea anxiously.

"Look, Mary Jane," said Michael, "if you need anything like that, I'll come down there and hook it up for you. I mean it. You just tell me when, I'll be there."

Twenty-five thousand dollars?

Mona's eyes had drifted to Rowan. Rowan was frowning just a little at the flowers, as if the flowers were talking to her in a quiet and secret tongue.

There followed a colorful description from Mary Jane of climbing swamp cypresses, of knowing just what electric wires to touch and not to touch, of purloined work gloves and boots. Maybe this girl was some kind of genius.

"What other stocks do you own?" asked Mona.

"What do you care at your age about the stock market?" asked Mary Jane with blithering ignorance.

"Good heavens, Mary Jane," Mona had said, trying to sound as much as she could like Beatrice, "I've always had a great obsession with the stock market. Business to me is an art. Everyone knows that about me. I plan someday to run my own mutual fund. I assume you know the term, mutual fund?"

"Well, sure I do," said Mary Jane, laughing at herself in an utterly agreeable and forgiving manner.

"I have, in the last few weeks, already completely designed my own portfolio," Mona said, and then she'd broken off, feeling dumb for having been baited like that by someone who probably was not even listening to her. Derision from the firm of Mayfair and Mayfair was one thing—and it would not last long—but from this girl it was another.

But the girl had really looked at her, and stopped just using her for a sounding board, while taking little peeping glances in between her own hasty words.

"Is that so?" asked Mary Jane. "Well, let me ask you something now. What about this Shopper's Channel on TV? I think this is going to go over like crazy? You know? I've put ten grand in the Shopper's Channel. You know what happened?"

"The stock's nearly doubled in the last four months," said Mona.

"You got it, that's right, now how did you know that? Well, you're some strange kid, aren't you now? And I thought you were one of those uptown girls, with that ribbon in your hair, you know, that you always wore, and going to Sacred Heart, you know? And I figured you wouldn't even talk to me."

A little pain had flared in Mona at that moment, pain and pity for this girl, for anybody who felt that cast out, that snubbed. Mona had never in her life suffered that lack of confidence. And this girl was interesting, putting it all together on her own, with far less nuts and bolts than Mona had.

"Hold it, please, darlings, let's not talk Wall Street," said Beatrice. "Mary Jane, how is Granny? You haven't told us a word. And it's four o'clock, and you have to leave soon if you're going to drive all the way back—"

"Oh, Granny's fine, Aunt Beatrice," said Mary Jane, but she had been looking straight at Mona. "Now, you know what happened to Granny after Mama came and got me and took me away to Los Angeles? I was six years old then, you know. Did you hear this story?"

"Yeah," said Mona.

Everybody had. Beatrice was still embarrassed about it. Celia stared at the girl as though she were a giant mosquito. Only Michael seemed uninformed.

What had happened was this: Mary Jane's grandmother, Dolly Jean Mayfair, had been slapped in the parish home after her daughter left with six-year-old Mary Jane. Dolly Jean was supposed to have died last year and been buried in the family tomb. And the funeral had been a big affair, only because when somebody called New Orleans, all the Mayfairs drove out there to Napoleonville, and beat their chests in grief and regret that they had let this old woman, poor Dolly Jean, die in a parish home. Most of them had never heard of her.

Indeed, none of them had really known Dolly Jean. Or at least they had not known her as an old lady. Lauren and Celia had seen her many times when they were all little girls, of course.

Ancient Evelyn had known Dolly Jean, but Ancient Evelyn had never left Amelia Street to ride to a country funeral, and no one had even thought of asking her about it.

Well, when Mary Jane hit town a year ago, and heard the story of her grandmother dying and being buried, she'd scoffed at it, even laughing in Bea's face.

"Hell, she's not dead," Mary Jane had said. "She came to me in a dream and said, 'Mary Jane, come get me. I want to go home.' Now I'm going back to Napoleonville, and you have to tell me where that parish home is."

For Michael's benefit, she had now repeated the entire tale, and the look of astonishment on Michael's face was becoming unintentionally comic.

"How come Dolly Jean didn't tell you in the dream where the home was?" Mona had asked.

Beatrice had shot her a disapproving look.

"Well, she didn't, that's a fact. And that's a good point, too. I have a whole theory about apparitions and why they, you know, get so mixed up."

"We all do," said Mona.

"Mona, tone it down," said Michael.

Just as if I'm his daughter now, thought Mona indignantly. And he still hasn't taken his eyes off Mary Jane. But it had been said affectionately.

"Honey, what happened?" Michael had pushed.

"Well, an old lady like that," Mary Jane had resumed, "she doesn't always know where she is, even in a dream, but she knew where she was from! This is exactly what happened. I walked into the door of that old folks' home, and there, slap-bang in the middle of the recreation room, or whatever they called it, was my grandmother and she looked up at me, right at me, and after all those years she said, 'Where you been, Mary Jane? Take me home, chère, I'm tired of waiting.' "

They had buried the wrong person from the old folks' home.

The real Granny Dolly Jean Mayfair had been alive, receiving but never laying eyes upon a welfare check every month with somebody else's name on it. A royal inquisition had taken place to prove it, and then Granny Mayfair and Mary Jane Mayfair had gone back to live in the ruins of the plantation house, and a team of Mayfairs had provided them with the basic necessities, and Mary Jane had stood outside, shooting her pistol at soft-drink bottles and saying that they'd be just fine, they could take care of themselves. She had some bucks she'd made on the road, she was kind of a nut about doing things her own way, no thank you kindly.

"So they let the old lady live with you in this flooded house?" Michael had asked so innocently.

"Honey, after what they did to her in the old folks' home out there, mixing her up with some other woman and putting her name on a slab and all, what the hell are they going to say to me about her living with me? And Cousin Ryan? Cousin Ryan of Mayfair and Mayfair? You know? He went down there and tore that town apart!"

"Yeah," said Michael. "I bet he did."

"It was all our fault," said Celia. "We should have kept track of these people."

"Are you sure you didn't grow up in Mississippi and maybe even Texas?" Mona had asked. "You sound like an amalgam of the whole South."

"What is an amalgam? See, that is where you have the advantage. You're educated. I'm self-educated. There's a world of difference between us. There are words that I don't dare pronounce and I can't read the symbols in the dictionary."

"Do you want to go to school, Mary Jane?" Michael had been getting more and more involved by the second, his intoxicatingly innocent blue eyes making a head-to-toe sweep about every four and one-half seconds. He was far too clever to linger on the kid's breasts and hips, or even her round little head, not that it had been undersized, just sort of dainty. That's how she'd seemed, finally, ignorant, crazy, brilliant, a mess, and somehow dainty.

"Yes, sir, I do," said Mary Jane. "When I'm rich I'll have a private tutor like Mona here is gettin' now that she's the designee and all, you know, some really smart guy that tells you the name of every tree you pass, and who was president ten years after the Civil War, and how many Indians there were at Bull Run, and what *is* Einstein's Theory of Relativity."

"How old are you?" Michael had asked.

"Nineteen and a half, big boy," Mary Jane had declared, biting her shiny white teeth into her lower lip, lifting one eyebrow and winking.

"This story about your granny, you're serious, this really happened? You picked up your granny and . . ."

"Darling, it all happened," said Celia, "exactly as the girl says. I think we should go inside. I think we're upsetting Rowan."

"I don't know," said Michael. "Maybe she's listening. I don't want to move. Mary Jane, you can care for this old lady all by yourself?"

Beatrice and Celia had immediately looked anxious. If Gifford had still been alive, and there, she too would have looked anxious. "Leaving that old woman out there!" as Celia had said so often of late.

And they had promised Gifford, hadn't they, that they would take care of it? Mona remembered that. Gifford had been in one of her hopeless states of worry about relatives far and wide, and Celia had said, "We'll drive out and check on her."

"Yes, sir, Mr. Curry, it all happened, and I took Granny home with me, and don't you know that the sleeping porch upstairs was just exactly the way we'd left it? Why, after thirteen years, the radio was still there, and the mosquito netting and the ice chest."

"In the swamps?" Mona had demanded. "Wait a minute."

"That's right, honey, that's exactly right."

"It's true," Beatrice had confessed dismally. "Of course, we got them fresh linen, new things. We wanted to put them in a hotel or a house or . . ."

"Well, naturally," said Celia. "I'm afraid this story almost made the papers. Darling, is your granny alone out there right now?"

"No, ma'am, she's with Benjy. Benjy's from the trappers live out that way—real crazy people, you know??? The kind that live in those shacks all made out of pieces of tin, and windows from salvage and even cardboard? I pay him below minimum wage to watch Granny and to cover the phones, but I don't take out any deductions."

"So what?" said Mona. "He's an independent contractor."

"You sure are smart," said Mary Jane. "Don't you think I know that? I was actually biting my lip on another little tidbit right at that point, you know??? That Benjy, bless his heart, has already discovered how to make some easy money in the French Quarter down here, you know?? Peddling nothing but what God give him."

"Oh my Lord," said Celia.

Michael laughed. "How old is Benjy?" he asked.

"Twelve years old this September," said Mary Jane. "He's all right. His big dream is to be a drug dealer in New York, and my big dream for him is to go to Tulane and become a medical doctor."

"But what do you mean, cover the phones?" asked Mona. "How many phones have you got? What are you actually doing down there?"

"Well, I had to spring for some money for the phones, that was an absolute necessity, and I've been calling my broker, naturally enough. Who else? And then there's another line that Granny can talk on to my mother, you know, my mother is never getting out of that hospital in Mexico."

"What hospital in Mexico?" asked Bea, utterly aghast. "Mary Jane, you told me two weeks ago how your mother died in California."

"I was trying to be polite, you know, save everybody the grief and the trouble."

"But what about the funeral?" Michael had asked, drawing close enough most likely to sneak a look down Mary Jane's tightly laced junk polyester blouse. "The old lady. Who *did* they bury?"

"Darlin', that's the worst part of it. Nobody ever found out!" said Mary Jane. "Don't worry about my mother, Aunt Bea, she thinks she's on the astral plane already. She might *be* on the astral plane for all I know. Besides, her kidneys are shot."

"Now, that's not exactly true about the woman in the grave," said Celia. "They believe it was . . ."

"Believe?" asked Michael.

Maybe big breasts are markers of power, Mona had thought as she watched the girl bend nearly double and laugh and laugh as she pointed at Michael.

"Look, that's all very sad about the woman in the wrong grave," said Beatrice. "But, Mary Jane, you have to tell me how to reach your mother!"

"Hey, you don't have a sixth finger," said Mona.

"Not now, precious," said Mary Jane. "My mother had some doctor in Los Angeles chop it off. That's what I was going to tell you. They did the same thing to—"

"Enough of this talk, really," said Celia. "I'm so worried for Rowan!"

"Oh, I didn't know," said Mary Jane. "I mean—"

"Same thing to whom?" asked Mona.

"Now that's another thing. When do you say 'whom' instead of 'who,' exactly?"

"I don't think you're at that stage yet," Mona had replied. "There are a lot of other basic things . . ."

"Enough, ladies and gentlemen!" Bea had declared. "Mary Jane, I'm going to call your mother."

"You're going to be so sorry, Aunt Bea. You know what kind a' doctor cut off my sixth finger in L.A.? It was a voodoo witch doctor from Haiti, and he did it on the kitchen table."

"But can't they dig up the wrong woman and find out once and for all who she was?" Michael asked.

"Well, they have a very good suspicion, but . . ." Celia had started.

"But what?" Michael had asked.

"Oh, it has to do with welfare checks," Beatrice had declared, "and that's none of our business. Michael, please forget about that dead woman!"

How *could* Rowan just ignore these proceedings? And here he was, calling Mary Jane by name, doing everything but eating Mary Jane up with a spoon. If this didn't snap Rowan to, then a tornado wouldn't do it.

"Well, Michael Curry, come to find out they'd been calling that dead lady Dolly Jean for some time before she passed on. Wasn't anybody in that place with a lick a' sense, if you ask me. I think one night they just started putting Granny in the wrong bed, and what do you know, the old lady in Granny's bed died, and there you have it. They buried some poor old stranger in the Mayfair grave!"

At that point Mary Jane had flashed her eyes on Rowan.

"She's listening!" Mary Jane had cried. "Yes, she is, swear to God. She's listening."

If it was true, no one else could see it or sense it. Rowan had remained oblivious to the eyes turning to her. Michael had flushed as though hurt by the kid's outburst. And Celia had studied Rowan, doubting, and grim.

"There's nothing wrong with her," Mary Jane had declared. "She'll snap right out of it, you watch. People like her, they talk when they want to. I can be like that."

Mona had wanted to say, Why don't you start now?

But in truth, she had wanted to believe that Mary Jane was right. This girl might just be some powerful witch after all, Mona had figured. If Mary Jane wasn't, she would still make it, somehow or other.

"Don't you worry none now about Granny," she said as she was "fixin' to go." She'd smiled and slapped her naked brown thigh. "Let me tell you something, it may have turned out for the best."

"Good Lord, how?" Bea had asked.

"Well, in all those years in that home, you know, they said she never said much of anything, just sort of talked to herself and acted like people were there who weren't and all that, and well now?? She knows who she is, you know??? She talks to me and she watches the soaps, and never misses 'Jeopardy' or 'Wheel of Fortune'?? I think it was all that commotion as well as anything else, and coming back to Fontevrault and finding things up in the attic? Did you know she could climb those steps?? Listen, she's fine, don't you worry about her, I'm getting cheese and graham crackers for her when I get home, and her and me will watch the late show, or the country-western channel, she likes that too, you know, 'Achy Breaky Heart' and all that stuff. Why, she can sing those songs. Never you mind. She's terrific."

"Yes, precious, but really . . ."

Mona had even sort of liked her for five minutes, a kid who could take care of an old woman like that, making it up every day with Band-Aids and hot wires.

Mona had walked out to the front with her, and watched her hop in her pickup truck, which had bare springs sticking out of the passenger seat, and roar off in a cloud of blue exhaust.

"We've got to take care of her," Bea had said. "We've got to sit down and talk about the Mary Jane situation very soon."

True, Mona had agreed. The Mary Jane Situation was a good label for it.

And though this girl clearly had evinced no remarkable powers on the spot, there was something exciting about her.

Mary Jane was spunky and there was something irresistible about the idea of showering her with Mayfair money and benefits, and trying to improve her. Why couldn't she come in and study with this tutor who was going to free Mona from the boredom of regular school forever? Beatrice had been chomping at the bit to buy Mary Jane some clothes before she left town, and no doubt had been sending her the crème de la crème of once-worn hand-me-downs.

And there was one other little secret reason that Mona liked Mary Jane, a reason which nobody would ever understand. Mary Jane had been wearing a cowboy hat. It was small and made of straw, and she'd let it fall down behind her shoulders on its strings, but it had been there for two minutes when she first walked up. And she'd popped it back on her head before she pulled hard on the stick shift of that old truck and rushed off, waving at everybody.

A cowboy hat. It had always been Mona's dream to wear a cowboy hat, especially when she was really rich and in control of things, and flying about the world in her own plane. Mona had for years pictured herself as a mogul in a cowboy hat, entering factories and banks and . . . well, Mary Jane Mayfair did have a cowboy hat. And with her braids on top of her head, and her slick, tight denim skirt, there was something all together about her. She had, in spite of everything, a sort of deliberate and successful style. Even her chipped and peeling purple fingernail polish had been part of it, giving her a kind of earthy seductiveness.

Well, it wouldn't be hard to verify that, would it?

"And those eyes, Mona," Beatrice had said as they walked back into the garden. "The child is adorable! Did you look at her? I don't know how I could ever . . . And her mother, her mother, oh, that girl always was insane, nobody should have ever let her run away with that baby. But there had been such bad blood between us and those Fontevrault Mayfairs."

"You can't take care of all of them, Bea," Mona had reassured her, "any more than Gifford could." But they would, of course. And if Celia and Beatrice didn't, well, Mona would. That had been one of the keenest revelations of that afternoon, that Mona was now part of the team; she wasn't going to let that kid not fulfill her dreams, not while she had breath in her little thirteen-year-old body.

"She's a sweet thing in her own way," Celia had admitted.

"Yeah, and that Band-Aid on her knee," Michael had muttered under his breath, not thinking. "What a girl. I believe what she said about Rowan."

"So do I," said Beatrice. "Only . . ."

"Only what?" Michael had asked desperately.

"Only what if she never makes up her mind to speak again!"

"Beatrice, shame on you," Celia had said, glancing pointedly at Michael.

"You think that Band-Aid's sexy, Michael?" Mona had asked.

"Well, er, yeah, actually. Everything about that girl was sexy, I guess. What does it matter to me?" He'd seemed sincere enough, and sincerely exhausted. He'd wanted to get back to Rowan. He'd been sitting with Rowan and reading a book, by himself, when they'd all come together.

For a while after that afternoon, Mona could have sworn, Rowan looked different, that her eyes were tighter now and then, and sometimes more open, as though she were posing a question to herself. Maybe Mary Jane's big gush of words had been good for Rowan. Maybe they ought to ask Mary Jane back, or maybe she'd just come back. Mona had found herself actually looking forward to it, or maybe just asking the new driver to fire up the monstrous stretch limo, pack the leather pockets with ice and drinks, and drive down there to that flooded house. You could do that when you had your own car. Hell, Mona had not gotten used to any of this.

For two or three days Rowan had seemed better, showing that little frown more and more, which was, after all, a facial expression.

But now? On this quiet, lonely, sticky sunny afternoon?

Mona thought that Rowan had slipped back. Even the heat did not touch her. She sat in the humid air, and the droplets of sweat appeared on her brow, with no Celia to boldly wipe them away, but Rowan didn't move to wipe them herself.

"Please, Rowan, talk to us," Mona said now in her frank, almost brash girlish voice. "I don't want to be the designee of the legacy! I don't even want to be the heiress if you don't approve of it." She leaned on her elbow, her red hair making a veil between her and the iron gates to the front garden. Felt more private. "Come on, Rowan. You know what Mary Jane Mayfair said. You're in there. Come on. Mary Jane said you could hear us."

Mona reached up for her own hair ribbon, to adjust it, to make her head stop itching. There was no hair ribbon. She hadn't worn her bow since her mother died. It was a little pearl-studded barrette, holding a clump of her hair too tight. Hell with it. She loosened it and let her hair slip down.

"Look, Rowan, if you want me to go, give me a sign. You know, like just do something weird. And I'll be out of here that quick."

Rowan was staring at the brick wall. She was staring at the bacon-'n'-eggs lantana—the wildly grown hedge of little brown and orange flowers. Or maybe she was just staring at the bricks.

Mona gave a sigh, a pretty spoiled and petulant thing to do, really. But then she had tried everything except throwing a tantrum. Maybe that's what somebody ought to do!

Only it can't be me, she thought dismally.

She got up, went to the wall, pulled off two sprigs of the lantana and brought them back, and put them before Rowan like an offering to a goddess who sits beneath an oak listening to people's prayers.

"I love you, Rowan," she said. "I need you."

For one moment her eyes misted. The burning green of the garden seemed to fold into one great veil. Her head throbbed slightly, and she felt some tightening in her throat and then a release that was worse than crying, some dim and terrible acknowledgment of all the terrible things that had come to pass.

This woman was wounded, perhaps beyond repair. And she, Mona, was the heiress who could bear a child now, and must indeed try to bear one, so that the great Mayfair fortune could be passed on. This woman, what would she do now? She could no longer be a doctor, that was almost certain; she seemed to care for nothing and no one.

And suddenly Mona felt as awkward and unloved and as unwelcome as she ever had in her life. She ought to get out of here. It was shameful that she had stayed so many days at this table, begging for forgiveness for once lusting after Michael, begging for forgiveness for being young and rich and able someday to have children, for having survived when both her mother, Alicia, and her Aunt Gifford, two women she loved and hated and needed, had died.

Self-centered! What the hell. "I didn't mean it with Michael," she said aloud to Rowan. "No, don't go into that again!"

No change. Rowan's gray eyes were focused, not dreaming. Her hands lay in her lap in the most natural little heap. Wedding ring so thin and spare it made her hands look like those of a nun.

Mona wanted to reach for one of her hands, but she didn't dare. It was one thing to talk for half an hour, but she couldn't touch Rowan, she couldn't force a physical contact. She didn't dare even to lift Rowan's hand and put the lantana in it. That was too intimate to do to her in her silence.

"Well, I don't touch you, you know. I don't take your hand, or feel it or try to learn something from it. I don't touch you or kiss you because if I was like you, I think I'd hate it if some freckle-faced, red-haired kid came around and did that to me."

Red hair, freckles, what had that to do with it, except to say, Yes, I slept with your husband, but you're the mysterious one, the powerful one, the woman, the one he loves and has always loved. I was nothing. I was just a kid who tricked him into bed. And wasn't as careful that night as I should have been. Wasn't careful at all, in fact. But not to worry, I've never been what anyone would call regular. He looked at me the way he looked later at that kid, Mary Jane. Lust, that was all. Lust and nothing more. And my period will finally come, like it always does, and my doctor will give me yet another lecture.

Mona gathered up the little sprigs of lantana there on the table, next to the china cup, and she walked away.

For the first time, as she looked up at the clouds moving over the chimneys of the main house, she realized it was a beautiful day.

Michael was in the kitchen, fixing the juices, or "brewing the concoction" as they had come to call it—papaya juice, coconut, grapefruit, orange. There was lots of undefinable slop and pulp all over.

It occurred to her, though she tried not to process the thought, that he looked healthier and handsomer with every passing day. He'd been working out upstairs. The doctors encouraged him. He must have gained fifteen good pounds since Rowan had woken up and climbed out of bed.

"She *does* like it," he said now, as if they'd been discussing this concoction all along. "I know she does. Bea said something about its being too acid. There's no evidence she finds it too acid." He shrugged. "I don't know," he said.

"I think," said Mona, "that she stopped talking because of me."

Mona stared at him, and then the tears came, wet and frightening. She didn't want to break down. She didn't want to make such a demand or display. But she was miserable. What the hell did she want from Rowan? She scarcely knew Rowan. It was as if she needed to be mothered by the designee of the legacy who had lost her power to carry on the line.

"No, honey," he said with the softest, most comforting smile.

"Michael, it's because I told her about us," she said. "I didn't mean to. It was the first morning I spoke to her. All this time, I've been scared to tell you. I thought she was just being quiet. I didn't . . . I don't . . . She never spoke after that, Michael. It's true, isn't it? It was after I came."

"Honey chile, don't torture yourself," he said, wiping up some of the sticky gunk from the counter. He was patient, reassuring, but he was too tired for all this, and Mona was ashamed. "She'd stopped talking the day before, Mona. I told you that. Pay attention." He gave her a little smile to mock himself. "I just didn't realize it then, that she'd quit talking." He stirred the juice again. "Well, now comes the big decision. Egg or no egg."

"Egg! You can't put an egg in fruit juice."

"Sure I can. Honey, you've never lived in Northern California, have you? This is a first-rate health-food special. And she needs the protein. But a raw egg can give you salmonella. Old problem. The family is split right down the middle on the subject of the raw egg. I should have asked Mary Jane her opinion last Sunday."

"Mary Jane!" Mona shook her head. "Damn the family," she said.

"I don't know about that," said Michael. "Beatrice thinks raw eggs are dangerous, and she has a point. On the other hand, when I was in high school, playing football, I used to pop a raw egg into a milkshake every morning. But Celia says . . ."

"Lord deliver me," said Mona, imitating Celia perfectly. "What does Aunt Celia know about raw eggs?"

She was so sick of the family discussing Rowan's tiny likes and dislikes, and Rowan's blood count, and Rowan's color, that if she found herself in one more pointless, ineffectual, and tiresome discussion, she would start screaming to be let out.

Maybe she had just had too much of it all, from the day they'd told her she was the heiress—too many people giving her advice, or asking after her as though *she* were the invalid. She'd written mock headlines on her computer:

GIRL KNOCKED ON HEAD BY WHOLE LOAD OF MONEY. Or, WAIF CHILD INHERITS BILLIONS AS LAWYERS FRET.

Naaah, you wouldn't "fret" in a headline today. But she liked the word.

She felt so terrible suddenly as she stood here in the kitchen that the tears spilled out of her eyes like they would from a baby, and her shoulders began to shake.

"Look, honey, she stopped the day before, I told you," he said. "I can tell you the last thing she said. We were sitting right there at the table. She'd been drinking coffee. She'd said she was dying for a cup of New Orleans coffee. And I'd made her a whole pot. It was about twenty-two hours from the time she woke up, and she hadn't slept at all. Maybe that was the problem. We kept talking. She needed her rest.

She said, 'Michael, I want to go outside. No, stay, Michael. I want to be alone for a while.' "

"You're sure that was the last thing she said?"

"Absolutely. I wanted to call everyone, tell them she was all right. Maybe *I* scared her! I'm the one, making that suggestion. And after that, I was leading her around, and she wasn't saying anything, and that's the way it's been since then."

He picked up what appeared to be a raw egg. He cracked it suddenly on the edge of the plastic blender and then pulled open the two halves of shell to let loose the icky white and yolk.

"I don't think you hurt her at all, Mona. I really, really doubt you did. I wish you hadn't told her. If you must know, I could have done without your telling her that I committed statutory rape on the living room couch with her cousin." He shrugged. "Women do that, you know. They tell afterwards." He gave her a bright reproving look, the sunlight glinting in his eyes. "We can't tell, but they can tell. But the point is, I doubt she even heard you. I don't think . . . she gives a damn." His voice trailed off.

The glass was foamy and faintly disgusting-looking.

"I'm sorry, Michael."

"Honey, don't—"

"No, I mean I'm okay. She's not okay. But I'm okay. You want me to take that stuff to her? It's gross, Michael, I mean gross. Like it is absolutely disgusting!"

Mona looked at the froth, the unearthly color.

"Gotta blend it," he said. He put the square rubber cap on the container, and pressed the button. Then came the ghastly sound of the blades turning as the liquid jumped inside.

Maybe it was better if you didn't *know* about the egg.

"Well, I put lots of broccoli juice in it this time," he said.

"Oh God, no wonder she won't drink it. Broccoli juice! Are you trying to kill her?"

"Oh, she'll drink it. She always drinks it. She drinks anything I put before her. I'm just thinking about what's in it. Now listen to me. If she wasn't listening when you made your confession, I'm not sure it came as a surprise. All that time she was in the coma, she heard things. She told me. She heard things people said when I was nowhere about. Of course, nobody knew about you and me and our little, you know, criminal activity."

"Michael, for chrissakes, if there is a crime of statutory rape in this state, you'd have to get a lawyer to look it up to be sure. The age of consent between cousins is probably ten, and there may even be a special law on the books lowering the age to eight for Mayfairs."

"Don't kid yourself, sweetheart," he said, shaking his head in obvious disapproval. "But what I was saying is, she heard the things you and I said to each other when we sat by the bed. We're talking about witches, Mona." He fell into his thoughts, staring off, brooding almost, looking intensely handsome, beefcake and sensitive.

"You know, Mona, it's nothing anybody said." He looked up at her. He was sad now, and it was very real, the way it is when a man of his age gets sad, and she found herself just a little frightened. "Mona, it was everything that happened to her. It was . . . perhaps the last thing that happened . . ."

Mona nodded. She tried to picture it again, the way he'd so briefly described it. The gun, the shot, the body falling. The terrible secret of the milk.

"You haven't told anyone, have you?" he said in a serious whisper. God help her if she had, she thought, she would have died at this moment, the way he was looking at her.

"No, and I never will," she said. "I know when to tell and when not to tell, but . . ."

He shook his head. "She wouldn't let me touch the body. She insisted on carrying it down herself, and she could hardly walk. Long as I live, I'm not going to get that sight out of my mind, ever. All the rest of it—I don't know. I can take it in stride, but something about the mother dragging the body of the daughter . . ."

"Did you think of it that way, like it was her daughter?"

He didn't answer. He just continued to look off, and gradually the hurt and trouble slipped away from his face, and he chewed his lip for a second, and then almost smiled.

"Never tell anyone that part," he whispered. "Never, never, never. No one needs to know. But someday, perhaps, she'll want to talk about it. Perhaps it's that, more than anything else, that's made her silent."

"Don't ever worry that I'll tell," she said. "I'm not a child, Michael."

"I know, honey, believe me, I know," he said with just the warmest little spark of good humor.

Then he was really gone again, forgetting her, forgetting them, and the huge glass of gunk, as he stared off. And for one second he looked as if he was giving up all hope, as if he was in a total despair beyond the reach of anyone, even maybe Rowan.

"Michael, for the love of God, she will be all right. If that's what it is, she'll get better."

He didn't answer right away, then he sort of murmured the words:

"She sits in that very place, not over the grave, but right beside it," he said. His voice had gotten thick.

He was going to cry, and Mona wouldn't be able to stand it. She wanted with all her heart to go to him and put her arms around him. But this would have been for her, not him.

She realized suddenly that he was smiling—for her sake, of course— and now he gave her a little philosophical shrug. "Your life will be filled with good things, for the demons are slain," he said, "and you will inherit Eden." His smile grew broader and so genuinely kind. "And she and I, we will take that guilt to our graves of whatever we did and didn't do, or had to do, or failed to do for each other."

He sighed, and he leaned on his folded arms over the counter. He looked out into the sunshine, into the gently moving yard, full of rattling green leaves and spring.

It seemed he had come to a natural finish.

And he was his old self again, philosophical but undefeated.

Finally he stood upright and picked up the glass and wiped it with an old white napkin.

"Ah, that's one thing," he said, "that is really nice about being rich."

"What?"

"Having a linen napkin," he said, "anytime you want it. And having linen handkerchiefs. Celia and Bea always have their linen handkerchiefs. My dad would never use a paper handkerchief. Hmmm. I haven't thought about that in a long time."

He winked at her. She couldn't stop herself from smiling. What a dope. But who the hell else could play off a wink like that with her? Nobody.

"You haven't heard from Yuri, have you?" he asked.

"I would have told you," she said dismally. It was agony to hear Yuri's name.

"Have you told Aaron that you haven't heard from him?"

"A hundred times, and three times this morning. Aaron hasn't heard anything, either. He's worried. But he's not going back to Europe, no matter what happens. He'll live out his days with us right here. He says to remember that Yuri is incredibly clever, like all the investigators of the Talamasca."

"You do think something has happened?"

"I don't know," she said dully. "Maybe he just forgot about me." It was too dreadful to contemplate. It couldn't have been that way. But one had to face things, didn't one? And Yuri was a man of the world.

Michael looked down into the drink. Maybe he would have the brains to see it was flat-out undrinkable. Instead he picked up a spoon and started to stir it.

"You know, Michael, that just may shock her out of her trance," Mona said. "I mean, while she's drinking it, right at that very moment, when half the glass is sliding down her throat, just tell her in a clear voice what's in it."

He chuckled, his deep-chested, fabulous chuckle. He picked up the jug of slop and poured a full, egregious glass of it.

"Come on, come out there with me. Come and see her."

Mona hesitated. "Michael, I don't want her to see both of us together, you know, standing side by side."

"Use a little of your own witchcraft, honey. She knows I am her slave till the day I die."

His expression changed again, very slowly. He was looking at her in a calm but almost cold fashion. And again there came over her a sense of how bereft he really was.

"Yeah, bereft," he said, and there was something almost mean in his smile. He didn't say anything more. He picked up the glass and went out the door.

"Let's go talk to the lady," he said over his shoulder. "Let's go read her mind together. Two heads, you know, and all that. Maybe we should do it again, Mona, on the grass, you know, you and me, and maybe she'd wake up."

Mona was shocked. Did he mean that? No, that wasn't the question. The question was, How could he say that?

She didn't answer him, but she knew what he felt. Or at least she thought she did. On some level she knew she couldn't really know, that things were painful for a man of his age in a different way from what they were for a young girl. She knew this in spite of so many people having told her this, more or less. It was a matter not of humility but logic.

She followed him out onto the flagstones and along the pool and then into the rear gates. His jeans were so tight, she could hardly stand it. His natural walk was a seductive swagger. *This is nice, think sexy thoughts! No way!* And his polo shirt wasn't exactly loose-fitting either. She loved the way it moved over his shoulders and back.

Can't stop it. She wished he hadn't made that bitter little joke. Do it on the grass! An awful restlessness took hold of her. Men were always complaining about how the sight of sexy women aroused them. Well, with her it was words as well as images. His tight jeans, and the sharp images that had invaded her mind after what he'd said.

Rowan was seated at the table, the way she'd been when Mona left her; the lantana was still there, the sprigs scattered a little, as if the wind had stirred them with one finger and then let them alone.

Rowan was frowning slightly, as if weighing something in her mind. Now that was always a good sign, Mona thought, but she would get Michael's hopes up if she talked about it. Rowan didn't seem to know that they were there. She was still looking at the distant flowers, at the wall.

Michael bent to kiss her on the cheek. He set the glass on the table. There was no change in her, except the breeze caught a few strands of hair. Then he reached down and he lifted her right hand and he placed her fingers around the glass.

"Drink it, honey," he said. He used the same tone he'd used to Mona, brusque and warm. Honey, honey, honey means Mona, Rowan, or Mary Jane, or any female being perhaps.

Would "honey" have been appropriate for the dead thing, buried in the hole with its father? Christ, if she had only laid eyes on one of them, for just a precious second! Yeah, and every Mayfair woman who laid eyes on him during his little rampage had paid with her life for it. Except Rowan. . . .

Whoa! Rowan was lifting the glass. Mona watched with a fearful fascination as she drank without ever moving her eyes from the distant flowers. She did blink naturally and slowly as she swallowed, but that was all. And the frown remained. Small. Thoughtful.

Michael stood watching her, hands in his pockets, and then he did a surprising thing. He talked about her to Mona, as if Rowan couldn't hear. This was the first time.

"When the doctor spoke to her, when he told her she should go in for tests, she just got up and walked off. It was like a person on a park bench in a big city. You'd think someone had sat down beside her, maybe too close to her. She was isolated like that, all alone."

He collected the glass. It looked more disgusting than ever. But to tell the truth, Rowan looked like she would have drunk anything that he'd put in her hand.

Nothing registered on Rowan's face.

"I could take her to the hospital for the tests, of course. She might go along. She's done everything else I've wanted her to do."

"Why don't you?" asked Mona.

"Because when she gets up in the morning she puts on her night-gown and her robe. I've laid out real clothes for her. She doesn't touch them. That's my cue. She wants to be in her nightgown and her robe. She wants to be home."

He was angry suddenly. His cheeks were red, and there was a frank twisting to his lips that said it all.

"The tests can't help her anyway," he continued. "All these vitamins, that's the treatment. The tests would only tell us things. Maybe it's none of our business now. The drink helps her."

His voice was tightening. He was getting angrier and angrier as he looked at Rowan. He stopped speaking.

He bent down suddenly and set the glass on the table, and laid his hands flat on either side of it. He was trying to look Rowan in the eye. He drew close to her face, but there was no change in her.

"Rowan, please," he whispered. "Come back!"

"Michael, don't!"

"Why not, Mona? Rowan, I need you now. I need you!" He banged the table hard with both hands. Rowan flinched, but did not otherwise change. "Rowan!" he shouted. He reached out for her as if he was going to take her by the shoulders and shake her, but he didn't.

He snatched up the glass and turned and walked away.

Mona stood still, waiting, too shocked to speak. But it was like everything he did. It had been the good-hearted thing to do. It had been rough, though, and sort of terrible to watch.

Mona didn't come away just yet. Slowly she sat down in the chair at the table, across from Rowan, the same place she'd taken every day.

Very slowly, Mona grew calm again. She wasn't sure why she stayed here, except it seemed the loyal thing to do. Perhaps she didn't want to appear to be Michael's ally. Her guilt just hung all over her all the time these days.

Rowan did look beautiful, if you stopped thinking about the fact that she didn't talk. Her hair was growing long, almost to her shoulders. Beautiful and absent. Gone.

"Well, you know," Mona said, "I'll probably keep coming until you give me a sign. I know that doesn't absolve me, or make it okay to be the pest of a shocked and mute person. But when you're mute like this, you sort of force people to act, to make choices, to decide. I mean, people can't just let you alone. It's not possible. It's not really kind."

She let out her breath, and felt herself relax all over.

"I'm too young to know certain things," she said. "I mean, I'm not going to sit here and tell you I understand what happened to you. That would be too stupid." She looked at Rowan; the eyes looked green now, as if picking up the tint of the bright spring lawn.

"But I . . . ah . . . care about what's happening to everybody, well, almost everybody. I know things. I know more than anybody except Michael or Aaron. Do you remember Aaron?"

That was a dumb question. Of course Rowan remembered Aaron, if she remembered anything at all.

"Well, what I meant to say was, there's this man, Yuri. I told you about him. I don't think you ever saw him. In fact, I'm sure you didn't. Well, he's gone, very gone, as it stands now, and I'm worried, and Aaron's worried, too. It's like things are at a standstill now, with you here in the garden like this, and the truth is, things never stand still—"

She broke off. This was worse than the other approach. There was no way to tell if this woman was suffering. Mona sighed, trying to be quiet about it. She put her elbows on the table. Slowly she looked up. She could have sworn that Rowan had been looking at her, and had only just looked away.

"Rowan, it's not over," she whispered again. Then she looked off, through the iron gates, and beyond the pool and down the middle of the front lawn. The crape myrtle was coming into bloom. It had been mere sticks when Yuri left.

She and he had stood out there whispering together, and he had said, "Look, whatever happens in Europe, Mona, I am coming back here to you."

Rowan *was* looking at her. Rowan was staring into her eyes.

She was too amazed to speak or move. And she was frightened to do either, frightened that Rowan would look away. She wanted to believe this was good, this was ratification and redemption. She had caught Rowan's attention, even if she had been a hopeless brat.

Gradually Rowan's preoccupied expression seemed to fade as Mona stared at her. And Rowan's face became eloquent and unmistakably sad.

"What's the matter, Rowan?" Mona whispered.

Rowan made a little sound, as if she were clearing her throat.

"It's not Yuri," Rowan whispered. And then her frown tightened, and her eyes darkened, but she didn't drift away.

"What is it, Rowan?" Mona asked her. "Rowan, what did you say about Yuri?"

It appeared for all the world as if Rowan thought she was still speaking to Mona, and didn't know that nothing was coming out.

"Rowan," Mona whispered. "Tell me. Rowan—" Mona's words stopped. She'd lost the nerve, suddenly, to speak her heart.

Rowan's eyes were still fixed on her. Rowan lifted her right hand and ran her fingers back through her pale ashen hair. Natural, normal, but the eyes were not normal. They were struggling . . .

A sound distracted Mona—men talking, Michael and someone else.

And then the sudden, alarming sound of a woman crying or laughing. For one second, Mona couldn't tell which.

She turned and stared through the gates, across the glaring pool. Her Aunt Beatrice was coming towards her, almost running along the flagstone edge of the water, one hand to her mouth and the other groping as if she were going to fall on her face. She was the one who was crying, and it was most certainly crying. Bea's hair was falling loose from her invariably neat twist on the back of her head. Her silk dress was blotched and wet.

Michael and a man in ominous plain dark clothes followed quickly, talking together as they did.

Great choked sobs were coming from Beatrice. Her heels sank into the soft lawn, but on she came.

"Bea, what is it?" Mona rose to her feet. So did Rowan. Rowan stared at the approaching figure, and as Beatrice rushed across the grass, turning her ankle and righting herself immediately, it was to Rowan that she reached out.

"They did it, Rowan," said Bea, gasping for breath. "They killed him. The car came up over the curb. They killed him. I saw it with my own eyes!"

Mona reached out to support Beatrice, and suddenly her aunt had put her left arm around Mona and was near crushing her with kisses while the other hand still groped for Rowan, and Rowan reached to take it and clasp it in both of hers.

"Bea, who did they kill, who?" Mona cried. "You don't mean Aaron."

"Yes," Bea answered, nodding frantically, her voice now dry and barely audible. She continued to nod, as Mona and Rowan closed against her. "Aaron," she said. "They killed him. I saw it. The car jumped the curb on St. Charles Avenue. I told him I'd drive him over here. He said no, he wanted to walk. The car deliberately hit him, I saw it. It ran over him three times!"

As Michael, too, put his arms around her, Bea slumped as if she would faint, and let herself fall to the ground. Michael collected her and held her and she sank, crying, against his chest. Her hair fell in her eyes, and her hands were still reaching, trembling, like birds that couldn't light.

The man in the ominous clothes was a policeman—Mona saw the gun and the shoulder holster—a Chinese American, with a tender and emotional face.

"I'm so sorry," he said with a distinct New Orleans accent. Mona had never heard such an accent from such a Chinese face.

"They killed him?" Mona asked in a whisper, looking from the policeman to Michael, who was slowly soothing Bea with kisses and a gentle hand that straightened her hair. In all her life Mona had never seen Bea cry like this, and for one moment two thoughts collided in her: Yuri must be dead already; and Aaron had been murdered, and this meant perhaps that they were all in danger. And this was terrible, unspeakably terrible above all for Bea.

Rowan spoke calmly to the policeman, though her voice was hoarse and small in the confusion, in the clattering of emotion.

"I want to see the body," said Rowan. "Can you take me to it? I'm a doctor. I have to see it. It will take me only a moment to dress."

Was there time for Michael to be amazed, for Mona to be flabbergasted? Oh, but it made sense, didn't it? Horrible Mary Jane had said, "She's listening. She'll talk when she's ready."

And thank God she had not sat still and silent through this moment! Thank God that she couldn't or didn't have to, and was with them now.

Never mind how fragile she looked, and how hoarse and unnatural her voice sounded. Her eyes were clear as she looked at Mona, ignoring the policeman's solicitous answer that perhaps it was better she did not see the body, the accident having been what it was.

"Bea needs Michael," said Rowan. She reached out and clasped Mona's wrist. Her hand was cool and firm. "I need you now. Will you go with me?"

"Yes," said Mona. "Oh yes."

Three

H<small>E HAD</small> promised the little man he would enter the hotel moments after. "You come with me," Samuel had said, "and everyone will see you. Now keep the sunglasses on your face."

Yuri had nodded. He didn't mind sitting in the car for the moment, watching people walk past the elegant front doors of Claridge's. Nothing had comforted him so much since he'd left the glen of Donnelaith as the city of London.

Even the long drive south with Samuel, tunneling through the night on freeways that might have been anywhere in the world, had unnerved him.

As for the glen, it was vivid in his memory and thoroughly gruesome. What had made him think it was wise to go there alone—to seek at the very roots for some knowledge of the Little People and the Taltos? Of course he had found exactly what he wanted. And been shot in the shoulder by a .38-caliber bullet in the process.

The bullet had been an appalling shock. He'd never been wounded before in such a fashion. But the truly unnerving revelation had been the Little People.

Slumped in the back of the Rolls, he suffered again a vivid memory of that sight—the night with its heavy rolling clouds and haunting moon, the mountain path wildly overgrown, and the eerie sound of the drums and the horns rising against the cliffs.

Only when he had seen the little men in their circle had he realized they were singing. Only then had he heard their baritone chants, their words thoroughly unrecognizable to him.

He wasn't sure he had believed in them until then—

Round in the circle they went, stunted, humpbacked, lifting their short knees, rocking back and forth, giving forth rhythmic bursts in the chants, some drinking from mugs, others from bottles. They wore their gunbelts over their shoulders. They fired their pistols into the great windy night with the riotous hilarity of savages. The guns did not roar. Rather they went off in tight bursts, like firecrackers. Worse, by far, were the drums, the awful pounding drums, and the few pipes whining and struggling with their gloomy melody.

When the bullet struck him, he thought it had come from one of them—a sentry perhaps. He had been wrong.

Three weeks had passed before he'd left the glen.

Now Claridge's. Now the chance to call New Orleans, to speak to Aaron, to speak with Mona, to explain why for so long he'd been silent.

As for the risk of London, as for the proximity of the Talamasca Motherhouse and those who were trying to kill him, he felt infinitely safer here than he had in the glen only moments before the bullet had knocked him on his face.

Time to go upstairs. To see this mysterious friend of Samuel's, who had already arrived, and who had not been described or explained to Yuri. Time to do what the little man wanted because the little man had saved Yuri's life, nursed him back to health, and wanted him to meet this friend who had, in this great drama, some mammoth significance.

Yuri climbed out of the car, the genial British doorman quickly coming to his assistance.

His shoulder ached; there was a sharp pain. When would he learn not to use his right arm! Maddening.

The cold air was fierce but momentary. He went directly into the lobby of the hotel—so vast, yet warm. He took the great curving staircase to his right.

The soft strains of a string quartet came from the nearby bar. The air was still all around him. The hotel calmed him and made him feel safe. It also made him feel happy.

What a wonder it was that all of these polite Englishmen—the doorman, the bellhops, the kindly gentleman coming down the stairs past him—took no visible notice of his dirty sweater or his soiled black pants. Too polite, he mused.

He walked along the second floor until he came to the door of the corner suite, which the little man had described to him, and finding the door open, he entered a small, inviting alcove rather like that of a gracious home, and which looked into a large parlor, dowdy yet luxurious as the little man had said it would be.

The little man was on his knees, piling wood into the fireplace. He had taken off his tweed jacket, and the white shirt pulled painfully over his stunted arms and hump.

"There, there, come in here, Yuri," he said, without so much as looking up.

Yuri stepped into the doorway. The other man was there.

And this man was as strange to behold as the little man, but in an entirely different fashion. He was outrageously tall, though not impossibly so. He had pale white skin and dark, rather natural-looking hair. The hair was long and free and out of keeping with the man's fine black wool suit and the dull sheen of the expensive white shirt that he wore, and his dark red tie. He looked decidedly romantic. But what did this mean? Yuri wasn't sure. Yet it was the word that came to his mind. The man did not look decisively athletic—he was not one of those freakish sports giants who excel in televised Olympic games or on noisy basketball courts—rather he looked romantic.

Yuri met the man's gaze with no trouble. There was nothing menacing in this extraordinary and rather formal figure. Indeed, his face was smooth and young, almost pretty for a man, with its long, thick eyelashes and full, gently shaped androgynous lips—and not intimidating. Only the white in his hair gave him an air of authority, which he clearly did not regularly enforce. His eyes were hazel and rather large, and they looked at Yuri wonderingly. It was altogether an impressive figure, except for the hands. The hands were a little too big, and there was an abnormality about the fingers, though Yuri wasn't sure what it was. Spidery thin they were, maybe that was the sum of it.

"You're the gypsy," said the man in a low, pleasing voice that was almost a little sensual and very unlike the caustic baritone of the dwarf.

"Come inside, sit down," said the dwarf impatiently. He had now lighted the fire and was fanning it with the bellows. "I sent for something to eat, but I want you to go into the bedroom when they bring it, I don't want you seen."

"Thank you," said Yuri quietly. He realized suddenly that he'd failed to remove his dark glasses. How bright the room was suddenly, even with its deep green velvet furniture and old-fashioned flowered curtains. An agreeable room, with the imprint of people upon it.

Claridge's. He knew the hotels of the world, but he had never known Claridge's. He had never lodged in London except at the Motherhouse, to which he could not go now.

"You're wounded, my friend told me," said the tall man, approaching him and looking down at him in such a kindly way that the man's height aroused no instinctive fear. The spidery hands were raised and extended as if, in order to see Yuri's face, the man had to frame it.

"I'm all right. It was a bullet, but your friend removed it. I would be dead if it wasn't for your friend."

"So he's told me. Do you know who I am?"

"No, I don't."

"Do you know what a Taltos is? That is what I am."

Yuri said nothing. He had no more suspected this than he had suspected that the Little People really existed. Taltos has meant Lasher—killer, monster, menace. He was too shocked to speak. He merely stared at the man's face, thinking that the man looked to be no more and no less, except for the hands, than a giant human.

"For the love of God, Ash," said the dwarf, "have some guile for once." He brushed off his pants. The fire was vigorous and splendid. He seated himself in a soft, rather shapeless chair that looked extremely comfortable. His feet didn't touch the ground.

It was impossible to read his deeply wrinkled face. Was he really so cross? The folds of flesh destroyed all expression. Indeed, the voice alone carried everything with the little man, who only occasionally made bright wide eyes as he spoke. His red hair was the appropriate cliché for his impatience and his temper. He drummed his short fingers on the cloth arms of the chair.

Yuri walked to the couch and took a stiff place at the very end of it, conscious that the tall one had gone to the mantel and was looking down at the fire. Yuri did not mean to stare rudely at this creature.

"A Taltos," said Yuri. His voice sounded acceptably calm. "A Taltos. Why do you want to talk to me? Why do you want to help me? Who are you, and why have you come here?"

"You saw the other one?" the tall man asked, turning and looking at Yuri with eyes that were almost shy in their openness, but not quite. This man might have been knock-dead beautiful if it hadn't been for the hands. The knuckles looked like knots.

"No, I never saw him," said Yuri.

"But you know for certain he was dead?"

"Yes, I know that for certain," said Yuri. The giant and the dwarf. He was not going to laugh at this, but it was horribly amusing. This creature's abnormalities made him pleasing to look at. And the little man's abnormalities made him seem dangerous and wicked. And it was all an act of nature, was it? It was somewhat beyond the scope of the range of accidents in which Yuri believed.

"Did this Taltos have a mate?" asked the tall one. "I mean another Taltos, a female?"

"No, his mate was a woman named Rowan Mayfair. I told your

friend about her. She was his mother, and his lover. She is what we call a witch in the Talamasca."

"Aye," said the little man, "and what we would call a witch as well. There are many powerful witches in this tale, Ashlar. There is a brood of witches. You have to let the man tell his story."

"Ashlar, that's your full name?" asked Yuri. It had been a jolt.

For hours before he'd left New Orleans, he had listened to Aaron summarize the tale of Lasher, the demon from the glen. St. Ashlar—that name had been spoken over and over again. St. Ashlar.

"Yes," said the tall one. "But Ash is the single-syllable version, which I heartily prefer. I don't mean to be impolite, but I so prefer the simple name Ash that often I don't answer to the other." This was said firmly but with courtesy.

The dwarf laughed. "I call him by his full name to make him strong and attentive," he said.

The tall one ignored this. He warmed his hands over the fire; with fingers splayed apart, they looked diseased.

"You're in pain, aren't you?" the man said, turning away from the fire.

"Yes. Excuse me, please, that I show it. The wound's in my shoulder, in such a place that every little movement pulls it. Will you forgive me that I slouch back on this sofa, and try to remain like this, looking lazy? My mind is racing. Will you tell me who you are?"

"I've done that, have I not?" asked the tall one. "You speak. What happened to you?"

"Yuri, I told you," said the dwarf, with rather good-natured impatience, "that this is my oldest confidant and friend in the world. I told you that he knew the Talamasca. That he knows more about it than any living being. Please trust him. Tell him what he wants to know."

"I trust you," said Yuri. "But to what purpose do I tell you my business, or of my adventures? What will you do with this knowledge?"

"Help you, of course," said the tall one slowly, with a gentle nod of his head. "Samuel says the men in the Talamasca are trying to kill you. This is hard for me to accept. I have always, in my own way, loved the Order of the Talamasca. I protect myself from it, as I do from anything which would constrict me in any way. But the men of the Talamasca have seldom been my enemies . . . at least not for very long. Who tried to hurt you? Are you sure these evil people came from the Order itself?"

"No, I'm not sure," said Yuri. "This is what happened, more or less. When I was an orphan boy, the Talamasca took me in. Aaron Lightner was the man who did it. Samuel knows who this man is."

"So do I," said the tall one.

"All my adult life I've served the Order, in a traveling capacity mostly, often performing tasks which I myself don't fully understand. Apparently, unbeknownst to me, my vows rested upon a loyalty to Aaron Lightner. When he went to New Orleans to investigate a family of witches, things somehow went wrong. This family was the Mayfair family, this family of witches. I read their history in old records of the Order before these records were closed to me. It was from Rowan Mayfair that the Taltos was born."

"Who or what was the father?" asked the tall one.

"It was a man."

"A mortal man. You're certain of this?"

"Without question, but there were other considerations. This family had been haunted for many, many generations by a spirit, both evil and good. This spirit took hold of the infant inside Rowan Mayfair, took possession of it and assisted its unusual birth. The Taltos, springing up full-grown from this woman, possessed the soul of the haunting spirit complete and entire. They called this creature Lasher in the family. I've never known any other name for him. Now this creature is dead, as I've told you."

The tall man was frankly amazed. He gave a little sympathetic shake of his head. He walked to the nearby armchair and sat down, turning politely towards Yuri, and crossing his long legs and ankles very much as Yuri had done. He sat very straight, as though never ashamed or uneasy about his height.

"From two witches!" said the tall one in a whisper.

"Absolutely," said Yuri.

"You say absolutely," said the tall one. "What can this mean?"

"There is genetic evidence, an abundance of it. The Talamasca has this evidence. The witch family carries an extraordinary set of genes within its various lines. Genes of the Taltos, which under the ordinary circumstances are never switched on by nature, but which in this case—either through witchcraft or possession—did indeed do their work to make the Taltos come into the world."

The tall man smiled. It surprised Yuri, because the smile so fired the face with expression and affection and simple delight.

"You speak like all the men from the Talamasca," said the tall one. "You speak like a priest in Rome. You speak as if you weren't born in these times."

"Well, I was educated on their documents in Latin," said Yuri. "Their story of this creature, Lasher, it went back to the sixteen hundreds. I read all of it, along with the story of this family—its rise to great wealth and power, its secret doings with this spirit, Lasher. And I have of course read a hundred such files."

"Have you?"

"Not stories of the Taltos," said Yuri, "if that's what you mean. I never heard the word until I was in New Orleans—until two members of the Order were killed there, trying to free this Taltos, Lasher, from the man who killed him. But I cannot tell that tale."

"Why? I want to know who killed him."

"When I know you better, when you've matched my confessions with your own."

"What can I confess? I'm Ashlar. I'm a Taltos. It's centuries since I've seen one single other member of my own species. Oh, there have been others. I've heard tell of them, chased after them, and in some instances almost found them. Mark, I say almost. But not in centuries have I touched my own flesh and blood, as humans are so fond of saying. Never in all this time."

"You're very old, that's what you're telling me. Our lifespan is nothing compared to yours."

"Well, apparently not," said the man. "I must be old. I have this white hair now, as you see. But then how am I to know how old I am, and what my decline may be, and how long it will take in human years? When I lived in happiness among my own, I was too young to learn what I would need for this long, lonely voyage. And God did not gift me with a supernatural memory. Like an ordinary man, I remember some things with haunting clarity; others are completely erased."

"The Talamasca knows about you?" asked Yuri. "It's crucial that you tell me. The Talamasca was my vocation."

"Explain how this changed."

"As I told you, Aaron Lightner went to New Orleans. Aaron is an expert on witches. We study witches."

"Understood," said the dwarf. "Get on with it."

"Hush, Samuel, mind your manners," said the tall one softly but seriously.

"Don't be an imbecile, Ash, this gypsy is falling in love with you!"

The Taltos was shocked and outraged. The anger flared in him beautifully and fully, and then he shook his head and folded his arms as if he knew how to deal with such anger.

As for Yuri, he was again stunned. It seemed the way of the world now—outrageous shocks and revelations. He was stunned and hurt because he had in some way warmed to this being far beyond the ways in which he'd warmed to the little man, which were, in the main, more intellectual.

He looked away, humiliated. He had no time now to tell the story of his own life—how he had fallen so totally under the dominance of Aaron Lightner, and the force and power which strong men often exerted over him. He wanted to say this was not erotic. But it was erotic, insofar as anything and everything is.

The Taltos was staring coldly at the little man.

Yuri resumed his story.

"Aaron Lightner went to help the Mayfair witches in their endless battles with the spirit Lasher. Aaron Lightner never knew whence this spirit came, or what it really was. That a witch had called it up in Donnelaith in the year 1665—that was known, but not much else about it.

"After the creature was made flesh, after it had caused the deaths of too many witches for me to count—only after all this did Aaron Lightner see the creature and learn from its own lips that it was the Taltos, and that it had lived in a body before, in the time of King Henry, meeting its death in Donnelaith, the glen which it haunted until the witch called it up.

"These things are not in any Talamasca file known to me. Scarcely three weeks have passed since the creature was slaughtered. But these things may be in secret files known to someone. Once the Talamasca learnt that Lasher had been reincarnated, or whatever in the name of God we should call it, they moved in on him and sought to remove him for their own purposes. They may have coldly and deliberately taken several lives in the process. I don't know. I know that Aaron had no part in their schemes, and felt betrayed by them. That is why I'm asking you: Do they know about you? Are you part of the Talamasca knowledge, because if you are, it is highly occult knowledge."

"Yes and no," said the tall one. "You don't tell lies at all, do you?"

"Ash, try not to say strange things," grumbled the dwarf. He too had sat back, letting his short, stumpy legs stretch out perfectly straight. He had knitted his fingers on his tweed vest, and his shirt was open at the neck. A bit of light flashed in his hooded eyes.

"I was merely remarking on it, Samuel. Have some patience." The tall man sighed. "Try not to say such strange things yourself." He looked a little annoyed and then his eyes returned to Yuri.

"Let me answer your question, Yuri," he said. The way he had spoken the name was warm and casual. "Men in the Talamasca today probably know nothing of me. It would take a genius to unearth what tales of us are told in Talamasca archives, if indeed such documents still exist. I never fully understood the status or the significance of this knowledge—the Order's files, as they call them now. I read some manuscript once, centuries ago, and laughed and laughed at the words in it. But in those times all written language seemed naive and touching to me. Some of it still does."

To Yuri, this was a fascinating point. The dwarf had been right, of course; he was falling under the sway of this being, he had lost his healthy reluctance to trust, but that was what this sort of love was about, wasn't it? Divesting oneself so totally of the customary feelings of alienation and distrust that the subsequent acceptance was intellectually orgasmic.

"What sort of language doesn't make you laugh?" asked Yuri.

"Modern slang," said the tall one. "Realism in fiction, and journalism which is filled with colloquialisms. It often lacks naiveté completely. It has lost all formality, and instead abides by an intense compression. When people write now, it is sometimes like the screech of a whistle compared to the songs they used to sing."

Yuri laughed. "I think you're right," he said. "Not so the documents of the Talamasca, however."

"No. As I was explaining, they are melodic and amusing."

"But then there are documents and documents. So you don't think they know about you now."

"I'm fairly certain they don't know about me, and as you tell your tale, it becomes very clear that they cannot possibly know about me. But go on. What happened to this Taltos?"

"They tried to take him away, and they died in the process. The man who killed the Taltos killed these men from the Talamasca. Before they died, however, when these men were seeking to take the Taltos into their custody, you might say, they indicated that they had a female Taltos, that they had for centuries sought to bring the male and the female together. They indicated it was the avowed purpose of the Order. The clandestine and occult purpose, I should say. This was demoralizing to Aaron Lightner."

"I can see why."

Yuri went on.

"The Taltos, Lasher, he seemed unsurprised by all this; he seemed to have figured it out. Even in his earlier incarnation, the Talamasca had tried to take him out of Donnelaith, perhaps to mate him with the female. But he didn't trust them and he didn't go with him. He was a priest in those days. He was believed to be a saint."

"St. Ashlar," said the dwarf more soberly, the voice seeming to rumble not from the wrinkles of his face but from his heavy trunk. "St. Ashlar, who always comes again."

The tall one bowed his head slightly, his deep hazel eyes moving slowly back and forth across the carpet, almost as if he were reading the rich Oriental design. He looked up at Yuri, head bowed, so that his dark brows shadowed his eyes.

"St. Ashlar," he said in a sad voice.

"Are you this man?"

"I'm no saint, Yuri. Do you mind that I call you by name? Let's not speak of saints, if you please . . ."

"Oh, please do call me Yuri. And I will call you Ash? But the point is, are you this same individual? This one they called the saint? You speak of centuries! And we sit here in this parlor, and the fire crackles, and the waiter taps at the door now with our refreshments. You must tell me. I can't protect myself from my own brothers in the Talamasca if you don't tell me and help me to understand what's going on."

Samuel slipped off the chair and proceeded towards the alcove. "Go into the bedroom, please, Yuri. Out of sight now." He swaggered as he went past Yuri.

Yuri rose, the shoulder hurting him acutely for a moment, and he walked into the bedroom, closing the door behind him. He found himself in a shadowy stillness, with soft, loose curtains filtering the subdued morning light. He picked up the telephone; quickly he punched the direct-dial number, followed by the country code for the United States.

Then he hesitated, feeling wholly unable to tell the protective lies that he would have to tell to Mona, eager to speak to Aaron and tell him what he knew, and half afraid he would be momentarily stopped from calling anyone.

Several times on the drive down from Scotland, he had found himself at public phones, experiencing the same dilemma, when the dwarf had commanded him to get in the car now.

What to tell his little love? How much to tell Aaron in the few moments he might have to speak with him?

In haste, he punched in the area code for New Orleans, and the number of the Mayfair house on St. Charles and Amelia, and he waited, a little worried suddenly that it might be the very middle of the night in America, and then realizing suddenly that indeed it was.

Rude and terrible mistake, whatever the circumstances. Someone had answered. It was a voice he knew but could not place.

"I'm calling from England. I'm so sorry. I'm trying to reach Mona Mayfair," he said. "I hope I haven't waked the house."

"Yuri?" asked the woman.

"Yes!" he confessed without obvious surprise that this woman had recognized his voice.

"Yuri, Aaron Lightner's dead," said the woman. "This is Celia, Beatrice's cousin. Mona's cousin. Everybody's cousin. Aaron's been killed."

There was a long pause in which Yuri did nothing. He didn't think or visualize anything or rush to any conclusion. His body was caught in a cold, terrible fear—fear of the implications of these words, that he would never, never see Aaron again, that they would never speak to each other, that he and Aaron—that Aaron was forever gone.

When he tried to move his lips, he found trouble. He did some senseless and stupid little thing with his hand, pinching the telephone cord.

"I'm sorry, Yuri. We've been worried about you. Mona's been very worried. Where are you? Can you call Michael Curry? I can give you the number."

"I'm all right," Yuri answered softly. "I have that number."

"That's where Mona is now, Yuri. Up at the other house. They will want to know where you are and how you are, and how to reach you immediately."

"But Aaron . . ." he said, pleadingly, unable to say more. His voice sounded puny to him, barely escaping the burden of the tremendous emotions that even clouded his vision and his equilibrium, his entire sense of who he was. "Aaron . . ."

"He was run over, deliberately, by a man in a car. He was walking down from the Pontchartrain Hotel, where he'd just left Beatrice with Mary Jane Mayfair. They were putting Mary Jane Mayfair up at the hotel. Beatrice was just about to go into the lobby of the hotel when she heard the noise. She and Mary Jane witnessed what happened. Aaron was run over by the car several times."

"Then it *was* murder," said Yuri.

"Absolutely. They caught the man who did it. A drifter. He was hired, but he doesn't know the identity of the man who hired him. He got five thousand dollars in cash for killing Aaron. He'd been trying to do it for a week. He'd spent half the money."

Yuri wanted to put down the phone. It seemed utterly impossible to continue. He ran his tongue along his upper lip and then firmly forced himself to speak. "Celia, please tell Mona Mayfair this for me, and Michael Curry too—that I am in England, I am safe. I will soon be in touch. I am being very careful. I send my sympathy to Beatrice Mayfair. I send to all . . . my love."

"I'll tell them."

He laid down the phone. If she said something more, he didn't hear it. It was silent now. And the soft pastel colors of the bedroom lulled him for a moment. The light filled the mirror softly and beautifully. All the fragrances of the room were clean.

Alienation, a lack of trust either in happiness or in others. Rome. Aaron coming. Aaron erased from life—not from the past, but utterly from the present and from the future.

He didn't know how long he stood there.

It began to seem that he had been planted by the dressing table for a long, long time. He knew that Ash, the tall one, had come into the room, but not to detach Yuri from the telephone.

And some deep, awful grief in Yuri was touched suddenly, disastrously perhaps, by the warm, sympatic voice of this man.

"Why are you crying, Yuri?"

It was said with the purity of a child.

"Aaron Lightner's dead," said Yuri. "I never called to tell him they'd tried to kill me. I should have told him. I should have warned him—"

It was the slightly abrasive voice of Samuel that reached him from the door.

"He knew, Yuri. He knew. You told me how he warned you not to come back here, how he said they'd come for him at any time."

"Ah, but I . . ."

"Don't hold on to it with guilt, my young friend," said Ash.

Yuri felt the big, spidery hands close tenderly on his shoulders.

"Aaron . . . Aaron was my father," Yuri said in a monotone. "Aaron was my brother. Aaron was my friend." Inside him the grief and the guilt boiled and the stark, awful terror of death became unendurable. It doesn't seem possible that this man is gone, totally gone from life, but it will begin to seem more and more possible, and then real, and then absolute.

Yuri might as well have been a boy again, in his mother's village in Yugoslavia, standing by her dead body on the bed. That had been the last time he'd known such pain as this; he couldn't bear it. He clenched his teeth, fearing that in an unmanly way he would cry out or even roar.

"The Talamasca killed him," said Yuri. "Who else would have done it? Lasher—the Taltos—is dead. He didn't do it. Lay all the murders upon them. The Taltos killed the women, but he did not kill the men. The Talamasca did it."

"Was it Aaron who killed the Taltos?" asked Ash. "Was he the father?"

"No. But he did love a woman there, and now perhaps her life too has been destroyed."

He wanted to lock himself in the bathroom. He had no clear image of what he meant to do. Sit on the marble floor, perhaps, with his knees up, and weep.

But neither of these two strange individuals would hear of it. In concern and alarm, they drew him back into the living room of the suite, and seated him on the sofa, the tall one being most careful not to hurt his shoulder, the little man rushing to prepare some hot tea. And bring him cakes and cookies on a plate. A feeble meal, but a particularly enticing one.

It seemed to Yuri that the fire was burning too fast. His pulse had quickened. Indeed, he felt himself breaking out in a sweat. He took off the heavy sweater, pulling it roughly over his neck, causing intense pain in his shoulder before he realized what he was doing, and before he realized he had nothing on under this sweater and was now sitting here bare-chested, with the sweater in his hands. He sat back and hugged the sweater, uncomfortable to be so uncovered.

He heard a little sound. The little man had brought him a white shirt, still wrapped around laundry cardboard. Yuri took it, opened it, unbuttoned it, and slipped it on. It was absurdly too big for him. It must have belonged to Ash. But he rolled up the sleeves and buttoned several of the buttons and was grateful to be concealed once more. It felt comforting, like a great pajama shirt. The sweater lay on the carpet. He could see the grass in it, the twigs and bits of soil clinging to it.

"And I thought I was so noble," he said, "not calling him, not worrying him, letting the wound heal and getting back on my feet before I reported in, to confirm to him that I was well."

"Why would the Talamasca kill Aaron Lightner?" asked Ash. He had retreated to his chair and was sitting with his hands clasped between his knees. Again, he was ramrod straight and unlikely and very handsome.

Good Lord, it was as if Yuri had been knocked unconscious, and was seeing all of this again for the first time. He noticed the simple black watchband around Ash's wrist, and the gold watch itself, with digital numbers. He saw the red-haired hunchback standing at the window, which he had opened a crack now that the fire was positively roaring. He felt the ice blade of the wind cleave through the room. He saw the fire arch its back and hiss.

"Yuri, why?" asked Ash.

"I can't answer. I had hoped somehow we were mistaken, that they hadn't had such a heavy hand in all this, that they hadn't killed innocent men. That it was a fanciful lie or something, that they had the female that they had always wanted. I couldn't think of such a tawdry purpose. Oh, I don't mean to offend you—"

"—of course not."

"I mean, I had thought their aims so lofty, their whole evolution so remarkably pure—an order of scholars who record and study, but never interfere selfishly in what they observe; students of the supernatural. I think I've been a fool! They killed Aaron because he knew about all this. And that's why they must kill me. They must let the Order sink back into its routines, undisturbed by all this. They must be watching at the Motherhouse. They must be anxious to prevent me entering it at all costs. They must have the phones covered. I couldn't call there or Amsterdam or Rome if I wanted to. They'd intercept any fax that I sent. They'll never let down this guard, or stop looking for me, till I'm dead.

"Then who will there be to go after them? To tell the others? To reveal the awful secret to the brothers and sisters that this Order is evil . . . that the old maxims of the Catholic Church perhaps have always been true. What is supernatural and not of God is evil. To find the male Taltos! To bring him together with the female . . ."

He looked up. Ash's face was sad. Samuel, leaning against the closed window, appeared, for all the fleshy folds of his face, sad and concerned as well. Calm yourself, he thought, make your words count. Do not lapse into hysteria.

He went on. "You speak of centuries, Ash," he said, "the way others speak of years. Then the female within the Talamasca might have lived for centuries. This might have been the only purpose always. Out of dark times, a web spun that is so evil and so perverse that modern men and women can't even conceive of it! It's too simple, all of these stupid men and women watching out for one single being—a Taltos, a creature that can breed with its mate so fast and so successfully that its kind would quickly overtake the world. I wonder what makes them so sure of themselves, the invisible and anonymous and secretive Elders of the Order, so sure that they themselves are not being—"

He paused. It had never occurred to him. Of course. Had he ever been in a room with a sentient being who wasn't human? Now he was, and who was to say how many such species lived in our comfortable little world, walking about, passing for human while servicing their own agenda in every respect? Taltos. Vampire. The aged dwarf, with his own clock and his own grudges and stories.

How quiet they both were. Had there been an unspoken decision to let him rave?

"You know what I would like to do?" Yuri asked.

"What?" asked Ash.

"Go to the Amsterdam Motherhouse and kill them, the Elders. But that's just it, I don't think I can find them. I don't think they are in the Amsterdam Motherhouse, or that they ever have been. I don't know who or what they are. Samuel, I want to take the car now. I have to go home here in London. I have to see the brothers and the sisters."

"No," said Samuel. "They'll kill you."

"They can't all be in it. That's my last hope; we are all dupes of a few. Now, please, I want to take the car outside London to the Mother-house. I want to walk inside quickly, before anyone is the wiser, and grab hold of the brothers and sisters, and make them listen. Look, I have to do this! I have to warn them. Why, Aaron's dead!"

He stopped. He realized he'd been frightening them, these two strange friends. The little man had his arms folded again, grotesquely, because they were so short and his chest was so big. The folded flesh of his forehead had descended in a frown. Ash merely watched him, not frowning, but visibly worrying.

"What do you care, either one of you!" said Yuri suddenly. "You saved my life when I was shot in the mountains. But nobody asked you to do this. Why? What am I to you?"

A little noise came from Samuel, as if to say, This is not worth an answer. Ash answered, however, in a tender voice.

"Maybe we are gypsies, too, Yuri," he said.

Yuri didn't answer, but he did not believe in the sentiments this man was describing. He didn't believe in anything, except that Aaron was dead. He pictured Mona, his little red-haired witch. He saw her, her remarkable little face and her great veil of red hair. He saw her eyes. But he could feel nothing for her. He wished with all his heart that she were here.

"Nothing, I have nothing," he whispered.

"Yuri," said Ash. "Please mark what I tell you. The Talamasca was not founded to search for the Taltos. This you can believe on my word. And though I know nothing of the Elders of the Order in this day and age, I have known them in the past; and no, Yuri, they were not Taltos then and I cannot believe they are Taltos now. What would they be, Yuri, females of our species?"

The voice went on unhurried and tender still, but profoundly forceful.

"A female Taltos is as willful and childlike as a male," said Ash. "A female would have gone at once to this creature, Lasher. A female, living only among females, could not have been prevented from doing it. Why send mortal men to capture such a prize and such a foe? Oh, I know to you I don't seem formidable, but you might be very surprised by my tales. Take comfort: your brothers and your sisters are not dupes of the Order itself. But I believe that you have hit upon the truth in your considerations. It is not the Elders who subverted the avowed purpose of the Talamasca, so that they might capture this creature, Lasher. It was some other small coterie of members who have discovered the secrets of the old breed."

Ash stopped. It was as if the air had been emptied of music suddenly. Ash was still regarding Yuri with patient, simple eyes.

"You have to be right," said Yuri softly. "I can't bear it if you are not."

"We have it in our power to discover the truth," said Ash. "The three of us together. And frankly, though I cared for you immediately upon meeting you, and would help because you are a fellow creature, and because my heart is tender to you in general, I must help you for another reason. I can remember when there was no Talamasca. I can remember when it was one man. I can remember when its catacombs enclosed a library no bigger than this room. I can remember when it became two members, and then three, and later five, and then it was ten. I can remember all these things, and those who came together to found it, I knew them and I loved them. And of course my own secret, my own story, is hidden somewhere in their records, these records being translated into modern tongues, and stored electronically."

"What he's saying," said Samuel, harshly but slowly for all his annoyance, "is that we don't want the Talamasca to be subverted. We don't want its nature to change. The Talamasca knows too much about us for such a thing to be tolerated. It knows too much about too many things. With me, it's no matter of loyalty, really. It's a matter of wanting to be left alone."

"I do speak of loyalty," said Ash. "I speak of love and of gratitude. I speak of many things."

"Yes, I see it now," said Yuri. He could feel himself growing tired—the inevitable finish to emotional tumult, the inevitable rescue, the leaden, defeated need for sleep.

"If they knew about me," said Ash in a low voice, "this little group would come for me as surely as they came for this creature, Lasher." He made a little accepting gesture. "Human beings have done this before. Any great library of secrets is dangerous. Any cache of secrets can be stolen."

Yuri had started to cry. He didn't make a sound. The tears never spilled. His eyes filled with water. He stared at the cup of tea. He'd never drunk it, and now it was cold. He took the linen napkin, unfolded it, and wiped his eyes. It was too rough, but he didn't care. He was hungry for the sweets on the plate, but didn't want to eat them. After a death, it seemed not proper to eat them.

Ash went on: "I don't want to be the guardian angel of the Talamasca," he said. "I never wanted this. But there have been times in the past when the Order has been threatened. I will not, if I can prevent it, see the Order hurt or destroyed."

"There are many reasons, Yuri," said Samuel, "why a little band of Talamasca renegades might try to trap this Lasher. Think what a trophy he would be. They are human beings perhaps who would capture a Taltos for no earthly reason. They are not men of science or magic or religion. They are not even scholars. But they would have this rare and indescribable creature; they would have it to look upon, to talk to, to examine and to know, and to breed under their watchful eyes, of course, inevitably."

"They would have it to chop it to pieces, perhaps," said Ash. "Lamentably, they would have it to stick it with needles and see if it screamed."

"Yes, it makes such good sense," said Yuri. "A plot from outside. Renegades or outsiders. I'm tired. I need to sleep in a bed. I don't know why I said such terrible things to you both."

"I do," said the dwarf. "Your friend's dead. I wasn't there to save *him.*"

"The man who tried to kill you," Ash said, "did you kill him?"

Samuel gave the answer. "No, *I* killed him. Not on purpose, really. It was either knock him off the cliff or let him fire another shot at the gypsy. I must confess I did it rather for the hell of it, as Yuri and I hadn't yet exchanged a single word. Here was this man aiming a gun at another man. The dead man's body is in the glen. You want to find it? It's a good chance the Little People left it right where it fell."

"Ah, it was like that," said Ash.

Yuri said nothing. Vaguely he knew that he should have found this body. He should have examined it, taken its identifying papers. But that really had not been feasible, given his wound and the awesome terrain. There seemed something just about the body being lost forever in the wilderness of Donnelaith, and about the Little People letting the body rot.

The Little People.

Even as he had fallen, his eyes had been on the spectacle of the tiny men, down in the little pocket of grass far below him, dancing like many twisted modern Rumplestiltskins. The light of the torches had been the last thing he saw before he lost consciousness.

When he'd opened his eyes to see Samuel, his savior, with the gunbelt and pistol, and a face so haggard and old that it seemed a tangle of tree roots, he had thought, They've come to kill me. But I've seen them. I wish I could tell Aaron. The Little People. I've seen them . . .

"It's a group from outside the Talamasca," said Ash, waking him abruptly from the unwelcome spell, pulling him back into this little circle. "Not from within."

Taltos, thought Yuri, and now I have seen the Taltos. I am in a room with this creature who is the Taltos.

Had the honor of the Order been unblemished, had the pain in his shoulder not been reminding him every moment of the shabby violence and treachery which had engulfed his life, how momentous it would have been to see the Taltos. But then this was the price of such visions, was it not? They always carried a price, Aaron had told him once. And now he could never, never discuss this with Aaron.

Samuel spoke next, a little caustic. "How do you know it's not a group from within the Talamasca?"

He looked nothing now like he had that night, in his ragged jerkin and breeches. Sitting by the fire, he had looked like a ghastly toad as he counted his bullets and filled the empty spaces in his belt and drank his whiskey and offered it over and over to Yuri. That was the drunkest Yuri had ever been. But it was medicinal, wasn't it?

"Rumplestiltskin," Yuri had said. And the little man had said, "You can call me that if you like. I've been called worse. But my name is Samuel."

"What language are they singing in?" *When will they stop with the singing, with the drums!*

"Our language. Be quiet now. It's hard for me to count."

Now the little man was cradled comfortably by the civilized chair, and swaddled in civilized garments, staring eagerly at the miraculous willowy giant, Ash, who took his time to answer.

"Yes," said Yuri, more to snap himself out of it than anything else. "What makes you think it's a group from outside?" Forget the chill and the darkness and the drums—the infuriating pain of the bullet.

"It's too clumsy," said Ash. "The bullet from a gun. The car jumping the curb and striking Aaron Lightner. There are many easy ways to kill people so that others hardly notice at all. Scholars always know this; they have learnt from studying witches and wizards and other princes of *maleficia*. No. They would not go into the glen stalking a man as if he were game. It is not possible."

"Ash, the gun is now the weapon of the glen," said Samuel derisively. "Why shouldn't wizards use guns if Little People use them?"

"It's the toy of the glen, Samuel," said Ash calmly. "And you know it. The men of the Talamasca are not monsters who are hunted and spied upon and must retreat from the world into a wilderness and, when sighted, strike fear in men's hearts." He went on with his reasoning. "It is not from within the Elders of the Talamasca that this menace has arisen. It is the worst nuisance imaginable—some small group of people from outside, who happened upon certain information and chose to believe it. Books, computer disks. Who knows? Perhaps these secrets were even sold to them by servants. . . ."

"Then we must seem like children to them," said Yuri. "Like monks and nuns, computerizing all our records, our files, gathering old secrets into computer banks."

"Who was the witch who fathered the Taltos? Who killed him?" demanded Ash suddenly. "You told me you'd tell me if I were to tell things to you. What more can I give you? I've been more than forthcoming. Who is this witch that can father a Taltos?"

"Michael Curry is his name," said Yuri. "And they'll probably try to kill him too."

"No, that wouldn't do for them, would it?" Ash said. "On the contrary, they will strive to strike the match again. The witch Rowan . . ."

"She can no longer bear," said Yuri. "But there are others, a family of others, and there is one so powerful that even—"

Yuri's head felt heavy. He raised his right hand and pressed it to his forehead, disappointed that his hand was so warm. Leaning forward made him feel sick. Slowly he eased back, trying not to pull or flick his shoulder, and then he closed his eyes. He reached into his pants pocket and pulled out his little wallet and opened it.

He slipped out of hiding the little school picture of Mona, very vividly colored; his darling with her smile, her even white teeth, her heap of coarse and beautiful red hair. Childwitch, beloved witch, but witch without question.

Yuri wiped his eyes again, and his lips. His hand was trembling so badly that Mona's lovely face was out of focus.

He saw the long, thin fingers of Ash touch the edges of the photograph. The Taltos was standing over him, one long arm behind him, braced against the back of the sofa, while with the other hand he steadied the picture and studied it in silence.

"From the same line as the Mother?" said Ash softly.

Suddenly Yuri pulled in the photograph and crushed it flat to his chest. He pitched forward, sick again, the pain in his shoulder immediately paralyzing him.

Ash politely withdrew and went to the mantel. The fire had gone down somewhat. Ash stood with his hands on the mantel shelf. His back was very straight, his bearing almost military, his full dark hair curling against his collar, completely covering his neck. From this vantage point, Yuri could see no white in his hair, only the deep dark locks, brownish black.

"So they'll try to get her," said Ash, with his back turned still, raising his voice as needed. "Or they will try to get her or some other witch in this family."

"Yes," said Yuri. He was dazed, yet maddened. How could he have thought that he did not love her? How could she have been so distant from him so suddenly? "They'll try to get her. Oh, my God, but we've given them an advantage," he said, only just realizing it, and realizing it completely. "Good God, we have played into their hands. Computers! Records! It's just what happened with the Order!"

He stood up. The shoulder was throbbing. He didn't care. He was still holding the picture, tight, under the cover of his palm, and pressed to the shirt.

"How so, played into their hands?" asked Ash, turning, the firelight flashing up on his face so that his eyes looked almost as green as Mona's and his tie looked like a deep stain of blood.

"The genetic testing!" Yuri said. "The whole family is going through the testing, so as never to match again a witch to a witch that might make the Taltos. Don't you see? There are records being compiled, genetic, genealogical, medical. It will be in these records who is a powerful witch and who is not. Dear God, they will know whom to single out. They'll know better than the foolish Taltos! They'll have a weapon in this knowledge he never had. Oh, he tried to mate with so many of them. He killed them. Each died without giving him what he wanted—the female child. But . . ."

"May I see the picture of the young red-haired witch again?" Ash asked timidly.

"No," said Yuri. "You may not."

The blood was throbbing in his face. He felt a wetness on his shoulder. He had torn the wound. He had a fever.

"You may not," he said again, staring at Ash.

Ash said nothing.

"Please don't ask me," Yuri said. "I need you, I need you very much to help me, but don't ask me to see her face, not now."

The two looked at each other. Then Ash nodded.

"Very well," he said. "Of course, I won't ask to see it. But to love a witch that strong is very dangerous. You know this, don't you?"

Yuri didn't answer. For one moment he knew everything—that Aaron was dead, that Mona might soon come to harm, that almost all that he had ever loved or cherished had been taken from him, almost all, that only a scant hope of happiness or satisfaction or joy remained to him, and that he was too weak and tired and hurt to think anymore, that he had to lie in the bed in the next room, which he had not even dared to glance at, the first bed he had seen in all this time since the bullet hit him and nearly killed him. He knew that never, never, should he have shown Mona's picture to this being who stood looking at him with deceptive softness and seemingly sublime patience. He knew that he, Yuri, might suddenly drop where he stood.

"Come on, Yuri," said Samuel to him with gruff gentleness, coming towards him with the usual swaggering walk. The thick, gnarled hand was reaching out for his. "I want you to go to bed now, Yuri. Sleep now. We'll be here with some hot supper for you when you wake up."

He let himself be led towards the door. Yet something stopped him, caused him to resist the little man, who was as strong as any full-sized man Yuri had ever known. Yuri found himself looking back at the tall one by the mantel.

Then he went into the bedroom and, to his own surprise, fell dazed upon the bed. The little man pulled off his shoes.

"I'm sorry," said Yuri.

"It's no bother," said the little man. "Shall I cover you?"

"No, it's warm in here, and it's safe."

He heard the door close, but he didn't open his eyes. He was already sliding away from here, away from everything, and in a spike of dream reality which caught him and shocked him awake, he saw Mona sitting on the side of her bed and telling him to come. The hair between her legs was red, but darker than the hair of her head.

He opened his eyes. For a moment he was only aware of a close darkness, a disturbing absence of light that ought to be there. Then gradually he realized Ash was standing beside him, and looking down at him. In instinctive fear and revulsion, Yuri lay still, not moving, eyes fixed forward on the wool of Ash's long coat.

"I won't take the picture while you sleep," said Ash in a whisper.

"Don't worry. I came to tell you that I must go north tonight, and visit the glen. I'll come back tomorrow and must find you here when I come."

"I haven't been very clever, have I?" asked Yuri. "Showing you her picture. I was a fool."

He was still staring at the dark wool. Then, right before his face, he saw the white fingers of Ash's right hand. Slowly he turned and looked up, and the nearness of the man's large face horrified him, but he made no sound. He merely peered up into the eyes that were fixed on him with a glassy curiosity, and then looked at the voluptuous mouth.

"I think I'm going mad now," said Yuri.

"No, you are not," said Ash, "but you must begin to be clever from now on. Sleep. Don't fear me. And remain here safe with Samuel until I return."

Four

THE MORGUE was small, filthy, made of little rooms with old white tile on the walls and on the floor, and rusted drains and creaking iron tables.

Only in New Orleans, she thought, could it be like this. Only here would they let a thirteen-year-old girl step up to the body and see it and start to cry.

"Go out, Mona," she said. "Let me examine Aaron."

Her legs were shaky, her hands worse. It was like the old joke: you sit there palsied and twisting and someone says, "What do you do for a living?" and you say, "I'm a ba-ba-ba-rain surgeon!"

She steadied herself with her left hand and lifted the bloody sheet. The car had not hurt his face; it was Aaron.

This was not the place to pay him reverence, to remember his multiple kindnesses and his vain attempts to help her. One image perhaps flared brightly enough to obscure the dirt, the stench, the ignominy of the once-dignified body in a heap on the soiled table.

Aaron Lightner at the funeral of her mother; Aaron Lightner taking her arm and helping her to move through the crowd of utter strangers who were her kin, to approach her mother's coffin, Aaron knowing that that was exactly what Rowan wanted to do, and had to do—look upon the lovely rouged and perfumed body of Dierdre Mayfair.

No cosmetic had touched this man who lay here beyond distinction and in profound indifference, his white hair lustrous as it had always been, the badge of wisdom side by side with uncommon vitality. His pale eyes were unclosed, yet unmistakably dead. His mouth had relaxed perhaps into its more familiar and agreeable shape, evidence of a life lived with amazingly little bitterness, rage, or sinister humor.

She laid her hand on his forehead, and she moved his head just a little to one side and then back again. She figured the time of death at less than two hours ago.

The chest was crushed. Blood soaked the shirt and the coat. No doubt the lungs had instantly collapsed, and even before that, the heart might have been ruptured.

Gently she touched his lips, prying them apart as if she were a lover teasing him, preparing to kiss him, she thought. Her eyes were moist, and the feeling of sadness was so deep suddenly that scents of Deirdre's funeral returned, the engulfing presence of perfumed white flowers. His mouth was full of blood.

She looked at the eyes, which did not look back at her. *Know you, love you!* She bent close. Yes, he had died instantly. He had died from the heart, not the brain. She smoothed his lids closed and let her fingers rest there.

Who in this dungeon would do a proper autopsy? Look at the stains on the wall. Smell the stench from the drawers.

She lifted the sheet back farther, and then ripped it aside, clumsily or impatiently, she wasn't sure which. The right leg was crushed. Obviously the lower portion and the foot had been detached and put back into the wool trouser. The right hand had only three fingers. The other two had been severed brutally and totally. Had someone collected the fingers?

There was a grinding sound. It was the Chinese detective coming into the room, the sound of dirt under his shoe making that awful noise against the tile.

"You all right, Doctor?"

"Yes," she said. "I'm almost finished." She went round to the other side. She laid her hand on Aaron's head, and on his neck, and she stood quiet, thinking, listening, feeling.

It had been the car accident, plain and savage. If he had suffered, no image of it hovered near him now. If he had struggled not to die, that too would be unknown forever. Beatrice had seen him try to dodge the car, or so she thought. Mary Jane Mayfair had reported, "He tried to get out of the way. He just couldn't."

Finally she drew back. She had to wash her hands, but where? She went to the sink, turned on the ancient faucet, and let the water flood over her fingers. Then she turned off the faucet and she shoved her hands in the pockets of her cotton coat, and she walked past the cop and back out into the small anteroom before the drawers of unclaimed corpses.

Michael was there, cigarette in hand, collar open, looking utterly wasted by grief and the burden of comfort.

"You want to see him?" she asked. Her throat still hurt, but this was of no importance to her whatsoever. "His face is all right. Don't look at anything else."

"I don't think so," said Michael. "I never was in this position before. If you say he's dead and the car hit him and there's nothing for me to learn, I don't want to see him."

"I understand."

"The smell's making me sick. It made Mona sick."

"There was a time when I was used to it," she said.

He drew close to her, gathering the back of her neck in his large, roughened hand, and then kissing her clumsily, wholly unlike the sweet and apologetic way he had kissed her all during her weeks of silence. He shuddered all over, and she opened her lips and kissed him back, and crushed him with her arms, or at least made an attempt to do so.

"I have to get out of here," he said.

She drew back only a step, and glanced into the other room, at the bloody heap. The Chinese cop had restored the covering sheet, out of respect perhaps, or procedure.

Michael stared at the drawers lining the opposite wall. Bodies inside made the abominable smell. She looked. There was one drawer partly open, perhaps because it couldn't be closed, and she could see the evidence of two bodies inside, the brown head of one facing up, and the molding pink feet of another lying directly on top of the first. There was green mold on the face, too. But the horror was not the mold; it was the two stacked together. The unclaimed dead, as intimate in their own way as lovers.

"I can't . . ." said Michael.

"I know, come on," she said.

By the time they climbed into the car, Mona had stopped crying. She sat staring out the window, so deep in thought she forbade any talk, any distraction. Now and then she turned and threw a glance at Rowan. Rowan met the glance and felt the strength of it, and the warmth. In three weeks of listening to this child pour out her heart—a lovely load of poetry which often became simply sound to Rowan in her somnambulant state—Rowan had come to love Mona completely.

Heiress, the one who will bear the child that will carry on the legacy. Child with a womb inside her, and the passions of an experienced woman. Child who had held Michael in her arms, who in her exuberance and ignorance had feared not at all for his battered heart, or that he might die at the pinnacle of passion. He hadn't died. He'd climbed out of invalidism and readied himself for the homecoming of his wife! And now the guilt lay on Mona, far too intoxicating, confusing all the mighty doses which she had had to swallow.

No one spoke as the car moved on.

Rowan sat next to Michael, in a little heap against him, resisting the urge to sleep, to sink back, to be lost again in thoughts that flowed with all the steadiness and imperturbability of a river, thoughts like the thoughts that had gently overlaid her for weeks, thoughts through which words and deeds had broken so slowly and so gently that they had hardly reached her at all. Voices speaking to you over the muffling rush of water.

She knew what she meant to do. It was going to be another terrible, terrible blow for Michael.

They found the house alive. Guards surrounded it once again. That was no surprise to any of them. And Rowan required no explanations. No one knew who had hired the man to run down Aaron Lightner.

Celia had come and had taken Bea in hand, letting her "cry it out" in Aaron's regular guest room on the second floor. Ryan Mayfair was in attendance, the man always prepared for court or church in his suit and tie, speaking cautiously of what the family must do now.

They were all looking at Rowan, of course. She had seen these faces at her bedside. She had seem them pass before her during her long hours in the garden.

She felt uncomfortable in the dress that Mona had helped her choose, because she could not remember ever seeing it before. But it didn't matter nearly as much as food. She was ravenously hungry, and they had laid out a full Mayfair-style buffet in the dining room.

Michael filled a plate for her before the others could do it. She sat at the head of the dining table and she ate, and she watched the others moving here and there in little groups. She drank a glass of ice water greedily. They were leaving her alone, out of respect or out of helplessness. What could they say to her? For the most part, they knew very little of what had actually taken place. They would never understand her abduction, as they called it, her captivity and the assaults that had been made upon her. What good people they were. They genuinely cared, but there was nothing they could do now, except leave her alone.

Mona stood next to her. Mona bent and kissed her cheek, doing this very slowly, so that at any time, Rowan might have stopped her. Rowan didn't. On the contrary, she took Mona's wrist, pulled her close, and kissed her back, loving the soft baby feel of her skin, thinking only in passing how Michael must have enjoyed this skin, to see, to touch, to penetrate.

"I'm going upstairs to sack out," Mona said. "I'll be there if you want me."

"I do want you," she said, but she said it in a low voice so that Michael perhaps wouldn't notice it. Michael was at her right, devouring a plate of food and a can of cold beer.

"Yeah, okay," said Mona. "I'll just be lying down." There was a look of dread in her face, weariness and sadness and dread.

"We need each other now," Rowan said, speaking the words as low as she could. The child's eyes fixed on her, and they merely looked at each other.

Mona nodded, then left, without even a quick farewell to Michael.

The awkwardness of the guilty, Rowan thought.

Someone in the front room laughed suddenly. It seemed that no matter what happened, the Mayfairs always laughed. When she had been dying upstairs, and Michael had been crying by her bed, there had been people in the house laughing. She remembered thinking about it, thinking about both sounds in a detached away, without alarm, without response. Drifting. The truth is, laughter always sounds more perfect than weeping. Laughter flows in a violent riff and is effortlessly melodic. Weeping is often fought, choked, half strangled, or surrendered to with humiliation.

Michael finished off the roast beef and the rice and gravy. He took down the last of the beer. Someone came quickly to put another can by his plate, and he picked this up and drank half of it immediately.

"This is good for your heart?" she murmured. He didn't respond.

She looked at her plate. She had finished her portion as well. Downright gluttonous.

Rice and gravy. New Orleans food. It occurred to her that she ought to tell him that during all these weeks she had loved it that he had given her food with his own hands. But what was the use of saying something like that to him?

That he loved her was as much a miracle as anything that had happened to her, as anything that had happened in this house to anyone. And it had all happened in this house, she mused, when you got right down to it. She felt rooted here, connected in some way she had never felt anywhere else—not even on the *Sweet Christine*, bravely plowing through the Golden Gate. She felt the strong certainty that this was her home, would never stop being that, and staring at the plate, she remembered that day when Michael and she had walked about the house together, when they'd opened the pantry and found all this old china, this precious china, and the silver.

And yet all of this might perish, might be blown away from her and from everyone else, by a tempest of hot breath, breath from the mouth of hell. What had her new friend, Mona Mayfair, said to her only hours ago? "Rowan, it's not finished."

No, not finished. And Aaron? Had they even called the Mother-house to let his oldest friends there know what had happened to him, or was he to be buried among new friends and conjugal kindred?

The lamps burned brightly on the mantel.

It was not yet dark outside. Through the cherry laurels, she could see the sky was the legendary purple. The murals gave off their reassuring colors to the twilight in the room, and in the magnificent oaks, the oaks that could comfort you even when no human being could, the cicadas had begun to sing, and the warm spring air rolled through the room, from windows that were open everywhere around them—here, and in the parlor, and perhaps in the back to the great unused pool, windows open to the garden graveyard where the bodies lay—the bodies of her only children.

Michael drank the last of the second beer, and gave the can the usual squeeze, and then laid it down neatly, as if the big table demanded such propriety. He didn't look at her. He stared out at the laurels brushing the colonettes of the porch, brushing the glass of the upper windows. Maybe he was looking at the purple sky. Maybe he was listening to the commotion of the starlings that swooped down at this hour in great flocks to devour the cicadas. It was all death, that dance, the cicadas swarming from tree to tree, and the flocks of birds crisscrossing the evening sky, just death, just one species eating another.

"That's all it is, my dear," she had said on the day of her awakening, her nightgown covered with mud, her hands covered with mud, her bare feet in the wet mud on the side of the new grave. "That's all it is, Emaleth. A matter of survival, my daughter."

Part of her wanted to return to the graves and the garden, to the iron table beneath the tree, to the *danse macabre* of the winged creatures high above, making the bold purple night throb with incidental and gorgeous song. Part of her didn't dare. If she walked out of here and went back to that table, she might open her eyes to discover that a night had passed away, perhaps more . . . Something as wretched and ugly as the death of Aaron would catch her again unawares and say to her, "Wake, they need you. You know what you must do." Had Aaron been there himself for a split second, disembodied and merciful, whispering it in her ear? No, it had been nothing so clear or personal.

She looked at her husband. The man slouching in the chair, crushing the hapless beer can into something round and almost flat, his eyes still settled on the windows.

He was both wondrous and dreadful—indescribably attractive to her. And the awful, shameful truth was that his bitterness and suffering had made him more attractive; it had tarnished him rather marvelously. He didn't look so innocent now, so unlike the man he really was inside. No, the inside had seeped through the handsome skin and changed the texture of him all over. It had lent a slight ferocity to his face, as well as many soft and ever-shifting shadows.

Saddened colors. He had told her something once about saddened colors, in the bright newlywed time before they knew their child was a goblin. He had said that when they painted houses in the Victorian times they used "saddened" colors. This meant darkening the colors somewhat; this meant somber, muted, complex. Victorian houses all over America had been painted in that way. That's what he'd said. And he had loved all that, those brownish reds and olive greens and steel grays, but here one had to think of another word for the ashen twilight and the deep green gloom, the shades of darkness that hovered about the violet house with its bright painted shutters.

She was thinking now. Was he "saddened"? Was that what had happened to him? Or did she have to find another word for the darker yet bolder look in his eye, for the manner in which his face yielded so little now, at first glance, yet was not for a moment mean or ugly.

He looked at her, eyes shifting and striking her like lights. Snap. Blue and the smile almost there. Do it again, she thought as he looked away. Make those eyes at me. Make them large and blue and really dazzling for a moment. Was it a handicap to have such eyes?

She reached out and touched the shadowy beard on his face, on his chin. She felt it all over his neck, and then she felt his fine black hair, and all the new coarser gray hair, and she sank her fingers into the curls.

He stared forward as if he were shocked, and then very cautiously he turned his eyes, without much turning his head, and looked at her.

She withdrew her hand, rising at the same time, and he stood up with her.

There was almost a throb in his hand as he held her arm. As he moved the chair back and out of her way, she let herself brush fully against him.

Up the stairs they went quietly.

The bedroom was as it had been all this time, very serene and overly warm, perhaps, with the bed never made but only neatly turned down so that she could at any moment sink back into it.

She shut the door and bolted it. He was already taking off his coat. She opened her blouse, pulling it out of the skirt with one hand and peeling it off and dropping it to the floor.

"The operation they did," he said. "I thought perhaps . . ."

"No, I'm healed. I want to do it."

He came forward and kissed her on the cheek, turning her head as he did it. She felt the blazing roughness of the beard, the coarseness of his hands, pulling a little hard on her hair as he bent her head back. She reached out and pulled at his shirt.

"Take it off," she said.

When she unzipped the skirt, it dropped to her feet. How thin she was. But she didn't care about herself or want to see herself. She wanted to see him. He was stripped now, and hard. She reached out and caught the black curling hair on his chest, and pinched his nipples.

"Ah, that's too hard," he whispered. He drew her against him, pushing her breasts right into the hair. Her hand came up, between his legs, finding him hard and ready.

She tugged on him as she climbed up on the bed, moving across it on her knees and then falling down on the cool cotton sheet and feeling his weight come down clumsily on top of her. God, these big bones crushing her again, this swarm of hair against us, this scent of sweet flesh and vintage perfume, this scratching, pushing, divine roughness.

"Do it, do it fast," she said. "We'll go slowly the second time. Do it, fill me up," she said.

But he needed no goading words.

"Do it hard!" she whispered between her teeth.

The cock entered her, its size shocking her, hurting her, bruising her. The pain was gorgeous, exquisite, perfect. She clenched the cock as best she could, the muscles weak and aching and not under her command—her wounded body betraying her.

Didn't matter. He battered her hard, and she came, giving no cue of cries or sighs. She was thoughtless, red-faced, hands flung out, and then tightening on him with all her might, on the very pain itself, as he drove into her repeatedly and then spent in great jerking motions that seemed to lift him off her and then abandon him to fall into her arms, wet and familiar and loved, desperately loved. Michael.

He rolled off. He wouldn't be able to do it so soon again. That was to be expected. His face was wet, the hair stuck to his forehead. She lay still in the cooling air of the room, uncovered and watching the slow movement of the fan blades near the ceiling.

The movement was so slow. Perhaps it was hypnotizing her. Be quiet, she said to her body, her loins, her inner self. She half dreamed, in fear, revisiting the moments in Lasher's arms and, mercifully, found them wanting. The savage, lustful god, yes, he might have seemed that; but this had been a man, and a brutal man with an immense and loving heart. It was so divinely rough, so divinely crude, so utterly blinding and bruising and simple.

He climbed out of the bed. She was certain he would sleep, and she herself knew she couldn't do it.

But he was up and dressing himself again, dragging clean clothes from the rods in the bathroom closet. He had his back to her, and when he turned around, the light from the bathroom shone on his face.

"Why did you do it!" he said. "Why did you leave with him!" It came like a roar.

"Shhhhh!" She sat up and put her finger to her lips. "Don't bring them all. Don't make them come. Hate me if you will . . ."

"Hate you? God, how can you say that to me? Day in and day out, I've told you that I love you!" He came towards the bed, and put his hands firmly on the footboard. He glowered over her, horrifically beautiful in his rage. "How could you leave me like that!" He whispered the cry. "How!"

He came round the side, and suddenly grabbed her by her naked arms, fingers hurting her skin unbearably.

"Don't do it!" she screamed back, struggling to keep her voice low, knowing how ugly it was, how filled with panic. "Don't hit me, I warn you. That's what he did, that's what he did over and over and over again. I'll kill you if you hit me!"

She pulled loose and rolled to the side, tumbling off the bed and pushing into the bathroom, where the cold marble tile burned her naked feet.

Kill him! Goddamn it, if you don't stop yourself you will, you will, with your power you'll kill Michael!

How many times had she tried it with Lasher, spitting it at him, the puny hatred, kill him, kill him, kill him, and he had only laughed. Well, this man would die if she struck with her invisible rage. He would die as surely as the others she had killed—the filthy, appalling murders that had shaped her life, brought her to this very house, this moment.

Terror. The stillness, the quietness of the room. She turned slowly and looked through the door and she saw him standing beside the bed, merely watching her.

"I ought to be afraid of you," he said. "But I'm not. I'm only afraid of one thing. That you don't love me."

"Oh, but I do," she said. "And I always did. Always."

His shoulders sagged for a minute, just a minute, and then he turned away from her. He was so hurt, but he would never again have the vulnerable look he had had before. He would never again have the pure gentleness.

There was a chair by the window to the porch, and he appeared to find it blindly and choose it indifferently as he sat down, still turned away from her.

And I'm about to hurt you again, she thought.

She wanted to go to him, to talk to him, to hold him again. To talk the way they had that first day after she'd come to herself, and buried her only daughter—the only daughter she'd ever have—beneath the oak. She wanted to open now with the kindling excitement she'd felt then, the utter love, thoughtless and rushed and without the slightest caution.

But it seemed as beyond reach now as words had been so soon after that.

She lifted her hands and ran them back hard through her hair. Then, rather mechanically, she reached for the taps in the shower.

With the water flooding down, she could think, perhaps clearly, for the first time. The noise was sweet and the hot water was luscious.

There seemed an impossible wealth of dresses to choose from. Absolutely confounding that there were so many in the closets. Finally she found a pair of soft wool pants, old pants she'd had eons ago in San Francisco, and she put those on, and on top a loose and deceptively heavy cotton sweater.

It was plenty cool enough now for the spring night. And it felt good to be dressed again in the clothes she herself had loved. Who, she wondered, could have bought all these pretty dresses?

She brushed her hair, and closed her eyes, and thought. "You are going to lose him, and with reason, if you do not talk to him now, if you do not once again explain, if you do not struggle against your own instinctive fear of words, and go to him."

She laid down the brush. He was standing in the doorway. She'd never shut the door all this while, and when she looked up at him, the peaceful, accepting look on his face was a great relief to her. She almost cried. But that would have been ludicrously selfish.

"I love you, Michael," she said. "I could shout it from the rooftops. I never stopped loving you. It was vanity and it was hubris; and the silence, the silence was the failure of a soul to heal and strengthen itself, or maybe just the necessary retreat that the soul sought as if it were some selfish organism."

He listened intently, frowning slightly, face calm but never innocent the way it had been before. The eyes were huge and glistening but hard and shadowed with sadness.

"I don't know how I could have hurt you just now, Rowan," he said. "I really don't. I just don't."

"Michael, no . . ."

"No, let me say it. I know what happened to you. I know what he did. I know. And I don't know how I could have blamed you, been angry with you, hurt you like that, I don't know!"

"Michael, I know," she said. "Don't. Don't, or you'll make me cry."

"Rowan, I destroyed him," he said. He had dropped his voice to a whisper the way so many people did when they spoke of death. "I destroyed him and it's not enough! I . . . I . . ."

"No, don't speak anymore. Forgive me, Michael, forgive me for your sake and my sake. Forgive me." She leant forward and kissed him, took the breath out of him deliberately so it would remain wordless. And this time when he folded her into his arms, it was full of the old kindness, the old cherishing warmth, the great protective sweetness that made her feel safe, safe as it had when they'd first made love.

There must have been something more lovely than falling in his arms like this, more lovely than merely being close to him. But she couldn't think what it was now—certainly not the violence of passion. That was there, obviously, to be enjoyed again and again, but this was the thing she'd never known with any other being on earth, this!

Finally he drew back, taking her two hands together and kissing them, and then flashing her that bright boyish smile again, precisely the one she thought sure she'd never receive again, ever. And then he winked and he said, his voice breaking:

"You really do still love me, baby."

"Yes," she said. "I learned how once, apparently, and it will have to be forever. Come with me, come outside, come out under the oak. I want to be near them for a while. I don't know why. You and I, we are the only ones who know that they're there together."

They slipped down the back stairs, through the kitchen. The guard by the pool merely nodded to them. The yard was dark as they found the iron table. She flung herself at him, and he steadied her. Yes, for this little while and then you'll hate me again, she thought.

Yes, you'll despise me. She kissed his hair, his cheek, she rubbed her forehead back and forth across his sharp beard. She felt his soft responsive sighs, thick and heavy and from the chest.

You'll despise me, she thought. But who else can go after the men who killed Aaron?

Five

T HE PLANE landed in Edinburgh's airport at 11:00 p.m. Ash was dozing with his face against the window. He saw the headlamps of the cars moving steadily towards him, both black, both German— sedans that would take him and his little entourage over the narrow roads to Donnelaith. It was no longer a trek one had to make on horseback. Ash was glad of it, not because he had not loved those journeys through the dangerous mountains, but because he wanted to reach the glen itself with no delay.

Modern life has made all impatient, he thought quietly. How many times in his long life had he set out for Donnelaith, determined to visit the place of his most tragic losses and reexamine his destiny again? Sometimes it had taken him years to make his way to England and then north to the Highlands. Other times it had been a matter of months.

Now it was something accomplished in a matter of hours. And he was glad of it. For the going there had never been the difficult or the cathartic part. Rather it was the visit itself.

He stood up now as this tentative young girl, Leslie, who had flown with him from America, brought his coat and a folded blanket and a pillow as well.

"Sleepy, my dearest?" he asked her, with gentle reproach. Servants in America baffled him. They did the strangest things. He would not have been surprised if she had changed into a nightgown.

"For *you*, Mr. Ash. The drive is almost two hours. I thought you might want it."

He smiled as he walked past her. What must it be like for her, he wondered. The nocturnal trips to far-flung places? Scotland must seem like any other place to which he had at times dragged her or his other attendants. No one could guess what this meant to him.

As he stepped out onto the metal stairway, the wind caught him by surprise. It was colder here even than it had been in London. Indeed, his journey had taken him from one circle of frost to another and then another. And with childish eagerness and shallow regret, he longed for the warmth of the London Hotel. He thought of the gypsy sleeping so beautifully against the pillow, lean and dark-skinned, with a cruel mouth and jet black eyebrows and lashes that curled upwards like those of a child.

He covered his eyes with the back of his hand and hurried down the metal steps and into the car.

Why did children have such big eyelashes? Why did they lose them later on? Did they need this extra protection? And how was it with the Taltos? He could not remember anything that he had ever known, per se, to be childhood. Surely for the Taltos there was such a period.

"Lost knowledge . . ." Those words had been given to him so often; he could not remember a time when he didn't know them.

This was an agony, really, this return, this refusal to move forward without a bitter consultation with his full soul.

Soul. You have no soul, or so they've told you.

Through the dim glass he watched young Leslie slip into the passenger seat in front of him. He was relieved that he had the rear compartment entirely to himself—that two cars had been found to carry him and his little entourage northward. It would have been unendurable now to sit close to a human, to hear human chatter, to smell a robust female human, so sweet and so young.

Scotland. Smell the forests; smell the sea in the wind.

The car moved away smoothly. An experienced driver. He was thankful. He could not have been tossed and pushed from side to side clear to Donnelaith. For a moment he saw the glaring reflection of the lights behind him, the bodyguards following as they always did.

A terrible premonition gripped him. Why put himself through this ordeal? Why go to Donnelaith? Why climb the mountain and visit these shrines of his past again? He closed his eyes and saw for a second the brilliant red hair of the little witch whom Yuri loved as foolishly as a boy. He saw her hard green eyes looking back at him out of the picture, mocking her little-girl hair with its bright colored ribbon. Yuri, you are a fool.

The car gained speed.

He could not see anything through the darkly tinted glass. Lamentable. Downright maddening. In the States, his own cars had untinted windows. Privacy had never been a concern to him. But to see the world in its natural colors, that was something he needed the way he needed air and water.

Ah, but maybe he would sleep a little, and without dreams.

A voice startled him—the young woman's, coming from the overhead speaker.

"Mr. Ash, I've called the Inn; they're prepared for our arrival. Do you want to stop for anything now?"

"No, I want only to get there, Leslie. Snuggle with the blanket and the pillow. It is a long way."

He closed his eyes. But sleep didn't come to him. This was one of those journeys when he would feel every minute, and every bump in the road.

So why not think of the gypsy again—his thin, dark face, the flash of his teeth against his lip, so white and perfect, the teeth of modern men. Rich gypsy, perhaps. Rich witch, that had come plain to him in the conversation. In his mind's eye he reached for the button of her white blouse in the photograph. He pulled it open to see her breasts. He gave them pink nipples, and he touched the blue veins beneath the skin which had to be there. He sighed and let a low whistle come from his teeth and turned his head to the side.

The desire was so painful that he forced it back, let it go. Then he saw the gypsy again. He saw his long dark arm thrown up over the pillow. He smelled again the woods and the vale clinging to the gypsy. "Yuri," he whispered in his fantasy, and he turned the young man over and bent to kiss his mouth.

This too was a fiery furnace. He sat up and forward and put his elbows on his knees and his face in his hands.

"Music, Ash," he said quietly, and then, settling back once more, his head against the window, his eyes large and struggling to see through the horrid dark glass, he began to sing to himself in a wee voice, a tiny falsetto, a song no one might understand but Samuel, and even Samuel might not know for sure.

It was 2:00 a.m. when he told the driver to stop. He could not continue. Beyond the dark glass lurked all the world that he had come here to see. He could wait no longer.

"We're almost there, sir."

"I know we are. You'll find the town only a few miles ahead. You're to go there directly. Settle into the Inn and wait for me. Now call the guards in the car behind us. Tell them to follow you in. I must be alone now here."

He didn't wait for the inevitable arguments or protests.

He stepped out of the car, slamming the door before the driver could come to his assistance, and with a little goodwill wave of his hand, he walked fast over the edge of the road and into the deep, cold forest.

The wind was not strong now. The moon, snared in clouds, gave an intermittent and filmy light. He found himself enveloped by the scents of the Scotch pines, the dark cold earth beneath his feet, the brave blades of early spring grass crushed beneath his shoe, the faint scent of new flowers.

The barks of the trees felt good beneath his fingers.

For a long time he moved on and on, in the dark, sometimes stumbling, sometimes catching hold of a thick tree trunk to steady himself. He didn't stop to catch his breath. He knew this slope. He knew the stars above, even though the clouds tried to obscure them.

Indeed, the starry heavens brought him a strange, painful emotion. When at last he stopped, it was upon a high crest. His long legs ached a little, as legs should perhaps. But being in this sacred place, this place which meant more to him than any other bit of land in the world, he could remember a time when his limbs would not have ached, when he could have hurried up the hill in big, loping steps.

No matter. What was a little pain? It gave him an insight into the pain of others. And humans suffered such terrible pain. Think of the gypsy asleep in his warm bed, dreaming of his witch. And pain was pain, whether physical or mental. Not the wisest of men or women or Taltos would ever know which was worse—the pain of the heart or the pain of the flesh.

At last he turned and sought even higher ground, climbing steadily up the slope even when it seemed impossibly steep, often reaching for a grip upon branches and firm rock to help himself.

The wind came up, but not strongly. His hands and feet were cold, but it was not a coldness he couldn't endure. Indeed, coldness had always refreshed him.

And indeed, thanks to Remmick he had his fur-collared coat; thanks to himself he had his warm wool clothes; thanks to heaven, perhaps, the pain in his legs grew no worse, only a little more annoying.

The ground crumbled a little. He could have fallen here, but the trees were like tall balusters keeping him safe, letting him go on and on rapidly.

At last he turned and found the path he had known would be here, winding up between two gently rising slopes where the trees were old, untouched, perhaps spared by all intruders for centuries.

The path descended into a small vale covered with sharp stones that hurt his feet, and made him more than once lose his balance. Then up again he went, thinking the slope quite impossible except for the fact that he'd climbed it before and he knew that his will would overcome the evidence of his senses.

At last he emerged into a small clearing, eyes fixed on the distant overhanging peak. The trees were so close he could not easily find the path now, or any simple footing. He moved on, crushing the smaller shrubbery as he went. And as he turned now to his right, he saw far below, beyond a great deep crevasse, the waters of the loch shining with the pale illumination of the moon, and farther still the high, skeletal ruins of a cathedral.

His breath went out of him. He had not known they had rebuilt so much. As he fixed his eyes on the scheme below, he made out the entire cross pattern of the church, or so it seemed, and a multitude of squat tents and buildings, and a few flickering lights that were no more than pinpoints. He rested against the rock, safely nestled, peeping, as it were, on this world, without any danger of tumbling and falling down to it.

He knew what that was, to fall and to fall, to reach and cry out and be unable to stop the fall, his helpless body gaining weight and speed with every few feet of bruising terrain beneath him.

His coat was torn. His shoes were wet from the snow.

For a moment all the smells of this land engulfed him and overpowered him so that he felt an erotic pleasure moving through him, gripping his loins and sending the coarse ripples of pleasure over his entire skin.

He closed his eyes and let the soft, harmless wind stroke his face, let it chill his fingers.

It's near, it's very near. All you have to do is walk on and up, and turn there before the gray boulder you can see right now under the naked moon. In a moment the clouds may again cover the light, but it will be no less easy for you.

A distant sound touched his ears. For a moment he thought perhaps he was imagining it. But there it was, the low beat of the drums, and the thin flat whine of the pipes, somber and without any rhythm or melody he could discern, which drew from him a sudden panic and then a low, pumping anxiety. The sounds grew stronger, or rather he allowed himself to hear them more truly. The wind rose, then died away; the drums came strong from the slopes below, the pipes whining on, and again he sought to find the pattern and, finding none, ground his teeth and pressed the heel of his palm to his right ear to shut the sound off finally.

The cave. Go on. Go up and go into it. Turn your back on the drums. What are the drums to you? If they knew you were here, would they play a true song to draw you in? Are the songs even known to them anymore?

He pushed up and on, and coming round the boulder, he felt the cold surface of the rock with both hands. Twenty feet ahead, perhaps more, lay the mouth of the cave, overgrown, concealed perhaps from any other climber. But he knew the random formations of stone above it. He walked higher, with one steep, heavy step after another. The wind whistled here among the pines. He pushed at the heavy overgrowth, letting the small branches scratch at his hands and face. He didn't care. At last he stepped into the blackness itself. And slumped, breathing heavily against the wall, and closing his eyes again.

No sound came to him from the depths. Only the wind sang as before, mercifully obscuring the distant drums if, indeed, they still made their awful ugly mayhem.

"I am here," he whispered. And the silence leapt back from him, curling perhaps into the very depths of the cave. Yet nothing gave an answer. Dare he say her name?

He took a timid step and then another. He moved on, with both hands upon the close walls, his hair brushing the roof overhead, until the passage broadened and the very echo of his footfalls told him that the roof was rising above him to a new height. He could see nothing.

For one moment fear touched him. Perhaps he had been walking with his eyes closed; he didn't know. Perhaps he had been letting his hands and ears guide him. And now, as he opened his eyes, as he sought to draw the light into them, there was only the blackness. He might have fallen, he was so afraid. A deep sense told him he was not alone. But he refused to run, refused to scramble out like some frightened bird, awkward, humiliated, perhaps even injuring himself in his haste.

He held fast. The darkness had no variation in it. The soft sound of his breath seemed to move out forever and ever.

"I'm here," he whispered. "I've come again." The words drifted away from him into nothingness. "Oh, please, once more, for mercy's sake . . ." he whispered.

Silence answered him.

Even in this cold, he was sweating. He felt sweat on his back under his shirt, and around his waist, beneath the leather belt that tightened around his wool pants. He felt the wetness like something greasy and filthy on his forehead.

"Why have I come?" he asked, and this time his voice was small and distant. Then he raised it as loud as he could. "In the hope that you would take my hand again, here, as you did before, and give me solace!" The swollen words, dying away, left him shaken.

What collected in this place was no tender apparition, but the memories of the glen which would never leave him. The battle, the smoke. He heard the cries! He heard her voice again from the very flames:

". . . cursed, Ashlar!" The heat and the anger struck his soul as it had struck his eardrums. He felt for a moment the old terror, and the old conviction.

". . . may the world around you crumble before your suffering is ended."

Silence.

He had to go back, he had to find the closer passage now. He would fall if he remained here, unable to see, unable to do anything but remember. In a panic, he pivoted and rushed forward, until he did feel the stone walls, harsh and closing in on him.

When at last he saw the stars, he breathed a sigh so deep that the tears threatened to come. He stood still, his hand over his heart, and the sound of the drums rose, perhaps because the wind had again died away, and there was nothing to prevent it from coming closer. A cadence had begun, quick and playful and then slow again, like the drums that beat for an execution.

"No, get away from me!" he whispered. He had to escape from this place. Somehow his fame and fortune had to assist him now to escape. He couldn't be stranded on this high peak, faced with the horror of the drums, with the pipes that now played a distinct and menacing melody. How could he have been so foolish as to come? And the cave lived and breathed just over his shoulder.

Help me. Where were those who obeyed his every command? He had been a fool to separate himself from them and climb to this terrible place alone. His pain was so sharp that he made a soft sound, like a child crying.

Down he went. He didn't care if he stumbled, or if his coat was torn, or if his hair was here and there caught. He ripped it loose and went on, the rocks beneath his feet hurting him but not stopping him.

The drums were louder. He must pass close by. He must hear these pipes and their nasal pulsing song, both ugly and irresistible. No, don't listen. Stop your ears. On down he climbed, and even though he had clamped his hands to his head, he could hear the pipes, and the grim old cadence, slow and monotonous and pounding suddenly as if it came from inside his brain, as if were emanating from his very bones, as if he were in the midst of it.

He broke into a run, falling once and ripping the fine cloth of his pants, and pitching forward another time to hurt his hands on the rocks and the torn bushes. But on he went, until quite suddenly the drums surrounded him. The pipes surrounded him. The piercing song ensnared him as if in loops of rope, and he turned round and round, unable to escape, and opening his eyes, saw through the thick forest the light of torches.

They did not know he was there. They had not caught his scent or heard him. Perhaps the wind had been on his side, and was with him now. He held to the trunks of two small pines as if they were the bars of a prison, and he looked down into the dark little space in which they played, dancing in their small and ludicrous circle. How clumsy they were. How horrid to him.

The drums and the pipes were a hideous din. He couldn't move. He could only watch as they jumped and pivoted and rocked back and forth, and one small creature, with long, shaggy gray hair, moved into the circle and threw up his small, misshapen arms, calling out above the howl of the music in the ancient tongue:

"O gods, have mercy. Have mercy upon your lost children."

Look, see, he told himself, though the music would not let him articulate these syllables even inside his imagination. Look, see, do not be lost in the song. See what rags they wear now, see the gunbelts over their shoulders. See the pistols in their hands, and now, now they draw their guns to shoot, and tiny flames burst from the barrels! The night cracks with guns! The torches nearly die in the wind, then bloom again like ghastly flowers.

He could smell burning flesh, but this was not real; it was only memory. He could hear screams.

"Curse you, Ashlar!"

And hymns, oh yes, hymns, and anthems in the new tongue, the Romans' tongue, and that stench, that stench of flesh consumed!

A loud sharp cry ripped through the din; the music came to a halt. Only one drum sounded perhaps two more dull notes.

He realized it had been his cry, and that they had heard him. Run, but why run? For what? Where? You don't need to run any longer. You are not of this place anymore! No one can make you be of it.

He watched in cold silence, his heart racing, as the little circle of men grew together, torches blazing very close to one another, and the small mob moved slowly towards him.

"Taltos!" They had caught his scent! The group scattered with wild cries, and then drew close to make one small body again.

"Taltos!" cried a rough voice. The torches moved closer and closer.

Now he could see their faces distinctly as they ranged about him, peering up, holding the torches high, the flames making ugly shadows on their eyes and their cheeks and their little mouths. And the smell, the smell of the burning flesh, it came from their torches!

"God, what have you done!" he hissed, making his two hands into fists. "Have you dipped them in the fat of an unbaptized child?"

There came a shriek of wild laughter, and then another, and finally a whole crackling wall of noise going up around him to enclose him.

He turned round and round.

"Despicable!" he hissed again, so angry that he cared nothing for his own dignity, or the inevitable distortions of his face.

"Taltos," said one who drew near. "Taltos."

Look at them, see what they are. He held his fists even tighter, prepared to fend them off, to beat them, and lift them and hurl them to right and left, if needs be.

"Aye, Aiken Drumm!" he cried, recognizing the old man, the gray beard dripping to the earth like soiled moss. "And Robin and Rogart, I see you."

"Aye, Ashlar!"

"Yes, and Fyne and Urgart; I see you, Rannoch!" And only now did he realize it. There were no women at all left among them! All the faces staring back at him were those of men, and men he'd known always, and there were no hags, no hags screaming with their arms outstretched. There were no more women among them!

He began to laugh. Was this absolutely true? Yes, it was! He walked forward, reaching out, and forcing them backwards. Urgart swung the torch near him, to hurt him or better illuminate him.

"Aaaahhh, Urgart!" he cried, and reached out, ignoring the flame, as if to grab the little man's throat and lift him.

With guttural cries they scattered, wild, in the darkness. Men, only men. Men, and no more than fourteen now at most. Only men. Oh, why in hell hadn't Samuel told him?

He sank down, slowly, to his knees. He laughed. And he let himself keel over and land upon the forest floor, so that he could see straight up through the lacy branches of the pines, the stars spread out gloriously above the fleece of the clouds, and the moon sailing gently northward.

But he should have known. He should have calculated. He should have known when last he'd come, and the women had been old and diseased, and thrown stones at him and rushed up to scream in his ears. He had smelled death all around him. He smelled it now, but it was not the blood smell of women. It was the dry, acid smell of men.

He turned over and let his face rest right against the earth. His eyes closed again. He could hear them scurrying around him.

"Where is Samuel?" one of them asked.

"Tell Samuel to come back."

"Why are you here? Are you free of the curse?"

"Don't speak to me of the curse!" he cried out. He sat up, the spell broken. "Don't speak to me, you filth." And this time he did catch hold, not of a little man, but of his torch, and holding the flaming brand close, he did catch the unmistakable smell of human fat burning. He threw it away in disgust.

"Damn you to hell, you cursed plague!" he cried.

One of them pinched his leg. A stone cut his cheek, but not deeply. Sticks were hurled at him.

"Where is Samuel?"

"Did Samuel send you here?"

And then the loud cackle of Aiken Drumm, riding over all. "We had a tasty gypsy for our supper, we did, till Samuel took him to Ashlar!"

"Where's our gypsy?" screamed Urgart.

Laughter. Shouts and cries of derision; guffaws and curses now. "May the devil take you home piece by piece!" cried Urgart. The drums had begun again. They were beating them with their fists, and a wild series of notes burst from the pipes.

"And you, all of you into hell," cried Ash. "Why don't I send you now?"

He turned and ran again, not sure at first of his direction. But the ascent had been steady and that was his best guide, and in the crunching of his feet, and in the crackling of the brush, and in the air rushing past him, he was safe from their drums, their pipes, their jeers.

Very soon soon he could no longer hear their music or their voices. Finally he knew he was alone.

PANTING, chest hurting him, legs aching and feet sore, he walked slowly until, after a very long time, he came to the road, and stepped out upon the asphalt as if from a dream, and stood again in the world he knew, empty and cold and silent as it was. Stars filled every quadrant of the heavens. The moon drew her veil and then lowered it again, and the soft breeze made the pines shiver ever so slightly, and the wind swept down as if urging him onward.

When he reached the Inn, Leslie, his little assistant, was waiting up for him. With a small cry of shock, she greeted him and quickly took the torn coat from him. She held his hand as they climbed the stairs.

"Oh, so warm," he said, "so very warm."

"Yes, sir, and the milk." There stood the tall glass by the bed. He drank it down. She was loosening the buttons of his shirt.

"Thank you, my dear, my little dear," he said.

"Sleep, Mr. Ash," she said.

He fell heavily on the bed, and felt the big feather comforter come down upon him, the pillow plumping beneath his cheek, the entire bed sweet and soft as it caught him and turned him in the first circle of sleep and drew him downward.

The glen, my glen, the loch, my loch, my land.

Betrayer of your own people.

IN THE morning he ate a quick breakfast in his room, as his staff prepared for an immediate return. No, he would not go down to see the Cathedral this time, he said. And yes, he had read the articles in the papers. St. Ashlar, yes, he had heard that tale, too. And the young Leslie was so puzzled.

"You mean, sir, that's not why we came here, to see the shrine of the saint?"

He only shrugged. "We'll be back someday, my dear."

Another time perhaps they would take that little walk.

By noon he had landed in London.

SAMUEL was waiting for him beside the car. He was cleanly attired in his tweed suit, with a fresh, stiff white shirt and tie, and looked the diminutive gentleman. Even his red hair was combed decently, and his face had the respectable look of an English bulldog.

"You left the gypsy alone?"

"He left while I slept," Samuel confessed. "I didn't hear him go out. He's gotten clean away. He left no message."

Ash thought for a long moment. "Probably just as well," he said. "Why didn't you tell me that the women were gone?"

"Fool. I wouldn't have let you go if there had been any women. You should have known. You don't think. You don't count the years. You don't use reason. You play with your toys and your money and all your fine things, and you forget. You forget and that's why you're happy."

The car carried them away from the airport and towards the city.

"Will you go home to your playground in the sky?" Samuel asked.

"No. You know I won't. I have to find the gypsy," he said. "I have to discover the secret in the Talamasca."

"And the witch?"

"Yes." Ash smiled and turned to Samuel. "I have to find the witch, too, perhaps. At least to touch her red hair, to kiss her white skin, to drink the scent of her."

"And—?"

"How will I know, little man?"

"Oh, you know. You know you do."

"Then let me in peace. For if it's to be, my days are finally numbered."

Six

I T WAS eight o'clock when Mona opened her eyes. She heard the clock strike the hour, slowly, in deep, rich tones. But it was another sound that had awakened her, the sharp ring of a phone. It must have been coming from the library, she reasoned, and it was too far away from her and had been ringing far too long for her to answer it. She turned over, nestling into the big velvet couch with its many loose pillows, and stared out the windows into the garden, which was flooded with the morning sun.

The sun was coming in the windows, actually, and making the floor amber and beautiful to look at right before the side porch.

The phone had stopped. Surely one of the new staff around here had answered it—Cullen, the new driver, or Yancy, the young boy about the house who was always up, they said, by 6:00 a.m. Or maybe even old Eugenia, who stared so solemnly at Mona now, every time their paths crossed.

Mona had fallen asleep here last night, in her new silk dress, right on the very couch of sin where she and Michael had done it together, and though she had tried her best to dream of Yuri—Yuri, who had called, leaving a message with Celia that indeed he was all right, and he would be in touch very soon with all of them—she had found herself thinking about Michael, thinking about those three tumbles, and how they'd been, very forbidden and perhaps the best erotic fling she'd scored so far.

It was not that Yuri had not been marvelous, the lover of her dreams. But the two had been so careful with each other; it had been lovemaking, yes, but in the safest way imaginable. And it had left Mona wishing that she had been more forthcoming on that last night about her usual rampant desires.

Rampant. She really loved that word. It suited her. "You are running rampant." That was the kind of thing Celia or Lily would say to her. And she would say, "I treasure the compliment, but I do get the point."

God, if only she'd talked to Yuri herself. Celia had told him to call First Street. Why hadn't he done it? She'd never know.

Even Uncle Ryan had been irritated. "We need to talk to this man. We need to talk him about Aaron."

And that was the really sad part, that it was Celia who'd told Yuri, and maybe nobody else in the world knew what Aaron had meant to Yuri, except Mona, in whom he'd confided, preferring to talk than to make love on their one and only stolen night. Where was he now? How was he? In those few hours of passionate exchange, he'd proven intensely emotional, black eyes glittering as he'd told her in stripped-down language—the very beautiful English of those for whom it is a second tongue—the key events of his tragic but amazingly successful life.

"You just can't tell a gypsy something like that, that his oldest friend's been run over by some maniac."

Then it hit her. The phone had been ringing. Perhaps that had been Yuri, and no one in this place could find her. No one had seen her come in here last night and collapse on the couch.

Of course, she'd been utterly captivated by Rowan, and had been since the first moment yesterday afternoon when Rowan had climbed to her feet and begun to speak. Why had Rowan asked her to stay here? What did Rowan have to say to her, to her alone, and in private? What was really on Rowan's mind?

Rowan was OK, that was certain. All afternoon long and into the evening, Mona had watched her gain strength.

Rowan had showed no signs of lapsing back into the silence that had imprisoned her for three weeks. On the contrary, she had taken easy command of the house, coming down alone late last night, after Michael had gone to sleep, to comfort Beatrice and persuade her to go up to bed in Aaron's old room. Beatrice had been leery of subjecting herself to "Aaron's things," only to confess finally that curling up in his bed, here in the guest bedroom, was exactly what she wanted to do.

"She'll smell the scent of Aaron all around her," Rowan had said to Ryan, almost absently, "and she'll feel safe."

That wasn't a normal comment, Mona had thought, but surely that was the trick of seeking your mate's bed after a death, and people had talked about that cure for grief being very good. Ryan had been so concerned about Bea, so concerned for everyone. But in Rowan's presence he had had the air of a general, all seriousness and capability, in the presence of the Chief of Staff.

Rowan had taken Ryan into the library, and for two hours, the door open for anyone who cared to stand in it or listen at it, they'd discussed everything from the plans for Mayfair Medical to various details about the house. Rowan wanted to see Michael's medical records. Yes, he seemed as sound now as he had been the day she met him. But she needed the records, and Michael, not wanting to argue, had referred her to Ryan.

"But what about your own recovery? They want you to go for tests, you know," Ryan had been saying as Mona came in for a final good-night.

Yuri had left his message at Amelia Street just before midnight, and Mona had experienced enough hate, love, grief, passion, regret, longing, and excruciating suspense to finally wear her out.

"I don't have time to take these tests," Rowan had been saying. "There are much more important things. For instance, what was found in Houston when you opened the room where Lasher had been keeping me?"

At that point Rowan had stopped because she'd seen Mona.

She'd risen to her feet as if she were greeting some important adult. Her eyes were brilliant now, and not so much cold anymore as serious, a real important distinction.

"I don't mean to disturb you," Mona had said. "I don't want to go home to Amelia," she'd said sleepily. "I was wondering if I could stay here—"

"I wish you would stay," said Rowan without hesitation. "I've kept you waiting for hours."

"Yes and no," said Mona, who would rather have been here than home.

"It's unforgivable," said Rowan. "Can we talk in the morning?"

"Yeah, sure," Mona had said, with an exhausted shrug. She's talking to me like I'm a grown woman, thought Mona, which is more than anybody else around here ever does.

"You *are* a woman, Mona Mayfair," Rowan had said, with a sudden, deeply personal smile. She'd immediately sat down again and resumed her conversation with Ryan.

"There should have been papers there, in my room in Houston, reams of scribbled writing. This was his writing, genealogies he had made before his memory deteriorated . . ."

Boy, Mona had thought, stepping away about as slowly as she

could—she's talking to Ryan of all people about Lasher, and Ryan still can't say that name, and now Ryan has to deal with hard evidence of what he still won't accept. Papers, genealogies, things written by the monster who killed his wife, Gifford.

But what Mona had realized in a flash was that she wasn't necessarily going to be shut out of all this. Rowan had just spoken to her again as if she were important. Everything was changed. And if Mona asked Rowan tomorrow or the day after what those papers were—Lasher's scribblings—Rowan might even tell her.

Incredible to have seen Rowan's smile, to have seen the mask of cold power broken, to have seen the gray eyes crinkle and glisten for an instant, to have heard the deep chocolate voice take on that extra little warmth that a smile can give it—amazing.

Mona had finally hurried out of sight. Quit while you're ahead. You're too sleepy to be eavesdropping, anyway.

The last thing she'd heard was Ryan saying in a strained voice that everything from Houston had been examined and cataloged.

Mona could still remember when all of those things had reached Mayfair and Mayfair. She could still remember that scent of him that came from the boxes. She could still—occasionally—catch that scent in the living room, but it was almost gone now.

She had flopped on the living room couch, too tired to think about it all just now.

All the others had left by that time. Lily was sleeping upstairs near Beatrice. Michael's Aunt Vivian had moved back to her own apartment on St. Charles Avenue.

The living room had been empty, the breeze floating in through the windows to the side porch. A guard had been walking back and forth out there, so Mona had figured, I don't have to close those windows, and facedown on the couch she had crashed, thinking Yuri, then Michael, and pushing her face into the velvet and going sound asleep.

They said when you grew older you couldn't sleep that way. Well, Mona was ready for it. That sort of blotto sleep always made her feel cheated, as if she'd checked out on the universe for a span of time that she herself could not control.

But at four o'clock she'd awakened, unsure of why.

The floor-length windows had been open still, and the guard was out there smoking a cigarette.

Sleepily she'd listened to the sounds of the night, the birds crying in the dark trees, the distant roar of a train along the waterfront, the sound of water splashing as in a fountain or a pool.

She must have listened for half an hour before the sound of the water began to prey on her. There was no fountain. Someone was swimming in the pool.

Half expecting to see some delicious ghost—poor Stella, for instance, or God only knew what other apparition—Mona had slipped out in her bare feet and crossed the lawn. The guard was nowhere in sight now, but that didn't mean much on a property of this size.

Someone had been swimming steadily back and forth across the pool.

Through the gardenia bushes, Mona had seen that it was Rowan, naked, and moving with incredible speed through lap after lap. Rowan took her breaths regularly, head to the side, the way professional swimmers do it, or the way that athletic doctors do it, who want to work the body and condition it, and maybe even heal it and bring it back into prime form.

No time to disturb her, Mona had thought, still sleepy, longing for the couch again, in fact, so sluggish she might have fallen down on the cool grass. Something about the scene had disturbed her, however; maybe that Rowan was nude, or that she swam so rapidly and so steadily; or maybe just that the guard was around and might be a peeping Tom in the bushes right now, which Mona didn't like.

Whatever, Rowan had known all about the guards on the property. She'd spent an hour with Ryan on that subject alone.

Mona had gone back to sleep.

Now, as she woke, it was Rowan she thought of, even before invoking the face of Yuri, or feeling routinely and religiously guilty about Michael, or at once reminding herself, rather like giving her own arm a cruel pinch, that Gifford and her mother were both dead.

She stared at the sunlight bathing the floor and the gold damask chair nearest the window. Maybe that was what this was all about. The lights had gone dim for Mona when Alicia and Gifford died, there was no doubt of it. And now, just because this woman was interested in her, this mysterious woman who meant so much to her for countless reasons, the lights were bright again.

Aaron's death was terrible, but she could handle it. In fact, what she felt more than anything else was the same selfish excitement she'd known yesterday at Rowan's first expression of interest, at her first confidential and respectful glance.

Probably wants to ask me if I want to go to boarding school, Mona thought. High heels lying there. She couldn't put those on again. But it was nice to walk on the bare boards at First Street. They were always polished now, with the new staff. Yancy, the houseman, buffed them for hours. Even old Eugenia had been working more and grumbling less.

Mona rose, straightened out the silk dress which was perhaps ruined now, she wasn't really sure. She walked over to the garden window and let the sun flood over her, warm and fresh, the air full of humidity and sweetness from the garden—all the things she usually took for granted, but which at First Street seemed doubly wonderful, and worth a moment's meditation before rushing headlong into the day.

Protein, complex carbos, vitamin C. She was famished. Last night there had been the usual groaning sideboard, with all the family coming to put their arms around Beatrice, but Mona had forgotten to eat.

"No wonder you woke up in the night, you idiot." When she failed to eat, she invariably had a headache. Now she thought again, suddenly, of Rowan swimming alone, and the thought disturbed her again—the nudity, the strange disregard for the hour and the presence of the guards. Hell, you idiot, she's from California. They do stuff like that out there night and day.

She stretched, spread her legs apart, touched her toes with her hands, and then leaned backwards, shaking her hair from side to side till it felt loose and cool again, and then she walked out of the room and back the long corridor, through the dining room and into the kitchen.

Eggs, orange juice, Michael's concoction. Maybe there was a goodly supply.

The smell of fresh coffee surprised her. Immediately she took a black china mug from the cupboard and lifted the pot. Very black, espresso, Michael's kind of coffee, the kind he'd loved in San Francisco. But she realized this wasn't what she wanted at all. She craved something cool and good. Orange juice. Michael always had bottles of it, mixed and ready, in the refrigerator. She filled the cup with orange juice, and carefully capped the jug to keep all the vitamins from dying in the air.

Suddenly she realized she wasn't alone.

Rowan was sitting at the kitchen table, watching her. Rowan was smoking a cigarette which she tapped now above a fine china saucer with flowers along the edge. She wore a black silk suit and pearl earrings, and there was a little string of pearls around her neck, too. It was one of those suits with a long curvaceous jacket, double-breasted and fully buttoned, with no blouse or shirt beneath it, only bare flesh to a discreet cleft.

"I didn't see you," Mona confessed.

Rowan nodded. "Do you know who bought these clothes for me?"

The voice was as chocolaty and smooth as it had been last night, after all the soreness had gone away.

"Probably the same person who bought this dress for me," said Mona. "Beatrice. My closets are bulging with stuff from Beatrice. And it's all silk."

"So are my closets," said Rowan, and there came again that bright smile.

Rowan's hair was brushed back from her face, but otherwise natural, curling loosely just above her collar; her eyelashes looked very dark and distinct, and she wore a pale violet-pink lipstick that carefully outlined a rather beautifully shaped mouth.

"You're really OK, aren't you?" asked Mona.

"Sit down here, will you?" said Rowan. She gestured to the chair at the other end of the table.

Mona obeyed.

An expensive fragrance emanated from Rowan, rather like citrus and rain.

The black silk suit was really terrific; in the days before the wedding, Rowan had never been seen in anything so deliberately sensual. Bea had a way of sneaking into people's closets and checking their sizes, not just by label but with a tape measure, and then dressing them up the way that she, Beatrice, thought they ought to look.

Well, with Rowan she'd done well.

And I've destroyed this blue dress, thought Mona. Just not ready for this kind of thing. Or those high heels she'd kicked off on the living room floor.

Rowan lowered her head as she crushed out her cigarette. A deep forward curl of ash-blond hair fell into the hollow of her cheek. Her face looked lean and awesomely dramatic. It was as if sickness and sorrow had given her the very gauntness for which starlets and models starve themselves to death.

For this sort of beauty, Mona was no contender. It was red hair and curves with her, and always would be. If you didn't like it, you wouldn't like Mona.

Rowan gave a soft laugh.

"How long have you been doing it?" asked Mona, taking a deep gulp of her coffee. It had just reached the right temperature. Delicious. In two minutes it would be too cold to drink. "Reading my mind, I mean. It's not consistent, is it?"

Rowan was caught off guard, but seemed faintly amused. "No, it's not consistent at all. I'd say it happens in flashes when you're sort of preoccupied, kind of slipping into your own reflections. It's like you suddenly strike a match."

"Yeah, I like that. I know what you're saying." Mona took a deep swallow of the orange juice, thinking how good it was, and how cold. For a moment her head hurt from the cold. She tried not to stare worshipfully at Rowan. This was like having a crush on a teacher, something that Mona had never known.

"When you look at me," said Rowan, "I can't read anything. Maybe it's your green eyes blinding me. Don't forget about them when you're making your tally. Perfect skin, red hair to die for, long and outrageously thick, and enormous green eyes. Then there's the mouth, and the body. No, I think your view of yourself is slightly blurred right now. Perhaps it's only that you're more interested in other things—the legacy, what happened to Aaron, when will Yuri come back?"

Clever words came to Mona's mind and faded away instantly. She had never in her life lingered before a mirror more than necessary. She had not looked in one this morning at all.

"Look, I don't have much time," Rowan said. She clasped her hands on the table. "I need to talk to you straight."

"Yes, do it," said Mona. "Please."

"I understand completely about your being the heiress. There is no malice between you and me. You're the finest conceivable choice. I knew this myself in my own instinctive fashion as soon as I came to grasp what had been done. But Ryan cleared up the matter completely. The tests and the profile are complete. You are the gifted daughter. You have the intelligence, the stability, the toughness. You have the perfect health. Oh, the extra chromosomes are there, all right, but they've been there in Mayfair women and men for centuries. There's no reason to expect that anything like what happened on Christmas will ever happen again."

"Yeah, that's what I figure," said Mona. "Besides, I don't have to marry anyone with the extra string, do I? I'm not in love with a member of the family. Oh, I know that's bound to change, you're thinking, but I mean at present there isn't any kind of childhood-sweetheart syndrome with someone loaded with deadly genes."

Rowan thought about this and then she nodded. She looked down into her coffee cup, then lifted it and took the last swallow and set the cup a little to the side.

"I don't hold any malice against you for what happened with Michael. You must understand that too."

"It's hard to believe. Because I think what I did was so wrong."

"Thoughtless perhaps, but not wrong. Besides, I think I understand just what happened. Michael doesn't talk about it. I'm not referring to the seduction anyway. I'm talking about the effect."

"If I did cure him, then I won't go to hell after all," said Mona. She pressed her lips together in a sad smile. There was more than a trace of guilt and self-loathing in her voice and face, and she knew it. But she was so relieved now, she couldn't put that part into words.

"You cured him, and perhaps you were meant to do this. Someday maybe we can talk together about the dreams you had, and the Victrola that materialized in the living room."

"Then Michael told you."

"No, you told me. All the times you thought about it out there, remembering the waltz from *La Traviata*, and the ghost of Julien telling you to do it. But this isn't important to me. It's only important that you not worry about my hating you anymore. You have to be strong to be the heiress, especially the way things are now. You can't be worried about the wrong things."

"Yes, you're right. You really don't hold it against me. I know you don't."

"You could have known sooner," said Rowan. "You're stronger than I am, you know. Reading people's thoughts and emotions, it's almost a trick. I always hated it when I was a child. It frightened me. It frightens lots of gifted children. But later on, I learned to use it in a subtle, almost subconscious way. Wait a beat after someone speaks to you, especially if the words are confusing. Wait a beat and you'll know what the person feels."

"You're right, it's like that, I've tried it."

"It gets better and stronger. I would think that knowing what you know—about everything—it would be easier for you. I was supposed to be disgustingly normal, an honors student with a passion for science, growing up with all the luxuries of a well-to-do only child. You know what you are."

She paused. She drew a cigarette out of the pack lying on the table. "You don't mind, do you?" she asked.

"No, not at all," said Mona. "I like the smell of cigarettes, always have."

But she stopped. She slipped the cigarette back in the pack. She laid the lighter beside it.

Then she looked at Mona, and her face seemed incidentally hard suddenly, as though she'd fallen deep in thought and forgotten to conceal her strong inner self.

The look was so cold and so quietly fierce that it made her seem sexless to Mona. It might be a man looking at her, this person with the gray eyes and the dark straight eyebrows and the soft blond hair. It might have been an angel. Surely, it was a beautiful woman. Mona was far too intrigued and excited by all this to let her eyes be forced away.

Almost at once the expression did soften, deliberately perhaps.

"I'm going to Europe," said Rowan. "I'm leaving in a little while."

"Why? Where are you going?" demanded Mona. "Does Michael know this?"

"No," she said. "And when he finds out, he'll be hurt again."

"Rowan, you can't do that to him, wait a second. Why are you going?"

"Because I have to. I'm the only one who can figure out this little mystery about the Talamasca. I'm the only one who can find out why Aaron died like he did."

"But Michael, you've got to take Michael with you, you've got to let him help. You leave him again, Rowan, and it's going to take more than a nubile thirteen-year-old to save his ego and whatever manhood he's got left."

Rowan listened to this, thoughtfully.

Mona instantly regretted what she'd said, then instantly thought she hadn't said it strongly enough.

"It's going to hurt," said Rowan.

"Oh, you're kidding yourself," said Mona. "Maybe he won't be waiting around here when you get back."

"Look, what would you do if you were me?" Rowan asked.

It took a second for this question to sink in. Mona took another big drink of the orange juice and then pushed the glass to the side. "You're really asking me?"

"There's no one I'd rather ask."

"Take him with you to Europe. Why not? What's he staying here for?"

"There are things," she said. "He's the only one who understands the kind of danger directed against the family. And there's the question of his own safety, but then I don't know just how critical that is."

"His safety? If the Talamasca guys want to hit him, they know where to find him if he just hangs around this house. Besides, Rowan, what about your own safety? You know more about all this than anyone except Michael. Don't you need him with you? You're really prepared to go over there alone?"

"I wouldn't be alone, I'd be with Yuri."

"Yuri?"

"He called again this morning, only a little while ago."

"Why didn't you tell me?"

"I'm telling you now," Rowan said coolly. "He had only a few minutes. He was in a pay booth in London. I persuaded him to meet me at Gatwick. I have only a few hours before I leave."

"You should have called me, Rowan, you should have . . ."

"Hold it, Mona. Yuri's purpose in calling was to warn you to stay close to your family and remain under guard. That's what's important here. He thinks there are people who may try to get hold of you, Mona. He was very serious. He wouldn't explain any more. He said things about the genetic testing, people accessing the records, figuring out that you were the most powerful witch in the clan."

"Yeah, well, I probably am. I figured that out a long time ago, but, Rowan, if they are after witches, why aren't they after you?"

"Because I can't give birth ever again, Mona. But you can. Yuri thinks they may want Michael also. Michael fathered Lasher. These evil people, whoever they are, will try to bring you together. I think Yuri's wrong."

"Why?"

"Mating two witches? Expecting the extra genes to throw a Taltos? It's as unlikely now as it ever was. You might say that breeding two witches is the long way of doing it. According to our records, the one and only successful attempt took three hundred years. There was intervention and purpose in that one success. I gave it my assistance at a crucial moment. Maybe it could not have happened without that."

"And Yuri thinks they'd try to force Michael and me to do that?"

All this while Rowan's gray eyes were fixed on her, scanning her, weighing her response to every word.

"I don't agree with him," said Rowan. "I think the villains of the piece killed Aaron to cover their tracks. That's why they've also tried to kill Yuri. That's why they may be arranging some sort of accidental death for me. On the other hand . . ."

"Then you are in danger! And what happened to Yuri? When did it happen, where?"

"This is my simple point," Rowan said. "We don't know the limits of the danger for anyone who's in any way involved. We can't know because we don't really know the motives of the killers. Yuri's theory, that they won't give up until they've bred a Taltos, is obviously the most pessimistic and the most inclusive. And that's what we should go with. You and Michael both have to be protected. And Michael is the only one in the family, really, who knows why. It's imperative you remain within the house."

"So you're leaving us together here? All cozy and comfortable under your own roof? Rowan, I want to say something to you that takes a lot of nerve."

"You shouldn't have any problem," said Rowan simply.

"You're underestimating Michael. You're selling him short in every respect. He's not going to go for this. And if you leave him without telling him, he's not likely to hang around and play the assigned role. If he does, what do you think the man in him is going to want? And if he does want to do it—sleep with me, that is—what do you think I am? Rowan, you're arranging all this as if we were pawns you're moving on a chess board. Rowan, we're not."

Rowan didn't answer. After a little pause, she smiled.

"You know, Mona, I wish I could take you with me," she said, "I wish you'd come."

"I will! Take me and Michael! The three of us should go."

"The family would never tolerate such a betrayal on my part," said Rowan. "And I couldn't do it to you myself."

"That's crazy, Rowan. Why are we having this conversation? Why are you asking me things like what I think about what's going on?"

"There are too many reasons, Mona, why you have to stay here with Michael."

"And what if we do get in the sack together?"

"That's up to you."

"Terrific, punch him out, and expect me to comfort him but not to—"

Absently, Rowan slipped out a cigarette, then stopped exactly as she had before, gave a little sigh, and pushed it back in the pack.

"I don't care if you smoke," said Mona. "I don't do it, due to my superior intelligence, but—"

"You'll care very soon."

"What do you mean by that?"

"Don't you know?"

Mona was flabbergasted. She didn't answer. "You're saying . . . oh God, I should have known."

She sat back. Still, there had been so many near misses in the past. She was always on the phone to her gynecologist. "I think I did it this time."

"It's no near miss," said Rowan. "Is it Yuri's child?"

"No," Mona answered. "That's impossible. Sir Galahad was too careful. I mean, that is flatly impossible."

"It's Michael's child."

"Yes. But are you certain I am pregnant? I mean, this was only a month ago, and . . ."

"Yes," said Rowan. "The witch and the doctor know the same thing."

"So this could be the Taltos," said Mona.

"Do you want a reason to get rid of it?"

"No, absolutely not. There's nothing on earth that's going to make me get rid of it."

"You're certain?"

"How certain do I have to be?" Mona asked. "Rowan, this is a Catholic family. We don't do away with babies. Besides, I wouldn't do away with this baby no matter who the father was. And if it's Michael's, that's all the more reason for everybody to be happy, because Michael's part of the family! You really don't know us so well, Rowan. You're not getting it, even now. If it's Michael's baby . . . if it's really there, that is . . ."

"Please finish."

"Why don't you finish for me?"

"No, I would like to hear you say it, if you don't mind."

"If it's Michael's, then Michael would be the father of the next generation that will inherit this house."

"Yes."

"And if the baby were a girl, I could designate it as the one to inherit everything, and . . . you and Michael could be its godparents and we could stand at the baptismal font together. We could stand there and then Michael would have a baby, and I'd have a father who I wanted for the baby that everyone will trust and love."

"I knew you would paint a more colorful description than I would," said Rowan softly, a little sadly. "That went beyond my expectations. You're right. There are still things about this family I have to learn."

"Color in St. Alphonsus Church, where Stella and Antha and Deirdre were baptized. And I think . . . I think they baptized you over there too."

"That they've never told me."

"Seems I heard it. Seems like something they would do."

"There's no chance that you might decide to get rid of it."

"You gotta be kidding! I want it. I'd want any baby of my own, be serious. Look, I'm going be so rich I can buy anything in the world, but there's no substitute in existence for my own baby. I can make that happen only one way. Oh, if you knew the family more, if you hadn't spent your life out there in California, you'd understand it's not even a question, unless, of course . . . But even then . . . ."

"Even then?"

"Let's worry about that when it happens. There must be indications, all kinds of little signs, if it's abnormal."

"Perhaps so. Perhaps not. When I carried Lasher, there were no signs until the moment came."

Mona wanted to respond, to say something, but she was too deep in her thoughts. Her own child. Her own child, and nobody, I mean nobody, was going to shove her around anymore. Her own child, and she would have passed over into adulthood regardless of age. Her own child. Suddenly she didn't think thoughts so much as she saw things. She saw a cradle. She saw a baby, a real live little baby, and she saw herself holding the emerald necklace and then she put the necklace around the baby's neck.

"What about Yuri?" asked Rowan. "Will he understand about this?"

Mona wanted to say yes. The truth was she didn't know. She thought of Yuri, quickly, sort of completely. He was sitting on the side of the bed that last night, and saying to her, "There are all sorts of very important reasons why you must marry among your people." She didn't want to think that she was thirteen and fickle. She realized suddenly that Yuri's understanding about the baby was the least of her worries, the very least.

Why, she hadn't even found out yet how they tried to kill Yuri. She hadn't even asked if he was hurt.

"An attempt was made to shoot him," said Rowan, "and the attempt failed. Unfortunately the assassin was killed by the person who foiled him. And the body won't be easy to find. We won't try to find the body anyway. We have a different plan."

"Listen, Rowan, whatever your plan, you've got to tell Michael all this. You can't just leave."

"I know."

"Why aren't you scared that these bad guys won't kill you and Yuri both?"

"I have a few weapons that are strictly my own. Yuri knows the Motherhouse completely. I think I can get into it. I can reach one of the very old members, one of the most trusted and revered. I need perhaps fifteen minutes with him to know whether this evil springs from the Order collectively, or from a small group."

"Can't be one person, Rowan. Too many people are dead."

"You're right, and three of their soldiers are dead. But it could be a very small group within the Order, or outsiders who have a connection within."

"You think you can get to the bad guys themselves?"

"Yes."

"Use me for bait!"

"And the child inside you too? If it is Michael's—"

"It is."

"Then they might want that more than they want you. Look, I don't want to speculate. I don't want to think of witches as some sort of rare commodity to those who know how to use them, of women in the family falling victim to a new species of mad scientist. I've had enough of mad science. I've had enough of monsters. I only want to end this. But you can't go. And neither can Michael. You have to be here."

Rowan pulled back the black silk of her jacket sleeve and looked at a small gold watch. Mona had never seen her wear this watch. Probably Beatrice had bought it too. It was delicate, the kind of watch women wore when Beatrice was a girl.

"I'm going to go upstairs and talk to my husband," said Rowan.

"Thank God," said Mona. "I'm going with you."

"No, please."

"I'm sorry. I'm going."

"For what reason?"

"To make sure you tell him everything that you should."

"All right, then let's go together. Maybe you're one jump ahead of me. You're going to give him the reason to cooperate. But let me ask you one more time, Jezebel. Are you sure this child is his?"

"It was Michael. I can tell you when it probably happened. It happened after Gifford's funeral. I took advantage of him again. I didn't think about precautions any more than I had the first time. Gifford was dead and I was possessed of the devil, I swear it. It was right after that that somebody tried to get in the library window and I smelled that scent."

Rowan said nothing.

"It was the man, wasn't it? He'd come for me after he'd been with my mother. Must have been that way. When he tried to get in, it woke me up. And then I went to her and she was already dead."

"Was it strong, the scent?"

"Very. Sometimes I can still smell it in the living room here, and upstairs in the bedroom. Can't you?"

Rowan didn't reply.

"I want you to do something just because I ask you," Rowan said.

"What's that?"

"Don't tell Michael about the baby until the usual tests have been done. There is someone you can confide in, isn't there, someone who can be like a mother? There must be."

"Don't worry about it," said Mona. "I have my secret gynecologist, I'm thirteen."

"Of course," said Rowan. "Look, whatever happens, I'm going to be back here before you have to tell anyone at all."

"Yeah, I hope so. Wouldn't that be something, if you could finish it that quick? But what if you never come back and Michael and I never know what happened to you or to Yuri?"

Rowan thought about this, apparently, and then she merely shrugged. "I'll come back," she said. "One more caution, if you don't mind."

"Hit me with it."

"If you do tell Michael about this baby, and then decide to get rid of it later, that will kill him. Twice before, this has been promised to him and taken away. If there's any doubt, any whatever, don't tell him till that doubt is resolved."

"I can't wait to tell him. I can get my doctor to see me this afternoon. I'll tell her I'm having a nervous breakdown and I'm on my way over. She's used to this stuff with me. When the tests come back okay, nothing's going to keep me from telling him. And nothing, I mean nothing, is going to keep a baby of mine from being born."

She was about to get up when she realized what she'd said, and that Rowan would never face this particular dilemma again. But Rowan seemed not at all offended by her words, and certainly not hurt. Her face was very quiet. She was looking at the cigarettes.

"Get out of here so I can smoke in peace, will you?" Rowan asked, smiling. "And then we'll wake up Michael. I have an hour and a half to make the plane."

"Rowan, I . . . I'm still sorry about doing it with him. I just can't be sorry about the child."

"Neither can I," said Rowan. "If he comes out of this with a child of his own, and a mother who'll let him love it, well, maybe he'll find a way to forgive everything as the years pass. Just remember. I'm still his wife, Jezebel. You've got the emerald and the baby. But Michael is still mine."

"Got it," said Mona. "I really like you, Rowan. I really, really like you. That's aside from loving you because you're my cousin and we're Mayfairs. If I wasn't pregnant I'd make you take me with you, for your sake and Yuri's and everybody else's."

"And how would you make me take you, Mona?"

"What were your words? Secret weapons of my own."

They looked at one another, and then slowly Rowan nodded and smiled.

Seven

THE HILL was muddy and cold, but never had Marklin made this slippery climb, either in winter or summer, when he had not loved it—to stand on Wearyall Hill beside the Holy Thorn and look down upon the quaint and picturesque town of Glastonbury. The country round was always green, even in winter, but now it had the new intense color of spring.

Marklin was twenty-three, and very fair, with blond hair and pale blue eyes, and thin clear skin that chilled easily. He wore a raincoat with a wool lining, and a pair of leather gloves, and a small wool cap on his head that fitted well and kept him warmer than one might expect from such a little article of clothing.

He'd been eighteen when Stuart had brought them here—he and Tommy both eager students, in love with Oxford, in love with Stuart and eager for every word that dropped from Stuart's lips.

All during their Oxford days, they had honored this place with regular visitations. They'd taken small, cozy little rooms at the George and Pilgrims Hotel, and walked High Street together perusing the bookshops and the stores that sold crystals and the Tarot, whispering to each other of their secret research, their keen scientific approach to things which others held to be purely mythological. The local believers, called variously the hippies of yore or the New Age fanatics, or the bohemians and artists who always seek the charm and tranquillity of such a place, held no charm for them.

They were for decoding the past, rapidly, with all the tools at their command. And Stuart, their instructor in ancient tongues, had been their priest, their magical connection to a true sanctuary—the library and the archives of the Talamasca.

Last year, after the discovery of Tessa, it had been on Glastonbury

Tor that Stuart had told them, "In you two, I have found everything I ever sought in a scholar, a pupil, or a novice. You are the first to whom I truly want to give all I know."

That had seemed a supreme honor to Marklin—something finer than any honors awarded him at Eton or Oxford, or anywhere in the wide world where his studies had carried him later on.

It had been a greater moment even than being accepted into the Order. And now, in retrospect, he knew that that acceptance had meant something only because it had meant everything to Stuart, who had lived all his life as a member of the Talamasca, and would soon die, as he so often said, within its walls.

Stuart was now eighty-seven, and perhaps one of the oldest active men alive in the Talamasca, if one could call tutoring in language an activity of the Talamasca, for it was more the special passion of Stuart's retirement. The talk of death was neither romantic or melodramatic. And nothing really had changed Stuart's matter-of-fact attitude to what lay ahead.

"A man of my age with his wits about him? If he isn't brave in the face of death, if he isn't curious, and rather eager to see what happens, well, then, he's wasted his life. He's a damned fool."

Even the discovery of Tessa had not infected Stuart with any last-ditch desperation to lengthen the time remaining to him. His devotion to Tessa, his belief in her, encompassed nothing so petty. Marklin feared Stuart's death far more than Stuart did. And Marklin knew now that he had overplayed his hand with Stuart, and that he must woo him back to the moment of commitment. To lose Stuart to death was inevitable; to lose Stuart before that time was unthinkable.

"You stand on the sacred ground of Glastonbury," Stuart had told them that day, when it all began. "Who is buried within this tor? Arthur himself, or only the nameless Celts who left us their coins, their weapons, the boats with which they traveled the seas that once made of this the isle of Avalon? We'll never know. But there are secrets which we can know, and the implications of these secrets are so vast, so revolutionary, and so unprecedented that they are worth our allegiance to the Order, they are worth any sacrifice we must make. If this is not so, then we are liars."

That Stuart now threatened to abandon Marklin and Tommy, that he had turned against them in his anger and revulsion, was something Marklin could have avoided. It had not been necessary to reveal every part of their plan to Stuart. And Marklin realized this now, that his refusal to assume full leadership himself had caused the rift. Stuart had Tessa . . . Stuart had made his wishes clear. But Stuart should never have been told what had really happened. That had been the error, and Marklin had only his own immaturity to blame, that he had loved Stuart so much he had felt compelled to tell Stuart everything.

He would get Stuart back. Stuart had agreed to come today. He was no doubt already here, visiting Chalice Well as he always did before coming to Wearyall Hill and leading them up on the tor itself. Marklin knew how much Stuart loved him. This breach would be repaired with an appeal from the soul, with poetry and with honest fervor.

That his own life would be long, that this was only the first of his dark adventures, Marklin had no doubt. His would be the keys to the tabernacle, the map to the treasure, the formula for the magic potion. He was utterly certain of it. But for this first plan to end in defeat would be a moral disaster. He would go on, of course, but his youth had been a chain of unbroken successes, and this too must succeed so that his ascent would lose no momentum.

I must win, I must always win. I must never attempt anything that I cannot do with utter success. This had always been Marklin's personal vow. He had never failed to keep it.

As for Tommy, Tommy was faithful to the vows the three had taken, faithful to the concept and the person of Tessa. There was no worry with Tommy. Deeply involved in his computer research, his precise chronologies and charts, Tommy was in no danger of disaffection for the very reasons that made him valuable; he was not the one to see the whole scheme, or to question the validity of it.

In a very basic sense, Tommy never changed.

Tommy was the same now as the boy whom Marklin had come to love in childhood—collector, collator, an archive unto himself, an appreciator and an investigator. Tommy without Marklin had never existed, as far as Marklin knew. They had first laid eyes upon each other at the age of twelve, in boarding school in America. Tommy's room had been filled with fossils, maps, animal bones, computer equipment of the most esoteric sort, and a vast collection of paperback science fiction.

Marklin had often thought that he must have seemed to Tommy to be one of the characters in those fantastic novels—Marklin himself hated fiction—and that Tommy had gone from an outsider to a featured player in a science fiction drama upon meeting Marklin. Tommy's loyalty had never, for even one moment, been in question. Indeed, during the years when Marklin had wanted his freedom, Tommy had been too close, always on hand, always at Marklin's service. Marklin had invented tasks for his friend, simply to give himself space to breathe. Tommy had never been unhappy.

Marklin was getting cold, but he didn't mind it.

Glastonbury would never be anything for him but a sacred place, though he believed almost nothing, literally, that was connected with it.

He would, each time he came to Wearyall Hill, with the private devotion of a monk, envision the noble Joseph of Arimathea planting his staff upon this spot. It did not matter to him that the present Holy Thorn had been grown from a scion of the ancient tree, now gone, any more than other specific detail mattered. He could in these places feel an excitement appropriate to his purpose, a religious renewal as it were, which strengthened him and sent him back into the world more ruthless than ever.

Ruthlessness. That was what was needed now, and Stuart had failed to see it.

Yes, things had gone dreadfully wrong, no doubt of it. Men had been sacrificed whose innocence and substance surely demanded a greater justice. But this was not entirely Marklin's fault. And the lesson to learn was that ultimately none of it mattered.

The time has come for me to instruct my teacher, Marklin thought.

Miles from the Motherhouse, in this open place, our meeting safely explained by our own customs of so many years, we will come together again as one. Nothing has been lost. Stuart must be given moral permission to profit by what has happened.

Tommy had arrived.

Tommy was always the second. Marklin watched Tommy's antique roadster slowing as it came down High Street. He watched as it found a parking place, and as Tommy shut the door, failing to lock it as always, and started his climb up the hill.

What if Stuart failed to show? What if he was nowhere near? What if he had truly abandoned his followers? Impossible.

Stuart was at the well. He drank from it when he came, he would drink from it before he left. His pilgrimages here were as rigid as those of an ancient Druid or Christian monk. From shrine to shrine to shrine traveled Stuart.

Such habits of his teacher had always aroused a tenderness in Marklin, as had Stuart's words. Stuart had "consecrated" them to a dark life of penetrating "the mystique and the myth, in order to lay hands upon the horror and the beauty at the core."

It seemed tolerable poetry both then and now. Only Stuart had to be reminded of it, Stuart had to be convinced in metaphors and lofty sentiments.

Tommy had almost reached the tree. He took his last steps carefully, for it was easy to lose one's footing in the slippery mud, and fall. Marklin had done it once, years ago, when they'd first begun their pilgrimages. This had meant a night at the George and Pilgrims Hotel while his clothes were thoroughly cleaned.

Not bad that it had happened; it had been a marvelous evening. Stuart had stayed down with him. They'd spent the night talking together, even though Marklin had been confined to a borrowed robe and slippers and a small, charming bedchamber, and both had longed in vain to climb the tor in the midnight, and commune with the spirit of the sleeping king.

Of course, Marklin had never for a moment in his life believed that King Arthur slept beneath Glastonbury Tor. If he had believed it, he would have taken a shovel and started digging.

Stuart had come late in life to his conviction that myth was only interesting when a truth lay behind it, and that one could find that truth, and even the physical evidence of it.

Scholars, thought Marklin, theirs is an inevitable flaw; words and deeds become the same to them. That was at the very basis of the confusion now. Stuart, at eighty-seven years of age, had had perhaps his first excursion into reality.

Reality and blood were intermingled.

Tommy at last took his place at Marklin's side. He blew on his cold fingers and then reached into his pockets for his gloves—a classic Tommy routine, to have walked up the hill without them, to have forgotten his gloves were even there until he saw Marklin's leather gloves, the very ones he'd long ago given Marklin.

"Where is Stuart?" Tommy asked. "Yes, gloves." He stared at Marklin, eyes enormous through his round, thick, rimless glasses, red hair clipped neatly short so that he might have been a lawyer or a banker. "Gloves, yes. Where is he?"

Marklin had been about to say that Stuart had not come, when in fact he saw Stuart beginning the very last leg of the ascent from his car, which he had brought as close as permissible up Wearyall Hill. Unlike Stuart to have done this.

But Stuart seemed otherwise unchanged—tall, narrow in his familiar greatcoat, with the cashmere scarf around his neck and streaming out behind him in the wind, his gaunt face looking as if it were carved out of wood. His gray hair resembled, as always, a jay's crest. It seemed in this last decade he had scarcely changed at all.

He looked right at Marklin as he drew near. And Marklin realized that he himself was trembling. Tommy stepped aside. Stuart stopped some six feet from both of them, his hands clenched, his thin face anguished as he confronted the two young men.

"You killed Aaron!" Stuart cried. "You, both of you. You killed Aaron. How in the name of God could you have done such a thing?"

Marklin was speechless, all his confidence and plans deserting him suddenly. He tried to stop the tremor in his hands. He knew if he spoke his voice would be frail and without any authority. He could not bear for Stuart to be angry, or disappointed in any way.

"Dear God, what have you done, both of you!" Stuart ranted. "And what have I done that I set this scheme into motion? Dear God, the blame is mine!"

Marklin swallowed, but kept his silence.

"You, Tommy, how could you have been a party to this!" Stuart continued. "And Mark. Mark, you, the very author of all of it."

"Stuart, you must hear me out!" Marklin declared before he could stop himself.

"Hear you out?" Stuart drew closer, his hands shoved into his coat pockets. "Hear you out, should I? Let me ask you a question, my brilliant young friend, my finest, my bravest hope! What's to stop you now from killing me, as you've done with Aaron and Yuri Stefano?"

"Stuart, it was for you that I did it," Marklin insisted. "If you would only listen, you'll understand. These are but flowers of the seeds you planted when we began this together. Aaron had to be silenced. That he had not reported back, that he had not come home to the Mother-house itself, was pure luck, Stuart! He might have any day, and Yuri Stefano would also have come. His visit to Donnelaith was a fluke. He might have come straight home from the airport."

"You speak of circumstance, you speak of detail!" Stuart said, taking yet another step towards them.

Tommy stood quiet, seemingly emotionless, his red hair tousled by the wind, eyes squinting behind his glasses. He watched Stuart steadily, his shoulder very close to Marklin's arm.

Stuart was beside himself.

"You speak of expediency, but you don't speak of life and death, my pupil," he insisted. "How could you do it! How could you bring an end to Aaron's life!"

And here Stuart's voice failed him, and the grief displayed itself, monstrous as the rage. "I would destroy you, Mark, if I could," said Stuart. "But I cannot do such things, and that is perhaps why I did not think that you could! But you've amazed me, Mark."

"Stuart, it was worth any sacrifice. What is sacrifice if it is not moral sacrifice!"

This horrified Stuart, but what else could Marklin do, other than take the plunge? Tommy really ought to say something, he thought, but he knew that when Tommy spoke, he would stand firm.

"I put an end to those who could have stopped us," said Mark. "That is all there is to it, Stuart. You grieve for Aaron because you knew him."

"Don't be a fool," said Stuart bitterly. "I grieve for innocent blood shed, I grieve for monstrous stupidity! Oh yes, that is what it was. Do you think the death of such a man will go unavenged within the Order? You think you know the Talamasca, you think with your shrewd young mind you could size it up in a matter of a few years. But all you've done is to learn its organizational weaknesses. You could live all your life in the Talamasca and not know the Talamasca. Aaron was my brother! It was my brother you killed! You have failed me, Mark. You have failed Tommy. You have failed yourself! You have failed Tessa."

"No," Mark said, "you don't speak the truth, and you know it. Look at me, Stuart, look into my eyes. You left it to me to bring Lasher here, you left it to me to step out of the library and plot everything. And to Tommy as well. Do you think this could have been orchestrated without us?"

"You miss a crucial point, don't you, Mark?" Stuart asked. "You failed. You did not rescue the Taltos and bring him here! Your soldiers were fools, and so it must be said of the general."

"Stuart, have patience with us," said Tommy. It was his usual matter-of-fact tone. "I knew the first day we spoke that this couldn't be accomplished without someone paying for it with his life."

"You never spoke such words to me, Tommy."

"Let me remind you," Tommy said in the same monotone manner, "you said that we were to render Yuri and Aaron powerless to interfere, and erase all evidence that the Taltos itself had been born into the Mayfair family. Now, how was this to be done except in the ways that we did it? Stuart, we have nothing to be ashamed of in our actions. What we seek makes these things utterly insignificant."

Marklin tried desperately to conceal his sigh of relief.

Stuart looked from Tommy to Marklin and then back again, and then out over the pale landscape of gently rolling green hills, and then up to the peak of Glastonbury Tor. He turned his back on them to face the tor, and he hung his head as if communing with some personal deity.

Marklin drew close, and he placed his hands very tentatively on Stuart's shoulders. He was far taller now than Stuart, and Stuart in old age had lost some of his earlier height. Marklin drew close to his ear.

"Stuart, the die was cast when we got rid of the scientist. There was no turning back. And the doctor . . ."

"No," said Stuart, shaking his head with dramatic emphasis. His eyes were narrow and fixed on the tor. "These deaths could have been blamed on the Taltos himself, don't you see? That was the beauty of it. The Taltos canceled the deaths of the two men who could have only misused the revelation granted to them!"

"Stuart," said Mark, very aware that Stuart had not sought to free himself from his light embrace. "You must understand that Aaron became the enemy of us when he became the official enemy of the Talamasca."

"Enemy? Aaron was never an enemy of the Talamasca! Your bogus excommunication broke his heart."

"Stuart," Marklin pleaded, "I can see now in retrospect that the excommunication was a mistake, but it has been our only mistake."

"There was no choice in the matter of the excommunication," said Tommy flatly. "It was either that or risk discovery at every turn. I did what I had to do, and I made it damned convincing. I could not have kept up a bogus correspondence between the Elders and Aaron. That would have been too much."

"I admit," said Marklin, "it was a mistake. Only loyalty to the Order might have kept Aaron quiet about the various things he'd seen and come to suspect. If we made an error, Stuart, the three of us made it together. We shouldn't have alienated him and Yuri Stefano. We should have tightened our hold, played our game better."

"The web was too intricate as it was," said Stuart. "I warn you, both of you. Tommy, come here. I warn you both! Do not strike against the Mayfair family. You have done enough. You have destroyed a man who was finer than any other I ever knew, and you did it for so small a gain that heaven will take its vengeance on you. But do not, for whatever remains to us now, strike against the family!"

"I think we already have," said Tommy in his usual practical voice. "Aaron Lightner had recently married Beatrice Mayfair. Besides, he had become so close to Michael Curry—indeed, to all of the clan—that the marriage was hardly required to cement the relationship. But there was a marriage, and to the Mayfairs marriage is a sacred bond, as we know. He had become one of them."

"Pray you're wrong," said Stuart. "Pray to heaven you're wrong. Risk the ire of the Mayfair witches, and God himself couldn't help you."

"Stuart, let us look at what must be done now," said Marklin. "Let's leave the hill and go down to the hotel."

"Never. Where others can hear our words? Never."

"Stuart, take us to Tessa. Let us discuss it there," pressed Marklin.

It was the key moment. Marklin knew it. He wished now that he had not said Tessa's name, not yet. He wished he had not played to this climax.

Stuart was eyeing both of them with the same deliberate condemnation and disgust. Tommy stood solidly, gloved hands clasped in front of him. The stiff collar of his coat rose to hide his mouth, and thereby leave nothing to scrutiny but his level, untroubled gaze.

Marklin himself was close to tears, or so he imagined. Marklin had actually never wept even once in his life that he could remember.

"Perhaps this is not the time to see her," Marklin said, hastening to repair the damage.

"Perhaps you should never see her again," said Stuart, voice small for the first time, eyes large and speculating.

"You don't mean what you say," said Mark.

"If I take you to Tessa, what's to stop you from doing away with me?"

"Oh, Stuart, you hurt us both; how can you ask this of us? We aren't without principle. We're simply dedicated to a common goal. Aaron had to die. So did Yuri. Yuri was never really one of the Order. Yuri left so easily and so quickly!"

"Yes, and neither of you were ever members either, were you?" Stuart asked. His manner was changing, hardening.

"We are dedicated to you and always have been," said Marklin. "Stuart, we waste our valuable time. Keep Tessa to yourself if you will. You will not shake my faith in her, or Tommy's. And we will move towards our goal. We cannot do otherwise."

"And what now is the goal?" Stuart demanded. "Lasher is gone now, as if he'd never existed! Or do you doubt the word of a man who would follow Yuri doggedly over land and sea only to finally shoot him?"

"Lasher is beyond destiny now," said Tommy. "I think we are all in agreement on that. What Lanzing saw couldn't be interpreted any other way. But Tessa is in your hands, as real as she was the day you discovered her."

Stuart shook his head. "Tessa is real, and Tessa is alone as she has always been alone. And the union shall not take place, and my eyes will close without ever seeing the miracle."

"Stuart, it is still possible," said Marklin. "The family, the Mayfair witches."

"Yes," cried Stuart, his voice out of control, "and strike them and they will destroy you. You have forgotten the very first warning I ever gave you. The Mayfair witches win over those who would hurt them. They always have! If not as individuals, they win as a family!"

They stood quiet for a moment.

"Destroy *you*, Stuart?" Tommy asked. "Why not the three of us, Stuart?"

Stuart was in despair. His white hair, blown back and forth by the wind, resembled the unkempt hair of a drunkard. He looked down at the earth beneath his feet, his hooked nose glistening as though it were nothing now but polished cartilage. An eagle of a man, yes, but not an elderly one, never that.

Marklin feared for him in the wind. Stuart's eyes were red and tearing. Marklin could see the map of blue veins spreading up from his temples. Stuart was trembling in every limb.

"Yes, you're right, Tommy," said Stuart. "The Mayfairs will destroy all of us. Why would they not?" He looked up and straight at Marklin. "And what is the greatest loss to me? Is it Aaron? Is it the marriage itself, of male and female Taltos? Is it the chain of memory we hoped to discover link by link to its earliest source? Or is it that you are damned now, both of you, for what you've done? And I have lost you. Let the Mayfairs come to destroy the three of us, yes, it will be justice."

"No, I don't want this justice," said Tommy. "Stuart, you can't turn on us."

"No, that you can't do," said Marklin. "You cannot call a defeat for us. The witches can bear the Taltos again."

"Three hundred years hence?" asked Stuart. "Or tomorrow?"

"Listen to me, sir, I beg you," said Marklin. "The spirit of Lasher possessed knowledge of what he had been, and what he could be, and what happened to the genes of Rowan Mayfair and Michael Curry happened under the spirit's knowing vigilance and to fulfill his purpose.

"But *we* have that knowledge now—of what a Taltos is, and perhaps was, and what can make it. And Stuart, *so do the witches!* For the first time, the witches know the destiny of the giant helix. And their knowing is as powerful as Lasher's knowing."

Stuart had no answer for this. Clearly he had not thought of it. He looked at Marklin a long time. Then he asked, "You believe this?"

"Their awareness is even more powerful, perhaps," said Tommy. "The telekinetic assistance that can be rendered by the witches themselves in the event of a birth can't be underestimated."

"Ever the scientist," said Marklin with a triumphant smile. The tide was changing. He could feel it, see it in Stuart's eyes.

"And one must remember," said Tommy, "that the spirit was addled and blundering. The witches are leagues from that, even at their most naive and ineffectual."

"That is a guess, Tommy."

"Stuart," Marklin pleaded. "We have come too far!"

"To put it another way," said Tommy, "our accomplishments here are by no means negligible. We verified the incarnation of the Taltos, and if we could get our hands on any notes written by Aaron before his death, we might verify what all suspect, that it was not incarnation but reincarnation."

"I know what we've done," said Stuart. "The good, the bad. You needn't make your summation for me, Tommy."

"Only to clarify," said Tommy. "And we have witches who know not only the old secrets now in abstract, but who believe in the physical miracle itself. We could not possibly have more interesting opportunities."

"Stuart, trust us again," said Marklin.

Stuart looked at Tommy and then back at Marklin. Marklin saw the old spark, the love.

"Stuart," he went on, "the killing is done. It's finished. Our other unwitting assistants can be phased out without their ever knowing the grand design."

"And Lanzing? He must know everything."

"He was a hireling, Stuart," said Marklin. "He never understood what he saw. Besides, he too is dead."

"We didn't kill him, Stuart," said Tommy, in an almost casual manner. "They found part of his remains at the foot of Donnelaith Crag. His gun had been fired twice."

"Part of his remains?" asked Stuart.

Tommy shrugged. "They said he'd been a meal for wild animals."

"But you can't be sure, then, that he killed Yuri."

"Yuri has never returned to the hotel," said Tommy. "His belongings are still unclaimed. Yuri is dead, Stuart. The two bullets were for Yuri. How Lanzing fell, or why, or if some animal attacked, those things we can't know. But Yuri Stefano is, for our purposes, gone."

"Don't you see, Stuart?" said Marklin. "Except for the escape of the Taltos, everything has worked perfectly. And we can withdraw now, and focus upon the Mayfair witches. We don't need anything further from the Order. If the interception is ever uncovered, no one will ever be able to trace it to us."

"You don't fear the Elders, do you?"

"There is no reason to fear the Elders," said Tommy. "The intercept continues to work perfectly. It always has."

"Stuart, we've learned from our errors," said Marklin. "But perhaps things have happened for a purpose. I don't mean in the sentimental sense. But look at the overall picture. All the right people are dead."

"Don't talk so crudely to me of your methods, either of you. What about our Superior General?"

Tommy shrugged. "Marcus knows nothing. Except that he will very soon be able to retire with a small fortune. He'll never put all the pieces together afterwards. No one will be able to. That's the beauty of the entire plan."

"We need a few more weeks at most," said Marklin. "Just to protect ourselves."

"I'm not so sure," said Tommy. "The smart thing may be to remove the intercepts now. We know everything the Talamasca knows about the Mayfair family."

"Don't be so hasty, so confident!" said Stuart. "What happens when your phony communications are finally discovered?"

"You mean *our* phony communications?" asked Tommy. "At the very worst, there'll be a little confusion, perhaps even an investigation. But no one could trace the letters or the interception itself to us. That's why it's very important that we remain loyal novices, that we do nothing now to arouse suspicion."

Tommy glanced at Marklin. It was working. Stuart's manner had changed. Stuart was giving the orders again . . . almost.

"This is all electronic," said Tommy. "There is no hard evidence of anything anywhere, except a few piles of paper in my flat in Regent's Park. Only you and Mark and I know where those papers are."

"Stuart, we need your guidance now!" said Marklin. "We go into the most exciting phase yet."

"Silence," said Stuart. "Let me look at you both, let me take your measure."

"Please do it, Stuart," said Marklin, "and find us brave and young, yes, young and stupid, perhaps, but brave and committed."

"What Mark means," said Tommy, "is that our position now is better than we could possibly have expected. Lanzing shot Yuri, then fell, fatally injuring himself. Stolov and Norgan are gone. They were never anything but a nuisance, and they knew too much. The men hired to kill the others don't know us. And we are here, where we began, at Glastonbury."

"And Tessa is in your hands, unknown to anyone but the three of us."

"Eloquence," said Stuart almost in a whisper. "That's what you give me now, eloquence."

"Poetry is truth, Stuart," said Marklin. "It is the highest truth, and eloquence is its attribute."

There was a pause. Marklin had to get Stuart down from this hill. Protectively, he put his arm around Stuart, and to his great relief, Stuart allowed this.

"Let's go down, Stuart," said Marklin. "Let's have our supper now. We're cold, we're hungry."

"If we had it to do over again," said Tommy, "we'd do it better. We didn't have to take those lives. It might have been more of a challenge, you know, to accomplish our purpose without really hurting anyone."

Stuart seemed lost in thought, only glancing at Tommy absently. The wind rose again, cuttingly, and Marklin shivered. If he was this cold, what must Stuart be feeling? They must go down to the hotel. They must break bread together.

"We are not ourselves, you know, Stuart," Marklin said. He was looking down at the town, and conscious that both of the others were staring at him. "When gathered together, we make a person whom none of us knows well enough, perhaps, a fourth entity which we should give a name, because he is more than our collective selves. Perhaps we must better learn to control him. But destroy him now? No, that we cannot do, Stuart. If we do, we all betray each other. It's a hard truth to face, but the death of Aaron means nothing."

He had played his final card. He had said the finest and the worst things that he'd had to say, here in the chill wind, and without real forethought, with only his instinct to guide him. Finally he looked at his teacher and at his friend, and saw that both had been impressed by these words, perhaps even more than he could have hoped.

"Yes, it was this fourth entity, as you call him, who killed my friend," said Stuart quietly. "You are right about that. And we know that the power, the future of this fourth entity, is unimaginable."

"Yes, exactly," said Tommy in a flat murmur.

"But the death of Aaron is a terrible, terrible thing! You will never, either of you, ever speak to me of it again, and never, never will you speak of it lightly to anyone."

"Agreed," said Tommy.

"My innocent friend," said Stuart, "who sought only to help the Mayfair family."

"No one in the Talamasca is really innocent," Tommy said.

Stuart appeared startled, at first enraged and then caught by this simple statement.

"What do you mean by this?"

"I mean that one cannot expect to possess knowledge which does not change one. Once one knows, then one is acting upon that knowledge, whether it is to withhold the knowledge from those who would also be changed, or to give it to them. Aaron knew this. The Talamasca is evil by nature; that's the price it pays for its libraries and inventories and computer records. Rather like God, wouldn't you say, who knows that some of his creatures will suffer and some will triumph, but does not tell his creatures what he knows? The Talamasca is more evil even than the Supreme Being, but the Talamasca creates nothing."

So very right, thought Marklin, though he could not have said such a thing aloud to Stuart, for fear of what Stuart would say in return.

"Perhaps you're right," said Stuart under his breath. He sounded defeated, or desperate for some tolerable point of view.

"It's a sterile priesthood," said Tommy, the voice once again devoid of all feeling. He gave his heavy glasses a shove with one finger. "The altars are barren; the statues are stored away. The scholars study for study's sake."

"Don't say any more."

"Let me talk of us, then," said Tommy, "that we are not sterile, and we will see the sacred union come about, and we will hear the voices of memory."

"Yes," said Marklin, unable to assume such a cold voice. "Yes, we are the real priests now! True mediators between the earth and the forces of the unknown. We possess the words and the power."

Another silence had fallen.

Could Marklin ever get them off this hill? He had won. They were together again, and he longed for the warmth of the George and Pilgrims. He longed for the taste of hot soup and ale, and the light of the fire. He longed to celebrate. He was wildly excited again.

"And Tessa?" asked Tommy. "How is it with Tessa?"

"The same," said Stuart.

"Does she know that the male Taltos is dead?"

"She never knew he was alive," said Stuart.

"Ah."

"Come on, teacher," said Marklin. "Let's go down now, to the hotel. Let's dine together."

"Yes," said Tommy, "we're all too cold now to speak anymore."

They began the descent, both Tommy and Marklin steadying Stuart in the slippery mud. When they had reached Stuart's car, they opted for the drive rather than the long walk.

"This is all very good," said Stuart, giving over the car keys to Marklin. "But I will visit Chalice Well as always before we go."

"What for?" asked Marklin, making his words quiet, and respectful, and seemingly expressive of the love he felt for Stuart. "Will you wash your hands in Chalice Well to cleanse the blood off them? The water is already bloody itself, teacher."

Stuart gave a little bitter laugh.

"Ah, but that is the blood of Christ, isn't it?" Stuart said.

"It's the blood of conviction," said Marklin. "We'll go to the well after dinner, and just before dark. I promise you that."

They drove down the hill together.

Eight

MICHAEL told Clem he wanted to leave by the front gate. He'd bring the suitcases out. There were only two of them—Rowan's and his. This was no vacation that required trunks and garment bags.

He looked at his diary before he closed it. There was a long statement there of his philosophy, written on Mardi Gras night, before he had ever dreamed that he would be awakened later by a plaintive gramophone song or by the vision of Mona dancing like a nymph in her white nightgown. Bow in hair, fresh and fragrant as warm bread, fresh milk, strawberries.

No, can't think anymore about Mona just now. Wait for the phone call in London.

Besides, it was the passage he wanted to read:

> And I suppose I do believe, in the final analysis, that a peace of mind can be obtained in the face of the worst horrors and the worst losses. It can be obtained by faith in change and in will and in accident; and by faith in ourselves, that we will do the right thing, more often than not, in the face of adversity.

Six weeks had passed since that night, when, in illness and in grief, he'd written those sentiments. He'd been a prisoner of this house then, and up until this very moment.

He closed the diary. He slipped it into his leather bag, tucked the bag under his arm, and picked up the suitcases. He went down the stairs, a bit nervous since neither hand was free to reach for the rail, reminding himself that he would suffer no dizzy spell now, or any other form of weakness.

And if he was wrong about that, well, then he would die in action.

Rowan stood on the porch talking to Ryan, and Mona was there, with tears in her eyes, peering up at him with renewed devotion. She looked as delectable in silk as in anything else; and when he looked at her now, he saw what Rowan had seen, saw it as he had once been the first to see it in Rowan—the new swell of the breasts, the higher color of the cheeks, and a brilliance in Mona's eyes, as well as a slightly different rhythm to her subtlest movements.

My child.

He'd believe it when she confirmed it. He'd worry about monsters and genes when he had to. He'd dream of a son or a daughter in his arms when there was a real chance of it.

Clem took the suitcases quickly, and carried them out the open gate. Michael liked this new driver so much better than the last, liked his good humor and his matter-of-fact ways. He made Michael think of musicians he'd known.

The trunk of the car was shut. Ryan kissed Rowan on both cheeks. Only now did Michael pick up Ryan's voice.

". . . anything further that you can tell me."

"Only that this situation won't last long. But don't for a moment think it's safe to let the guards go. And don't let Mona out alone under any circumstances."

"Chain me to the walls," said Mona with a shrug. "They would have done it to Ophelia if she hadn't drowned in the stream."

"Who?" asked Ryan. "Mona, so far I have taken this whole thing very well indeed, considering the fact that you are thirteen years old and—"

"Chill, Ryan," she said. "Nobody's taking it better than I am."

She smiled in spite of herself. Ryan stood baffled, staring at her.

This was the moment, Michael figured. He couldn't endure a long Mayfair goodbye. And Ryan was confused enough.

"Ryan, I'll be in touch with you as soon as possible," he said. "We'll see Aaron's people. Learn what we can. Come home."

"Now, can you tell me *exactly* where you're going?"

"No, can't do it," said Rowan. She had turned and was headed right out of the gate.

Mona suddenly clattered down the steps after her. "Hey, Rowan!" she said, and Mona flung her arms around Rowan's neck and kissed her.

For one moment Michael was terrified that Rowan would not respond, that she'd stand like a statue beneath the oaks, neither acknowledging this sudden desperate hug, nor trying to free herself from it. But something entirely different happened. Rowan held Mona tight, kissing Mona's cheek and then smoothing her hair, and even laying her hand on Mona's forehead.

"You're going to be all right," Rowan said. "But do everything that I've told you to do."

Ryan followed Michael down the steps.

"I don't know what to say except good luck," Ryan said. "I wish you could tell me more about all this, what you're *really* doing."

"Tell Bea we had to go," said Michael. "I wouldn't tell the others any more than you have to."

Ryan nodded, obviously full of suspicion and concern, but basically stymied.

Rowan was already in the car. Michael slipped in beside her. In seconds they were sliding away beneath the lowering tree branches, and Mona and Ryan made a little picture, standing together in the gate, both waving, Mona's hair like a starburst, and Ryan clearly baffled as ever and highly uncertain.

"Seems he's doomed," said Rowan, "to run things for a coterie who will never tell him anything that's really happening."

"We tried once," said Michael. "You should have been there. He doesn't want to know. And he will do exactly what you tell him. Mona? Will she? I have no idea. But he will."

"You're still angry."

"No," he said. "I stopped being angry when you gave in."

But this wasn't true. He was still hurt to the quick that she had planned to leave without him, that she had seen him not as a companion on this trip, but as some keeper of the house, and of the baby inside Mona.

Well, hurt wasn't anger, was it?

She'd turned away. She was looking forward, and so he felt maybe it was safe to look at her. She was too thin still, far too thin, but her face had never been more lovely to him. The black suit she wore, the pearls, the high heels—all of it had given her a deceptively wicked glamour. But she had not needed these things. Her beauty lay in her purity—in the bones of her face, in the dark straight eyebrows that so vividly determined her expression, and in her soft long mouth which he wanted to kiss now with a brutal male desire to waken her, part her lips, make her soften all over in his arms again, have her.

That was the only way, ever, to have her.

She lifted her hand and pressed the button for the leather privacy panel to go up behind the driver. Then she turned to Michael.

"I was wrong," she said, without rancor or pleading. "You loved Aaron. You love me. You love Mona. I was wrong."

"You don't have to go into this," he answered. It was hard for him to look her in the eye, but he was determined to do it, to calm himself inside, to stop being hurt or mad or whatever this was right now.

"But there's something you have to understand," she said. "I don't plan to be kind and law-abiding with these people who killed Aaron. I don't intend to answer to anyone about what I do—even to you, Michael."

He laughed. He looked into her large, cold gray eyes. He wondered if this was what her patients had seen as they looked up, right before the anesthesia began to work on them.

"I know that, honey," he said. "When we get there, when we meet Yuri, I want to know, that's all, what he knows. I want to be there with you both. I'm not claiming to have your capabilities, or your nerve. But I want to be there."

She nodded.

"Who knows, Rowan?" he asked. "Maybe you'll find a purpose for me." The wrath had come out. It was too late now to draw back in. He knew that his face had gone red. He looked away from her.

When she spoke this time, it was a secret voice he'd never heard her use except with him, and in the past months it had gained a new depth of feeling.

"Michael, I love you. But I know you're a good man. I'm no longer a good woman."

"Rowan, you don't mean that."

"Oh yes, I do. I've been with the goblins, Michael. I've been down into the inner circle."

"And you've come back," he said, looking at her again, trying to put the lid on these feelings that were about to explode out of him. "You're Rowan again, and you're here, and there are things to live for other than vengeance."

That was it, wasn't it? He had not roused her from her waking sleep. It had been Aaron's death that had done the trick, bringing her back to all of them.

If he didn't think of something else quick, he was going to lose his temper again, the hurt was so intense, it was so out of his control.

"Michael, I love you," she said. "I love you very much. And I know what you've suffered. Don't think I don't know, Michael."

He nodded. He'd give her that much, but maybe he was lying to both of them.

"But don't think you know what it's like to be the person I am. I was there at the birth, I was the mother. I was the cause, you might say, I was the crucial instrument. And I paid for that. I paid and I paid and I paid. And I'm not the same now. I love you as I always did, my love for you was never in question. But I'm not the same and I can't be the same, and I knew it when I was sitting out there in the garden, unable to answer your questions or look at you or put my arms around you. I knew it. And yet I loved you, and I love you now. Can you follow what I'm saying?"

Again he nodded.

"You want to hurt me, and I know you do," she said.

"No, not hurt you. Not that. Not hurt you, just . . . just . . . rip your little silk skirt off, perhaps, and tear off that blazer that's been so skillfully painted on and make you know I'm here, I'm Michael! That's shameful, isn't it? It's disgusting, isn't it? That I want to have you the only way I can, because you shut me out, you left me, you . . ."

He stopped. This had sometimes happened to him before, that in the midst of cresting anger, he had seen the futility of what he was doing and saying. He had seen the emptiness of anger itself, and realized in a moment of utter practicality that he could not continue like this, that if he did, nothing would be accomplished except his own misery.

He sat still and he felt the anger leave him. He felt his body grow relaxed and almost tired. He sat back against the back of the seat. And then he looked at her again.

She'd never turned away. She looked neither frightened nor sad. He wondered if, in her secret heart, she was bored and wishing him safe at home as she plotted the next steps she would take.

Clear away these thoughts, man, because if you don't, you can't love her again, ever.

And he did love her. There wasn't any doubt suddenly. He loved her strength, he loved her coldness. That's how it had been in her house on Tiburon, when they'd made it beneath the bare beam roof, when they had talked and talked, with no possible inkling of how they had, all their lives, been moving towards one another.

He reached out and touched her cheek, very aware that her expression hadn't changed, that she seemed as totally in control as she ever had.

"I do love you!" he whispered.

"I know," she said.

He laughed under his breath.

"You do?" he asked. He felt himself smile, and it felt good. He laughed silently and shook his head. "You know it!" he said.

"Yes," she said with a little nod. "I'm afraid for you, always have been. It's not because you aren't strong, aren't capable, aren't everything you ought to be. I'm afraid because there's a power in me that you don't have, and there's a power in these others—these enemies of ours who killed Aaron—a power that comes from a total lack of scruples." She flicked a bit of dust off the tight little skirt. When she sighed, the soft sound of it seemed to fill up the car, rather like her perfume.

She lowered her head, a small gesture that made her hair go very soft and longish around her face. And as she looked up, her brows seemed especially long and her eyes both pretty and mysterious.

"Call it witch power, if you will. Maybe it's as simple as that. Maybe it's in the genes. Maybe it's a physical capability to do things that normal people can't do."

"Then I have it," he said.

"No. Coincidentally, perhaps, you have the long helix," she said.

"Coincidentally, like hell," he said. "He chose me for you, Rowan. Lasher did that. Years ago when I was a kid and I stopped at the gate of that house, he chose me. Why do you think he did that? Not because he ever thought I'd be a good man and destroy his hard-won flesh, no, that wasn't it. It was for the witch in me, Rowan. We come from the same Celtic root. You know we do. And I'm the worker's son and so I don't know my story. But it goes back to the same beginnings as yours. The power's there. It was there in my hands when I could read the past and the future in people's touch. It was there when I heard the music played by a ghost especially to lead me to Mona."

She gave a small frown, and her eyes grew small for one tiny instant and then large again and wondering.

"I didn't use that power to bring Lasher down," he said. "I was too scared to use it. I used my strength as a man, and the simple tools, as Julien had told me I would. But the power's there. It has to be. And if that's what it takes for you to love me, I mean really love me, then I can reach down inside me and find out just what that power can do. That has always been my option."

"My innocent Michael," she said, but it had the tone of a query rather than a declaration.

He shook his head. He leant forward and kissed her. It was not the best thing to do, perhaps, but he couldn't stop himself. He held her by the shoulders, and he did press her back against the seat and cover her mouth with his mouth. He felt her instant response, the way her body was united at once in passion, arms sliding up around his back, mouth kissing him back, back arching as if she would press her entire self against him.

When he let her go, it was only because he had to.

The car was moving swiftly along the freeway. The airport loomed ahead. And there was no time now for the passion he felt, for the consummation of anger and hurt and love that he needed so desperately.

This time it was she who reached out for him, who clasped his head in her hands, and kissed him.

"Michael, my love," she said, "my one and only love."

"I'm with you, darling," he said. "And don't ever try to change it. What we have to do—for Aaron, for Mona, for the baby, for the family, for God knows what—we do together."

IT WASN'T until they were over the Atlantic that he tried to sleep. They'd eaten their gluttonous fill, and drunk a little too much, and talked for an hour about Aaron. Now the cabin was dark and silent, and they bundled beneath a loose half-dozen blankets.

They needed sleep, he figured. Aaron would advise them to sleep now, wouldn't he?

They'd land in London after eight hours, and it would be early morning there, though it was really night to their bodies, and there would be Yuri, eager to hear and entitled to hear how Aaron had died. Pain. Grief. The inevitable.

He was slipping off, not certain whether he was going right straight into a nightmare or into something as bright and meaningless as a bad cartoon, when he felt her touch his arm.

He let his head roll on the leather seat as he turned to her. She lay back beside him, hand clasping his hand.

"If we see this through," she whispered, "if you don't back off from what I do, if I don't shut you . . ."

"Yes . . ."

"Then nothing will ever come between us. Nobody ever will. And anything you might have with a girl bride will be forfeit."

"I want no girl brides," he said. "I never did. I didn't dream of other women while you were gone from me. I love Mona in my own way, and always will, but that's part of who we are, all of us. I love her and I want the child. I want the child so much I don't even want to talk about it. It's too soon. I'm too desperate. But I want only you, and that's been true since the first day I was with you."

She closed her eyes, her hand still warm and tight on his arm, and then it slipped away rather naturally, as if she'd gone to sleep. Her face looked serene and utterly perfect.

"You know, I've taken life," he said in a whisper. But he wasn't sure she was awake still. "I've taken life three times, and I've walked away from those deeds without regret. That changes anyone."

No answer from her lips.

"I can do it again," he said, "if I have to."

Her lips moved.

"I know that you can," she said softly, not opening her eyes, still lying there as if in deep sleep. "But you see, I'm going to do it whether I have to or not. I have been mortally offended."

She drew in close and kissed him again.

"We're not going to make it to London," he said.

"We're the only ones in the entire first-class cabin," she said, raising her eyebrows, and then kissing him again. "I was once riding on a plane when a certain sort of love was made known to me. It was Lasher's first kiss, you might say. It had a wild, electric quality to it. But I want your arms. I want your cock. I want your body! I can't wait until London. Give it to me."

Enough said, he thought. Thank God she'd opened the blazer, or he might have torn the buttons in proverbial romantic fashion.

Nine

I T WAS not so changed. It stood in its forest or park, without locked
gates or dogs to protect it, a great manor house of fine arched
windows and myriad chimneys, luxuriously large and luxuriously well
cared for. One could imagine those times, looking at it. Their brutality
and darkness, their particular fire—all this drew breath and hissed in
the empty night.

Only the cars lining the gravel drive, the cars parked in the open
garages in long rows, betrayed the modern age. Even the wires and
cables ran underground.

He walked through the trees, and then up close to the foundations
and along the stones, searching for the doors he remembered. He wore
no suit or coat now, but only simple clothes, long workman's pants of
brown corduroy and a thick sweater made from wool, the favorite of
seamen.

The house seemed to grow to immense size as he approached it.
Sprinkled throughout were weak and lonely lights, but lights nevertheless. Scholars in their cells.

Through a series of small barred windows he saw a cellar kitchen.
Two lady cooks in white were setting aside the kneaded bread to let
it rise. And white flour covered their hands and the pale wood of the
counter. The smell of coffee came up to him from this room—very rich
and fresh. There had been a door . . . a door for deliveries and such.
He walked along, out of the helpful illumination of the windows,
feeling the stone wall with his hands, and then coming to a door,
though it was one that had not been lately used, and it seemed quite
impassable.

It was worth a try. And he had come equipped. Perhaps it was not
wired with alarms as any door of his own would have been. Indeed, it
looked neglected and forlorn and when he studied it, he saw that it had

no lock at all, but merely old hinges, very rusted, and a simple latch.

To his amazement, it opened to his touch, and made a yawning creak that startled him and unnerved him. There was a stone passage and a small stairway leading upwards. Fresh foot tracks on the stairs. A gush of warm and faintly stale air, the indoor air of winter.

He entered and pushed the door closed. A light leaked down the stairs from above, illuminating a carefully written sign that said DO NOT LEAVE THIS DOOR OPEN

Obediently, he made sure that it was shut and then turned and made his way upwards, emerging into a large, darkly paneled corridor.

This was the hall he remembered. He walked along, not trying to hide the sound of his tennis shoes or to conceal himself in the shadows. Here was the formal library he remembered—not the deep archive of priceless and crumbling records, but the daily reading room, with long oak tables and comfortable chairs, and heaps of magazines from throughout the world, and a dead fireplace, still warm beneath his foot, with a few scattered embers still glowing among its charred logs and ashes.

He had thought the room was empty, but on closer inspection he saw an old man dozing in a chair, a heavyset individual with a bald head and small glasses on the end of his nose, a handsome robe over his shirt and trousers.

It would not do to begin here. An alarm could be too easily sounded. He backed out of the room, careful to be silent this time and feeling lucky that he had not waked this man, and then he went on to a large stairway.

Bedchambers began on the third floor in olden times. Would it be the same now? He went all the way up. It was certainly likely.

When he reached the end of the corridor on the third floor, he turned down another small hall and spied light beneath a door, and decided upon that as his beginning.

Without knocking, he turned the knob and let himself into a small but elegant bedroom. The sole occupant was a woman with gray hair, who looked up from her desk with obvious but fearless amazement.

This was just what he had hoped for. He approached the desk.

There was a book open there under her left hand, and with her right she'd been underlining words in it.

It was Boethius. *De topicis differentiis*. And she had underlined the sentence, "Syllogism is discourse in which, when certain things have been laid down and agreed to, something other than the things agreed to must result by means of the things agreed to."

He laughed. "Excuse me," he said to the woman.

She was looking up at him, and had not moved at all since he entered.

"It's true but it's funny, isn't it? I had forgotten."

"Who are you?" she asked.

The gravel in her voice, the age of it perhaps, startled him. Her gray hair was heavy and worn in an old-fashioned bun on the back of her head rather than the sexless bob of the present fashion.

"I'm being rude, I know," he said. "I always know when I'm being rude, and I beg your pardon."

"Who are you?" she asked again in almost precisely the same tone of voice as before, except that she put a space after each word for emphasis.

"*What* am I?" he asked. "That's the more important question. Do you know what I am?"

"No," she said. "Should I?"

"I don't know. Look at my hands. See how long and thin they are."

"Delicate," she said in the same gravelly voice, her eyes moving only very quickly to his hands and then back to his face. "Why have you come in here?"

"My methods are those of a child," he said. "That is my only way of operating."

"So?"

"Did you know that Aaron Lightner was dead?"

She held his gaze for a moment and then slipped back in her chair, her right hand releasing the green marker. She looked away. It was a dreadful relevation to her.

"Who told you?" she asked. "Does everyone know?"

"Apparently not," he said.

"I knew he wouldn't come back," she said. She pursed her mouth so that the heavy lines above her lips were very defined and dark for a moment. "Why have you come here to tell me this?"

"To see what you would say. To know whether or not you had a hand in killing him."

"What?"

"You heard what I said, did you not?"

"Killing him?" She rose slowly from her chair and gave him a cruel look, especially now that she realized how very tall he was. She looked to the door—indeed, she seemed about ready to move towards it—but he lifted his hand, gently, asking for her patience.

She weighed this gesture.

"You're saying Aaron was killed by someone?" she asked. Her

brows grew heavy and wrinkled over the silver frames of her glasses.

"Yes. Killed. Deliberately run over by a car. Dead."

The woman closed her eyes this time, as if, unable to leave, she would allow herself to feel this appropriately. She looked straight ahead, dully, with no thought of him standing there, apparently, and then she looked up.

"The Mayfair witches!" she said in a harsh, deep whisper. "God, why did he go there?"

"I don't think it was the witches who did it," he said.

"Then who?"

"Someone from here, from the Order."

"You don't mean what you're saying! You don't know what you're saying. No one of us would do such a thing."

"Indeed I do know what I'm saying," he said. "Yuri, the gypsy, said it was one of you, and Yuri wouldn't lie in such a matter. Yuri tells no lies as far as I can tell, none whatsoever."

"Yuri. You've seen Yuri. You know where he is?"

"Don't you?"

"No. One night he left, that's all anyone knows. Where is he?"

"He is safe, though only by accident. The same villains who killed Aaron have tried to kill him. They had to."

"Why?"

"You're innocent of all this?" He was satisfied.

"Yes! Wait, where are you going?"

"Out, to find the killers. Show me the way to the Superior General. I used to know the way, but things change. I must see him."

She didn't wait to be asked twice. She sped past him and beckoned for him to follow. Her thick heels made a loud sound on the polished floor as she marched down the corridor, her gray head bowed, and her hands swinging naturally at her sides.

It seemed forever that they walked, until they had reached the very opposite end of the main corridor. The double doors. He remembered them. Only in former times they had not been cleaned and polished to such a luster. They'd been layered with old oil.

She pounded on the door. She might wake the entire house. But he knew no other way to do this.

When the door opened, she went inside, and then turned very pointedly to reveal to the man within that she was with another.

The man within looked out warily, and when he saw Ash, his face was transformed from amazement to shock and immediate secrecy.

"You know what I am, don't you?" said Ash softly.

He quickly forced his way into the room and closed the doors behind him. It was a large office with an adjoining bedroom. Things were vaguely messy, lamps scattered and dim, fireplace empty.

The woman was watching him with the same ferocious look. The man had backed up as if to get clear of something dangerous.

"Yes, you know," said Ash. "And you know that they killed Aaron Lightner."

The man was not surprised, only deeply alarmed. He was large and heavily built, but in good health, and he had the air of an outraged general who knows that he is in danger. He did not even try to pretend to be surprised. The woman saw it.

"I didn't know they were going to do it. They said you were dead, you'd been destroyed."

"I?"

The man backed up. The man was now in terror. "I was not the one who gave the order to kill Aaron. I don't even know the purpose of the order, or why they wanted you here. I know next to nothing."

"What does all this mean, Anton?" the woman asked. "Who is this person?"

"Person. Person. What an inappropriate word," said the man called Anton. "You're looking at something that . . ."

"Tell me what part you played in it," Ash said.

"None!" he said. "I'm the Superior General here. I was sent here to see that the wishes of the Elders were carried out."

"Regardless of what those wishes were?"

"Who are you to question me?"

"Did you tell your men to bring the Taltos back to you?"

"Yes, but that's what the Elders told me to do!" said the man. "What are you accusing me of? What have I done that you should come here, demanding answers of me? The Elders picked those men, not I." The man took a deep breath, all the while studying Ash, studying the small details of his body. "Don't you realize my position?" the man asked. "If Aaron Lightner's been harmed, don't you realize it's the will of the Elders?"

"You accept this. Does anyone else?"

"No one else knows, and no one is meant to know," said the man indignantly.

The woman let out a small gasp. Perhaps she hoped that Aaron was not dead after all. Now she knew.

"I have to tell the Elders you're here," said the man. "I must report your appearance at once."

"How will you do that?"

The man gestured to the fax machine on the desk. The office was large. Ash had scarcely noticed. The fax was a plain-paper fax, replete with many glowing lights and trays for paper. The desk was full of drawers. Probably one of these harbored a gun.

"I'm to notify them immediately," said the man. "You'll have to excuse me now."

"I don't think so," said Ash. "You are corrupt. You are no good. I can see this. You sent men from the Order to do harm."

"I was told by the Elders."

"Told? Or paid?"

The man was silent. In a panic he looked to the woman. "Call for help," he said. He looked at Ash. "I said they were to bring you back. What happened was not my doing. The Elders said I was to come here and do what I had to do, at all costs."

Once again, the woman was visibly shocked. "Anton," she said in a whisper. She didn't move to pick up the phone.

"I give you one final chance," said Ash, "to tell me something that will prevent me from killing you." This was a lie. He realized it as soon as the words were out of his mouth, but on the other hand, perhaps the man would say something.

"How dare you!" said the man. "I have but to raise my voice and help will come to me."

"Then do it!" said Ash. "These walls are thick. But you should try it."

"Vera, call for help!" he cried.

"How much did they pay you?" asked Ash.

"You know *nothing* about it."

"Ah, but I do. You know what I am, but very little else. Your conscience is decrepit and useless. And you're afraid of me. And you lie. Yes, you lie. In all probability you were very easy to corrupt. You were offered advancement and money, and so you cooperated with something you knew to be evil."

He looked at the woman, who was plainly horrified.

"This has happened before in your Order," he said.

"Get out of here!" said the man. He cried out for help, his voice sounding very big in the closed room. He cried again, louder.

"I intend to kill you," said Ash.

The woman cried, "Wait." She had her hands out. "You can't do things this way. There's no need. If some deliberate harm came to Aaron, then we must call the Council immediately. The house is filled this time of year with senior members. Call the Council now. I'll go with you."

"You can call them when I am gone. You are innocent. I don't intend to kill you. But you, Anton, your cooperation was necessary for what took place. You were bought, why don't you admit this to me? Who bought you? Your orders did not come from the Elders."

"Yes, they did."

The man tried to dart away. Ash reached out, easily catching hold of the man due to the uncommon length of his arms, and he wrapped his fingers very tightly around the man's throat, more tightly perhaps than a human being could have done. He began to squeeze the life out of the man, doing it as rapidly as he could, hoping his strength was sufficient to break the man's neck, but it wasn't.

The woman had backed away. She'd snatched up the telephone and was now speaking into it frantically. The man's face was red, eyes bulging. As he lost consciousness, Ash squeezed tighter and tighter until he was very sure the man was dead, and would not rise from the floor gasping for breath, as it sometimes happened. He let the man drop.

The woman dropped the telephone receiver.

"Tell me what happened!" she cried. It was almost a scream. "Tell me what happened to Aaron! Who are you?"

Ash could hear people running in the hallway.

"Quickly, I need the number through which I can reach the Elders."

"I can't give you that," she said. "That's known only to us."

"Madam, don't be foolish. I have just killed this man. Do as I ask you."

She didn't move.

"Do it for Aaron," he said, "and for Yuri Stefano."

She stared at the desk, her hand rising to her lips, and then she snatched up a pen, wrote something fast on a piece of white paper, and thrust it towards him.

There was a pounding on the double doors.

He looked at the woman. There was no time to talk further.

He turned and opened the doors, to face a large group of men and women who had only just come to a halt, to range round him and look at him.

Here were some who were old and others quite young, five women, four men, and a boy very tall, but still almost beardless. The old gentleman from the library stood among them.

He closed the doors behind him, hoping to delay the woman.

"Do you—any of you—know who I am?" Ash asked. Quickly he looked from face to face, eyes darting back and forth until he was certain he had memorized the features of each person. "Do you know what I am? Answer me, please, if you know."

Not a single one gave him anything but a puzzled expression. He could hear the lady crying inside the room, a thick, heavy sobbing rather like her speaking voice, roughened with age.

Alarm was now spreading through the group. Another young man had arrived.

"We have to go in," said one of the women. "We have to see what's happened inside."

"But do you know me? You!" Ash spoke to the latecomer now. "Do you know what I am and why I might have come here?"

None of them did. None of them knew anything. Yet they were people of the Order, scholars all, not a service person among them. Men and women in the prime of life.

The woman in the room behind him tugged at the knobs of the doors, then flung them open. Ash stepped to the side.

"Aaron Lightner's dead!" she cried. "Aaron's been murdered."

There were gasps, small cries of dismay and surprise. But all around, there was innocence. The old man from the library looked mortally wounded by this news. Innocent.

It was time to get away.

Ash pushed through the loose gathering quickly and decisively and made for the stairs, going down two by two before anyone followed. The woman screamed for them to stop him, to not let him escape. But he had too good a head start, and his legs were so much longer than theirs.

He reached the side exit before his pursuers found the top of the little stairway.

He went out into the night and walked fast across the wet grass, and then, glancing back, began to run. He ran until he had reached the iron fence, which he easily vaulted, and then he walked up to his car and made a hasty gesture for his driver to open the door for him and then take off out of here.

He sat back as the car moved faster and faster on the open highway.

He read the fax numbers written by the woman on a piece of paper. It was a number outside of England, and if memory served him right, it was in Amsterdam.

He pulled loose the phone hooked beside him on the wall of the car, and he punched in the number for the long-distance operator.

Yes, Amsterdam.

He memorized the number, or tried to, at least, and then he folded the paper and put it into his pocket.

WHEN he returned to the hotel, he wrote down the fax number, ordered supper, then bathed at once, and watched patiently as the hotel waiters laid out for him a large meal on a linen-draped table. His assistants, including the pretty young Leslie, stood anxiously by.

"You're to find me another place of residence as soon as it's daybreak," he told Leslie. "A hotel as fine as this one, but something much larger. I need an office and several lines. Come back for me only when everything is arranged."

The young Leslie seemed overjoyed to be so commissioned and empowered, and off she went with the others in tow. He dismissed the waiters, and began to consume the meal of sumptuous pasta in cream sauce, lots of cold milk, and the meat of a lobster, which he did not like, but which was, nevertheless, white.

Afterwards he lay on the sofa, quietly listening to the crackling of the fire and hoping perhaps for a gentle rainfall.

He also hoped that Yuri would return. It wasn't likely. But he had insisted they remain here at Claridge's on the chance that Yuri would trust them again.

At last Samuel came in, so drunk that he staggered. His tweed jacket was slung over his shoulder, and his white shirt was rumpled. Only now did Ash see that the shirt was specially made, as the suit had been, to fit Samuel's grotesque body.

Samuel lay down by the fire, awkward as a whale. Ash got up, gathered some soft pillows from the couch, and put them beneath Samuel's head. The dwarf opened his eyes, wider than usual, it seemed. His breath was fragrant from drink. His breath came in snorts, but none of this repelled Ash, who had always loved Samuel.

On the contrary, he might have argued to anyone in the world that Samuel had a rocklike, carven beauty, but what would have been the use?

"Did you find Yuri?" Samuel asked.

"No," said Ash, who remained down on one knee, so that he could speak to Samuel almost in a whisper. "I didn't look for him, Samuel. Where would I begin in all of London?"

"Aye, there is no beginning and no end," said Samuel with a deep and forlorn sigh. "I looked wherever I went. Pub to pub to pub. I fear he'll try to go back. They'll try to kill him."

"He has many allies now," said Ash. "And one of his enemies is dead. The entire Order has been alerted. This must be good for Yuri. I have killed their Superior General."

"Why in the name of God did you do that?" Samuel forced himself up on his elbow and struggled to gain an upright position, but Ash had finally to help him.

Samuel sat there with his knees bent, scowling at Ash.

"Well, I did it because the man was corrupt and a liar. There cannot be corruption in the Talamasca that isn't dangerous. And he knew what I was. He believed me to be Lasher. He pleaded the Elders as his cause when I threatened his life. No loyal member would have mentioned the Elders to anyone outside, or said things that were so defensive and obvious."

"And you killed him."

"With my hands, the way I always do. It was quick. He didn't suffer much, and I saw many others. None of them knew what I was. So what can one say? The corruption is near the top, perhaps at the very top, and has not by any means penetrated to the rank and file. If it has, it has penetrated in some confused form. They do not know a Taltos when they see one, even when given ample opportunity to study the specimen."

"Specimen," said Samuel. "I want to go back to the glen."

"Don't you want to help me, so that the glen remains safe so that your revolting little friends can dance and play the pipes, and kill unsuspecting humans and boil the fat from their bones in cauldrons?"

"You have a cruel tongue."

"Do I? Perhaps so."

"What will we do now?"

"I don't know the next step. If Yuri hasn't returned by morning, I suppose that we should leave here."

"But I like Claridge's," Samuel grumbled. He keeled over, eyes closing the moment he hit the pillow.

"Samuel, refresh my memory," Ash said.

"About what?"

"What is a syllogism?"

Samuel laughed. "Refresh your memory? You never knew what a syllogism was. What do you know about philosophy?"

"Too much," said Ash. He tried to remember it himself. All men are beasts. Beasts are savage. Therefore all men are savage.

He went into the bedroom and lay down on the bed.

For one moment, he saw again the pretty-haired witch, Yuri's beloved. He imagined that her naked breasts were pressed gently against his face, and that her hair covered them both like a great mantle.

Then he was fast asleep. He dreamed he was walking through the doll museum in his building. The marble tile had just been polished, and he could see all the many colors, and how colors changed depending upon what color was right beside them. All the dolls in their glass cases began to sing—the modern, the antique, the grotesque, the beautiful. The French dolls danced, and swung their little bell-shaped dresses as they did so, their round little faces full of glee, and the magnificent Bru dolls, his queens, his most treasured queens, sang high soprano, their paperweight eyes glistening in the fluorescent lights. Never had he heard such music. He was so happy.

Make dolls that can sing, he thought in his dream, dolls that can really sing—not like the old ones that were bad mechanical toys, but dolls with electronic voices that will sing forever. And when the world ends, the dolls will still sing in the ruins.

Ten

"THERE'S no question," said Dr. Salter. She set down the manila folder on the edge of the desk. "But it didn't happen six weeks ago."

"Why do you say that?" said Mona. She hated this little examining room because it didn't have any windows. Made her feel she was going to smother.

"Because you're almost three months along, that's why." The doctor approached the table. "Here, you want to feel it yourself? Give me your hand."

Mona let the doctor lift her wrist and then place her hand on her own belly.

"Press hard. You feel that? That's the baby. Why do you think you're wearing that loose thing? You can't stand anything tight against your waist, now, can you?"

"Look, my aunt bought me these clothes. They were hanging there, or it was hanging there." What was it, damn it, oh yeah, linen, black for funerals, or for looking nifty with fancy high-heeled black-and-white string shoes. "I can't be that pregnant," said Mona. "That's just not possible."

"Go home and check your computer log, Mona. You are."

Mona sat up, and jumped down from the table, smoothing down the black skirt and quickly slipping into the fancy shoes. No need to lace or unlace, though if Aunt Gifford had seen her stuffing her foot like that into an expensive shoe, she would have screamed.

"I gotta go," she said. "I'm expected at a funeral."

"Not that poor man who married your cousin, the one killed by the car?"

"Yep, that poor man. Listen, Annelle. Can we do one of those tests where you see the fetus?"

"Yes, and it will confirm exactly what I've been telling you—that you're twelve weeks along. Now listen, you have to take all the supplements I'm giving you. A thirteen-year-old body is not ready to have a baby."

"Okay, I want to make an appointment for that test where we look at it." Mona started for the door, and had her hand on the knob when she stopped. "On second thought," she said, "I'd rather not."

"What's the matter?"

"I don't know. Let's just leave it alone in there for a while. Tests can be scary, can't they?"

"My God, you're turning white."

"No, I'm not, I'm just going to faint like women in the movies."

She went out, passing through the small, carpeted outer office, and out the door, though the doctor was calling to her. The door swished shut heavily, and she hurried through the glass-enclosed lobby.

The car was waiting at the curb. Ryan stood beside it, arms folded. Dressed in dark blue for the funeral, he looked almost the same as always, except that his eyes were watery now, and he was plainly very tired. He opened the door for her.

"Well, what did Dr. Salter say?" he asked. He turned to look at her, up and down and with care.

She really wished everybody would stop looking at her.

"I'm pregnant all right," said Mona. "Everything's OK. Let's get out of here."

"We're going. Are you unhappy? Perhaps this has all begun to sink in."

"Of course I'm not unhappy. Why would I be unhappy? I'm thinking about Aaron. Has Michael or Rowan called?"

"No, not yet. They're probably asleep right now. What's the matter, Mona?"

"Ryan, chill, OK? People keep asking me what's the matter. Nothing's the matter. Things are just happening . . . awfully fast."

"You have a very uncharacteristic look on your face," said Ryan. "You look frightened."

"Naw, just wondering what it's going to be like. My own child. You did tell everybody, didn't you? No sermons or lectures."

"It wasn't necessary," he said. "You're the designee. No one is going to say anything to you. If anyone were likely, it would be me. But I can't bring myself to make the requisite speeches, to issue the usual warnings and reservations."

"Good," she said.

"We've lost so many, and this is a brand-new life, and I see it rather like a flame, and I keep wanting to cup my hands around it and protect it."

"You're flipping out, Ryan. You're really tired. You need to rest for a while."

"Do you want to tell me now?"

"Tell you what?"

"The identity of the father, Mona. You do plan to tell us, don't you? Is it your cousin David?"

"No, it's not David. Forget about David."

"Yuri?"

"What is this? Twenty questions? I know who the father is, if that's what you're wondering, but I don't want to talk about it now. And the identity of the father can be confirmed as soon as the baby's born."

"Before then."

"I don't want any needles going into this baby! I don't want any threat to it. I told you I know who the father is. I'll tell you when it's . . . when I think it's time."

"It's Michael Curry, isn't it?"

She turned and glared at him. Too late now to field the question. He had seen it in her face. And he looked so exhausted, so without the usual backbone. He was like a man on strong medicine, a little punchy, and more open than usual. Good thing they were in the limo, and he wasn't driving. He would go straight into a fence.

"Gifford told me," he said, speaking slowly, in the same druggy fashion. He looked out the window. They were driving slowly down St. Charles Avenue, the prettiest stretch of newer mansions and very old trees.

"Come again?" she asked. "Gifford told you? Ryan, are you OK?" What would happen to this family if Ryan went off his rocker? She had enough to worry about as it was. "Ryan, answer me."

"It was a dream I had last night," he said, turning to her finally. "Gifford said the father was Michael Curry."

"Was Gifford happy or sad?"

"Happy or sad." He pondered. "Actually, I don't remember."

"Oh, so that's great," said Mona. "Even now that she's dead, no one is paying attention to what she says. She comes in a dream, and you don't even pay attention."

This startled him, but only a little. He took no offense, as far as she could tell. When he looked at her, his eyes were remote and very peaceful.

"It was a nice dream, a good dream. We were together."

"What did she look like?" There was really something wrong with him. I'm alone, she thought. Aaron's been murdered. Bea needs our sympathy; Rowan and Michael haven't called in yet, we're all scared, and now Ryan is drifting, and maybe, just maybe, that is all for the best.

"What did Gifford look like?" she asked again.

"Pretty, the way she always looked. She always looked the same to me, you know, whether she was twenty-five or thirty-five, or fifteen even. She was my Gifford."

"What was she doing?"

"Why do you want to know?"

"I believe in dreams. Ryan, please tell me. Think back—was Gifford doing anything?"

He shrugged, and gave a little smile. "She was digging a hole, actually. I think it was under a tree. I believe it was Deirdre's oak. Yes, that's what it was, and the dirt was piled high all around her."

For a moment Mona didn't answer. She was so shaken she didn't trust her voice.

He drifted away again, looking out the window, as if he'd already forgotten they were talking.

She felt a pain in her head, very sharp, through both temples. Maybe the movement of the car was making her sick. That happened when you were pregnant, even if the baby was normal.

"Uncle Ryan, I can't go to Aaron's funeral," she said suddenly. "The car is making me feel sick. I want to go, but I can't. I have to go home. I know it sounds stupid and self-centered, but . . ."

"I'll take you right home," he said gallantly. He reached up and pressed the intercom. "Clem, take Mona to First Street." He shut off the intercom. "You did mean First Street, didn't you?"

"Yeah, I certainly did," said Mona. She had promised Rowan and Michael she would move in immediately, and she had. Besides, it was more home than Amelia Street, with her mother gone, and her father dead drunk now, only getting up occasionally at night to look for his bottles or his cigarettes, or his dead wife.

"I'm going to call Shelby to stay with you," said Ryan. "If Beatrice didn't need me, I'd stay with you myself."

He was very concerned. This certainly was a whole new ball game. He was positively doting on her, the way he used to do when she was very little, and Gifford would dress her in lace and ribbons. She should have known he would react like this. He loved babies. He loved children. They all did.

And I'm not a child anymore to them, not at all.

"No, I don't need Shelby," she said. "I mean, I want to be alone. Just alone up there, with only Eugenia. I'll be all right. I'll take a nap. That's a beautiful room up there, to nap in. I've never been there alone before. I have to think and sort of feel things. And besides, the fences are being patrolled by a force equivalent to the French Foreign Legion. Nobody's going to get in there."

"You don't mind being in the house itself alone?"

Obviously he was not thinking of intruders, but old stories, stories that had always excited her in the past. They now seemed remote, romantic.

"No, why should I?" she said impatiently.

"Mona, you are some young woman," he said, and he smiled in a way that she'd seldom seen him smile. Perhaps it took exhaustion and grief to bring him to the point where something so spontaneous could happen with him. "You're not afraid of the baby, and not afraid of the house."

"Ryan, I was never afraid of the house. Never. And as for the baby, the baby's making me sick right now. I'm going to throw up."

"But you're afraid of something, Mona," he said sincerely.

She had to make this good. She couldn't go on like this, with these questions. She turned to him and put her right hand on his knee.

"Uncle Ryan, I'm thirteen. I have to think, that's all. There's nothing wrong with me, and I don't know what scared or frightened means, except for what I have read of those words in the dictionary, OK? Worry about Bea. Worry about who killed Aaron. That's something to worry about."

"OK, Mona dear," he said with another smile.

"You miss Gifford."

"You didn't think I would?" He looked out the window again, not waiting for an answer. "Now, Aaron is with Gifford, isn't he?"

Mona shook her head. He was really bad off. Pierce and Shelby must know how their father needed them.

They had just turned the corner of First Street.

"You have to tell me the minute that Rowan or Michael calls," Mona said. She gathered her handbag and prepared to jump out. "And . . . and kiss Bea for me . . . and . . . Aaron."

"I will," he said. "You're sure you can stay here alone? What if Eugenia isn't here?"

"That would be too much to hope for," she said over her shoulder. Two young uniformed guards were at the gate, and one of them had just unlocked it for her. She gave him a nod as she passed.

When she reached the front door, she put her key into the lock, and was inside within seconds. The door closed as always with a deep, muffled, heavy sound, and she collapsed against it with her eyes shut.

Twelve weeks, that was flat-out impossible! This baby had started when she slept with Michael the second time. She knew it! She knew it as surely as she knew anything else. Besides, there just wasn't anybody between Christmas and Mardi Gras! No, twelve weeks was out of the question!

Crisis! Think.

She headed for the library. They had brought her computer over last night and she'd set it up, creating a small station to the right of the big mahogany desk. She flopped in the chair now, and at once booted the system.

Quickly she opened a file: /WS/MONA/SECRET/Pediatric.

"Questions that must be asked," she wrote. "How fast did Rowan's pregnancy progress? Were there signs of accelerated development? Was she unusually sick? No one knows these answers because no one knew at that time that Rowan was pregnant. Did Rowan appear pregnant? Rowan must still know the chronology of events. Rowan can clarify everything, and wash away these stupid fears. And of course there was the second pregnancy, the one no one else knows about, except Rowan and Michael and me. Do you dare ask Rowan about this second . . ."

Stupid fears. She stopped. She sat back and rested her hand on her belly. She didn't press down to feel the hard little lump that Dr. Salter had let her feel. She simply opened her fingers and clasped her belly loosely, realizing that it was altogether bigger than it had ever been.

"My baby," she whispered. She closed her eyes. "Julien, help me, please."

But she felt no answer coming to her. That was all past.

She wanted so to talk to Ancient Evelyn, but Ancient Evelyn was still recovering from the stroke. She was surrounded by nurses and equipment in her bedroom at Amelia Street. She probably didn't even know that they'd brought her home from the hospital at all. It would be too maddening to sit there babbling out her heart to Ancient Evelyn and then realize that Ancient Evelyn couldn't understand a word she said.

No one, there is no one. Gifford!

She went to the window, the very one that had been opened that day so mysteriously, perhaps by Lasher, she'd never know. She peered out through the green wooden shutters. Guards on the corner. A guard across the street.

She left the library, walking slowly, falling into a dragging rhythm almost, though she didn't know why, except that she was looking at everything that she passed, and when she stepped out into the garden, it seemed gloriously green and crowded to her, with the spring azaleas almost ready to bloom, and the ginger lilies laden with buds, and the crape myrtles filled with tiny new leaves, making them enormous and dense.

All the bare spaces of winter had been closed. The warmth had unlocked everything, and even the air breathed a sigh of relief.

She stood at the back garden gate, looking at Dierdre's oak, and the table where Rowan had sat, and the fresh green grass growing there, brighter and more truly green than the grass around it.

"Gifford?" she whispered. "Aunt Gifford." But she knew she didn't want a ghost to answer her.

She was actually afraid of a revelation, a vision, a horrible dilemma. She placed her hand on her belly again and just let it stay there, warm, tight.

"The ghosts are gone," she said. She realized she was talking to the baby as well as herself. "That's finished. We aren't going to need those things, you and I. No, never. They've gone to slay the dragon, and once the dragon's dead, the future's ours—yours and mine—and you'll never even have to know all that happened before, not till you're grown and very bright. I wish I knew what sex you were. I wish I knew the color of your hair—that is, if you have any. I should give you a name. Yes, a name."

She broke off this little monologue.

She had the feeling someone had spoken to her—somebody very close had whispered something—just a tiny fragment of a sentence— and it was gone, and she'd couldn't catch it now. She even turned around, spooked suddenly. But of course no one was near her. The guards were around the periphery. Those were their instructions, un-less they heard an alarm sound in the house.

She slumped against the iron post of the gate. Her eyes moved over the grass again and up over the thick black arms of the oak. The new leaves burst forth in brilliant mint-green clusters. The old leaves looked dusty and dark and ready perhaps to dry up and drop away. The oaks of New Orleans were never really barren, thank heaven. But in spring they were reborn.

She turned around and looked to her right, towards the very front of the property. Flash of a blue shirt beyond the front fence. It was more quiet than she'd ever known it to be. Possibly even Eugenia had gone to Aaron's funeral. She hoped so.

"No ghosts, no spirits," she said. "No whispers from Aunt Gifford."

Did she really want there to be any? Suddenly, for the first time in her life, she wasn't so sure. The whole prospect of ghosts and spooks confused her.

Must be the baby, she thought, and one of those mysterious mental changes that comes over you, even this early, guiding you to a sedentary, unquestioning existence. Spirits were not the thing, now. The baby was everything. She'd read plenty on these physical and mental changes last night in her new books on pregnancy, and she had plenty more to read.

The breeze stole through the shrubbery as it always had, grabbing loose petals and leaves and little blossoms here and there, and tumbling them across the purple flags, then dying away to nothing. A slow warmth rose from the ground.

She turned and walked back inside, and through the empty house to the library.

She sat down at the computer and began to write.

"You would not be human if you did not have these doubts and suspicions. How can you not wonder whether or not the baby is all right, under these circumstances? Undoubtedly, this fear has some hormonal origin, and it is a survival mechanism. But you are not a mindless incubator. Your brain, though flooded with new chemicals and combinations of chemicals, is still your brain. Look at the facts.

"Lasher guided the earlier disaster from the beginning. Without the intervention of Lasher, Rowan might have had a completely healthy and beautiful . . ."

She stopped. But what did that mean, Lasher's intervention?

The phone rang, startling her, even hurting her a little. She reached for it hastily, not wanting it to ring again.

"Mona here, start talking," she said.

There was a laugh on the other end. "That's a hell of a way to answer, kid."

"Michael! Thank God. I *am* pregnant, Dr. Salter says there is absolutely no doubt."

She heard him sigh. "We love you, sweetheart," he said.

"Where are you?"

"We're in some frightfully expensive hotel in a French-style suite full of fruitwood chairs standing on tiptoe. Yuri is well, and Rowan is examining this gunshot wound of his. It's become infected. I want you to wait on talking to Yuri. He's overexcited, and talking out of his head a little, but otherwise OK."

"Yeah, sure. I don't want to tell him now about this baby."

"No, that wouldn't be good at all."

"Give me your number."

He gave her the number.

"Honey, are you okay?"

Here we go again, even he can tell that you're worried about it. And he knows why you might be worried. But don't say anything! No, not one word. Something inside her closed up, fearful suddenly of Michael, the very person she'd wanted so to talk to, the very person, along with Rowan, whom she'd felt she could trust.

Play this carefully.

"Yeah, I'm fine, Michael. Ryan's office has your number?"

"We're not going to disappear, honey."

She realized she was staring at the screen, at the questions she had so intelligently and logically listed:

How fast did Rowan's pregnancy progress? Were there signs of accelerated development?

Michael would know these answers. No, don't let on.

"I'm going to go, honey. I'll call you later. We all love you."

" 'Bye, Michael."

She hung up the phone.

She sat quiet for a long time, then began to type rapidly:

"It is too early to ask them stupid questions about this baby, too early to have fears which may affect your health and your peace of mind, too early to worry Rowan and Michael, who have on their minds much more important things . . ."

She broke off.

There had been a whisper near her! It was like somebody right next to her. She looked around and then rose and walked across the room, looking back at it to make certain of what she already knew. There had been no one there, no wispy spooks, no shadows even. Her fluorescent desk lamp had taken care of that.

Guards outside on Chestnut? Maybe. But how could she hear them whispering through eighteen inches of solid brick?

Minutes ticked past.

Was she afraid to move? This is crazy, Mona Mayfair. Who do you think it is? Gifford, or your own mother? Oncle Julien come again? Doesn't he deserve a rest now? Maybe this goddamned house was just plain haunted, and always had been, by all kinds of spirits, like the ghost of the upstairs maid from 1859 or that of a coachman who fell to his death tragically from the roof in 1872. Could be. The family didn't write down everything that happened. She started to laugh.

Proletarian ghosts in the Mayfair house on First Street? Ghosts who weren't blood kin? Boy, what a scandal! Nah, there weren't any ghosts here at all.

She looked at the gilt frame of the mirror, the dark brown marble mantel, the shelves of old decaying books. A calm descended on her, kind of comfortable and nice. She loved this place best of all, she thought, and there wasn't any spirit gramophone playing, and no faces in the mirror. You belong here. You're safe. You're home.

"Yes, you and me, kid," she said, talking to the baby again. "This is our house now, with Michael and with Rowan. And I promise you, I will come up with an interesting name."

She sat down again, and began to type as fast as before:

"Nerves on edge. Imagining things. Eat protein, vitamin C for nerves and for general overall condition. Hearing voices whispering in my ear, sounds like . . . sounds like, unsure, but think it sounds like someone singing or even humming! Kind of maddening. Could be a ghost or a deficiency in vitamin B.

"Aaron's funeral is presently underway. This no doubt contributes to overall jumpiness."

Eleven

Y ou're certain this was a Taltos?" Rowan asked. She had put away the bandages and the antiseptic, and washed her hands. She stood in the bathroom door of the suite, watching Yuri as he walked back and forth, a dark, gangly, and unpredictable figure against the carefully fringed silks and abundant ormolu of the room.

"Oh God, you don't believe me. It was a Taltos."

"This could have been a human who had a reason for deceiving you," she said. "The height alone does not necessarily mean—"

"No, no, no," Yuri said, in the same crazed and manic tone in which he'd been talking since he'd found them at the airport. "It wasn't human. It was . . . it was beautiful and hideous. Its knuckles were enormous, and its fingers, they were so long. The face could have been human, certainly. Very, very handsome man, yes. But this was Ashlar, Rowan, the very one. Michael, tell her the story. St. Ashlar, from the oldest church in Donnelaith. Tell her. Oh, if only I had Aaron's notes. I know he made them. He wrote down the story. Even though we were excommunicated by the Order, he wouldn't have failed to write everything down."

"He did make notes, son, and we have them," said Michael. "And I've told her everything I know as well."

Michael had already explained this twice, if Rowan wasn't mistaken. The endless repetition and circumlocutions of the day had worn on her. She was badly jet-lagged. Her entire constitution had been aged and weakened, she knew that now, if there had ever been any real hope to the contrary. Thank God she had slept on the plane.

Michael sat against the arm of the fancy French couch, with his socked feet crossed on the gold pillows. He had taken off his jacket, and his chest, in the turtleneck sweater, looked massive, as though it housed a heart that would beat triumphantly for another fifty years. He shot a secretive, commiserating glance at Rowan.

Thank God you are here, she thought. Thank God. Michael's calm voice and manner were beyond reassuring. She could not imagine herself here without him.

Another Taltos. Another one of them! God, what secrets does this world harbor, what monsters are camouflaged amid its forests, its big cities, its wilderness, its seas? Her mind played tricks on her. She could not clearly picture Lasher. The figure was all out of proportion. His strength seemed supernatural. That was not accurate. These creatures were not all-powerful. She tried to banish these jarring memories, of Lasher's fingers bruising her arms, and the back of his hand striking her so hard that she lost consciousness. She could feel that moment of disconnection, and the moment of awakening, when, stunned, she'd found herself trying to crawl, for safety, under the bed. But she had to snap out of this, had to concentrate and make Yuri concentrate.

"Yuri," she said in her most quiet and unobtrusive authoritarian manner, "describe the Little People again. Are you certain—"

"The Little People are a wild race," said Yuri, words coming in a rush as he pivoted, hands out, as if to hold a magic glass in which he saw the images of all that he described. "They're doomed, said Samuel. They have no women anymore. They have no future. They will die out, unless a female Taltos comes among them, unless some female of their kind is found in some other remote part of Europe or the British Isles. And this happens. Mark my words, it happens. Samuel told me. Or a witch, don't you see? A witch? The wise women in those parts never go near the glen. The tourists and the archaeologists go and come in groups and by day."

They had been over this, but Rowan had begun to realize that each time he told it, he added something, threw in some new and possibly important detail.

"Of course, Samuel told me all this when he thought I was going to die in that cave. When the fever broke, he was as surprised as I was. And then Ash. Ash has no duplicity in him whatsoever. You cannot imagine the candor or simplicity of this being. Man, I want to say man. Why not man, as long as you remember that he is a Taltos? No human could be so direct, unless he was an idiot. And Ash is not an idiot."

"Then he wasn't lying when he told you he wanted to help you," said Rowan, watching him keenly.

"No, he wasn't lying. And he wants to protect the Talamasca, why I can't tell you. It all has to do with the past, and perhaps the archives, the secrets, though what is really in those archives nobody knows now. Oh, if I could only trust that the Elders were not part of it. But a witch, don't you see, a witch of Mona's power is simply too valuable to Ash and to Samuel. I should never, never have told them about Mona. Oh, I was a fool to tell them all about the family. But you see, this Samuel, he saved my life."

"But did this Taltos say he had no mate?" asked Michael. "If 'mate' is the proper word?"

"That was plainly obvious. He came here because Samuel told him that a Taltos—Lasher, with you, Rowan!—had appeared at Donnelaith. Ash came immediately from someplace far off, I don't know where. Ash is rich. He has bodyguards, attendants, he travels in a little motorcade, so Samuel tells me. Samuel talks too freely, really, for his own good."

"But he didn't mention a female Taltos?"

"No. Both of them gave me the distinct impression that they did not know of the existence of a female Taltos! Rowan, don't you see, the Little People are dying, and the Taltos is damned near extinct. God, Ash could be the only one living, now that Lasher is gone. Imagine it! You see what Mona means to these two?"

"All right, you want my opinion?" asked Michael. He reached for the coffeepot on the tray beside him and refilled his cup, holding it like a mug, without the saucer. "We've done all we can about Ashlar and Samuel." He looked at Rowan as he spoke. "There is a one-in-ten chance, perhaps, that we can locate them at Claridge's even—"

"No, you must not approach them," said Yuri. "You must not even let them know that you are here. Especially not you."

"Yeah, I understand," said Michael nodding, "but—"

"No, you don't understand," said Yuri, "or you don't believe me. Michael, these creatures can tell a witch when they see it, male or female. They know. They do not require modern medical tests to know that you have the chromosomes which are so precious to them. They know you, by scent perhaps, and surely by sight."

Michael gave a little shrug, as if to say he was reserving judgment, but he wouldn't push this now.

"Okay, so I don't go over there to Claridge's right now. But it's awfully hard not to do that, Yuri. I mean, you're saying that Ash and Samuel are only five minutes away from this hotel."

"God, I hope they are gone. And I hope they are not gone to New Orleans. Why did I tell them? Why was I not more clever? Why was I so foolish in my gratitude and in my fear?"

"Stop blaming yourself for this," said Rowan.

"The guards are quadrupled in New Orleans," said Michael. His relaxed posture hadn't changed. "Let's just leave the subject of Ashlar and Samuel for a moment, and go back to the Talamasca. Now, we were making a list of the oldest members in London, ones who could either be trusted or must surely have smelled a rat."

Yuri sighed. He was very near to a small satin chair by the window, one dressed in the same high-pitched moiré as the draperies, so that it was scarcely visible at all. He flopped down on the edge of it, putting his hands over his mouth. He let out his breath again slowly. His hair was rumpled.

"Okay," said Yuri. "The Talamasca, my refuge, my life. Ah, the Talamasca." He counted now upon his right fingers. "We had Milling, he's bedridden, there's no way to get to him. I don't want to call him and agitate him. Then there was . . . there was . . ."

"Joan Cross," said Michael. He picked up the yellow pad from the coffee table. "Yeah, Joan Cross. Seventy-five years old, invalid. Wheelchair. Declined to be appointed Superior General due to crippling arthritis."

"Not the devil himself could subvert Joan Cross," said Yuri, words tumbling faster than ever. "But Joan is too self-absorbed. She spends all her time in the archives. She wouldn't notice now if the members were running around naked."

"Then the next one, Timothy Hollingshed," said Michael, reading it from the pad.

"Yes, Timothy, if only I knew him better. No, the one we should select is Stuart Gordon. Did I say Stuart Gordon? I said Stuart Gordon before, didn't I?"

"No, you didn't, but it's quite all right to say it now," said Rowan. "Why Stuart Gordon?"

"He's eighty-seven and he still teaches, at least within the Order itself. Stuart Gordon's closest friend was Aaron! Stuart Gordon may know all about the Mayfair witches. Why, he almost certainly knows! I remember him telling me once in passing, last year it was, that Aaron had been near to the family too long. I swear on my soul that nothing could corrupt Stuart Gordon. He's the man we should take into our confidence."

"Or at least draw out," said Rowan under her breath.

"You have another name here," said Michael. "Antoinette Campbell."

"She's younger, much younger. But if Antoinette is corrupted, then so is God. But Stuart—if there is anyone on that list who may be an

Elder, and we never know who they are, you see, it would be Stuart Gordon! That's our man."

"We'll save the other names. We shouldn't contact more than one of these people at a time."

"So what do you lose by contacting Gordon now by telephone?" asked Michael.

"He lets them know he's alive," said Rowan. "But perhaps that's inevitable." She was watching Yuri. How would he ever handle a key phone conversation with anyone in this state? Indeed, the sweat had broken out on him again. He was shaking. She'd gotten him clean clothes, but they were already soaked with sweat.

"Yes, it's inevitable," said Yuri, "but if they don't know where I am, there's no danger. I can get more out of Stuart in five minutes than anyone else I can think of, even my old friend Baron in Amsterdam. Let me make this call."

"But we cannot forget," said Rowan, "that he may be in on the conspiracy. It may be the entire Order. It may be all of the Elders."

"He would rather die than hurt the Talamasca. He has a pair of brilliant novices who might even help us. Tommy Monohan, he's some sort of computer genius. He might be of great assistance in tracing down the corruption. And then there's the other one, the blond one, the pretty one, he has a strange name, Marklin, that's it, Marklin George. But Stuart must judge this situation."

"And we are not to trust Stuart until we know that we can."

"But how will we know?" Yuri looked at Rowan.

"There are ways to know," she said. "You're not going to call from here. And when you do, I want you to say certain things. You cannot open up to this man, you understand, no matter how much you trust him."

"Tell me what to say," said Yuri. "But you realize Stuart may not talk to me. No one may talk to me. I am excommunicated, remember? Unless, of course, I appeal to him as Aaron's friend. That's the key with Stuart! He loved Aaron so much."

"Okay, the phone call is a crucial step," said Michael, "we've got that. Now the Motherhouse, can you draw a plan of the house, or give me the info and I'll draw the plan for your approval? What do you think?"

"Yes, that is an excellent idea," said Rowan. "Draw a plan. Show us the location of the archives, the vaults, the exits, everything."

Yuri was on his feet again, as though someone had shoved him forward. He was looking around.

"Where is the paper? Where is the pencil?"

Michael picked up the phone and asked for the front desk.

"We'll get those things," said Rowan. She took Yuri's hands. They were moist and shaking still. His black eyes were frenzied, darting from object to object. He did not want to look at her. "Take it easy," she said, gripping his hands firmly, thinking *Calm,* and drawing closer, until he had to look right into her eyes.

"I am rational, Rowan," he said. "Believe me. I am only . . . only fearing for Mona. I made a hideous blunder. But how often does one meet such beings? I never laid eyes on Lasher, not for one moment, I was not there when he told his tale to Michael and to Aaron. I never saw him! But I saw these two, and not in some cloud of vapor! They were with me as you are with me, they were in a room!"

"I know," she said. "But it's not your fault, all this, that you told them about the family. You must let this go. Think about the Order. What else can you tell us? What about the Superior General?"

"Something's wrong with him. I don't trust him. He is too new. Oh, if you could have seen this creature Ash, you would not have believed your eyes."

"Why not, Yuri?" she asked.

"Ah, yes. Yes, you saw the other one. You knew the other one."

"Yes, in every sense. What makes you certain this one is older, that he's not trying to confuse you with those easy statements he made?"

"Hair. In his hair, two white streaks. Means age. I could tell it."

"White streaks," she said. This was new information. How much more could Yuri spill if they continued to question him? She lifted her hands to her head, as if to say, Where were these streaks of white hair?

"No, here, from the temples, the graying pattern of humans. These streaks alarmed Samuel as soon as he saw them. The face? The face is that of a man of thirty. Rowan, the lifespan of these beings is unknown. Samuel described Lasher as a newborn."

"That's what he was," said Rowan. She realized suddenly that Michael was watching her. He'd gotten to his feet and was standing near the door, arms folded.

She turned to face him. She blotted all thought of Lasher from her mind.

"There is no one who can help us with this, is there?" Michael said. He was speaking only to her.

"No one," she said. "Haven't you known that all along?"

He didn't answer, but she knew what he was thinking. It was as if he wanted her to know. He was thinking that Yuri was cracking. Yuri had to be protected now. And they had counted more upon Yuri, for judgment, direction, help.

The bell sounded. Michael searched in his pocket and drew out some pound notes as he went to the door.

How extraordinary, she thought, that he remembers such things, that he keeps everything going. But she had to get a grip on herself. Lasher's fingers biting into her arm. Her entire body convulsed suddenly and she reached for the place where he'd hurt her again and again and again. Heed your own advice, Doctor. Be calm.

"Now, Yuri, you have to sit down and draw pictures," said Michael. He had the paper and the pencils.

"What if Stuart doesn't know that Aaron is dead?" asked Yuri. "I don't want to be the one to tell him this. God, they must know. They know, don't they, Rowan?"

"Pay attention," said Rowan gently. "I've explained to you before. Ryan's office did not call the Talamasca. I insisted that they wait. The excommunication gave me my excuse. I wanted time. Now we can use their ignorance to our advantage. We have to plan this telephone conversation."

"There's a good-sized desk in the other room," said Michael. "This little Louis Quinze thing will fall apart if we try to use it."

She smiled. He'd said he loved French furniture, but everything in this room seemed to be prancing. The gilded moldings were bubbling up and down the paneled walls as if they were made of neon lights. Hotel rooms, she had been in so many of them. All she could think of when she'd arrived was, Where are the doors, where are the phones, does the bathroom have a window for possible escape? Another flash of Lasher's hand closing on her arm. She flinched. Michael was watching her.

Yuri was staring off. He hadn't seen her shut her eyes, and then struggle to catch her breath.

"They know," Yuri said. "Their newspaper clippers will have seen it in the New Orleans papers. Mayfair. They will have seen it, and faxed the clippings home. They know everything," he said. "Absolutely everything. All my life is in their files."

"All the more reason," said Michael, "to set to work now."

Rowan stood still. *He's gone, he's dead, he can't hurt you. You saw his remains, you saw them covered with earth when you put Emaleth with him. You saw.* She had folded her arms and she was rubbing her elbows. Michael was speaking to her, but she hadn't caught the words.

She looked at Michael.

"I have to see this Taltos," she said. "If he exists, I have to see him."

"It's too dangerous," said Yuri.

"No, it isn't. I have a small plan. It will take us only so far, but it is a plan. You said that Stuart Gordon was Aaron's friend?"

"Yes, for years they worked together. You want us to take Stuart into our confidence? You want to trust Ash that he has told us the truth?"

"You said that Aaron had never heard the word 'Taltos' until it came from Lasher's lips?"

"That's correct," said Michael.

"You can't contact those two, you can't do it!" said Yuri frantically.

"Michael, the drawing can wait. I have to call Claridge's."

"No!" cried Yuri.

"I'm not a fool," she said with a small smile. "Under what name are these odd-sized persons registered?"

"I don't know."

"Describe them," said Michael. "Say the name Samuel. Yuri said everyone knew him, they treated him as if he were a jolly little Father Christmas. The sooner we make this call the better. They could have already left."

"Aaron never knew what a Taltos was, he never read anything or heard anything—"

"That's right," said Yuri. "Rowan, what are you thinking?"

"All right. I make my call first," said Rowan. "Then you make yours. We should go now."

"Don't you want to tell me what you mean to do?" asked Michael.

"Let's see if we can reach these two. It all falls apart if we can't reach them, and we're back to the starting line. Let's go."

"I don't have to draw pictures?" asked Yuri. "You said something about pictures."

"Not now, get your jacket, come on," said Michael. But Yuri looked as helpless and confused as he had all morning. Michael took the jacket off the chair and put it over Yuri's shoulders. He looked at Rowan.

Her heart was pounding. *Taltos.* Got to make this call.

Twelve

MARKLIN had never seen the house in such an uproar. This was a test of his talent to dissemble to the max. The council room was crowded with members, but the meeting had not been called to order. No one noticed him as he passed in the corridor. The noise was deafening under the arched wooden ceilings. But this commotion was a blessing. No one seemed to care about one novice and his reactions, or what he did or where he went.

They had not even awakened him to let him know what was happening. He'd stumbled onto all of this when he'd finally opened his door and discovered several members "patrolling" the hallway. He and Tommy had scarcely exchanged words.

But by now Tommy had reached Regent's Park and disconnected the fax interception. All physical evidence of the false communications was being destroyed.

And where was Stuart? Not in the library, not in the parlors, not in the chapel praying for his beloved Aaron, not in the council room, either.

Stuart could not break under this pressure! And if he was gone, if he was gone to be with Tessa . . . But no, he would not have fled. Stuart was with them again. Stuart was their leader, and it was three against the world.

The big case clock in the hallway said 11:00 a.m., the face of the bronze moon smiling above the ornate numerals. In the noise, the chimes were nearly inaudible. When would they begin formal deliberations?

Did he dare to go up to Stuart's room? But wouldn't that be natural for him? Stuart was his tutor within the Order. Wouldn't that be the right thing to do? And what if Stuart was in panic again, crumbling, questioning everything? What if Stuart turned on him again, as he had on Wearyall Hill, and he did not have Tommy to help him bring Stuart back?

Something had just happened. He could hear it in the council room. He took a few steps, until he found himself in the north door. Members were taking their seats around the huge oak table. And there was Stuart, Stuart looking straight at him—a sharp-beaked bird with small, round blue eyes, in the usual somber, almost clerical clothes.

Dear God, Stuart stood beside the empty chair of the Superior General. He had his hand on the back of the chair. They were all looking at Stuart. They had appointed Stuart to take over! Of course.

Marklin reached to cover his imprudent but inevitable smile with a curled hand and a muffled cough. Too perfect, he thought, it's as though the powers that be were on our side. After all, it might have been Elvera, or Joan Cross. It might have been old Whitfield. But it was Stuart! Brilliant! Aaron's oldest friend.

"Come inside, all of you, be seated, please," said Stuart. He was extremely nervous, Marklin could see it. "You must forgive me," said Stuart, forcing a polite smile which was certainly not required and was hardly appropriate. *Dear God, he's not going to be able to pull this off!* "I have not quite recovered yet from my shock. But you know I've been appointed to take over. We're waiting at this very moment for communication from the Elders."

"Surely they've answered, Stuart," said Elvera. Surrounded by cronies, she had been the star all morning, the witness to Anton Marcus's murder, the one who had conversed with the mysterious man who had entered the building and asked strange questions of those he encountered, and then coldly and methodically strangled Marcus to death.

"There is no answer yet, Elvera," said Stuart patiently. "Sit down there, all of you over there. It's time for this meeting to begin."

At last the room felt silent. The giant table was surrounded by curious faces. Dora Fairchild had been crying, and looked it. So had Manfield Cotter. So had others whom Marklin didn't even know. All friends of Aaron Lightner, or worshipers, to be more correct.

No one here had really known Marcus. His death had horrified everyone, of course. But grief was not a problem there.

"Stuart, has the Mayfair family answered?" came another question. "Do we have any more information about what happened to Aaron?"

"Patience, all of you. I will post the information as soon as it's received. What we know now is that something had gone terribly wrong within this house. Intruders have come and gone. Perhaps there have been other breaches of security. We do not know if all these events are connected."

"Stuart," said Elvera, raising her voice shrilly. "This man asked me if I knew that Aaron was dead! He walked into my room and started talking about Aaron!"

"Of course it's connected," said Joan Cross. Joan had been in a wheelchair for a year now; she looked impossibly frail, even her short white hair was thinning, but her voice was impatient and domineering as it had always been. "Stuart, our first priority is to determine the identity of this killer. We have the authorities telling us the fingerprints are untraceable. But we know that this man might have come from the Mayfair family. They do not."

"Yes . . . all connected somehow, doesn't it seem?" Stuart was actually stammering. "But we have no further indication. That is what I meant." Suddenly his deep-set eyes fixed upon Marklin, who sat almost at the far end of the table, looking calmly at him.

"Gentlemen, to tell you the truth," said Stuart, tearing his eyes away and searching the faces around him, "I'm completely inadequate to take Anton's place. I think . . . I think I should pass the scepter to Joan, if it's all right with the entire assembly. I can't continue!"

Stuart, how could you! Marklin stared at the table, trying to conceal his disappointment just the way he'd tried moments ago to conceal his triumphant smile. You're in the driver's seat, he thought bitterly, but you can't handle it. You're stepping down when you are needed to block the very communication that will hasten things. You are a fool.

"I have no alternative!" said Stuart loudly, as if he were speaking only to his novice. "Gentlemen, I'm too . . . I'm too upset over Aaron's death to be of use."

Interesting statement, wise statement, thought Marklin. Stuart had always taught them, if you have some secret you must keep from the psychics around you, think something close to the truth.

Stuart had risen. He was giving the chair to Joan Cross. There were cries of "Aye!" and approval coming from all sides. Even Elvera was nodding. Young Crawford, one of Joan's pupils, was maneuvering her wheelchair into position at the head of the table. Stuart stood back, near the wall. Stuart was going to try to slip out!

Not without me, thought Marklin, but how could he leave now? Stuart wasn't going to get away from him, he wasn't going to get a chance to flee to that secret place where he kept Tessa. No, that was not going to happen.

Once again, there was a hubbub. One of the old men was complaining that in this emergency the Elders present should identify themselves. Someone else had told the old man to be silent, not to mention such a thing again.

Stuart was gone! Quickly, Marklin slipped out of the chair and hurried through the north doorway. He could see Stuart leagues ahead of him, it seemed, moving towards the Superior General's office. Marklin didn't dare call out. There were two younger members with Stuart—Ansling and Perry, both secretarial assistants. They had been a threat to the operation since the beginning, though neither had had the wits to realize that anything had been wrong.

Suddenly the trio disappeared through the double doors and closed them. Marklin stood alone in the empty hall.

A gavel sounded in the council room, or something very like it. Marklin stared at the doors. On what pretext could he enter? To offer his help, his condolences? Everyone knew he was devoted to Stuart. Good God, what should he do under normal circumstances, if he wasn't . . . Don't think about it, don't ever clearly dwell upon it, not here, not within these halls.

He glanced at his watch. What were they doing? If Stuart had resigned the position, why was he in that office at all? Perhaps the fax was feeding out a message from the Elders. Tommy had had time to stop the interception. Or perhaps Tommy had written the communication that might be coming in.

At last he couldn't stand it any longer. He marched forward, rapped on the doors, and opened them without waiting for permission.

The two young men were alone in the office, Perry seated at Marcus's desk, talking on the telephone, and Ansling hovering above him, obviously trying to follow the call. The fax was silent. The doors to Anton's bedroom were closed.

"Where is Stuart?" Marklin asked loudly and directly, though both men gestured for him to be silent.

"Where are you now, Yuri?" said Perry into the receiver.

Yuri!

"You shouldn't be here," said Ansling. "Everyone should be in the council room!"

"Yes, yes . . ." Perry was saying, clearly humoring the man on the other end of the line.

"Where is Stuart?" demanded Marklin.

"I can't tell you."

"You will tell me!" said Marklin.

"That's Yuri Stefano on the phone," said Ansling, obviously very ambivalent about what he was revealing, glancing anxiously now from

Perry to Marklin. "Stuart's gone to meet him. He told Stuart that he had to come alone."

"Where? How did he leave?"

"Well, down the Superior General's private stairs, I imagine," said Ansling. "How should I know?"

"Shut up, both of you!" said Perry. "Ah, God, he's just rung off!" He slammed down the receiver. "Marklin, get out of here."

"Don't speak to me in that tone, you idiot," said Marklin furiously. "Stuart's my tutor. What private stairs?"

He went right past them, ignoring their indignant and imperious voices, moving through the bedroom and then seeing the perfect cutout of a doorway in the paneling, the unmarked door itself pushed only a few inches ajar. He shoved it back. There was the stairway! Damn!

"Where's he gone to meet Yuri?" he shouted to Ansling, who had only just entered the room.

"Get away from that passage," Perry said. "Get out of this bedroom now. You don't belong in the Superior General's bedroom."

"What's the matter with you, Marklin!" said Ansling. "The last thing we need now is insubordination. Go back to the council room at once."

"I asked you a question. I want to know where my tutor has gone."

"He didn't tell us, and if you'd shut up and stayed out of this, I might have gotten it out of Yuri Stefano myself."

Marklin stared at the two angry, frightened young men. Idiots, he thought, idiots. I hope they blame you and your sniveling, subservient kind for everything. I hope they expel you. He turned and went down the hidden stairs.

A long, narrow passage wound round the corner before leading to a small door. It opened directly to the park, as he knew it would. He had never even noticed this door! There were so many. A few scattered steppingstones led off across the lawn in the direction, more or less, of the garage.

He broke into a run, but he knew it was useless. When he reached the cars, the attendant was on his feet.

"They've asked everyone to stay in, sir, until the meeting's over."

"Stuart Gordon. Did he take a staff car?"

"No, sir, his own, sir. But his orders were that no one else should leave without express permission, sir, that's what he said."

"I'm sure!" said Marklin furiously. He went directly to his own Rolls, and slammed the door on the attendant who had followed him. He hit thirty before he reached the gates.

On the highway he quickly accelerated to sixty, then seventy, eighty. But Stuart was long gone. And he could not know whether Stuart had even taken the highway—whether it was to Tessa or to Yuri that Stuart had gone. And since he had no idea whatsoever where Tessa was, or Yuri, he was following nothing and no one!

"Tommy, I need you," he said aloud. He reached for the car phone and, with his thumb, punched in the number of the secret digs in Regent's Park.

No answer.

Tommy might have already disconnected everything. Oh, why hadn't they made a plan to meet in London? Surely Tommy would realize the error. Surely Tommy would wait there.

The loud screech of a horn startled him. He slammed down the phone. He had to pay attention to what he was doing. He floored the accelerator and passed the truck in front of him, pushing the Rolls to its top speed.

Thirteen

IT WAS an apartment in Belgravia, not far from Buckingham Palace, and expertly fitted with everything he required. Georgian furnishings surrounded him, a great deal of fine new white marble, and soft shades of peach, lemon, oyster white. A staff of expert clerks had been retained to do his bidding, stringently efficient-looking men and women who set to work immediately preparing the fax machine for him, the computer, the phones.

He saw that the near-unconscious Samuel was put to bed properly in the largest of the bedrooms, and then he took possession of the office, seating himself at the desk to read through the papers quickly, and absorb whatever he could of the story of the murder outside London, the man who had been strangled by a mysterious intruder with very large hands.

The articles made no mention of his height. Curious. Had the Talamasca decided to keep this secret, and if so, why?

"Surely Yuri has seen this," he thought, "if Yuri is functioning at all normally." But then, how could he know whether or not Yuri was?

Messages were already coming in from New York.

Yes, these were things he had to attend to. He couldn't pretend even for one day, really, that the company could run without him.

The young Leslie, who apparently never slept, looked radiant as she waited upon him, receiving yet another few pages from a clerk, and placing them to one side.

"Your lines are connected, sir," she said. "Anything else?"

"Dearest," he said, "see that a great roast is prepared in the kitchen for Samuel. He'll be a bear when he opens his eyes."

He was already punching in the direct line to Remmick in New York as he continued speaking to her.

"See to it that my car and driver are ready for me whenever I need them. Fill the refrigerators with fresh milk, and buy some cheeses for me, soft double- and triple-cream cheeses. All manner of the best Camembert and Brie that you can find. But you must send out for all this. I need you here. Tell me immediately if Claridge's calls with a message, and if you don't hear from them, call every hour on the hour, you understand?"

"Yes, Mr. Ash!" she said zealously, and at once began to scribble everything on a notebook which she held two inches from her eyes.

In a twinkling, she had vanished.

But he was to see her rushing about with marvelous energy every time he glanced up.

It was three o'clock when she came to the desk, with all the enthusiasm of a schoolgirl.

"Claridge's, sir, they want to talk to you personally. Line two."

"Excuse me," he said, pleased to see that she at once backed away.

He picked up the lighted line.

"Yes, this is Ashlar, you are calling me from Claridge's?"

"No. This is Rowan Mayfair. I got your number from Claridge's about five minutes ago. They said you'd left this morning. Yuri is with me. He's afraid of you, but I have to talk you. I have to see you. Do you recognize my name?"

"Absolutely, Rowan Mayfair," he said softly. "Will you tell me where I can meet you, please? Yuri is unharmed?"

"First tell me why you're willing to meet me. What precisely do you want?"

"The Talamasca is full of treachery," he said. "Last night I murdered their Superior General." No response from her. "The man was part of the conspiracy. The conspiracy is connected with the Mayfair family. I want to restore order to the Talamasca so that it will go on being the Talamasca, and also because I vowed once that I would always look out for the Talamasca. Rowan Mayfair, do you know Yuri is in danger? That this conspiracy is a threat to his life?"

Silence on the other end of the line.

"I haven't lost you, have I?" he asked.

"No. I was just thinking about the sound of your voice."

"The Taltos you bore did not live past infancy. His soul had not been at peace before he was born. You cannot think of me in those terms, Rowan Mayfair, even if my voice reminds you of him."

"How did you kill the Superior General?"

"I strangled him. I did it as mercifully as I could. There was a purpose to what I did. I wanted to expose the conspiracy to the entire Order, so that the innocent might know, as well as the guilty. However, I do not think the problem involves the whole Order, only a few." Silence. "Please let me come to you. I will come alone if you like. We can meet in a crowded place. Perhaps you know you've reached me in Belgravia. Tell me where you are."

"Yuri is meeting with a member of the Talamasca right now. I can't leave him."

"You must tell me where this meeting is taking place." Quickly he stood up and motioned to the doorway. The clerk appeared immediately. "I need my driver!" he whispered. "Now!" He lifted the mouthpiece again. "Rowan Mayfair, this meeting could be dangerous to Yuri. It could be a very, very bad mistake."

"But that man too is coming alone," said Rowan. "And we will see him before he sees us. His name is Stuart Gordon. Does that name mean anything to you?"

"I have heard the name. The man is very old, that's all I can tell you."

Silence. "Do you know anything else about him, anything that would make it likely that he would know about you?"

"No, nothing," he said. "Stuart Gordon and other members of the Talamasca do go from time to time to the glen of Donnelaith. But they have never seen me there. Or anywhere. They have never laid eyes upon me."

"Donnelaith? You're sure it was Gordon?"

"Yes. I am very sure. Gordon used to appear there often. The Little People have told me. The Little People steal things from the scholars during the night. They take their knapsacks, or whatever they can snatch in a moment. I know the name Stuart Gordon. The Little People are careful not to kill the scholars from the Talamasca. It makes trouble to kill them. They don't kill the people of the countryside, either. But they kill other people who wander in with binoculars and rifles. They tell me who comes to the glen."

Silence.

"Please trust me," said Ash. "This man I killed, Anton Marcus, he was corrupt and unscrupulous. I never do these things on impulse. Please accept my word that I am not a danger to you, Rowan Mayfair. I must talk to you. If you will not let me come—"

"Can you find the corner of Brook Street and Spelling?"

"I know where it is," he said. "Are you there now?"

"Yes, more or less. Go to the bookshop. It's the only bookshop on the corner. I'll see you when you arrive there, and I'll come to you. Oh, and do hurry. Stuart Gordon should be here soon."

She rang off.

He hurried down the two flights of steps, Leslie following, asking all the requisite questions: Did he want his guards? Should she go along?

"No, dear, stay here," he said. "Brook and Spelling, just up from Claridge's," he told the driver. "Do not follow me, Leslie." He climbed into the back of the car.

He did not know whether he should take the car to the very meeting place. Surely Rowan Mayfair would see it and memorize its license, if such a thing was even necessary with a Rolls-Royce stretch limousine. But why should he worry? What had he to fear from Rowan Mayfair? What had she to gain from hurting him?

It seemed he was missing something, something extremely important, some probability that would make itself known to him only with pondering and time. But this line of thinking made his head ache. He was far too eager to see this witch. He would go the way of the child.

The limousine bumped and shoved its way through the busy London traffic, arriving at the destination, two busy shopping streets, in less than twelve minutes. "Please stay here, near at hand," he said to the driver. "Keep your eyes on me, and come to me if I call you. You understand?"

"Yes, Mr. Ash."

Fancy shops dominated the corner of Brook and Spelling. Ash got out, stretched his legs for a moment, walked slowly to the edge of the corner, and scanned the crowd, ignoring the inevitable gawkers and the few persons who made loud, good-natured remarks to him about his height.

There was the bookshop, catercorner from him. Very fancy, with polished wood window frames and brass fixtures. It was open, but there was no one standing outside.

He crossed the intersection boldly, walking against the traffic, infuriating a couple of drivers, but he reached the other corner, naturally, unharmed.

There was a small crowd inside the bookshop. None of them witches. But she had said that she would see him and that she would meet him here.

He turned around. His driver was holding the position, in spite of the traffic going around him, with all the arrogance of a chauffeur at the wheel of a monstrous limousine. That was good.

Quickly, Ash surveyed the shops on Brook to his left, and then, looking across, down the length of Spelling, taking the shops and the passersby one by one.

Against the crowded window of a dress shop stood a man and woman. Michael Curry and Rowan Mayfair. It had to be.

His heart quite literally stood still.

Witches. Both of them.

Both of them were looking at him, and they had witches' eyes, and they gave off that very faint sheen that witches always possessed in his eyes.

He marveled. What was it that made the sheen? When he touched them, if he did indeed do that, they would be warmer than other humans, and if he put his ear to their heads, he would hear a low, organic sound that he could not detect in other mammals or people who were not witches. Though occasionally, very occasionally, he had heard this soft, whispering murmur from the body of a living dog.

Good God in heaven, what witches! It had been so long since he had seen witches of this power, and he had never seen witches with more. He didn't move. He merely looked at them, and tried to pull loose from their staring eyes. No easy thing. He wondered if they could tell it. He remained composed.

The man, Michael Curry, was Celtic to the core. He might have been from Ireland, and not America. There was nothing about him that was not Irish, from his curly black hair to his blazing blue eyes and the wool hunting jacket, which he wore for fashion, obviously, and his soft flannel pants. He was a big man, a strong man.

The father of the Taltos, and its murderer! He remembered it with a dull shock. Father . . . killer.

And the woman?

She was very thin and extremely beautiful, though in a completely modern way. Her hair was simple, yet lustrous and alluring, around her narrow face. Her clothes, too, were seductive, calculatedly skimpy, indeed almost flamboyantly erotic. Her eyes were far more frightening than those of the man.

Indeed, she possessed the eyes of a man. It was as though that part of her face had been removed from a male human and put there, above the soft, long, womanish mouth. But he often saw this seriousness, this aggressiveness, in modern females. It's just that this was, well, a witch.

Both were enthralled.

They did not speak to each other, or move. But they were together, one figure slightly overlapping the other. The wind didn't carry their scent to him. It was blowing in the other direction, which meant, strictly speaking, that they ought to catch his.

The woman suddenly broke the stillness, but only with the slight movement of her lips. She had whispered something to her companion. But he remained silent, studying Ash as before.

Ash relaxed all over. He let his hands hang naturally at his sides, which he seldom did, due to the length of his arms. But they must see he concealed nothing. He walked back across Brook Street, very slowly, giving them time to run if they wanted it, though he prayed to God they would not.

He moved towards them slowly on Spelling. They did not move. Suddenly one of the pedestrians bumped him accidentally and dropped an entire paper sack of small items to the pavement with a crash. The sack broke. The items were scattered.

"Now of all times," he thought, but quickly he smiled, and dropped down on one knee and began to pick up everything for the poor individual. "I'm so very sorry," he said.

It was an elderly woman, who gave him a cheery laugh now, and told him that he was too tall to bend down to do such things as this.

"I don't mind at all. It was my fault," he said, shrugging. He was close enough to the witches, perhaps, for them to hear him, but he could not show fear.

The woman had a large canvas bag over her arm. Finally he had gathered up all of the little bundles and deposited them in the canvas bag. And away she went, waving to him as he waved cordially and respectfully to her.

The witches hadn't moved. He knew it. He could feel them watching him. He could feel the same power which caused the sheen to them in his vision, perhaps the same energy. He didn't know. There was now at most twenty feet between them.

He turned his head and looked at them. He had his back to the traffic, and he could see them clearly in front of the plate-glass window full of dresses. How fearsome they both looked. The light emanating from Rowan had become a very subtle glow in his eyes, and now he did smell her—bloodless. A witch who could not bear. The scent of the man was strong, and the face was more terrible, filled with suspicion and perhaps even wrath.

It chilled him, the way they looked at him. But everyone cannot love you, he thought with a small smile. Not even all witches can love you. That is far too much to ask. The important thing was that they had not run away.

Again, he started to walk towards them. But Rowan Mayfair startled him. She gestured with a pointing finger, and a hand held close to her breast, for him to look across the street.

Perhaps this is a trick. They mean to kill me, he thought. The idea amused him, but only partially. He looked as she had directed. He saw a coffee shop opposite. And the gypsy was just emerging, with an elderly man at his side. Yuri looked ill, worse than ever, and his haphazard jeans and shirt were far too light for the chilly air.

Yuri saw Ash at once. He stepped clear of the busy entrance. He stared at Ash madly, or so it seemed. Poor soul, he is crazy, thought Ash, truly. The elderly man was talking very intently to Yuri, and did not seem to notice that Yuri was looking away.

This elderly man. It had to be Stuart Gordon! He wore the somber, old-fashioned clothes of the Talamasca, wingtip shoes and very narrow lapels, and the vest to match his coat. Almost precious. Yes it was Gordon, surely, or another member of the Talamasca. There could be no mistake.

How Gordon pleaded with Yuri, how distraught he seemed. And Yuri stood not one foot from this man. This man could at any moment kill Yuri in any of a half-dozen secret ways.

Ash started across the street, dodging one car and forcing another to a hasty and noisy stop.

Suddenly, Stuart Gordon realized that Yuri was being distracted. Stuart Gordon was annoyed. He wanted to see what distracted Yuri. He turned just as Ash bore down upon him, reaching the curb, and reaching out to grab Stuart Gordon's arm.

The recognition was indisputable. He knows what I am, thought Ash, and his heart sank slightly for this man. This man, this friend of Aaron Lightner, was guilty. Yes, without question, the man knew him, and gazed up into his face with mingled horror and a deep secretive recognition.

"You know me," said Ash.

"You killed our Superior General," said the man, but this he had latched upon in desperation. The confusion and recognition went far beyond anything which had happened only last night. Gordon went into a panic and began to claw at Ash's fingers. "Yuri, stop him, stop him."

"Liar," said Ash, "look at me. You know full well what I am. You know about me. I know you do, don't lie to me, guilty man."

They had become a spectacle. People were cutting out into the street to get around them. Others had stopped to watch.

"Get your hands off me now!" said Stuart Gordon furiously, teeth clenched, face coloring.

"Just like the other," said Ash. "Did you kill your friend Aaron Lightner? What about Yuri? You sent the man who shot him in the glen."

"I know only what I was told about these things this morning!" said Stuart Gordon. "You must release me."

"Must I?" said Ash. "I'm going to kill you."

The witches were beside him. He glanced to his right and saw Rowan Mayfair at his elbow. Michael Curry stood right beside her, eyes full of venom as before.

The sights of the witches struck new terror in Gordon.

Holding tight to Gordon, Ash glanced to the corner and quickly raised his left hand for his driver. The man was out of the car, and had been watching the whole proceedings. He slid behind the wheel at once, and the car was turning to come down the street.

"Yuri! You're not going to let him do this to me, are you?" Gordon demanded. Desperate, brilliant, counterfeit indignation.

"Did you kill Aaron?" Yuri asked. This one was almost insane now, and Rowan Mayfair moved to restrain him as he pressed in on Gordon. Gordon began to writhe in courageous fury, scratching again at Ash's fingers.

The long Rolls-Royce jolted to a halt beside Ash. The driver stepped out immediately.

"Can I help you, Mr. Ash?"

"Mr. Ash," said the terrified Gordon, who stopped his vain struggling. "What sort of name is 'Mr. Ash'?"

"Sir, there's a policeman coming," said the driver. "Tell me what you want me to do."

"Let's get out of here, please," said Rowan Mayfair.

"Yes, all of us, come." Ash turned and dragged Stuart, stumbling, off the sidewalk.

As soon as the back door of the car was open, he flung the helpless Gordon into the backseat. He slipped in beside him, forcing him to the far side. Michael Curry had slipped in the front, beside the driver, and Rowan climbed in now across Ash, her skin burning him as it touched his leg, and took the jumpseat opposite, as Yuri collapsed beside her. The car lurched, then took off.

"Where shall I take you, sir?" the driver called out. The glass panel was sliding down. Now it had vanished into the back of the front seat and Michael Curry had turned and was peering past Yuri, right into Ash's eyes.

These witches, their eyes, thought Ash desperately.

"Just get out of here," said Ash to the driver.

Gordon reached for the door handle.

"Lock the doors," said Ash, but he didn't wait for the familiar electronic click. He clamped his right hand on Gordon's right arm.

"Let go of me, you bastard!" declared Gordon, with low thundering authority.

"You want to tell me the truth now?" asked Ash. "I'm going to kill you the way I killed your henchman Marcus. What can you tell me that will prevent me from doing it?"

"How dare you, how can you . . ." Stuart Gordon began again.

"Stop lying," said Rowan Mayfair. "You're guilty, and you didn't accomplish this alone. Look at me."

"I will not!" said Gordon. "The Mayfair witches," he said bitterly, all but spitting out the words. "And this thing, this thing you've conjured from the swamps, this Lasher, is it your avenger, your Golem?"

The man was suffering exquisitely. His face was white with shock. But he was far from defeated.

"All right," said Ash quietly. "I'm going to kill you, and the witches can't stop me. Do not think that they can."

"No, you won't!" said Gordon, turning so that he might face Ash as well as Rowan Mayfair, his head back against the upholstered corner of the car.

"And why is that?" asked Ash gently.

"Because I have the female!" whispered Gordon.

Silence.

Only the sounds of traffic around them as the car moved speedily and belligerently ahead.

Ash looked at Rowan Mayfair. Then at Michael Curry, peering back at him from the front seat. And finally at Yuri, across from him, who seemed unable to think or to speak. Ash let his eyes return to Gordon.

"I've always had the female," said Gordon, in a small, heartfelt, yet sardonic voice. "I did this for Tessa. I did it to bring the male to Tessa. That was my purpose. Now let go of me, or you will never lay eyes on Tessa, any of you. Especially not you, Lasher, or Mr. Ash, whoever you may be. Whatever you call yourself! Or am I tragically mistaken, and do you have a harem of your own?"

Ash opened his fingers, stretching them, letting them frighten Gordon, and then withdrawing them and laying his hand in his lap.

Gordon's eyes were red and teary. Still stiff with outrage, he pulled out a huge, rumpled hankerchief and blew his tender-looking beak of a nose.

"No," said Ash quietly. "I'm going to kill you now, I think."

"No! You'll never see Tessa!" snapped Gordon.

Ash leaned over him, very close to him. "Then take me to her, please, immediately, or I *will* strangle you now."

Gordon was silent, but only for a moment.

"Tell your driver to go south," he said. "Out of London, towards Brighton. We're not going to Brighton, but that will do for now. It's an hour and a half."

"Then we have time to talk, don't we?" asked the witch, Rowan. Her voice was deep, almost husky. She made a dazzle in Ash's vision, glinting slightly in the dark car. Her breasts were small but beautifully shaped beneath the black silk lapels of the deep-cut jacket. "Tell me how you could do it," she said to Gordon. "Kill Aaron. You're a man like Aaron, yourself."

"I didn't do it," said Gordon bitterly. "I didn't want it done. It was a stupid, stupid, and vicious thing to do. And it happened before I could stop it. Same with Yuri and the gun. I had nothing to do with it. Yuri, in the coffee shop, when I told you I was concerned for your life, I meant it. There are some things which are simply beyond my control."

"I want you to tell us everything now," said Michael Curry. He looked at Ash as he spoke. "We really can't restrain our friend here. And we wouldn't even if we could."

"I'm not telling you anything more," said Gordon.

"That's foolish," said Rowan.

"No, it isn't," said Gordon. "It's the only move I have. Tell you what I know before you reach Tessa, and when you have her, you'll do away with me at once."

"I'll probably do it anyway," said Ash. "You are buying a few hours of life."

"Not so quick. There are many things I can tell you. You have no idea. You'll need much more than a few hours."

Ash didn't reply.

Gordon's shoulders slumped. He took a deep breath, eyeing his captors one by one again, and then returning to Ash. Ash had drawn back until he too was in the corner. He did not wish to be near this human, this feisty and vicious human whom he knew that he would eventually kill.

He looked at his two witches. Rowan Mayfair sat with her hand on her knee, much as Ash did, and she raised her fingers now in a rolling gesture, begging him, perhaps, to be patient.

The snap of a lighter startled Ash.

"Mind if I smoke, Mr. Ash, in your fancy car?" asked Michael Curry from the front seat. His head was already bowed over the cigarette and the tiny flame.

"Please, do what you wish," said Ash with a cordial smile.

To his amazement, Michael Curry smiled back at him.

"There's whiskey in this car," said Ash. "There is ice and water. Would any of you care for a drink?"

"Yeah," said Michael Curry with a little sigh, exhaling the cigarette. "But in the name of virtue, I'll wait till after six."

And this witch can father the Taltos, Ash thought, studying Michael Curry's profile and his slightly crude but charmingly proportioned features. His voice had a lust in it that surely extended to many things, thought Ash. Look at the way he is watching the buildings as we pass them. He misses nothing.

Rowan Mayfair continued to look only at Ash.

They had just left the city proper.

"This is the right way," said Gordon, in a thick voice. "Keep going until I tell you."

The old man looked away as if he were merely checking their position, but then his forehead struck the window hard, and he began to weep.

No one spoke. Ash merely looked at his witches. Then he thought of the photograph of the red-haired one, and when he let his eyes drift to Yuri, who sat directly opposite, beside Rowan, he saw that Yuri's eyes were closed. He had curled up against the side of the car, his head turned away from them, and he too was shedding tears, without making much of a sound.

Ash leant forward to lay a comforting hand on Yuri's leg.

Fourteen

I T WAS one o'clock, perhaps, when Mona woke up in the upstairs front bedroom, her eyes turned towards the oaks outside the window. Their branches were filled with bright Resurrection ferns, once again green from the recent spring rain.

"Phone for you," said Eugenia.

Mona almost said, God, I'm glad someone's here. But she didn't like admitting to anyone that she'd been spooked in the famous house earlier, and that her dreams had been deeply disturbing to her.

Eugenia looked askance at Mona's big, billowy white cotton shirt. So what was wrong? It was loungewear, wasn't it? In the catalogs, they called them Poet's Shirts.

"Oughtn't be sleepin' in your pretty clothes!" declared Eugenia. "And look at those beautiful big sleeves all rumpled, and that lace, that delicate lace."

If only she could say *Buzz off.* "Eugenia, it's meant to be rumpled."

There was a tall glass of milk, frosty, luscious looking, in Eugenia's hand. And in the other, an apple on a small white plate.

"Who's this from?" asked Mona, "the Evil Queen?"

Of course, Eugenia didn't know what she was talking about, but it didn't matter. Eugenia pointed to the phone again. Mona was about to pick up the phone when her mind, veering back to the dream, discovered the dream was gone. Like a veil snatched away, it left nothing but a faint memory of texture and color. And the very strange certainty that she must name her daughter Morrigan, a name she'd never heard before.

"And what if you're a boy?" she asked.

She picked up the receiver.

It was Ryan. The funeral was over, and the Mayfair crowd was arriving at Bea's house. Lily was going to stay there for a few days, and so would Shelby and Aunt Vivian. Cecilia was uptown, seeing to Ancient Evelyn, and was doing well.

"Could you offer some old-fashioned First Street hospitality to Mary Jane Mayfair for a while?" asked Ryan. "I can't take her down to Fontevrault till tomorrow. And besides, I think it would be good if you got to know her. And naturally, she's half in love with First and Chestnut and wants to ask you a thousand questions."

"Bring her over," said Mona. The milk tasted good! It was just about the coldest milk she'd ever tasted, which killed all the ickiness of it, which she had never much liked. "I'd welcome her company," she went on. "This place is spooky, you are right."

Instantly she wished she hadn't admitted it, that she, Mona Mayfair, had been spooked in the great house.

But Ryan was off on the track of duty and organization and simply continued to explain that Granny Mayfair, down at Fontevrault, was being cared for by the little boy from Napoleonville, and that this was a good opportunity to persuade Mary Jane to get out of that ruin, and to move to town.

"This girl needs the family. But she doesn't need any more of this grief and misery just now. Her first real visit has for obvious reasons been a disaster. She's in shell shock from the accident. You know she saw the entire accident. I want to get her out of here—"

"Well, sure, but she'll feel closer to everybody afterwards," said Mona with a shrug. She took a big, wet, crunchy bite of the apple. God, was she hungry. "Ryan, have you ever heard of the name Morrigan?"

"I don't think so."

"There's never been a Morrigan Mayfair?"

"Not that I remember. It's an old English name, isn't it?"

"Hmmm. Think it's pretty?"

"But what if the baby is a boy, Mona?"

"It's not, I know," she said. And then caught herself. How in the world could she know? It was the dream, wasn't it, and it also must have been wishful thinking, the desire to have a girl child and bring her up free and strong, the way girls were almost never brought up.

Ryan promised to be there within ten minutes.

Mona sat against the pillows, looking out again at the Resurrection ferns and the bits and pieces of blue sky beyond. The house was silent all around her, Eugenia having disappeared. She crossed her bare legs, the shirt easily covering her knees with its thick lace hem. The sleeves were horribly rumpled, true, but so what? They were sleeves fit for a pirate. Who could keep anything like that neat? Did pirates? Pirates must have gone about rumpled. And Beatrice had bought so many of these things! It was supposed to be "youthful," Mona suspected. Well, it was pretty. Even had pearl buttons. Made her feel like a . . . a little mother!

She laughed. Boy, this apple was good.

Mary Jane Mayfair. In a way, this was the only person in the family that Mona could possibly get excited about seeing, and on the other hand, what if Mary Jane started saying all kinds of wild and witchy things? What if she started running off at the mouth irresponsibly? Mona wouldn't be able to handle it.

She took another bite of the apple. This will help with vitamin deficiencies, she thought, but she needed the supplements Annelle Salter had prescribed for her. She drank the rest of the milk in one Olympian gulp.

"What about 'Ophelia'?" she said aloud. Would that be right, to name a girl child after poor mad Ophelia, who had drowned herself after Hamlet's rejection? Probably not. Ophelia's my secret name, she thought, and you're going to be called Morrigan.

A great sense of well-being came over her. Morrigan. She closed her eyes and smelled the water, heard the waves crashing on the rocks.

A SOUND woke her, abruptly. She'd been asleep and she didn't know how long. Ryan was standing beside the bed, and Mary Jane Mayfair was with him.

"Oh, I'm sorry," said Mona, swinging her legs over the side of the bed and coming round to greet them. Ryan was already backing out of the room.

"I presume you know," he said, "that Michael and Rowan are in London. Michael said he would call you." Then he was off, headed down the stairs.

Here stood Mary Jane.

What a change from the afternoon she'd come spouting diagnoses of Rowan. But one had to remember, thought Mona, that those diagnoses had been correct.

Mary Jane's yellow hair was hanging loose and splendid, like flax, over her shoulders, and her big breasts were poking against the tight fit of a white lace dress. There was a little mud, from the cemetery, probably, on her beige high-heeled shoes. She had a tiny, mythical Southern waist.

"Hey there, Mona, I hope this doesn't hang you up, my being here," she said, immediately grabbing Mona's right hand and pumping it furiously, her blue eyes glittering as she looked down at Mona from her seemingly lofty height of about five foot eight inches in the heels. "Listen, I can cut out of here any time you don't want me. I'm no stranger to hitchhiking, I can tell you. I'll get to Fontevrault just fine. Hey, lookie, we're both wearing white lace, and don't you have on the most darlin' little smock? Hey, that's just adorable, you look like a white lace bell with red hair. Hey, can I go out there on the front porch?"

"Yeah, sure, I'm glad to have you here," said Mona. Her hand had been sticky from the apple, but Mary Jane hadn't noticed.

Mary Jane was walking past her.

"You have to push up that window," said Mona, "then duck. But this is really not a dress, it's some kind of shirt or something." She liked the way it floated around her. And she loved the way that Mary Jane's skirts flared from that tiny waist.

Well, this was no time to be thinking about waists, was it?

She followed Mary Jane outside. Fresh air. River breeze.

"Later on, I can show you my computer and my stock-market picks. I've got a mutual fund I've been managing for six months, and it's making millions. Too bad I couldn't afford to actually buy any of the picks."

"I hear you, darlin,' " said Mary Jane. She put her hands on the front porch railing and looked down into the street. "This is some mansion," she said. "Yeah, it sure is."

"Uncle Ryan points out that it is not a mansion, it is a town house, actually," said Mona.

"Well, it's some town house."

"Yeah, and some town."

Mary Jane laughed, bending her whole body backwards, and then she turned to look at Mona, who had barely stepped out on the porch.

She looked Mona up and down suddenly, as if something had made an impression on her, and then she froze, looking into Mona's eyes.

"What is it?" asked Mona.

"You're pregnant," said Mary Jane.

"Oh, you're just saying that because of this shirt or smock or whatever."

"No, you're pregnant."

"Well, yeah," said Mona. "Sure am." This girl's country voice was infectious. Mona cleared her throat. "I mean, everybody knows. Didn't they tell you? It's going to be a girl."

"You think so?" Something was making Mary Jane extremely uneasy. By all rights, she should have enjoyed descending upon Mona and making all kinds of predictions about the baby. Isn't that what self-proclaimed witches did?

"You get your test results back?" asked Mona. "You have the giant helix?" It was lovely up here in the treetops. Made her want to go down into the garden.

Mary Jane was actually squinting at her, and then her face relaxed a little, the tan skin without a single blemish and the yellow hair resting on her shoulders, full but sleek.

"Yeah, I have the genes all right," said Mary Jane. "You do too, don't you?"

Mona nodded. "Did they tell you anything else?"

"That it probably wouldn't matter, I'd have healthy children, everybody always did in the family, 'cept for one incident about which nobody is willing to talk."

"Hmmmmm," said Mona. "I'm still hungry. Let's go downstairs."

"Yeah, well, I could eat a tree!"

Mary Jane seemed normal enough by the time they reached the kitchen, chattering about every picture and every item of furniture she saw. Seemed she'd never been *in* the house before.

"How unspeakably rude that we didn't invite you," said Mona. "No, I mean it. We weren't thinking. Everybody was worried about Rowan that afternoon."

"I don't expect fancy invitations from anybody," said Mary Jane. "But this place is beautiful! Look at these paintings on the walls."

Mona couldn't help but take pride in it, the way Michael had refurbished it, and it occurred to her suddenly, as it had upwards of fifty million times in the last week, that this house would someday be hers. Seemed it already was. But she mustn't presume on that, now that Rowan was OK again.

Was Rowan ever going to be really OK? A flash of memory came back to her, Rowan in that sleek black silk suit, sitting there, looking at her, with the straight dark eyebrows and the big, hard, polished gray eyes.

That Michael was the father of her baby, that *she* was pregnant with a baby, that this connected her to both of them—these things suddenly jarred her.

Mary Jane lifted one of the curtains in the dining room. "Lace," she said in a whisper. "Just the finest, isn't it? Everything here is the best of its kind."

"Well, I guess that's true," said Mona.

"And you, too," said Mary Jane, "you look like some kind of princess, all dressed in lace. Why, we're both dressed in lace. I just love it."

"Thanks," said Mona, a little flustered. "But why would somebody as pretty as you notice somebody like me?"

"Don't be crazy," said Mary Jane, sweeping past her into the kitchen, hips swinging gracefully, high heels clicking grandly. "You're just a gorgeous girl. I'm pretty. I know I am. But I like to look at other girls who are pretty, always have."

They sat together at the glass table. Mary Jane examined the plates that Eugenia set out for them, holding hers up to the light.

"Now this is real bone china," she said. "We got some of this at Fontevrault."

"Really, you still have those sorts of things down there?"

"Darlin', you'd be amazed what's in that attic. Why, there's silver and china and old curtains and boxes of photographs. You should see all that. That attic's real dry and warm too. Sealed tight up there. Barbara Ann used to live up there. You know who she was?"

"Yeah, Ancient Evelyn's mother. And my great-great-grandmother."

"Mine too!" declared Mary Jane triumphantly. "Isn't that something."

"Yep, sure is. Part of the entire Mayfair experience. And you should look at the family trees where it gets all crisscrossed, like if I were to marry Pierce for instance, with whom I share not only that great-great-grandmother, but also a great-grandfather, who also pops up . . . damn, it's the hardest thing to keep track of. There comes a point in the life of every Mayfair when you spend about a year drawing family trees everywhere, trying just to keep it clear in your mind who is sitting next to you at the family picnic, know what I mean?"

Mary Jane nodded, eyebrows raised, lips curled in a smile. She wore a kind of smoky violet lipstick, to die for. My God, I am a woman now, Mona thought. I can wear all that junk, if I want to.

"Oh, you can borry all my things, if you want," said Mary Jane. "I've got an overnight case??? You know??? Just full of cosmetics that Aunt Bea bought for me, and all of them from Saks Fifth Avenue, and Bergdorf Goodman in New York."

"Well, that's very sweet of you." *Mind reader, be careful.*

Eugenia had taken some veal out of the refrigerator, little tender cuts for scallopini, which Michael had set aside for Rowan. She was frying these now, the way Michael had taught her, with sliced mushrooms and onions, already prepared, from a little plastic sack.

"God, that smells good, doesn't it?" said Mary Jane. "I didn't mean to read your mind, just happens."

"I don't care about that, it doesn't matter. As long as we both know it's very hit-and-miss, and easy to misunderstand."

"Oh, absolutely," said Mary Jane.

Then she looked at Mona again, the way she had looked at her upstairs. They were sitting opposite each other, just the way that Mona and Rowan sat, only Mona was in Rowan's place now, and Mary Jane was in Mona's. Mary Jane had been looking at her silver fork, and suddenly she just stopped moving and narrowed her eyes again and looked at Mona.

"What's the matter?" asked Mona. "You're looking at me like something's the matter."

"Everybody just looks at you when you're pregnant, they always do, soon as they know."

"I know that," said Mona. "But there's something different in the way you're looking at me. Other people are giving me swoony, loving looks, and looks of approbation, but you—"

"What's approbation?"

"Approval," said Mona.

"I got to get an education," said Mary Jane, shaking her head. She set the fork down. "What is this silver pattern?"

"Sir Christopher," said Mona.

"You think it's too late for me to ever be a truly educated person?"

"No," said Mona, "you're too smart to let a late start discourage you. Besides, you're already educated. You're just educated in a different way. I've never been the places you've been. I've never had the responsibility."

"Yeah, well, I didn't always want that myself. You know, I killed a man? I pushed him off a fire escape in San Francisco and he fell four stories into an alley and cracked open his head."

"Why did you do it?"

"He was trying to hurt me. He'd shot me up with heroin and he was giving it to me and telling me that him and me were going to be lovers together. He was a goddamned pimp. I pushed him off the fire escape."

"Did anyone come after you?"

"No," said Mary Jane, shaking her head. "I never told that story to anybody else in this family."

"I won't either," said Mona. "But that kind of strength isn't unusual in this family. How many girls, do you think, had been turned out by this pimp? That's the phrase for it, isn't it?"

Eugenia was serving them and ignoring them. The veal did look OK, well browned and juicy, with a light wine sauce.

Mary Jane nodded. "Lots of girls. Idiots," she said.

Eugenia had set down a cold salad of potatoes and peas, another Michael Curry gentleman's special, tossed in oil and garlic. Eugenia plopped a big spoon of it on Mary Jane's plate.

"Do we have any more milk?" asked Mona. "What are you drinking, Mary Jane?"

"Coca-Cola, please, Eugenia, if you don't mind, but then I can certainly get up and get it myself."

Eugenia was outraged at the suggestion, especially coming from an unknown cousin who was obviously a perfect rube. She brought the can and the glass of ice.

"Eat, Mona Mayfair!" Eugenia said. She poured the milk from the carton. "Come on now."

The meat tasted awful to Mona. She couldn't figure why. She loved this kind of food. As soon as it had been set before her, it had begun to disgust her. Probably just the usual bout of sickness, she thought, and that proves I'm on schedule. Annelle had said it would happen at just about six weeks. That is, before she'd declared the baby was a three-month-old monster.

Mona bowed her head. Little wisps of that last dream were catching hold of her, very tenacious and full of associations that were just moving away from her at jet speed as soon as she tried to catch them, and hold them, and open up the dream itself.

She sat back. She drank the milk slowly. "Just leave the carton," she said to Eugenia, who hovered over her, wrinkled and solemn, glaring at her, and at her untouched plate.

"She'll eat what she needs to eat, won't she?" asked Mary Jane, helpfully. Sweet kid. She was already gobbling her veal, and noisily stabbing every bit of mushroom and onion she could find with her fork.

Eugenia finally ambled off.

"Here, you want this?" said Mona. "Take it." She pushed the plate towards Mary Jane. "I never touched it."

"You sure you don't want it?"

"It's making me sick." She poured herself another glass of milk. "Well, I was never much of a milk lover, you know, probably because the refrigerator in our house never kept it cold. But that's changing. Everything's changing."

"Oh yeah, like what?" Mary Jane asked, rather wide-eyed. She chugalugged her entire Coke. "Can I get up and get another one?"

"Yes," said Mona.

She watched Mary Jane as she bounced towards the refrigerator. Her dress had just enough flare to remind you of a little girl's. Her legs looked beautifully muscled, thanks to the high heels, though they had looked beautifully muscled the other day when she'd been wearing flat shoes.

She flopped back down and starting devouring Mona's offering.

Eugenia poked her head in the door from the butler's pantry.

"Mona Mayfair, you didn't eat nothin'. You live on potato chips and junk!"

"Get out of here!" Mona said firmly. Eugenia vanished.

"But she's trying to be maternal and all," said Mary Jane. "Why did you yell at her?"

"I don't want anybody to be maternal with me. And besides, she's not. She's a pest. She thinks . . . she thinks I'm a bad person. It's too long to explain. She's always scolding me about something."

"Yeah, well, when the father of the baby is Michael Curry's age, you know, people are either going to blame him or you."

"How did you know that?"

Mary Jane stopped gobbling, and looked at Mona.

"Well, it is him, isn't it? I kinda figured you were sweet on him, first time I come here. I didn't mean to make you mad. I thought you were happy about it. I keep getting this vibe that you're really happy that he's the father."

"I'm not sure."

"Oh, it's him," said Mary Jane. She jabbed the fork through the last piece of veal, picked it up, and stuffed it in her mouth and chewed it lustily, her smooth brown cheeks working furiously without so much as a line or a wrinkle or any real distortion. This was one beautiful girl. "I know," she said, as soon as she had swallowed a wad of chewed meat big enough to catch in her windpipe and choke her to death.

"Look," said Mona. "This is something I haven't told anybody yet, and . . ."

"Everybody knows it," said Mary Jane. "Bea knows it. Bea told me. You know what's going to save Bea? That woman is going to get over her grief for Aaron on account of one simple reason. She never stops worrying about everybody else. She's real worried about you and Michael Curry, because he's got the genes, as everybody knows, and he's Rowan's husband. But she says that gypsy you fell in love with is just all wrong for you. He belongs with another kind of woman, somebody wild and homeless and without a family, like himself."

"She said all that?"

Mary Jane nodded. Suddenly she spied the plate of bread which Eugenia had set out for them, slices of plain white bread.

Mona didn't consider bread like that fit for consumption. She only ate French bread, or rolls, or something properly prepared to accompany a meal. Sliced bread! Sliced *white* bread!

Mary Jane grabbed the top slice, mushed it together, and started sopping up veal juice.

"Yeah, she said all that," said Mary Jane. "She told Aunt Viv and she told Polly and Anne Marie. Didn't seem to know that I was listening. But I mean, this is what is going to save her, that she's got so much on her mind about the family, like coming down to Fontevrault and making me leave."

"How could they all know this about me and Michael?"

Mary Jane shrugged. "You're asking me? Darlin', this is a family of witches, you're supposed to know that better than I do. Any number of ways they could have found out. But, come to think of it, Ancient Evelyn spilled the beans to Viv, if I am not mistaken. Something about you and Michael being here alone?"

"Yeah," said Mona with a sigh. "So big deal. I don't have to tell them. So much for that." But if they started being mean to Michael, if they started treating him any differently, if they started . . .

"Oh, I don't think you have to worry about that, like I said, when it's a man that age and a girl your age, they blame one or the other, and I think they blame you. I mean, not in a mean way or anything, they just say things like, 'Whatever Mona wants, Mona gets,' and 'Poor Michael,' and you know, stuff like, 'Well, if it got him up off that bed and to feeling better, maybe Mona's got the healing gift.'"

"Terrific," said Mona. "Actually, that's exactly the way I feel myself."

"You know, you're tough," said Mary Jane.

The veal juice was gone. Mary Jane ate the next slice of bread plain. She closed her eyes in a deliberate smile of satiation. Her lashes were all smoky and slightly violet, rather like her lipstick actually, very subtle however, and glamorous and beautiful. She had a damned near perfect face.

"Now I know who you look like!" cried Mona. "You look like Ancient Evelyn, I mean in her pictures when she was a girl."

"Well, that makes sense, now doesn't it?" said Mary Jane, "being's we're come down from Barbara Ann."

Mona poured the last of the milk into her glass. It was still wonderfully cold. Maybe she and this baby could live on milk alone, she wasn't sure.

"What do you mean, I'm tough?" asked Mona. "What did you mean by that?"

"I mean you don't get insulted easily. Most of the time, if I talk like this, you know, completely open-like, with no secrets, like really trying to get to know somebody??? You know??? I offend that person."

"Small wonder," said Mona, "but you don't offend me."

Mary Jane stared hungrily at the last thin, forlorn slice of white bread.

"You can have it," said Mona.

"You sure?"

"Positive."

Mary Jane grabbed it, tore the middle of it, and started rolling the soft bread into a ball. "Boy, I love it this way," she said. "When I was little??? You know??? I used to take a whole loaf, and roll it all into balls!"

"What about the crust?"

"Rolled it into balls," she said, shaking her head with nostalgic wonder. "Everything into balls."

"Wow," said Mona flatly. "You know, you really are fascinating, you're the most challenging combination of the mundane and mysterious that I've ever run across."

"There you go, showing off," said Mary Jane, "but I know you don't mean any harm, you're just teasing me, aren't you? Did you know that if mundane started with a *b*, I'd know what it meant?"

"Really? Why?"

"Because I'm up to *b* in my vocabulary studies," said Mary Jane. "I've been working on my education in several different ways, I'd like to know what you think about it. See, what I do is, I get a big-print dictionary??? You know???? The kind for old ladies with bad eyes??? And I cut out the *b* words, which gives me some familiarity with them right there, you know, cutting out each one with the definition, and then I throw all the little balls of paper . . . oops, there we go again," she laughed. "Balls, more balls."

"So I notice," said Mona. "We little girls are just all obsessed with them, aren't we?"

Mary Jane positively howled with laughter.

"This is better than I expected," said Mona. "The girls at school appreciate my humor, but almost no one in the family laughs at my jokes."

"Your jokes are real funny," said Mary Jane. "That's because you're a genius. I figure there are two kinds, ones with a sense of humor and those without it."

"But what about all the *b* words, cut out, and rolled into balls?"

"Well, I put them in a hat, you know??? Just like names for a raffle."

"Yeah."

"And then I pick them out one at a time. If it's some word nobody ever uses, you know, like *batrachian*?? I just throw it away. But if it's a good word like *beatitude*—'a state of utmost bliss'???? Well, I memorize it right on the spot."

"Hmmm, that sounds like a fairly good method. Guess you're more likely to remember words that you like."

"Oh yeah, but really, I remember almost everything, you know?? Being as smart as I am?" Mary Jane popped the bread ball into her mouth and started pulverizing the frame of crust.

"Even the meaning of *batrachian*?" asked Mona.

" 'A tailless leaping amphibian,' " Mary Jane answered. She nibbled on the crust ball.

"Hey, listen, Mary Jane," said Mona, "there's plenty of bread in this house. You can have all you want. There's a loaf right over there on the counter. I'll get it for you."

"Sit down! You're pregnant, I'll git it!" Mary Jane declared. She jumped up, reached for the bread, caught it by its plastic wrapping, and brought it down on the table.

"How about butter? You want some butter? It's right here."

"No, I've conditioned myself to eat it without butter, to save money, and I don't want to go back to butter, because then I'll miss the butter and the bread won't taste so good." She tore a slice out of the plastic, and scrunched up the middle of it.

"The thing is," said Mary Jane, "I will forget *batrachian* if I don't use it, but *beatitude* I will use, and not forget."

"Gotcha. Why were you looking at me in that way?"

Mary Jane didn't answer. She licked her lips, tore loose some fragments of soft bread, and ate them. "All this time, you remembered that we were talking about that, didn't you?"

"Yes."

"What do you think about your baby?" asked Mary Jane, and this time she looked worried and protective, sort of, or at least sensitive to what Mona felt.

"Something might be wrong with it."

"Yeah." Mary Jane nodded. "That's what I figure."

"It's not going to be some giant," said Mona quickly, though with each word, she found it more difficult to continue. "It's not some monster or whatever. But maybe there's just something wrong with it, the genes make some combination and . . . something could be wrong."

She took a deep breath. This might be the worst mental pain she'd ever felt. All her life she'd worried about things—her mother, her father, Ancient Evelyn, people she loved. And she'd known grief aplenty, especially of late. But this worrying about the baby was wholly different; it aroused a fear so deep in her that it was agony. She found she'd put her hand on her belly again. "Morrigan," she whispered.

Something stirred inside her, and she looked down by moving her eyes instead of her head.

"What's wrong?" asked Mary Jane.

"I'm worrying too much. Isn't it normal to think that something's wrong with your baby?"

"Yeah, it's normal," said Mary Jane. "But this family has got lots of people with the giant helix, and they haven't had horrible deformed little babies, have they? I mean, you know, what's the track record of all this giant-helix breeding?"

Mona hadn't answered. She was thinking, What difference does it make? If this baby's not right, if this baby's . . . She realized she was looking off through the greenery outside. It was still early afternoon. She thought of Aaron in the drawerlike crypt at the mausoleum, lying one shelf up from Gifford. Wax dummies of people, pumped with fluid. Not Aaron, not Gifford. Why would Gifford be digging a hole in a dream?

A wild thought came to her, dangerous and sacrilegious, but not really so surprising. Michael was gone. Rowan was gone. Tonight she could go out there into the garden alone, when no one was awake on the property, and she could dig up the remains of those two that lay beneath the oak; she could see for herself what was there.

Only trouble was, she was frightened to do it. She had seen plenty of scenes in horror movies over the years in which people did that sort of thing, traipsed off to the graveyard to dig up a vampire, or went at midnight to discover just who was in what grave. She had never believed those scenes, especially if the person did it by herself or himself. It was just too frightening. To dig up a body, you had to have a lot more balls than Mona had.

She looked at Mary Jane. Mary Jane had finished her feast of bread, apparently, and she just sat there, arms folded, looking steadily at Mona in a manner that was slightly unnerving, Mary Jane's eyes having taken on that dreamy luster that eyes have when the mind has drifted, a look that wasn't vacant but deceptively seriously focused.

"Mary Jane?" she said.

She expected to see the girl startle, and wake up, so to speak, and immediately volunteer what she had been thinking. But nothing like that happened. Mary Jane just kept looking at her in exactly the same fashion, and she said:

"Yes, Mona?" without a single change in her face.

Mona stood up. She went towards Mary Jane, and stood right beside her, looking down at her, and Mary Jane continued to look at her with the same large and frightening eyes.

"Touch this baby, here, touch it, don't be shy. Tell me what you feel."

Mary Jane turned the gaze on Mona's belly, and she reached out very slowly, as if she was going to do what Mona had asked her to do, and then suddenly she jerked her hand back. She rose from the chair, moving away from Mona. She looked worried.

"I don't think we should do it. Let's not do witchcraft with this baby. You and I are young witches," she said. "You know, we really are. What if witchcraft can, you know??? Have an effect on it???"

Mona sighed. Suddenly she didn't want to talk about this anymore; the feeling of fear was too draining and too damned painful, and there had been quite enough.

The only person in the world who could answer her questions was Rowan, and she was going to have to ask them, sooner or later, because she could feel this baby now, and that was flat-out impossible, really, to feel a baby moving like this, just this tiny, tiny movement, even, when a baby was only six or even ten or even twelve weeks.

"Mary Jane, I have to be alone right now," she said. "I'm not being rude. It's just this baby has me worried. That is the simple truth."

"You sure are sweet to explain this to me. You go right ahead. I'm going upstairs if it's okay. Ryan??? He put my suitcase in Aunt Viv's room, you know??? I'm going to be in there."

"You can use my computer if you want," said Mona. She turned her back to Mary Jane and looked out again in the garden. "It's in the library, there are plenty of open programs. It boots right to WordStar, but you can go to Windows or Lotus 1-2-3 simply enough."

"Yeah, I know how to do that, you take it easy, Mona Mayfair, you call me if you need me."

"Yeah, I will. I . . ." She turned around. "I really like having you here, Mary Jane," she said. "There's no telling when Rowan or Michael will come back."

What if they never came back? The fear was growing, including all things at random that came into her mind. Nonsense. They were coming back. But of course they had gone to look for people who might very well want to hurt them. . . .

"Don't you worry now, darlin'," said Mary Jane.

"Yeah," said Mona again, pushing open the door.

She wandered out on the flagstones and off towards the back garden. It was still early and the sun was high and falling down on the lawn beneath the oak, as it would be, really, until late in the day. Best, warmest time in the back garden.

She walked out on the grass. This had to be where they were buried. Michael had added earth to this place, and the newest, tenderest grass grew here.

She went down on her knees, and stretched out on the earth, not caring that it was getting on her beautiful white shirt. There were so many of them. That's what it meant to be rich, and she was already feeling it, having so many of everything, and not having to wear shoes with holes. She pressed her cheek to the cool mud and grass, and her billowing right sleeve was like a big white parachute fallen beside her from heaven. She closed her eyes.

Morrigan, Morrigan, Morrigan . . . The boats came across the sea, torches lifted. But the rocks looked so dangerous. Morrigan, Morrigan, Morrigan. . . . Yeah, this was the dream! The flight from the island to the north coast. The rocks were the danger, and the monsters of the deep who lived in the lochs.

She heard the sound of someone digging. She was wide awake and staring across the grass at the distant ginger lilies, at the azaleas.

No one was digging. Imagination. You want to dig them up, you little witch, she said to herself. She had to admit it was fun playing little witches with Mary Jane Mayfair. Yeah, glad she'd come. Have some more bread.

Her eyes slid closed. A beautiful thing happened. The sun struck her eyelids, as if some big branch or cloud had just freed it, and the light made the darkness brilliant orange, and she felt the warmth creeping all over her. Inside her, in the belly that she could still sleep on, the thing stirred again. *My baby.*

Someone was singing the nursery rhyme again. Why, that must be the oldest nursery rhyme in the world. That was Old English, or was it Latin?

Pay attention, said Mona. I want to teach you how to use a computer before you are four years old, and I want you to realize that there's nothing stopping you from being anything you ever want to be, you're listening?

The baby laughed and laughed. She turned somersaults and stretched her tiny arms and hands and laughed and laughed. It looked like a tiny "tailless leaping amphibian." Mona couldn't stop laughing either. "That's what you are!" she said to the baby.

And then the voice of Mary Jane said—in a pure dream now, and on some level Mona knew it, yes, because Mary Jane was all dressed up like Ancient Evelyn, in old lady clothes, a gabardine dress and string shoes, this was definitely a dream—the voice of Mary Jane said, "There's more to it than that, darlin'. You better make up your mind real soon."

Fifteen

Look, forget what you did, bolting," said Tommy. They were driving back to the Motherhouse, because Tommy insisted. "We have to behave as if we are guilty of nothing. All the evidence is gone now, the route destroyed. They can't trace any phone to any other phone. But we have to go back there and we have to behave as if nothing's happened, and we have to show our concern over the death of Marcus, that's all."

"I'll tell them I was so worried about Stuart," said Marklin.

"Yes, that's exactly what you should tell them. You were worried about Stuart. Stuart was under such a terrible strain."

"Maybe they didn't even notice, I mean, maybe the older ones took no notice that I was even gone."

"And you didn't find Stuart, and now you've come back home. Got it? You have come back home."

"And then what?"

"That depends on them," said Tommy. "Regardless of what happens, we must remain there so as not to arouse suspicion. Our attitude is simply, 'What has happened? Won't anyone explain?' "

Marklin nodded. "But where is Stuart?" he asked. He chanced a glance at Tommy. Tommy was as calm as he'd been at Glastonbury, when Marklin would have fallen on his knees before Stuart and begged him to come back.

"He's gone to meet Yuri, that's all. Stuart isn't under suspicion, Mark. You're the one who may be under suspicion because of the way you bolted. Now get a grip, old man, we have to play this well."

"For how long?"

"How should I know?" asked Tommy, same calm voice. "At least until we have some natural reason to leave again. Then we go back to my place in Regent's Park and we decide. Is the game up? What do we have to lose by remaining in the Order? What do we have to gain?"

"But who was it that killed Anton?"

Tommy shook his head. He was watching the road now, as if Marklin needed a pilot. And Marklin wasn't so sure that he didn't. If he hadn't known this route by heart, he wasn't sure he could have made it.

"I'm not sure we should go back there," said Marklin.

"That's foolish. They haven't an inkling of what really happened."

"How do you know?" asked Marklin. "My God, Yuri could have told them! Tommy, will you use your head? Perhaps it's not a healthy sign to be so calm in the face of this. Stuart went to see Yuri, and Yuri may be at the Motherhouse himself by now."

"You don't think Stuart had the sense to tell Yuri to stay away? That there was some sort of conspiracy, and that Stuart didn't know the extent of it?"

"I think you would have the sense to do that, and perhaps I would, but I don't know about Stuart."

"And so what if Yuri is there? They know about the conspiracy, they just don't know about us! Stuart wouldn't tell Yuri about us, no matter what happened. You're the one who's not thinking. What does Yuri have to tell? He'll fill them in on whatever happened in New Orleans, and if that goes into the records . . . You know, I think I'm going to regret that I destroyed the intercept."

"I don't regret it!" said Marklin. He was becoming irritated by Tommy's businesslike manner, his absurd optimism.

"You're afraid you can't pull it off, aren't you?" asked Tommy. "You're afraid you'll crack like Stuart. But, Marklin, you have to realize Stuart has been in the Talamasca all his life. What is the Talamasca to you or to me?" Tommy gave a little flat laugh. "Boy, they made a mistake with us, didn't they, brother?"

"No, they didn't," said Marklin. "Stuart knew just what he was doing, that we'd have the nerve to carry out schemes that he could never realize. Stuart didn't make a mistake. The mistake was that somebody killed Anton Marcus."

"And neither of us stayed around long enough to find out about this person, this crime, this fortuitous incident. You do realize it's fortuitous, don't you?"

"Of course I do. We're rid of Marcus. That's that. But what happened at the moment of the murder? Elvera talked to the killer. The killer said things about Aaron."

"Wouldn't it be simply marvelous if the intruder was one of the Mayfair family? A top-notch witch? I tell you, I want to read that whole file on the Mayfair Witches from cover to cover. I want to know everything about those people! I was thinking. There must be some way to lay claim to Aaron's papers. You know Aaron. He wrote down everything. He must have left cartons of papers. They must be in New Orleans."

"You're moving too far ahead! Tommy, Yuri may be there. Stuart may have cracked. They may know everything."

"I doubt it seriously," said Tommy, with an air of one who wants to meditate on more important things. "Marklin, the turn!"

Marklin had almost missed it, and when he swerved, it was into the path of another car, but the car gave way, and Marklin raced forward. Within seconds he was away from the highway and going down the country road. He relaxed, realizing only then that he had braced himself so hard for an accident that his jaw was aching from the clenching of his teeth.

Tommy was glaring at him.

"Look, ease up on me!" Marklin said suddenly, feeling the heat behind his eyes which always meant that he was perfectly furious, and had not completely realized it. "I'm not the problem here, Tommy. They are! Now back off. We play it naturally. We both know what to do."

Tommy turned his head slowly as they went through the front gates of the park.

"Everybody in the Order must be here. I've never seen this many cars," said Marklin.

"We'll be lucky," said Tommy, "if they haven't commandeered our quarters for some deaf and blind octogenarian from Rome or Amsterdam."

"I hope they have. It's a perfect excuse to turn everything over to the old guard and very considerately clear out."

Marklin brought the car to a halt, several yards from the busy attendant who was directing the car in front of them to a parking spot quite far away, on the other side of the hedge. In all these years, Marklin had never seen cars packed side by side on the other side of the hedge.

He got out, and tossed the keys to the attendant. "Will you park, please, Harry?" he said. He peeled off several pound notes, a bribe sufficient to waive all objections to this breach of custom, and headed towards the front doors of the house.

"Why in the hell did you do that?" Tommy said, catching up with him. "Try to follow the rules, will you? Fade into the woodwork. Say nothing. Do nothing to attract attention, are we agreed?"

"You're too nervous yourself," said Marklin crossly.

The front doors stood open. The hall was choked with men and women, thick with cigar smoke, and positively roaring with voices. It had the air of a crowded wake or intermission at the theatre.

Marklin stopped. Every instinct in him told him not to go in. And all his life he had believed in his instincts, as surely as he believed in his intelligence.

"Come on, man," said Tommy, between his teeth. He urged Marklin forward.

"Oh, hello," said a bright-faced old gentleman who turned to greet them. "And who are you?"

"Novices," said Marklin. "Tommy Monohan and Marklin George. Are novices allowed to come in?"

"Of course, of course," said the man, stepping aside. The crowd pressed in behind him, faces turning towards him and then away indifferently. A woman was whispering to a man on the other side of the doorway, and when her eyes met Marklin's, she made a small noise of surprise and distress.

"This is all wrong," said Marklin under his breath.

"You should all be here, of course," the jolly man was saying, "all the young ones should be here. When something like this happens, everyone is called home."

"Why, I wonder," said Tommy. "Nobody liked Anton."

"Shut up," said Marklin. "It's quite remarkable, isn't it, the way that people—you and I for instance—respond to stress."

"No, unfortunately, it's not remarkable at all."

They edged their way through the press. Strange faces to the right and left. People everywhere were drinking wine and beer. He could hear French, Italian, even people speaking Dutch.

There sat Joan Cross, in the first of the formal parlors, surrounded by faces unknown to Marklin, but all of them in serious conversation. No Stuart.

"You see?" said Tommy, whispering in his ear. "They're doing what comes naturally after someone dies—gathering, talking, as if it were a party. Now that's what we have to do. What comes naturally. You understand?"

Marklin nodded, but he didn't like it, no, not at all. He glanced back once, trying to find the door, but the door had been closed, apparently, and the crowd blocked his view in any event. He could see nothing. Indeed, it struck him as strange that there were so many foreign faces, and he wanted to say something to Tommy, but Tommy had moved away.

Tommy was chatting with Elvera, nodding as Elvera explained something to him. She looked as dowdy as ever, with her dark gray hair knotted at the nape of her neck, and her rimless glasses halfway down her nose. Enzo stood beside her, that devious-looking Italian. Where the hell was his twin?

How dreadful to spend one's life in this place, he thought. Did he dare to ask about Stuart? Certainly he didn't dare to ask about Yuri, though of course he knew. Ansling and Perry had told him about Yuri's call. Oh God, what was he to do? And where were Ansling and Perry?

Galton Penn, one of the other novices, was pushing his way towards Marklin.

"Hey, there, Mark. What do you think of all this?"

"Well, I don't know that people are talking about it here," said Marklin. "But then I haven't really listened."

"Let's talk about it now, man, before they forbid all conversation on the subject. You know the Order. They haven't a clue as to who killed Marcus. Not a clue. You know what we're all thinking? There's something they don't want us to know."

"Like what?"

"That it was some supernatural agency, what else? Elvera saw something that horrified her. Something bad happened. You know, Mark, I'm very sorry for Marcus and all, but this is the most exciting thing that's ever happened since I was received."

"Yes, I know what you mean," Mark answered. "Haven't seen Stuart, have you?"

"No, not at all, not since this morning, when he declined to take charge. Were you here when that happened?"

"No. I mean yes," said Mark. "I was wondering if he went out or what."

Galton shook his head. "You hungry? I am. Let's get some chow."

This was going to be rough, very rough. But if the only people who spoke to him were bright-faced imbeciles like Galton, he would do just fine, just fine indeed.

Sixteen

THEY'D been on the road over an hour, and it was almost dark, the sky clabbering with silvery clouds, and a drowsy look coming over the great expanses of rolling hills and bright green farmland, neatly cut into patterns as if the landscape were covered with a great patchwork quilt.

They made a pit stop in a little one-street village with several black and white half-timbered houses and a small, overgrown cemetery. The pub was more than inviting. It even had the proverbial dart board and a couple of men playing darts, and the smell of the beer was wonderful.

But this was hardly the time to stop for a drink, thought Michael.

He stepped outside, lit a fresh cigarette, and watched with quiet fascination the formal gentleness with which Ash guided his prisoner into the pub and inevitably towards the bathroom.

Across the street, Yuri stood at a phone booth, talking rapidly, having made his connection to the Motherhouse, apparently, and Rowan stood beside him, arms folded, watching the sky or something in it, Michael couldn't be sure which. Yuri was upset again, wringing his right hand as he held the receiver with the left, nodding over and over again. It was plain that Rowan was listening to his words.

Michael leaned back against the plaster wall, and drew in on the smoke. It always amazed him how tiring it was to simply ride in a car.

Even this journey, with its agonizing suspense, was no different ultimately, and now that darkness had closed off the lovely country-side, he would grow more sleepy, he figured, no matter what was yet to come.

When Ash and his prisoner emerged from the pub, Gordon looked resentful and desperate. But obviously he'd been unable to solicit help, or had not dared to try.

Yuri hung up the phone. It was his turn to disappear into the pub now; he was still anxious, if not crazed. Rowan had been watching him attentively during the drive, that is, when she was not riveted to Ash.

Michael watched Ash as he returned Gordon to the backseat. He didn't try to disguise the fact that he was staring. That seemed unnecessarily cumbersome. The thing about the tall man was this: he did not in any way appear hideous, as Yuri had averred. The beauty was there, and rather spectacular, but the hideousness? Michael couldn't see it. He saw only a graceful frame, and easy, efficient movements that indicated both alertness and strength. The man's reflexes were amazing. He'd proved that when Stuart Gordon had reached again for the lock of the door when they were stopped at a crossroads about a half hour back.

The man's soft black hair reminded him all too much of Lasher; too silky, too fine, too much body to it, he didn't know for certain. The white streaks added a kind of high luster to the whole figure. The face was far too big-boned to be feminine in any conventional sense, but it was delicate, the long nose redeemed perhaps by the fact that the eyes were so large and set so wide apart. The skin was mature skin and not baby-fine. But the real allure of the man was mixed up with his voice and his eyes. His voice could have talked you into anything, Michael thought, and the eyes were highly persuasive as well.

Both bordered on a childlike simplicity, but were not ultimately simple. The effect? The man seemed some sort of angelic being, infinitely wise and patient and yet resolved, without question, to murder Stuart Gordon exactly as he had said that he would.

Of course, Michael wasn't assuming anything about the age of this creature. It was pretty hard not to think he was human, just different, unaccountably strange. Of course, Michael knew he wasn't. He knew it by a hundred little details—the size of Ash's knuckles, the curious way he widened his eyes now and then so that he looked awestruck, and above all perhaps by the absolute perfection of his mouth and teeth. The mouth was baby-soft, impossible for a man with that skin, really, or at least highly improbable, and the teeth were as white as some sort of flashing advertisement that had been shamelessly retouched.

Michael didn't for a moment believe this creature was ancient, or that he was the great Saint Ashlar of the Donnelaith legends, the ancient king who had converted to Christianity in the last days of the Roman Empire in Britain, and allowed his pagan spouse, Janet, to be burnt at the stake.

But the grim tale he had believed when Julien had told it to him. And this was one of the many Ashlars, no doubt—one of the mighty

Taltos from the glen—a being of the very same ilk as the one that Michael had slaughtered.

These things were not disputed by any part of his mind.

He had experienced too much for him to doubt. It was only that he couldn't believe the tall, beautiful man was that old St. Ashlar himself. Perhaps he just didn't want it to be so, for very good reasons that made sense within these elaborate frameworks which he'd now totally accepted.

Yes, you are living now with a whole series of completely new realities, he thought. Maybe this is why you're taking it all calmly. You've seen a ghost; you've listened to him; you know he was there. He told you things you could have never manufactured or imagined. And you've seen Lasher and you've heard his long plea for sympathy, and that was also something completely unimaginable for you, something filled with new information and strange details that you can still remember with puzzlement, now that the misery you were feeling when Lasher told it is over, and Lasher lies buried under the tree.

Oh yeah, don't forget, the burying of the body, dropping the head down in the hole beside it, and then finding the emerald, picking it up, and holding it in the dark while the decapitated body lay down there in the wet earth, ready to be covered up.

Perhaps you can become accustomed to anything, he figured. And he wondered if that was what had happened to Stuart Gordon. He had no doubt that Stuart Gordon was guilty, dreadfully and inexcusably guilty of everything. Yuri had no doubt. But how had the man managed to betray his values?

Michael had to admit he himself had always had a susceptibility to this very kind of Celtic darkness and mystery. His very love of Christmas had its roots in some irrational longing for rituals born in these isles, perhaps. And the tiny Christmas ornaments he had so lovingly collected over the years were all in some way emblematic of old Celtic gods, and a worship overlaid on pagan secrets.

His love of the houses he'd restored had brought him at times as close to this atmosphere of old secrets, old designs and a dormant knowledge to be revealed as one could ever get in America.

He realized he understood Stuart Gordon in a way. And very soon the figure of Tessa would explain Gordon's sacrifices and terrible mistakes, very clearly.

Whatever, Michael had been through so much that his calm now was only inevitable.

Yes, you've been through these things, and you've been used by them and battered by them, and now you stand here, by the village pub in this small, picture-postcard village, with its gently sloping stone street, and you think about all this without emotion—that you are with something that is not human, but is as intelligent as any human, and is soon to meet a female of its kind, an event of such enormous significance that no one really wants to touch upon it, perhaps only out of respect for the man who is supposed to die.

It's hard to ride in a car for an hour with a man who is supposed to die.

He'd finished the cigarette. Yuri had just come out of the pub. They were ready to push off.

"You did reach the Motherhouse?" Michael asked quickly.

"Yes, and I reached more than one person. I made four different calls and reached four different individuals. If these four, my oldest and closest friends, are part of it, then I despair."

Michael gave Yuri's thin shoulder a squeeze. He followed Yuri to the car.

Another thought came to him, that he wasn't going to think about Rowan and her reactions to the Taltos any more now than he had all the way down here, when a deep, instinctive possessiveness had almost caused him to demand that they stop the car, that Yuri climb in the front, so that he could sit by his wife.

No, he wasn't going to give in to this. He couldn't any way in the world know what Rowan was thinking or feeling as she looked at this strange creature. A witch he might be, by genetic profile, and perhaps by some peculiar heritage of which he knew nothing. But he wasn't a mind reader. And he had been aware from the very first moments of their encounter with Ashlar that Rowan would probably not be harmed by making love to this strange creature, because now that she could not have children, she could not suffer the sort of terrible hemorrhage which had brought down Lasher's Mayfair victims one by one.

As for Ash, if he was lusting after Rowan, he was keeping it a gentlemanly secret, but then the creature was driving towards a female of his species, who was perhaps one of the last female Taltos in the world.

And then there's the immediate consideration, isn't there, he thought as he slipped into the passenger seat and firmly shut the door. Are you going to stand by and let this giant of a man murder Stuart Gordon? You know perfectly well you can't do that. You can't watch somebody be murdered. That's impossible. The only time you've ever done it, it happened so quick, with the crack of the gun, that you scarcely had time to breathe.

Of course, you have killed three people yourself. And this misguided bastard, this crazed man who claims to have a goddess under lock and key, has killed Aaron.

They were leaving the little village, which had all but disappeared into the gathering shadows. How tender, how manageable, how tame this landscape. At any other time he would have asked them to stop so that they could walk for a while along the road.

When he turned to the side, he was surprised to discover that Rowan had been watching him. That she was sitting to the side herself and had brought her leg up on the seat right behind him, apparently so that she could look at him. Of course her half-naked legs looked glorious, but so what? She had pulled her skirt down properly. It was no more than a fashionable flash of nylon-covered thigh.

He stretched out his arm along the old leather upholstery, and he laid his left hand on her shoulder, which she allowed, quietly looking at him with her immense and secretive gray eyes, and giving him something far more intimate than a smile.

He had avoided her the entire time they were in the village, and now he wondered why he had done that. Why? On impulse, he decided to do something rude and vulgar.

He leaned over, reaching out to cup the back of her head with his hand, and he kissed her quickly, and then settled back. She could have avoided it, but she didn't. And when her lips had touched him, he had felt a sharp little pain inside, that now began to glow and to increase in intensity. *Love you! Dear God, give it a chance again!*

And no sooner had that reprimand come into his mind than he realized he wasn't talking to her at all; he was talking to himself *about* her.

He settled back, looking out the windshield, watching the dark sky thicken and lose the last of its porcelain luster, and leaning his head to the side, he closed his eyes.

There was nothing stopping Rowan from falling madly in love with this being who could not wring monstrous babies from her, nothing but her marriage vows and her will.

And Michael realized he was not sure of either one. Perhaps he would never be sure again.

Within twenty minutes the light was gone. Their headlights forged through the darkness, and this might have been any highway, any-where in the world.

Finally Gordon spoke up. The next road right, and left on the one immediately following.

The car turned off into the weald, into the high dark trees, a mixture of beech and oak it seemed, with even some light flowering fruit trees that he could not clearly see. The blossoms looked pink here and there in the headlights.

The second side road was unpaved. The woods grew thicker. Maybe this was the remnant of an ancient forest, the kind of grand, Druid-infested woods that had once covered all of England and Scotland, possibly all of Europe, the kind of forest that Julius Caesar had cleared away with ruthless conviction so that the gods of his enemies would either flee or die.

The moon was fairly bright. He could see a little bridge now as they drew closer, and then came another turn, and they were driving along the borders of a small and peaceful lake. Far across the water stood a tower, perhaps a Norman keep. It was a sight so romantic that surely the poets of the last century had gone mad for the place, he thought. Perhaps they had even built it, and it was one of those beautiful shams which were thrown up everywhere as the recent love for the Gothic transformed architecture and style worldwide.

But as they drew closer, as they swung round and came near to the tower, Michael saw it more clearly. And realized that it was a rounded Norman tower, rather large, with perhaps three stories rising to its battlements. The windows were lighted. The lower portion of the building was shrouded by trees.

Yes, that was exactly what it was, a Norman tower—he had seen many in his student years, wandering the tourists' roads over all England. Perhaps on some summer sabbatical which he could no longer remember he had even seen this one.

It didn't seem so. The lake, the giant tree to the left, all of this was too nearly perfect. Now he could see the foundations of a larger structure, wandering away in crumbling lumps and pieces, worn down by rain and wind, no doubt, and further blurred by mounds of wild ivy.

They drove through a thick copse of young oaks, losing track of the building altogether, and then emerged, surprisingly close to it, and Michael could see a couple of cars parked in front of it, and two tiny electric lights flanking a very large door.

All very civilized, it seemed, livable. But how marvelously preserved it was, unmarred by any visible modern addition. Ivy crawled over the rounded and mortared stone, up above the simple arch of the doorway.

No one spoke.

The driver stopped the car finally, in a small graveled clearing.

Michael at once got out and looked around. He could see a lush and wild English garden spreading towards the lake and towards the forest, banks of flowers just coming into bloom. He knew their dim shapes, but they had closed up in the darkness, and who knew what glory would be all around when the sun rose?

Were they going to be here when the sun rose?

An enormous larch tree stood between them and the tower, a tree that was surely one of the oldest Michael had ever seen.

He walked towards its venerable trunk, realizing that he was walking away from his wife. But he couldn't do otherwise.

And when he finally stood under the tree's great spreading branches, he looked up at the façade of the tower, and saw a lone figure in the third window. Small head and shoulders. A woman, her hair loose or covered with a veil, he couldn't be certain.

For one moment the entire scene overwhelmed him—the dreamy white clouds, the high light of the moon, the tower itself in all its rough grandeur.

Though he could hear the crunch of the others coming, he didn't step out of the way, or move at all. He wanted to stand here, to see this—this serene lake to his right, water interrupted and framed now by the delicate fruit trees with their pale, fluttering flowers. Japanese plum, most likely, the very kind of tree that bloomed all over Berkeley, California, in the springtime, sometimes making the very light in the small streets a rosy pink.

He wanted to remember all this. He wanted never to forget it. Perhaps he was still weakened by jet lag, maybe even going predictably crazy like Yuri. He didn't know. But this, this was some image that spoke of the entire venture, of its horrors and revelations—the high tower and the promise of a princess within it.

The driver had switched off the headlamps. The others were walking past him. Rowan stood at his side. He looked one more time across the lake and then at the enormous figure of Ash walking in front of him, Ash's hand still clamped to Stuart Gordon, and Stuart Gordon walking as if he would soon collapse—an elderly gray-haired man, the tendons of his thin neck looking woefully vulnerable as he moved into the light of the doorway.

Yes, this was the quintessential moment, he thought, and it hit him rather like somebody slamming him with a boxing glove, that a female Taltos lived in this tower, like Rapunzel, and that Ash was going to kill the man he was guiding towards the door.

Maybe the memory of this moment—these images, this soft chilly night—maybe this was all he would salvage from this experience. It was a very real possibility.

Ash wrested the key with a firm but slow gesture from Stuart

Gordon, and slipped the key into a large iron lock. The door opened with modern efficiency and they entered a lower hall, electrically heated and filled with large, comfortable furnishings, massive Renaissance Revival pieces with bulbous but beautifully carved legs, claws for feet, and tapestried fabrics, worn but still very pretty, and genuinely old.

Medieval paintings hung on the walls, many with the high imperishable gloss of true egg tempera. A suit of armor stood, covered with dust. And other treasures were heaped here and there in careless luxury. This was the den of a poetic man, a man in love with England's past, and perhaps fatally alienated from the present.

A staircase came down into the room, on their left, following the curve of the wall as it descended. Light shone down from the room above and, for all Michael knew, from the room above that.

Ash let go of Stuart Gordon. He went to the foot of the stairs. He laid his right hand on the crude newel post and began to go up.

Rowan followed him immediately.

Stuart Gordon seemed not to realize that he was free.

"Don't hurt her," he cried suddenly, viciously, as though it was the only thing he could think of to say. "Don't touch her without her permission!" he pleaded. The voice, issuing from the skeletal old face, seemed the last reservoir of his masculine power. "You hurt my treasure!" he said.

Ash stopped, looking at Gordon thoughtfully, and then again he started to climb.

They all followed, finally even Gordon, who pushed past Michael rudely, and then shoved Yuri out of his way. He caught up with Ash at the head of the stairway and disappeared out of Michael's sight.

When they finally reached the top, they found themselves in another large room as simple as the one below it, its walls the walls of the tower, except for two small rooms, skillfully built of old wood, and roofed over—bathrooms perhaps, closets, Michael couldn't tell. They seemed to melt back into the stone behind them. The great room had its share of soft couches and sagging old chairs, scattered standup lamps with parchment shades making distinct islands in the darkness, but the center was wonderfully bare. And a single real iron chandelier, a circle of melting candles, revealing a great pool of polished floor beneath it.

It took a moment for Michael to realize the room held another partially concealed figure. Yuri was already looking at this figure.

Across the circle from them, at the far end of the diameter, so to speak, sat a very tall woman at a stool, apparently working on a loom. One small gooseneck lamp illuminated her hands, but not her face. A small bit of her tapestry was revealed, and Michael could see that it was very intricate and full of muted color.

Ash stood stock-still, staring at her. The woman stared back. It was the long-haired woman Michael had seen at the window.

The others made no move. Gordon rushed towards her.

"Tessa," he said, "Tessa, I'm here, my darling." The voice was speaking in a realm of its own, the others forgotten.

The woman rose, towering over the frail figure of Gordon as he embraced her. She yielded with a sweet, delicate sigh, her hands rising to gently touch Gordon's thin shoulders. In spite of her height, she was so slight of build that she seemed the weaker one. With his arms around her, he brought her forward into the brighter light, into the circle.

There was something grim in Rowan's expression. Yuri was enthralled. Ash's face was unreadable. He merely watched as the woman came closer and closer and now stood beneath the chandelier, the light gleaming on the top of her head and on her forehead.

Perhaps on account of her sex, the woman's height seemed truly monstrous.

Her face was perfectly round, flawless, rather like that of Ash, but not so long or deeply defined. Her mouth was tender and tiny, and her eyes, though big, were timid and without unusual color. Blue eyes, however, kind, and fringed, like those of Ash, with long, luxuriant lashes. A great mane of white hair grew back from her forehead, falling about her almost magically. It seemed motionless and soft, more a cloud than a mane, perhaps, and so fine that the light made the mass of it appear faintly transparent.

She wore a violet dress, beautifully smocked just beneath her breasts. The sleeves were gorgeously old-fashioned, gathered around the small of her upper arms and then ballooning to the cuffs that fitted tightly at the wrists.

Dim thoughts of Rapunzel came to Michael—or more truly of every speck of romance that he had ever read—a realm of fairy queens and princes of unambiguous power. As the woman drew near to Ash, Michael couldn't help but see that her skin was so pale it was almost white. A swan of a princess she seemed, her cheeks firm and her mouth glistening slightly, and her lashes very vivid around her glowing blue eyes.

She frowned, which made a single pucker in her forehead, and seemed like a baby about to bawl.

"Taltos," she whispered. But this was said without the slightest alarm. Indeed, she looked almost sad.

Yuri let out a tiny, faint gasp.

Gordon was transformed with astonishment, as if nothing had actually prepared him for this meeting to take place. He seemed for a moment almost young, eyes fired with love and with rapture.

"This is your female?" asked Ash softly. He was gazing at her, even smiling slightly, but he had not moved to greet her or touch her outstretched hand. He spoke slowly.

"This is the female for whom you murdered Aaron Lightner, for whom you tried to kill Yuri, the female to whom you would have brought the male Taltos at any cost?"

"What are you saying!" said Gordon in a timorous voice. "You dare to hurt her, either with words or actions, I'll kill you."

"I don't think so," said Ash. "My dearest," he said to the woman, "can you understand me?"

"Yes," she said softly, in a tiny bell of a voice. She shrugged and threw up her hands, almost in the manner of an ecstatic saint. "Taltos," she said, and gave a small sad shake of her head, and frowned again with almost dreamy distress.

Had the doomed Emaleth been so fair and feminine?

With a shock, Michael saw Emaleth's face collapse as the bullets struck it, saw the body fall over backwards! Was this why Rowan was crying, or was she merely tired and wondering, eyes watering slightly as she watched Ash looking down at the woman and the woman looking up. What must this be for her?

"Beautiful Tessa," Ash said with a slight rise of his eyebrows.

"What's wrong?" asked Gordon. "Something is wrong—for both of you. Tell me what's wrong." He moved closer, but stopped, obviously not willing to step between them. His voice was rich and sorrowful now. It had the quality of an orator, or of someone who knew how to affect his listeners. "Oh, God in heaven, this is not what I imagined—to meet here in this place, surrounded by those who can't truly grasp the meaning."

But he was too full of emotion for there to be any artifice in what he was saying or doing at all. His gestures were no longer hysterical. They were tragic.

Ash stood as still as ever, smiling at Tessa very deliberately, and then nodding with pleasure as her little mouth opened and expanded, and her cheeks grew small and plump with her own smile.

"You're very beautiful," Ash whispered, and then he raised his hand to his lips, and kissed his fingers and gently placed this kiss on her cheek.

She sighed, stretching her long neck and letting her hair tumble down her back, and then she reached out for him, and he took her in his arms. He kissed her, but there was no passion in it. Michael could see it.

Gordon came between them, circling Tessa's waist with his left hand and gently drawing her back.

"Not here, I beg you. Oh, please, not as if it were in a common brothel."

He let go of Tessa and approached Ash, hands clasped as if praying, peering up without fear now, caught in something more crucial to him even than his own survival.

"What is the place for the wedding of the Taltos?" he said reverently, voice rich and imploring. "What is the holiest place in England, where St. Michael's line runs over the crest of the hill, and the ruined tower of the ancient Church of St. Michael is a sentinel still?"

Ash regarded him almost sadly, composed, merely listening, as the impassioned voice continued.

"Let me take you there, both of you, let me see the wedding of the Taltos on Glastonbury Tor!" His voice dropped low and the words came evenly, almost slowly. "If I see this, if I see the miracle of the birth there on the sacred mountain, in the place where Christ himself came to England—where old gods have fallen and new gods risen, where blood was shed in the defense of the sacred—if I see this, the birth of the offspring, full-grown and reaching out to embrace its parents, the very symbol of life itself, then it doesn't matter whether I go on living, or whether I die."

His hands had risen as if he held the sacred concept in them, and his voice had lost all its hysteria, and his eyes even were clear and almost soft.

Yuri watched with obvious suspicion.

Ash was the picture of patience, but for the first time Michael saw a deeper and darker emotion behind Ash's eyes and even his smile.

"Then," said Gordon, "I will have seen the thing that I was born to see. I will have witnessed the miracle of which poets sing and old men dream. A miracle as great as any ever made known to me from the time my eyes could see to read, and my ears could hear the tales told to me, and my tongue could form words that would express the strongest inclinations of my heart.

"Grant me these last precious moments, the time to travel there. It's not far. Scarcely a quarter of an hour from here—a mere few minutes for us all. And on Glastonbury Tor, I will give her over to you, as a father would a daughter, my treasure, my beloved Tessa, to do what you both desire."

He stopped, looking to Ash desperately still, and deeply saddened, as if behind these words were some complete acceptance of his own death.

He took no notice of Yuri's plain though silent contempt.

Michael was marveling at the transformation in the old man, the sheer conviction.

"Glastonbury," Stuart whispered. "I beg you. Not here." And finally, he shook his head. "Not here," he whispered, and then fell silent.

Ash's face did not change. And then, very gently, as if breaking a terrible secret to a tender heart, one for which he had compassion, he said:

"There can be no union, there can be no offspring." He took his time with the words. "She is old, your beautiful treasure. She is barren. Her fount is dried."

"Old!" Stuart was baffled, disbelieving. "Old!" he whispered. "Why, you're mad, how can you say this?" He turned helplessly to Tessa, who watched him without pain or disappointment.

"You're mad," said Stuart again, his voice rising. "Look at her!" he cried out. "Look at her face, her form. She's magnificent. I've brought you together with a spouse of such beauty that you should fall to your knees and give me your thanks!" Suddenly he was stricken, disbelieving and yet slowly being crushed.

"Her face will be that way, perhaps, the day she dies," Ash said with his characteristic mildness. "I have never seen the face of a Taltos that was different. But her hair is white, completely white, not a single live strand remains in it. No scent comes from her. Ask her. Humans have used her again and again. Or perhaps she has wandered longer even than I. Her womb is dead within her. Her fount is dried."

Gordon gave no further protest. He had clapped his hands over his lips, the little steeple of his fingers collapsed to shut in his pain.

The woman looked a little puzzled, but only vaguely disturbed. She stepped forward and put her long, slender arm lightly around the shivering Gordon, and addressed her words very distinctly to Ash.

"You judge me for what men have done to me, that they used me in every village and every town I entered, that over the years they made the blood flow again and again, until there was no more?"

"No, I don't judge you," Ash said earnestly and with great concern. "I don't judge you, Tessa. Truly I do not."

"Ah!" Once again she smiled, brightly, almost brilliantly, as if this was a reason to be supremely happy.

She looked at Michael suddenly, and then at the shadowy figure of Rowan near the stairway. Her expression was eager and loving.

"I'm saved from these horrors here," she said. "I'm loved in chastity by Stuart. This is my refuge." She stretched out her hands to Ash. "Won't you stay with me, talk to me?" She tugged him towards the center of the room. "Won't you dance with me? I hear music when I look into your eyes."

She drew Ash closer. She said with deep, true feeling, "I'm so glad you've come."

Only now did she look at Gordon, who had slipped away, forehead furrowed, fingers still pressed to his lips, stepping backwards and finding a heavy old wooden chair. He sank down on it, and rested his head against the hard planks that made up the back of it, and turned wearily to the side. The spirit had gone out of him. It seemed his very life was leaving him.

"Dance with me," said Tessa. "All of you, don't you want to dance?" She flung out her arms and threw back her head and shook out her hair, which did indeed look like the lifeless white hair of the very very old.

She turned round and round until her long, full, violet skirts swung out around her, making a bell, and she was dancing on tiptoe with small slippered feet.

Michael couldn't take his eyes off her, off the subtle swaying movements with which she made a great circle, leading with her right foot, and then bringing the other close to it, as though it were a ritual dance.

As for Gordon, it was too painful even to look at him, and this disappointment seemed far more important to him than his life. Indeed, it was as if the fatal blow had already been struck.

Ash, too, stared rapt at Tessa—touched perhaps, worried certainly, and maybe even miserable.

"You lie," Stuart said. But it was a desperate, broken murmur. "You're telling a terrible and abominable lie."

Ash didn't bother to answer him. He smiled and nodded at Tessa.

"Stuart, my music. Please play my music. Play my music for . . . for Ash!" She gave Ash a great bow and another smile, and he too bowed and reached out to take her hands.

The figure in the chair was incapable of movement, and, once again in a murmur, he said, "It's not true," but he didn't believe his own denial.

Tessa had begun to hum a song, turning again in a circle.

"Play the music, Stuart, play it."

"I'll play it for you," said Michael in a low voice. He turned, looking for some possible source, hoping against hope it wasn't an instrument, a harp, a fiddle, something that required a player, because if it was, then he could not rise to the moment.

He felt heartbroken himself, impossibly sad, unable to enjoy the great relief he ought to have been feeling. And for one moment his eyes moved over Rowan, and she too seemed lost in sadness, veiled in it, her hands clasped, her body very upright against the stair railing, her eyes following the dancing figure who had begun to hum a distinct melody, something that Michael knew and loved.

Michael discovered the machines—modern stereo components, designed to look almost mystically technical, with hundreds of tiny digital screens, and buttons, and wires snaking in all directions to speakers hung at random intervals along the wall.

He bent down, tried to read the name of the tape inside the player.

"It's what she wants," said Stuart, staring still at the woman. "Just start it. She plays it all the time. It is her music."

"Dance with us," said Tessa. "Don't you want to dance with us?" She moved towards Ash, and this time he could not resist. He caught her hands, and then embraced her as a man might embrace a woman for a waltz, in the modern intimate position.

Michael pressed the button.

The music began low, the throb of bass strings plucked slowly—flowing out of the many speakers; then came trumpets, smooth and lustrous, over the shimmering tones of a harpsichord, descending in the same melodic line of notes and now taking the lead, so that the strings followed.

At once Ash guided his partner into wide graceful steps, and a gentle circle.

This was Pachelbel's Canon, Michael knew it at once, played as he'd never heard it, in a masterly rendition, with the full brass perhaps intended by the composer.

Had there ever been a more plaintive piece of music, anything more frankly abandoned to romance? The music swelled, transcending the constraints of the baroque, trumpets, strings, harpsichord now singing their overlapping melodies with a heartrending richness so that the music seemed both timeless and utterly from the heart.

It swept the couple along, their heads bending gently, their wide steps graceful and slow and in perfect time with the instruments. Ash was smiling now, as fully and completely as Tessa. And as the pace quickened, as the trumpets began to delicately trill the notes, with perfect control, as all voices blended magnificently in the most jubilant moments of the composition, faster and faster they danced, Ash swinging Tessa along almost playfully, into bolder and bolder circles. Her skirts flared freely, her small feet turned with perfect grace, heels clicking faintly on the wood, her smile ever more radiant.

Another sound was now blended into the dance—for the canon, when played like this, was surely a dance—and slowly Michael realized it was the sound of Ash singing. There were no words, only a lovely openmouthed humming, to which Tessa quickly added her own, and their faultless voices rose above the dark lustrous trumpets, effortlessly traveling the crescendos, and now, as they turned faster, their backs very straight, they almost laughed in what seemed pure bliss.

Rowan's eyes had filled with tears as she watched them—the tall, regal man and the lithesome, graceful fairyqueen, and so had the eyes of the old man, who clung to the arm of his chair as if he were very close to the limit of his resources.

Yuri seemed torn inside, as if he would lose control finally. But he remained motionless, leaning against the wall, merely watching.

Ash's eyes were now playful, yet adoring, as he rocked his head and swayed more freely, and moved even more quickly.

On and on they danced, spinning along the edge of the pool of light, into shadow and out of it, serenading one another, Tessa's face as ecstatic as that of a little girl whose greatest wish has been granted her.

It seemed to Michael that they should withdraw—Rowan, Yuri, and he—and leave them to their poignant and gentle union. Perhaps it was the only embrace they'd ever really know with each other. And they seemed now to have forgotten their watchers, and whatever lay ahead of them.

But he couldn't go. No one moved to go, and on and on the dance went until the rhythm slowed, until the instruments played more softly, warning that they would soon take their leave, and the overlapping lines of the canon blending in one last full-throated voice and then slacking, drawing away, the trumpet giving forth a final mournful note, and then silence.

The couple stopped in the very center of the floor, the light spilling down over their faces and their shimmering hair.

Michael rested against the stones, unable to move, only watching them.

Music like that could hurt you. It gave you back your disappointment, and your emptiness. It said, *Life can be this. Remember this.*

Silence.

Ash lifted the hands of the fairyqueen, looking at them carefully as he did so. Then he kissed her upturned palms and he let her go. And she stood staring at him, as if in love, perhaps not with him, perhaps with the music and the dance and the light, with everything.

He led her back to her loom, gently urging her to sit again on her stool, and then he turned her head so that her eyes fell on her old task, and as she peered at the tapestry, she seemed to forget that he was there. Her fingers reached for the threads, and began immediately to work.

Ash drew back, careful not to make a sound, and then he turned and looked at Stuart Gordon.

No plea or protest came from the old man, fallen to one side in the chair, his eyes moving without urgency from Ash to Tessa and then to Ash again.

The awful moment had come, perhaps. Michael didn't know. But surely some story, some long explanation, some desperate narrative would forestall it. Gordon had to try. Somebody had to try. Something had to happen to save this miserable human being; simply because he was that, something had to prevent this imminent execution.

"I want the names of the others," said Ash in the usual mild fashion. "I want to know who your cohorts were, both within and outside the Order."

Stuart took his time in answering. He didn't move, or look away from Ash. "No," he said finally. "Those names I will never give you."

It sounded as final as anything Michael had ever heard. And the man, in his pain, seemed beyond any form of persuasion.

Ash began to walk calmly towards Gordon.

"Wait," said Michael. "Please, Ash, wait."

Ash stopped, politely looking to Michael.

"What is it, Michael?" he asked, as if he could not possibly presume to know.

"Ash, let him tell us what he knows," Michael said. "Let him give us his story!"

Seventeen

EVERYTHING was changed. Everything was easier. She lay in Morrigan's arms and Morrigan lay in hers and—

It was evening when she opened her eyes.

What a great dream that had been. It was as if Gifford and Alicia and Ancient Evelyn had been with her, and there was no death and no suffering, and they had been together, dancing even, yes, dancing, in a circle.

She felt so good! Let it fade; the feeling remained with her. The sky was Michael's violet.

And there was Mary Jane standing over her, looking so goddamned cute with her flaxen yellow hair.

"You're Alice in Wonderland," said Mona, "that's who you are. I should nickname you Alice."

Going to be perfect, I promise you.

"I cooked the supper," said Mary Jane. "I told Eugenia to take the night off, hope you don't mind, when I saw that pantry I went crazy."

" 'Course I don't mind," said Mona. "Help me up, you're a real cousin."

She jumped up refreshed, feeling so light and free, like the baby tumbling inside, the baby with its long red hair swishing in the fluid, like a teeny rubbery doll with the teensiest little knobby knees . . .

"I cooked yams, rice, and baked oysters in cheese, and broiled chicken with butter and tarragon."

"Wherever did you learn to cook like that?" asked Mona. Then she stopped and threw her arms around Mary Jane. "There's nobody like us, is there? I mean, you know your blood, don't you?"

Mary Jane beamed at her. "Yeah, it's just wonderful. I love you, Mona Mayfair."

"Oh, I'm so glad to hear it," said Mona.

They had reached the kitchen doors, and Mona peered inside.

"God, you did cook a big supper."

"You better believe it," said Mary Jane proudly, again displaying her perfect white teeth. "I could cook when I was six years old. My mama was living with this chef then?? You know?? And then later on, I worked in a fancy restaurant in Jackson, Mississippi. Jackson's the capital, remember? This was a place where the senators ate. And I told them, 'You want me to work here, then you let me watch when the cook's doing things, you let me learn what I can.' What do you want to drink?"

"Milk, I'm starving for it," said Mona. "Don't run inside yet. Look, it's the magic time of twilight. This is Michael's favorite time."

If only she could remember in the dream who had been with her. Only the feeling of love lingered, utterly comforting love.

For a moment she worried fiercely for Rowan and Michael. How would they ever solve the mystery of who killed Aaron? But together they could probably defeat anybody, that is, if they really cooperated, and Yuri, well, Yuri's destiny had never been meant to involve itself with hers.

Everybody would understand when the time came.

The flowers had begun to glow. It was as if the garden were singing. She slumped against the door frame, humming with the flowers, humming as if the song were being made known to her by some remote part of her memory where beautiful and delicate things were never forgotten, but only securely stored. She could smell some perfume in the air—ah, it was the sweet olive trees!

"Honey, let's eat now," said Mary Jane.

"Very well, very well!" Mona sighed, threw up her arms and said farewell to the night, and then went inside.

She drifted into the kitchen, as if in a delicious trance, and sat down at the lavish table that Mary Jane had set for them. She'd taken out the Royal Antoinette china, the most delicate pattern of all, with fluted and gilded edges to the plates and saucers. Clever girl, such a wonderful clever girl. How unboring of her to have found the very best china by instinct. This cousin opened up a whole vista of possibilities, but how adventuresome was she, really? And how naive of Ryan to have dropped her off here, and left the two of them alone!

"I never saw china like that," Mary Jane was saying, bubbling away. "It's just like it's made of stiff starch cloth. How do they do it?" Mary Jane had just come back with a carton of milk and a box of powdered chocolate.

"Don't put that poison in the milk, please," said Mona, as she snatched the carton, tore it open, and filled her glass.

"I mean, how can they make china that's not flat, I don't get it, unless the china's soft like dough before they bake it, but even then—"

"Haven't the faintest idea," said Mona, "but I have always adored this pattern. Doesn't look good in the dining room. It's overshadowed by the murals. But looks absolutely splendid on this kitchen table, and how smart of you to have found the Battenburg lace table mats. I'm starving again, and we just had lunch. This is glorious, let's pig out now."

"We didn't just have lunch, and you didn't eat a thing," said Mary Jane. "I was scared to death you might mind me touching these things, but then I thought, 'If Mona Mayfair minds, I'll just slap-bang put them all away, like I found them.'"

"My darling, the house is ours for now," said Mona triumphantly.

God, the milk was good. She'd splashed it on the table, but it was so good, so good, so good.

Drink more of it.

"I am, I'm drinking it," she said.

"You're telling me," said Mary Jane, sitting down beside her. All the serving bowls were full of delectable and scrumptious things.

Mona heaped the steaming rice on her plate. Forget the gravy. This was wonderful. She began to eat it, not waiting for Mary Jane to serve herself, who was too busy dropping spoon after spoon of dirty chocolate powder into her own milk.

"Hope you don't mind. I just love chocolate. I can't live for too long without chocolate. There was a time when I made chocolate sandwiches, you know???? You know how to do that? You slap a couple Hershey bars between white bread, and you put sliced bananas and sugar too, and I'm telling you, that's delicious."

"Oh, I understand, might feel the same way if I wasn't pregnant. I once devoured an entire box of chocolate-covered cherries." Mona ate one big forkful of the rice after another. No chocolate could equal this. The chocolate-covered cherries had faded to an idea. And now the funniest thing. The white bread. It looked good too. "You know, I think I need complex carbohydrates," she said. "That's what my baby is telling me."

Laughing, or was it singing?

No problem; this was all so simple, so natural; she felt in harmony with the whole world, and it wouldn't be difficult to bring Michael and Rowan in harmony also. She sat back. A vision had taken hold of her, a vision of the sky speckled with all the visible stars. The sky was arched overhead, black and pure and cold, and people were singing, and the stars were magnificent, simply magnificent.

"What's that song you're humming?" asked Mary Jane.

"Shhh, hear that?"

Ryan had just come in. She could hear his voice in the dining room. He was talking to Eugenia. How marvelous to see Ryan. But he sure as hell wasn't taking Mary Jane out of here.

As soon as he stepped in the kitchen, Mona felt so sorry for him with his tired expression. He was still wearing his somber funeral suit. Ought to wear seersucker, the way the other men did this time of year. She loved the men in their seersucker suits in summer, and she loved the old ones who still wore the straw hats.

"Ryan, come join us," she said, chewing another huge mouthful of rice. "Mary Jane's cooked a feast."

"Just you sit right down here," said Mary Jane, hopping to her feet, "and I'll serve your plate, Cousin Ryan."

"No, I can't, dear," he said, being punctiliously polite to Mary Jane, because she was the country cousin. "I'm rushing. But thank you."

"Ryan is always rushing," said Mona. "Ryan, before you go, take a little walk outside, it's simply beautiful. Look at the sky, listen to the birds. And if you haven't smelled the sweet olives, it's time to do it now!"

"Mona, you're stuffing yourself with that rice. Is this going to be that kind of pregnancy?"

She tried not to go into spasms of laughter.

"Ryan, sit down, have a glass of wine," she said. "Where's Eugenia? Eugenia! Don't we have some wine?"

"I don't care for any wine, Mona, thank you." He made a dismissing gesture to Eugenia, who appeared for one moment in the lighted door, gnarled, angry, disapproving, and then slipped away.

Ryan looked so handsome in spite of his obvious crossness—a man who'd been polished all over with a big rag. She started to laugh again. Time for a gulp of milk, no, drink the whole glass. Rice and milk. No wonder people from Texas ate these two things together.

"Cousin Ryan, won't take a second—" said Mary Jane. "Just you let me fill you a plate."

"No, Mary Jane, thank you. Mona, there's something I have to tell you."

"Right now, during dinner? Oh, well, shoot. How bad can it be?" Mona poured some more milk from the carton, slopping a bit on the glass table. "After everything that's already happened? You know, the problem with this family is entrenched conservatism. I wonder if that is redundant. What do you think?"

"Miss Piggy," said Ryan dourly, "I am talking to you."

Mona went into hysterics. So did Mary Jane.

"I think I got a job as a cook," said Mary Jane, "and all I did to that rice was throw in some butter and garlic."

"It's the butter!" declared Mona, pointing at Mary Jane. "Where's the butter? That's the secret, slop butter on everything." She picked up a slice of ordinarily pukey white bread, and carved out a glomp of oozy warm butter from the print slowly melting on the saucer.

Ryan was looking at his watch, the infallible signal that he would remain in this spot no more than four more minutes. And God bless us all, he had not said one word about taking Mary Jane away.

"What is it, big boy?" asked Mona. "Hit me with it. I can take it."

"I don't know if you can," he said in a low voice.

That sent her into another reel of laughter. Or maybe it was the blank expression on Ryan's face. Mary Jane couldn't stop giggling. She stood beside Ryan, with her hand over her mouth.

"Mona, I'm off," he said, "but there are several boxes of papers up in the master bedroom. These are things that Rowan wanted, writings that came out of her last room in Houston." He gave a pointed look to Mary Jane, as if to say, She is not to know about all that.

"Oh yeah, writings," said Mona. "I heard you talking about it last night. You know, I heard a funny story, Ryan, that when Daphne Du Maurier, you know who she was?"

"Yes, Mona."

"Well, when she was writing *Rebecca,* it began as an experiment to see how long she could go on without naming her first-person narrator. Michael told me this. It's true. And you know by the end of the book the experiment didn't matter. But you never do know the name of Maxim de Winter's second wife in that novel, or in the movie. Did you see the movie?"

"What's the point?"

"Well, you're like that yourself, Ryan, you're going to go to the grave without ever saying Lasher's name." Again, she broke into laughter.

Mary Jane laughed and laughed as though she knew everything.

There is nothing funnier than someone laughing at a joke, except for someone who does not even crack a smile and stares at you with a face full of outrage.

"Don't touch the boxes," said Ryan solemnly. "They belong to

Rowan! But there is something I must tell you, about Michael, something I found in a genealogy in those papers. Mary Jane, please do sit down and eat your supper."

Mary Jane sat down.

"Right, genealogies," said Mona. "Wow, maybe Lasher knew things we didn't know. Mary Jane, genealogy is not a special interest with this family, it's a full-time obsession. Ryan, your four minutes are nearly up."

"What four minutes?"

She was laughing again. He had to leave. She was going to get sick, laughing like this.

"I know what you're gonna say," said Mary Jane, who jumped up again out of her chair, as though for truly serious conversations she had to be standing. "You're going to say Michael Curry is a Mayfair. I told you!"

All the vitality drained out of Ryan's face.

Mona drank down the fourth glass of milk. She had finished her rice, and lifting the serving bowl, she tipped it and let a new little mountain of soft, steaming rice grains fall on her plate.

"Ryan, stop staring at me," she said. "What is it about Michael? Is Mary Jane right? Mary Jane said Michael was a Mayfair the first time she met him."

"He is," declared Mary Jane. "I saw the resemblance right away, and you know who he looks like? He looks like that opera singer."

"What opera singer?" asked Ryan.

"Yeah, what opera singer?"

"Tyrone MacNamara, the one that Beatrice has pictures of, you know????? Those engravings on her wall???? Julien's father???? Well, Ryan, he must be your great-grandfather. I saw a passel a' cousins at the genealogical laboratory looked like that, Irish as can be, you never noticed? Of course you didn't, but then y'all have got Irish blood, French blood—"

"And Dutch blood," said Ryan in a terse, uncomfortable little voice. He looked at Mona, and then back at Mary Jane. "I have to go."

"Wait a second, is that it?" Mona demanded. She gulped down her mouthful of rice, took another drink of milk. "Is that what you were going to tell me? Michael is a Mayfair?"

"There is a mention," Ryan said, "in those papers, that apparently pertains to Michael, explicitly."

"God damn, you don't mean it," said Mona.

"You all are sooooo divinely inbred!" said Mary Jane. "It's like royalty. And here sits the Czarina herself!"

"I'm afraid you're right," said Ryan. "Mona, have you taken any medicine?"

"Certainly not, would I do that to my daughter?"

"Well, I have no choice but to go," he said. "Do try to behave yourselves. Remember the house is surrounded by guards. I don't want you going out, and please don't devil Eugenia!"

"Shucks," said Mona. "Don't leave. You're the life of the party. What do you mean 'devil Eugenia'?"

"When you've returned to your senses," said Ryan, "would you please call me? And what if this child is a boy? Certainly you aren't going to risk his life with one of those tests to determine gender."

"He's not a boy, silly," said Mona. "She's a girl and I've already named her Morrigan. I'll call you. Okay? Okay."

And away he went, hurrying in his own special quiet way of hurrying. Kind of like the way nuns hurry, or doctors. With a minimum of sound and fuss.

"Don't touch those papers," he called out from the butler's pantry.

Mona relaxed, took a deep breath. That was the last adult scheduled to be looking in on them, as far as she knew.

And what was this about Michael? "God, you think it's true? Hey, Mary Jane, when we're finished, let's go up and look at those papers."

"Oh, Mona, I don't know, he just said those were Rowan's papers, didn't he just say that? 'Don't touch those papers.' Mona, have some cream gravy. Don't you want the chicken? That's the best chicken I ever fixed."

"Cream gravy! You didn't say it was cream gravy. Morrigan doesn't want meat. Doesn't like meat. Look, I have a right to look at those papers. If *he* wrote things, if *he* left anything in writing."

"Who's *he*?"

"Lasher. You know who he is. Don't tell me your Granny didn't tell you."

"She told me, all right, you believe in him?"

"Believe in him, dollface, he almost attacked me. I almost became a statistic like my mother and Aunt Gifford and all those other poor dead Mayfair women. Of course I believe in him, why he's . . ." She caught herself pointing to the garden, in the direction of the tree. No, don't tell her that, she'd sworn to Michael, never tell anyone, buried out there, and the other one, the innocent one, Emaleth, the one that had to die, though she'd never done anything to anyone ever.

Not you, Morrigan, don't you worry, baby girl!

"Long story, no time for it," she said to Mary Jane.

"I know who Lasher is," said Mary Jane. "I know what happened.

Granny told me. The others didn't come right out and say he was killing the women. They just said Granny and I had to come to New Orleans and stay with everybody else. Well, you know? We didn't do it and nothing happened to us!"

She shrugged and shook her head.

"That could have been a terrible mistake," said Mona. The cream gravy tasted wonderful with the rice. Why all this white food, Morrigan?

The trees were filled with apples, and their meat was white, and the tubers and roots we pulled from the earth were white and it was paradise. Oh, but look at the stars. Was the unspoiled world really unspoiled, or were the everyday menaces of nature so terrible that everything was just as ruined then as it was now? If you live in fear, what does it matter . . .

"What's the matter, Mona?" said Mary Jane. "Hey, snap out of it."

"Oh, nothing, actually," said Mona. "I just had a flash of the dream I had out there in the garden. I was having a hell of a conversation with somebody. You know, Mary Jane, people have to be educated to understand one another. Like right now, you and I, we are educating each other to understand each other, you get what I mean?"

"Oh yeah, exactly, and then you can pick up your phone and call me down at Fontevrault and say, 'Mary Jane, I need you!' and I'd just leap up and get in the pickup and take off and be at your side."

"Yes, that's it, exactly, you know I really, really meant it, you'd know all kinds of things about me, and I'd know all kinds of things about you. It was the happiest dream I ever had. It was such a . . . such a happy dream. We were all dancing. A bonfire that big would normally scare me. But in the dream I was free, just perfectly free. I didn't care about anything. We need another apple. The invaders didn't invent death. That's a preposterous notion, but one can see why everybody thought that they had . . . well, sort of, everything depends on perspective, and if you have no sure concept of time, if you don't see the basic relevance of time, and of course hunter-gatherer people did and so did agricultural people, but perhaps those in tropical paradises don't ever develop that kind of relationship because for them there are no cycles. The needle's stuck on heaven. You know what I mean?"

"What *are* you talking about?"

"Well, pay attention, Mary Jane! And you'll know! It was that way in the dream, the invaders had invented death. No, I see now, what they had invented was *killing*. That's a different thing."

"There's a bowl full of apples over there, you want me to get you an apple?"

"Right, later. I want to go upstairs to Rowan's room."

"Well, lemme finish my meal," pleaded Mary Jane. "Don't go without me. Matter of fact, I don't know if we have any right to go up there at all."

"Rowan won't mind, Michael might mind. But you know???" said Mona, imitating Mary Jane. "It doesn't matter???"

Mary Jane nearly fell out of the chair laughing. "You are the worst child," she said. "Come on. Chicken's always better cold, anyway."

And the meat from the sea was white, the meat of the shrimps and the fishes, and of the oysters and the mussels. Pure white. The eggs of gulls were beautiful, because they were all white outside, and when you broke them open one great golden eye stared at you, floating in the clearest fluid.

"Mona?"

She stood still in the door to the butler's pantry. She closed her eyes. She felt Mary Jane grip her hand.

"No," she said with a sigh, "it's gone again." Her hand moved to her belly. She spread her fingers out over the rounded swelling, feeling the tiny movements within. Beautiful Morrigan. Hair as red as my hair. *Is your hair so very red, Mama?*

"Can't you see me?"

In Mary Jane's eyes I see you.

"Hey, Mona, I'm going to get you a chair!"

"No, no, I'm okay." She opened her eyes. A lovely surge of energy shot through her. She stretched out her arms and ran, through the pantry and the dining room and down the long hall, and then up the stairway.

"Come on, let's go!" she was shouting.

It felt so good to run. That's one of the things she missed from childhood, and she hadn't even known it, just running, running all the way down St. Charles Avenue as fast as she could with her arms out. Running upstairs two at a time. Running around the block just to see if you could do it without stopping, without fainting, without having to throw up.

Mary Jane came pounding after her.

The door to the bedroom was closed. Good old Ryan. Probably locked it.

But no. When she opened it, the room was dark. She found the light switch, and the overhead chandelier went on, pouring a bright light over the smooth bed, the dressing table, the boxes.

"What's that smell?" asked Mary Jane.

"You smell it, don't you?"

"Sure do."

"It's Lasher's smell," she whispered.

"You mean it?"

"Yes," said Mona. There was the pile of brown cardboard boxes. "What's it like to you, the smell?"

"Hmmmm, it's good. Kind of makes you want butterscotch or chocolate or cinnamon, or something like that. Wooof. Where's it coming from? But you know what?"

"What?" asked Mona, circling the pile of boxes.

"People have died in this room."

"No kidding. Mary Jane, anybody could have told you that."

"What do you mean? About Mary Beth Mayfair, and Deirdre and all that. I heard all that when Rowan was sick in here, and Beatrice called down to get Granny and me to come to New Orleans. Granny told me. But somebody else died in here, somebody that smelled sort of like him. You smell it? You smell the three smells? The one smell is the smell of him. The other smell is the smell of the other one. And the third smell is the smell of death itself."

Mona stood very still, trying to catch it, but for her the fragrances must have been mingled. With a sharp, nearly exquisite pain, she thought of what Michael had described to her, the thin girl that was not a girl, not human. Emaleth. The bullet exploded in her ears. She covered them.

"What's the matter, Mona Mayfair?"

"Dear God, where did it happen?" Mona asked, still holding tight to her ears and squinching her eyes shut, and then opening them only to look at Mary Jane, standing against the lamp, a shadowy figure, her eyes big and brilliantly blue.

Mary Jane looked around, mostly with her eyes, though she did turn her head a little, and then she began to walk along the bed. Her head looked very round and small beneath her soft, flattened hair. She moved to the far side of the bed, and stopped. Her voice was very deep when she spoke.

"Right here. Somebody died right here. Somebody who smelled like him, but wasn't him."

There was a scream in Mona's ears, so loud, so violent it was ten times as terrible as the imagined gunshot. She clutched her belly. *Stop it, Morrigan, stop it. I promise you . . .*

"Goodness, Mona, you going to be sick?"

"No, absolutely not!" Mona shuddered all over. She began to hum a little song, not even asking herself what it was, just something pretty, something perhaps that she made up.

She turned and looked at the heap of irresistible boxes.

"It's on the boxes, too," said Mona. "You smell it real strong here? From him. You know, I have never gotten another single member of this family to admit that they could smell that smell."

"Well, it's just all over the place," said Mary Jane. She stood at Mona's side, annoyingly taller, and with more pointed breasts. "It's more all over these boxes, too, you're right. But look, all these boxes are taped up."

"Yes, and marked in neat black felt-tip pen, by Ryan, and this one, conveniently enough, says, 'Writings, Anonymous.' " She gave a soft laugh, nothing as giddy as before. "Poor Ryan. 'Writings, Anonymous.' Sounds like a psychology support group for books who don't know their authors."

Mary Jane laughed.

Mona was delighted, and broke into giggles. She went round the boxes, and eased down on her knees, careful not to shake the baby. The baby was still crying. The baby was flip-flopping like crazy. It was the smell, wasn't it? As much as all the foolish talk and imagining and picturing. She hummed to the baby . . . then sang softly:

" 'Bring flowers of the fairest, bring flowers of the rarest, from garden and woodland and hillside and dale!' " It was the gayest, sweetest hymn she knew, one that Gifford had taught her to sing, the hymn from the Maytime. " 'Our full hearts are swelling, our glad voices telling the tale of the loveliest rose of the dale!' "

"Why, Mona Mayfair, you've got a voice."

"Every Mayfair has a voice, Mary Jane. But really I haven't. Not like my mother did, or Gifford. You should have heard them. They were real sopranos. My voice is low."

She hummed the tune now without the words, picturing the forests, and the green land, and flowers. " 'Oh, Mary, we crown thee with blossoms today, queen of the angels, queen of the May. Oh, Mary, we crown thee with blossoms today . . .' "

She rocked on her knees, her hand on her belly, the baby rocking gently with the music, her red hair all around her now, looking magnificent in the water of the womb, as if it were orange ink dropped into water, billowing out, that weightless, that translucent, that beautiful. Such tiny feet and tiny fingers. *What color are your eyes, Morrigan?*

I can't see my eyes, Mama, I can see only what you see, Mama.

"Hey, wake up, I'm scared you're gonna fall."

"Oh yes. I'm glad you called me back, Mary Jane, you did right to call me back, but I pray to heaven and the Blessed Mary Ever Virgin that this baby has green eyes like mine. What do you think?"

"Couldn't be a better color!" Mary Jane declared.

Mona laid her hands on the cardboard box in front of her. This was the right one. It reeked of him. Had he written these sheets in his own blood? And to think his body was down there. I ought to dig up that body. I mean, everything is changed now, Rowan and Michael are going to have to accept that, either that or I'm simply not going to tell them, I mean, this is an entirely new development and this one concerns *me*.

"What bodies are we going to dig up?" asked Mary Jane with a puckered frown.

"Oh, stop reading my mind! Don't be a Mayfair bitch, be a Mayfair witch. Help me with this box."

Mona ripped at the tape with her fingernails and pried back the cardboard.

"Mona, I don't know, this is somebody else's stuff."

"Yesssss," said Mona. "But this somebody else is part of my heritage, this somebody else has her own branch on this tree, and up through the tree from its roots runs this potent fluid, our lifeblood, and he was part of it, he lived in it, you might say, yes, ancient, and long-lived and forever, sort of like trees. Mary Jane, you know trees are the longest-lived things on earth?"

"Yeah, I know that," she said. "There's trees down near Fontevrault that are so big???? I mean there's cypress trees down there with knees sticking up out of the water?"

"Shhhh," said Mona. She had pushed back all the brown wrapping—this thing was packed like it had to carry the Marie Antoinette china all the way to Iceland—and she saw the first page of a loose stack covered in a thin plastic, and bound with a thick rubber band. Scrawl, all right, spidery scrawl, with great long *l*'s and *t*'s and *y*'s, and little vowels that were in some cases no more than dots. But she could read it.

She made her hand a claw and tore the plastic.

"Mona Mayfair!"

"Guts, girl!" said Mona. "There's a purpose to what I do. Will you be my ally and confidante, or do you wish, right now, to abandon me? The cable TV in this house gets every channel, you can go to your room, and watch TV, if you don't want to be with me, or take a swim outside, or pick flowers, or dig for bodies under the tree—"

"I want to be your ally and confidante."

"Put your hand on this, then, country cousin. You feel anything?"

"Oooooh!"

"He wrote it. You are looking at the writing of a certified nonhuman! Behold."

Mary Jane was kneeling beside her. She had her fingertips on the page. Her shoulders were hunched, her flaxen hair hanging down on both sides of her face, spectacular as a wig. Her white eyebrows caught the light against her bronzed forehead, and you could practically see every hair. What was she thinking, feeling, seeing? What was the meaning of the look in her eyes? This kid is not stupid, I'll say that for her, she's not stupid. Trouble is . . .

"I'm so sleepy," Mona said suddenly, realizing it as soon as she said it. She put her hand to her forehead. "I wonder if Ophelia went to sleep before she drowned."

"Ophelia? You mean Hamlet's Ophelia?"

"Oh, you know what I mean," she said. "That's just great. You know, Mary Jane, I just love you."

She looked at Mary Jane. Yes, this was the Ultimate Cousin, the Cousin who could be a Great Friend, the Cousin who could know everything that Mona knew. And nobody, really, nobody knew everything that Mona knew.

"But I'm so drowsy." She let herself fall gently to the floor, stretching out her legs and then her arms until she lay flat, looking up at the bright, pretty chandelier. "Mary Jane, would you go through that box? If I know Cousin Ryan, and I do, the genealogy is marked."

"Yeah," said Mary Jane.

How refreshing that she had stopped arguing.

"No, I'm not arguing, I figure we've gone this far, and beings this is the writing of a certified nonhuman being, beings we've gone this far . . . well, the point is, I can put it all back when we're through."

"Precisely," said Mona, laying her cheek against the cool floor. The smell was very strong in the floorboards! "And beings," she said, imitating Mary Jane, but without malice, no, no malice whatsoever, "and beings that knowledge is precious, one has to get it where one can."

Wow, the most incredible thing had happened. She'd closed her eyes and the hymn was singing itself. All she had to do was listen. She wasn't pushing these words out, these notes, it was just unfolding, like she was in one of those brain experiments where they zap part of your brain with an electrode and wham, you see visions, or you smell the creek on the hill behind your house when you were a little kid!

"That's what both of us have to realize, that witchcraft is an immense science," she said drowsily, talking easily over the pretty hymn, since it sang itself now. "That it is alchemy and chemistry and brain science, and that those things collected make up magic, pure lovely magic. We haven't lost our magic in the age of science. We have discovered a whole new bunch of secrets. We're going to win."

"Win?"

Oh Mary we crown thee with blossoms today, queen of the angels, queen of the May, oh Mary we crown thee . . . "Are you reading the pages, Mary Jane?"

"Well, hey, lookie, he has a whole folder here of Xerox copies. 'Inventory in Progress: Relevant Pages, incomplete genealogy.' "

Mona rolled over on her back again. For a moment she didn't know where they were. Rowan's room. There were tiny prisms in the crystal baubles above. The chandelier that Mary Beth had hung there, the one from France, or had it been Julien? Julien, where are you? Julien, how did you let this happen to me?

But the ghosts don't answer unless they want to, unless they have a reason of their own.

"Well, I'm reading this here incomplete genealogy."

"You got it?"

"Yeah, the original and a Xerox. Everything here is in duplicate. Original and Xerox. Little packets like. What he's got circled here is Michael Curry, all right, and then all this stuff about Julien sleeping with some Irish girl, and that girl giving up her baby to Margaret's Orphanage, and then becoming a Sister of Mercy, Sister Bridget Marie, and the baby girl, the one in the orphanage, marrying a fireman named Curry, and him having a son, and then him, something, Michael! Right here."

Mona laughed and laughed. "Oncle Julien was a lion," she said. "You know what male lions do, when they come to a new pride? They kill all the young, so that the females go into heat at once, and then they sire as many young as they can. It's the survival of the genes. Oncle Julien knew. He was just improving the population."

"Yeah, well, from what I heard, he was pretty picky about who got to survive. Granny told me he shot our great-great-great-grandfather."

"I'm not sure that's the right number of 'greats.' What else do all those papers say?"

"Well, sugar plum, to tell you the truth, I couldn't have made this out if somebody hadn't marked it. There's just all kinds of things here. You know what this is like? It's like the writing that people do when they're high on drugs and they think they're being brilliant and the next day, lo and behold, they look at the tablets and see they've written little bitty jagged lines, like the lines, you know??? That make up an electrocardiogram?"

"Don't tell me you've been a nurse?"

"Yeah, for a while, but that was at this crazy commune where they made us all take an enema every day to get rid of the impurities in our system."

Mona started to laugh again, a lovely sleepy laugh. "I don't think a commune of the Twelve Apostles could have made me do that," she said.

This chandelier was damned near spectacular. That she had lived this long without lying on the floor and looking up at one of these things was just inexcusable. The hymn was still going, only this time, miracle of miracles, it was being played on some instrument, like a harp perhaps, and each note merged with the next note. She could almost not feel the floor under her, when she concentrated on the music and on the lights above.

"You didn't stay in that commune, did you?" she asked drowsily. "That sounds horrible."

"Sure didn't. I made my mother leave. I said, lookie, you leave with me or I cut out of here on my own. And as I was about twelve years old at the time, she wadn't about to let that happen. Lookie, here's Michael Curry's name again. He drew a circle around it."

"Lasher did? Or Ryan?"

"You got me. This is the Xerox, I can't tell. No, I see, the circle's drawn on the Xerox. Must have been Ryan, and this says something about 'waerloga.' Well, you know??? That probably means 'warlock.' "

"Right you are," said Mona. "That's Old English. I have at one time or another looked up the derivation of every single word that pertains to witches and witchcraft."

"Yeah, so have I. Warlock, right you are. Or it means, don't tell me, it means somebody who knows the truth all the time, right?"

"And to think it was Oncle Julien who wanted me to do this, that's the puzzle, but then a ghost knows his own business and Oncle Julien maybe didn't know. The dead don't know everything. The evil people do, whether they're dead or alive, or at least they know enough to tangle us up in such a web we can never escape. But Julien didn't know that Michael was his descendant. I know he didn't. He wouldn't have told me to come."

"To come where, Mona?"

"To this house on Mardi Gras night, to sleep with Michael, to make this baby that only Michael and I could have made, or maybe you too could have made it with Michael, perhaps, because you can smell that smell coming up out of these boxes, that smell of him?"

"Yeah, maybe I could, Mona. You never know."

"Right, sweets, you never know. But I got him first. I got Michael while the door was open before Rowan came home. Just slipped through the cracks, and wham! This baby, this marvelous little baby."

Mona turned over and lifted her head, resting her chin on her hands, elbows on the carpet.

"Mary Jane, you have to know everything."

"Yeah, I do," said Mary Jane. "I want to. I'm kind of worried about you."

"Me? Don't worry. I couldn't be better. I'm thirsty for some more milk, but otherwise, I'm fine. Look, I can still lie on my belly, well, actually no." She sat up. "That wasn't so comfortable, guess I have to kiss that goodbye for a while, you know, sleeping on your stomach?"

Mary Jane's brows had gone together in a very serious expression. She looked so cute! No wonder men were so damned patronizing to women. Did Mona look cute this way?

"Little witches!" said Mona in a hissing whisper, and she made her fingers flutter beside her hair.

Mary Jane laughed. "Yeah, little witches," she said. "So it was the ghost of Oncle Julien told you to come up here and sleep with Michael, and Rowan was nowhere around."

"Exactly, nowhere around. And Oncle Julien had more than a heavy hand in it, I tell you. The thing is, I fear he has gone to heaven and left us to our own devices, but then that is fine. I wouldn't want to have to explain this to him."

"Why wouldn't you?"

"It's a new phase, Mary Jane. You might say it's witchcraft in our generation. It's got nothing to do with Julien or Michael or Rowan and the way that they would have solved things. It's something else altogether."

"Yeah, I see."

"You do, don't you?"

"Yep. You're really sleepy. I'm going to go get you some milk."

"Oh, that would be divine."

"You just lie down and go on to sleep, darlin'. Your eyes look really bad. Can you see me at all?"

"Sure, I can, but you're right. I'm just going to sleep right here. And, Mary Jane, take advantage of the situation."

"Oh, you're too young for that, Mona."

"No, silly, I didn't mean that," said Mona, laughing. "Besides, if I'm not too young for men, I'm not too young for girls either. As a matter of fact, I'm curious about doing it with a girl, or a woman perhaps, a beautiful woman like Rowan. But what I meant was, the boxes are opened. Take advantage of that fact, and read what you can out of them."

"Yeah, maybe I'll do that. I can't really read his handwriting, but I can read hers. And she's got stuff here."

"Yeah, read it. If you're going to help me, you have to read it. And down in the library, Mary Jane, the file on the Mayfair Witches. I know you said you read it, but did you really read it?"

"You know, Mona? I'm not sure I really did."

Mona turned over on her side, and closed her eyes.

And as for you, Morrigan, let's go back, way, way back, none of this foolishness about invaders and Roman soldiers, way back to the plain, and tell me how it all began. Who is the dark-haired one that everyone so loves? "Good night, Mary Jane."

"Listen, before you fly away here, darlin', who would you say is your very best trusted next of kin?"

Mona laughed. She almost forgot the question, then woke with a start.

"Aaah, you are, Mary Jane."

"Not Rowan and Michael?"

"Absolutely not. They must now be perceived as the enemy. But there are things I have to ask Rowan, I have to know from her, but she doesn't have to know what's going on with me. I have to think out the purpose for my questions. As for Gifford and Alicia, they're dead, and Ancient Evelyn is too sick, and Ryan is too dumb. And Jenn and Shelby are too innocent. And Pierce and Clancy are simply hopeless, and why ruin normal life for them? Have you ever put much of a premium on normal life?"

"Never."

"I guess I'm depending upon you, then, Mary Jane. 'Bye now, Mary Jane."

"Then what you're saying is, you don't want me to call Rowan or Michael in London and ask their advice."

"Good heavens, no." Six circles had formed, and the dance was beginning. She didn't want to miss it. "You mustn't do that, Mary Jane. You absolutely musn't. Promise me you won't, Mary Jane. Besides, its the middle of the night in London and we don't know what they're doing, do we? God help them. God help Yuri."

Mona *was* floating away. Ophelia, with the flowers in her hair, moving steadily downstream. The branches of the trees came down to stroke her face, to touch the water. No, she was dancing in the circle, and the dark-haired one was standing in the very center and trying to tell them, but everyone was laughing and laughing. They loved him, but they knew he had a habit of going on and on, with such foolish worries . . .

"Well, I am worried about you, Mona, I should tell you . . ."

Mary Jane's voice was very far away. Flowers, bouquets of flowers. That explains everything, why I have dreamed gardens all my life, and drawn pictures of gardens with crayons. Why are you always drawing gardens, Mona, Sister Louise asked me. I love gardens, and First Street's garden was so ruined until they cleared it and changed it, and now, all clipped and kept, it harbors the worst secret of all.

No, Mother, don't . . .

No, the flowers, the circles, *you talk!* This dream was going to be as good as the last one.

"Mona?"

"Let me go, Mary Jane."

Mona could barely hear her; besides, it didn't make any difference what she said.

And that was a good thing, too, because this was what came out of Mary Jane's mouth, far, far away . . . before Mona and Morrigan began to sing.

". . . you know, Mona Mayfair, I hate to tell you this, but that baby's grown since you went to sleep out by the tree!"

Eighteen

I THINK we should leave now," said Marklin.

He lay on Tommy's bed, his head resting on his clasped hands, studying over and over the knots in the wood of the bed's coffered canopy.

Tommy sat at the desk, feet crossed on the black leather ottoman. This room was larger than Marklin's, with a southern exposure, but he had never resented it. He had loved his own room. Well, he was ready now to get out of it. He had packed everything of importance in one suitcase, and hidden it under his own bed.

"Call it a premonition. I don't want to stay here," he said. "There's no reason to stay longer."

"You're being fatalistic and a bit silly," said Tommy.

"Look, you've wiped the computers. Stuart's quarters are absolutely impenetrable, unless we want to risk breaking in the doors, and I don't like being under a curfew."

"The curfew is for everyone, may I remind you, and if we were to leave now, we wouldn't make it to the door without a dozen questions. Besides, to walk out before the memorial service would be blatantly disrespectful."

"Tommy, I can't endure some tenebrious ceremony in the small hours of the morning, with a lot of preposterous speeches about Anton and Aaron. I want to go now. Customs; rituals. These people are fools, Tommy. It's too late to be anything but frank. There are back stairs; there are side stairs. I'm for leaving here immediately. I have things on my mind. I have work to do."

"I want to do what they asked us to do," said Tommy, "which is what I intend to do. Observe the curfew they have asked us to observe. And go down when the bell is sounded. Now, please, Marklin, if you have nothing insightful or helpful to say, be quiet, will you?"

"Why should I be quiet? Why do you want to stay here?"

"All right, if you must know, we may have a chance during the memorial, or whatever it is, to find out where Stuart is keeping Tessa."

"How could we find out that?"

"Stuart's not a rich man, Marklin. He's bound to have a home somewhere, a place we've never seen, some ancestral manse or something. Now, if we play our cards right, we can ask a few questions about this subject, out of concern, of course, for Stuart. Have you got a better idea?"

"Tommy, I don't think Stuart would hide Tessa in a place that was known to be his home. He's a coward, perhaps, a melodramatic lunatic even, but he's not stupid. We are not going to find Stuart. And we are not going to find Tessa."

"Then what do we do?" asked Tommy. "Abandon everything? With what we know?"

"No. We leave here. We go back to Regent's Park. And we think. We think about something far more important to us now than anything the Talamasca can offer."

"Which is?"

"We think, Tommy, about the Mayfair witches. We go over Aaron's last fax to the Elders. And we study the File, we study it closely for every clue as to which of the clan is most useful for our purposes."

"You're going too fast," said Tommy. "What do you mean to do? Kidnap a couple of Americans?"

"We can't discuss it here. We can't plan anything. Look, I'll wait till the damned ceremony starts, but then I'm leaving, I'm stepping out at the first opportunity. You can come later if you like."

"Don't be stupid," said Tommy. "I don't have a car. I have to go with you. And what if Stuart's at the ceremony? Have you thought of that?"

"Stuart's not coming back here. He has better sense. Now, listen, Tommy. This is my final decision. I'll stay for the beginning of the ceremony, I'll pay my respects, chat with a few of the members, that sort of thing. And then I'm out of here! And on, on to my rendezvous with the Mayfair witches, Stuart and Tessa be damned."

"All right, I'll go with you."

"That's better. That's intelligent. That's my practical Tommy."

"Get some sleep then. They didn't say when they'd call us. And you're the one who's going to drive."

Nineteen

THE TOPMOST room of the tower. Yuri sat at the round table, looking down into the cup of steaming Chinese tea before him. The condemned man himself had made the tea. Yuri didn't want to touch it.

All his life in the Talamasca, he had known Stuart Gordon. He had dined countless times with Gordon and Aaron. They had strolled the gardens together, gone to the retreats in Rome together. Aaron had talked so freely with Gordon. The Mayfair witches and the Mayfair witches and the Mayfair witches. And now it was Gordon.

Betrayed him.

Why didn't Ash kill him now? What could the man give that would not be contaminated, not perverted by his madness? It was almost a certainty that his helpers had been Marklin George and Tommy Monohan. But the Order would discover the truth on that score. Yuri had reached the Motherhouse from the phone booth in the village, and the mere sound of Elvera's voice had brought him to tears. Elvera was faithful. Elvera was good. Yuri knew that the great chasm that had opened between him and the Talamasca had already begun to close. If Ash was right, that the conspiracy had been small, and indeed that seemed to be the case—that the Elders were not involved—then Yuri must be patient. He must listen to Stuart Gordon. Because Yuri had to take back to the Talamasca whatever he learned tonight.

Patience. Aaron would want it thus. Aaron would want the story known, and recorded for others to know. And Michael and Rowan, were they not entitled to the facts? And then there was Ash, the mysterious Ash. Ash had uncovered Gordon's treachery. If Ash had not appeared in Spelling Street, Yuri would have accepted Gordon's pretense of innocence, and the few foolish lies Gordon had told while they sat in the café.

What went on in Ash's mind? He was overwhelming, just as Yuri had told them. Now they knew. They saw for themselves his remarkable face, the calm, loving eyes. But they mustn't forget that he was a menace to Mona, to any of the Mayfair family—

Yuri forced himself to stop thinking about this. They needed Ash too much just now. Ash had somehow become the commander of this operation. What would happen if Ash withdrew and left them with Gordon? They couldn't kill Gordon. They couldn't even scare him, at least Yuri didn't think so. It was impossible to gauge how much Rowan and Michael hated Gordon. Unreadable. Witches. He could see that now.

Ash sat on the other side of the circle, his monstrous hands clasped on the edge of the old, unfinished wood, watching Gordon, who sat to his right. He did hate Gordon, and Yuri saw it by the absence of something in Ash's face, the absence of compassion, perhaps? The absence of the tenderness which Ash showed to everyone, absolutely everyone else.

Rowan Mayfair and Michael Curry sat on either side of Yuri, thank God. He could not have endured to be close to Gordon. Michael was the wrathful one, the suspicious one. Rowan was taken with Ash. Yuri had known she would be. But Michael was taken with no one just yet.

Yuri could not touch this cup. It might as well have been filled with the man's urine.

"Out of the jungles of India," said Stuart, sipping his own tea, in which he had poured a large slug of whiskey. "I don't know where. I don't know India. I know only that the natives said she'd been there forever, wandering from village to village, and that she'd come to them before the war, and that she spoke English and that she didn't grow old, and the women of the village had become frightened of her."

The whiskey bottle stood in the middle of the table. Michael Curry wanted it, but perhaps he could not touch the refreshments offered by Gordon either. Rowan Mayfair sat with her arms folded. Michael Curry had his elbows on the table. He was closer to Stuart, obviously trying to figure him out.

"I think it was a photograph, her undoing. Someone had taken a picture of the entire village, together. Some intrepid soul with a tripod and a wind-up camera. And she had been in that picture. It was one of the young men who uncovered it among his grandmother's possessions when the grandmother died. An educated man. A man I'd taught at Oxford."

"And he knew about the Talamasca."

"Yes, I didn't talk much to my students about the Order, except for those who seemed as if they might want to . . ."

"Like those boys," said Yuri.

He watched the light jump in Stuart's eye, as if the lamp nearby had jumped, and not Stuart.

"Yes, well, those boys."

"What boys?" asked Rowan.

"Marklin George and Tommy Monohan," said Yuri.

Stuart's face was rigid. He lifted the mug of tea with both hands and drank deeply.

The whiskey smelled medicinal and sickening.

"Were they the ones who helped you with this?" asked Yuri. "The computer genius and the Latin scholar?"

"It was my doing," said Stuart, without looking at Yuri. He was not looking at any of them. "Do you want to hear what I have to say, or not?"

"They helped you," said Yuri.

"I have nothing to say on the subject of my accomplices," Gordon said, looking coldly at Yuri now, and then back again into empty space, or the shadows along the walls.

"It was the two young ones," said Yuri, though Michael was gesturing to him to hold back. "What about Joan Cross, or Elvera Fleming, or Timothy Hollingshed?"

Stuart made an impatient and disgusted gesture at the mention of these names, hardly realizing how this might be interpreted in relation to the boys.

"Joan Cross doesn't have a romantic bone in her body," Stuart said suddenly, "and Timothy Hollingshed has always been overrated due simply to his aristocratic background. Elvera Fleming is an old fool! Don't ask me these questions anymore. I won't be made to speak of my accomplices. I won't be made to betray them. I'll die with that secret, be assured."

"So this friend," said Ash, his expression patient but surprisingly cold, "this young man in India, he wrote to you, Mr. Gordon."

"Called me, as a matter of fact, told me he had a mystery for me. He said he could get her to England, if I'd take over once she arrived. He said that she couldn't really fend for herself. She seemed mad, and then not mad. No one could quite analyze her. She spoke of times unknown to the people around her. And when he'd made inquiries, with a view to sending her home, he found she was a legend in that part of India. I have a record of it all. I have our letters. They are all here.

There are copies in the Motherhouse as well. But the originals are here. Everything I value is in this tower."

"You knew what she was when you saw her?"

"No. It was extraordinary. I found myself enchanted by her. Some selfish instinct dominated my actions. I brought her here. I didn't want to take her to the Motherhouse. It was most peculiar. I couldn't have told anyone what I was doing or why, except for the obvious fact that I was so charmed by her. I had only lately inherited this tower from my mother's brother, an antiquarian who had been my family mentor. It seemed the perfect place.

"The first week, I scarcely left at all. I had never been in the company of such a person as Tessa. There was a gaiety and simplicity in her which gave me inexpressible happiness."

"Yes, I'm sure," said Ash softly, with a trace of a smile. "Please go on with your story."

"I fell in love with her." He paused, eyebrows raised, as if amazed by his own words. He seemed excited by the revelation. "I fell completely in love with her."

"And you kept her here?" asked Yuri.

"Yes, she's been here ever since. She never goes out. She's afraid of people. It's only when I've been here a long while that she'll talk, and then she tells her amazing tales.

"She's seldom coherent, or I should say chronological. The little stories always make sense. I have hundreds of recordings of her talking, lists of Old English words and Latin words which she has used.

"You see, what became clear to me almost immediately was that she was speaking of two different lives, a very long one which she was living now, and a life she'd lived before."

"Two lives? Then you mean, simply, reincarnation."

"After a long while, she explained," said Gordon. He was now so passionately involved in his tale, he seemed to have forgotten the danger to him. "She said that all her kind had two lives, sometimes more," he went on. "That you were born knowing all you needed to know to survive, but then gradually an earlier life came back to you, and bits and pieces of others. And it was the memory of this earlier life that kept you from going mad among human beings."

"You had realized," asked Rowan, "by this time, that she wasn't human. She would have fooled me."

"No. Not at all. I thought she was human. Of course, there were strange characteristics to her—her translucent skin, her tremendous height, and her unusual hands. But I didn't think, 'No, this being isn't human.'

"It was she who said that she wasn't human. She said it more than once. Her people lived before humans. They had lived thousands of years in peace on islands in the northern seas. These islands were warmed by volcanic springs from the depths, by geysers of steam, and pleasant lakes.

"And this she knew, not because she herself had lived at that time, but because others she had known in her first lifetime could remember a former life in this paradise, and that was how her people knew their history, through the inevitable and always singular remembrance of earlier lives.

"Don't you see? It was incredible, the idea that everyone would come into this world with some distinct and valuable historical memories! It meant that the race knew more of itself than humans could possibly know. It knew of earlier ages from, so to speak, firsthand experience!"

"And if you bred Tessa to another of her race," said Rowan, "you would have a child who could remember an earlier life—and then perhaps another child and another life remembered."

"Exactly! The chain of memory would be established, and who knows how far back it would go, for each one, remembering some earlier existence, remembered the tales of those he had known and loved in that time who remembered having lived before!"

Ash listened to all this without comment, or any perceptible change of emotion. None of it seemed to surprise him or offend him. Yuri almost smiled. It was the same simplicity he'd observed in Ash at Claridge's, when they had first spoken.

"Someone else might have dismissed Tessa's claims," said Gordon, "but I recognized the Gaelic words she used, the bits of Old English, the Latin, and when she wrote down the runic script, I could read it! I knew she told the truth."

"And this you kept to yourself," said Rowan, neutrally, as if merely trying to quell Gordon's annoying emotion and get back on track.

"Yes! I did. I almost told Aaron about it. The more Tessa talked, the more she spoke of the Highlands, of early Celtic rituals and customs, of Celtic saints even, and the Celtic church.

"You do know that our church in England then was Celtic or Briton or whatever you want to call it, founded by the Apostles themselves, who had come from Jerusalem to Glastonbury. We had no connection with Rome. It was Pope Gregory and his henchman, St. Augustine, who thrust the Roman church on Britain."

"Yes, but then you did not tell Aaron Lightner?" asked Ash, raising his voice just slightly. "You were saying . . . ?"

"Aaron had already gone to America. He had gone there to make contact once more with the Mayfair witches, and to pursue other paths in psychic investigation. It was no time to question Aaron about his early research. And then, of course, I had done something wrong. I had taken a woman entrusted to me as a member of the Order, and I had kept her for myself, almost a prisoner. Of course, there has never been anything stopping Tessa from leaving, nothing but her own fear. But I had closeted this woman away. I had told the Order nothing about it."

"But how did you make the connection?" asked Ash. "Between Tessa and the Mayfair witches?"

"Oh, it wasn't that difficult at all. One thing followed upon another. As I said, Tessa's speech was full of references to archaic Highland customs. She spoke over and over of the circles of stones built by her people and later used by the Christians for bizarre rituals to which their priests could never put a stop.

"You know our mythology, surely all of you, some of you. The ancient myths of Britain are full of mythic giants. Our stories say the giants built the circles, and so did Tessa. Our giants lingered long after their time in the dark and remote places, in the caves by the sea, in the caves of the Highlands. Well, Tessa's giants, hunted from the earth, almost annihilated, also survived in secret places! And when they did dare to appear among human beings, they incited both worship and fear. It was the same, she said, with the Little Folk, whose origins had been forgotten. They were revered on the one hand, and feared on the other. And often the early Christians of Scotland would dance and sing within the circle of stones, knowing that the giants had once done this—indeed, had built the circles for that purpose—and they would, by their music, lure the giants from hiding, so that the giants came down to join the dance, at which point these Christians would slaughter them to satisfy the priests, but not before using them to satisfy old gods."

"How do you mean, 'using them'?" asked Rowan.

Gordon's eyes glazed slightly, and his voice dropped to a soft, nearly pleasant tone, as if the mere mention of these things could not but evoke a sense of wonder.

"Witchcraft, that is what we are talking about—early, blood-drenched witchcraft, in which superstition, under the yoke of Christianity, reached back into a pagan past for magic, to do *maleficia*, or to gain power, or only to witness a dark secret rite which thrilled them as criminal acts have always thrilled humankind. I longed to corroborate Tessa's stories.

"Without confiding in anyone, I went to the very cellars of the Motherhouse, the places where the oldest unexamined material on British folklore had been stored. These were manuscripts that had been deemed 'fanciful' and 'irrelevant' by the scholars, like Aaron, who had spent years translating old documents. This material did not exist in our modern inventory or our modern computer banks. One had to touch the crumbling pages with one's own hand.

"Oh, what I found! Crumbling quartos and books of beautifully illustrated parchment, the works of Irish monks and the Benedictines and the Cistercians, complaining of the mad superstition of the common people, and filled with tales of these giants and these Little Folk, and how the common people persisted in believing in them, in luring them out, in using them in various ways.

"And right there, mixed in with these ranting condemnations, were tales of giant saints! Giant knights and kings!

"Here, at Glastonbury, only a little way from where we sit now, a giant of seven feet was unearthed in former times, and declared to be King Arthur. What was this but one of Tessa's giants, I ask you? Such creatures have been found all over Britain.

"Oh, a thousand times I was tempted to call Aaron. How Aaron would have loved these stories, especially those which had come directly from the Highlands and its haunted lochs and glens.

"But there was only one person in this world in whom I could confide. And that was Tessa.

"And as I brought home my carefully excavated stories, Tessa recognized these rituals, these patterns—indeed, the names of saints and kings. Of course, Tessa didn't speak with sophisticated words. It came in fragments from her, how her people had become a sacred quarry, and could save themselves from torture and death only by rising to power and gaining sway over the Christians, or by fleeing deeper and deeper into the great forests which still covered the mountains in those years, and into the caves and the secret valleys where they struggled to live in peace."

"And this you never told Aaron," said Yuri.

Gordon ignored the words. He continued:

"Then, in a painful voice, Tessa confessed to me that she had once suffered horribly at the hands of Christian peasants, who had imprisoned her and forced her to receive man after man from all the villages round. The hope was that she would give birth to another giant like herself, a giant who would spring from the womb, speaking, knowing, and growing to maturity within hours—a creature which the villagers might then have killed before her eyes!

"It had become a religion to them, don't you see? Catch the Taltos, breed it, sacrifice the offspring. And Christmas, that time of ancient pagan rituals, had become their favorite period for the sacred game. From this hideous captivity Tessa had finally escaped, having never given birth to the sacrificial creature, and only suffering a flow of blood from the seed of each human man."

He stopped, his brows knit. His face became sad, and he looked at Ash.

"This is what hurt my Tessa? This is what dried the fount?" It wasn't so much a question as a confirmation of what had been revealed earlier, only Ash, feeling no need, apparently, to confirm it, did not speak.

Gordon shuddered.

"She spoke of horrible things!" he said. "She talked of the males lured down into the circles, and of the village maidens offered to them; but if the giant was not born to such a maiden, death would surely result. And when enough maidens had died that the people doubted the power of this male giant, he was then burnt as the sacrifice. Indeed, he was always burnt, whatever the outcome, or whether or not he had fathered a sacrificial offspring, because the males were so greatly feared."

"So they didn't fear the women," said Rowan. "Because the women didn't bring death to the human men who lay with them."

"Exactly," said Gordon. "However!" He held up his finger with a little delighted smile. "However! It did now and then happen, yes! That the male giant or the female giant did parent, as it were, the magical child of its own race. And there would be this newborn giant for all to behold.

"No time was more propitious for such a union than Christmas, December Twenty-fifth, the feast of the old solar god! And it was said then—when a giant was born—that the heavens had once again copulated with the earth, and out of the union had come a great magic, as had happened at the First Creation; and only after great feasting, and singing of the Christmas songs, was the sacrifice carried out in Christ's name. Now and then a giant fathered or mothered many such offspring, and Taltos mated with Taltos, and the fires of sacrifice filled the glens, the smoke rising to heaven, bringing an early spring and warm winds and good rains, and making the crops grow."

Gordon broke off, turning enthusiastically to Ash. "You must know all of this. You yourself could give us links in the chain of memory. Surely you too have lived an earlier life. You could tell us things which no human can ever discover in any other way. You can tell them with clarity and power, for you're strong, and not addled, like my poor Tessa! You can give us this gift."

Ash said nothing. But his face had darkened, and Gordon seemed not at all aware of it.

He's a fool, thought Yuri. Perhaps that is what great schemes of violence always require—a romantic fool.

Gordon turned to the others, even to Yuri, to whom he appealed now. "Don't you understand? Surely you understand now what such possibilities meant to me?"

"What I know," said Yuri, "is that you didn't tell Aaron. And you didn't tell the Elders, either, did you? The Elders never knew. Your brothers and sisters never knew!"

"I told you. I could trust no one with my discoveries, and frankly, I would not. They were mine. Besides, what would our beloved Elders have said, if 'said' is even appropriate for their endless silent communications! A fax would have come through directing me to bring Tessa to the Motherhouse at once, and to—No, this discovery was mine by right. I had found Tessa."

"No, you lie to yourself and everyone else," said Yuri. "Everything that you are is because of the Talamasca."

"That's a contemptible thought! Have I given the Talamasca nothing? Besides, it was never my idea to hurt our own members! The doctors involved, yes, I agreed to this, though again I would never have proposed it."

"You did kill Dr. Samuel Larkin?" asked Rowan in her low, expressionless voice, probing but not meaning to alarm him.

"Larkin, Larkin . . . Oh, I don't know. I get confused. You see, my helpers had some very different notions from mine, about what was required to keep the whole thing secret. You might say I went along with the more daring aspects of the plan. In truth, I can't imagine simply killing another human being."

He glared at Ash, accusingly.

"And your helpers, their names?" asked Michael. His tone was not unlike Rowan's, low-key, entirely pragmatic. "The men in New Orleans, Norgan and Stolov, you invited those men to share these secrets?"

"No, of course not," declared Gordon. "They weren't really members, any more than Yuri here was a member. They were merely investigators for us, couriers, that kind of thing. But by that time it had . . . it had gotten out of hand, perhaps. I can't say. I only know my friends, my confidants, they felt they could control those men with secrets and money. That's what it's always about, corruption—secrets and money. But let's get away from all that. What matters here is the discovery itself. That is what is pure and what redeems everything."

"It redeems nothing!" said Yuri. "For gain you took your knowledge! A common traitor, looting the archives for personal gain."

"Nothing could be farther from the truth," declared Gordon.

"Yuri, let him go on," said Michael quietly.

Gordon calmed himself with remarkable will, appealing to Yuri again in a manner that infuriated Yuri.

"How can you think that my goals were other than spiritual?" asked Gordon. "I, who have grown up in the shadow of Glastonbury Tor, who all his life has been devoted to esoteric knowledge, only for the light it brings into our souls?"

"It was spiritual gain, perhaps," said Yuri, "but it was gain, personal gain. And that is your crime."

"You try my patience," said Gordon. "Perhaps you should be sent from this room. Perhaps I should say nothing more . . ."

"Tell your story," said Ash calmly. "I'm growing impatient."

Gordon stopped, gazed at the table, one eyebrow raised, as if to say he need not settle for this ultimatum.

He looked at Ash coldly.

"How did you make the connection?" asked Rowan. "Between all of this and the Mayfair witches?

"I saw a connection at once. It had to do with the circle of stones. I had always known the original tale of Suzanne, the first Mayfair, the witch of the Highlands who had called up a devil in the circle of stones. And I had read Peter van Abel's description of that ghost and how it pursued him, and taunted him, and evinced a will far stronger than any human haunt.

"The account of Peter van Abel was the first record of the Mayfair witches which Aaron translated, and it was to me, naturally, that he came with many question about the old Latin. Aaron was always coming to me in those days for assistance."

"How unfortunate for him," said Yuri.

"Naturally it occurred to me, what if this Lasher were the soul of another species of being seeking to reincarnate? How well it fitted the whole mystery! And Aaron had only lately written from America that the Mayfair family faced its darkest hour when the ghost who would be made flesh was threatening to come through.

"Was this the soul of a giant wanting its second life? At last my discoveries had become too momentous. I had to share them. I had to bring into this those I trusted."

"But not Stolov and Norgan."

"No! My friends . . . my friends were of an entirely different ilk. But you're confusing me. Stolov and Norgan weren't involved then. No. Let me continue."

"But they were in the Talamasca, these friends," said Rowan.

"I will tell you nothing of them except that they were . . . they were young men in whom I believed."

"You brought these friends here, to the tower?"

"Indeed not," said Stuart. "I'm not that much of a fool. Tessa I revealed to them, but in a spot chosen by me for the purpose, in the ruin of Glastonbury Abbey, on the very spot where the skeleton of the seven-foot giant had been unearthed, only to be later reinterred.

"It was a sentimental thing, my taking her there, to stand over the grave of one of her own. And there I allowed her to be worshiped by those whom I trusted to help with my work. They had no idea that her permanent abode was less than a mile away. They were never to know.

"But they were dedicated and enterprising. They suggested the very first scientific tests. They helped me obtain with a syringe the first blood from Tessa, which was sent to various laboratories for anonymous analysis. And then we had the first firm proof that Tessa was not human! Enzymes, chromosomes, it was all quite beyond me. But they understood it."

"They were doctors?" Rowan asked.

"No. Only very brilliant young men." A shadow passed over his face, and he glanced viciously at Yuri.

Yes, your acolytes, Yuri thought. But he said nothing. If he interrupted again, it would be to kill Gordon.

"Everything was so different at that point! There were no plots to have people killed. But then, so much more was to happen."

"Go on," said Michael.

"My next step was obvious! To return to the cellars, to all the abandoned folklore, and research only those saints of exceedingly great size. And what should I come upon but a pile of hagiography—manuscripts saved from destruction at the time of Henry VIII's ghastly suppression of the monasteries, and dumped in our archives along with thousands of other such texts.

"And . . . And among these treasures was a carton marked by some long-dead secretary or clerk: 'Lives of the Scottish Saints.' And the hastily scribbled subtitle: 'Giants'!

"At once I happened upon a later copy of an early work by a monk at Lindisfarne, writing in the 700s, who told the tale of St. Ashlar, a saint of such magic and power that he had appeared among the Highlanders in two different and separate eras, having been returned by God to earth, as was the Prophet Isaiah, and who was destined, according to legend, to return again and again."

Yuri looked at Ash, but Ash said nothing. Yuri couldn't even remember whether Gordon had ever understood Ash's name. But Gordon was already staring at Ash, and then said quickly:

"Could this be the very personage for whom you were named? Could it be that you know of this saint yourself, through your remembrances or those you heard from others, assuming you have known others like yourself?" Gordon's eyes blazed.

Ash didn't answer. The silence this time was stony. Something changed again in Ash's face. Was it pure hatred that he felt for Gordon?

Gordon at once resumed his account, his shoulders hunched and his hands working now in his excitement.

"I was overcome with enthusiasm when I read that St. Ashlar had been a giant of a being, standing perhaps seven feet tall, that St. Ashlar had come from a pagan race whom he himself had helped to exterminate—"

"Get on with it," said Ash softly. "How did you connect this with the Mayfair witches? How did men come to die as the result?"

"All right," said Gordon patiently, "but you will perhaps grant this dying man one request."

"Perhaps not," said Ash. "But what is it?"

"You will tell me whether or not these tales are actually known to you, whether you yourself have remembrances of these early times?"

Ash made a gesture that Gordon should continue.

"Ah, you are cruel, my friend," said Gordon.

Ash was becoming deeply angry. It was plain to see. His full black hair and smooth, almost innocent mouth rendered his expression all the more menacing. He was like an angel gathering its anger. He did not respond to Gordon's words.

"You brought home these tales to Tessa?" asked Rowan.

"Yes," said Gordon, ripping his eyes off Ash finally and looking to her. A little false smile came over his mouth as he continued—as if to say, Now we will answer the question of the pretty lady in the first row.

"I did bring the tale home to Tessa; over supper, as always, I told her of my reading. And the history of this very saint, she knew! Ashlar, one of her own people, and a great leader, a king among them, who had converted to Christianity, betraying his own kind. I was triumphant. Now I had this name to track through history.

"And the following morning I was back at the archives and hard at work. And then, and then . . . came my momentous discovery, that for which other scholars of the Talamasca would give their eyeteeth, if only they knew."

He paused, glancing from one face after another, and even to Yuri finally, his smile full of pride.

"This was a book, a codex of vellum, such as I had never seen in my long life of scholarship! And never dreamed that I would see 'St. Ashlar,' that was the name carved on the cover of the wood box which contained it. 'St. Ashlar.' That was the name of the saint that leapt from the dust and the shadows as I went along the shelves with my electric torch."

Another pause.

"And beneath that name," said Gordon, again looking from one to the other to enlarge the drama. "Beneath, in runic script, were the words, 'History of the Taltos of Britain!' and in Latin: 'Giants in the Earth!' As Tessa was to confirm for me that very night with a simple nod of her head, I had hit upon the crucial word itself."

"Taltos. 'That is what we are,' she said.

"At once I left the tower. I drove back to the Motherhouse. I went down into the cellar. Other records I had always examined within the house, in the libraries or wherever I chose. When has such scholarship ever attracted anyone's notice? But *this* I had to possess."

He rose, resting his knuckles on the table. He looked at Ash, as if Ash would move to stop him. Ash's face was dark, and some imperceptible change had rendered it utterly cold.

Gordon drew back, turned, and then went directly to a big carved cabinet against the wall, and took out of it a large rectangular box.

Ash had watched him calmly, not anticipating an attempt at escape, or confident that he could catch Gordon if Gordon had run for the stairway.

And now Ash stared at the box as Gordon set it down before them. It seemed something was building in Ash, something that might explode.

Good God, the document is genuine, thought Yuri.

"See," Gordon said, his fingers resting on the oiled wood as if on the sacred. "St. Ashlar," he said. And again he translated the rest.

"And what do you think is in this box, all of you? What would you guess?"

"Get on with it, please, Gordon," said Michael, throwing a pointed glance at Ash.

"I shall!" Gordon declared in a whisper, and then, opening the box, he drew out a huge book with stiff leather covers, and laid it down in front of him, as he pushed the box aside.

At once he opened the cover and revealed the title page on the vellum, beautifully illustrated in crimson and gold and royal blue. Tiny miniatures speckled the Latin text. He turned the page carefully. Yuri saw more gorgeous writing and more fine, tiny illustrations whose beauty could only be studied by someone looking through a glass.

"Behold, for you have never in your life seen such a document. For it was written by the saint himself.

"It is the history of the Taltos from their earliest beginnings; the history of a race annihilated; and his own confession that he himself—priest, miracle worker, saint if you will—is not human, but one of the lost giants. It is his plea, to Saint Columba himself, the great missionary to the Picts, abbot and founder of the Celtic monastery on Iona, to believe that the Taltos are not monsters, but beings with immortal souls, creatures made by God, who can share in Christ's grace—it is too magnificent!"

Suddenly Ash rose to his feet, and snatched the book away from Gordon, tearing it loose from Gordon's very hands.

Gordon stood frozen by his chair, Ash standing over him.

The others rose slowly to their feet. When a man is this angry, one must respect his anger, or at least acknowledge it, thought Yuri. They stood quietly gazing up at him as he continued to glare at Gordon as if he would kill the man now.

To see the mild face of Ash disfigured with rage was a terrible thing to behold. This is what angels look like, thought Yuri, when they come with their flaming swords.

Gordon was slowly yielding from outrage to plain terror.

When Ash finally began to speak, it was in a soft whisper, the voice of his former gentleness, yet loud enough for all of them to hear:

"How dare you take this into your possession?" The voice rose in its anger. "You are a thief as well as a killer! You dare!"

"And you would take it from me?" demanded Gordon with blazing eyes. He threw his anger in the face of Ash's anger. "You would take it from me as you will take my life? Who are you to take it? Do you know what I know of your own people?"

"I wrote it!" declared Ashlar, his face now flushed with his rage. "It's mine, this book!" he whispered, as if he didn't dare to speak aloud.

"I inscribed every word," he said. "I painted every picture. It was for Columba that I did this, yes! And it is mine!" He stepped back, clutching the book against his chest. He trembled and blinked his eyes for a moment and then spoke again in his soft voice: "And all your talk," he said, "of your research, of remembered lives, of . . . chains of memory!"

The silence quivered with his anger.

Gordon shook his head. "You're an impostor," he said.

No one spoke.

Gordon remained firm, his face almost comic in its insolence. "Taltos, yes," he said, "St. Ashlar, never! Your age would be beyond calculation!"

No one spoke. No one moved. Rowan's eyes were searching Ash's face. Michael watched all, it seemed, as Yuri did.

Ash gave a deep sigh. He bowed his head slightly, still holding tight to the book. His fingers relaxed ever so slightly around the edges of it.

"And what do you think," he asked sadly, "is the age of that pathetic creature who sits at her loom below?"

"But it was of the remembered life that she spoke, and other remembered lives related to her in her—"

"Oh, stop it, you miserable old fool!" Ash pleaded softly. His breath came haltingly, and then at last the fire started to drain from his face.

"And this you kept from Aaron Lightner," he said. "This you kept from the greatest scholars of your Order, for you and your young friends to weave a filthy plot to steal the Taltos! You are no more than the peasants of the Highlands, the ignorant, brutish savages that lured the Taltos into the circle to kill him. It was the Sacred Hunt all over again."

"No, never to kill!" cried Gordon. "Never to kill. To see the coupling! To bring Lasher and Tessa together on Glastonbury Tor!" He began to weep, choking, gasping, his voice half strangled as he went on. "To see the race rise again on the sacred mountain where Christ himself stood to propagate the religion that changed the whole world! It was not to kill, never to kill, but to bring back to life! It's these witches who have killed, these here who destroyed the Taltos as if he were nothing but a freak of nature! Destroyed him, coldly and ruthlessly, and without a care for what he was, or might become! They did it, not I!"

Ash shook his head. He clutched the book ever more tightly.

"No, you did it," said Ash. "If only you had told your tale to Aaron Lightner, if only you had given him your precious knowledge!"

"Aaron would never have cooperated!" Gordon cried. "I could

never have made such a plan. We were too old, both of us. But those who had the youth, the courage, the vision—they sought to bring the Taltos safely together!"

Again Ash sighed. He waited, measuring his breaths. Then again he looked at Gordon.

"How did you learn of the Mayfair Taltos?" Ash demanded. "What was the final connection? I want to know. And answer me now or I will rip your head from your shoulders and place it in the lap of your beloved Tessa. Her stricken face will be the very last thing you see before the brain inside sputters and dies."

"Aaron," said Gordon. "It was Aaron himself." He was trembling, perhaps on the verge of blacking out. He backed up, eyes darting from right to left. He stared at the cabinet from which he'd taken the book.

"His reports from America," said Gordon, moving closer to the cabinet. "The Council was convened. The information was of critical importance. A monstrous child had been born to the Mayfair witch, Rowan. It had happened on Christmas Eve. A child that had grown within hours perhaps to the size of a man. Members throughout the world were given the description of this being. It was a Taltos, I knew it! And only I knew."

"You evil man," whispered Michael. "You evil little man."

"You call me that! You, who destroyed Lasher! Who killed the mystery as if he were a pedestrian criminal to be dispatched by you to hell in a barroom brawl?"

"You and the others," said Rowan quickly. "You did this on your own."

"I've told you we did." He took another step towards the cabinet. "Look, I won't tell you who the others were, I told you."

"I mean the Elders weren't any part of it," said Rowan.

"The excommunications," said Gordon, "were bogus. We created an intercept. I didn't do it. I don't even understand. But it was created, and we let through only those letters to and from the Elders that did not pertain to this case. We substituted our own exchanges for those between Aaron or Yuri and the Elders, and those from the Elders to them. It wasn't difficult—the Elders, with their penchant for secrecy and simplicity, had left themselves wide open for such a trick."

"Thank you for telling us this," said Rowan gravely. "Perhaps Aaron suspected it."

Yuri could scarcely bear the kindness with which she was speaking to the villain, giving him comfort, when he should have been strangled then and there.

Then she said, "What else can we get out of him?" She looked at Ash. "I think we're finished with him."

Gordon understood what was happening. She was giving Ash permission to kill him. Yuri watched as, slowly, Ash set down the precious book again and turned to face Gordon, his hands free now to carry out the sentence which he himself had imposed.

"You know nothing," Gordon declared suddenly. "Tessa's words, her history, the tapes I made. Only I know where they are."

Ash merely stared at him. His eyes had grown narrow, and his eyebrows came together now in a scowl.

Gordon turned, looking to the left and the right.

"Here!" he cried. "I have another important thing which I shall voluntarily show you."

He dashed to the cabinet again, and when he spun around, he held a gun in both hands, pointing it at Ash, and then at Yuri, and then at Rowan and Michael.

"You can die by this," said Gordon. "Witches, Taltos, all of you! One bullet from this through your heart, and you are as dead as any man!"

"You can't shoot all of us," said Yuri, moving around the edge of the table.

"Don't you dare, or I will shoot!" Gordon screamed.

It was Ash who made the swift move to close the gap between himself and the man. But Gordon turned to face him again, and cocked the gun. Ash didn't stop, but the gun didn't go off, either.

With a grimace, Gordon brought the gun close to his own chest, his shoulders suddenly hunched, the other hand opening and closing. "God in heaven!" he gasped. The gun fell to the floor, clattering on the bare boards.

"You," he said, glaring at Rowan. "You, witch, Mayfair witch!" he cried. "I knew it would be you. I told them. I knew it—" Bent near double, he shut his eyes, and collapsed against the cabinet. It seemed he would fall forward, but then he slipped to the floor. With his right hand he pushed vainly at the floorboards, as if trying to lift himself. Then his body went entirely limp, and his eyelids slid down halfway over his eyes, giving them the dull look of the dead.

He lay there, with only the most haphazard and tawdry air of finality.

Rowan stood as before, without a single outward sign that she had caused it. But she had, Yuri knew, and he could see that Michael knew. He could see it in the way that Michael looked at her—without condemnation, but with a quiet awe. Then a sigh came out of Michael. He took his handkerchief out of his pocket and mopped his face with it.

He turned his back on the dead man, shaking his head, and he moved away, into the shadows, near to the window.

Rowan merely stood there, her arms folded now, her eyes fixed on Gordon's.

Perhaps, thought Yuri, she sees something that we don't see. She senses something we can't sense.

But it really didn't matter. The bastard was dead. And for the first time, Yuri could breathe. He could express a long sigh of relief, so different from the mournful whisper of sound that had just come from Michael.

He is dead, Aaron. He is dead. And the Elders were not part of it. And they will find out, they will surely find out, who his helpers were, if they were those proud young novices.

It seemed a foregone conclusion to Yuri that those young men— Marklin George and Tommy Monohan—were guilty. Indeed, the whole scheme seemed the work of the young, rash and ruthless and full of waste—and perhaps it had been truly beyond the old man's imagining.

No one moved. No one spoke. They all stood there, paying some sort of dark homage to the dead body, perhaps. Yuri wanted to feel relief, but he felt none.

Then Ash went to Rowan, very deliberately and formally, and touching her arms lightly with his long fingers, he bent to kiss her on both cheeks. She looked up, into his eyes, as if she'd been dreaming. Hers was the unhappiest expression Yuri had ever seen.

Ash withdrew and then turned to Yuri. He waited, without speaking. They were all waiting. What was there to say? What must happen now?

Yuri tried to plan, but it was quite impossible.

"Will you go home now, to the Order?" Ash finally asked.

"Yes," said Yuri with a quick nod. "I'll go home to the Order!" He whispered, "I've already alerted them to everything. I called them from the village."

"I saw you," said Ash.

"I spoke with Elvera and with Joan Cross. I have no doubt it was George and Monohan who helped him, but they'll find out."

"And Tessa," said Ash with a little sigh. "Can you take Tessa under your roof?"

"You would let me do it?" Yuri asked. "Of course we would take her. We would shelter her and care for her forever. But you would let this happen?"

"What other place is safe for her?" said Ash, rather frankly sad now, and weary. "She does not have long to live. Her skin is as thin as the vellum pages of my book. She will probably die very soon. But how soon, I have no idea. I don't know how long any of us have to live. We died so often by violence. In the very early days, we believed that was the only way that people died. Natural death, we didn't know what it—"

He broke off, scowling, dark eyebrows beautifully curved beneath the scowl and along the ridge over the end of the large eyes.

"But you take her," he resumed. "You'll be kind to her."

"Ash," said Rowan softly. "You will give them incontrovertible evidence of the Taltos! Why would you do such a thing?"

"That's the best thing that could happen," said Michael. His vehemence caught Yuri off guard. "Do it, do it for Aaron's sake," said Michael. "Take her there, to the Elders. You've done your best to blow the lid off the whole conspiracy. Give them the precious information!"

"And if we're wrong," said Rowan, "if it was not a mere handful of men . . ." She hesitated, looking down at the small, desolate dead body of Gordon. "Then what do they have?"

"Nothing," said Ash softly. "A creature who will die soon, and become once again legend, no matter how many scientific tests are taken with her gentle forbearance, no matter how many photographs or tapes are made. Take her there, Yuri, I ask you. Make her known to the Council. Make her known to everyone. Destroy the secrecy so cruelly used by Gordon and his friends."

"And Samuel?" asked Yuri. "Samuel saved my life. What will Samuel do when he discovers they have her in their very possession?"

Ash pondered, eyebrows rising very gracefully, face softened with thought, and very much the way it had been when Yuri first saw it, the countenance of a large, loving man, perhaps more human than humans, he would never know.

Such a lovely thought, suddenly, that he who lives forever becomes ever more compassionate. But it wasn't true. This being had taken life, and would have killed Gordon if Rowan hadn't somehow forced Gordon's heart to come to a fatal stop. This being might move heaven and earth to get to Mona, Mona the witch, who could make another Taltos.

How in God's name was he to protect Mona?

It was too confusing suddenly, too overwhelming. Of course he would take Tessa with him; he would call them now and beg them to come, and they would, and he would be home again, and he would talk to the Elders once more, and they would be his guardians and his friends. They would help him know what to do. They would take the decisions from his shoulders.

"And I will protect Mona," said Rowan quietly.

He was startled. The gifted witch had been reading his thoughts. How much could she read in all their hearts and souls? How much could the Taltos beguile her and fool her?

"I am no enemy to Mona Mayfair," said Ash, apparently catching on easily. "You have been wrong on this from the beginning. I would not endanger the life of a child. I would force myself upon no woman. You have worries enough. Leave Mona Mayfair to these two witches who love her and will take care of her. Leave the family to them. That is what the Elders will tell you, no doubt, when you do reach them. Let the family heal the family. Let the Order cleanse itself."

Yuri wanted to answer. But he didn't know what to say. *I want this so much to be true?*

Suddenly Ash came towards him, and covered Yuri's face gently in kisses. Yuri looked up, overcome with love, and then, clamping his hand behind Ash's neck, he put his lips to Ash's mouth.

The kiss was firm and chaste.

Somewhere in the back of his mind were Samuel's careless words, that he had fallen in love with Ash. He didn't care. That was the thing about trust. Trust brought such a relief to one, such a lovely feeling of being connected, and that is how you let down your guard, and you can be destroyed.

"I'll take the body now," Ash said. "I'll put it somewhere where men aren't likely to find it."

"No," said Yuri. He was looking right into Ash's large, calm eyes. "I've already spoken to the Motherhouse, as I said. When you're a few miles away, call them. Here, I'll get the number for you. Tell them to come here. We will take care of the body of Stuart Gordon, along with everything else."

He moved away from Ash and stood at the foot of the crumpled body. How puny in death Gordon looked, Gordon the scholar whom everyone had so admired, the friend of Aaron, and the mentor to the boys. Yuri bent down, and without disturbing anything else about the body, slipped his hand in the inside pocket of Gordon's jacket, and found there the inevitable stash of small white cards.

"Here, this is the number of the Motherhouse," he said to Ash as he righted himself, and put a single card in Ash's hand. He looked back at the body. "There's nothing to connect anyone to this dead man," he said. And, realizing it suddenly, the wonderful truth of it, he almost laughed.

"How marvelous," he announced. "He is simply dead, with no mark on him of violence. Yes, call the number and they will come. They'll take us all home."

He turned and looked at Rowan and Michael. "I'll contact you soon."

Rowan's face was sad and unreadable. Michael was plainly anxious.

"And if you don't," said Michael, "then we'll know that we were wrong."

Yuri smiled and shook his head. "I understand now, I understand how it could happen; I see the weaknesses, the charm." He looked about the tower room. Part of him hated it so much; part of him saw it as a sanctuary to deadly romanticism; part of him could not endure the thought of waiting for rescue. But he was too tired, really, to think of anything else, or to do it in any other way.

"I'll go talk to Tessa," said Rowan. "I'll explain that Stuart is very very ill, and that you're going to stay with her until help comes."

"Oh, that would be too good of you," said Yuri. And then, for the first time, he felt his full exhaustion. He sat down on the chair at the table.

His eyes fell on the book or codex, as Stuart had called it so properly or so pedantically, he wasn't sure which.

He saw the long fingers of Ash close on either side of it, picking it up. And then Ash held it again to his chest.

"How can I reach you?" Yuri asked him.

"You can't," said Ash. "But in the days that follow, I promise, I will contact you."

"Please don't forget your promise," said Yuri wearily.

"I must warn you about something," said Ash softly, thoughtfully, holding the book as if it were some sort of sacred shield. "In the months and years to come," he continued, "you may see my likeness here and there, in the normal course of your life, as you happen to pick up a newspaper or a magazine. Don't ever try to come to me. Don't ever try to call me. I am well guarded in ways you cannot dream of. You will not succeed in reaching me. Tell the same to your Order. I will never acknowledge, to any one of them, the things I've told you. And for the love of God, please warn them not to go to the glen. The Little People are dying out, but until they do, they can be most dangerous. Warn them all: stay away from the glen."

"Then you are saying that I can tell them what I've seen."

"Yes, you'll have to do that, you'll have to be utterly open with them. Otherwise you can't go home."

Yuri looked up at Rowan and then at Michael. They drew close, one on either side of him. He felt Rowan's hand touch his face as she kissed him. He felt Michael's hand on his arm.

He didn't say anything. He couldn't. He had no more words. Perhaps he had no more tears.

But the joy in him was so alien to his expectations, it was so wonderous that he longed to tell them to let them know. The Order would come to get him. The disastrous treachery was finished. They were coming, his brothers and sisters, and he could lay bare the horrors and the mysteries he'd seen.

He didn't look up as they left him. He heard them descending the winding staircase. He heard the distant sound of the front door. He also heard soft voices just beneath him.

Slowly he climbed to his feet. He went down the steps to the second floor.

Beside the loom, in the shadows, Tessa stood like a great sapling, her hands pressed together, nodding her head as Rowan spoke too softly for Yuri to hear. Then Rowan gave the woman her kisses of parting, and quickly walked towards the stairs.

"Goodbye, Yuri," she said gently as she passed him, and she turned with her hand on the rail. "Yuri, tell them everything. Make sure the file on the Mayfair witches is finished, just as it should be."

"Everything?" he asked.

"Why not?" she asked with a strange smile. And then she disappeared.

Quickly he looked to Tessa. He'd forgotten about Tessa for those few moments. And Tessa was bound to be miserable when she saw Stuart. Dear God, how would he stop her from going upstairs?

But Tessa was at her loom again, or her tapestry frame, perhaps that's what it was, and she was sewing and singing a little to herself, or making of her normal respiration a little song.

He drew close to her, afraid of disturbing her.

"I know," she said now, looking up at him, smiling sweetly and brightly, with a round and radiant face. "Stuart's died now, and gone, perhaps to heaven."

"She told you?"

"Yes, she did."

Yuri looked out the window. He did not know what he actually saw in the darkness. Was it the gleaming water of the lake? He couldn't tell.

But then, without mistake, he saw the headlights of a car moving away. Through the dark pockets of forest, the lights flashed and then the car disappeared.

For a moment he felt deserted, and horribly exposed. But they would make the call for him, of course they would. They were probably making the call right now. Then there would be no record on the phone here, connecting those who were to come, and those with whom he and the woman would go.

Suddenly he was so tired. Where was the bed in this place? He wanted to ask, but he didn't. He stood merely watching her at her sewing, listening to her humming, and when finally she looked up, she smiled again.

"Oh, I knew it was coming," she said. "I knew it every time I looked at him. I've never known it to fail with your kind. Sooner or later, you all grow weak and small and you die. It took me years to realize it, to realize that no one escaped it. And Stuart, poor dear, he was so very weak, I knew the death would come for him at any time."

Yuri said nothing. He felt a powerful aversion to her, so powerful that he struggled with all his being to disguise it, lest she feel some chill, lest she be hurt. Dimly he thought of his Mona; he saw her aflame with human life, fragrant and warm and continuously surprising. He wondered, did the Taltos see humans that way? Rougher? Wilder? Were we coarse animals to them, animals perhaps of volatile and dangerous charm? Rather like lions and tigers are to us?

Mona. In his mind, he caught a handful of Mona's hair. He saw her turn to look at him, green eyes, lips smiling, words coming rapidly with a lovely American vulgarity and charm.

He felt more certain than ever that he would never see Mona again.

He knew that that was what was meant for her, that her family enfold her, that someone of her own mettle, within her own clan, should be her inevitable love.

"Let's not go upstairs," Tessa said now in a confidential whisper. "Let's let Stuart be dead by himself. It's all right, don't you think? After they're dead, I don't think they mind what you do."

Slowly Yuri nodded, and looked back out into the secretive night beyond the glass.

Twenty

SHE STOOD in the dark kitchen, deliciously full. All the milk was gone, every single drop of it, and the cream cheese, and the cottage cheese, and butter too. That's what you call a clean sweep. Oops, forgot something, thin slices of yellow processed cheese, gag me with a spoon, full of chemicals and dye. Ugh, yuk. She chewed them up, gone, thank you.

"You know, darling, if you had turned out to be an idiot . . ." she said.

That was never a possibility, Mother, I am you and I am Michael. And in a very real way, I am everyone who has been speaking to you from the beginning, and I am Mary Jane.

She burst into laughter, all alone, in the dark kitchen, leaning against the refrigerator. What about ice cream! Shit, she almost forgot!

"Well, honey, you drew a good hand," she said. "You couldn't have drawn better. And am I to presume you did not miss a single syllable . . ."

Häagen-Dazs vanilla! Pints! Pints!

"Mona Mayfair!"

Who was that calling? Eugenia? Don't want to talk to her. Don't want her to disturb me or Mary Jane.

Mary Jane was still in the library, with the papers she'd sneaked out of Michael's desk, or was it Rowan's, now that Rowan was back in circulation? Never mind, it was all kinds of medical stuff and lawyer business, and papers relating to things that had happened only three weeks ago. Mary Jane, once introduced to the various files and histories, had proved insatiable. The history of the family was now her ice cream, so to speak.

"Now, the question is, do we share *this* ice cream with Mary Jane, in cousinly fashion, or do we gobble it?"

Gobble it.

It was time to tell Mary Jane! The time had come. When she'd passed the door just a few minutes ago, before the final raid on the kitchen, Mary Jane had been mumbling things about those dead doctors, God help them, Dr. Larkin and the one out in California, and the chemical autopsies on the dead women. The key thing was to remember to put that stuff back so that neither Rowan nor Michael was unduly alarmed. After all, these things were not being done casually, there was a purpose, Mary Jane was the one upon whom she had fully to depend!

"Mona Mayfair."

It was Eugenia calling, what a nuisance. "Mona Mayfair, it's Rowan Mayfair on the phone, all the way from England, calling you!"

Scold, scold. What she needed was a tablespoon for this ice cream, even if she had almost finished the entire pint. There was one more pint to go.

Now, whose were those little feet coming tippy-tap in the dark, someone running through the dining room? Morrigan clicked her tiny tongue in time with the tippy-tapping.

"Why, it's my beloved cousin, Mary Jane Mayfair."

"Shhhh." Mary Jane put a finger to her lips. "She's looking for you. She's got Rowan on the phone. Rowan wants to talk to you, she said for us to wake you up."

"Pick it up in the library and take the message, I can't risk talking to her. You've got to fool her. Tell her we're fine, I'm in the bathtub or something, and ask about everybody. Like how's Yuri and how's Michael and is she all right?"

"Got it." And off went the teeny tiny feet, tippy-tapping on the floor.

She scraped up the last of that pint and threw the container in the sink. What a messy kitchen! And all my life I have been so neat, and now look, I'm corrupted by money. She tore open the next pint.

Once again came the magic feet. Mary Jane, ripping into the butler's pantry, and flying around the edge of the door, with her corn-yellow hair and her long thin brown legs, and her teensy waist and her white lace skirts swinging like a bell.

"Mona!" she said in a whisper.

"Yeah!" Mona whispered back. What the hell. She ate another big spoon of the ice cream.

"Yes, but Rowan said she had momentous news for us," said Mary

Jane, very obviously aware of the import of this message. "That she would tell us all when she saw us, but that right now she had something she had to do. Same for Michael. Yuri's okay."

"You did a splendid job. What about the guards outside?"

"She said to keep them, not to change anything. Said she'd already called Ryan and told him. Said for you to stay inside and rest, and do whatever your doctor tells you."

"Practical woman, intelligent woman. Hmmmmm . . ." Well, this second carton was empty already. Enough is enough. She started to shiver all over. So coooold! Why hadn't she gotten rid of those guards?

Mary Jane reached out and rubbed Mona's arms. "You okay, darlin'?" Then Mary Jane's eyes dropped to Mona's stomach and her face went blank with fear. She lowered her right hand, wanting to touch Mona's stomach, but she didn't dare.

"Listen, it's time to tell you everything," said Mona. "To give you your choice right now. I was going to lead you into it step by step, but that's not fair and it's not necessary. I can do what I have to do, even if you don't want to help me, and maybe you'd be better off not helping. Either we go now and you help me, or I go alone."

"Go where?"

"That's just it. We're clearing out of here, right now. Guards or no guards. You can drive, can't you?"

She pushed past Mary Jane and into the butler's pantry. She opened the key cabinet. Look for the Lincoln insignia. The limo was a Lincoln, wasn't it? When Ryan had bought it for her, he'd said she should never be in a limousine that was not black and was not a Lincoln. Sure enough, there were the keys! Michael had his keys and the keys to Rowan's Mercedes, but the keys to the limo were right here, where Clem was supposed to leave them.

"Well, sure, I can drive," said Mary Jane, "but whose car are we taking?"

"Mine. The limousine. Only we're not taking the driver with it. You ready? We're counting on the driver being fast asleep out back. Now, what do we need?"

"You're supposed to tell me everything, and give me my choice."

Mona stopped. They were both in the shadows. The house was dark all around them, light pouring in from the garden, from the big zone of blue illumination that was the pool. Mary Jane's eyes were huge and round, making her nose look tiny and her cheeks very smooth. Tendrils of her hair moved behind her shoulders, but mostly it was corn silk. The light struck the cleft of her breasts.

"Why don't *you* tell *me*?" said Mona.

"OK," said Mary Jane. "You're going to have it, no matter what it is."

"Right you are."

"And you're not lettin' Rowan and Michael kill it, no matter what it is."

"Right you are!"

"And the best place for us to go is where nobody will be able to find us."

"Right you are!"

"Only the only place I know is Fontevrault. And if we cut loose every skiff at the landing, the only way they can get out there into the basin after us is to bring in their own boat, if they even think of coming down that way."

"Oh, Mary Jane, you genius! Right you are!"

Mama, I love you, Mama.

And I love you too, my little Morrigan. Trust in me. Trust in Mary Jane.

"Hey, don't faint on me! Lissen, I'm going to go get pillows, blankets, stuff like that. You got any cash?"

"Heaps, twenty-dollar bills in the drawer by the bed."

"You sit down, come in here with me, and sit down." Mary Jane led her through the kitchen and to the table. "Put your head down."

"Mary Jane, don't freak out on me, don't, no matter what it looks like."

"Just you rest till I come back."

And away went the clicky high heels, running through the house.

The song started again, so sweet, so pretty, the song of flowers and the glen.

Stop, Morrigan.

Talk to me, Mother, and Oncle Julien brought you here to sleep with my father, but he didn't know what would happen, but you understand, Mother, you said you understood, that the giant helix was in this case not allied to any ancient evil, but was purely an expression of a genetic potential in you and in Father that had always been there . . .

Mona tried to answer, but it wasn't necessary, the voice went on and on, singsong and soft and very rapid.

Hey, slow down. You sound like a bumblebee when you do that.

". . . immense responsibility, to survive and to give birth, and to love me, Mother, don't forget to love me, I need you, your love, above all things, without which I may lose in my frailty the very will to live . . ."

They were all gathered together in the stone circle, shivering, crying, the tall dark-haired one had come, trying to quiet them. They drew in close to the fire.

"But why? Why do they want to kill us?"

And Ashlar said, "It is their way. They are warlike people. They kill those who are not of their clan. It is as important as eating or drinking or making love is to us. They feast on death."

"Look," she said aloud. The kitchen door had just slammed. Be quiet, Mary Jane! Don't bring Eugenia down here. But we've got to be scientific about this, I should have been recording all this on the computer, typing it in as I see it, but it's almost impossible to accurately record when surrendering to a trance. When we reach Fontevrault, we will have Mary Jane's computer. Mary Jane, the godsend.

Mary Jane had come back, shutting the kitchen door quietly this time, thank heaven.

"That is what the others have to understand," said Mona, "that this is not from hell, but from God. Lasher was from hell, one could say that, you know, speaking metaphysically or metaphorically, I mean religiously or poetically, but when a creature is born this way of two human beings, both of whom contain a mysterious genome, then it's from God. Who else but God? Emaleth was the child of rape, but not this child. Well, at least the mother wasn't the one who got raped."

"Shhh, les us get out of here. I told the guards that I'd seen somebody funny out front, and that I was driving you up to your house to get you some clothes and then to the doctor. Come on!"

"Mary Jane, you are a genius."

But when she stood up, the world swam. "Holy God."

"I have you, now you hold on to me. Are you in pain?"

"Well, no more than anybody would be, with a nuclear explosion going on in her womb. Let's get out of here!"

They crept out down the alley, Mary Jane steadying her when she needed it, but she was doing all right hanging on to the gate and to the fence, and then they were in the carport. And there was the big sleek limousine, and bless her heart, Mary Jane had started the engine, and the door was open. Here we go.

"Morrigan, stop singing! I have to think, tell her about the gate-opener. You have to press the little magic twanger."

"I know that! Get in."

Roar of the engine, and the rusty, creaky sound of the gate rolling back.

"You know, Mona, I've got to ask you something. I've got to. What if this thing can't be born without your dying?"

"Shhhh, bite your tongue, cousin! Rowan didn't die, did she, and she gave birth to one and the other! I'm not dying. Morrigan won't let me."

No, Mother, I love you. I need you, Mother. Don't talk of dying. When you talk of death, I can smell death.

"Shhhhhh. Mary Jane, is the best place Fontevrault? You're sure? Have we considered all the possibilities, perhaps a motel somewhere . . ."

"Lissen, Granny's there, and Granny can be completely trusted, and that little boy staying with her will light out of there soon as I give him one of these twenty-dollar bills."

"But he can't leave his boat at the landing, not for someone else to—"

"No, he won't do that, honey, don't be silly, he'll take his pirogue up home to his place! He doesn't come by the landing. He lives up near town. Now just you sit back and rest. We've got a stash of things at Fontevrault. We have the attic, all dry and warm."

"Oh yes, that would be wonderful."

"And when the sun comes up in the morning, it will come into all the attic windows . . ."

Mary Jane hit the brakes. They were already at Jackson Avenue.

"Sorry, honey, this car is so powerful."

"You're having trouble? God, I never sat up here before, with the whole damned stretch behind me. This is weird, like driving a plane."

"No, I'm not having trouble!" Mary Jane took the turn onto St. Charles. " 'Cept with these creepy drunken New Orleans drivers. It's midnight, you know. But this is a cinch to drive, actually, especially if you've driven an eighteen-wheeler, which I certainly have."

"And where the hell did you do that, Mary Jane?"

"Arizona, honey, had to do it, had to steal the truck, but that's another story."

Morrigan was calling her, singing again, but in that rapid humming voice. Singing to herself, perhaps.

I can't wait to see you, to hold you! I love you more for what you are! Oh, this is destiny, Morrigan, this eclipses everything, the whole world of bassinets and rattles and happy fathers, well, he will be happy eventually, when he comes to understand that the terms now have changed utterly . . .

The world spun. The cold wind swept down over the plain. They were dancing in spite of it, trying desperately to keep warm. Why had the warmth deserted them? Where was their homeland?

Ashlar said, "This is our homeland now. We must learn the cold as well as we learned the warmth."

Don't let them kill me, Mama.

Morrigan lay cramped, filling the bubble of fluid, her hair falling around her and under her, her knees pressed against her eyes.

"Honey, what makes you think anyone will hurt you?"

I think it because you think it, Mama. I know what you know.

"You're talking to that baby?"

"I am, and it's answering me."

Her eyes were closing when they hit the freeway.

"Just you sleep now, darlin'. We're burning up the miles, honey, this thing does ninety and you can't even feel it."

"Don't get a ticket."

"Honey, don't you think a witch like me can handle a policeman? They never finish writing the ticket!"

Mona laughed. Things couldn't have worked out better. Really, they couldn't have.

And the best was yet to come.

Twenty-one

THE BELL tolling . . .

He was not really dreaming; he was planning. But when he did this on the edge of sleep, Marklin saw images vividly, saw possibilities that he could not see any other way.

They would go to America. They would take with them every scrap of valuable information which they had amassed. To hell with Stuart and with Tessa. Stuart had deserted them. Stuart had disappointed them for the last time. They would carry with them the memory of Stuart, Stuart's belief and conviction, Stuart's reverence for the mystery. But that would be all of Stuart that they would ever need.

They would set up some small apartment in New Orleans, and begin their systematic watch of the Mayfair witches. This might take years. But both of them had money. Marklin had real money, and Tommy had the unreal kind that expressed itself in multimillions. Tommy had paid for everything so far. But Marklin could support himself, no problem. And the families could chew on some excuse about an informal sabbatical. Perhaps they would even enroll in courses at the nearby university. Didn't matter.

When they had their sights on the Mayfairs, the fun would begin again.

The bell, dear God, that bell . . .

Mayfair witches. He wished he were in Regent's Park now, with the entire file. All those pictures, Aaron's last reports, still in Xerox typescript. Michael Curry. Read Aaron's copious notes on Michael Curry. This was the man who could father the monster. This was the man whom Lasher had chosen in childhood. Aaron's reports, hasty, excited, full of concern finally, had been clear on that point.

Was it possible for an ordinary man to learn a witch's powers? Oh, if only it were a matter of mere diabolic pact! What if a transfusion of the witch's blood could give him the telepathic abilities? Sheer nonsense, more than likely. But think of the power of the two of them— Rowan Mayfair, the doctor and the witch; Michael Curry, who had fathered the beautiful beast.

Who had called it the beautiful beast? Was that Stuart? Where the hell was Stuart? Damn you, Stuart. You ran like a ruptured duck. You left us, Stuart, without so much as a phone call, a hasty word of parting, a hint of where and when we might meet.

Go on without Stuart. And speaking of Aaron, how could they get his papers from this new wife in America?

Well, everything rested upon one thing. They had to leave here with an unblemished reputation. They had to ask for a leave of absence, without arousing the least suspicion.

With a start, he opened his eyes. Had to get out of here. Didn't want to spend another minute. But there was the bell. It had to be the signal for the memorials. Listen to it, tolling, an awful, nerve-racking sound.

"Wake up, Tommy," he said.

Tommy was slumped over in the chair by the desk, snoring, a tiny bit of drool on his chin. His heavy tortoiseshell glasses had reached the very tip of his rounded nose.

"Tommy, it's the bell."

Marklin sat up, straightened his clothes as best he could. He climbed off the bed.

He shook Tommy by the shoulder.

For one moment Tommy had that baffled, annoyed look of the just-awakened, and then the common sense returned.

"Yes, the bell," he said calmly. He ran his hands over his sloppy red hair. "At last, the bell."

They took turns washing their faces. Marklin took a bit of Kleenex, smeared it with Tommy's toothpaste, and cleaned his teeth by hand. He needed to shave, but there was no time for it. They'd go to Regent's Park, get everything, and leave for America on the first flight out.

"Leave of absence, hell," he said now. "I'm for leaving, just going. I don't want to go back to my own room to pack. I'm for heading out of here immediately. The hell with the ceremony."

"Don't be so foolish," Tommy murmured. "We'll say what we have to say. And we'll learn what we can learn. And then we'll leave at the appropriate and less conspicuous time."

Damn!

A knock sounded at the door.

"We're coming!" Tommy said, with a little raising of his eyebrows. He straightened his tweed jacket. He looked both mussed and hot.

Marklin's own wool blazer was badly rumpled. And he'd lost his tie. Well, the shirt looked all right with the sweater. Would have to do, wouldn't it? The tie was in the car, perhaps. He'd ripped it off when he was driving away the first time. He should never, never have come back.

"Three minutes," came the voice through the door. One of the old ones. The place was going to be choked with them.

"You know," said Marklin, "none of this was bearable even when I thought of myself as a dedicated novice. Now I find it simply outrageous. Being awakened at four in the morning . . . Good God, it's actually five . . . for a mourning ceremony. It's as stupid as those modern-day Druids, dressed up in sheets, who carry on at Stonehenge on the summer solstice, or whenever the hell they do it. I may let you say the appropriate words for us. I may wait in the car."

"The hell you will," said Tommy. He took several swipes at his dry hair with the comb. Useless.

They went out of the room together, Tommy stopping to lock the door. The hall was predictably cold.

"Well, you can do that if you wish," said Marklin, "but I'm not coming back up to this floor. They can have whatever I've left in my room."

"That would be perfectly stupid. You'll pack as if you were leaving for normal reasons. Why the hell not?"

"I can't stay here, I tell you."

"And what if you've overlooked something in your room, something that would blow the lid off the entire affair?"

"I haven't. I know I haven't."

The corridors and the staircase were empty. Possibly they were the last of the novices to hear the bell.

A soft whisper of voices rose from the first floor. As they came to the foot of the steps, Marklin saw it was worse than he could have imagined.

Look at the candles everywhere. Everyone, absolutely everyone, dressed in black! All the electric lights had been put out. A sickening gush of warm air surrounded them. Both fires were blazing. Good heavens! And they had draped every window in the house with crepe.

"Oh, this is too rich!" Tommy whispered. "Why didn't someone tell us to dress?"

"It's positively nauseating," said Marklin. "Look, I'm giving it five minutes."

"Don't be a blasted fool," said Tommy. "Where are the other novices? I see old people, everywhere, old people."

There must have been a hundred in small groups, or simply standing alone against the dark oak-paneled walls. Gray hair everywhere. Well, surely the younger members were here somewhere.

"Come on," said Tommy, pinching Marklin's arm and pushing him into the hall.

A great supper was spread on the banquet table.

"Good Lord, it's a goddamned feast," Marklin said. It made him sick to look at it—roast lamb and beef, and bowls of steaming potatoes, and piles of shiny plates, and silver forks. "Yes, they're eating, they're actually eating!" he whispered to Tommy.

A whole string of elderly men and women were quietly and slowly filling their plates. Joan Cross was there in her wheelchair. Joan had been crying. And there was the formidable Timothy Hollingshed, wearing his innumerable titles on his face as he always did, arrogant bastard, and not a penny to his name.

Elvera passed through the crowd with a decanter of red wine. The glasses stood on the sideboard. Now that is something I can use, thought Marklin, I can use that wine.

A sudden thought came to him of being free from here, on the plane to America, relaxed, his shoes kicked off, the stewardess plying him with liquor and delicious food. Only a matter of hours.

The bell was still tolling. How long was that going to go on? Several men near him were speaking Italian, all of them on the short side. There were the old grumbly British ones, the friends of Aaron's, most of them now retired. And there was a young woman—well, at least she seemed young. Black hair and heavily made-up eyes. Yes, when you looked you saw they were senior members, but not merely the decrepit class. There stood Bryan Holloway, from Amsterdam. And there, those anemic and pop-eyed male twins who worked out of Rome.

No one was really looking at anyone, though people did talk to each other. Indeed, the air was solemn but convivial. From all around came soft murmurs of Aaron this, and Aaron that . . . always loved Aaron, adored Aaron. Seems they had forgotten Marcus entirely, and well they should, thought Marklin, if only they knew how cheaply Marcus had been bought out.

"Have some wine, please, gentlemen," said Elvera softly. She gestured to the rows and rows of crystal glasses. Old stemware. All the old finery. Look at the antique silver forks with their deep encrustations. Look at the old dishes, dragged from some vault somewhere perhaps, to be loaded with fudge and iced cakes.

"No, thank you," said Tommy, tersely. "Can't eat with a plate and a glass in my hands."

Someone laughed in the low roar of whispers and murmurs. Another voice rose above the others. Joan Cross sat solitary in the midst of the gathering, her forehead resting in her hand.

"But who are we mourning?" asked Marklin in a whisper. "Is it Marcus or Aaron?" He had to say something. The candles made an irritating glare, for all the swimming darkness around him. He blinked. He had always loved this scent of pure wax, but this was overpowering, absurd.

Blake and Talmage were talking together rather heatedly in the corner. Hollingshed joined them. As far as Marklin knew, they were in their late fifties. Where were the other novices? No other novices. Not even Ansling and Perry, the officious little monsters. What does your instinct tell you? Something is wrong, very wrong.

Marklin went after Elvera, quickly catching her elbow.

"Are we supposed to be here?"

"Yes, of course you are," said Elvera.

"We're not dressed."

"Doesn't matter. Here, do have a drink." This time she put the glass in his hand. He set down his plate on the edge of the long table. Probably a breach of etiquette, nobody else had done it. And, God, look at this spread. There was a great roasted boar's head, with the apple in its mouth, and the suckling pig surrounded by fruit on its steaming silver platter. The mingled fragrances of the meat were delicious, he had to admit it. He was getting hungry! How absurd.

Elvera was gone, but Nathan Harberson was very close to him, looking down at him from his lofty mossback height.

"Does the Order always do this?" Marklin asked. "Throw a banquet when someone dies?"

"We have our rituals," said Nathan Harberson in an almost sad voice. "We are an old, old order. We take our vows seriously."

"Yes, very seriously," said one of the pop-eyed twins from Rome. This one was Enzo, wasn't it? Or was it Rodolpho? Marklin couldn't remember. His eyes made you think of fish, too large for expression, indicative only of illness, and to think it had struck both of them. And when the twins both smiled as they were doing now, they looked rather hideous. Their faces were wrinkled, thin. But there was supposed to be some crucial difference between them. What was it? Marklin could not recall.

"There are certain basic principles," said Nathan Harberson, his velvety baritone voice growing a little louder, a little more confident, perhaps.

"And certain things," said Enzo, the twin, "are beyond question with us."

Timothy Hollingshed had drawn near and was looking down his aquiline nose at Marklin, as he always did. His hair was white and thick, like Aaron's had been. Marklin didn't like the look of him. It was like looking at a cruel version of Aaron, much taller, more ostentatiously elegant. God, look at the man's rings. Positively vulgar, and every one was supposed to have its history, replete with tales of battle, treachery, vengeance. When can we leave here? When will all this end?

"Yes, we hold certain things sacred," Timothy was saying, "just as if we were a small nation unto ourselves."

Elvera had returned. "Yes, it isn't merely a matter of tradition."

"No," said a tall, dark-haired man with ink-black eyes and a bronzed face. "It's a matter of a deep moral commitment, of loyalty."

"And of reverence," said Enzo. "Don't forget reverence."

"A consensus," said Elvera, looking straight at him. But then they were *all* looking at him. "On what is of value, and how it must be protected at all costs."

More people had pressed into the room, senior members only. A predictable increase in soft chatter. Someone laughing again. Didn't people have the sense not to laugh?

There is something just flat-out wrong with this, that we're the only novices, thought Marklin. And where was Tommy? Suddenly in a panic, he realized he had lost sight of Tommy. No, there he was, eating grapes from the table like some sort of Roman plutocrat. Ought to have the decency not to do that.

Marklin gave a quick, uneasy nod to those clustered around him and pushed through a tight press of men and women, and, nearly tripping over someone's foot, landed finally at Tommy's side.

"What the hell's the matter with you?" Tommy demanded. He was looking at the ceiling. "For God's sake, relax. We'll be on the plane in a few hours. Then we'll be in . . ."

"Shhh, don't say anything," said Marklin, conscious that his voice was no longer normal, no longer under his control. If he had ever been this apprehensive in his life, he didn't remember it.

For the first time he saw that the black cloth had been draped everywhere along the walls. The two clocks of the great hall were covered! And the mirrors, the mirrors were veiled in black. He found these things totally unnerving. He had never seen such old-fashioned funeral trappings. When people in his family had died, they'd been cremated. Someone called you later to tell you that it had been done. That was precisely what had happened with his parents. He'd been at school, lying on his bed, reading Ian Fleming, when the call came, and he had only nodded and gone on reading. *And now you've inherited everything, absolutely everything.*

Suddenly he was thoroughly sick from the candles. He could see the candelabra everywhere, such costly silver. Some of them were even encrusted with jewels. God, how much money did this Order have stashed away in its cellars and its vaults? A small nation indeed. But then it was all the fault of fools like Stuart, who had long ago willed his entire fortune to the Order, and must surely have changed that will, all things considered, of course.

All things. Tessa. The plan. Where was Stuart now—with Tessa?

The talk grew louder and louder. There was the tinkling of glasses. Elvera came again and poured more wine into his glass.

"Drink up, Mark," she said.

"Do behave, Mark," whispered Tommy, unpleasantly close to his face.

Marklin turned. This wasn't his religion. This wasn't his custom, to stand about feasting and drinking in black clothes at dawn!

"I'm going now!" he suddenly declared. His voice seemed to explode from his mouth and echo throughout the room!

Everybody else had gone silent.

For one second, in the ringing stillness, he almost gave in to a scream. The desire to scream was more pure in him than ever in childhood. To scream in panic, in horror. He didn't know which.

Tommy pinched his arm, and pointed.

The double doors to the dining hall had been opened. Ah, so that was the reason for the silence. Dear God, had they brought the remains of Aaron home?

The candles, the crepe—it was the very same in the dining hall, another cavern of grimness. He was determined not to enter, but before he could act upon this decision, the crowd moved him slowly and solemnly towards the open doorway. He and Tommy were being almost carried along.

Don't want to see any more, want to leave here . . .

The press loosened as they passed through the doors. Men and women were filing around the long table. Someone *was* laid out on the table. God, not Aaron! Can't look at Aaron. *And they know you can't look at him, don't they? They are waiting for you to panic, and for Aaron's wounds to bleed!*

Horrible, stupid. He clutched Tommy's arm again, and heard Tommy's correction. "Do be still!"

At last they had come to the edge of the grand old table. This was a man in a dusty wool jacket, with mud on his shoes. Look, mud. This was no corpse properly laid out.

"This is ludicrous," said Tommy under his breath.

"What sort of funeral is this!" he heard himself say aloud.

Slowly he leant over so that he could see the dead face that was turned away from him. Stuart. Stuart Gordon, dead and lying on this table—Stuart's impossibly thin face, with its bird-beak of a nose, and his lifeless blue eyes. Dear God, they had not even closed his eyes! Were they all insane?

He backed away awkwardly, colliding with Tommy, feeling his heel on Tommy's toe, and then the swift removal of Tommy's foot. All thought seemed beyond him. A dread took hold of him totally. Stuart is dead, Stuart is dead, Stuart is dead.

Tommy was staring at the body. Did he know it was Stuart?

"What is the meaning of this?" Tommy asked, his voice low and full of wrath. "What's happened to Stuart . . ." But the words had little conviction. His voice, always a monotone, was now weak with shock.

The others drew in all around them, pressing them right against the table. Stuart's limp left hand lay right near them.

"For the love of heaven," said Tommy angrily. "Someone close his eyes."

From one end of the table to the other, the members surrounded it, a phalanx of mourners in black. Or were they mourners? Even Joan Cross was there, at the head of the table, arms resting on the arms of her wheelchair, her reddened eyes fixed upon them!

No one spoke. No one moved. The first stage of silence had been the absence of speech. This was the second stage, the absence of movement, with members so still he could not even hear anyone draw breath.

"What's happened to him!" demanded Tommy.

Still no one answered. Marklin could not fix his gaze on anything; he kept looking at the small dead skull, with its thin covering of white hair. *Did you kill yourself, you fool, you crazed fool? Is that what you did? At the first chance of discovery?*

And suddenly, very suddenly, he realized that all the others were not looking at Stuart, they were looking at Tommy and at him.

He felt a pain in his chest as though someone had begun to press on his breastbone with impossibly strong hands.

He turned, desperately searching the faces around him—Enzo, Harberson, Elvera, and the others, staring at him with malign expressions, Elvera herself staring straight up into his eyes. And right beside him, Timothy Hollingshed, staring coldly down at him.

Only Tommy did not stare at him. Tommy stared across the table, and when Marklin looked to see what had so distracted him, what had made him oblivious to the perfect horror of all this, he saw that Yuri Stefano, clothed in proper funereal black, was standing only a few feet away.

Yuri! Yuri was here, and had been here all along! Had Yuri killed Stuart? Why in the name of God hadn't Stuart been clever, why hadn't he known how to deflect Yuri? The whole point of the intercept, of the bogus excommunication, was that Yuri would never, never be able to reach the Motherhouse again. And that idiot Lanzing, to have let Yuri escape from the glen.

"No," said Elvera, "the bullet found its mark. But it wasn't fatal. And he's come home."

"You were Gordon's accomplices," said Hollingshed disdainfully. "Both of you. And you and only you are left."

"His accomplices," said Yuri from the other side of the table. "His bright ones, his geniuses."

"No!" said Marklin. "This is not true! Who is accusing us?"

"Stuart accused you," said Harberson. "The papers scattered all through his tower house accused you, his diary accused you, his poetry accused you, Tessa accused you."

Tessa!

"How dare you enter his house!" thundered Tommy, red with rage as he glared about him.

"You don't have Tessa, I don't believe you!" Marklin screamed. "Where is Tessa? It was all for Tessa!" And then, realizing his terrible error, he realized in full what he already knew.

Oh, why hadn't he listened to his instinct! His instinct had told him to leave, and now his instinct told him, without question—*It is too late.*

"I'm a British citizen," said Tommy under his breath. "I won't be detained here for any sort of vigilante court."

At once the crowd shifted and moved against them, pushing them slowly from the head of the table, towards the foot. Hands had taken hold of Marklin's arms. That unspeakable Hollingshed had hold of him. He heard Tommy protest once more, "Let me go," but it was now utterly impossible. They were being pressed into the corridor and down it, the soft thudding of feet on the waxed boards echoing up beneath the wooden arches. It was a mob which had caught him, a mob from which he couldn't conceivably escape.

With a loud metallic shuffle and crack, the doors of the old elevator were thrown back. Marklin was shoved inside, turning frantically, a claustrophobia gripping him that again pushed him to scream.

But the doors were sliding shut. He and Tommy stood pressed against each other, surrounded by Harberson, Enzo, Elvera, the dark-haired tall one, and Hollingshed and several other men, strong men.

The elevator was clattering and wobbling its way down. Into the cellars.

"What are you going to do to us?" he demanded suddenly.

"I insist upon being taken to the main floor again," said Tommy disdainfully. "I insist upon immediate release."

"There are certain crimes we find unspeakable," said Elvera softly, her eyes fixed on Tommy now, thank heaven. "Certain things which, as an order, we cannot possibly forgive or forget."

"Which means what, I'd like to know!" said Tommy.

The heavy old elevator stopped with a shattering jolt. Then it was out into the passage, the hands hurting Marklin's arms.

They were being taken along some unknown route in the cellars, down a corridor supported with crude wooden beams, rather like a mineshaft. The smell of the earth was around them. All the others were beside them or behind them now. They could see two doors at the end of this passage, large wooden doors inset beneath a low arch, and bolted shut.

"You think you can detain me here against my will?" said Tommy. "I'm a British citizen."

"You killed Aaron Lightner," said Harberson.

"You killed others in our name," said Enzo. And there was his brother beside him, repeating in a maddening echo the very same words.

"You besmirched us in the eyes of others," said Hollingshed. "You did unspeakable evil in our name!"

"I confess to nothing," said Tommy.

"We don't require you to confess," said Elvera.

"We don't require anything of you," said Enzo.

"Aaron died believing your lies!" said Hollingshed.

"God damn it, I will not stand for this!" roared Tommy.

But Marklin could not bring himself to be indignant, outraged, whatever it was he ought to be, that they were holding him prisoner, forcing him now towards the doors.

"Wait a minute, wait, please, don't. Wait," he stammered. He begged. "Did Stuart kill himself? What happened to Stuart? If Stuart were here, he would exonerate us, you can't really think that someone of Stuart's years . . ."

"Save your lies for God," said Elvera softly. "All night long we've examined the evidence. We've spoken with your white-haired goddess. Unburden your soul of the truth to us, if you wish, but don't bother us with your lies."

The figures closed ranks tightly against them. They were being moved closer and closer to this chamber or room or dungeon, perhaps, Marklin couldn't know.

"Stop!" he cried suddenly. "In the name of God! Stop! There are things you don't know about Tessa, things you simply don't understand."

"Don't cater to them, you idiot!" snarled Tommy. "Do you think my father won't be asking questions! I'm not a bloody orphan! I have a huge family. Do you think—"

A strong arm gripped Marklin about the waist. Another was clamped around his neck. The doors were being opened inward. Out of the corner of his eye, he saw Tommy struggling, knee bent, foot kicking at the men behind him.

An icy gust of air rose from the open doors. Blackness. I cannot be locked in blackness. I cannot!

And finally he screamed. He couldn't hold it back any longer. He screamed, the terrible cry begun before he was pushed forward, before he felt himself topple from the threshold, before he realized he was plunging down and down into the blackness, into the nothingness, that Tommy was falling with him, cursing them, threatening them, or so it seemed. It was quite impossible to know. His scream was echoing too loudly off the stone walls.

He'd struck the ground. The blackness was outside him and also within. Then the awakening to pain throughout his limbs. He lay among hard and jagged things, cutting things. Dear God! And when he sat upright, his hand fell on objects which crumbled and broke and gave off a dull ashen smell.

He squinted in the single shaft of light that fell down upon him, and looking upwards, he realized with horror that it came from the door through which he'd fallen, over the heads and shoulders of the figures who filled it in black silhouette.

"No, you can't do it!" he screamed, scrambling forward in the darkness, and then, without compass points or touchstones of any kind, climbing to his feet.

He couldn't see their darkened faces; he couldn't make out even the shapes of their heads. He'd fallen many feet, many, perhaps thirty feet, even. He didn't know.

"Stop it, you can't keep us here, you can't put us here!" he roared, raising his hands to them, imploring them. But the figures had stepped back out of the lighted opening, and with horror he heard a familiar sound. It was the hinges creaking as the light died, and the doors were closed.

"Tommy, Tommy, where are you?" he cried desperately. The echo frightened him. It was locked in with him. It had nowhere to go but up against him, against his ears. He reached out, patting the floor, touching these soft, broken, crumbling things, and suddenly he felt something wet and warm!

"Tommy!" he cried with relief. He could feel Tommy's lips, his nose, his eyes. "Tommy!"

Then, in a split second, longer in duration, perhaps, than all his life, he understood everything. Tommy was dead. He'd died in the fall. And they had not cared that he might. And they were never coming back for Marklin, never. Had the law, with its comforts and its sanctions, been a possibility, they would not have thrown either one of them from such a height. And now Tommy was dead. He was alone in this place, in the dark, beside his dead friend, clinging to him now, and the other things, the things round which his fingers curled, were bones.

"No, you can't do it, you can't countenance such a thing!" His voice rose again in a scream. "Let me out of here! Let me out!" Back came the echo, as if these cries were streamers rising and then tumbling back down upon him. "Let me out!" His cries ceased to be words. His cries grew softer and more full of agony. And their terrible sound gave him a strange comfort. And he knew it was the last and only comfort he'd ever know.

He lay still, finally. Beside Tommy, fingers locked around Tommy's arm. Perhaps Tommy wasn't dead. Tommy would wake up, and they would search this place together. Perhaps that's what they were supposed to do. There was a way out, and the others meant for him to find it; they meant him to walk through the valley of death to find it, but they didn't mean to kill him, not his brothers and sisters in the Order, not Elvera, dear Elvera, and Harberson and Enzo, and his old teacher Clermont. No, they were incapable of such things!

At last he turned over and climbed to his knees, but when he tried to rise to his feet, his left ankle gave out from under him in a flash of pain.

"Well, I can crawl, damn it!" he whispered. "I can crawl!" He screamed the words. And crawl he did, pushing the bones away from him, the debris, the crumbled rock or bone or whatever it was. Don't think about it. Don't think about rats, either. Don't think!

His head was suddenly struck, or so it seemed, by a wall.

Within sixty seconds he had traveled along that wall, and along another and another, and finally another. The room was no more than a shaft, it was so small.

Oh, well, don't have to worry about getting out, it seems, not till I feel better and I can stand up and look for some other opening, something other than a passage, a window perhaps. After all, there's air, fresh air.

Just rest awhile, he thought, snuggling close to Tommy again, and pressing his forehead against Tommy's sleeve, rest and think what to do. It is absolutely out of the question that you could die like this, you, this young, die like this, in this dungeon, thrown here by a pack of evil old priests and nuns, impossible . . . Yes, rest, don't confront the entire issue, just yet. Rest . . .

He was drifting. How stupid of Tommy to have utterly alienated his stepmother, to have told her he wanted no further contact. Why, it would be six months, a year even . . . No, the bank would be looking for them, Tommy's bank, his bank, when he didn't draw his quarterly check, and when was that? No, this couldn't be their final decision, to bury them alive in this awful place!

He was startled wide awake by a strange noise.

Again came the noise, and then again. He knew what that was, but he couldn't identify it. Damn, in utter darkness, he could not identify even the direction. He must listen. There was a series of sounds, actually, picture it, try to picture it, and then he did.

Bricks being fitted into place, and mortar troweled over them. Bricks and mortar, high above.

"But that's absurd, absolutely absurd. It's medieval, it's utterly outrageous. Tommy, wake up. Tommy!" He would have screamed again, but it was too humiliating, that those bastards up there would hear him, that they'd hear him roaring as they bricked up the bloody door.

Softly, he cried against Tommy's arm. No, this was temporary, a contrivance to make them miserable, contrite, before turning them over to the authorities. They didn't mean for them to remain here, *to die here!* It was some sort of ritual punishment and only meant to frighten him. But of course, the awful part was that Tommy was dead! But still, he'd be glad to say that this had been an accident. When they came, he'd be entirely cooperative. The point was to get out! That's what he'd wanted to do all along, get out!

I can't die like this, it's unthinkable that I should die like this, it's impossible, all my life forfeit, my dreams taken from me, the greatness I only glimpsed with Stuart and with Tessa . . .

Somewhere in the back of his mind, he knew there were awful flaws in his logic, fatal flaws, but he continued, constructing the future, their coming, telling him they had only meant to scare him, and that it had been an accident, Tommy's dying, they hadn't known the drop was so dangerous, foolish of them, murderous, vengeful liars and fools. The thing was to be ready, to be calm, to sleep perhaps, sleep, listening to the sounds of the brick and the mortar. No, these sounds have stopped. The door is sealed, perhaps, but that doesn't matter. There have to be other ways into this dungeon, and other ways out. Later he'd find them.

For now, best to cling to Tommy, just to snuggle close to him and wait till the initial panic was gone, and he could think what to do next.

Oh, how foolish of him to have forgotten Tommy's lighter. Tommy never smoked any more than he did, but Tommy always carried that fancy lighter, and would snap it for pretty girls lifting cigarettes to their lips.

He felt in Tommy's pockets, pants, no, jacket, yes. He had it, the little gold lighter. Pray it had fluid or a cartridge of butane, or whatever the hell made it burn.

He sat up slowly, hurting the palm of his left hand on something rough. He snapped the light. The little flame sputtered and then grew long. The illumination swelled around him, revealing the small chamber, cut deep, deep into the earth.

And the jagged things, the crumbling things, were bones, human bones. There lay a skull beside him, sockets staring at him, and there another, oh God! Bones so old, some had turned to ashes, bones! And Tommy's dead, staring face, red blood drying on the side of his mouth and on his neck, where it had run down into his collar. And before him and beside him and behind him, bones!

He dropped the lighter, his hands flying to his head, his eyes closing, his mouth opening in an uncontrollable and deafening scream. There was nothing but the sound and the darkness, the sound emptying from him, carrying all his fear and his horror heavenward, and he knew in his soul he would be all right, he would be all right, if only he did not stop screaming, but let the scream pour forth from him, louder and louder, and forever, without cease.

Twenty-two

APLANE rarely ever fully insulated you. Even in this plane, so lavishly upholstered, with its deep chairs and large table, you know you were in a plane. You know you were thirty-eight thousand feet over the Atlantic, and you could feel the small ups and downs as the plane rode the wind, rather like a great vessel rides the sea.

They sat in the three chairs grouped around the table. At the three points of an invisible equilateral triangle. One chair had been specially made for Ash, that was obvious, and he'd been standing by that chair when he had gestured for Rowan and Michael to take the other two.

Other chairs, along the windowed walls of the cabin, were empty, big upturned gloved hands waiting to hold you firm and tight. One of them was larger than the others. For Ash, no doubt.

The colors were caramel, gold. Everything streamlined and near perfect. The young American woman who had served the drinks, perfect. The music, for the little while it had played, Vivaldi, perfect.

Samuel, the astonishing little man, slept in a rear cabin, curled up in bed, holding tight to the bottle he'd brought from the flat in Belgravia, and demanding a bulldog which Ash's servants had not procured for him. "You said, Ash, that I was to have anything I wanted. I heard you tell them. Well, I wanted a bulldog! And I want a bulldog now."

Rowan lay back in the chair, holding the backs of her arms.

She didn't know how long it had been since she'd slept. Sometime before they reached New York, she'd have to sleep. Right now she was curiously electrified, staring at the two men opposite her—at Michael, who smoked his little stub of a cigarette, holding it in two fingers, the red brand of the lighted end facing inwards.

And Ash, in another one of those long, full-cut, double-breasted silk coats, all the rage, with sleeves turned up carelessly, white shirt cuffs adorned with gold and stone cufflinks that made her think of opals, though she realized she was not much of an expert on precious or semiprecious stones or anything of that sort. Opals. His eyes had a rather opalescent quality, or so she had thought several times. His pants were loose, rather like pajamas, but that too was fashionable. He had brought up his foot, disrespectfully, on the edge of the leather, his leather, and on his right wrist he wore a thin gold bracelet without any obvious use, a thin band of metal, glittering and looking maddeningly sexual to her, though why she couldn't explain.

He lifted his hand, ran it back through his dark hair, running the little finger through the white streak as if he didn't want to forget it, leave it out, but collect it with all the other dark waves. It made his face come alive for her again, just this little movement, and the way his eyes scanned the room and then stopped on her.

She herself hardly noticed what she'd taken hastily from her suitcase. Something red, something soft, something loose and short that barely touched her knees. Michael had put the pearls around her neck, a small, neat necklace. It had surprised her. She'd been so dazed then.

Ash's servants had packed up everything else.

"I didn't know whether or not you wanted us to get Samuel a bulldog," the young one, Leslie, had said several times, very distressed that she'd displeased the boss.

"It doesn't matter," Ash had said finally, hearing her, perhaps for the first time. "In New York we will get Samuel bulldogs. He can keep his bulldogs in the garden on the roof. Do you know, Leslie, there are dogs who live on the rooftops of New York who have never, never been to the street below?"

What must she think he is? Rowan had wondered. What do they all think he is? Is it to his advantage that he is blindingly rich? Or blindingly handsome?

"But I wanted a bulldog tonight," the little man had fussed until he'd passed out again, "and I want it now."

The little man had on first sight terrified Rowan. What was that, witch genes? Witch knowledge? Or was it the physician in her, horrified by the folds of flesh slowly covering his entire face? He was like a great variegated and living piece of stone. What if a surgeon's scalpel removed those folds, revealing eyes, a full, correctly shaped mouth, the bones under the cheeks, the chin? What would his life become?

"Mayfair witches," he'd said when he saw them, Rowan and Michael.

"Does everyone in this part of the world know us?" Michael had asked testily. "And does our reputation always go before us? When I get home, I mean to read up on witchcraft, to study it in earnest."

"Very good idea," Ash had said. "With your powers, you can do many things."

Michael had laughed. They liked each other, these two. She could see it. They shared certain attitudes. Yuri had been so frenzied, shattered, so young.

All the way back from the grim confrontation at Stuart Gordon's tower, Michael had told them the long story related to him by Lasher, of a life lived in the 1500s, and of Lasher's strange account of earlier memories, of his sense that he had lived even before that. There had been nothing clinical in the telling—rather a ragged outpouring of the tale which he and Aaron alone had known. He had told it once before to Rowan, yes, and she remembered it more as a series of images and catastrophes than words.

To have heard it again in the black limousine, flying over the miles towards London, was to see it again and in greater detail. Lasher the priest, Lasher the saint, Lasher the martyr, and then, a hundred years later, the beginning of Lasher the witch's familiar, the invisible voice in the dark, a force of wind lashing the fields of wheat, and the leaves from the trees.

"Voice from the glen," the little man had said in London, jabbing his thumb to point at Michael.

Was it? She wondered. She knew the glen, she would never forget it, forget being Lasher's prisoner, being dragged up through the ruins of the castle, never forget the moments when Lasher had "recalled" everything, when the new flesh had reclaimed his mind and severed it from whatever true knowledge a ghost can possess.

Michael had never been there. Maybe someday they would, together, visit that place.

Ash had told Samuel to go to sleep as they drove for the airport. The little man had drunk another pint of whiskey, with a lot of grunting and groaning and occasional belching, and had been comatose when carried onto the plane.

Now they were flying over the Arctic.

She closed and opened her eyes. The cabin shimmered.

"I would never hurt this child Mona," said Ash suddenly, startling her, waking her more fully. He was watching Michael with quiet eyes.

Michael took a final drag off the stubby little cigarette, and crushed it out in the big glass tray so that it became a hideous little worm. His fingers looked large, powerful, dusted with dark hair.

"I know you wouldn't," said Michael. "But I don't understand it all. How can I? Yuri was so frightened."

"That was my fault. Stupidity. This is why we have to talk to each other, we three. There are others reasons as well."

"But why trust us?" asked Michael. "Why befriend us at all? You're a busy man, some sort of billionaire, obviously."

"Ah, well, we have that in common then, too, don't we?" said Ash, earnestly.

Rowan smiled.

It was a fascinating study in contrasts, the deep-voiced man with the flashing blue eyes and the dark, almost bushy eyebrows; and the tall one, so beguilingly slender, with graceful movements of the wrist that made you almost dizzy. Two exquisite brands of masculinity, both bound up with perfect proportions and fierce personality, and both men—as big men often do—seemed to luxuriate in a great self-confidence and inner calm.

She looked at the ceiling. In her exhaustion, things were distorted. Her eyes were dry and she would have to sleep soon, simply have to, but she couldn't now. Not now.

Ash spoke again.

"You have a tale to tell which no one can hear but me," said Ash. "And I want to hear it. And I have a tale to tell that I will tell only to you. Is it that you don't want my confidence? That you don't want my friendship or ever, possibly, my love?"

Michael considered this. "I think I want all that, since you ask," said Michael, with a little shrug and laugh. "Since you ask."

"Gotcha," said Ash softly.

Michael laughed again, just a low little rumble. "But you know, don't you, that I killed Lasher? Yuri told you this. You hold this against me, that I killed one of you?"

"He was not one of me," said Ash, smiling kindly. The light glinted on the white streak coming from his left temple. A man of thirty, perhaps, with elegant gray streaks, a sort of boy genius of the corporate world, he must have seemed, prematurely rich, prematurely gray. Centuries old, infinitely patient.

It gave her a small warm burst of pride, suddenly, that she had killed Gordon. Not him.

She had done it. It was the first time in all her sad life that she had enjoyed using the power, condemning a man to death with her will, destroying the tissues inside him, and she had confirmed what she had always suspected, that if she really wanted to do it, if she really cooperated with it, rather than fighting this power, it could work awfully fast.

"I want to tell you things," Ash said. "I want you to know them, the story of what happened and how we came to the glen. Not now, we're all too tired, surely. But I want to tell you."

"Yeah," said Michael, "and I want to know." He was reaching into his pocket, pulling the pack halfway up and then shaking loose the cigarette. "I want to know all about you, of course. I want to study the book, if you still mean to let us do that, see the book."

"All that is possible," said Ash, with an easy gesture, one hand resting on his knee. "You are a veritable tribe of witches. We are close, you and I. Oh, it isn't terribly complicated, really. I have learned to live with a profound loneliness. I forget about it for years and years. Then it surfaces, the desire to be placed in context by somebody else. The desire to be known, understood, evaluated morally by a sophisticated mind. That was always the lure of the Talamasca, from the beginning, that I could go there and confide in my scholars, that we would talk late into the night. It's lured many another secretive nonhuman. I'm not the only one."

"Well, that's what all of us need, isn't it?" asked Michael, glancing at Rowan. There passed another one of those silent, secret moments, rather like an invisible kiss.

She nodded.

"Yes," Ash agreed. "Human beings very seldom survive without that kind of exchange, communication. Love. And our breed was such a loving breed. It took so long for us to come to understand aggression. We always seem like children when humans first meet us, but we're not children. It's a different kind of mildness. There's a stubbornness in it, a desire to be gratified at once, and for things to remain simple."

He fell silent. Then he asked, very sincerely, "What really troubles you? Why did you both hesitate when I asked you to come with me to New York? What went through your minds?"

"Killing Lasher," said Michael. "It was a matter of survival with me, no more, no less. There was one witness, one man present who could understand and forgive, if a forgiving witness is required. And that man's dead."

"Aaron."

"Yeah, he wanted to take Lasher, but he understood why I didn't let him. And those other two men, well, that, we could say, was self-defense . . ."

"And you suffer over these deaths," said Ash gently.

"Lasher, that was the deliberate murder," said Michael, as if he were speaking to himself. "The thing had hurt my wife; it had taken my child somehow, taken my child. Though what that child would have been, who can say? There are so many questions, so many possibilities. And it had preyed upon the women. Killed them, in its drive to propagate. It could no more live with us than could some plague or insect. Coexistence was unthinkable, and then there was—to use your word— the context, the way it had presented itself from the beginning, in ghostly form, the way it had . . . used me from the start."

"Of course I understand you," Ash said. "Were I you, I would have killed him too."

"Would you?" asked Michael. "Or would you have spared him because he was one of the very few of your kind left on the earth? You would have had to feel that, a species loyalty."

"No," said Ashlar. "I don't think you understand me, I mean in a very basic way. I have spent my life proving to myself that I am as good as human. Remember. To Pope Gregory himself I once made the case that we had souls. I am no friend to a migrant soul with a thirst for power, an aged soul that had usurped a new body. This arouses no such loyalty in me."

Michael nodded as if to say *I see.*

"To have spoken with Lasher," said Ash, "to have talked about his remembrances, that might have given me considerable pause. But no, I would have felt no loyalty to him. The one thing that the Christians and the Romans never believed was that murder is murder, whether it is a human murder or a murder of one of us. But I believe it. I have lived too long to hold foolish beliefs that humans aren't worthy of compassion, that they are 'other.' We are all connected; everything is connected. How and why, I couldn't tell you. But it's true. And Lasher had murdered to reach his ends, and if this one evil could be stamped out forever, only this one . . ." He shrugged and his smile came back, a little bitter perhaps, or only sweet and sad. "I always thought, imagined, dreamed, perhaps, that if we did come back, if we had again our chance on the face of the earth, we could stamp out that one crime."

Michael smiled. "You don't think that now."

"No," said Ash, "but there are reasons for not thinking about such possibilities. You'll understand when we can sit down and talk together in my rooms in New York."

"I hated Lasher," said Michael. "He was vicious and he had vicious habits. He laughed at us. Fatal error, perhaps. I'm not entirely certain. I also believed that others wanted me to kill him, others both alive and dead. Do you believe in destiny?"

"I don't know."

"What do you mean, you don't know?"

"I was told centuries ago that to be the lone survivor of my people was my destiny. It's happened. But does that mean it was really destiny? I was cunning; I had survived winters and battles and unspeakable tribulations. So I continued to survive. Destiny, or survival? I don't know. But whatever the case, this creature was your enemy. Why do you need my forgiveness now for what you did?"

"That isn't really the worry," said Rowan. She spoke before Michael could answer. She remained curled in the chair, head to one side against the leather. She could see both of them comfortably, and they were both looking at her. "At least I don't think it's Michael's worry."

He didn't interrupt her.

"His worry," she said, "is something that I've done, which he himself could not do."

Ash waited, just as Michael waited.

"I killed another Taltos, a female," Rowan said.

"A female?" Ash asked softly. "A true female Taltos?"

"Yes, a true female, my own daughter by Lasher. I killed her. I shot her. I killed her as soon as I realized what she was and who she was, and that she was there, with me. I killed her. I feared her as much as I'd feared him."

Ash appeared fascinated, but in no way disturbed.

"I feared a match of male and female," said Rowan. "I feared the cruel predictions he'd made and the dark future he'd described, and I feared that somewhere out there, among the other Mayfairs, he'd fathered a male, and the male would find her and they would breed. That would have been his victory. In spite of all I suffered and what Michael had suffered, and all the Mayfair witches, from the beginning, for this . . . this coupling, this triumph of the Taltos."

Ash nodded.

"My daughter had come to me in love," said Rowan.

"Yes," Ash whispered, obviously eager for her to go on.

"I shot my own daughter," she said. "I shot my own lonely and unprotected girl. And she'd cured me, she'd come to me with her milk and given me this and healed me of the trauma of her birth.

"That's what worries me and what worries Michael, that you should know this, that you'll discover it, that you, who want to be close to us, will be horrified when you discover that a female might have been within your grasp if I hadn't snuffed out her life."

Ash had leant forward in the chair, his elbows resting on his knee, one finger curled beneath his soft lower lip, pressing into it. His eyebrows were raised, coming together in a frown only slightly, as he peered into her face.

"What would you have done?" Rowan asked. "If you had discovered her, my Emaleth?"

"This was her name!" he whispered, amazed.

"The name her father gave her. Her father had forced me and forced me, though the miscarriages were killing me. And finally, for some reason, this one, Emaleth, was strong enough to be born."

Ash sighed. He sat back again, putting his arm on the edge of the leather arm of the chair, and he studied her, but he seemed neither devastated or angry. But then, how could one know?

For one split second, it seemed madness to have told him, to have told him here, of all places, on his own plane, flying silently through the sky. But then it seemed simply inevitable, something that had to be done, if anything was to progress, if anything was to come of their knowing each other, if love was in fact already growing between them out of what they'd already witnessed and heard.

"Would you have wanted her?" Rowan asked. "Would you have, perhaps, moved heaven and earth to get to her, to save her, to take her away safely, and father the tribe again?"

Michael was afraid for her, she could see it in his eyes. And she realized as she looked at both of them that she wasn't really saying all this just for them. She was talking for her own sake, the mother who had shot the daughter, pulled the trigger. She flinched suddenly, eyes shut tight, shuddering, her shoulders rising, and then sitting back in the chair, head to one side. She'd heard the body drop on the floor, she'd seen the face collapse before that, she'd tasted the milk, the thick sweet milk, almost like a white syrup, so good to her.

"Rowan," said Ash gently, "Rowan, Rowan, don't suffer these things again on my account."

"But you would have moved heaven and earth to get to her," Rowan said. "It's why you came to England when Samuel called you, when he told you Yuri's story. You came because a Taltos had been seen in Donnelaith."

Slowly Ash nodded. "I can't answer your question. I don't know the answer. Yes, I would have come, yes. But tried to take her away? I don't know."

"Oh, come now, how could you not want it?"

"You mean how could I not want to make the tribe again?"

"Yes."

He shook his head and looked down, thoughtfully, the finger curled beneath his lip again, elbow on the arm of the chair.

"What strange witches you are, both of you," he whispered.

"How so?" asked Michael.

Ash rose to his feet suddenly, his head almost touching the top of the cabin. He stretched and then turned his back, walking a few steps, head bowed, before he turned around.

"Listen, we cannot answer each other's questions this way," he said. "But what I can tell you now is I am glad the female is dead. I am glad it's dead!" He shook his head, and placed his hand on the sloped back of the chair. He was looking off, hair falling down over his eyes, rather wild now, so that he looked especially gaunt and dramatic, and rather like a magician, perhaps. "So help me, God," he said. "I'm relieved, I'm relieved that you tell me in the same breath it was there and that it is no more."

Michael nodded. "I think I'm beginning to see."

"Do you?" asked Ash.

"We can't share this earth, can we, the two tribes so apparently similar and so utterly unalike?"

"No, we can't share it," Ash said, shaking his head with emphasis. "What race can live with any other? What religion with any other? War is worldwide; and the wars are tribal, no matter what men say they are! They are tribal, and they are wars of extermination, whether it be the Arabs against the Kurds, or the Turks and the Europeans, or the Russian fighting the Oriental. It's never going to stop. People dream that it will, but it can't, as long as there are people. But of course, if my kind came again, and if the humans of the earth were exterminated, well, then, my people could live in peace, but then, doesn't every tribe believe this of itself?"

Michael shook his head. "It doesn't have to be strife," he said. "It is conceivable that all tribes stop fighting each other."

"Conceivable, yes, but not possible."

"One breed doesn't have to reign over another," insisted Michael. "One breed doesn't even have to know about the other."

"You mean that we should live in secret?" Ash asked. "Do you know how quickly our population doubles itself and then triples and then quadruples? Do you know how strong we are? You can't know how it was, you have never seen the Taltos born knowing, you've never seen it grow to its full height in those first few minutes or hours or days or however long it takes; you've never seen it."

"I've seen it," said Rowan. "I've seen it twice."

"And what do you say? What would come of my wanting a female? Of grieving for your lost Emaleth and seeking to find a replacement for her? Of troubling your innocent Mona with the seed that might make the Taltos or might make her die?"

"I can tell you this," said Rowan, taking a deep breath. "At the moment I shot Emaleth, at that moment there wasn't the slightest doubt in my mind that she was a threat to my breed, and that she had to die."

Ash smiled; he nodded. "And you were right."

They were all silent. Then Michael spoke.

"You have our worst secret now," he said.

"Yes, you have it," said Rowan softly.

"And I wonder," said Michael, "if we have yours."

"You will," said Ash. "We should sleep now, all of us. My eyes hurt me. And the corporation waits with a hundred small tasks which only I can perform. You sleep now, and in New York I'll tell you everything. And you will have all my secrets, from the worst to the least."

Twenty-three

ONA, wake up."
She heard the swamp before she actually saw it. She heard the bullfrogs crying, and the night birds, and the sound of water all around her, murky, still, yet still moving somewhere, in a rusted pipe perhaps, or against the side of a skiff, she didn't know. They had stopped. This must be the landing.

The dream had been the strangest yet. She had had to pass an examination, and she that passed would rule the world, so Mona had to answer every question. From every field the questions had come, on science, mathematics, history, the computer she so loved, the stocks and bonds, the meaning of life, and that had been the hardest part, because she'd felt so alive that she could not begin to justify it. *You know, you just know that it is magnificent to be alive.* Had she scored the perfect one hundred percent? Would she rule the world?

"Wake up, Mona!" Mary Jane whispered.

Mary Jane couldn't see that Mona's eyes were open. Mona was looking through the glass window at the swamp, at the ragged, tilting trees, sickly and strung with moss, at the vines snarled like ropes around the huge old cypresses. Out there in the light of the moon she could see patches of water through the covering of still duckweed, and the knees of the cypress trees, so many dangerous spikes sticking up all around the thick trunks of the old trees. And black things, little black things flying in the night. Could be roaches, but don't think about it!

Her back ached. As she tried to sit forward, she felt heavy and achy all over, and wanting more milk. They'd stopped twice for milk, and she wanted more. They had cartons and cartons in the ice chest, best to get to the house. Then drink it.

"Come on, honey, you get out and wait for me right here, and I'm going to hide this car where nobody's likely to see it."

"Hide this car, this enormous car?"

Mary Jane opened the door and helped her out, and then stood back, obviously horrified again looking at her, and trying not to show it. The light came from inside the car on Mary Jane's face.

"Lord, Mona Mayfair, what if you die?"

Mona grasped Mary Jane's wrist as she stood up, her feet squarely planted on the soft earth thick with dredged white shells, glowing beneath her. There went the pier, out into the dark.

"Stop saying that, Mary Jane, but I'll give you something to think about, just in case it happens," said Mona. She tried to lift the sack of groceries from the floor, but she could not bend down that far.

Mary Jane had just lighted the lantern. She turned around and the light went up into her eyes, making her ghastly. It shone on the weathered shack behind her and on the few feet of dilapidated pier, and on the tendrils of moss that hung down from the dead-looking branches right above her.

God, there were so many flying things in the dark.

"Mona Mayfair, your cheekbones are sticking right out of your face!" said Mona. "I swear to God, I can see your teeth through the skin around your mouth."

"Oh, stop it, you're being crazy. It's the light. You look like a ghost yourself." Whoa, she felt horrible. Weak, and full of aching. Even her feet ached.

"And you wouldn't believe the color of your skin, my God, you look like somebody sunk in a bath of milk of magnesia."

"I'm okay. I can't lift this stuff."

"I'll get it, you rest there against that tree, that's the tree I told you about, the cypress tree, oldest one in these parts, you see this was the pond out here, the little pond???? You know??? Where the family would go rowing??? Here, take the lantern, the handle doesn't get hot."

"It looks dangerous. In the western movies, they are always throwing a lantern like that into the barn where the hero has been trapped by the bad guys. It breaks and sets the barn on fire every time. I don't like it."

"Well, nobody's going to do that out here," shouted Mary Jane over her shoulder, as she moved one sack after another, plunking them down on the shells. "And there isn't any hay, besides, and if there was, it would be soggy."

The headlights of the car bored into the swamp, deep into the endless forest of trunks, thick and thin, and the wild broken palmetto and jagged banana. The water breathed and sighed and trickled again, for all its stagnant stench and motionlessness.

"Jesus Christ, this is a wild place," Mona whispered, but in a way she loved it. She loved even the coolness of the air here, languid and soft, not moving with a breeze, but nevertheless stirred, perhaps by the water.

Mary Jane let the heavy ice chest drop.

"No, lookie, get over to one side, and when I get in the car and turn it around like to go back out, you look yonder where the light shines and you'll see Fontevrault!"

The door slammed, the tires churned the gravel.

The big car backed up to the right, and the beams slid over the spindly phantom trees, and lo and behold, lo and behold, she saw it—enormous, and listing horribly in the light, its attic gable windows flashing and winking out as the car made its circle.

The night went dark, but what she had seen remained, a great black hulk against the sky, impossible. The house was falling.

She almost screamed, though why she wasn't certain. They couldn't be going to that house, not a house leaning like that, a crippled house. A house underwater was one thing, but a house like that? But even as the car drove away, with a small, healthy blast of white smoke, she saw that there were lights in this impossible ruin. She could see through the upstairs fanlight in the center of the porch, way back, deep inside, lights. And when the last sound of the car was gone, she thought for a moment that she heard something like the playing of a radio.

The lantern was bright enough, but this was country dark, pitch black. There was nothing but the lantern and that dim, glowing coal of light inside the collapsing mansion.

Dear God, Mary Jane doesn't realize this damned place has keeled over in her absence! We've got to get Granny out, assuming that Granny has not already been unceremoniously dumped into the drink! And what drink, what slime! The smell was the greenest smell she had ever smelled, oh, but when she looked up, the sky was that glowing pink that it can be in the Louisiana night, and the disappearing trees stuck their futile little branches out to connect with each other, and the moss became translucent, veils and veils of moss. The birds, listen to the birds crying. The very topmost branches were thin and covered over with webs, silvery webs, were they spiders or silkworms?

"I do see the charm of this place," she said. "If only that house wasn't about to topple."

Mama.

I'm here, Morrigan.

There was a sound on the road behind her. Christ, Mary Jane was running towards her, all alone in the dark. The least she could do was turn around and hold up the lantern. Her back ached now almost unbearably, and she wasn't even lifting anything or trying to reach anything, just holding up this awfully heavy lantern.

And is this theory of evolution supposed to account for absolutely every species on the planet at this time? I mean, there is no secondary theory, perhaps, of spontaneous development?

She shook herself awake all over. Besides, she didn't know the answer to that question. Truth was, evolution had never seemed logical to her. *Science has reached a point where once again various kinds of beliefs, once condemned as metaphysical, are now entirely possible.*

Mary Jane came right out of the blackness, running like a little girl, clasping her high-heeled shoes together in the fingers of her right hand. When she got to Mona, she stopped, bent over double, and caught her breath and then looked at Mona.

"Jesus Christ, Mona Mayfair," she said with anxious gasps, her pretty face gleaming with a thin polish of sweat, "I've got to get you to that house pronto."

"Your pantyhose are split to pieces."

"Well, I should hope so," said Mary Jane. "I hate them." She picked up the ice chest and started running down the pier. "Come on, Mona, hurry it up. You're going to die on me right here."

"Will you stop that? The baby can hear you!"

There was a loud noise, a splash. Mary Jane had heaved the ice chest into the boat. So that meant there *was* a boat. Mona tried to hurry across the creaky, splintery boards, but each step was excruciating for her. Then, quite suddenly, she felt the real thing, had to be. A pain like a whip wrapping around her back and her waist, or what was left of her waist. She stopped, biting down hard not to shout.

Mary Jane was running back to the boat already with her second load.

"I want to help," said Mona, but she could barely get out the last word. She walked slowly to the edge of the pier, thinking she was glad she had on her flat slippers, though she couldn't really remember thinking to put them on, and then she saw the wide shallow pirogue as Mary Jane put in the last of the sacks, and all the tumbling pillows and blankets.

"Now gimme that lantern and you stay right there till I back her up."

"Mary Jane, I'm kind of, well, sort of, scared of the water? I mean I feel real clumsy, Mary Jane, I don't know if I should climb into the boat."

The pain flashed again. *Mama, I love you, I'm afraid.*

"Well, don't be afraid, shut up!" said Mona.

"What did you say?" asked Mary Jane.

Mary Jane jumped in the big metal pirogue, grabbed the long stick that was somehow anchored to the side, and then backed up the boat with some quick dipping pushes. The lantern stood at the very front, like there was a little bench or something especially for it. All the stuff was behind her.

"Come on now, honey, just step into it, quick-like, yeah, that's right, both feet."

"Oh God, we're going to drown."

"Now, darlin', that's plain silly, this water isn't six feet deep here! We'll get filthy, but we won't drown."

"I could easily drown in six feet of water," said Mona. "And the house, Mary Jane, look at the house."

"What about it?"

The world mercifully ceased to rock and roll. Mona was hurting Mary Jane's hand, probably. And now Mary Jane had to let go. Okay, easy! Mary Jane had both hands on the pole, and they were moving away from the pier.

"But, Mary Jane, look, Mary Jane," said Mona.

"Yeah, that's it, honey, we don't go but fifty feet, you just stand still, real still. This is a big, steady pirogue. Nothing's going to make it tip. You can kneel down if you want, or even sit down, but at this point I would not recommend the bother."

"The house, Mary Jane, the house, it's tilted to one side."

"Darlin', it's been like that for fifty years."

"I knew you'd say that. But what if it sinks, Mary Jane! God, I can't stand the sight of it! It's horrible, something that big tilting like that, it's like . . ."

Another flash of pain, small and mean and deep, for all its quickness.

"Well, stop looking at it!" Mary Jane said. "You will not believe this, but I myself, with a compass and a piece of glass, have actually measured the angle of the tilt, and it is less than five degrees. It's just all the columns make those vertical lines and look like they're about to fall over."

She lifted the pole, and the flat-bottomed boat slipped forward fast on its own momentum. The dreamy night closed all around them, leafy and soft, vines trailing down from the boughs of a listing tree that looked as if it might fall too.

Mary Jane dug the pole in again and shoved hard, sending the boat flying towards the immense shadow looming over them.

"Oh my God, is that the front door?"

"Well, it's off the hinges now, if that's what you mean, but that's where we're headed. Honey, I'm going to take you right up to the staircase inside. We're going to tie this boat right there like always."

They had reached the porch. Mona put her hands over her mouth, wanting to cover her eyes, but knowing she'd fall if she did. She stared straight up at the wild vines tangled above them. Everywhere she looked she saw thorns. Must have been roses once, and maybe would be again. And there, look, blossoms glowing in the dark, that was wisteria. She loved wisteria.

Why don't the big columns just fall, and had she ever seen columns so wide? God, she'd never, when looking at all those sketches, ever dreamed the house was on this scale, yes, it was, absolutely Greek Revival grandeur. But then she'd never actually known anyone who really lived here, at least not a person who could remember.

The beading of the porch ceiling was rotted out, and a hideous dark hole gaped above that could just harbor a giant python, or what about a whole nest of roaches? Maybe the frogs ate the roaches. The frogs were singing and singing, a lovely sound, very strong and loud compared to the more gentle sound of garden cicadas.

"Mary Jane, there are no roaches here, are there?"

"Roaches! Darlin', there are moccasins out here, and cottonmouth snakes, and alligators now, lots of them. My cats eat the roaches."

They slid through the front door, and suddenly the hallway opened up, enormous, filled with the fragrance of the wet soaked plaster and the glue from the peeling wallpaper, and the wood itself, perhaps, oh, there were too many smells of rot and the swamp, and living things, and the rippling water which cast its eerie light all over the walls and the ceiling, ripples upon ripples of light, you could get drugged by it.

Suddenly she pictured Ophelia floating away on her stream, with the flowers in her hair.

But look. You could see through the big doors into a ruined parlor and, where the light danced on the wall there, the sodden remnant of a drapery, so dark now from the water it had drunk up that the color was no longer visible. Paper hung down in loose garlands from the ceiling.

The little boat struck the stairs with a bump. Mona reached out and grabbed the railing, sure it would wobble and fall, but it didn't. And a good thing, too, because another pain came round her middle and bit deep into her back. She had to hold her breath.

"Mary Jane, we've got to hurry."

"You're telling me. Mona Mayfair, I'm so scared right now."

"Don't be. Be brave. Morrigan needs you."

"Morrigan!"

The light of the lantern shivered and moved up to the high second-floor ceiling. The wallpaper was covered with little bouquets, faded now so that only the white sketch of the bouquet remained, glowing in the dark. Great holes gaped in the plaster, but she could not see anything through them.

"The walls are brick, don't you worry about a thing, every single wall, inside, out, brick, just like First Street." Mary Jane was tying up the boat. Apparently they were beached on an actual step. They were steady now. Mona clung to the railing, as fearful of getting out as of staying in the little boat.

"Go on upstairs, I'll bring the junk. Go up and straight back and say hello to Granny. Don't worry about your shoes, I got plenty of dry shoes. I'll bring everything."

Cautiously, moaning a little, she reached over, took hold of the rail with both hands, and stepped up out of the boat, hoisting herself awkwardly until she found herself standing securely on the tread, with dry stairway ahead of her.

If it hadn't been tilting, it would have felt perfectly secure, she thought. And quite suddenly she stood there, one hand on the railing, one on the soft, spongy plaster to her left, and looking up, she felt the house around her, felt its rot, its strength, its obdurate refusal to fall down into the devouring water.

It was a massive and sturdy thing, giving in only slowly, perhaps stopped at this pitch forever. But when she thought of the muck, she didn't know why they weren't both sucked right down now, like bad guys on the run in motion-picture quicksand.

"Go on up," said Mary Jane, who had already hurled one sack up on the step above Mona. Crash, bang, slam. The girl was really moving.

Mona began to walk. Yes, firm, and amazingly dry by the time she reached the very top, dry as if the sun of the spring day had been fiercely hot, trapped in here, and bleaching the boards, look, yes, bleaching it as surely as if it were driftwood.

At last she stood on the second floor, estimating the angle to be less than five degrees, but that was plenty enough to drive you mad, and then she narrowed her eyes the better to see to the very end of the hallway. Another grand and lovely door with sidelights and fanlight, and electric bulbs strung on crisscrossing wire, hanging from the ceiling. Mosquito netting. Was that it? Lots and lots of it, and the soft electric light, nice and steady, shining through it.

She took several steps, clinging to the wall still, which did indeed feel hard and dry now, and then she heard a soft little laugh coming from the end of the hall, and as Mary Jane came up with the lantern in hand and set it down beside her sack at the top of the stairs, Mona saw a child standing in the far doorway.

It was a boy, very dark-skinned, with big inky eyes and soft black hair and a face like a small Hindu saint, peering out at her.

"Hey, you, Benjy, come help me here with all this. You gotta help me!" shouted Mary Jane.

The boy sauntered forward, and he wasn't so little as he came closer. He was maybe almost as tall as Mona, which wasn't saying much, of course, since Mona hadn't broken five feet two yet, and might never.

He was one of those beautiful children with a great mysterious mingling of blood—African, Indian, Spanish, French, probably Mayfair. Mona wanted to touch him, touch his cheek and see if his skin really felt the way it looked, like very, very fine tanned leather. Something Mary Jane had said came back to her, about him selling himself downtown, and in a little burst of mysterious light, she saw purple-papered rooms, fringed lampshades, decadent gentlemen like Oncle Julien in white suits, and of all things, herself in the brass bed with this adorable boy!

Craziness. The pain stopped her again. She could have dropped in her tracks. But quite deliberately she picked up one foot and then the other. There were the cats, all right, good Lord, witches' cats, big, long-tailed, furry, demon-eyed cats. There must have been five of them, darting along the walls.

The beautiful boy with the gleaming black hair carried two sacks of groceries down the hall ahead of her. It was even sort of clean here, as if he'd swept and mopped.

Her shoes were sopping wet. She was going to go down.

"That you, Mary Jane? Benjy, is that my girl? Mary Jane!"

"Coming, Granny, I'm coming, what are you doing, Granny?"

Mary Jane ran past her, holding the ice chest awkwardly, with her elbows flying out and her long flaxen hair swaying.

"Hey, there, Granny!" She disappeared around the bend. "What you doing now?"

"Eating graham crackers and cheese, you want some?"

"No, not now, gimme a kiss, TV broken?"

"No, honey, just got sick of it. Benjy's been writing down my songs as I sing them. Benjy."

"Listen, Granny, I got to go, I got Mona Mayfair with me. I've got to take her up to the attic where it's really warm and dry."

"Yes, oh yes, please," Mona whispered. She leant against the walls which tilted away from her. Why, you could lie right on a tilted wall like this, almost. Her feet throbbed, and the pain came again.

Mama, I am coming.

Hold on, sweetheart, one more flight of steps to climb.

"You bring Mona Mayfair in here, you bring her."

"No, Granny, not now!" Mary Jane came flying out of the room, big white skirts hitting the doorjamb, arms out to reach for Mona.

"Right on up, honey, right straight, come on around now."

There was a rustling and a clatter, and just as Mary Jane turned Mona around and pointed her to the foot of the next stairs, Mona saw a tiny little woman come scuttling out of the back room, gray hair in long loose braids with ribbons on the end of them. She had a face like wrinkled cloth, with amazing jet black eyes, crinkled with seeming good humor.

"Got to hurry," Mona said, moving as quickly as she could along the railing. "I'm getting sick from the tilt."

"You're sick from the baby!"

"You go on ahead, and turn on those lights," shouted the old woman, clamping one amazingly strong and dry little hand to Mona's arm. "Why the hell didn't you tell me this child was pregnant, God, this is Alicia's girl, like to died when they cut off that sixth finger."

"What? From me, you mean?" Mona turned to look into the little wrinkled face with the small lips pressed tight together as the woman nodded.

"You mean I had a sixth finger?" asked Mona.

"Sure did, honey, and you almost went to heaven when they put you under. Nobody ever told you that tale, about the nurse giving you the shot twice? About your heart nearly stopping dead, and how Evelyn came and saved you!"

Benjy rushed by, headed up the stairs, his bare feet sounding dusty on the bare wood.

"No, nobody ever told me! Oh God, the sixth finger."

"But don't you see, that will help!" declared Mary Jane. They were headed up now, and it only looked like one hundred steps to the light up there, and the thin figure of Benjy, who, having lighted the lights, was now making his slow, languid descent, though Mary Jane was already hollering at him.

Granny had stopped at the foot of the steps. Her white nightgown touched the soiled floor. Her black eyes were calculating, taking Mona's measure. A Mayfair, all right, thought Mona.

"Get the blankets, the pillows, all that," said Mary Jane. "Hurry up. And the milk, Benjy, get the milk."

"Well, now, just wait a minute," Granny shouted. "This girl looks like she doesn't have time to be spending the night in that attic. She ought to go to the hospital right now. Where's the truck? Your truck at the landing?"

"Never mind that, she's going to have the baby here," said Mary Jane.

"Mary Jane!" roared Granny. "God damn it, I can't climb these steps on account of my hip."

"Just go back to bed, Granny. Make Benjy hurry with that stuff. Benjy, I'm not going to pay you!!!!"

They continued up the attic steps, the air getting warmer as they ascended.

It was a huge space.

Same crisscross of electric lights she'd seen below, and look at the steamer trunks and the wardrobes tucked into every gable. Every gable except for one, which held the bed deep inside, and next to it, an oil lamp.

The bed was huge, built out of those dark, plain posts they used so much in the country, the canopy gone, and only the netting stretched over the top, veil after veil. The netting veiled the entrance to the gable. Mary Jane lifted it as Mona fell forward on the softest mattress.

Oh, it was all dry! It was. The feather comforter went *poof* all around her. Pillows and pillows. And the oil lamp, though it was treacherously close, made it into a little tent of sorts around her.

"Benjy! Get that ice chest now."

"*Chère,* I just carry that ice chest to the back porch," the boy said, or something like it, the accent clearly Cajun. Didn't sound like the old woman at all. She just sounds like one of us, thought Mona, a little different maybe . . .

"Well, just go git it," Mary Jane said.

The netting caught all the golden light, and made a beautiful solitary place of this big soft bed. Nice place to die, maybe better than in the stream with the flowers.

The pain came again, but this time she was so much more comfortable. What were you supposed to do? She'd read about it. Suck in your breath or something? She couldn't remember. That was one subject she had not thoroughly researched. Jesus Christ, this was almost about to happen.

She grabbed Mary Jane's hand. Mary Jane lay beside her, looking down into her face, wiping her forehead now with something soft and white, softer than a handkerchief.

"Yes, darlin', I'm here, and it's getting bigger and bigger, Mona, it's just not, it's . . ."

"It will be born," Mona whispered. "It's mine. It will be born, but if I die, you have to do it for me, you and Morrigan together."

"What!"

"Make a bier of flowers for me—"

"Make a what?"

"Hush up, I'm telling you something that really matters."

"Mary Jane!" Granny roared from the foot of the steps. "You come down here and help Benjy carry me up now, girl!"

"Make a raft, a raft, all full of flowers, you know," Mona said. "Wisteria, roses, all those things growing outside, swamp irises . . ."

"Yeah, yeah, and then what!"

"Only make it fragile, real fragile, so that as I float away on it, it will slowly fall apart in the current, and I'll go down into the water . . . like Ophelia!"

"Yeah, okay, anything you say! Mona, I am scared now. I am really scared."

"Then be a witch, 'cause there's no changing anybody's mind now, is there?"

Something broke! Just as if a hole had been poked through it. Christ, was she dead inside?

No, Mother, but I am coming. Please be ready to take my hand. I need you.

Mary Jane had drawn up on her knees, her hands slapped to the sides of her face.

"In the name of God!"

"Help it! Mary Jane! Help it!" screamed Mona.

Mary Jane shut her eyes tight and laid her hands on the mountain of Mona's belly. The pain blinded Mona. She tried to see, to see the light in the netting, and to see Mary Jane's squeezed-shut eyes, and feel her hands, and hear her whispering, but she couldn't. She was falling. Down through the swamp trees with her hands up, trying to catch the branches.

"Granny, come help!" screamed Mary Jane.

And there came the rapid patter of the old woman's feet!

"Benjy, get out!" the old woman screamed. "Go back downstairs, out, you hear me?"

Down, down through the swamps, the pain getting tighter and tighter. Jesus Christ, no wonder women hate this! No joke. This is horrible. God help me!

"Lord, Jesus Christ, Mary Jane," Granny cried. "It's a walking baby!"

"Granny, help me, take her hand, take it. Granny, you know what she is?"

"A walking baby, child. I've heard of them all my life, but never seen one. Jesus, child. When a walking baby was born out there in the swamps, to Ida Bell Mayfair, when I was a child, they said it stood taller than its mother as soon as it came walking out, and Grandpère Tobias went down there and chopped it up with an ax while the mother was laying there in the bed, screaming! Haven't you never heard of the walking babies, child? In Santo Domingo they burned them!"

"No, not this baby!" wailed Mona. She groped in the dark, trying to open her eyes. Dear God, the pain. And suddenly a small slippery hand caught hers. *Don't die, Mama.*

"Oh, Hail Mary, full of grace," said Granny, and Mary Jane started the same prayer, only one line behind her, as if it were a reel. "Blessed art thou among women, and blessed is . . ."

"Look at me, Mama!" the whisper was right by her ear. "Look at me! Mama, I need you, help me, make me grow big, big, big."

"Grow big!" cried the women, but their voices were a long way off. "Grow big! Hail Mary, full of grace, help her grow big."

Mona laughed! That's right, Mother of God, help my walking baby!

But she was falling down through the trees forever, and quite suddenly someone grabbed both her hands, yes, and she looked up through the sparkling green light and she saw her own face above her! Her very own face, pale and with the same freckles and the same green eyes, and the red hair tumbling down. Was it her own self, reaching down to stop her fall, to save her? That was her own smile!

"No, Mama, it's me." Both hands clasped her hands. "Look at me. It's Morrigan."

Slowly she opened her eyes. She gasped, trying to breathe, breathe against the weight, trying to lift her head, reach for her beautiful red hair, raise up high enough just to . . . just to hold her face, hold it, and . . . kiss her.

Twenty-four

It was snowing when she awoke. She was in a long cotton gown they'd given her, something very thick for the New York winters, and the bedroom was very white and quiet. Michael slept soundly against the pillow.

Ash worked below in his office, or so he had told her that he would. Or maybe he had finished his tasks and gone to sleep as well.

She could hear nothing in this marble room, in the silent, snowy sky above New York. She stood at the window, looking out at the gray heavens, and at the ways the flakes became visible, emerging distinct and small to fall heavily on the roofs around her, and on the sill of the window, and even in soft graceful gusts against the glass.

She had slept six hours. That was enough.

She dressed as quietly as possible, putting on a simple black dress from her suitcase, another new and expensive garment chosen by another woman, and perhaps more extravagant than anything she might have bought for herself. Pearls and pearls. Shoes that laced above the instep, but with dangerously high heels. Black stockings. A touch of makeup.

And then she walked through the silent corridors. Press the button marked *M,* they had said, and you will see the dolls.

The dolls. What did she know of dolls? In childhood they had been her secret love, one which she had always been ashamed to confess to Ellie and Graham, or even to her friends. She had asked for chemistry sets at Christmastime, or a new tennis racket, or new stereo components for her room.

Wind howled in the elevator shaft as if it were a chimney. She liked the sound.

The elevator doors slid open, revealing a cab of wood paneling and ornate mirrors, which she scarcely recalled from this morning, when they'd arrived just before dawn. They had left at dawn. They had arrived at dawn. Six hours had been given back to them. It was evening for her body and she felt it, alert, ready for the night.

Down she went, in mechanical silence, listening to the howling, thinking how utterly ghostly it was, and wondering if Ash liked it too.

There must have been dolls in the beginning, dolls she didn't remember. Doesn't everybody buy them for girls? Perhaps not. Perhaps her loving foster mother had known of the witches' dolls in the trunk in the attic, made of real hair and real bone. Maybe she had known that there was one doll for every Mayfair witch of past years. Maybe dolls gave Ellie the shivers. And there are people who are, regardless of background, taste, or religious beliefs, simply afraid of dolls.

Was she afraid of dolls?

The doors opened. Her eyes fell on glass cases, brass fittings, the same pristine and shining marble floors. A brass plaque on the wall said simply, THE PRIVATE COLLECTION.

She stepped out, letting the door rush closed behind her, realizing that she stood in a vast, brilliantly lighted room.

Dolls. Everywhere she looked, she saw their staring glass eyes, their flawless faces, their mouths half open with a look of frank and tender awe.

In a huge glass case right before her stood a doll of some three feet in height, made of bisque, with long mohair tresses and a dress of finely tailored faded silk. This was a French beauty from the year 1888, made by Casimir Bru, said the little card beneath it, greatest dollmaker perhaps in the world.

The doll was startling, whether one liked it or not. The blue eyes were thick and filled with light and perfectly almond-shaped. The porcelain hands of pale pink were so finely wrought they seemed about to move. But it was the doll's face, of course, her expression, that so captivated Rowan. The exquisitely painted eyebrows were ever so slightly different, giving movement to its gaze. Curious and innocent and thoughtful it looked.

It was a nonpareil of its kind, one couldn't doubt it. And whether or not she'd ever wanted dolls, she felt a desire to touch this one now, to feel its round and brightly rouged cheeks, to kiss, perhaps, its slightly parted red lips, to touch with the tip of her right finger the subtly shaped breasts pressed so erotically beneath its tight bodice. Its golden hair had thinned with the ages, obviously. And its fancy little leather shoes were worn and cracked. But the effect remained timeless, irresistible, "a joy forever." She wished she could open the case and hold it in her arms.

She saw herself rocking it, rather like a newborn, and singing to it, though it was no infant. It was just a little girl. Little blue beads hung from its perfectly fashioned ears. A necklace hung about its neck, fancy, a woman's perhaps. Indeed, when one considered all the aspects of it, it was no child at all, really, but a sensual little woman of extraordinary freshness, perhaps a dangerous and clever coquette.

A little card explained its special features, that it was so very large, that it wore its original garments, that it was perfect, that it had been the first doll ever purchased by Ash Templeton. And no further identification for Ash Templeton was given or apparently required.

The first doll. And he had told her briefly, when he explained about the museum, that he had seen it when it was new in the window of a Paris shop.

No wonder it had caught his eye and his heart. No wonder he had lugged it with him for a century; no wonder he'd founded his enormous company as some sort of tribute to it, to bring, as he had said, "its grace and beauty to everyone in new form."

There was nothing trivial about it, and something sweetly mysterious. Puzzled, yes, quizzical, reflective, a doll with things on her mind.

In seeing this, I understand all of it, she thought.

She moved on, through the other displays. She saw other French treasures, the work of Jumeau and Steiner and others whose names she'd never remember, and hundreds upon hundreds of little French girlies with round moonlike faces and tiny red mouths and the same almond eyes. "Oh, what innocents you are," she whispered. And here came the fashion dolls, in their bustles and exquisite hats.

She could have spent hours wandering here. There was infinitely more to see than she had imagined. And the quiet was so enticing, the vision outside the windows of the unceasing snow.

But she was not alone.

Through several banks of glass, she saw that Ash had joined her, and had been watching her, perhaps for some time. The glass faintly distorted his expression. When he moved, she was glad.

He came towards her, making no sound at all on the marble, and she saw that he held the beautiful Bru in his hands.

"Here, you may hold it," he said.

"It's fragile," she whispered.

"It's a doll," he said.

It evoked the strongest feeling, just cupping its head in the palm of her left hand. There came a little delicate sound from its earrings, tinkling against the porcelain neck. Its hair was soft, yet brittle, and the stitching of the wig was visible in many spots.

Ah, but she loved its tiny fingers. She loved its lace stockings and its silk petticoats, very old, very faded, apt to tear at her touch.

Ash stood very still, looking down at her, face rested, almost annoyingly handsome, streaked hair brushed to a luster, hands a little steeple beneath his lips. His suit was white silk today, very baggy, fashionable, probably Italian, she honestly didn't know. The shirt was black silk, and the tie white. Rather like a decorative rendition of a gangster, a tall, willowy man of mystery, with enormous gold cuff links, and preposterously beautiful black-and-white wingtip shoes.

"What does the doll make you feel?" he asked innocently, as if he really wanted to know.

"It has virtue to it," she whispered, frightened of her voice being louder than his. She placed it in his hands.

"Virtue," he repeated. He turned the doll and looked at her, and made a few very quick and natural gestures of grooming her, moving her hair, adjusting the ruffles of her dress. And then he lifted her and tenderly kissed her and lowered her slowly, gazing down at her again. "Virtue," he said. He looked at Rowan. "But what does it make you feel?"

"Sad," she said, and turned away, placing her hand on the case beside her, looking at the German doll, infinitely more natural, sitting inside in a small wooden chair. MEIN LEIBLING, said the card. She was far less decorative and overdone. She was not the coquette of anyone's imagination, yet she was radiant, and as perfect as the Bru in her own way.

"Sad?" he asked.

"Sad for a kind of femininity that I've lost or never had. I don't regret it, but the feeling is sadness, sadness for something perhaps I dreamed about when I was young. I don't know."

And then, looking at him again, she said, "I can have no more children. And my children were monsters to me. And my children are buried together beneath a tree."

He nodded. His face was very eloquent of sympathy, so he said not a word.

There were other things she wanted to say—that she had not guessed there was such craft or beauty in the realm of dolls, that she had not guessed they could be so interesting to look at, or that they were so different, one from the other, that they had such a frank and simple charm.

But beneath these thoughts, running deep in the coldest place in her heart, she was thinking, Their beauty is sad beauty, and I don't know why, and so is yours.

She felt suddenly that if he were to kiss her now, if he were so inclined, she would yield very easily, that her love for Michael wouldn't stop her from yielding, and she hoped and prayed that there was no such thought in his mind.

Indeed, she wasn't going to allow time for it. She folded her arms and walked past him into a new and unexplored area, where the German dolls ruled. Here were laughing and pouting children, homely little girls in cotton frocks. But she didn't see the exhibits now. She couldn't stop thinking that he was just behind her, watching her. She could feel his observation, hear the faint sound of his breath.

Finally, she looked back. His eyes surprised her. They were too charged with emotion, too full of obvious conflict, and very little if any struggle to hide it from her.

If you do this, Rowan, she thought, you will lose Michael forever. And slowly she lowered her gaze and walked softly, slowly away.

"It's a magical place," she said over her shoulder. "But I'm so eager to talk to you, to hear your story, I could savor it more truly at another time."

"Yes, of course, and Michael's awake now, and Michael should be almost finished with breakfast. Why don't we go up? I am ready for the agony. I am ready for the strange pleasure of recounting it all."

She watched as he set the big French doll back in her glass cabinet. And once again his thin fingers made quick, busy gestures to groom her hair and her skirts. Then he pressed a kiss to his fingers and gave this to the doll. And he shut the glass and turned the small golden key, which he then put away.

"You are my friends," he said, turning to face Rowan. He reached past her and pressed the button for the tower. "I think I am coming to love you. A dangerous thing."

"I don't want it to be dangerous," she said. "I'm too deep under your spell to want our knowledge of each other to wound or disappoint. But tell me, as to the present state of things, do you love us *both*?"

"Oh yes," he said, "or I would beg you on bended knee to let me make love to you." His voice fell to a whisper. "I would follow you to the ends of the earth."

She turned away, stepping into the elevator, her face hot and her mind swimming for the moment. She saw one grand flash of the dolls in their finery before the doors slid shut.

"I'm sorry that I told you this," he whispered timidly. "It was a dishonest thing to do, to tell you and to deny it, it was wrong."

She nodded. "I forgive you," she whispered. "I'm too . . . too flattered. Isn't that the right word?"

"No, 'intrigued' is the word you want," he said. "Or 'tantalized,' but you're not really flattered. And you love him so wholeheartedly that I feel the fire of it when I'm with you. I want it. I want your light to shine on me. I should never have said those words."

She didn't answer. If she'd thought of an answer, she might have said it, but nothing really came to her mind. Except that she couldn't imagine being severed from Ash right now, and she didn't think that Michael could, either. In a way, it seemed that Michael needed Ash more than she did, though Michael and she had not had a moment, really, to talk of these things.

When the doors opened, she found herself in a large living room, with the floor tiled in rose- and cream-colored marbles, with the same kind of large, snug leather furnishings that had been on the plane. These chairs were softer, larger, yet remarkably similar, as if designed for comfort.

And once again, they gathered around a table, only this time it was very low, and set out with a dozen or more little offerings of cheeses and nuts and fruits and breads that they might eat as the hours passed.

A tall, cold glass of water was all she required just now.

Michael, his horn-rimmed glasses on, and wearing a battered tweed Norfolk jacket, sat bent over the day's *New York Times*.

Only when they were both seated did he tear himself away, fold the paper neatly, and put it to the side.

She didn't want him to take off the glasses. They were too appealing to her. And it struck her, suddenly, making her smile, that she rather liked having these two men with her, one on either side.

Vague fantasies of a ménage à trois flitted through her mind, but such things, as far as she knew, never really worked, and she could not imagine Michael either tolerating it or participating in it in any way. Sweeter, really, to think of things precisely the way they were.

You have another chance with Michael, she thought. You know you do, no matter what he may think. Don't throw away the only love that's ever really mattered to you. Be old enough and patient enough for kinds of love, seasons of it, be quiet in your soul so that when happiness comes again, if it ever does, you will know.

Michael had put away his glasses. He'd sat back, his ankle on his knee.

Ash had also relaxed into his chair.

We are the triangle, she thought, and I am the only one with bare knees, and feet tucked to the side as if I have something to conceal.

That made her laugh. The smell of the coffee distracted her. She realized the pot and cup were right in front of her, easy to reach.

But Ash reached to pour for her before she could do it, and he put the cup in her hand. He sat at her right, closer to her than he'd been in the plane. They were all closer. And it was the equilateral triangle again.

"Let me just talk to you," Ash said suddenly. He'd made his fingers into the little steeple again and was pushing at his lower lip. There came the tiny scowl to the very inside tips of his eyebrows, and then it melted, and the voice went on, a bit sad. "This is hard for me, very hard, but I want to do it."

"I realize that," said Michael. "But why do you want to do it? Oh, I'm dying to hear your story, but why is it worth the pain?"

He thought for a moment, and Rowan could hardly bear to see the tiny signs of stress in his hands and his face.

"Because I want you to love me," Ash said softly.

Once again, she was speechless, and faintly miserable.

But Michael just smiled in his usual frank fashion and said, "Then tell us everything, Ash. Just . . . shoot."

Ash laughed at once. And then they all fell silent, but it was an easy silence.

And he began.

Twenty-five

ALL TALTOS are born knowing things—facts of history, whole legends, certain songs—the necessity for certain rituals, the language of the mother, and the languages spoken around her, the basic knowledge of the mother, and probably the mother's finer knowledge as well.

Indeed, these basic endowments are rather like an uncharted vein of gold in a mountain. No Taltos knows how much can be drawn from this residual memory. With effort, amazing things can be discovered within one's own mind. Some Taltos even know how to find their way home to Donnelaith, though why no one knows. Some are drawn to the far northern coast of Unst, the northernmost island of Britain, to look out over Burrafirth at the lighthouse of Muckle Flugga, searching for the lost land of our birth.

The explanation for this lies in the chemistry of the brain. It's bound to be disappointingly simple, but we won't understand it until we know precisely why salmon return to the river of their birth to spawn, or why a certain species of butterfly finds its way to one tiny area of forest when it comes time to breed.

We have superior hearing; loud noises hurt us. Music can actually paralyze us. We must be very, very careful of music. We know other Taltos instantly by scent or sight; we know witches when we see them, and the presence of witches is always overwhelming. A witch is that human which cannot—by the Taltos—be ignored.

But I'll come to more of these things as the story goes on. I want to say now, however, that we do *not,* as far as I know, have two lives, as Stuart Gordon thought, though this might have been a mistaken and oft-repeated belief about us among humans for some time. When we explore our deepest racial memories, when we go bravely into the past, we soon come to realize these cannot be the memories of one particular soul.

Your Lasher was a soul who had lived before, yes. A restless soul refusing to accept death, and making a tragic, blundering reentry into life, for which others paid the price.

By the time of King Henry and Queen Anne, the Taltos was a mere legend in the Highlands. Lasher did not know how to probe the memories with which he was born; his mother had been merely human, and he set his mind upon becoming a human, as many a Taltos has done.

I want to say that, for me, actual life began when we were still a people of the lost land, and Britain was the land of winter. And we knew about the land of winter, but we never went there, because our island was always warm. My constitutional memories were all of that land. They were filled with sunlight, and without consequence, and they have faded under the weight of events since, under the sheer weight of my long life and my reflections.

The lost land was in the northern sea, within very dim sight of the coast of Unst, as I've indicated, in a place where the Gulf Stream of that time apparently made the seas fairly temperate as they struck our shores.

But the sheltered land in which we actually developed was, I believe now when I remember it, nothing less than the giant crater of an immense volcano, miles and miles in width, presenting itself as a great fertile valley surrounded by ominous yet beautiful cliffs, a tropical valley with innumerable geysers and warm springs rising bubbling from the earth, to make small streams and finally great clear and beautiful pools. The air was moist always, the trees that grew about our little lakes and riverets immense, the ferns also of gigantic size, and the fruit of all kinds and colors—mangos, pears, melons of all sizes—always abundant, and the cliffs hung with vines of wild berry and grape, and the grass forever thick and green.

The best fruit was pears, which are nearly white. The best food from the sea was the oyster, the mussel, the limpet, and these were white too. There was a breadfruit that was white once you peeled it. There was milk from the goats, if you could catch them, but it wasn't as good as milk from your mother or the other women who would let those they loved have their milk.

Scarcely ever did the winds come into the valley, sealed off as it was, except for two or three passes, from the coasts. The coasts were dangerous, for though the water was warmer than on the coast of Britain, it was nevertheless cold, and the winds violent, and one could be swept away. Indeed, if a Taltos wanted to die, which I was told did happen, that Taltos would go out and walk into the sea.

I think, though I'll never know, that ours *was* an island, very large, yet an island. It was the custom of some very white-haired ones to walk completely around it, along the beaches, and I was told that this trek took many many days.

Fire we had always known, because there were places up in the mountains where fire breathed right out of the earth. Hot earth itself, molten lava, came in a tiny trickle from some of these places, running down to the sea.

We had always known how to get fire, keep it alive, feed it, and make it last. We used fire to light up the longer nights of winter, though we had no name for it, and it wasn't cold. We used fire occasionally to cook big feasts, but most of the time this wasn't necessary. We used fire in the circle sometimes when the birth was happening. We danced around fire, and sometimes played with it. I never beheld a hurtful incident in which any of us was injured by fire.

How far the winds of the earth can carry seeds, birds, twigs, branches, uprooted trees, I have no idea, but that which loved heat thrived in this land, and this is where we began.

Now and then, someone among us told of visiting the islands of Britain—known now as the Shetlands or the Orkneys—or even the coast of Scotland. The islands of winter, that's what we called them, or, more literally, the islands of the bitter cold. This was always an exciting tale. Sometimes a Taltos was washed out, and somehow managed to swim to the land of winter, and make a raft there for the return home.

There were Taltos who went to sea deliberately to seek adventure, in hollow log boats, and if they did not drown, they would often come home, half dead from the cold, and never travel to the land of winter again.

Everybody knew there were beasts in that land, covered with fur, that would kill you if they could. And so we had a thousand legends and ideas and wrong notions and songs about the snows of winter, and the bears of the forests, and ice that floated in great masses in the lochs.

Once in a very great while, a Taltos would commit a crime. He or she would couple without permission and make a new Taltos that was not, for one reason or another, welcome. Or someone would willfully injure another, and that one would die. It was very rare. I only heard of it. I never saw it. But those outcasts were taken to Britain in the large boats, and left there to die.

We did not know the actual cycle of the seasons, by the way, for to us even the summer in Scotland felt fatally cold. We reckoned time in moons only, and we did not have a concept, as I recall, of a year.

Of course there was a legend you will hear all over the planet, of a time before the moon.

And that was the legendary time before time, or so we thought, but no one actually remembered it.

I can't tell you how long I lived in this land before it was destroyed. I knew the powerful scent of the Taltos in that land, but it was as natural as air. Only later did it become distinct, to mark the difference between Taltos and human.

I remember the First Day, as do all Taltos. I was born, my mother loved me, I stayed for hours with my mother and father, talking, and then I went up to the high cliffs just below the lip of the crater, where the white-haired ones sat, who talked and talked. I nursed from my mother for years and years. It was known that the milk would dry if a woman didn't let others drink from her breasts, and not come again till she gave birth. Women didn't want ever for the milk to dry, and they loved having the men nurse from them; it gave them divine pleasure, the sucking, the stimulation, and it was a common custom to lie with a woman and let the suckling, in one form or another, be the extent of the love. The semen of the Taltos was white, of course, like the semen of human beings.

Women, of course, nursed from women, and teased men that their nipples had no milk. But then our semen was thought to be like milk, not as tasty but in its own way just as nourishing and good.

One game was for the males to find a female alone, pounce upon her, and drink her milk, until others heard her protests and came and drove us away. But no one would have thought of making another Taltos with that woman! And if she really didn't want us sucking her milk, well, within a reasonable amount of time we stopped.

The women would every now and then gang up on other women also. And beauty had much to do with the allure of those who were sought for this kind of pleasure; personality was always mixed with it; we had distinct personalities, though everyone was pretty much always in a good mood.

There were customs. But I don't remember laws.

Death came to Taltos through accidents. And as Taltos are playful by nature, indeed physically rough and reckless, many Taltos were always dying of accidents, of having slipped from a cliff or choked on a peach pit, or being attacked by a wild rodent, which attack then caused bleeding which could not be stopped. Taltos rarely if ever broke their bones when they were young. But once a Taltos's skin had lost its baby softness and there were perhaps a few white hairs in his head, well, then he could be killed by falling from the cliffs. And it was during those years, I think, that most Taltos died. We were a people of the white-haired, and the blond, the red, and the black-haired. We didn't have many people of the mixed hair, and of course the young greatly outnumbered the old.

Sometimes a pestilence came over the valley that greatly diminished our numbers, and the stories of the pestilence were the saddest that we were ever told.

But I still don't know what the pestilence *was*. Those which kill humans do not apparently kill us.

I could "remember" pestilence, and nursing sick ones. I was born knowing how to get fire and carry it safely back to the valley. I knew how to make fire so that I did not have to go to get it, though getting it from someone else was the easiest way. I was born knowing how to cook mussels and limpets with fire. I knew how to make black paste for painting from ashes of fire.

But to return to the subject of death, there was no murder. The idea that one Taltos had the power to kill another was not generally believed. Indeed, if you did quarrel and push someone off a cliff, and that person fell and died, it was still an "accident." You hadn't really done it, though others might condemn you for your appalling carelessness and even send you away.

The white-haired ones who liked to tell tales had been alive the longest, certainly, but no one thought of them as old. And if they lay down one night and failed to wake in the morning, it was assumed they had died of a blow from an accident that had not been observed. The white-haired ones often had very thin skin, so thin you could almost see the blood running under it; and often they had lost their scent. But other than that, we didn't know age in any particular.

To be old was just to know the longest and the best stories, to have stories to relate from Taltos who were gone.

Tales were told in loose verses, or were sung as songs, or sometimes merely poured forth in a rush, with lavish images and rhythms and little bits and pieces of melody and much laughter. Telling, telling was joyful; telling was glorious; telling was the spiritual side of life.

The material side of life? I'm not sure there was one, in the strict sense. There was no ownership, except perhaps of musical instruments or pigments for painting, but even these were fairly liberally shared. Everything was easy.

Now and then a whale would be washed ashore, and when the meat had rotted, we would take the bones and make things of them, but to us, these were toys. Digging in the sand was fun, digging loose rocks to make them tumble downhill was fun. Even carving little shapes and circles into the bone with a sharp stone or another bone—this was fun.

But telling, ah, that took respectable talent, and true remembering, and remembering not only in one's own head, but remembering what other people had remembered and told as well.

You see what I am driving at. Our assumptions about life and death were founded upon these special conditions and notions. Obedience was natural to Taltos. To be agreeable was apparently natural. Seldom was there a rebel or a visionary, until the human blood became mixed with ours.

There were very few white-haired women, perhaps one to every twenty men. And these women were much sought after, for their fount was dried, like that of Tessa, and they wouldn't birth when they gave themselves to the men.

But in the main, childbirth killed the women, though we never said so at the time. It weakened women, and if a woman did not die by the fourth or fifth birth, she would almost always fall asleep later and die. Many women did not care to give birth at all, or would do it only once.

Birth always followed the true coupling of a pair of true Taltos. It was only later, when we mingled with humans, that women were worn out, like Tessa, by having bled again and again. But the Taltos descended from human origins have many traits entirely peculiar to them which I will recount in time. And who knows but that Tessa didn't have offspring? It is entirely possible, as you know.

Generally, birth was something that a woman did want to do. But not for a long time after she was born. Men wanted to do it all the time, because they enjoyed it. But no one who thought of coupling did not know that a child would be born from it, as tall as his own mother, or taller, and so no one thought to do it just for fun.

Just for fun was woman making love to woman in many ways, and man making love to man; or man finding a white-haired beauty who was free now for pleasure. Or one male being approached by several young virgins, all eager to bear his child. Fun was occasionally finding the woman who could bear six and seven children without injury. Or the young woman who, for reasons no one knew, could not bear at all. Nursing from the breasts of women was exquisite pleasure; to gather in groups to do this was splendid, the woman who gave her breasts often going into a sensuous trance. Indeed, women could derive complete pleasure in this way, reaching satisfaction with scarcely any other contact at all.

I don't remember rape; I don't remember execution; I don't remember grudges that lasted very long.

I remember pleading and arguments and much talk, and even some quarreling over mates, but always it was in the realm of songs or words.

I do not remember bad tempers or cruelty. I do not remember uneducated souls. That is, all were born knowing some concept of gentleness, goodness, the value of happiness, and a strong love of pleasure and a desire for others to share that pleasure, for the pleasure of the tribe to be assured.

Men would fall deeply in love with women, and vice versa. They would talk for days and nights; then finally the decision would be made to couple. Or argument would prevent this from ever taking place.

More women were born than men. Or so it was said. But no one really counted. I think more women were born, and that they died much more easily; and I think this is one reason the men felt so utterly tender to the women, because they knew the women were likely to die. The women passed on the strength of their bodies; simple women were cherished because they were gay all the time, and glad to be living and not afraid of giving birth. In sum, the women were more childlike, but the men were simple too.

Deaths by accident were invariably followed by a ceremonial coupling and a replacement of the dead one; and times of pestilence gave way to times of rampant and orgiastic mating, as the tribe sought to repopulate the land.

There was no want. The land never became crowded. Never did people quarrel over fruit or eggs or milk animals. There was too much of everything. It was too warm and lovely, and there were too many pleasant things to do.

It was paradise, it was Eden, it was the golden time that all peoples speak of, a time before the gods became angry, a time before Adam ate the fatal apple, a time of bliss and plenty. The only point is, I remember it. I was there.

I do not remember any concept of laws.

I remember rituals—dances, songs, forming the circles, and each circle moving in the opposite direction from the one inside it, and I remember the men and the women who could play pipes and drums, and even stringed harps that were small and sometimes made of shells. I remember a band of us carrying torches along the most treacherous cliffs, just to see if we could do it and not fall.

I remember painting, that those who liked to do it did it on the cliffs, and in the caves that surrounded the valley, and that sometimes we would go on a day's journey to visit all the caves.

It was unseemly to paint too much at any one given time; each artist mixed his or her own colors from earth, or from her blood, or from the blood of a poor fallen mountain goat or sheep, and from other natural things.

At several intervals I remember the whole tribe coming together to make circle after circle after circle. It is conceivable the whole population was then gathered. Nobody knew.

At other times we gathered in small, single circles and made the chain of memory as we knew it—not what Stuart Gordon has described to you.

One would call out, "Who remembers from long, long ago?" And someone would venture, telling a tale of white-haired ones long gone, whom he had heard tell when he was newborn. Those tales he would relate now, offering them as the oldest, until someone raised his voice and told tales that he could place before those.

Others would then volunteer their earliest recollections; people would argue with or add to or expand the stories of others. Many sequences of events would be put together and fully described.

That was a fascinating thing—a sequence, a long period of events linked by one man's vision or attitude. That was special. That was our finest mental achievement, perhaps, other than pure music and dance.

These sequences were never terribly eventful. What interested us was humor or a small departure from the norm, and of course beautiful things. We loved to talk of beautiful things. If a woman was born with red hair, we thought it a magnificent thing.

If a man stood taller than the others, this was a magnificent thing. If a woman was gifted with the harp, this was a magnificent thing. Terrible accidents were very, very briefly remembered. There were some stories of visionaries—those who claimed to hear voices and to know the future—but that was very infrequent. There were tales of the whole life of a musician or an artist, or of a red-haired woman, or of a boatbuilder who had risked his life to sail to Britain and had come home to tell the tale. There were tales of beautiful men and women who had never coupled, and they were much celebrated and sought after, though as soon as they did couple, they lost this charm.

The memory games were most often played in the long days—that is, those days on which there was scarcely three hours of darkness. Now, we had some sense of seasons based on light and dark, but it had never become terribly important because nothing much changed in our lives from the long days of summer to the shorter days of winter. So we didn't think in terms of seasons. We didn't keep track of light and dark. We frolicked more on the longer days, but other than that, we didn't much notice. The darkest days were as warm as the longest for us; things grew in profusion. Our geysers never ceased to be warm.

But this chain of memory, this ritual telling and recounting, it is important to me now for what it later became. After we migrated to the land of bitter cold, this was our way of knowing ourselves and who we had been. This was crucial when we struggled to survive in the Highlands. We, who had no writing of any kind, held all our knowledge in this way.

But then? In the lost land? It seemed like a pastime. A great game.

The most serious thing that happened was birth. Not death—which was frequent, haphazard, and generally deemed to be sad but meaningless—but the birth of a new person.

Anyone who did not take this seriously was considered to be a fool.

For the coupling to happen, the guardians of the woman had to consent that she could do it, and the men had to agree that they would give permission to the particular man.

It was known always that the children resembled the parents, that they grew up at once, possessing characters of one or the other, or both. And so the men would argue vehemently against a male of poor physique seeking to couple, though everyone was entitled by custom to do it at least once.

As for the woman, the question was, did she understand how hard it might be to bear the child? She would have pain, her body would be greatly weakened, she might even bleed afterwards, she might even die when the child came out of her, or die later on.

It was also deemed that some physical combinations were better than others. In fact, this was the cause of what we might have called our disputes. They were never bloody, but they could be very noisy, with Taltos shouting finally, and some foot-stomping, and so forth and so on. Taltos loved to outshout each other, or to rail at one another in a great, speedy buzz of language until the other was exhausted and couldn't think.

And very, very seldom, there was one prime male or female considered to be so perfect of limb and fair of face, so tall, so well proportioned, that coupling with him or her to produce a beautiful offspring was a great honor; and this did lead to contests and games. Indeed, there was a whole realm of these.

But those are the only painful or difficult things I remember, and I won't tell of them now. Maybe because the only time I knew desperation was in these games. Also, we lost those rituals when we traveled to the land of bitter winter. We had too many real sorrows to contend with from then on.

When the couple had finally obtained permission—I remember once having to beg permission of twenty different people, and having to argue and wait for days on end—the tribe would gather, forming the circle, and then another and another, quite far back, until people felt it was no fun anymore because it was too far away to see.

The drums and the dancing would begin. If it was night, the torches would appear. And the couple would embrace and play lovingly with each other for as long as they could before the final moment had to come. This was a slow feast. To go on for an hour, that was lovely, to go on for two hours was sublime. Many could not go on more than half an hour. Whatever, when the consummation came, it too held the couple for an amazing period of time. How long? I don't know. More, I think, than humans or Taltos born of humans could endure. Perhaps an hour, perhaps more.

When at last the couple fell back away from each other, it was because the new Taltos was about to be born. The mother would swell painfully. The father would then help to take the long, ungainly child out of the mother and to warm it with his hands, and to give it to its mother's breasts.

All drew in to watch this miracle, for the child, commencing as a being of perhaps twenty-four to thirty-six inches, very slender and delicate, and apt to be damaged if not carefully handled, began to elongate and enlarge at once. And over the next fifteen minutes or less, it would often grow to full and majestic height. Its hair would pour down, and its fingers stretch, and the tender bones of its body, so flexible and strong, would make the big frame. The head would grow to three times its birth size.

The mother lay as dead after, sleeping the mother's thin sleep. But the offspring lay with her, talking to her, and the mother sometimes never really slipped into dreams, but talked and sang to the young one, though she was always groggy and often humorous, and she would draw from the young one the first memories, so that the young one wouldn't forget.

We do forget.

We are very capable of forgetting. And to tell is to memorize, or to imprint. To tell is to strike out against the awful loneliness of forgetting, the awful ignorance of it, the sadness. Or so we thought.

This offspring, whether male or female, and most often it was female, caused great joy. It meant more to us than the birth of a single being. It meant the life of the tribe was good; the life of the tribe would go on.

Of course, we never doubted it would, but there were always some legends that at times it had not, that at times women had coupled and runtish offspring had been born to them, or nothing, and that the tribe had dwindled to a very few. Pestilence now and then sterilized the women, and sometimes the men too.

The offspring was much loved and cared for by both parents, though if it was a daughter, it might be taken away after a while to a place where only women lived. In general, the offspring was the bond of love between the man and the woman. They did not seek to love each other in any other or private way. Childbearing being what it was, we had no concept of marriage or monogamy, or of remaining with one woman. On the contrary, it seemed a frustrating, dangerous, and foolish thing to do.

It did sometimes happen. I'm sure it did. A man and a woman loved each other so much that they would not be parted. But I don't remember it happening myself. Nothing stood between one seeing any woman or any man, and love and friendship were not romantic; they were pure.

There are many things more about this life I could describe—the various kinds of songs we sang, the nature of arguments, for there were structures to them, the types of logic that held currency with us, which you would probably find proposterous, and the types of awful errors and blunders young Taltos inevitably made. There were small mammalian animals—very like monkeys—on the island, but we never thought of hunting them or cooking them or eating them. Such an idea would have been vulgar beyond tolerance.

I could describe also the kinds of dwellings we built, for they were many, and the scant ornaments we wore—we did not like clothing or need it or want to keep something so dirty next to our skin—I could describe our boats and how bad they were, and a thousand such things.

There were times when some of us crept to the place where the women lived, just to see them in each other's arms, making love. Then the women would discover us and insist that we go away. There were places in the cliffs, grottoes, caves, small alcoves near bubbling springs, which had become veritable shrines for making love, for both men and men, and women and women.

There was never boredom in this paradise. There were too many things to do. One could romp for hours on the seashore, swim even, if one dared. One could gather eggs, fruit, dance, sing. The painters and the musicians were the most industrious, I imagine, and then there were the boatbuilders and the hut builders too.

There was great room for cleverness. I was thought to be very clever. I discerned patterns in things which others did not notice, that certain mussels in the warm pools grew faster when the sun shone on the pools, and that some mushrooms thrived best in the dark days, and I liked to invent systems—such as simple lifts of vines and twig baskets, by which fruit could be sent down from the tops of trees.

But as much as people admired me for this, they also laughed at it. It really wasn't necessary to do things like this, it was supposed.

Drudgery was unheard of. Each day dawned with its myriad possibilities. No one doubted the perfect goodness of pleasure.

Pain was bad.

That is why the birth aroused such reverence and such caution in all of us, for it involved pain for the woman. And understand the woman Taltos was no slave of the man. She was often as strong as the male, arms just as long, and just as limber. The hormones in her formed a totally different chemistry.

And the birth, involving both pleasure and pain, was the most significant mystery of our lives. Actually, it was the only significant mystery of our lives.

You have now what I wanted you to know. Ours was a world of harmony and true happiness, it was a world of one great mystery and many small, wondrous things.

It was paradise, and there was never a Taltos born, no matter how much human blood ran in his veins from whatever corrupt lineage, who did not remember the lost land, and the time of harmony. Not a single one.

Lasher most surely remembered it. Emaleth most surely remembered it.

The story of paradise is in our blood. We see it, we hear the songs of its birds, and we feel the warmth of the volcanic spring. We taste the fruit; we hear the singing; we can raise our voices and make the singing. And so we know, we know what humans only believe, that paradise can come again.

Before we move on to the cataclysm and the land of winter, let me add one thing.

I do believe there were bad ones among us, those who did violence. I think there were. There were those who killed perhaps, and those who were killed. I'm sure it must have been that way. It had to be. But no one wanted to talk about it! They would leave such things out of the tales! So we had no history of bloody incidents, rapes, conquests of one group of men by another. And a great horror of violence prevailed.

How justice was meted out, I don't know. We didn't have leaders in the strict sense, so much as we had collections of wise ones, people who drew together out of presence and formed a loose elite, so to speak, to whom one might appeal.

Another reason I believe that violence must have happened was that we had definite concepts of the Good God and the Evil One. Of course the Good God was he or she (this divinity was not divided) who had given us the land and our sustenance and our pleasures; and the Evil One had made the terrible land of bitter cold. The Evil One delighted in accidents which killed Taltos; and now and then the Evil One got into a Taltos, but that was really rare!

If there were myths and tales to this vague religion, I never heard them told. Our worship was never one of blood sacrifice or appeasement. We celebrated the Good God in songs and verses, and in the circle dances always. When we danced, when we made the child, we were close to the Good God.

Many of these old songs come back to me all the time. Now and then I go down in the early evening, and I walk through the streets of New York, solitary, amid the crowds, and I sing all of these songs that I can then remember, and the feeling of the lost land returns to me, the sound of the drums and the pipes, and the vision of men and women dancing in the circle. You can do that in New York, no one pays any attention to you. It's really amusing to me.

Sometimes others in New York who are singing to themselves, or mumbling loudly, or chattering, will come near to me, chatter at me, or sing towards me, and then drift off. In other words, I am accepted by the crazies of New York. And though we are all alone, we have each other for those few moments. The twilight world of the city.

Afterwards, I go out in my car and give coats and wool scarves to those who don't have them. Sometimes I send Remmick, my servant, to do this. Sometimes we bring in the street people to sleep in the lobby, to feed them and bed them down. But then one will fight with another, perhaps even knife another, and out they all must go, into the snow again.

Ah, but that brings me to one other pitfall of our life in the lost land. How could I have forgotten? There were always those Taltos who were caught in music and couldn't get out. They could be caught by the music of others, so that others had to be made to stop the music in order to release them. They could be caught in their own song, and truly sing until they fell dead. They could dance until they fell dead.

I often fell into great spells of singing and dancing and rhyming, but

I always woke out of it, or the music came to a ceremonial finish, or I grew weary perhaps, or lost the rhythm. Whatever, I was never in any danger of death. Many did as I did. But there were always deaths in this manner.

Everyone felt that the Taltos who died dancing or singing had gone to the Good God.

But nobody talked much about it. Death just wasn't a fit subject for Taltos. All unpleasant things were forgotten. That was one of our basic ideals.

I'd been alive a long time by the time of the cataclysm. But I don't know how to measure. Let me estimate twenty or thirty years.

The cataclysm was entirely a thing of nature. Later, men told tales of Roman soldiers or the Picts driving us from our island. No such thing happened at all. In the lost land, we never laid eyes on human beings. We knew no other people. We knew only ourselves.

A great upheaval of the earth caused our land to tremble and begin to break apart. It started with vague rumblings, and clouds of smoke covering the sky. The geysers began to scald our people. The pools were so hot we couldn't drink from them. The land moved and groaned both day and night.

Many Taltos were dying. The fish in the pools were dead, and the birds had fled the cliffs. Men and women went in all directions seeking a place that was not turbulent, but they did not find it, and some came running back.

At last, after countless deaths, all the tribe built rafts, boats, dugouts, whatever they could, to make the journey to the land of bitter cold. There was no choice for us. Our land grew more tumultuous and treacherous with every day.

I don't know how many remained. I don't know how many got away. All day and all night, people built boats and went into the sea. The wise ones helped the foolish ones—that was really the way we divided old from young—and on about the tenth day, as I would calculate it now, I sailed with two of my daughters, two men whom I loved, and one woman.

And it is really in the land of winter, on the afternoon that I saw my homeland sink into the sea, on that afternoon, that the history of my people really began.

Then began their trials and their tribulations, their real suffering, and their first concept of valor and sacrifice. There began all the things human beings hold sacred, which can only come from difficulty, struggle, and the growing idealization of bliss and perfection, which can only flourish in the mind when paradise is utterly lost.

It was from a high cliff that I saw the great cataclysm reach its conclusion; it was from that height that I saw the land break into pieces and sink into the sea. It was from there that I saw the tiny figures of Taltos drowning in that sea. It was from there that I saw the giant waves wash the foot of the cliffs and the hills, and crash into the hidden valleys, and flood the forests.

The Evil One has triumphed, said those who were with me. And for the first time the songs we sang and the tales we recited became a true lament.

It must have been late summer when we fled to the land of bitter cold. It was truly cold. The water striking the shores was cold enough to knock a Taltos unconscious. We learned immediately that it would never be warm.

But the full breath of winter was something of which we had not truly dreamed. Most of the Taltos who escaped the lost land died the first winter. Some who remained bred furiously to reestablish the tribe. And as we had no real idea that winter was going to come again, many more died the following winter, too.

Probably we caught on to the cycle of the seasons by the third or fourth year.

But those first years were times of rampant superstition, endless chattering and reasoning as to why we had been cast out of the lost land, and why the snow and wind came to kill us, and whether or not the Good God had turned against us.

My penchant for observation and making things elevated me to the undisputed leader. But the entire tribe was learning rapidly about such things as the warm carcasses of dead bears and other large animals, and then the good warmth from their furry skins. Holes were warmer obviously than caves, and with the horns of a dead antelope we could dig deep underground homes for ourselves, and roof them over with tree trunks and stones.

We knew how to make fire, and very soon got good at it, because we didn't find any fire to be had for nothing, simply breathing out of the rock. Different Taltos at different times developed similar kinds of wheels, and crude wagons were soon fashioned to carry our food, and those who were sick.

Gradually, those of us who had survived all the winters of the land of bitter cold began to learn very valuable things which had to be taught to the young. Paying attention mattered for the first time. Nursing had become a means of survival. All women gave birth at least once, to make up for the appalling rate of death.

If life had not been so hard, this would have been seen perhaps as a time of great creative pleasure. I could list the various discoveries that were made.

Suffice it to say we were hunter-gatherers of a very primitive sort, though we did not eat the meat of animals unless we were really starving, and that we progressed erratically in a completely different fashion from human beings.

Our large brains, our enhanced verbal capacity, the strange marriage in each of us of instinct and intelligence—all this made us both more clever and more clumsy, more insightful and more foolish in many respects.

Of course, quarrels broke out among us, as the result of scarcity or questions of judgment—whether to go this way or that to seek game. Groups broke off from the main group and went their own way.

I had by this time become accustomed to being the leader, and did not frankly trust anybody else to do it. I was known simply by name, Ashlar, as no titles were required among us, and I exerted tremendous influence over the others, and lived in terror of their getting lost, being eaten by wild animals, or fighting each other in harmful ways. Battles, quarrels, they were now daily occurences.

But with each passing winter we had greater and greater skills. And as we followed the game south, or moved in that direction simply by instinct or by accident, I don't know, we came into warmer lands of fairly extended summer, and our true reverence for, and reliance upon, the seasons began.

We began to ride the wild horses for fun. It was great sport to us. But we didn't think that horses could really be tamed. We did all right with the oxen to pull our carts, which, in the beginning, of course, we had pulled ourselves.

Out of this came our most intense religious period. I invoked the name of the Good God every time chaos came upon us, striving to put our lives back in order. Executions took place sometimes twice a year.

There's so much I could write or say about those centuries. But in a very real sense they constitute a unique time—between the lost land and the coming of human beings—and much of what was deduced, surmised, learned, memorized, was shattered, so to speak, when the humans came.

It is enough to say that we became a highly developed people, worshiping the Good God largely through banquets and dances as we had always done. We still played the game of memory, and still kept to our strict rules of conduct, though now men "remembered" at birth how to be violent, to fight, to excel and to compete, and women were born remembering fear.

And certain strange events had had an incredible impact upon us, far greater than anyone realized at the time.

Other men and women were afoot in Britain. We heard of them from other Taltos—and that they were loathsome and as mean as animals. The Taltos had slaughtered them in self-defense. But the strange people, who were not Taltos, had left behind pots made of brittle earth, painted with pretty pictures, and weapons made of magical stone. They had also left behind curious little creatures like monkeys, though hairless and very helpless, who might be their young.

This settled the question that they were bestial, for in our minds only the beasts had helpless little young. And even the young of the beasts weren't as helpless as these little creatures.

But Taltos took mercy on them; they nourished them on milk and kept them, and finally, having heard so much about them, we bought about five of these little creatures, who by that time were no longer crying all the time, and actually knew how to walk.

These creatures didn't live long. What, thirty-five years, perhaps, but during that time they changed dramatically; they went from little wriggling pink things to tall, strong beings, only to become wizened, withered old things. Purely animal, that was our conjecture, and I don't think we treated these primitive primates any better than they might have treated dogs.

They were not quick-witted, they didn't understand our very rapid speech; indeed, it was quite a discovery that they could understand if we spoke slowly, but they had no words, apparently, of their own.

Indeed, they were born stupid, we thought, with less innate knowledge than the bird or the fox; and though they gained greater reasoning power, they always remained fairly weak, small, and covered with hideous hair.

When a male of our kind mated with a female of them, the female bled and died. The men made our women bleed. They were crude and clumsy, besides.

Over the centuries we came upon such creatures more than once, or bought them from other Taltos, but we never saw them in any organized force of their own. We supposed them to be harmless. We had no name for them, really. They taught us nothing, and they made us cry with frustration when they couldn't learn anything from us.

How sad this is, we thought, that these big animals look so much like Taltos, even walking upright and having no tails, but they have no minds.

Meanwhile, our laws had become very strict. Execution was the ultimate punishment for disobedience. It had become a ritual, though never a celebrated one, in which the offending Taltos was quickly dispatched with deliberate and severe blows to the skull.

Now, the skull of a Taltos stays resilient long after other bones in his body have become hard. But the skull can be crushed easily, if one knows how to do it, and we had—unfortunately—learned.

But death still horrified us. Murder was a very infrequent crime. The death penalty was for those who threatened the entire community. Birth was still our central sacred ceremony, and when we found good places to settle, which argued for permanence, we frequently selected places for our religious circle dancing, and we laid out stones to mark these places, sometimes very, very large stones, in which we took pride.

Ah, the circles of stones! We became, though we never thought of it that way, the people of the stone circles all over the land.

When we were forced to a new territory—either by starvation or because another band of Taltos was coming towards us whom none of us liked, and with whom no one wanted to live in close quarters—we got in the custom of making a new circle at once. Indeed, the diameter of our circle and the weight of its stones became a claim upon a certain area, and the sight of a very large circle built by others was a sign to us that this was their land and we should move on.

Anybody foolish enough to disregard a sacred circle? Well, they would be given no peace and quiet till they decamped. Of course, it was scarcity that imposed these rules often. A great plain could support very few hunters, really. Good spots on lakes and rivers and on the coast were better, but no place was paradise, no place was the endless fountain of warmth and plenty that had been the lost land.

Claims of sacred protection were asserted against invaders or squatters. And I remember myself carving a figure of the Good God, as I perceived God—with both breasts and a penis—upon an immense stone in one of these circles, a plea to other Taltos that they must respect our holy circle and therefore our land.

When there was a true battle, born of personality and misunderstanding, and rank greed for a particular portion of the earth, the invaders would knock down the stones of those who lived there, and make a new circle entirely of their own.

To be driven out was exhausting, but in a new home the desire to build a larger, more imposing circle burnt hot. We would find stones, we vowed, so large that no one could ever dislodge them, or would ever try.

Our circles spoke of our ambition and our simplicity—of the joy of the dance and our willingness to fight and die for the territory of the tribe.

Our basic values, though unchanged since the days of the lost land, had hardened somewhat around certain rituals. It was mandatory for all to attend the birth of a new Taltos. It was the law that no woman could give birth more than twice. It was the law that reverence and sensuality attend these births; indeed, a great sexual euphoria was often sustained.

The new Taltos was seen as an omen; if not perfect of limb and form, beautiful to behold, and full sized, a terrible fear came over the land. The perfect newborn was the blessing of the Good God as before, but you see, our beliefs had darkened; and as they darkened, as we drew all the wrong conclusions from purely natural events, so did our obsession with the great circles darken, our belief in them as pleasing to the Good God, and as morally essential for the tribe.

At last came the year when we settled on the plain.

This was in the south of Britain, now known as Salisbury, where the climate was beautiful to us, and the best we had ever been able to find. The time? Before the coming of human beings.

We knew by then that the winter would always be with us; we did not think it possible to escape the winter anywhere in the world. If you think about this, it's a perfectly logical assumption. Alas! The summers were longest and sweetest in this part of Britain, I knew this firsthand now, and the forests were thick and full of deer, and the sea was not far away.

Herds of wild antelope wandered the plain.

Here we decided that we would build our permanent home.

The idea of moving all the time, to avoid arguments or to chase the food supply, had long since lost its appeal. We had become, to some extent, a people of settlements. The search was on among all our peoples for permanent refuge and a permanent place to perform the sacred singing, the sacred memory game, and the sacred dance, and of course the ritual of the birth.

We had deeply resented our last invasion, and had only left after endless argument (Taltos always try words first), some pushing and shoving, and finally a lot of ultimatums, such as "All right, if you are determined to crowd these woods, then we shall leave them!"

We held ourselves to be vastly superior to the other tribes for any number of reasons, and certainly because we had so many who had lived in the lost land, and many, many still with white hair. We were in many respects the most clearly organized group, and we had the most customs. Some of us had horses now, and could manage to ride them. Our caravan was comprised of many wagons. And we had good-sized herds and flocks of sheep, goats, and a form of wild cattle that no longer exists.

Others poked fun at us, especially for riding horses, off which we fell repeatedly, but in general other Taltos held us in awe, and came running to us for help in bad times.

Now, upon the Salisbury Plain, determining that it would be ours forever, we chose to make the greatest circle of stones ever seen in the world.

By this time, too, we knew that the very making of the circle united the tribe, organized it, kept it from mischief, and made the dances all the more joyous, as stone after stone was added, and the circle grew ever more impressive to behold.

This great undertaking, the building of the biggest circle in the world, shaped several centuries of our existence, and pushed us forward rapidly in terms of inventiveness and organization. The search for the sarsens, or the sandstone, as it is now called, the means of bringing the boulders back, of dressing them and erecting them, and finally laying in place the lintels—this consumed us; it became a justification for life itself.

The concept of fun and play was almost gone from us now. We were survivors of the bitter cold. The dance had been sanctified. Everything had been sanctified. Yet this was a great and thrilling time.

Those who would share our life joined us, and we grew to such a number that we could resist invasion; indeed, the very first monstrous stone of our great plan inspired such inspiration that other Taltos came to worship, to join our circle or to watch it, rather than to steal part of the plain.

The building of the circle became the backdrop against which our development took place.

During these centuries our life reached its highest peak. We built our encampments all over the plain, in easy walking distance of our great circle, and gathered our animals into small stockades. We planted the elderberry and the blackthorn around our encampments, and these encampments became forts.

We arranged for the orderly burial of the dead; indeed, we built some graves beneath the ground during this time. Indeed, all the consequences of permanent settlement played themselves out. We did not begin to make pottery, but we bought a great deal of it from other Taltos who claimed to have bought it from the short-lived hairy people who came to the coast in boats made of animal skin.

Soon tribes came from all over Britain to make the living circle of the dance within our standing stones.

The circles became great winding processions. It was deemed to be good luck to give birth within our circle. And much trade and prosperity came our way.

Meanwhile, other large circles were being erected in our land. Vast, marvelous circles, but none, absolutely none, to rival our own. Indeed, sometime during this productive and wondrous era, it became known that ours was indeed the circle of circles; people did not seek to rival it, but rather only to see it, to dance in it, to join the procession weaving in and out of the various doorways formed by the lintels and the standing stones.

To travel to another circle, to dance with the tribe there, became a regular event. At such gatherings we learnt much from each other, and celebrated great chains of memory, swapping tales and reinforcing the details of the most cherished stories, and correcting the legends of the lost land.

We would go in bands to see the circle which is now called Avebury, or to see other circles farther south, near Stuart Gordon's beloved Glastonbury Tor. We went north to worship at others.

But all the while, ours was the most magnificent, and when Ashlar and his people came to visit the circle of another tribe, it was considered to be a great honor, and we were asked for advice, and begged to remain, and given fine gifts.

Of course, you know that our circle became Stonehenge. Because it and many others of our sacred rings are standing even today. But let me explain what may be obvious only to scholars of Stonehenge. We did not build the whole thing that is there now, or is believed to have been there at one time.

We built only two circles of sarsens, quarried in other areas, including the distant Marlborough Downs, but mainly at Amesbury, which is very near to Stonehenge. The inner circle had ten standing stones, and the outer thirty. And the placing of the lintels atop these stones was a matter of great debate. From the beginning, we opted for the lintels. But I never much appreciated them. I had dreamed of a circle of stones to imitate a circle of men and women. Each stone was to be roughly twice the size of a Taltos, and as wide as a Taltos is tall. That was my vision.

But to others of the tribe, the lintels gave the impression of shelter, reminding them of the great volcanic cone which had once protected the tropical valley of the lost land.

It was later peoples who built the circle of blue stones, and many other formations at Stonehenge. At one time, all of our beloved open-air temple was enclosed into some sort of wooden edifice by savage human tribes. And I do not care to think of the bloody rites practiced there. But this was not our doing.

As to the emblems carved upon the sarsens, we used only one, upon a central stone which is long gone. It was a symbol of the Good God with breasts and phallus, and it was deeply etched and within reach of a Taltos, so that he or she might trace it in the dark by touch.

Later, human beings put other carvings upon the sarsens, just as they put Stonehenge to other use.

But I can tell you that no one—Taltos, human, or other species—has ever happened upon our great circle who did not to some extent respect it or come to feel the presence of the sacred when within it. Long before it was ever completed, it became a place of inspiration, and it has been one ever since.

In this monument you have the essence of our people. It is the only great monument we were ever to build.

But to fully appreciate what we were, remember, we retained our values. We deplored death and did not celebrate it. We made no blood sacrifice. We did not see war as glorious so much as chaotic and unpleasant. And the high expression of our art was the singing and dancing circles assembled in and around Stonehenge.

At their greatest height, our birth festivals and festivals of memory or music would include thousands of Taltos, come from far and wide. It was impossible to count the circles formed, or to measure the widest of them. It is impossible to say how many hours and days these rituals went on.

Imagine it, if you will, the vast snowy plain, the clear blue sky, smoke rising from the encampments and the huts built near to the stone circle, for warmth and food and drink. See the Taltos, men and women all, and of my height, with hair long, often to the waist or even to the ankles, wearing carefully sewn skins and furs and high boots of leather, and linking hands to form these beautiful, simple configurations as the voices rose in song.

Ivy leaves, mistletoe, holly, whatever was green in winter, we wore in our hair, and brought with us, and laid upon the ground. The branches of the pine or whatever tree did not lose their leaves.

And in summer we brought flowers aplenty; and indeed, deputations were kept going all day and night into the woodlands to find flowers and fresh green boughs.

The singing and the music alone were magnificent. One did not tear oneself from the circles easily. Indeed, some people never left of their own accord, and small fires were made within the margins between moving lines of dancers, for warmth. Some danced and sang and embraced others until they fell down in a faint or dead.

In the beginning we had no one presiding, but that changed. I was called upon to go into the center, to strike the strings of the harp, to begin the dance. And after I had spent many hours there, another came to stand in my place, and later another and another, each new singer or musician making a music which the others imitated, taking the new song out from small circle to big circle, like the ripples in a pond from a falling stone.

At times, many great fires were constructed beforehand, one in the center and others at various points, so that the dancers would pass near to them often as they followed the circular path.

The birth of the Taltos in our circle was for the newborn an event unrivaled even in the lost land. For there the circles had been voluntary and spontaneous and small. But here the new creature opened its eyes upon an enormous tribe of its own kind, and heard a chorus like that of angels, and dwelt within that circle, being suckled and stroked and comforted for the first days and nights of life.

Of course, we were changing. As our innate knowledge changed, we changed. That is, what we learned changed the genetic makeup of the newborn.

Those born in the time of the circles had a stronger sense of the sacred than we old ones did, and were frankly not so given to rampant humor or irony or suspicion as we were. Those born in the time of the circles were more aggressive, and could murder when they had to, without giving way to tears.

Had you asked me then, I would have said our kind would rule forever. Had you said, "Ah, but men will come who will slaughter people for fun, who will rape and burn and lay waste simply because it is what they do for a living," I would not have believed it. I would have said, "Oh, but we'll talk to them, we'll tell all our stories and memories and ask them to tell theirs, and they'll start dancing and singing, and they'll stop fighting or wanting things they shouldn't have."

When human beings did come down on us, we assumed, of course, that they would be simple little hairy people, of the gentle ilk of the amiable, grunting little traders who sometimes came to the coast in boats of skin to sell us goods and then went away.

We heard tales of raids and massacres but we could not believe these. After all, why would anyone do such things?

And then we were amazed to discover that the human beings coming into Britain had smooth skin like ours, and that their magic stone had been hammered into shields and helmets and swords, that they had brought their own trained horses with them by the hundreds, and on horseback they rode us down, burning our camps, piercing our bodies with spears, or chopping off our heads.

They stole our women and raped them until they died of the bleeding. They stole our men and sought to enslave them, and laughed at them and ridiculed them, and in some instances drove them mad.

At first their raids were very infrequent. The warriors came by sea, and descended upon us by night from the forests. We thought each raid was the last.

Often we fought them off. We were not by nature as fierce as they, by any means, but we could defend ourselves, and great circles were convened to discuss their metal weapons and how we might make our own. Indeed, we imprisoned a number of human beings, invaders all, to try to pry the knowledge from them. We discovered that when we slept with their women, whether willing or unwilling, they died. And the men had a deep, inveterate hatred of our softness. They called us "the fools of the circle," or "the simple people of the stones."

The illusion that we could hold out against these people crumbled almost in the space of one season. We only learned later that we'd been saved from earlier annihilation by one simple fact: we didn't have much that these people wanted. Principally, they wanted our women for pleasure, and some of the finer gifts which pilgrims had brought to the circle shrine.

But other tribes of Taltos were flocking onto the plain. They'd been driven from their homes along the coast by the human invaders, who inspired in them only deathly fear. Their mounts gave these human beings a fanatical sense of power. Humans enjoyed these invasions. Massacre was sport to them.

We fortified our camps for the winter. Those who had come to join us replaced many of the fighting men we had lost.

Then the snow came; we had plenty to eat, and we had peace. Maybe the invaders didn't like the snow. We didn't know. There were so many of us gathered together, and we had lifted from the dead so many spears and swords, that we felt safe.

It was time for the winter birth circle to be convened, and it was most important, as so many had been killed in the last year. Not only must we make new Taltos for our villages; we had to make them to send to other villages where the inhabitants had been burnt out.

Many had come from far and wide for the winter birth circle, and we heard more and more tales of slaughter and woe.

However, we were many. And it was our sacred time.

We formed the circles, we lit the sacred fires; it was time to declare to the Good God that we believed the summer would come again, to make birth happen now as an affirmation of that faith, and an affirmation that the Good God wanted us to survive.

We had had perhaps two days of singing and dancing and birthing, of feasting and drinking, when the tribes of human beings descended on the plain.

We heard the enormous rumble of the horses before we saw them; it was a roar like the sound of the crumbling of the lost land. Horsemen came from all sides to attack us; the great sarsens of the circles were splashed with our blood.

Many Taltos, drunk on music and erotic play, never put up any resistance at all. Those of us who ran to the camps put up a great fight.

But when the smoke had cleared, when the horsemen were gone, when our women had been taken by the hundreds in our own wagons, when every encampment had been burnt to the ground, we were only a handful, and we had had enough of war.

Indeed, the horrors we'd seen we never wanted to witness again. The newborns of our tribe had all been slain, to the last one. They had blundered into death in the first days of their lives. Few women remained to us, and some had given birth too many times in the past.

By the second nightfall after the massacre, our scouts came back to tell us what we had feared was true: the warriors had set up their camps in the forest. They were building permanent dwellings; indeed, there was talk of their villages dotting the southern landscape.

We had to go north.

We had to return to the hidden valleys of the Highlands, or places too inaccessible for these cruel invaders. Our journey was a long one, lasting the rest of the winter, in which birth and death became daily occurrences, and more than once we were attacked by small bands of humans, and more than once we spied upon their settlements and learned of their lives.

We massacred more than one band of the enemy. Twice we raided lowland forts to rescue our men and women, whose singing we could hear from great distances.

And by the time we discovered the high valley of Donnelaith, it was spring, the snow was melting, the rich forest was green again, the loch was no longer frozen, and we soon found ourselves in a hideaway accessible to the outside world only by a winding river whose route was so circuitous that the loch itself could not be seen from the sea. Indeed, the great cove through which a seafarer enters it appears to all eyes as a cave.

Understand, the loch in later times became a port. Men did much by that time to open it to the sea.

But in those times we found ourselves hidden and safe at last.

We had many rescued Taltos with us. And the stories they told! The human beings had discovered the miracle of birth with us! They were spellbound by the magic of it; they had tortured the Taltos women and men mercilessly, trying to force them to do it, and then had screamed in delight and thrilling fear when the new Taltos appeared. They had worried some of these women to death. But many of our kind had resisted, refusing to be so violated; some women had found ways to take their own lives. Many had been killed for struggling, for attacking every human who came near them, and finally for trying repeatedly to escape.

When humans discovered that the newborns could breed immediately, they forced them to do it, and the newborns, muddled and frightened, did not know what to do but comply. The humans knew the power of music over the Taltos, and how to use it. The humans thought the Taltos sentimental and cowardly, though what the words were for it then, I don't now know.

In sum, a deep hatred grew between us and the warriors. We thought them animals, of course, animals that could talk and make things, perfect horrors, actually, aberrations that might destroy all beautiful life. And they thought us amusing and relatively harmless monsters! For it soon became apparent that the wide world was filled with people of their height or even smaller, who bred and lived as they did, and not with people like us.

From our raids we had gathered many objects which these people had brought from far and wide. The slaves repeated tales of great kingdoms with walls about them, of palaces in lands of desert sand and jungle, of warring tribes and of great congregations of people in encampments of such size that one could not imagine it. And these encampments had names.

All of these people, as far as we knew, bred in the human way. All had tiny, helpless babies. All brought them up half-savage and half-intelligent. All were aggressive, liked to war, liked to kill. Indeed, it was perfectly obvious to me that the most aggressive among them were the survivors, and they had weeded out over the centuries anyone who was not aggressive. So they had had a hand in making themselves what they were.

Our early days in the glen of Donnelaith—and let me say here that *we* gave it that name—were days of intense pondering and discussion, of building the finest circle that we could, and of consecration and prayer.

We celebrated the birth of numerous new Taltos, and these we schooled vigorously for the ordeals that lay ahead. We buried many who died of old wounds, and some women who died from childbearing, as always happens, and we buried others who, having been driven from the plain of Salisbury, simply did not want to live.

It was the worst time of suffering for my people, even worse than the massacre itself had been. I saw strong Taltos, white-haired ones, great singers, abandon themselves completely to their music, and fall at last without breath into the high grass.

Finally, when a new council had been appointed, of newborns and wiser Taltos, of the white-haired and of those who wanted to do something about all this, we came to the one very logical position.

Can you guess what it was?

We realized that humans had to be annihilated. If they weren't, their warring ways would destroy all that had been given us by the Good God. They were burning up life with their cavalry and their torches and swords. We had to stamp them out.

As for the prospect that they existed all over distant lands in great numbers, well, we bred much faster than they did—was that not so? We could replace our slain very quickly. They took years to replace a fallen warrior. Surely we could outnumber them as we fought against them, if only . . . if only we had the stomach for the fight.

Within a week, after endless argument, it was decided that we did not have the stomach for the fight. Some of us could do it; we were so angry and full of hate and irony now that we could ride down upon them and hack them to pieces. But in the main, Taltos simply could not kill in this way; they could not match the malicious lust of humans for killing. And we knew it. Humans would win by sheer meanness and cruelty in the end.

Of course, since that time, and possibly a thousand times before it, a people has been annihilated because it lacked aggression; it could not match the cruelty of another tribe or clan or nation or race.

The one real difference in our case was that we knew it. Whereas the Incas were slaughtered in ignorance by the Spanish, we understood much more of what was involved.

Of course, we were certain of our superiority to humans; we were baffled that they didn't appreciate our singing and stories; we did not believe that they knew what they were doing when they struck us down.

And realizing that we really couldn't match them in combat, we assumed that we could reason with them, we could teach them, we could show them how much more pleasant and agreeable life was if one did not kill.

Of course, we had only just begun to understand them.

By the end of that year, we had ventured out of the glen to take a few human prisoners, and from these we learned that things were far more hopeless than we thought. Killing lay at the very basis of their religion; it was their sacred act!

For their gods they killed, sacrificing hundreds of their own kind at their rituals. Indeed, death was the very focus of their lives!

We were overcome with horror.

We determined that life would exist for us within the glen. As for other Taltos tribes, we feared the worst for them. In our little forays to find human slaves, we had seen more than one village burnt out, more than one field of wasting, sinewy Taltos bones being scattered by the winter wind.

As the years passed, we remained secure in the glen, venturing out only with the greatest care. Our bravest scouts traveled as far as they dared.

By the end of the decade, we knew that no Taltos settlements remained in our part of Britain. All the old circles were now abandoned! And we also came to find out from the few prisoners we took—which was not easy—that we were hunted now, and very much in demand to be sacrificed to the humans' gods.

Indeed, massacres had become a thing of the past. Taltos were hunted strictly for capture, and only killed if they refused to breed.

It had been discovered that their seed brought death to human women, and on that account the males were kept in unbearable bondage, laden with metal chains.

Within the next century the invaders conquered the earth!

Many of the scouts who went out to seek other Taltos, and bring them into the glen, simply never came back. But there were always young ones who wanted to go, who had to see life beyond the mountains, who had to go down to the loch and travel to the sea.

As the memories were passed on in our blood, our young Taltos became even more warlike. They wanted to slaughter a human! Or so they thought.

Those wanderers who did return, and frequently with at least a couple of human prisoners, confirmed our most terrible fears. From one end of Britain to the other, the Taltos was dying out. Indeed, in most places it was no more than legend, and certain towns, for the new settlements were nothing less than that, would pay a fortune for a Taltos, but men no longer hunted for them, and some did not believe anymore that there had ever been such strange beasts.

Those who were caught were wild.

Wild? we asked. What in the name of God is a wild Taltos?

Well, we were soon told.

In numerous encampments, when it came time for sacrifice to the gods, the chosen women, often fanatically eager for it, were brought to embrace a prisoner Taltos, to arouse his passion, and then to die by his seed. Dozens of women met their deaths in this fashion, precisely as human men were being drowned in cauldrons, or decapitated, or burnt in horrid wicker cages for the gods of the human tribes.

But over the years some of these women had not died. Some of them had left the sacred altar alive. And a few of these, within a matter of weeks, had given birth!

A Taltos came out of their bodies, a wild seed of our kind. This Taltos invariably killed its human mother, not meaning to, of course, but because she could not survive the birth of such a creature. But this didn't always happen. And if the mother lived long enough to give her offspring milk, which she had aplenty, this Taltos would grow, within the customary time of three hours, to full size.

In some villages this was counted as a great omen of good fortune. In others it was disaster. Human beings could not agree. But the name of the game had become to get a pair of such human-mothered Taltos and to make them breed more Taltos, and to keep a stock of these prisoners, to make them dance, to make them sing, to make them give birth.

Wild Taltos.

There was another way that wild Taltos could be born. A human man now and then made one grow in the body of a Taltos woman! This poor prisoner, being kept for pleasure, did not suspect at first that she had conceived. Within weeks her child was born to her, growing to full height as she knew it would, only to be taken from her and imprisoned, or put to some grisly use.

And who were the mortals who could breed with Taltos in this way? What characterized them? In the very beginning we did not know; we could not perceive any visible signs. But later, as more and more mixture occurred, it became clear to us that a certain kind of human was more prone than any other, either to conceive or to father the Taltos, and that was a human of great spiritual gifts, a human who could see into people's hearts, or tell the future, or lay healing hands upon others. These humans to our eyes became quite detectable and finally unmistakable.

But this took centuries to develop. Blood was passed back and forth.

Wild Taltos escaped their captors. Human women swelling monstrous with Taltos fled to the glen to hope of shelter. Of course we took them in.

We learned from these human mothers.

Whereas our young were born within hours, their young took a fortnight to a month, depending upon whether or not the mother knew of the child's existence. Indeed, if the mother knew and was to address the child, quiet its fears, and sing to it, the growth was greatly accelerated. Hybrid Taltos were born knowing things their human ancestors had known! In other words, our laws of genetic inheritance embraced the acquired knowledge of the human species.

Of course, we had no such language then to discuss these things. We only knew that a hybrid might know how to sing human songs in human tongues, or to make boots such as we had never seen, very skillfully, from leather.

In this way, all manner of human knowledge passed into our people.

But those wild ones, born in captivity, were always full of the Taltos memories too, and conceived a hatred for their human tyrants. They broke for freedom as soon as they could. To the woods they fled, and to the north, possibly to the lost land. Some unfortunates, we learned later, went home to the great plain and, finding no refuge, survived hand-to-mouth in the nearby forest, or were captured and killed.

Some of these wild Taltos inevitably bred with each other. As fugitives they found one another; or within captivity they were bred. They could always breed with the pure Taltos prisoner, giving birth in the pure way, immediately; and so a fragile race of Taltos was hanging on in the wildernesses of Britain, a desperate minority of outcasts, incessantly searching for their ancestors and for the paradise of their memories, and carrying in their veins human blood.

Much, much human blood came into the wild Taltos during these centuries. And the wild Taltos developed beliefs and habits of their own. They lived in the green treetops, often painting themselves entirely green for camouflage, making the paint of several natural pigments, and clothing themselves when they could in ivy and leaves.

And it was these, or so it was claimed, who somehow created the Little People.

Indeed, the Little People may have always lived in the shadows and hidden places. We had glimpsed them surely in our early years, and during the time of our rule of Britain, they had kept themselves entirely away from us. They were but a kind of monster in our legends. We scarcely noticed them any more than hairy human beings.

But now tales came to our ears that they had begun with the spawning of Taltos and human—that when the conception occurred but the development failed, a hunchbacked dwarf was born, rather than the wiry and graceful Taltos.

Was this so? Or did they spring from the same root as we did? Were we cousins of each other in some time before the lost land, when perhaps we had mingled in some earlier paradise? The time before the moon? Was that the time of our branching off, one tribe from the other?

We didn't know. But at the times of hybrids, and experiments of this sort, of wild Taltos seeking to discover what they could or could not do, or who could breed with whom, we did learn that these horrid little monsters, these malicious, mischievous, and strange Little People, could breed with us. Indeed, if they could seduce one of us into coupling with them, man or woman, the offspring was more often than not a Taltos.

A compatible race? An evolutionary experiment closely related to us?

Again, we were never to know.

But the legend spread, and the Little People preyed upon us as viciously as human beings. They set traps for us; they tried to lure us with music; they did not come in warrior bands; they were sneaks, and they tried to entrance us with spells which they could cast by the powers of their minds. They wanted to make the Taltos. They dreamed of becoming a race of giants, as they called us. And when they caught our women, they coupled with them until they died; and when they caught our men, they were as cruel to them to make them breed as humans.

Over the centuries the mythology grew; the Little People had once been as we were, tall and fair. They had once had our advantages. But demons had made them what they were, cast them out, made them suffer. They were as long-lived as we were. Their monstrous little offspring were born as quickly and as fully developed proportionately as ours were.

But we feared them, we hated them, we did not want to be used by them, and we came to believe the stories that our children could be like them if not given milk, if not loved.

And the truth, whatever it was, if anyone ever knew, was buried in folklore.

In the glen the Little People still hang on; there are few natives of Britain who do not know of them. They go by countless names, lumped with other creatures of myth—the fairies, the Sluagh, the Ganfers, the leprechauns, the elves.

They are dying out now in Donnelaith, for a great many reasons. But they live in other dark, secret places still. They steal human women now and then to breed, but they are no more successful with humans than we are. They long for a witch—a mortal with the extra sense, the type that, with one of them, often conceives or fathers the Taltos. And when they find such creatures, they can be ruthless.

Never believe that they won't hurt you in the glen, or in other glens and remote woods and valleys. They would do it. And they would kill you and burn the fat of your bodies on their torches for the sheer joy of it.

But this is not their story.

Another tale can be told of them, by Samuel, perhaps, should he ever be moved to tell it. But then Samuel has a tale all his own of his wanderings away from the Little People, and that would make a better adventure, I think, than their history.

Let me return to the wild Taltos now, the hybrids who carried the human genes. Banding together outside the glen, whenever possible, they exchanged the memories, the tales, and formed their own tiny settlements.

And periodically we went in search of them and brought them home. They bred with us; they gave us offspring; we gave them counsel and knowledge.

And surprisingly enough, they never stayed! They would come to the glen from time to time to rest; but they had to return to the wild world, where they shot arrows at humans, and fled through the forests laughing afterwards, believing themselves to be the very magical creatures, sought for sacrifice, which humans believed them to be.

And the great tragedy, of course, of their desire to wander is that inevitably they carried the secret of the glen to the human world.

Simpletons, that is what we are in a true sense. Simpletons, that we did not see that such a thing would have to happen, that these wild ones, when finally captured, would tell tales of our glen, sometimes to threaten their enemies with the prospect of vengeance from a secret nation, or out of sheer naiveté, or, that the tale having been told to other wild Taltos who had never seen us, would be passed on by them.

Can you see what happened? The legend of the glen, of the tall people who gave birth to children who could walk and speak at birth, began to spread. Knowledge of us was general throughout Britain. We fell into legend with the Little People. And with other strange creatures whom humans seldom saw, but would have given anything to capture.

And so the life we'd built in Donnelaith, a life of great stone towers or brochs, from which we hoped someday to successfully defend ourselves against invasions, of the old rituals carefully preserved and carried out, of the memories treasured, and of our values, our belief in love and birth above all things held sacred—that life was in mortal danger from those who would hunt for monsters for any reason, from those who only wanted to "see with their own eyes."

Another development took place. As I said earlier, there were always those born in the glen who wanted to leave. It was deeply impressed upon them that they must remember the way home. They must look at the stars and never forget the various patterns that could guide them home. And this became a part of innate knowledge very rapidly because we deliberately cultivated it, and this cultivation worked. In fact, it worked amazingly well, opening up to us all kinds of new possibilities. We could program into the innate knowledge all manner of practical things. We put it to the test by questioning the offspring. It was quite astonishing. They knew the map of Britain as we knew it and preserved it (highly inaccurate), they knew how to make weapons, they knew the importance of secrecy, they knew the fear and hatred of human beings and how best to avoid them or triumph over them. They knew the Art of the Tongue.

Now, the Art of the Tongue, as we called it, was something we never thought of until the humans came. But it was essentially talking and reasoning with people, which we did with each other all the time. Now, basically we speak among ourselves much, much faster than humans, sometimes. Not always. Just sometimes. It sounds to humans like a whistling or a humming, or even a buzzing. But we can talk more in human rhythm, and we had learned how to speak to humans on their level, that is, to confuse them and entangle them in logic, to fascinate them and to influence them somewhat.

Obviously this Art of the Tongue wasn't saving us from extinction.

But it could save a lone Taltos discovered by a pair of humans in the forest, or a Taltos man taken prisoner by a small human clan with no ties to the warrior people who had invaded the land.

Anyone venturing out must know the Art of the Tongue, of speaking slowly to humans, on their level, and doing it in a convincing way. And inevitably some of those who left decided to settle outside.

They built their brochs, that is, our style of tower, of dry stone without mortar, and lived in wild and isolated places, passing for humans to those new peoples who happened to pass their home.

It was a sort of clan existence that developed defensively, and in scattered locales.

But inevitably these Taltos would reveal their nature to humans, or humans would war on them, or someone would learn of the magical Taltos birth, and again talk of us, talk of the glen, would circulate among hostile men.

I myself, having ever been inventive and forward-looking and refusing to give up, ever—even when the whole lost land was exploding, I did not give up—more or less thought ours was a lost cause. We could, for the present, defend the glen, that was true, when outsiders did occasionally break in on us, but we were essentially trapped!

But the question of those who passed for human, those who lived among human beings, pretending to be an old tribe or clan—that fascinated me. That got me to thinking . . . What if we were to do this? What if, instead of shutting human beings out, we slowly let them in, leading them to believe that we were a human tribe too, and we lived in their midst, keeping our birth rituals secret from them?

Meantime great changes in the outside world held a great fascination for us. We wanted to speak to travelers, to learn.

And so, finally, we devised a dangerous subterfuge . . .

Twenty-six

YURI Stefano here. Can I help you?"

"Can you help me! God, it's good to hear your voice," said Michael. "We've been separated less than forty-eight hours, but the Atlantic Ocean is between us!"

"Michael. Thank God you called me. I didn't know where to reach you. You're still with Ash, aren't you?"

"Yes, and we will be for another two days, I think. I'll tell you all about it, but how are things with you?"

"It's over, Michael. It's over. All the evil is gone, and the Talamasca is itself again. This morning I received my first communication from the Elders. We're taking serious measures to see that this sort of interception can never happen again. I have my work cut out for me, writing my reports. The new Superior General has recommended that I rest, but that's impossible."

"But you have to rest some of the time, Yuri. You know you do. We all do."

"I sleep for four hours. Then I get up. I think about what happened. I write. I write for maybe four, five hours. Then I sleep again. At mealtimes they come and get me. They make me go downstairs. It's nice. It's nice to be back with them. But what about you, Michael?"

"Yuri, I love this man. I love Ash the way I loved Aaron. I've been listening to him talk for hours. It's no secret, what he's telling us, of course, but he won't let us record any of it. He says that we should take away only what we naturally remember. Yuri, I don't think this man will ever hurt us or anyone connected with us. I'm sure of it. You know, it's one of those situations. I've put my trust in him. And if he does come to hurt us, for any reason, well, that's going to be what happens."

"I understand. And Rowan? How is she?"

"I think she loves him too. I know she does. But how much and in what way, well, that's her story. I never could speak for Rowan. We're going to stay here, as I said, for another two days, maybe more, then we have to go back down south. We're a little worried about Mona."

"Why?"

"It's nothing terrible. She's run off with her cousin Mary Jane Mayfair—this is a young woman you've not had the pleasure of meeting—and they're a bit too young to be running around without any parental supervision."

"Michael, I've written a letter to Mona. I had to write it. You know, before I left New Orleans, I pledged my heart to Mona. But Mona is too young for such a pledge, and now that I am home, back with the Order, I realize more than ever how unsuited I am to court Mona. I've sent my letter to the Amelia Street address, but I fear that Mona will, for a little while at least, be angry with me."

"Yuri, Mona has other things on her mind right now. This is probably the best decision you could have made. We forget that Mona is thirteen. Everybody forgets it. And certainly Mona forgets it. But you've done the right thing. Besides, she can contact you if she wants to, can't she?"

"Yes, I am here. I am safe. I am home."

"And Tessa?"

"Well, they took her away, Michael. That's the Talamasca for you. I'm sure that's what happened to her. She was surrounded by a very courtly group of companions and invited to go with them, probably to Amsterdam. I kissed her goodbye before she left. There was some talk of a nice place for her where she could rest, and where all her memories and stories would be recorded. No one seems to know how to calculate her age. No one knows if what Ash has said is true, that she will die soon."

"But she's happy, and the Talamasca has taken care of her."

"Yes, absolutely. Of course, if she ever wants to leave, she can leave. That's our way. But I don't think Tessa thinks in those terms. I think she drifted for years—how many years, no one knows—from one protector to another. She didn't grieve too long for Gordon, by the way. She says that she doesn't care to dwell on unpleasant things."

Michael laughed. "I understand. Believe me. Look, I've got to go back now. We're having some supper together, and then Ash is going to go on with his story. It's beautiful here where we are. Snowing and cold, but beautiful. Everything that surrounds Ash reflects his personality. It's always that way. The buildings we choose for ourselves, they're always reflections of us. This place is filled with colored marble and with paintings, and with . . . with things that interest him. I don't suppose I should talk about it much. He does want his privacy, to be left in peace after we leave him."

"I know. I understand. Listen, Michael, when you see Mona, you must tell her something for me . . . that . . . you must tell her that I . . ."

"She'll understand, Yuri. Mona has other things on her mind right now. It's an exciting time for her. The family wants her to leave Sacred Heart, to start studying with private tutors. Her IQ is off the charts, just as she always said it was. And she is the heir to the Mayfair legacy. I think for the next few years Mona will be spending a lot of time with Rowan and with me, studying, traveling, getting sort of the ideal education for a lady of what . . . how shall I say, great expectations. I'm going to go now. I'll call you again from New Orleans."

"Please do this, please. I love both of you. I love . . . the three of you. Will you tell the others for me, Ash and Rowan?"

"Yes. By the way, those cohorts, those helpers of Gordon?"

"It's all finished. They're gone, and they can never hurt the Order again. I'll talk to you soon, Michael."

"Goodbye, Yuri."

Twenty-seven

EVERYBODY always told him the Fontevrault Mayfairs were crazy. "That's why they come to you, Dr. Jack." Every single one of them was mad, said the town, even the rich kin in New Orleans.

But did he have to find it out for himself on an afternoon like this, when it was as dark as night, and half the streets in town were flooded out?

And bringing out a little newborn baby in such a storm, wrapped up in smelly little blankets and lying in a plastic ice chest, no less! And Mary Jane Mayfair expecting him just to make out the birth certificate right there in his office.

He'd demanded to see the mother!

Of course, if he'd known she was going to drive this limousine like this over these shell roads, right through this storm, and that he'd end up holding this baby in his arms, he would have insisted on following her in his pickup.

When she'd pointed to the limousine, he'd thought the woman had a driver. And this was a brand-new car, too, twenty-five feet long if it was a foot, with a moon roof and tinted glass, a compact disc player, and a goddamned telephone. And this teen Amazon queen at the wheel—in her dirty white lace dress, with mud spattered on her bare legs and her sandals.

"And you mean to tell me," he shouted over the rain, "that with a big car like this, you couldn't have brought this baby's mother to the hospital?"

The baby looked fine enough, thank God for that, about a month premature, he figured, and undernourished, of course! But otherwise okay and sleeping right now, deep in the ice chest with all the stinky little blankets around it, as he held the thing on his knees. Why, these blankets actually reeked of whiskey.

"Good heavens, Mary Jane Mayfair, slow down!" he said finally. The branches were making a racket on the top of the car. He flinched as the clumps of wet leaves slapped right against the windshield. He could hardly stand it, the way she ran right over the ruts! "You're going to wake the baby."

"That baby's just fine, Doctor," said Mary Jane, letting her skirt fall all the way back down her thighs to her panties. This was a notorious young woman, nobody had to tell him that. He'd been pretty damn sure this was her baby and she was going to make up some cock-and-bull story about its having been left on the doorstep. But no, there was a mother out there in those swamps, praise God. He was going to put this in his memoirs.

"We're almost there," Mary Jane called out, half smashing a thicket of bamboo on their left, and rolling right on past it. "Now, you got to carry the baby in the boat, all right, Doctor?"

"What boat!" he shouted. But he knew damn good and well what boat. Everybody had told him about this old house, that he ought to drive out to Fontevrault Landing just to see it. You could hardly believe it was standing, the way the west side had sunk, and to think this clan insisted upon living there! Mary Jane Mayfair had been slowly cleaning out the local Wal-Mart for the last six months, fixing the place up for herself and her grandmother. Everybody knew about it when Mary Jane came to town in her white shorts and T-shirts.

She was a pretty girl, though, he had to give her that much, even with that cowboy hat. She had the most high-slung and pointed pair of breasts he'd ever seen, and a mouth the color of bubble gum.

"Hey, you didn't give this baby whiskey to keep it quiet, did you?" he demanded. The little tucker was just snoring away, blowing a big bubble with its tiny little pink lips. Poor child, to grow up in this place. And she hadn't let him even examine this baby, saying Granny had done all that! Granny, indeed!

The limousine had come to a halt. The rain was teeming. He could scarcely see what looked like a house up ahead, and the great fan leaves of a green palmetto. But those were electric lights burning up there, thank God for that. Somebody'd told him they didn't have any lights out here.

"I'll come round for you with the umbrella," she said, slamming the door behind her before he could say they should wait till the rain slacked off, and then his door flew open and he had no choice but to pick up this ice chest like a cradle.

"Here, put the towel over it, little guy will get wet!" Mary Jane said. "Now run for the boat."

"I will walk, thank you," he said. "If you'll just kindly lead the way, Miss Mayfair!"

"Don't let him fall."

"I beg your pardon! I delivered babies in Picayune, Mississippi, for thirty-eight years before I ever came down to this godforsaken country."

And just why did I come? he thought to himself as he had a thousand times, especially when his new little wife, Eileen, born and raised in Napoleonville, wasn't around to remind him.

Lord in heaven, it was a great big heavy aluminum pirogue, and it didn't have a motor! But there was the house, all right, the entire thing the color of driftwood, with the purple wisteria completely wrapped around the capitals of those upstairs columns, and making its way for the balusters. At least the tangle of trees was so thick in this part of the jungle that he was almost dry for a moment. A tunnel of green went up to the tilting front porch. Lights on upstairs, well, that was a relief. If he had had to see his way around this place by kerosene lamp, he would have gone crazy. Maybe he was already going crazy, crossing this stretch of duckweed slop with this crazy young woman, and the place about to sink any minute.

"That's what's going to happen," Eileen had said. "One morning we'll drive by there, and there won't be any house, whole thing, lock, stock, and barrel, will have sunk into the swamp, you mark my words, it's a sin, anybody living like that."

Carrying the ice chest and its quiet little contents with one hand, he managed to get into the shallow boat, thrilled to discover that it was full of about two inches of water. "This is going to sink, you should have emptied it out." His shoes filled up to the ankles immediately. Why had he agreed to come out here? And Eileen would have to know every last detail.

"It's not going to sink, this is a sissy rain," said Mary Jane Mayfair, shoving on her long pole. "Now hang on, please, and don't let the baby get wet."

The girl was past all patience. Where he came from, nobody talked to a doctor like that! The baby was just fine under the towels, and pissing up a storm for a newborn.

Lo and behold, they were gliding right over the front porch of this dilapidated wreck and into the open doorway.

"My God, this is like a cave!" he declared. "How in the world did a woman give birth in this place? Will you look at that. There are books in there on the top shelf of that bookcase, right above the water."

"Well, nobody was here when the water came in," said Mary Jane, straining as she pushed on the pole.

He could hear the *thonk-thonk* of it hitting the floorboards beneath them.

"And I guess lots of things are still floating around in the parlor. Besides, Mona Mayfair didn't have her baby down here, she had it upstairs. Women don't have their babies in the front room, even if it isn't underwater."

The boat collided with the steps, tossing him violently to the left, so that he had to grab the slimy wet banister. He leapt out, immediately stamping both his feet to make sure the steps weren't going to sink under him.

A warm flood of light came from upstairs, and he could hear, over the hiss and roar of the rain, another sound, very fast, *clickety, clickety, clickety.* He knew that sound. And with it, a woman's voice humming. Kind of pretty.

"Why doesn't this stairway just float loose from the wall?" he asked. He started up, the ice-chest cradle beginning to feel like a sack of rocks to him. "Why doesn't this whole place just disintegrate?"

"Well, in a way, I guess it is," said Mary Jane, "only it's taking a couple hundred years, you know???" She went thumping up the steps in front of him, pushing right in his way as she hit the second-floor hall, and then turning around and saying, "You come with me, we got to go up to the attic."

But where was that *clickety, clickety, clickety* coming from? He could hear somebody humming, too. But she didn't even give him a chance to look around, rushing him to the attic steps.

And then he saw old Granny Mayfair at the very top in her flowered flannel gown, waving her little hand at him.

"Hey, there, Dr. Jack. How's my handsome boy? Come give me a kiss. Sure am glad to see you."

"Glad to see you too, Grandma," he said coming up, though Mary Jane once again shoved right past him, with the firm admonition that he was to hold tight to the baby. Four more steps and he'd be glad to set this bundle down. How come he was the one who'd wound up carrying it, anyway?

At last he reached the warm, dry air of the attic, the little old lady standing on tiptoe to press her lips to his cheeks. He did love Grandma Mayfair, he had to admit that much.

"How you doing, Grandma, you taking all your pills?" he asked.

Mary Jane picked up the ice chest as soon as he set it down, and ran off with it. This wasn't such a bad place, this attic; it was strung with electric lights, and clean clothes hanging on the lines with wooden clothespins. Lots of comfortable old furniture scattered around, and it didn't smell too much like mold; on the contrary, it smelled like flowers.

"What is that 'clickety-clickety' sound I'm hearing on the second floor down there?" he asked as Grandma Mayfair took his arm.

"You just come in here, Dr. Jack, and do what you got to do, and then you fill out that baby's birth certificate. We don't want any problems with the registration of this baby's birth, did I ever tell you about the problems when I didn't register Yancy Mayfair for two months after he was born, and you wouldn't believe the trouble I got into with the city hall and them telling me that . . ."

"And you delivered this little tyke, did you, Granny?" he asked, patting her hand. His nurses had warned him the first time she came in that it was best not to wait till she finished her stories, because she didn't. She'd been at his office the second day he opened up, saying none of the other doctors in this town were ever going to touch her again. Now that was a story!

"Sure did, Doctor."

"The mama's over there," said Mary Jane, pointing to the side gable of the attic, all draped in unbleached mosquito netting as if it were a tent with its peaked roof, and the distant glowing rectangle of the rain-flooded window at the end of it.

Almost pretty, the way it looked. There was an oil lamp burning inside, he could smell it, and see the warm glow in the smoky glass shade. The bed was big, piled with quilts and coverlets. It made him sad, suddenly, to think of his own grandmother years and years ago, and beds like that, so heavy with quilts you couldn't move your toes, and how warm it had been underneath on cold mornings in Carriere, Mississippi.

He lifted the long, thin veils and lowered his head just a little as he stepped under the spine of the gable. The cypress boards were bare here, and dark brownish red and clean. Not a leak anywhere, though the rainy window sent a wash of rippling light over everything.

The red-haired girl lay snug in the bed, half asleep, her eyes sunken and the skin around them frighteningly dark, her lips cracked as she took her breaths with obvious effort.

"This young woman should be in a hospital."

"She's worn out, Doctor, you would be too," said Mary Jane, with her smart tongue. "Why don't you get this over with, so she can get some rest now?"

At least the bed was clean, cleaner than that makeshift bassinet. The girl lay nestled in fresh sheets, and wearing a fancy white shirt trimmed in old-fashioned lace, with little pearl buttons. Her hair was just about the reddest he'd ever seen, and long and full and brushed out on the pillow. The baby's might be red like that someday, but right now it was a bit paler.

And speaking of the baby, it was making a sound at last in its little ice-chest bed, thank God. He was beginning to worry about it. Granny Mayfair snatched it up into her arms, and he could tell from the way she lifted it that the baby was in fine hands, though who wanted to think of a woman that age in charge of everything? Look at this girl in the bed. She wasn't even as old as Mary Jane.

He drew closer, went down with effort on his knees, since there was nothing else to do, and he laid his hand on the mother's forehead. Slowly her eyes opened, and surprised him with their deep green color. This was a child herself, should never have had a baby!

"You all right, honey?" he asked.

"Yes, Doctor," she said in a bright, clear voice. "Would you fill out the papers, please, for my baby?"

"You know perfectly well that you should—"

"Doctor, the baby's born," she said. She wasn't from around here. "I'm not bleeding anymore. I'm not going anywhere. As a matter of fact, I am fine, better than I expected."

The flesh beneath her fingernails was nice and pink. Her pulse was normal. Her breasts were huge. And there was a big jug of milk, only half drunk, by the bed. Well, that was good for her.

Intelligent girl, sure of herself, and well bred, he thought, not country.

"You two leave us alone now," he said to Mary Jane and the old woman, who hovered right at his shoulders like two giant angels, the little baby whining just a little, like it had just discovered again that it was alive and wasn't sure it liked it. "Go over there so I can examine this child, and make sure she's not hemorrhaging."

"Doctor, I took care of that child," said Granny gently. "Now do you think I would let her lie there if she was hemorrhaging?" But she went away, bouncing the baby in her arms, pretty vigorously, he thought, for a newborn.

He thought sure the little mother was going to put up a fuss, too, but she didn't.

There was nothing to do but hold this oil lamp himself, if he wanted to make sure everything was all right. This was hardly going to be a thorough examination.

She sat up against the pillows, her red hair mussed and tangled around her white face, and let him turn back the thick layer of covers. Everything nice and clean, he had to hand it to them. She was immaculate, as though she'd soaked in the tub, if such a thing was possible, and they had laid a layer of white towels beneath her. Hardly any discharge at all now. But she was the mother, all right. Badly bruised from the birth. Her white nightgown was spotless.

Why in the world didn't they clean up the little one like that, for God's sake? Three women, and they didn't want to play dolls enough to change that baby's blankets?

"Just lie back now, honey," he said to the mother. "The baby didn't tear you, I can see that, but it would have been a damned sight easier for you if it had. Next time, how about trying the hospital?"

"Sure, why not?" she said in a drowsy voice, and then gave him just a little bit of a laugh. "I'll be all right." Very ladylike. She'd never be a child again now, he thought, pint-sized though she was, and just wait till this story got around town, though he wasn't about to tell Eileen one word of it.

"I told you she was fine, didn't I?" asked Granny, pushing aside the netting now, the baby crying a little against her shoulder. The mother didn't even look at the baby.

Probably had enough of it for the moment, he thought. Probably resting while she could.

"All right, all right," he said, smoothing the cover back. "But if she starts to bleed, if she starts running a fever, you get her down into that limousine of yours and get her into Napoleonville! You go straight on in to the hospital."

"Sure thing, Dr. Jack, glad you could come," said Mary Jane. And she took his hand and led him out of the little tent enclosure, away from the bed.

"Thank you, Doctor," said the red-haired girl, softly. "Will you write it all out, please? The date of birth and all, and let them sign it as witnesses?"

"Got a wooden table for you to write on right here," said Mary Jane. She pointed to a small makeshift desk of two pine boards laid over two stacks of old wooden Coke bottle crates. It had been a long time since he'd seen Coke crates like that, the kind they used to use for the little bottles that used to cost a nickel. Figured she could probably sell them at a flea market these days to a collector. Lots of things around here she could sell. He spied the old gas sconce on the wall just above him.

It broke his back to lean over and write like this, but it wasn't worth complaining about. He took out his pen. Mary Jane reached up and tipped the naked light bulb towards him.

There came that sound from downstairs, *clickety-clickety-clickety*. And then a whirring sound. He knew those noises.

"What is that sound?" he asked. "Now let's see here, mother's name, please?"

"Mona Mayfair."

"Father's name?"

"Michael Curry."

"Lawfully wedded husband and wife."

"No. Just skip that sort of thing, would you?"

He shook his head. "Born last night, you said?"

"Ten minutes after two this morning. Delivered by Dolly Jean Mayfair and Mary Jane Mayfair. Fontevrault. You know how to spell it?"

He nodded. "Baby's name?"

"Morrigan Mayfair."

"Morrigan, never heard of the name Morrigan. That a saint's name, Morrigan?"

"Spell it for him, Mary Jane," the mother said, her voice very low, from inside the enclosure. "Two *r*'s, Doctor."

"I can spell it, honey," he said. He sang out the letters for her final approval.

"Now, I didn't get a weight . . ."

"Eight pounds nine ounces," said Granny, who was walking the baby back and forth, patting it as it lay on her shoulder. "I weighed it on the kitchen scale. Height, regular!"

He shook his head again. He quickly filled in the rest, made a hasty copy on the second form. What was the point of saying anything further to them?

A glimmer of lightning flashed in all the gables, north and south and east and west, and then left the big room in a cozy, shadowy darkness. The rain teemed softly on the roof.

"Okay, I'm leaving you this copy," he said, putting the certificate in Mary Jane's hand, "and I'm taking this one to mail it into the parish from my office. In a couple of weeks you'll get the official registration of your baby. Now, you should go ahead and try to nurse that child a little, you don't have any milk yet, but what you have is colostrum and that . . ."

"I told her all that, Dr. Jack," said Granny. "She'll nurse the baby soon as you leave, she's a shy little thing."

"Come on, Doctor," said Mary Jane, "I'll drive you back."

"Damn, I wish there was another way to get home from here," he said.

"Well, if I had a broom, we'd fly, now, wouldn't we?" asked Mary Jane, gesturing for him to come on as she started her thin-legged march to the stairway, loose sandals clopping on the boards.

The mother laughed softly to herself, a girl's giggle. She looked downright normal for a moment, with a bit of rosy color in her cheeks. Those breasts were about to burst. He hoped that baby wasn't a snooty little taster and lip-smacker. When you got right down to it, it was impossible to tell which of these young women was the prettiest.

He lifted the netting and stepped up again to the bed. The water was oozing out of his shoes, just look at it, but what could he do about it? It was running down the inside of his shirt, too.

"You feel all right, don't you, honey?" he asked.

"Yes, I do," she said. She had the jug of milk in her arms. She'd been drinking it in big gulps. Well, why not? But she sure as hell didn't need it. She threw him a bright schoolgirl smile, just about the brightest he'd ever seen, showing a row of white teeth, and just a sprinkle of freckles on her nose. Yes, pint-sized, but just about the prettiest redhead he'd ever laid eyes on.

"Come on, Doctor," Mary Jane positively shouted at him. "Mona's got to get her rest, and that baby's going to start yowling. 'Bye now, Morrigan, 'bye, Mona, 'bye, Granny."

Then Mary Jane was dragging him right through the attic, only stopping to slap on her cowboy hat, which she had apparently taken off when they'd come in. Water poured off the brim of it.

"Hush, now, hush," said Granny to the baby. "Mary Jane, you hurry now. This baby's getting fussy."

He was about to say they ought to put that baby in its mother's arms, but Mary Jane would have pushed him down the steps if he hadn't gone. She was all but chasing him, sticking her little breasts against his back. Breasts, breasts, breasts. Thank God his field was geriatrics, he could never have taken all this, teenage mothers in flimsy shirts, girls talking at you with both nipples, damned outrageous, that's what it was.

"Doctor, I'm going to pay you five hundred dollars for this visit," she said in his ear, touching it with her bubble-gum lips, "because I know what it means to come out on an afternoon like this, and you are such a nice, agreeable . . ."

"Yeah, and when will I see that money, Mary Jane Mayfair?" he asked, just cranky enough to speak his mind after all this. Girls her age. And just what was she likely to do if he turned around and decided to cop a feel of what was in that lace dress that she had just so obligingly mashed up against him? He ought to bill her for a new pair of shoes, he thought, just look at these shoes, and she could get those rich relatives in New Orleans to pay for it.

Oh, now wait a minute now. If that little girl upstairs was one of those rich Mayfairs come down here to—

"Now don't you worry about a thing," Mary Jane sang out, "you didn't deliver the package, you just signed for it."

"What are you talking about?"

"And now we have to get back in that boat!"

She hurried on to the head of the lower steps, and he sloshed and padded right behind her. Well, the house didn't tilt that much, he figured, once you were inside of it. *Clickety, clickety, clickety,* there it was again. Guess you could get used to a tilted house, but the very idea of living in a place that was half flooded was perfectly—

The lightning let go with a flash like midday, and the hall came to life, wallpaper, ceilings, and transoms above the doors, and the old chandelier dripping dead cords from two sockets.

That's what it was! A computer. He'd seen her in the split second of white light—in the back room—a very tall woman bent over the machine, fingers flying as she typed, hair red as the mother up in the bed, and twice as long, and a song coming from her as she worked, as if she was mumbling aloud whatever she was composing on the keyboard.

The darkness closed down around her and her glowing screen and a gooseneck lamp making a puddle of yellow light on her fluttering fingers.

Clickety, clickety, clickety!

Then the thunder went off with the loudest boom he'd ever heard, rattling every piece of glass left in the house. Mary Jane's hands flew to her ears. The tall young thing at the computer screamed and jumped up out of her chair, and the lights in the house went out, complete and entire, pitching them all into deep, dull afternoon gloom that might as well have been evening.

The tall beauty was screaming her head off. She was taller than he was!

"Shhhh, shhhh, Morrigan, stop!" shouted Mary Jane, running towards her. "It's just the lightning knocked out the power! It will go back on again!"

"But it's dead, it's gone dead!" the young girl cried, and then, turning, she looked down and saw Dr. Jack, and for one moment he thought he was losing his faculties. It was the mother's head he saw way up there on this girl's neck, same freckles, red hair, white teeth, green eyes. Good grief, like somebody had just pulled it right off the mother and plunked it down on this creature's neck, and look at the size of this beanpole! They couldn't be twins, these two. He himself was five foot ten, and this long, tall drink of water was at least a foot taller than that. She wasn't wearing anything but a big white shirt, just like the mother, and her soft white legs just went on forever and ever. Must have been sisters. Had to be.

"Whoa!" she said, staring down at him and then marching towards him, bare feet on the bare wood, though Mary Jane tried to stop her.

"Now you go back and sit down," said Mary Jane, "the lights will be on in a jiffy."

"You're a man," said the tall young woman, who was really a girl, no older than the pint-sized mother in the bed, or Mary Jane herself. She stood right in front of the doctor, scowling at him with red eyebrows, her green eyes bigger than those of the little one upstairs, with big curling lashes. "You are a man, aren't you?"

"I told you, this is the doctor," said Mary Jane, "come to fill out the birth certificate for the baby. Now, Dr. Jack, this is Morrigan, this is the baby's aunt, now Morrigan, this is Dr. Jack, sit down now, Morrigan! Let this doctor get about his business. Let's go, Doctor."

"Don't get so theatrical, Mary Jane," declared the beanpole girl, with a great spreading smile. She rubbed her long, silky-looking white hands together. Her voice sounded exactly like that of the little mother upstairs. Same well-bred voice. "You have to forgive me, Dr. Jack, my manners aren't what they should be yet, I'm still a little rough all over at the edges, trying to ingest a little more information, perhaps, than God ever intended for anyone of my ilk, but then we have so many different problems which we have to solve, for example, now that we have the birth certificate, we do have that, do we not, Mary Jane, that is what you were trying to make plain to me when I so rudely interrupted you, was it not, what about the baptism of this baby, for if memory serves me right, the legacy makes quite a point of the matter that the baby must be baptized Catholic. Indeed, it seems to me that in some of these documents which I've just accessed and only skimmed, that baptism is a more important point actually than legal registration."

"What *are* you talking about?" asked Dr. Jack. "And where in God's name did they vaccinate you, RCA Victor?"

She let out a pretty peal of laughter, clapping both of her hands together, very loudly, her red hair rippling and shaking out from her shoulders as she shook her head.

"Doctor, what are *you* talking about!" she said. "How old are you? You're a fairly good-sized man, aren't you, let me see, I estimate you are sixty-seven years old, am I right? May I see your glasses?"

She snatched them off his nose before he could protest, peering through them into his face. He was flabbergasted; he was also sixty-eight. She became a fragrant blur before his naked eyes.

"Oh, now this is major, really, look at this," she said. And quickly put the glasses back on the bridge of his nose with perfect aim, flaring into detail again, with plump little cheeks and a cupid's bow of a mouth just about as perfect as he'd ever seen. "Yes, it makes everything just a fraction bigger, doesn't it, and to think this is but one of the more common everyday inventions I'm likely to encounter within the first few hours of life, eyeglasses, spectacles, am I correct? Eyeglasses, microwave oven, clip-on earrings, telephone, NEC MultiSync 5D computer monitor. It would seem to me that later on, at a time of reflection on all that's taken place, one ought to be able to discern a certain poetry in the list of those objects which were encountered first, especially if we are right that nothing in life is purely random, that things only have the appearance from different vantage points of being random and that ultimately as we better calibrate all our tools of observation, we'll come to understand that even the inventions encountered on two stories of an abandoned and distressed house, do cluster together to form a statement about the occupants that is far more profound than anyone would suppose at first thought. What do *you* think!"

Now it was his turn to let out the peal of laughter. He slapped his leg. "Honey, I don't know what I think about that, but I sure do like the style with which you say it!" he declared. "What did you say your name was, you the one that baby's named after, Morrigan, don't tell me you're a Mayfair, too."

"Oh yes, sir, absolutely, Morrigan Mayfair!" she said, throwing up her arms like a cheerleader.

There was a glimmer, then a faint purring sound, and on came the lights, and the computer behind them in the room began to make its grinding, winding, start-up noises.

"Ooops, there we go!" she said, red hair flying about her shoulders. "Back on line with Mayfair and Mayfair, until such time as Mother Nature sees fit to humble all of us, regardless of how well we are equipped, configured, programmed, and installed. In other words, until lightning strikes again!"

She dashed to the chair before the desk, took up her place before the screen, and began typing again, just as if she'd completely forgotten he was standing there.

Granny shouted from upstairs, "Mary Jane, go on, this baby's hungry!"

Mary Jane pulled on his sleeve.

"Now wait just a minute," he said. But he had lost the amazing young woman, totally and completely, he realized that, just as he realized that she was purely naked under the white shirt, and that the light of her gooseneck lamp was shining right on her breast and her flat belly and her naked thighs. Didn't look like she had any panties on, either. And those long bare feet, what big bare feet. Was it safe to be typing on a computer in a lightning storm in your bare feet? Her red hair just flooded down to the seat of the chair.

Granny shouted from above.

"Mary Jane, you got to get this baby back by five o'clock!"

"I'm going, I'm going, Dr. Jack, come on!"

" 'Bye there, Dr. Jack!" shouted the beanpole beauty, suddenly waving at him with her right hand, which was at the end of an amazingly long arm, without even taking her eyes off the computer.

Mary Jane rushed past him and jumped in the boat. "You coming or not?" she said. "I'm pulling out, I got things to do, you want to be stuck here?"

"Get that baby *where* by five o'clock?" he demanded, coming to his senses, and thinking about what that old woman had just said. "You're not taking that baby out again to be baptized!"

"Hurry up, Mary Jane!"

"Anchors aweigh!" Mary Jane screamed, pushing the pole at the steps.

"Wait a minute!"

He took the leap, splashing into the pirogue as it rocked against the balusters and then the wall. "All right, all right. Just slow down, will you? Get me to the landing without dumping me into the swamp, would you do that, please?"

Clickety, clickety, clickety.

The rain had slacked up a bit, praise God. And a little bit of sun was even breaking through the heavy gray clouds just enough to shine on the drops!

"Now, here, Doctor, you take this," said Mary Jane, as he climbed into the car. It was a fat envelope just full of bills, and, he saw by the way she ruffled them with her thumb, all new twenties. He eyeballed that to be a thousand. She slammed the door and ran around to the other side.

"Now that's just too much money, Mary Jane," he said, but he was thinking Weed Eater, lawn mower, brand-new electric shrub clippers, *and* Sony color TV, and there wasn't a reason in the world to declare this on his taxes.

"Oh, shut up, you keep it!" she said. "Coming out on a day like this, you earned it." There went her skirt, back down to her thighs. But she couldn't hold a candle to that flaming darling upstairs, and what would it be like to get his hands on something like that, just for five minutes, something that young and that sleek and fresh and that beautiful, with those long long legs! Hush now, you old fool, you're going to give yourself a heart attack.

Mary Jane threw the car into reverse, wheels whirring in the wet shells of the road, and then made a dangerous one-hundred-eighty-degree turn and headed off over the familiar potholes.

He looked back at the house one more time, the big hulk of rotting columns and wood towering over the cypresses, with the duckweed muck lapping at its half-sunk windows, and then at the road ahead. Boy, he was glad to get out of here.

And when he got home and his little wife Eileen said, "What all did you see out there at Fontevrault, Jack?" what was he going to tell her? Not about the three prettiest young women he'd ever seen under one roof, that's for sure. And not about this wad of twenty-dollar bills in his pocket, either.

Twenty-eight

W^E INVENTED a human identity for ourselves.

We "became" an ancient tribe called the Picts, tall because we came from the northern countries where men grow tall, and we were eager to live in peace with those who would not disturb us.

Of course, we had to go about this very gradually. Word went out before we did. There was a waiting period at first, during which no strangers were admitted to the glen; then occasional travelers were let through, and from these we gleaned valuable knowledge. Then we ventured out, declaring ourselves to be the Picts and offering enlightened friendship to those whom we encountered.

Over time, in spite of the legend of the Taltos, which was always around, and gained some new impetus every time some poor Taltos was captured, we succeeded with this ruse. And our security improved not through battlements, but through our slow integration with human beings.

We were the proud and reclusive Clan of Donnelaith, but others would receive hospitality at our brochs. We did not speak of our gods much. We did not encourage questions about our private ways or our children.

But we lived as noblemen; we held the concepts of honor, and pride in our homeland.

It began to work rather beautifully. And with the doors of the glen open finally, new learning came to us for the first time directly from outside elements. We quickly learned to sew, to weave, and weaving proved a trap for the obsessive Taltos. Men, women, all of us would weave. We would weave for days and nights on end. We could not stop ourselves.

The only remedy was to pull away and turn to some other new craft and master it. Working with metals. We learned this. And though we never did more than forge a few coins and make arrowheads, we nevertheless went mad for a while with it.

Writing also had come to us. Other peoples had come to the shores of Britain, and unlike the uncouth warriors who had destroyed our world of the plain, these people wrote things on stone, on tablets, and on sheepskin especially worked by them to be permanent and beautiful to see and touch.

The writing on these stones, tablets, and scrolls of vellum was Greek and Latin! And we learnt it from our slaves as soon as the first marvelous connection between symbol and word was made. And then later from the traveling scholars who came into the valley.

Indeed, it became an obsession to many of us, myself in particular, and we read and wrote incessantly, translating our own tongue, which is far older than any in Britain, into written words. We made a script called Ogham, and it formed our secret writings. You can see this script on many a stone in the north of Scotland, but no one today can decipher it.

Our culture, the name we took, that of the Pictish people, and our art and our writing continue in modern times to be a complete mystery. You'll see the reason for that soon—for the loss of the Pict culture.

As a practical point, I wonder sometimes what became of those dictionaries which I so laboriously completed, working months on end without stopping except to collapse for a few hours of sleep or send out for food.

They were hidden away in the souterrains or earth houses which we built beneath the floor of the glen, the ultimate hiding place in case humans ever swept down on us again. Also hidden were many of the manuscripts in Greek and Latin from which I studied in those early days.

Another great trap for us, something which could entrance us, was mathematics, and some of the books that came into our possession were concerned with theorems of geometry which set us talking for days and days, and drawing triangles in the mud.

The point is that these were exciting times for us. The subterfuge gave us a perfect access to new developments. And though we had all the time to watch and chastise the foolish young Taltos that they weren't to confide in the newcomers or fall in love with their men and women, we generally came to know much of the Romans who had come into Britain, and to realize that these Romans had punished the Celtic barbarians who had inflicted such atrocities on us.

Indeed, these Romans put no faith in the local superstitions about the Taltos. They spoke of a civilized world, vast and full of great cities.

But we feared the Romans as well. For though they built magnificent buildings, the likes of which we'd never seen, they were more skilled at war than the others. We heard lots of stories of their victories. Indeed, they had refined the art of war and made it even more successful at destroying lives. We kept to the remote glen. We never wanted to meet them in battle.

More and more traders brought their books to us, their scrolls of vellum, and I read avidly their philosophers, their playwrights, their poets, their satirists, and their rhetoricians.

Of course, no one of us could grasp the actual quality of their lives, the ambience, to use the modern word, their national soul, their character. But we were learning. We knew now that all men were not barbarians. Indeed, this was the very word the Romans used for the tribes that were filling Britain from all sides, tribes which they had come here to subdue in the name of a mighty empire.

The Romans, by the way, never did reach our glen, though for two hundred years they campaigned in Britain. The Roman Tacitus wrote the story of Agricola's early campaign which reached Scotland. In the next century the Antonine Wall was built, a marvel to the barbarian tribes who resisted Rome, and very near it for forty-five miles the Military Way, a great road on which not only the soldiers passed, but traders bringing all manner of goods from the sea, and tantalizing evidence of other civilizations.

Finally the Roman Emperor himself, Septimus Severus, came to Britain to subdue the Scottish tribes, but even he never penetrated our strongholds.

For many years after that the Romans remained, providing much strange booty for our little nation.

By the time they withdrew from those lands, and gave them up to the barbarians at last, we were no longer really a hidden people. Hundreds of human beings had settled in our valley, paying homage to us as the lords, building their smaller brochs around our larger ones, and seeing us as a great, mysterious, but altogether human family of rulers.

It was not easy always to maintain this ruse. But nowhere was the life of the times more suited to it. Other clans were springing up in their remote strongholds. We were not a country of cities, but of small feudal holdings. Though our height and our refusal to intermarry were deemed unusual, we were in every other way completely acceptable.

Of course the key was never, never to let the outsiders see the birth ritual. And in this the Little People, needing our protection from time to time, became our sentries.

When we chose to make the circle amid the stones, all lesser clans of Donnelaith were told that our priests could only preside over our family rites in the strictest privacy.

And as we grew bolder, we let the others come, but only in far-reaching outer circles. Never could they see what the priests did in the very heart of the assembly. Never did they see the birth. They imagined it was only some vague worship of sky and sun and wind and moon and stars. And so they called us a family of magicians.

Of course, all this depended upon considerable peaceful cooperation with those who lived in the glen, and this remained stable for centuries.

In sum, we passed for people, in the midst of people. And other Taltos partook of our subterfuge, declaring themselves Picts, learning our writing and taking it, with our styles of building and ornament, to their strongholds. All Taltos who truly wanted to survive lived in this way, fooling human beings.

Only the wild Taltos continued to flash about in the forests, risking everything. But even they knew the Ogham script and our many symbols.

For example, if a lone Taltos lived in the forest, he might carve a symbol on a tree to let other Taltos know that he was there, a symbol without meaning for human beings. One Taltos seeing another in an inn might approach and offer him some gift, which was in fact a brooch or pin with our emblems.

A fine example of this is the bronze pin with a human face, discovered many centuries later by modern peoples in Sutherland. Humans do not realize, when they write about this pin, that it is a picture of an infant Taltos emerging from the womb, its head huge, its small arms still folded, though ready to unfold and grow, rather like the wings of a new butterfly.

Other symbols we carved into rock, at the mouths of caves or upon our sacred stones, represented fanciful conceptions of the animals of the lost land of tropical abundance. Others had purely personal meanings. Pictures of us as fierce warriors were deceptive, and skillfully made to actually show people meeting in peace, or so we imagined.

The art of the Picts is the common name given to all of this. And that tribe has become the great mystery of Britain.

What was our worst fear? The worst threat, so to speak? Enough time had passed that we did not fear human beings who really knew anything about us. But the Little People knew and the Little People longed to breed with us, and though they needed us, to protect them, they still occasionally caused us trouble.

But the true threats to our peace came from witches. Witches— those singular humans who caught our scents, and could somehow breed with us, or were the descendants of those who had bred with us. For the witches—who were always very rare, of course—passed on, from mother to daughter and father to son, the legends of our kind, and the lovely, mad notion that if they could ever couple with us, they could make monsters of size and beauty who might never die. And other fanciful propositions inevitably grew up around this idea—that if they drank the blood of the Taltos, the witches could become immortal. That if they killed us, with the proper words and the proper curses, they could take our power.

And the most awful aspect of all this, the only real, true part of it, was that the witches could often tell on sight we were not mere tall humans, but real Taltos.

We kept them out of the glen. And when traveling abroad, we took great pains to avoid the village witch, or the sorcerer who lived in the wood. But they of course had reason to fear us too, for we too knew them infallibly on sight and, being very clever and very rich, we could make plenty of trouble for them.

But when a witch was about, it was a dangerous game. And all that was required to make it worse was one clever or ambitious witch determined to find the true Taltos of the Highlands among the tall clans that dwelt there.

And now and then there was the worst challenge, a powerful spellbinding witch capable of luring Taltos out of their dwellings, of wrapping them up in charms and music, and drawing them to her rituals.

Occasionally there would be talk of a Taltos found elsewhere. There would be talk of hybrid births; there would be whispers of witches and Little People and magic.

By and large, we were safe in our strongholds.

The glen of Donnelaith was now known to the world. And as the other tribes squabbled with one another, our valley was left in peace, not because people feared that monsters dwelt there, but only because it was the stronghold of respectable noblemen.

It was in those years a grand life, but a life with a lie at its core. And many a young Taltos could not endure it. Off he would go into the world, and never return. And sometimes hybrid Taltos came to us who knew nothing of who or what had made them.

Very gradually, over time, a rather foolish thing happened. Some of us even intermarried with human beings.

It would happen in this way. One of our men would go on a long pilgrimage, perhaps, and come upon a lone witch in a dark wood with whom he fell in love, a witch who could bear his offspring without difficulty. He would love this witch; she would love him; and being a ragged poor creature, she would throw herself upon his mercy. He would bring her home; she might at some point in the distant future bear him another child before she died. And some of these hybrids married other hybrids.

Sometimes, too, a beautiful female Taltos would fall in love with a human man, and forsake everything for him. They might be together for years before she would bear, but then a hybrid would be born, and this would unite the little family even more closely, for the father saw his likeness in the child, and laid claim to its loyalty, and it of course was a Taltos.

So that is how the human blood in us was increased. And how our blood came into the human Clan of Donnelaith that eventually survived us.

Let me pass over in silence the sadness we often felt, the emotions we evinced at our secret rituals. Let me not try to describe our long conversations, pondering the meaning of this world, and why we had to live among humans. You are both outcasts now. You know it. And if God is merciful and you really don't, well, then, you can still imagine it.

What is left of the glen today?

Where are the countless brochs and wheelhouses which we built? Where are our stones with their curious writing and strange serpentine figures? What became of the Pictish rulers of that time, who sat so tall on their horses, and impressed the Romans so much with their gentle manner?

As you know, what is left at Donnelaith is this: a quaint inn, a ruined castle, an immense excavation that is slowly revealing a giant cathedral, tales of witchcraft and woe, of earls who died untimely deaths, and of a strange family, gone through Europe to America, carrying with them an evil strain in the blood, a potential to give birth to babies or monsters, an evil strain evidenced by the glow of witches' gifts, a family wooed for that blood and those gifts by Lasher—a wily and unforgiving ghost of one of *our* people.

How were the Picts of Donnelaith destroyed? Why did they fall as surely as the people of the lost land and the people of the plain? What happened to them?

It was not the Britons, the Angles, or the Scots who conquered us. It was not the Saxons or the Irish, or the German tribes who invaded the island. They were far too busy destroying each other.

On the contrary, we were destroyed by men as gentle as ourselves, with rules as strict as our own, and dreams as lovely as our dreams. The leader they followed, the god they worshipped, the savior in whom they believed was the Lord Jesus Christ. He was our undoing.

It was Christ himself who brought an end to five hundred years of prosperity. It was his gentle Irish monks who brought about our downfall.

Can you see how it might happen?

Can you see how vulnerable we were, we, who in the solitude of our stone towers would play at weaving and writing like little children, who would hum or sing all day long for the love of it? We, who believed in love and in the Good God, and refused to hold death sacrosanct?

What was the pure message of the early Christians? Of both the Roman monks and the Celtic monks who came to our shores to preach the new religion? What is the pure message, even today, of those cults which would consecrate themselves anew to Christ and his teachings?

Love, the very thing we believed in!

Forgiveness, the very thing we thought practical. Humility, the virtue we believed, even in our pride, to be far more noble than the raging hubris of those who warred endlessly upon others. Goodness of heart, kindness, the joy of the just—our old values. And what did the Christians condemn? The flesh, the very thing that had always been our downfall! The sins of the flesh, which had caused us to become monsters in the eyes of humans, copulating in great ceremonial circles and bringing forth full-grown offspring.

Oh, we were ripe for it. Oh, it was made for us!

And the trick, the sublime trick, was that at its core Christianity not only embraced all this, but managed somehow to sacralize death and at the same time redeem that sacralization.

Follow my logic. Christ's death had not come in battle, the death of the warrior with the sword in his hand; it had been a humble sacrifice, an execution which could not be avenged, a total surrender on the part of the Godman to save his human children! But it was death, and it was everything!

Oh, it was magnificent! No other religion could have had a chance with us. We detested pantheons of barbarian gods. We laughed at the gods of the Greeks and Romans. The gods of Sumer or India we would have found just as alien and distasteful. But this Christ, why, my God, he was the ideal of every Taltos!

And though he had not sprung full-grown from his mother's womb, he had nevertheless been born of a virgin, which was just as miraculous! Indeed, the birth of Christ was just as important as his submissive crucifixion! It was our way, it was the triumph of our way! It was the God to whom we could give ourselves without reservation!

Lastly, let me add the *pièce de résistance.* These Christians, too, had been once hunted and persecuted and threatened with annihilation. Diocletian, the Roman emperor, had subjected them to these things. And refugees came seeking shelter in our glen. We gave it to them.

And the Christians won our hearts. When we spoke to them, we came to believe that possibly the world was changing. We believed that a new age had dawned and that our elevation and restoration were now at least conceivable.

The final seduction was simple.

A lone monk came into the glen for refuge. He had been chased thither by ragged wandering pagans and begged shelter. Of course we would never refuse such a person, and I brought him into my own broch and into my own chambers, to pick his brains about the outside world, as I hadn't ventured out in a while.

This was the mid-sixth century after Christ, though I didn't know it. If you would picture us then, see men and women in long, rather simple robes trimmed in fur, embroidered with gold and jewels; see the men with their hair trimmed above the shoulders. Their belts are thick, and their swords are always near at hand. The women cover their hair with silk veils beneath simple gold tiaras. See our towers very bare, yet warm and snug, and filled with skins and comfortable chairs, and raging fires to keep us warm. See us as tall, of course, all of us tall.

And see me in my broch alone with this little yellow-haired monk in brown robes, eagerly accepting the good wine I offered him.

He carried with him a great bundle which he was eager to preserve, he said, and first off, he begged me that I give him a guard to escort him home to the island of Iona in safety.

There had been three in his party originally, but brigands had murdered the other two, and now he was wretchedly alone, dependent upon the goodwill of others, and must get his precious bundle to Iona, or lose something more valuable than his own life.

I promised to see that he reached Iona safely. Then he introduced himself as Brother Ninian, named for the earlier saint, Bishop Ninian, who had converted many pagans at his chapel or monastery, or whatever it was, at Whittern. This bishop had already converted a few wild Taltos.

Young Ninian, a very personable and beautiful Irish Celt, then laid out his invaluable bundle and revealed its contents.

Now, I had seen many books in my time, Roman scrolls and the codex, which was now the popular form. I knew Latin. I knew Greek. I had even seen some very small books called *cathachs* which Christians wore as talismans when they rode into battle. I had been intrigued by the few fragments of Christian writing I had beheld, but I was in no way prepared for the treasure which Ninian revealed to me.

It was a magnificent altar book that he carried with him, a great illustrated and decorated account of the Four Gospels. Its front cover was decorated with gold and jewels, it was bound in silk, and its pages were painted with spectacular little pictures.

At once I fell on this book and virtually devoured it. I began to read the Latin aloud, and though there were some irregularities in it, in the main I understood it, and began to run with the story like someone possessed—nothing very extraordinary, of course, for a Taltos. It felt like singing.

But as I turned the vellum pages, I marveled not only at the tale which was being told to me, but also at the incredible drawings of fanciful beasts and of little figures. It was an art which I loved truly, from having done my own similar form of it.

Indeed, it was very like much art of that time in the islands. Later ages would say it was crude, but then come to love the complexity and ingenuity of it.

Now, to understand the effect of the gospels themselves, you have to remind yourself of how very different they were from any literature which had come before them. I don't include the Torah of the Hebrews, because I didn't know it, but the gospels are even different from that.

They were different from everything! First off, they concerned this one man, Jesus, and how he had taught love and peace and been hounded, persecuted, tormented, and then crucified. A confounding story! I couldn't help but wonder what the Greeks and the Romans thought of it. And the man had been a humble person, with only the most tenuous of connections to ancient kings, that was obvious. Unlike any god of whom I'd ever heard, this Jesus had told his followers all sorts of things which they had been charged to write down and teach to all nations.

To be born again in spirit was the essence of the religion. To become simple, humble, meek, loving, that was the gist of it.

Now step back a moment and see the whole picture. Not only was this god amazing and this story amazing; the whole question of the relationship of the tale to writing was amazing.

As you can tell from this narrative, the one thing we had once shared with our barbarian neighbors was that we distrusted writing. Memory was sacred to us, and we thought that writing was not good for it. We knew how to read and write. But we still distrusted it. And here was this humble god who quoted from the sacred book of the Hebrews, connected himself with its innumerable prophecies concerning a messiah, and then charged his followers to *write about him.*

But long before I'd finished the last gospel, pacing, reading aloud, holding the big altar book in two arms, with fingers curled over the tops of the pages, I came to love this Jesus for the strange things that he said, the way he contradicted himself, and his patience with those who killed him. As for his resurrection, my first conclusion was that he was as long-lived as were we—the Taltos. And that he had put one over on his followers because they were mere humans.

We had to do such tricks all the time, to assume different identities when speaking to human neighbors, so that they would become confused and fail to realize that we were living for centuries.

But I soon realized through Ninian's zealous instructions—and he was a joyful and ecstatic monk—that Christ had in fact risen from the dead. And truly ascended into heaven.

I saw in something of a mystical flash the whole picture—this god of love, martyred for love, and the radical nature of his message. In a mad way, the thing gripped me because it was so utterly unbelievable. Indeed, the entire combination of elements was cumbersome and preposterous.

And another fact—all Christians believed the world would end soon. And apparently—this emerged slowly from my conversations with Ninian—they always had! But preparing for this end of the world was also the essence of the religion. And the fact that the world hadn't ended yet discouraged nobody.

Ninian spoke feverishly of the growth of the church since Christ's time, some five hundred years before, of how Joseph of Arimathea, his dear friend, and Mary Magdalene, who had bathed his feet and dried them with her own hair, had come to England in the southern part, and founded a church on a sacred hill in Somerset. The chalice from Christ's last supper had been brought to that spot, and indeed a great spring flowed blood-red year-round from the magical presence of Christ's blood having been poured into it. And the staff of Joseph, having been put into the ground of Wearyall Hill, had grown into a hawthorn which had never ceased to flower.

I wanted to go there at once, to see the sacred place where Our Lord's own disciples had set foot on our own island.

"Oh, but please," cried Ninian, "my good-hearted Ashlar, you've promised to take me home to my monastery on Iona."

There the abbot, Father Columba, was expecting him. Many books such as this were being made in monasteries all over the world, and this copy was most important for study at Iona.

I had to meet this Columba. He sounded as strange as Jesus Christ! Perhaps you know the story. Michael, probably you know it.

This is how Ninian described Columba. Columba was born of a rich family, and might have in the scheme of things become King of Tara. Instead he became a priest and founded many Christian monasteries. But then he got into a battle with Finnian, another holy man, over whether or not he, Columba, had had a right to make a copy of the Psalter of St. Jerome, another holy book, which Finnian had brought to Ireland. A quarrel over the possession of the book? The right to copy?

It had led to blows. Three thousand men had died as a result of this dispute, and Columba had been blamed for it. He had accepted this judgment, and off he had gone to Iona, very near our coast, in order to convert *us,* the Picts, to Christianity. It was his plan to save three thousand pagan souls to exactly make up for the three thousand men who had died as the result of his quarrel.

I forget who got the copy of the Psalter.

But Columba was now at Iona and, from there, was sending missionaries everywhere. Beautiful books such as this were being made in these Christian compounds, and all were invited into this new faith. Indeed, Christ's church was for the salvation of everyone!

And it soon became clear that though Columba and many missionary priests and monks like him had been kings or persons of royal blood, the rule of the monasteries was extraordinarily severe, demanding constant mortification of the flesh and self-sacrifice.

For example, if a monk spilled milk while helping to serve at community meals, he must go into the chapel during the singing of Psalms and lie on his face, prostrate, until twelve of them had been completely finished. Monks were beaten when they broke their vows of silence. Yet nothing could restrain the rich and powerful of the earth from flocking into these monasteries.

I was dumbfounded. How could a priest who believed in Christ get into a war in which three thousand died! Why would the sons of kings submit to being lashed for common offenses? But, ah, it had a simple potency to it, a captivating logic.

I set out with Ninian and two of my recent sons to go to Iona. Of course we kept up our masquerade as human beings. Ninian thought we were human beings.

But as soon as I arrived at Iona, I became further spellbound by the monastery itself and the personality of Columba.

It was a magnificent island, forested and green, with splendid views from its cliffs, where the openness and cleanness of the sea brought peace to the soul immediately.

In fact, a wondrous calm descended upon me. It was as if I had found again the lost land, only now the dominant themes were penance and austerity. But the harmony was there, the faith in the sheer goodness of existence.

Now the monastery was Celtic, and not at all like the Benedictine monasteries which later covered Europe. It was made of a great circular enclosure—the vallum, as it was called—which suggested a fort, and the monks lived in small, simple huts, some no more than ten feet wide inside. The church itself was not grand, but a humble wooden structure.

But never was a complex of buildings more in keeping with its natural setting. It was a place to listen quietly to the birds, to walk, to think, to pray, to talk with the enchanting and friendly and truly gracious Columba. This man had royal blood; I had long been a king. Ours was the north country of Ireland and Scotland; we knew each other; and something in me touched the saint as well—the sincerity of the Taltos, the foolish way of coming directly to the point, an easy outpouring of enthusiasm.

Columba soon convinced me that the harsh monastic life and the mortification of the flesh were the keys to the love which Christianity demanded of a man. This love was not a sensual thing. This love was spiritually elevated beyond expression through the body.

He longed to convert my entire tribe, or my clan. He longed to see me an ordained priest among my people.

"But you don't know what you're saying," I said. And then, binding him under the seal of the confessional—that is, to eternal confidentiality—I told him the tale of my long life, of our secret and miraculous way of giving birth, of how it seemed that many of us seemed capable of living an endless life of eternal youth, unless accident or disaster or some specific pestilence destroyed us.

Some things I did not tell. I did not tell that I had once been the leader of the great circle dances at Stonehenge.

But all the rest I told, even of the lost land, and how we had lived in our glen for so many hundreds of years, passing from secrecy to a masquerade as human beings.

All this he listened to with great fascination. Then he said an amazing thing. "Can you prove these things to me?"

I realized that I could not. The only way any Taltos can prove he is a Taltos is by coupling with another and producing the offspring.

"No," I said, "but look well at us. Look at our height."

This he dismissed; there were tall men in the world. "People have for years known of your clan; you are King Ashlar of Donnelaith, and they know you are a good ruler. If you believe these things about yourself, it is because the devil has put them into your imagination. Forget them. Proceed to do what God wants you to do."

"Ask Ninian, the whole tribe is of this height."

But he'd heard of that, very tall Picts in the Highlands. It seems my own ruse was working!

"Ashlar," he said, "I've no doubt of your goodness. Once again, I counsel you to disregard these illusions as coming from the devil."

Finally I agreed, for one reason. I felt that it made no difference whether he believed me or not about my past. What mattered was that he had recognized a soul in me.

Michael, you know that this was a great point in Lasher's tale—that, alive in the time of Henry, he wanted to believe that he had a soul, that he would not accept that he could not be a priest of God the same as a human.

I know this awful dilemma. All who are outsiders in their own way know it. Whether we talk of legitimacy, of a soul, of citizenship, or of brotherhood or sisterhood, it is all the same, we long to be seen as true individuals, as inherently valuable inside as any other.

This I longed for too, and I made the terrible error of accepting Columba's advice. I forgot what I knew to be true.

There on Iona, I was received into the Christian faith. I was baptized, and so were my sons. Another baptism was to follow, but for me and my sons it was only ceremonial. On that island, removed from the mists of the Highlands, we became Christian Taltos.

I spent many days at the monastery. I read all the books that were in it; I was charmed by the pictures, and very soon took to making copies of them. With official permission, of course. I copied a psalter, then a gospel, amazing the monks with my typical Taltos obsessive behavior. I drew strange beasts in brilliant colors by the hour. I made the priests laugh sometimes with bits of poetry I copied out. I pleased them with my good Greek and Latin.

What community had ever been more like the Taltos? Monk children is what they seemed, surrendering the entire concept of sophisticated adulthood to serve the abbot as their lord, and thereby serve their Lord Himself, the Crucified Christ who had died for them.

These were happy, happy days.

Gradually I began to see what many a heathen prince had come to see in Christianity: absolute redemption of everything! All my suffering made sense in light of the woes of the world and Christ's mission to save us from sin. All the disasters I'd witnessed had done nothing but improve my soul and school it for this moment. My monstrousness, indeed the monstrousness of all the Taltos, would be accepted by this church, surely, for all were welcome into it, regardless of race, it was an utterly open faith, and we could submit as well as any human being to the baptism of water and the spirit, to the vows of poverty, chastity, obedience.

The stringent rules, which bound even laymen to purity and restraint, would help us to control our terrible urge to procreate, our terrible weaknesses for dance and for music. And the music we would not lose; we would, within the constraints of the monastic life—which for me at this point was synonymous with the Christian life—sing our greatest and most joyful songs ever!

In sum, if this church accepted us, if it embraced us, all our past and future sufferings would have meaning. Our true loving nature would be allowed to flower. No subterfuge would be required any longer. The church would not let the old rituals be forced upon us. And those who dreaded the birthing now, as I did, out of age and experience and seeing so many young die, could consecrate themselves to God in chastity.

It was perfect!

At once, with a small escort of monks, I returned to the glen of Donnelaith and drew all my people together. We must pledge our allegiance to Christ, I told them, and I told them why, in long rippling speeches, not too fast for my human companions to understand, talking passionately of the peace and harmony that would be restored to us.

I also spoke of the Christian belief in the end of the world. Very soon all this horror would be over! And then I spoke of heaven, which I imagined to be like the lost land, except that no one would want to make love, everyone would be singing with the choirs of angels.

We must all now confess our sins and prepare to be baptized. For a thousand years I had been the leader, and all must follow me. What greater guidance could I give my people?

I stood back at the end of this speech. The monks were overcome with emotion. So were the hundreds of Taltos gathered in the glen around me.

At once began the heated discussions for which we were known—all in the human Art of the Tongue—the endless debates and telling of little tales and relating of this to that, and drawing memories into it where they seemed to pertain, and beneath it all the great theme: we could embrace Christ. He was the Good God! He was our God. The souls of the others were as open to Christ as was my soul.

A great many at once declared their faith. Others spent the afternoon, the evening, and the night examining the books I'd brought back, arguing somewhat about the things they'd heard, and there were some very fretful whispers about its being contrary to our nature to be chaste, absolutely contrary, and that we could never live with marriage.

Meantime I went out to the human beings of Donnelaith and preached this great conversion to them as well, and the monks followed me. We called all the clans of the valley together.

And in our great gathering ground, amid the stones, hundreds declared their desire to come to Christ, and indeed, some of the humans confessed they had already converted, maintaining it as a secret for their own protection.

I was very struck by this, particularly when I found that some human families had been Christian for three generations. "How very like us you are," I thought, "but you don't know it."

It seemed then that all were on the verge of conversion. En masse, we begged the priests to begin the baptisms and the blessings.

But one of the great women of our tribe, Janet, as we had come to call her, a name very current then, raised her voice to speak out against me.

Janet too had been born in the lost land, which she mentioned now quite openly before the human beings. Of course they didn't know what she meant. But we did. And she reminded me that she had no white streaks in her hair, either. In other words, we were wise and young, both of us, the perfect combination.

I had had one son by Janet, and truly loved her. I had spent many, many nights at play in her bed, not daring to have coitus, of course, but nursing from her rounded little breasts, and exchanging all kinds of other clever embraces that gave us exquisite pleasure.

I loved Janet. But there had never been any doubt in my mind that Janet was fierce in her own beliefs.

Now she stepped forth and condemned the new religion as a pack of lies. She pointed out all its weaknesses in terms of logic and consistency. She laughed at it. She told many stories which made Christians look like braggarts and idiots. The story of the gospel she declared unintelligible.

The tribe was immediately split. So loud was the talk that I could not even tell how many were for Janet's point of view or against it. Violent verbal quarrels ensued. Once again we undertook our marathon debates, which no human being could watch without realizing our differences.

The monks withdrew to our sacred circle. There they consecrated the earth to Christ, and prayed for us. They did not fully understand yet how different we were, but they knew we were not like other people.

At last a great schism occurred. One third of the Taltos refused utterly to be converted, and threatened battle with the others if we tried to make the glen a haven of Christianity. Some evinced a great fear of Christianity and the strife it would cause among others. Others simply did not like it, and wanted to keep to our own ways and not live in austerity and penance.

The majority wanted to convert, and we did not wish to give up our homes—that is, to leave the glen and go elsewhere. To me, such a possibility was unthinkable. I was the ruler here.

And like many a pagan king, I expected my people to follow me absolutely in my conversion.

The verbal battles progressed to physical pushing and shoving and threats, and I saw within an hour that the entire future of the valley was threatened.

But the end of the world was coming. Christ had known this and come to prepare us. The enemies of Christ's church were the enemies of Christ!

Bloody skirmishes were being fought in the grasslands of the glen. Fires broke out.

Accusations were flung out. Humans who had always seemed loyal suddenly turned on Taltos and accused them of wretched perversity, of having no lawful marriage, no visible children, and of being wicked magicians.

Others declared that they had long suspected the Taltos of evil things, and now was the time to have it out. Where did we keep our young? Why did no one ever see any children among us?

A few crazed individuals, for reasons of their own, shouted the truth. A human who had mothered two Taltos pointed at her Taltos husband and told all the world what he was, and that if we were to sleep with human women we would soon annihilate them.

The frenzied zealots, of whom I was the most outspoken one, declared that these things no longer mattered. We, the Taltos, had been welcomed into the church by Christ and Father Columba. We would give up the old licentious habits, we would live as Christ would have us live.

There followed more confusion. Blows were struck. Screams rang out.

Now I saw how three thousand people could die in an argument over the right to copy a book! Now I perceived everything.

But too late. The battle had already commenced. All rushed to their brochs to take up arms and to defend their positions. Armed men poured out of doors, attacking their neighbors.

The horror of war, the horror I had sought to hide from all these years in Donnelaith, was now upon us. It had come through my conversion.

I stood confounded, my sword in my hand, hardly knowing what to make of it. But the monks came to me. "Ashlar, lead them to Christ," they said, and I became as many a zealot king before me. I led my converts against their brothers and sisters.

But the real horror was yet to come.

When the battle was over, the Christians still stood in the majority, and I saw, though it did not register very clearly yet, that most of them were human. The majority of the Taltos elite, never very numerous anyway, thanks to our rigid control, had been slaughtered. And only a band of some *fifty of us* remained, the oldest, the wisest, in some ways the most dedicated, and we were all still convinced of our conversion.

But what were we to do with the few humans and Taltos who had not come over to us, who had not been killed only because the killing had stopped before everyone was dead? Now gathered from the battlefield, wounded, limping, these rebels, with Janet as their leader, cursed us. They would not be driven from the glen, they declared, they would die where they stood in opposition to us.

"You, Ashlar, look at what you've done," Janet declared. "Look, everywhere on the bodies of your brothers and sisters, men and women who have lived since the time before the circles! You have brought about their death!"

But no sooner had she laid on me this terrible judgment than the zealous human converts began to demand: "How could you have lived since the time before the circles? What were you, if you were not human beings?"

At last one of the boldest of these men, one who had been a secret Christian for years, came up and slit open my robe with his sword, and I, baffled as Taltos often are by violence, found myself standing naked in the circle.

I saw the reason. They would see what we were, if our tall bodies were the bodies of men. Well, let them see, I announced. I stepped out of the fallen robe. I laid my hand upon my testicles in the ancient fashion, to swear an oath—that is, testify—and I swore that I would serve Christ as well as any human.

But the tide had turned. The other Christian Taltos were losing their nerve. The sight of the slaughter had been appalling to them. They had begun to weep, and to forget the Art of the Tongue, and to talk in the high, rapid speech of our kind, which quickly terrified the humans.

I raised my voice, demanding silence, and demanding allegiance. I had put back on my slashed robe, for all that it mattered. And I walked back and forth in the circle, angry, using the Art of the Tongue as well as I'd ever used it.

What would Christ say to us on account of what we had done? What was the crime here, that we were a strange tribe? Or that we had murdered our own in this dispute? I wept with great gestures and tore my hair, and the others wept with me.

But the monks were now filled with fear, and the human Christians were filled with fear. What they had suspected all their lives in the glen was almost revealed to them. Once again the questions flew. Our children, where were they?

At last another Taltos male, whom I greatly loved, stepped forward and declared that from this moment forth he was, in the name of Christ and Virgin, celibate. Other Taltos made the same pledge, women and men both.

"Whatever we were," the Taltos women declared, "does not matter now, for we will become the Brides of Christ and make our own monastery here in the spirit of Iona."

Great cries rang out, of joy and agreement, and those humans who had always loved us, who loved me as their king, rallied quickly around us.

But the danger hung in the air. At any moment the bloody swords might clash again, and I knew it.

"Quickly, all of you, pledge yourselves to Christ," I declared, seeing in this Taltos vow of celibacy our only chance for survival.

Janet cried out for me to cease with this unnatural and evil plan. And then, in a great volley of words, rushing sometimes too fast and sometimes too slow, she spoke of our ways, of our offspring, our sensuous rites, our long history, everything that I was now prepared to sacrifice.

It was the fatal mistake.

At once the human converts descended upon her and bound her hand and foot, as those who sought to defend her were cut down. Some of the converted Taltos tried to flee, and they were immediately cut down, and another vicious battle broke out, in which cottages and huts were set aflame and people ran hither and thither in panic, screaming for God to help us. "Kill all the monsters," was the cry.

One of the monks declared it was the end of the world. Several of the Taltos did also. They dropped to their knees. Humans, seeing those Taltos in that submissive posture, at once killed those whom they did not know, or feared or disliked, sparing only those few who were beloved of everyone.

Only I and a handful were left—those who had been most active in the leadership of the tribe, and had magnetic personalities. We fought off the few who had the stamina to attack us, subduing others with mere ferocious looks or vociferous condemnations.

And at last—when the frenzy had peaked, and men fell under the burden of their swords, and others screamed and wept over the slain, only five of us remained—Taltos dedicated to the Christ—and all those who would not accept Christ, except for Janet, had been annhilated.

The monks called for order.

"Speak to your people, Ashlar. Speak or all is lost. There will be no Donnelaith, and you know it."

"Yes, speak," said the other Taltos, "and say nothing that will frighten anyone. Be clever, Ashlar."

I was weeping so hard this task seemed utterly beyond me. Everywhere I looked I saw the dead, hundreds born since the circle of the plain, dead and gone now, into eternity, and perhaps into the flames of hell without Christ's mercy.

I fell to my knees. I wept until I had no more tears, and when I stopped, the valley was still.

"You are our king," said the human beings. "Tell us that you are no devil, Ashlar, and we will believe you."

The other Taltos with me were desperately afraid. Their fate hung now with mine. But they were those most known to the human population and most revered. We did have a chance, that is, if I did not despair and seal the fate of all of us.

But what was left of my people? What? And what had I brought into my valley?

The monks came close. "Ashlar, God tries those whom He loves," they said. And they meant it. Their eyes were filled with sadness too. "God tests those whom he would make saints," they said, and heedless of what others might think of our monstrousness, our sinfulness, they threw their arms around me, and stood firm against the rest, risking their own safety.

Now Janet, held tight by her captors, spoke:

"Ashlar, you are the betrayer of your people. You have brought death to your own in the name of a foreign god. You have destroyed the Clan of Donnelaith, which has lived in this glen since time immemorial."

"Stop the witch!" someone cried.

"Burn her," said another. And another and another.

And even as she continued to speak, there was whispering, and those going to prepare a stake in the stone circle.

All this I saw from the corner of my eye, and so did she, and still she kept her courage.

"I curse you, Ashlar. I curse you in the eyes of the Good God."

I couldn't speak, and yet I knew that I had to. I had to speak to save myself, the monks, my followers. I had to speak if I was to stop the death of Janet.

Wood had been dragged to the stake. Coal was being thrown down. Humans, some of whom had always feared Janet and every female Taltos whom they could not have, had brought torches.

"Speak," whispered Ninian beside me. "For Christ, Ashlar."

I closed my eyes, I prayed, I made the Sign of the Cross, and then I made my plea to all to listen.

"I see before me a chalice," I declared, speaking softly but loud enough for all to hear. "I see the Chalice of Christ's blood which Joseph of Arimathea brought to England. I see the blood of Christ emptied into the Well; I see the water run red, and I know its meaning.

"The blood of Christ is our sacrament and our nourishment. It shall forever replace the cursed milk we sought from our women in lust; it shall be our new sustenance and our portion.

"And in this awful slaughter today, may Christ receive our first great act of self-sacrifice. For we loathe this killing. We loathe it and we always have. And we do it only to the enemies of Christ, that His kingdom may come on earth, that he may rule forever."

It was the Art of the Tongue as best I knew it, and it was said with eloquence and tears, and it left the entire mob of human and Taltos alike cheering and praising Christ and throwing their swords to the ground and tearing off their finery, their bracelets, their rings, and declaring themselves to be born again.

And at that moment, as they had come from my lips, I knew these words were lies. This religion was a deceiving thing, and the body and blood of Christ could kill as surely as poison.

But we were saved, we who stood there exposed as monsters. The crowd no longer wanted our death. We were safe—all except for Janet.

They dragged her now to the stake, and though I protested, weeping and begging, the priests said no, that Janet must die, that she might die as a lesson to all those who would refuse Christ.

The fire was lighted.

I threw myself to the ground. I couldn't bear it. Then, leaping up, I ran at the slowly gathering blaze, only to be pulled back and held against my will.

"Ashlar, your people need you!"

"Ashlar, set an example!"

Janet fixed her eyes on me. The fire licked at her rose-colored gown, at her long yellow hair. She blinked to clear her eyes of the rising smoke, and then she cried out to me:

"Cursed, Ashlar, cursed for all time. May death elude you forever. May you wander—loveless, childless—your people gone, until our miraculous birth is your only dream in your isolation. I curse you, Ashlar. May the world around you crumble before your suffering is ended."

The flames leapt up, obscuring her fair face, and a low roar came from the rapidly burning timbers. And then came her voice again, louder, full of agony and full of courage.

"A curse on Donnelaith, a curse on its people forever! A curse on the Clan of Donnelaith. A curse on Ashlar's people."

Something writhed within the flames. I did not know if it was Janet in her final pain, or some trick of light and shadow and flickering.

I had fallen to my knees. I couldn't stop the tears and I couldn't look away. It was as if I had to go as far as I could with her into her pain, and I prayed to Christ, "She knows not what she says, take her to heaven. For her kindnesses to others, for her goodness to her people, take her to heaven."

The flames leapt heavenward, and then at once began to die away, revealing the stake, the smoldering heap of wood and burnt flesh and bone that had been this gracious creature, older and wiser than I was.

The glen was still. Nothing remained of my people now but five males who vowed to be celibate Christians.

Lives that had existed for centuries had been snuffed out. Torn limbs, severed heads, and mutilated bodies lay everywhere.

The human Christians wept. We wept.

A curse on Donnelaith, she had said. A curse. But, Janet, my darling Janet, I prayed, what more can happen to us!

I collapsed on the ground.

At that moment I wanted no more of life. I wanted no more of suffering or death, or of the best of intentions resulting in abominable ruin.

But the monks came to me, lifting me to my feet. My followers called to me. I was to come, they said, to behold a miracle that had happened before the ruined and burnt-out tower that had once been the home of Janet and those closest to her.

Dragged there, dazed, unable to speak, I was gradually made to understand that an old spring, long dried, had come to life, clear water bubbling up from the earth once again, and cutting its path through the old dried bed, between hillocks and the roots of the trees and into a great drift of wildflowers.

A miracle!

A miracle. I pondered. Should I point out that that stream had come and gone a number of times in the century? That the flowers were blooming yesterday and the day before because the earth there was already damp, presaging the little fount which had now at last broken through the surface again?

Or should I say:

"A miracle."

I said, "A sign from God."

"Kneel, all," cried Ninian. "Bathe in this holy water. Bathe away the blood of those who wouldn't accept God's grace and have gone now to eternal perdition."

Janet burning in hell forever, the pyre that will never go out, the voice that will curse me still crying . . .

I shuddered and all but fainted again, but I fell on my knees.

In my soul, I knew that this new faith must sweep me up, it must consume my whole life, or I was lost forever!

I had no more hope, no more dreams; I had no more words, and no more thirst for anything! This had to save me, or I should die in this very spot now, by sheer will, never speaking or moving or taking nourishment again until death stole over me.

I felt the cold water slapped against my face. I felt it running down into my robes. The others had gathered. They too were bathing. The monks had begun to sing the ethereal psalms which I had heard on Iona. My people, the humans of Donnelaith crying and sad, and eager for the same grand redemption, took up the song, in the old-fashioned way, singing the lines right after the monks, until voices everywhere were raised in praise of God.

We were all baptized in the Name of the Father, and of the Son, and of the Holy Ghost.

The Clan of Donnelaith was Christian thereafter. All human save for five Taltos.

Before the following morning a few more Taltos were discovered, mostly very young women who had been shielding two almost new-born males in their house, from which they had seen the whole tragedy, including Janet's execution. They were six altogether.

The Christian humans brought them to me. They would not speak, either to accept or deny Christ, but looked at me in terror. What should we do?

"Let them go, if they will," I said. "Let them flee the valley."

No one had the stomach for any more blood or death. And their youth and their simplicity and their innocence made a shield around them. As soon as the new converts stepped back, these Taltos fled, with nothing but the clothes on their backs, right into the forest.

In the days that followed, we five males who were left did win the entire goodwill of the people. In the fervor of their new religion, they praised us that we had brought Christ to them, and honored us for our vows of celibacy. The monks prepared us with instructions day and night to accept Holy Orders. We pored over our holy books. We prayed constantly.

Work was begun upon the church, a mighty Roman-style building of dry stone, with rounded arch windows and a long nave.

And I myself led a procession through the old circle, at which we effaced any symbols from olden times, and carved into the rocks new emblems, from the Altar Book of the Gospels.

These were the fish, which stood for Christ, the dove, which stood for the Apostle John, the lion for Mark, the ox for Luke, and the man for Matthew. And in a little Taltos fury we carved other biblical scenes into the flatter stones, and moved into the cemetery, putting crosses upon the old graves, in the style of the crosses of the book, very ornate and ornamented.

It was a brief interlude in which something returned of the old fervor that had once taken hold of all of us on the Salisbury Plain. But we were only five now, and not an entire tribe, five who had renounced their own nature to please God and the human Christians, five who had been cast in the role of saints in order not to be massacred.

But a dark terror lurked inside me and in the others. How long would this uneasy truce last? Would not the slightest sin topple us from our pedestals?

Even as I prayed to God to help me, to forgive me for all my errors, to bind me to him as a good priest, I knew that we five could not remain in Donnelaith much longer.

And I could not endure it myself! Even at my prayers, and during the singing of psalms with the monks, I heard Janet's curse in my ears, I saw my people covered in blood. Christ, give me faith, I prayed, yet in my secret heart I did not believe that the only path for my kind was one of such renunciation and chastity. How could it be? Did God mean for us to die out?

This was not self-sacrifice, it was a form of utter denial. For Christ, we had become no one!

Yet the love of Christ burned hot in me. It burned desperately. And a very strong personal sense of my Savior developed in me as it has in Christians always. Night after night in my meditations I envisioned the Chalice of Christ, the holy hill on which Joseph's hawthorn bloomed, the blood in the water of Chalice Well. I made a vow to go in pilgrimage to Glastonbury.

There were rumblings from outside the glen. Men had heard of the Holy Battle of Donnelaith, as it had come to be called. They had heard of the tall celibate priests with strange powers. Monks had written to other monks, passing on the story.

The legends of the Taltos came alive. Others who had lived as Picts in small communities had now to flee their homes as their pagan neighbors taunted and threatened them, and as Christians came to plead with them to renounce their wicked ways and become "holy fathers."

Wild Taltos were found in the forest; there were rumors of the magic birth having been witnessed in this or that town. And the witches were on the prowl, boasting that they could make us reveal ourselves, and render us powerless.

Other Taltos, richly dressed and armed to the teeth, and now exposed for what they were, came in heavily defended groups to the glen and cursed me for what I had done.

Their women, beautifully clothed, and guarded on all sides, spoke of Janet's curse, having heard whispers of this, no doubt from the

Taltos who had fled Donnelaith, and demanded that I repeat the curse to all, and hear their judgments.

I refused. I said nothing.

Then, to my horror, these Taltos repeated the entire curse to me, for indeed they already knew it.

"Cursed, Ashlar, cursed for all time. May death elude you forever. May you wander—loveless, childless—your people gone, until our miraculous birth is your only dream in your isolation . . . May the world around you crumble before your suffering is ended."

It had become a poem to them which they could recite, and they spat at my feet when they were finished.

"Ashlar, how could you forget the lost land?" the women demanded. "How could you forget the circle of Salisbury Plain?"

These brave few walked amid the ruins of the old brochs; the human Christians of Donnelaith looked on them with cold eyes and fear, and sighed with relief when they took their final leave of the valley.

Over the months that followed, some Taltos came who had accepted Christ and wanted to become priests. We welcomed them.

All over northern Britain, the quiet time for my people had ended.

The race of the Picts was fast disappearing. Those who knew the Ogham script wrote terrible curses on me, or they carved into walls and stones their newfound Christian beliefs with fervor.

An exposed Taltos might save himself by becoming a priest or a monk, a transformation which not only appeased the populace but greatly exhilarated it. Villages wanted a Taltos priest; Christians of other tribes begged for a celibate Taltos to come and say the special Mass for them. But any Taltos who did not play this game, who did not renounce his pagan ways, who did not claim the protection of God, was fair game for anyone.

Meantime, in a great ceremony, some five of us, and four who had come later, accepted Holy Orders. Two female Taltos who had come into the glen became nuns in our community, and dedicated themselves to caring for the weak and the sick. I was made Father Abbot of the monks of Donnelaith, with authority over the glen and even the surrounding communities.

Our fame grew.

There were times when we had to barricade ourselves in our new monastery to escape the pilgrims who came "to see what a Taltos was" and to lay hands on us. Word got around that we could "cure" and "work miracles."

Day after day, I was urged by my flock to go to the sacred spring, and bless the pilgrims there who had come to drink the holy water.

Janet's broch had been torn down. The stones from her home, and what metal could be melted down from her plate and few bracelets and rings, were put into the building of the new church. And a cross was erected at the holy stream, inscribed with Latin words to celebrate the burning of Janet and the subsequent miracle.

I could barely look at this. Is this charity? Is this love? But it was more than plain that for the enemies of Christ, justice could be as bitter as God chose to make it.

But was all this God's plan?

My people destroyed, our remnants turned into sacred animals? I pleaded with our monks from Iona to discourage all these beliefs! "We are not a magical priesthood!" I declared. "These people are on the verge of declaring that we have magical powers!"

But to my utter horror the monks said that it was God's will.

"Don't you see, Ashlar?" said Ninian. "This is why God preserved your people, for this special priesthood."

But all that I had envisioned had been laid waste. The Taltos had not been redeemed, they had not discovered a way to live on the earth at peace with men.

The church began to grow in fame, the Christian community became enormous. And I feared the whims of those who worshiped us.

At last I set aside each day an hour or two when my door was locked and no one might speak to me. And in the privacy of my cell, I began a great illustrated book, using all the skill I had acquired from my teacher on Iona.

Done in the style of the Four Gospels, it was to be, complete with golden letters on every page, and tiny pictures to illustrate it, the story of my people.

My book.

It was the book which Stuart Gordon found in the crypts of the Talamasca.

For Father Columba, I wrote every word, lavishing on it my greatest gift for verse, for song, for prayer, as I described the lost land, our wanderings to the southern plain, the building of our great Stonehenge. In Latin, I told all I knew of our struggles in the world of men, of how we'd suffered and learned to survive, and how at last my tribe and clan had come to this—five priests amid a sea of humans, worshiped for powers we did not possess, exiles without a name, a nation, or a god of our own, struggling to beg salvation from the god of a people who feared us.

"Read my words here, Father," I wrote, "you who would not listen to them when I tried to speak them. See them here inscribed in the language of Jerome, of Augustine, of Pope Gregory. And know that I tell the truth and long to enter God's church as what I truly am. For how else will I ever enter the Kingdom of Heaven?"

Finally my task was complete.

I sat back, staring at the cover to which I myself had affixed the jewels, at the binding which I myself had fashioned from silk, at letters which I myself had written.

At once I sent for Father Ninian, and laid the book before him. I sat very still as Ninian examined the work.

I was too proud of what I'd done, too certain now that somehow our history would find some redeeming context in the vast libraries of church doctrine and history. "Whatever else happens," I thought, "I have told the truth. I have told how it was, and what Janet chose to die for."

Nothing could have prepared me for the expression on Ninian's face when he closed the volume.

For a long moment he said nothing, and then he began to laugh and laugh.

"Ashlar," he said, "have you lost your mind, that you would expect me to take this to Father Columba!"

I was stunned. In a small voice I said, "I've given it all my effort."

"Ashlar," he said, "this is the finest book of its kind I've ever beheld; the illustrations are perfectly executed, the text written in flawless Latin, replete with a hundred touching phrases. It is inconceivable that a man could have created this thing in less than three to four years, in the solitude of the scriptorium at Iona, and to think that you have done it here within the space of a year is nothing short of miraculous."

"Yes?"

"But the contents, Ashlar! This is blasphemy. In the Latin of Scripture, and in the style of an Altar Book, you have written mad pagan verses and tales full of lust and monstrousness! Ashlar, this is the proper form for Gospels of the Lord, and psalters! Whatever possessed you to write your frivolous stories of magic in this manner?"

"So that Father Columba would see these words and realize they were true!" I declared.

But I had already seen his point. My defense meant nothing.

Then, seeing me so crushed, he sat back and folded his hands and looked at me.

"From the first day I came into your house," he said, "I knew your simplicity and your goodness. Only you could have made such a foolish blunder. Put it aside; put your entire history aside once and for all! Devote your extraordinary talent to the proper subjects."

For a day and a night I thought on it.

Wrapping my book carefully, I gave it again to Ninian.

"I am your abbot here at Donnelaith," I said, "by solemn appointment. Well, this is the last order I shall ever give you. Take this book to Father Columba as I've told you. And tell him for me that I have chosen to go away on a pilgrimage. I don't know how long I will be gone, or where. As you can see from this book, my life has already spanned many lifetimes. I may never lay eyes on him again, or on you, but I must go. I must see the world. And whether I shall ever return to this place or to Our Lord, only He knows."

Ninian tried to protest. But I was adamant. He knew that he had to make a journey home to Iona soon anyway, and so he gave in to me, warning me that I did not have Columba's permission to go away, but realizing that I did not care about this.

At last he set out with the book, and a strong guard of some five human beings.

I never saw that book again until Stuart Gordon laid it out on the table in his tower at Somerset.

Whether it ever reached Iona I don't know.

My suspicion is that it did, and it may have remained at Iona for many years, until all those who knew what it was, or knew who'd written it or why it was there, were long gone.

I was never to know whether Father Columba read it or not. The very night after Ninian went on his way, I resolved to leave Donnelaith forever.

I called the Taltos priests together into the church and bade them lock the doors. The humans could think what they liked, and indeed this did make them naturally restless and suspicious.

I told my priests that I was leaving.

I told them that I was afraid.

"I do not know if I have done right. I believe, but I do not know," I said. "And I fear the human beings around us. I fear that any moment they might turn on us. Should a storm come, should a plague sweep through the land, should a terrible illness strike the children of the more powerful families—any of these disasters could provoke a rebellion against us.

"These are not our people! And I have been a fool to believe that we could ever live in peace with them.

"Each of you, do what you will, but my advice to you as Ashlar, your leader since the time we left the lost land, is go away from here. Seek absolution at some distant monastery, where your nature is not known, and ask permission to practice your vows in peace there. But leave this valley.

"I myself shall go on a pilgrimage. First to Glastonbury, to the well there where Joseph of Arimathea poured the blood of Christ into the water. I will pray there for guidance. Then I will go to Rome, and then perhaps, I do not know, to Constantinople to see the holy icons there which are said to contain the very face of our Christ by magic. And then to Jerusalem to see the mountain where Christ died for us. I herewith renounce my vow of obedience to Father Columba."

There was a great outcry, and much weeping, but I stood firm. It was a very characteristic Taltos way of ending things.

"If I am wrong, may Christ lead me back to his fold. May he forgive me. Or . . . may I go to hell," I said with a shrug. "I'm leaving."

I went to prepare for my journey . . .

BEFORE these parting words to my flock, I had taken all of my personal possessions out of my tower, including all my books, my writings, my letters from Father Columba, and everything of any importance to me, and I had hidden these in two of the souterrains I had built centuries ago. Then I took the last of my fine clothes, having given up all else for vestments and for the church, and I dressed in a green wool tunic, long and thick and trimmed in black fur, and put around it my only remaining girdle of fine leather and gold, strapped on my broadsword with its jeweled scabbard, placed on my head an old hood of fur, and a bronze helmet of venerable age. And thus garbed as a nobleman, a poor one perhaps, I rode out, with my possessions in a small sack, to leave the glen.

This was nothing as ornate and heavy as my kingly raiment had been, and nothing as humble as a priest's robes. Merely good clothing for travel.

I rode for perhaps an hour through the forest, following old trails known only to those who had hunted here.

Up and up I went along the heavily wooded slopes towards a secret pass that led to the high road.

It was late afternoon, but I knew I would reach the road before nightfall. There would be a full moon, and I meant to travel until I was too tired to go further.

It was dark in these dense woods, so dark, I think, that people of this day and age cannot quite imagine it. This was a time before the great forests of Britain had been destroyed, and the trees here were thick and ancient.

It was our belief that these trees were the only living things that were older than us in the whole world—for nothing we had ever beheld lived as long as trees or Taltos. We loved the forest and we had never feared it.

But I had not been in the darkest forest for very long when I heard the voices of the Little People.

I heard their hisses and whispers and laughter.

Samuel had not been born in that time, so he was not there, but Aiken Drumm and others alive today were among these that called, "Ashlar, the fool of the Christians, you've betrayed your people." Or, "Ashlar, come with us, make a new race of giants and we shall rule the world," and other such things. Aiken Drumm I have always hated. He was very young then, and his face was not so gnarled that one couldn't see his eyes. And as he rushed through the undergrowth, shaking his fist at me, his face was full of malevolence.

"Ashlar, you leave the glen now after destroying everything! May Janet's curse be upon you!"

Finally they all fell back and away for a simple reason. I was coming close to a cave on the mountainside, about which I had—for simple reasons—entirely forgotten.

Without even thinking, I'd chosen the path that ancient tribes had taken to worship there. In the time when the Taltos lived on the Salisbury Plain, these tribes had filled this cave with skulls, and later peoples revered it as a place of dark worship.

In recent centuries the peasants had sworn that a door was open inside this cave by which one might hear the voices of hell, or the singing of heaven.

Spirits had been seen in the nearby wood, and witches sometimes braved our wrath to come here. Though there had been times when we rode up the hills in fearsome bands to drive them out, we had not in the last two hundred years much bothered with them.

I myself had only been up this way a couple of times in all my life, but I had no fear of the cave at all. And when I saw that the Little People were afraid, I was relieved to be rid of them.

However, as my horse followed the old trail closer and closer to the cave, I saw flickering lights playing in the thick darkness. I came to see there was a crude dwelling in the mountainside, made out of a cave itself perhaps, and covered over with stones, leaving only a small door and a window, and a hole higher up through which the smoke passed.

The light flickered through the cracks and crevices of the crude wall.

And there, many feet above, was the path to the great cave, a yawning mouth altogether hidden now by pine and oak and yew trees.

I wanted to keep clear of the little house as soon as I saw it. Anyone who would live in the vicinity of this cave had to be trouble.

The cave itself vaguely intrigued me. Believing in Christ, though I had disobeyed my abbot, I did not fear pagan gods. I did not believe in them. But I was leaving my home. I might not ever come back. And I wondered if I should not visit the cave, perhaps even rest there a while, hidden, and safe from the Little People.

Twenty-nine

N ow listen to me, both of you," she said without taking her eyes off the road. "This is the point where I am going to take over. I've thought this over since I was born, and I know exactly what we need to do. Is Granny asleep back there?"

"Sound asleep," said Mary Jane from the jump seat, where she was stretched out sideways, so she could see Morrigan behind the wheel.

"What do you mean," asked Mona, "that you are going to take over?"

"Just exactly this," said Morrigan, both her hands together at the top of the wheel, gripping it easily on account of the fact that they had been going ninety miles an hour for quite some time now, and no cop, obviously, was going to stop them. "I've been listening to you argue and argue, and you're stuck on things that are utterly beside the point, sort of moral technicalities."

Morrigan's hair was tangled and falling all over her shoulders and her arms, a brighter red, as far as Mona could tell, but in the same family as her own hair. And the uncanny resemblance between their faces was enough to completely unnerve Mona if she let herself stare too long at Morrigan. As for the voice, well, the big danger was obvious. Morrigan could pretend to be Mona on the phone. She had done it with ease when Uncle Ryan had finally called Fontevrault. What a hilarious conversation that had been! Ryan had asked "Mona" very tactfully if she was taking amphetamines, and reminded her gently that anything ingested might hurt the baby. But the point was, Uncle Ryan had never guessed that the fast-talking and inquisitive female on the other end of the line was not Mona.

They were all dressed in their Easter Sunday best, as Mary Jane had called it earlier, including Morrigan, whom they had outfitted in the fashionable shops of Napoleonville. The white cotton shirtwaist dress would have been ankle length on Mona or even Mary Jane. On Morrigan it came to the knee; the waist was cinched really tight, and the plain V neck, the symbol of matronly good sense, became against her fairly well-developed breasts a plunging neckline. It was the old story; put a plain, simple dress on a flamboyantly beautiful girl, and it becomes more eye-catching than gold foil or sable. Shoes had been no problem, once they had faced that she was a size ten. One size larger and they would have had to put her in men's lace-ups. As it was, she had stiletto heels and had danced around the car in them for fifteen minutes, before Mona and Mary Jane had laid firm hands on her, told her to shut up, don't move, and get in. Then she had demanded to drive. Well, it wasn't the first time . . .

Granny, in Wal-Mart's best cotton knit pantsuit, slept beneath her baby-blue thermal blanket. The sky was blue, the clouds magnificently white. Mona wasn't sick anymore at all, thank God, just weak. Dismally weak.

They were now one half hour from New Orleans.

"Like what moral technicality?" asked Mary Jane. "This is a question of safety, you know, and what do you mean, 'take over'?"

"Well, I'm talking about something inevitable," said Morrigan, "but let me break it to you in stages."

Mona laughed.

"Ah, you see, Mother is smart enough to know, of course, to see the future as a witch might, I suppose, but you, Mary Jane, persist in being a cross between a disapproving aunt and the devil's advocate."

"You sure you know the meaning of all those words?"

"My dear, I have imbibed the entire contents of two dictionaries. I know all the words my mother knew before I was born, and a great many my father knew. How else would I know what a socket wrench is, and why the trunk of this car contains an entire set of them?

"Now back to the crisis of the moment: Where do we go, which house? And all of that nonsense?"

Immediately she answered her own questions.

"Well, my thinking is that whose house we go to is not all that fired important. Amelia Street would be a bad idea, simply because it is loaded with other people, as you have thrice described, and though it may be Mother's house in a sense, it truly belongs to Ancient Evelyn. Fontevrault is too far away. We are not going back, I don't care what happens! An apartment is a hideout which I cannot, in my anticipatory anxiety, abide! I will not choose some small impersonal lodgings obtained under false pretenses. I cannot live in boxes. First Street does belong to Michael and Rowan, that's true, but Michael is my father! What we need is at First Street. I need Mona's computer, her records, the papers Lasher scribbled out, any notes my father has made in his copy of the famous Talamasca file, everything which is presently in that house, and to which Mona has acknowledged access. Well, not Lasher's scribblings, but again, that is a technicality. I claim the rights of breed to take those notes. And I do not have a single scruple about reading Michael's diary if I do find it. Now don't start screaming, both of you!"

"Well, just slow down for one thing!" shouted Mary Jane. "And I get a creepy feeling in my bones from the way you say those words, 'take over.'"

"And let's think this out a little further," said Mona.

"You have reminded each other enough in my presence that the name of the game is survival," Morrigan replied. "I need this knowledge—diaries, files, records—for survival. And First Street is empty now, we know that, and we can make our preparations in peace for Michael and Rowan's homecoming. So I will make the decision here and now that that is where we go, at least until Michael and Rowan have returned and we have apprised them of the situation. If my father then wishes to banish me from the house, we seek an appropriate dwelling, or put into operation Mother's plan to obtain funds for the complete restoration of Fontevrault. Now, do you have all this in your memories?"

"There are guns in that house," said Mary Jane, "she has told you that. Guns upstairs, downstairs. These people are going to be scared of you. This is their house. They're going to start screaming! Don't you understand? They think that Taltos are evil beings, evil! Trying to take over the world!"

"I am a Mayfair!" declared Morrigan. "I am the daughter of my father and my mother. And the hell with guns. They are not going to aim a gun at me. That's perfectly absurd, and you are forgetting that they are not expecting me to be there at all, and will be utterly unprepared when you search them for guns, as if they would be carrying guns at all, and furthermore you will be there, both of you, to protect me, and speak for me, and to issue dire warnings that they are not to harm me, and please remember for more than five consecutive minutes at a stretch that I have a tongue in my mouth with which to protect myself, that nothing in this situation is analogous to any that existed before, and that it is best to settle in there, where I can examine everything I should examine, including this famous Victrola, and the backyard—there you go, stop screaming, both of you!"

"Just don't dig up the bodies!" Mona cried.

"Right, leave those bodies under the tree!" declared Mary Jane.

"Absolutely, I will. I shall. I told you. No digging up bodies. Bad, bad idea. Morrigan is sorry. Morrigan won't do it. Morrigan has promised Mona and Mary Jane. No time for bodies! Besides, what are these bodies to me?" Morrigan shook her head, making her red hair tumble and tangle and then giving it a vigorous and determined toss. "I am the child of Michael Curry and Mona Mayfair. And that is what matters, isn't it?"

"We're scared, that's all!" Mary Jane declared. "Now, if we turn around right now, and we go back to Fontevrault—"

"No. Not without the appropriate pumps, scaffolding, jacks, and lumber to straighten out that house. I shall have a sentimental attachment to it all of my life, of course, but at this time I simply cannot remain there! I am dying to see the world, don't both of you understand, the world is not Wal-Mart and Napoleonville and the latest issues of *Time*, *Newsweek*, and *The New Yorker*. I cannot remain waiting any longer. Besides, for all you know, they are home now, Rowan and Michael, and I am for an immediate confrontation. No doubt they will make the records available to me, even if in their secret hearts they have opted for extermination."

"They're not home," said Mona. "Ryan said two more days."

"Well, then, what are you all so afraid about?"

"I don't know," cried Mona.

"Then First Street it is, and I don't want to hear another word about it. There is a guest room, is there not? I'll stay in there. And I want all this squabbling to stop. We can then obtain a secure home base of our own at our leisure. Besides, I want to see this house, I want to see the house the witches built. Do not either of you understand the degree to which my being and my fate are connected to this house, this house designed to perpetuate the line with the giant helix? Why, if we strip away most of the clouding sentiment, it is perfectly obvious that Stella, Antha, and Deirdre died so that I might have life, and the bumbling literalist dreams of this evil spirit, Lasher, have resulted in an incarnation he could never foresee, but which is now my destiny. I am tenacious of life, I am tenacious of position!"

"Okay," Mona said, "but you have to be quiet, and you have to not speak to the guards, and you cannot answer the phone again!"

"Yeah, the way you grab for a phone when it rings," said Mary Jane, "any phone at all, is just downright loco."

Morrigan gave a shrug. "What you fail to realize is that each day achieves for me an enormous series of developments. I am not the girl I was two days ago!" She flinched suddenly, and gave a little groan.

"What's the matter, what's wrong?" asked Mona.

"The memories, the way they come. Mother, turn on the tape recorder, will you? You know, it's the strangest thing, the way some of them fade, and some of them don't and it's as if they are memories from lots and lots of people, people like me, I mean. I see Ashlar through everybody's eyes . . . The glen is the same glen in the Talamasca file, I know it. Donnelaith. I can hear Ashlar say it."

"Speak loud," said Mary Jane, "so I can hear you."

"This is about the stones again, we're not in the glen yet, we're near the river, and the men are dragging the stones out onto the rolling logs. I tell you that there are no accidents in this world, nature is sufficiently random and lush for things to happen almost inevitably. This may not make sense at first, but what I am saying is this—that out of all the chaos and pain of resistant and defiant witches has come the moment when this family must become a family of humans and Taltos. The strangest feelings come over me. I have to go there, to see that place. And the glen. The circle is smaller, but it's ours too, Ashlar has consecrated both circles, and the stars overhead are in the winter configuration. Ashlar wants the dark woods to shelter us, to lie between us and the hostile world. I am tired. Sleepy."

"Don't let go of the wheel," said Mary Jane. "Describe this man, Ashlar, again. Is he always the same, I mean, in both circles and both times?"

"I think I'm going to cry. I keep hearing the music. We have to dance when we get there."

"Where?"

"First Street, anywhere. The glen. The plain. We have to dance in a circle. I'll show you, I'll sing the songs. You know? Something terrible has happened more than once, to my people! Death and suffering, they have become the norm. Only the very skilled avoid them; the very skilled see human beings for what they are. The rest of us are blinded."

"Is he the only one with a name?"

"No, just the one whose name everyone knows, everyone. Like a magnet drawing everyone's emotions. I don't want to . . ."

"Take it easy," said Mona. "When we get there you can write it all out again, you can have peace and quiet, two whole days before they come."

"And who will I be by that time?"

"I know who you are," said Mona. "I knew who you were when you were in me. You're me and Michael, and something else, something powerful and wondrous, and part of all the other witches, too."

"Talk, honey," said Mary Jane. "Tell us, tell us about him and everybody making the little chalk dolls. I want to hear about that, burying the dolls at the foot of the stones. You remember what you said?"

"I think I do. They were dolls with breasts and penises."

"Well, you never mentioned that before."

"They were sacred dolls. But there must be a purpose to this, a redemption for this pain, I . . . I want the memories to let go, but not before I take everything of value from them. Mary Jane, would you please, honeybunch, grab a Kleenex there and wipe my eyes? I am saying this for the record, pay attention. This is stream of consciousness. We are taking the long stone to the plain. Everybody is going to dance and sing around it for a long time, before they begin to make the scaffolding out of logs by which we'll make it stand upright. Everyone has been carving their dolls. You can't tell the difference, each doll looks somehow like every one of them. I am sleepy. I'm hungry too. I want to dance. Ashlar is calling everyone to attention."

"Fifteen more minutes and we pull in the back gate," said Mary Jane. "So just keep your teary little peepers open."

"Don't say a word to the guards," said Mona. "I'll handle them. What else do you remember? They're bringing the stone to the plain. What's the name of the plain? Say it in their language."

"Ashlar calls it simply 'the flat land' and 'the safe land' or 'the grass land.' To say it right I have to speak it very, very fast, to you it will sound like whistling. But everyone knows those stones. I know everyone does. My father knows them, has seen them. God, do you suppose there is another of me anywhere in this whole world? Don't you think there has to be? Another me besides those buried under the tree? I can't be the only one alive!"

"Settle down, honey," said Mary Jane. "There's a lot of time to find out."

"We are your family," said Mona. "Remember that. Whatever else you are, you are Morrigan Mayfair, designated by me to be heir to the legacy, and we have a birth certificate, a baptismal certificate, and fifteen Polaroid photographs with my solemn word on a sticker label pasted to the back of each of them."

"Somehow or other that sounds insufficient," said Morrigan, crying now, making a pout like a baby, the tears making her blink. "Hopelessly contrived, possibly legally irrelevent." The car moved on, in its own lane, but they had come into Metairie, the traffic was getting heavy. "Perhaps a videotape is required, what do you think, Mother? But nothing in the end will suffice, will it, but love? Why do we speak of legal things at all?"

"Because they're important."

"But, Mother, if they don't love—"

"Morrigan, we'll do a videotape at First Street, soon as we get there. And you will have your love, mark my words. I'll get it for you. I won't let anything go wrong this time."

"What makes you think that, given all your reservations and fears, and desires to hide from prying eyes?"

"I love you. That's why I think it."

The tears were springing from Morrigan's eyes as if from a rainspout. Mona could hardly bear it.

"They will not have to use a gun, if they don't love me," Morrigan said.

Unspeakable pain, my child, this.

"Like hell," said Mona, trying to sound very calm, very controlled, very much the woman. "Our love is enough, and you know it! If you have to forget them, you do it. We are enough, don't you dare say we're not, not enough for now, you hear me?" She stared at this graceful gazelle, who was driving and crying at the same time, passing every laggard in her path. *This is my daughter.* Mine has always been monstrous ambition, monstrous intelligence, monstrous courage, and now a monstrous daughter. But what *is* her nature, besides brilliant, impulsive, loving, enthusiastic, super-sensitive to hurts and slights, and given to torrents of fancy and ecstasy? What *will* she do? What does it mean to remember ancient things? Does it mean you possess them and know from them? What *can* come of this? You know, I don't really care, she thought. I mean not now, not when it's beginning, not when it's so exciting.

She saw her tall girl struck, the body crumple, her own hands out to shield her, taking the head to her breasts. *Don't you dare hurt her.*

It was all so different now.

"All right, all right," Mary Jane interjected. "Lemme drive, this is really getting crowded."

"You are out of your mind, Mary Jane," cried Morrigan, shifting forward in the seat and pressing on the accelerator to pass the car threatening on the left. She lifted her chin, and took a swat at her tears with the back of her hand. "I am steering this car home. I wouldn't miss this for anything!"

Thirty

WHAT was it like in the cave, I wondered. The voices of hell I had no desire to hear, but what about the singing of heaven?

I thought it over, and then decided to pass by. I had a long journey ahead of me. It was too early for rest. I wanted to be away from here.

I was about to set off and go around this part of the slope, when a voice called to me.

It was a woman's voice, very soft and seemingly without a source, and I heard it say:

"Ashlar, I've been waiting for you."

I turned, looking this way and that. The darkness was unnerving. The Little People, I thought, one of their women, determined to seduce me. Again I determined to be on my way, but the call came again, soft as a kiss:

"Ashlar, King of Donnelaith, I am waiting for you."

I looked at the little hovel, with its lights flickering in the dimness, and there I saw a woman standing. Her hair was red, and her skin very pale. She was human, and a witch, and she carried the very faint scent of a witch, which could mean, but might not, that she had the blood of the Taltos in her.

I should have gone on. I knew it. Witches were always trouble. But this woman was very beautiful and in the shadows my eyes played tricks on me, so that she looked somewhat like our lost Janet.

As she came towards me, I saw that she had Janet's severe green eyes and straight nose, and a mouth that might have been carved from marble. She had the same small and very round breasts, and a long graceful neck. Add to this her beautiful red hair, which has ever been a lure and a delight to the Taltos.

"What do you want of me?" I said.

"Come lie with me," she said. "Come into my house. I invite you."

"You're a fool," I said. "You know what I am. I lie with you and you'll die."

"No," she said. "Not I." And she laughed, as so many witches had before her. "I shall bear the giant by you."

I shook my head. "Go your way, and be thankful I'm not easily tempted. You're beautiful. Another Taltos might help himself. Who is there to protect you?"

"Come," she said. "Come into my house." She drew closer, and in the few feeble rays of light that broke through the branches, the long, very golden light of the last of the day, I saw her beautiful white teeth, and how her breasts looked beneath her fine lace blouse, and above her painfully tight leather girdle.

Well, it wouldn't hurt just to lie with her, just to put my lips on her breasts, I thought. But then. She is a witch. Why do I allow myself to even think of this?

"Ashlar," she said, "we all know your tale. We know you are the king who betrayed your kind. Don't you want to ask the spirits of the cave how you might be forgiven?"

"Forgiven? Only Christ can forgive me my sins, child," I said. "I'm going."

"What power has Christ to change the curse that Janet has laid upon you?"

"Don't taunt me anymore," I said. I wanted her. And the angrier I became, the less I cared about her.

"Come with me," she said. "Drink the brew that I have by the fire, and then go into the cave, and you will see the spirits who know all things, King Ashlar."

She came up to the horse, and laid her hand on mine, and I felt the desire rising in me. She had a witch's penetrating eyes; and the soul of Janet seemed to look out of them.

I had not even made up my mind when she'd helped me from my horse, and we were walking together through the thick bracken and elderberry.

The little hut was a rank and frightening place! It had no windows. Above the fire, a kettle hung on a long skewer. But the bed was clean, and laid with skillfully embroidered linen.

"Fit for a king," she said.

I looked about, and I saw a dark open doorway opposite that by which we'd come in.

"That is the secret way to the cave," she said. She kissed my hand suddenly, and pulling me down onto the bed, she went to the kettle and filled a crude earthen cup with the broth inside it.

"Drink it, Your Majesty," she said. "And the spirits of the cave will see you and hear you."

Or I will see them and hear them, I thought, for God only knows what she had put in it—the herbs and oils which made witches mad, and likely to dance like Taltos under the moon. I knew their tricks.

"Drink, it's sweet," she said.

"Yes," I replied. "I can smell the honey."

And while I was looking into the cup and resolving not to take a drop, I saw her smile, and as I smiled back, I realized I was lifting the cup, and suddenly I drank a deep swallow of it. I closed my eyes.

"What if?" I whispered. "What if there *is* magic in it?" I was faintly amused and already dreaming.

"Now lie with me," she said.

"For your sake, no," I replied, but she was taking off my sword and I let her do it. Getting up long enough only to bolt her door, I fell back on the bed and pushed her down beneath me. I dragged her blouse loose from her breasts, and thought I would weep at the mere sight of them. Ah, the Taltos milk, how I wanted it. She was not a mother, this witch, she would have no milk, Taltos or human. But the breasts, the sweet breasts, how I wanted to suckle them, to bite the nipples and pull at them, and lick at them with my tongue.

Well, that won't do her any harm, I thought, and when she is moist and hot with desire, I'll place my fingers between her hidden hairy lips and make her shiver.

At once I began to suckle her. I began to kiss her and nuzzle against her. Her skin was firm and young and smelled young. And I loved the sound of her soft sighs, and the way her white belly felt to my cheek, and the way her nether hair looked, when I pulled down her skirt, and found it red, like the hair of her head, flaming and softly curly.

"Beautiful, beautiful witch," I whispered.

"Take me, King Ashlar," she said.

I sucked hard on her breast, letting my cock suffer, thinking, no, I will not kill her. She is a fool, but she does not deserve to die for it. But she pulled my cock between her legs, she pressed its tip against her hair, and quite suddenly, as many a male has done, I decided that if she really wanted it so, I would do as she asked of me.

I came in her hard, with as little care as I would have had for a Taltos, riding her, and loving it. She flushed and wept and cried out to spirits whose names I didn't know.

Immediately it was over. Sleepily she looked at me from the pillow, a triumphant smile on her lips. "Drink," she said, "and go into the cave." And she closed her eyes to sleep.

I downed the rest of the cup. Why not? I had gone this far. What if there was something in that remote darkness, one last secret my own land of Donnelaith had to give me? God knew the future held trials, pain and probably disillusionment.

I climbed off the bed, put my sword back on, buckling everything properly so that I was ready should I meet with trouble, and then, taking a crude lump of wax with a wick, which she kept at hand, I lighted the wick, and I entered the cave by this secret doorway.

I went up and up in the darkness, feeling my way along the earthen wall, and finally I came to a cool and open place, and from there, very far off, I could see a bit of light stealing in from the outside world. I was above the cave's main entrance.

I went on up. The light went before me. With a start, I came to a halt. I saw skulls gazing back at me. Rows and rows of skulls! Some of them so old they were no more than powder.

This had been a burial place, I reasoned, of those people that save only the heads of the dead, and believe that the spirits will talk through those heads, if properly addressed.

I told myself not to be foolishly frightened. At the same time I felt curiously weakened.

"It is the broth you drank," I whispered. "Sit down and rest."

And I did, leaning against the wall to my left, and looking into the big chamber, with its many masks of death grinning back at me.

The crude candle rolled out of my hand, but did not go out. It came to rest in the mud, and when I tried to reach for it, I couldn't.

Then slowly I looked up and I saw my lost Janet.

She was coming towards me through the chamber of the skulls, moving slowly, as if she were not real, but a figure in a dream.

"But I am awake," I said aloud.

I saw her nod, and smile. She stepped before the feeble little candle.

She wore the same rose-colored robe that she had the day they had burnt her, and then I saw to my horror that the silk had been eaten away by fire, and that her white skin showed through the jagged tears in it. And her long blond hair, it was burnt off and blackened on the ends, and ashes smudged her cheeks and her bare feet and her hands. Yet she was there, alive, and near to me.

"What is it, Janet?" I said. "What would you say to me now?"

"Ah, but what do you say to me, my beloved King? I followed you from the great circle in the southland up to Donnelaith and you destroyed me."

"Don't curse me, fair spirit," I said. I climbed to my knees. "Give me that which will help all of us! I sought the path of love. It was the path to ruin."

A change came over her face, a look of puzzlement and then awareness.

She lost her simple smile, and taking my hand, she spoke these words as if they were our secret.

"Would you find another paradise, my lord?" she asked. "Would you build another monument such as you left on the plain for all time? Or would you rather find a dance so simple and full of grace that all the peoples of the world could do it?"

"The dance, Janet, I would. And ours would be one great living circle."

"And would you make a song so sweet that no man or woman of any breed could ever resist it?"

"Yes," I said. "And sing we would, forever."

Her face brightened and her lips parted. And with a look of faint amazement, she spoke again.

"Then take the curse I give you."

I began to cry.

She gestured for me to be still, but with patience. Then she spoke this poem or song in the soft, rapid voice of the Taltos:

> Your quest is doomed, your path is long,
> Your winter just beginning.
> These bitter times shall fade to myth
> And memory lose its meaning
> But when at last her arms you see,
> Outstretched in bold forgiveness,
> Shrink not from what the earth would do
> When rain and winds do till it.
> The seed shall sprout, the leaves unfurl,
> The boughs shall give forth blossoms,
> That once the nettles tried to kill, and
> Strong men sought to trample.
> The dance, the circle, and the song,
> Shall be the key to heaven,
> As ways that once the mighty scorned
> Shall be their final blessing.

The cave grew dim, the little candle was dying, and with a subtle farewell gesture of her hand, she smiled again, and disappeared completely.

It seemed the words she'd spoken were carved in my mind as if engraved on the flat stones of the circle. And I saw them, and fixed them for all time, even as the last reverberation of her voice left me.

The cave was dark. I cried out, and groped in vain for the candle. But quickly climbing to my feet, I saw that my beacon was the fire burning in the little hut far back down the tunnel by which I'd entered.

Wiping at my eyes, overcome with love for Janet and a terrible confusion of sweetness and pain, I hurried into the small warm room and saw the red-haired witch there, on her pillow.

For one moment it was Janet! And not this gentle spirit who had just looked at me with loving eyes, and spoken verses that promised some remission.

It was the burnt one, the suffering and dying woman, her hair full of small flames, her bones smoldering. In agony she arched her back and tried to reach for me. And as I cried out and reached to snatch her from her own flames, it was the witch again, the red-haired one who had brought me into her bed and given me the potion.

Dead, white, quiet forever in death, the blood staining her gathered skirts, her little hut a tomb, her fire a vigil light.

I made the Sign of the Cross.

I ran out of the place.

But nowhere in the dark wood could I find my horse, and within moments I heard the laughter of the Little People.

I was at my wits' end, frightened by the vision, uttering prayers and curses. Fiercely I turned on them, challenging them to come out, to fight, and was in a moment surrounded. With my sword I struck down two and put the others to flight, but not before they had torn and dragged from me my green tunic, ripped away my leather girdle, and stolen my few belongings. My horse, too, they had taken.

A vagabond with nothing left to me but a sword, I did not go after them.

I made for the high road by instinct, and by the stars, which a Taltos can always do, and as the moon rose, I was walking south away from my homeland.

I didn't look back on Donnelaith.

I did go on to the summerland, as it was called, to Glastonbury, and I did stand on the sacred hill where Joseph had planted the hawthorn. I washed my hands in Chalice Well. I drank from it. I crossed Europe to find Pope Gregory in the ruins of Rome, I did go on to Byzantium, and finally to the Holy Land.

But long before my journey took me even to Pope Gregory's palace amid the squalid ruins of Rome's great pagan monuments, my quest had changed, really. I was not a priest anymore. I was a wanderer, a seeker, a scholar.

I could tell you a thousand stories of those times, including the tale of how I finally came to know the Fathers of the Talamasca. But I cannot claim to know their history. I know of them what you know, and what has been confirmed now that Gordon and his cohorts have been discovered.

In Europe I saw Taltos now and then, both women and men. I thought that I always would. That it would always be a simple thing, sooner or later, to find one of my own kind and to talk for the night by a friendly fire of the lost land, of the plain, of the things we all remembered.

There is one last bit of intelligence I wish to communicate to you.

In the year 1228, I finally returned to Donnelaith. It had been too long since I had laid eyes on a single Taltos. I was beginning to feel a fear on this account, and Janet's curse and her poetry were ever in my mind.

I came as a lone Scotsman wandering through the land, eager to talk to the bards of the Highlands about their old stories and legends.

My heart broke when I saw that the old Saxon church was gone and a great cathedral now stood upon the very spot, at the entrance of a great market town.

I had hoped to see the old church. But who could not be impressed by this mighty structure, and the great glowering castle of the Earls of Donnelaith that guarded the whole valley?

Bending my back, and pulling my hood up high to disguise my height, I leaned on my cane as I went down to give thanks that my tower still stood in the glen, along with many of the stone towers built by my people.

I cried tears of gratitude again when I discovered the circle of stones, far from the ramparts, standing as it always had in the high grass, imperishable emblems of the dancers who had once gathered there.

The great shock came, however, when I entered the cathedral and, dipping my hand into the water fount, looked up to see the stained-glass window of St. Ashlar.

There was the very image of myself in the glass, clothed in a priest's robes, with long flowing hair such as I had worn in those days, and peering down at my own true self with dark eyes so like my own they frightened me. Stunned, I read the prayer inscribed in Latin.

St. Ashlar Beloved of Christ
And the Holy Virgin Mary
Who will come again

Heal the sick
Comfort the afflicted
Ease the pangs
Of those who must die

Save us
From everlasting darkness
Drive out the demons from the valley.
Be our guide
Into the Light.

For a long time I was overcome with tears. I could not understand how this could have happened. Remembering to play the cripple still, I went to the high altar to say my prayers, and then to the tavern.

There I paid the bard to play all the old songs he knew, and none of them were familiar to me. The Pict language had died out. No one knew the writing on the crosses in the churchyard.

But this saint, what could the man tell me about him, I asked.

Was I truly Scots, the bard asked.

Had I never heard of the great pagan King Ashlar of the Picts, who had converted this entire valley to Christianity?

Had I never heard of the magic spring through which he worked his miracles? I had only to go down the hill to see it.

Ashlar the Great had built the first Christian church on this spot, in the year 586, and then set out for Rome on his first pilgrimage, being murdered by brigands before he had even left the valley.

Within the shrine his holy relics lay, the remnants of his bloody cloak, his leather belt, his crucifix, and a letter to the saint himself from none other than St. Columba. In the scriptorium I might see a psalter which Ashlar himself had written in the style of the great monastery at Iona.

"Ah, I understand it all," I said. "But what is the meaning of this strange prayer, and the words 'who will come again'?"

"Ah, that, well now, that's a story. Go to Mass tomorrow morning and look well at the priest who celebrates. You will see a young man of immense height, almost as tall as yourself, and such men are not so uncommon here. But this one is Ashlar come again, they say, and they tell the most fantastic story of his birth, how he came from his mother speaking and singing, and ready to serve God, seeing visions of the Great Saint and the Holy Battle of Donnelaith and the pagan witch Janet burnt up in the fire as the town converted in spite of her."

"This is true?" I asked, in quiet awe.

How could it be? A wild Taltos, born to humans who had no idea they carried the seed in their blood? No. It could not have been. What humans could make the Taltos together? It must have been a hybrid, sired by some mysterious giant who had come in the night and coupled with a woman cursed with the witches' gifts, leaving her with his monster offspring.

"It has happened three times before in our history," said the bard. "Sometimes the mother does not even know she's with child, other times she is in her third or her fourth month. No one knows when the creature inside her shall start to grow and become the image of the saint, come again to his people."

"And who were the fathers of these children?"

"Upstanding men of the Clan of Donnelaith, that's who they were, for St. Ashlar was the founder of their family. But you know there are so many strange tales in these woods. Each clan has its secrets. We're not to speak of it here, but now and then such a giant child is born who knows nothing of the Saint. I have seen one of these with my own eyes, standing a head taller than his father moments after he left his mother to die at the hearthside. A frantic thing, crying in fear, and possessed of no visions from God, but wailing for the pagan circle of stones! Poor soul. They called it a witch, a monster. And do you know what they do with such creatures?"

"They burn them."

"Yes," came his answer. "It's a terrible thing to see. Especially if the poor creature is a woman. For then she is judged to be the devil's child, without trial, for she cannot possibly be Ashlar. But these are the Highlands, and our ways have always been very mysterious."

"Have you yourself ever laid eyes on the female thing?" I asked.

"No," he said. "Never. But there are some who say they have known those who have seen it. There is talk among the sorcerers, and those who cling to the pagan ways. People dream that they will bring the female and the male together. But we should not speak of these things. We suffer those witches to live because now and then they can cure. But no one believes their stories, or thinks them proper for the ears of Christian people."

"Ah, yes," I said. "I can well imagine." I thanked him.

I did not wait for morning Mass to see the strange, tall priest.

I caught his scent as soon as I approached the rectory, and when he came to the door, having caught mine, we stood staring at one another. I rose to my full height, and of course he had done nothing to disguise his own. We merely stood there, facing one another.

In him I saw the old gentleness, the eyes almost timid, and the lips soft, and the skin as fresh and free of blemish as that of a baby. Had he really been born of two human beings, two powerful witches perhaps? Did he believe his destiny?

Born remembering, yes, born knowing, yes, and thank God for him it had been the right time that he remembered—and the right battle, and the right place. And now he followed the old profession they had marked for us hundreds of years ago.

He came towards me. He wanted to speak. Perhaps he could not believe his eyes, that he was looking upon one exactly like him.

"Father," I asked in Latin, so that he was most likely to answer, "was it really from a human mother and father you came?"

"How else?" he asked, quite clearly terrified. "Go if you will to my parents themselves. Ask them." He grew pale, and was trembling.

"Father," I said, "where is your like among women?"

"There is no such thing!" he declared. But now he could scarcely keep himself from running away from me. "Brother, where have you come from?" he asked. "Here, seek God's forgiveness for your sins, whatever they are."

"You have never seen a woman of our kind?"

He shook his head. "Brother, I am the chosen of God," he explained. "The chosen of St. Ashlar." He bowed his head, humbly, and I saw a blush come to his cheeks, for obviously he'd committed a sin of pride in announcing this.

"Farewell, then," I said. And I left him.

I left the town and I went again to the stones; I sang an old song, letting myself rock back and forth in the wind, and then I made for the forest.

Dawn was just rising behind me when I climbed the wooded hills to find the old cave. It was a desolate spot, dark as it had been five hundred years before, with no sign now of the witch's hovel.

In the early light, cold and bitter as that of a winter's eve, I heard a voice call me.

"Ashlar!"

I turned around and I looked at the dark woods.

"Ashlar the cursed, I see you!"

"It's you, Aiken Drumm," I cried. And then I heard his mean laughter. Ah, the Little People were there, garbed in green so that they would blend with the leaves and the bracken. I saw their cruel little faces.

"There's no tall woman here for you, Ashlar," cried Aiken Drumm. "Nor will there ever be. No men of your ilk but a mewling priest born of witches, who falls to his knees when he hears our pipes. Here! Come. Take a little bride, a sweet morsel of wrinkled flesh, and see what you beget! And be grateful for what God gives you."

They had begun to beat their drums. I heard the whining of their song, discordant, ghastly, yet strangely familiar. Then came the pipes. It was the old songs we had sung, the songs we taught them!

"Who knows, Ashlar the cursed?" he cried out. "But your daughter by one of us this morn might be a female! Come with us; we have wee women aplenty to amuse you. Think, a daughter, Your Royal Majesty! And once again the tall people would rule the hills!"

I turned and ran through the trees, not stopping till I had cleared the pass and come once more to the high road.

Of course Aiken Drumm spoke the truth. I had found no female of my kind in all of Scotland. And that was what I'd come to seek.

And what I would seek for another millennium.

I did not believe then, on that cold morning, that I would never lay eyes again upon a young or fertile female Taltos. Oh, how many times in the early centuries had I seen my female counterparts and turned away from them. Cautious, withdrawn, I would not have fathered a young Taltos to suffer the confusion of this strange world for all the sweet embraces of the lost land.

And now where were they, these fragrant darlings?

The old, the white of hair, the sweet of breath, the scentless, these I had seen many a time and would see again—creatures wild and lost, or wrapped in a sorceress's dreams, they had given me only chaste kisses.

In dark city streets once I caught the powerful scent, only to be maddened, unable ever to find soft folds of hot and secret flesh from which it emanated.

Many a human witch I've lured to bed, sometimes warning her of the dangers of my embrace, and sometimes not, when I believed her strong, and able to bear my offspring.

Across the world I've gone, by every means, to track the mysterious ageless woman of remarkable height, with memories of long ago, who greets men who come to her with sweet smiles and never bears their children.

She is human or she is not there at all.

I had come too late, or to the wrong place, or plague took the beauty many years ago. War laid waste that town. Or no one knows the story.

Would it always be so?

Tales abound of giants in the earth, of the tall, the fair, the gifted.

Surely they are not all gone! What became of those who fled the glen? Are no wild female Taltos born into the world of human parents?

Surely somewhere, in the deep forest of Scotland or the jungles of Peru, or the snowy wastes of Russia, there lives a family of Taltos, a clan, in its warm and well-defended tower. The woman and the man have their books, their memories to share, their games to play, their bed in which to kiss and and play, though the act of coitus must, as always, be approached with reverence.

My people can't be gone.

The world is huge. The world is endless. Surely I am not the last. Surely that has not been the meaning of Janet's terrible words, that I should wander through time, mateless forever.

Now you know my story.

I could tell many tales. I could tell of my journeys through many lands, my years in various occupations; I could tell of the few male Taltos I met over the years, of the stories I heard of our lost people who had once lived in this or that fabled village.

The story you tell is the story you choose to tell.

And this is the story we share, Rowan and Michael.

You know now how the clan of Donnelaith came into being. You know how the blood of the Taltos came to be in the blood of humans. You know the tale of the first woman ever burnt in the beautiful valley. And the sad account of the place to which the Taltos brought such misery, not once, but again and again, if all our stories are history.

Janet, Lasher, Suzanne, her descendants, even to Emaleth.

And you see now that when you raised your gun, when you lifted it, Rowan, and you fired the shots that brought down this child, the girl who had given you her milk, it was no small act of which you need ever be ashamed, but destiny.

You have saved us both. You have saved us all perhaps. You have saved me from the most terrible dilemma I could ever know, and one which I may be not meant to know.

Whatever the case, don't weep for Emaleth. Don't weep for a race of strange, soft-eyed people, long ago driven from the earth by a stronger species. This is the way of the earth, and we are both of it.

What other strange, unnamed creatures live within the cities and jungles of our planet? I have glimpsed many things. I have heard many stories. The rain and wind till the earth, to use Janet's words. What next shall spring from some hidden garden?

Could we now live together, the Taltos, the human, in the same world? How would such be possible? This is a world where human races battle endlessly, where people of one faith still slaughter people of another. Religious wars rage from Sri Lanka to Bosnia, from Jerusalem to American cities and towns where Christians still, in the name of Jesus Christ, bring death in his name to their enemies, to their own, even to little children.

Tribe, race, clan, family.

Deep within us all are the seeds of hate for what is different. We do not have to be taught these things. We have to be taught *not* to give in to them! They are in our blood; but in our minds is the charity and the love to overcome them.

And how would my gentle people fare today, if they did come back, as foolish now as they were then, unable to meet the ferocity of men, yet frightening even the most innocent humans with their bold eroticism? Would we choose tropical islands on which to play our sensuous games, to do our dances and fall into our spells of dancing and singing?

Or would ours be a realm of electronic pastimes, of computers, films, games of virtual reality, or sublime mathematical puzzles—studies suited to our minds, with their love of detail and their inability to sustain irrational states such as wrath or hatred? Would we fall in love with quantum physics the way we once fell in love with weaving? I can see our kind, up night and day, tracing the paths of particles through magnetic fields on computer screens! Who knows what advances we might make, given those toys to preoccupy us?

My brain is twice the size of the human brain. I do not age by any known clock. My capacity to learn modern science and modern medicine cannot be imagined.

And what if there rose among us but one ambitious male or female, one Lasher, if you will, who would the supremacy of the race restore, what then might happen? Within the space of one night, a pair of Taltos could breed a battalion of adults, ready to invade the citadels of human power, ready to destroy the weapons which humans know how to use so much better, ready to take the food, the drink, the resources of this brimming world, and deny it to those less gentle, less kind, less patient, in retribution for their eons of bloody dominance.

Of course, I do not wish to learn these things.

I have not spent my centuries studying the physical world. Or the uses of power. But when I choose to score some victory for myself—this company you see around you—the world falls back from me as if its obstacles were made of paper. My empire, my world—it is made of toys and money. But how much more easily it could be made of medicines to quiet the human male, to dilute the testosterone in his veins, and silence his battle cries forever.

And imagine, if you will, a Taltos with true zeal. Not a dreamer who has spent his brief years in misted lands nourished on pagan poetry, but a visionary who, true to the very principles of Christ, decided that violence should be annihilated, that peace on earth was worth any sacrifice.

Imagine the legions of newborns who could be committed to this cause, the armies bred to preach love in every hamlet and vale and stamp out those, quite literally, who spoke against it.

What am I finally? A repository for genes that *could* make the world crumble? And what are you, my Mayfair witches—have you carried those same genes down through the centuries so that we may finally end the Kingdom of Christ with our sons and our daughters?

The Bible names this one, does it not? The beast, the demon, the Antichrist.

Who has the courage for such glory? Foolish old poets who live in towers still, and dream of rituals on Glastonbury Tor to make the world new again.

And even for that mad old man, that doddering fool, was murder not the first requisite of his vision?

I have shed blood. It is on my hands now for vengeance's sake, a pathetic way to heal a wound, but one to which we turn again and again in our wretchedness. The Talamasca is whole again. Not worth the price, but done. And our secrets are safe for the present.

We are friends, you and I, I pray, and we will never hurt each other. I can reach for your hands in the dark. You can call out to me, and I'll answer.

But what if something *new* could happen? Something wholly new? I think I see it, I think I imagine . . . But then it escapes me.

I don't have *the answer.*

I know I shall never trouble your red-haired witch, Mona. I shall never trouble any of your powerful women. Many centuries have passed since lust or hope has tricked me into that adventure.

I am alone, and if I am cursed, I've forgotten it.

I like my empire of small, beautiful things. I like the playthings that I offer to the world. The dolls of a thousand faces are my children.

In a small way they are my dance, my circle, my song. Emblems of eternal play, the work perhaps of heaven.

Thirty-one

AND THE dream repeats itself. She climbs out of bed, runs down the stairs. "Emaleth!" The shovel is under the tree. Who would ever bother to move it?

She digs and digs, and there is her girl, with the long slack hair and the big blue eyes.

"Mother!"

"Come on, my darling."

They're down in the hole together. Rowan holds her, rocking her. "Oh, I'm so sorry I killed you."

"It's all right, Mother Dear," she says.

"It was a war," Michael says. "And in a war, people are killed, and then afterwards . . ."

She woke, gasping.

The room was quiet beneath a faint drone of heat from the small vents along the floor. Michael slept beside her, his knuckles touching her hip as she sat there, hands clasped to her mouth, looking down at him.

No, don't wake him. Don't put him through the misery again. But she knew.

When all the talk was over and done with, when they'd had their dinner and their long walk through the snowy streets, when they'd talked till dawn and breakfasted and talked some more and vowed their eternal friendship, she knew. She should never never have killed her girl. There was no reason for it.

How could that doe-eyed creature, who had comforted her so, in that kindly voice, milk spilling from her breasts, hhhmmm, the taste of the milk, how could that trembling creature have hurt anyone?

What logic had made her lift the gun, what logic had made her pull the trigger? Child of rape, child of aberration, child of nightmare. But child still. . . .

She climbed out of the bed, finding her slippers in the dark, and reaching for a long white negligee on the chair, another one of these strange garments which filled her suitcase, full of the perfume of another woman.

Killed her, killed her, killed her, this tender and trusting thing, full of knowledge of long-ago lands, of valley and glen and plains and who knew what mysteries? Her comfort in the dark, when she'd been tied to the bed. *My Emaleth.*

A pale white window was hung in the darkness at the far end of the hallway, a great rectangle of glowing night sky, light spilling on the long path of colored marble.

To that light she moved, the negligee ballooning out, her feet making a soft skittering tap on the floor, her hand out for the button of the elevator.

Take me down, down, down to the dolls. Take me out of here. If I look from that window, I'll jump. I'll open the glass, and I'll look out over the endless lights of the largest city in the world, and I'll climb up and put my arms out, and then I'll drop down into the ice-cold darkness.

Down, down, down with you, my daughter.

All the images of his tale went through her mind, the sonorous timbre of his voice, his gentle eyes as he spoke. And she is now debris beneath the roots of the oak, something erased from the world without a jot of ink upon a piece of paper, without a hymn sung.

The doors closed. The wind sounded in the shaft, that faint whistling, like wind in mountains perhaps, and as the cab descended, a howling as if she were in a giant chimney. She wanted to crumple and fall on the floor, to go limp without will or purpose or fight anymore, just to sink into the darkness.

No more words to say, no more thoughts. No more to know or to learn. I should have taken her hand, I should have held her. So easy it would have been to keep her, tender, against my breasts, my darling, my Emaleth.

And all those dreams that sent you out the door with him—of cells within cells the like of which no human had ever seen, of secrets gleaned from every layer and fiber gently plied from willing hands, willing arms, willing lips pressed to sterile glass, and droplets of blood given with the smallest frown, of fluids and maps and schemes and X rays made without a pinch of hurt, all to tell a new tale, a new miracle, a new beginning—all that, with her, would have been possible! A drowsy feminine thing that would not have hurt any mortal being, so easy to control, so easy to care for.

The doors opened. The dolls have been waiting. The gold light of the city comes through a hundred high windows, caught and suspended in squares and rectangles of gleaming glass, and the dolls, the dolls wait and watch with hands uplifted. Tiny mouths ever on the verge of greeting. Little fingers hovering in the stillness.

Silently she walked through the dolls, corridor after corridor of dolls, eyes like pitch-black holes in space, or gleaming buttons in a glint of light. Dolls are quiet; dolls are patient; dolls are attentive.

We've come back to the Bru, the queen of the dolls, the big cold bisque princess with her almond eyes and her cheeks so rosy and round, her eyebrows caught forever in that quizzical look, trying vainly to understand what? The endless parade of all these moving beings who look at her?

Come to life. Just for a moment come to life. Be mine. Be warm. Be alive.

Out from under the tree in the dark, walk again as if death were a part of the tale you could have erased, as if those fatal moments could be omitted forever. No stumbling in this wilderness. No false steps.

Hold you in my arms.

Her hands were splayed out on the cold glass of the case. Her forehead pressed against it. The light made two crescent moons in her eyes. The long mohair tresses lay flat and heavy against the silk of her dress, as if they were moist with the dampness of the earth, the dampness of the grave perhaps.

Where was the key? Had he worn it on a chain around his neck? She couldn't remember. She longed to open the door, to take the doll in her arms. To hold it tight for one moment against her breast.

What happens when grief is this mad, when grief has blotted out all other thoughts, feelings, hopes, dreams, wonder?

Finally exhaustion comes. The body says return to sleep, lie down now to rest, not torment. Nothing's changed. The dolls stare as the dolls will always stare. And the earth eats at what is buried inside of it as it always has. But a kind weariness overtakes the soul, and it seems possible, just possible, to wait to weep, to wait to suffer, to wait to die and lie down with them, to have it finished, because only then is all guilt gone, washed away, when you are as dead as they are.

· · ·

HE WAS there. He was standing before the glass. You couldn't mistake him for anyone else. There is no one else that tall, and even if it weren't for that, she knew his face too well now, the line of his profile.

He'd heard her in the dark, walking back down the corridor. But he didn't move. He was just leaning there against the window frame and watching the light gather outside, watching the blackness fade and turn to milk and the stars dissolve as though melted in it.

What did he think? That she'd come to seek him out?

She felt shattered inside, weak. Unable to reason what to do, needing perhaps to walk across the floor, to stand beside him and look down on the smoky gloom of early roofs and towers, on lights twinkling along hazy streets, and smoke rising and curling from a hundred stacks and chimneys.

She did this. She stood beside him.

"We love each other now," he said. "Don't we?"

His face was so sad. It hurt her. It was a fresh hurt, touching her right in the midst of the old pain, something immediate that could bring the tears where before there had only been something as black and empty as horror.

"Yes, we do, we love each other," she said. "With our whole hearts."

"And we will have that," he said. "Won't we?"

"Yes, always. For as long as we live. We are friends and we will always be, and nothing, nothing will ever break the promises between us."

"And I'll know you're there, it's as simple as that."

"And when you don't want to be alone anymore, come. Come and be with us."

He turned for the first time, as if he had not really wanted to look at her. The sky was paling so fast, the room just filling up and opening wide, and his face was weary and only slightly less than perfect.

One kiss, one chaste and silent kiss, and no more, just a tight clasp of fingers.

And then she was gone, drowsy, aching, glad of the day spilling down over the soft bed. Now I can sleep, daylight at last, now I can sleep, tumbling under the soft covers, next to Michael again.

Thirty-two

I<small>T WAS</small> too cold to be out, but winter would not let go its hold upon New York. And if the little man wanted to meet at the Trattoria, so be it.

Ash didn't mind the walk. He did not want to be alone in his lonely tower rooms, and he was fairly certain that Samuel was on his way, and could not be persuaded to return.

He enjoyed the crowds on Seventh Avenue rushing in the early dusk, bright shop windows full of lavishly colored Oriental porcelains, ornate clocks, bronze statues, and rugs of wool and silk—all the gift merchandise sold in this part of midtown. Couples were hurrying to dinner so that they might make the curtain at Carnegie Hall for a young violinist who was causing a worldwide sensation. Lines at the ticket office were long. The fancy boutiques had not yet closed; and though the snow fell in tiny little flakes, it could not possibly cover either asphalt or sidewalks due to the continuous thunder of human feet.

No, this is not a bad time to be walking. This is a bad time for trying to forget that you have just embraced your friends, Michael and Rowan, for the last time until you hear from them.

Of course they don't know that that is the rule of the game, the gesture his heart and his pride would require, but more than likely, they would not have been surprised. They had spent four days, all told, with him. And he was as unsure of their love now as he had been the very first moment in London when he had laid eyes on them.

No, he did not want to be alone. Only problem was, he should have dressed for anonymity and the freezing wind, but he had dressed for neither. People stared at a seven-foot-tall man with dark wavy hair who wore a violet silk blazer in such weather. And the scarf was yellow.

How mad of him to have thrown on these decidedly private-realm clothes and then rushed out into the street wearing them.

But he had changed before Remmick gave him the news: Samuel had packed and gone; Samuel would meet him at the Trattoria. Samuel had left behind the bulldog, that it might be his New York dog, if Ash didn't mind. (Why would Ash mind a dog that both drooled and snored, but then Remmick and the young Leslie undoubtedly would be the ones to endure the brunt of this. The young Leslie was now a permanent fixture in the tower offices and rooms, much to her glee.) Samuel would get another dog in and for England.

The Trattoria was already packed, he could see this through the glass, patrons shoulder to shoulder along its winding bar and at its innumerable little tables.

But there was Samuel, as promised, puffing on a small damp cigarette (he murdered them the way Michael did), and drinking whiskey from a heavy little glass, and watching for him.

Ash tapped on the window.

The little man took him in, head to toe, and shook his head. The little man himself was spruce in his new style, tweed with waistcoat, brand-new shirt, shoes shined like mirrors. There was even a pair of brown leather gloves lying like two ghost hands, all collapsed and mashed, on the table.

It was impossible to know what feelings were concealed behind the folds and wrinkles of Samuel's flesh, but the neatness and style of the overall figure argued for something other than the bleary, drunken, grumbling melodrama of the last forty-eight hours.

That Michael had found Samuel so amusing was a blessing. Indeed, one night they had drunk each other under the table, telling jokes, while Rowan and Ash had only smiled indulgently, to be left at last with the awful tension of knowing that if they went to bed more would be lost than gained—unless Ash thought of himself, and only himself entirely.

Not in Ash's nature.

"Not in my nature to be alone, either," he thought. There was a leather portmanteau beside Samuel's glass. Leaving.

Ash pushed very gently past those entering and exiting, giving a little nod and a point of the finger to Samuel to let the harried doorman know he was expected.

The cold died away at once, and with the loud crash of voices and pots and pans, dishes and shuffling feet, there came the warm air like a fluid oozing around him. Inevitably heads turned, but the marvelous thing about any restaurant crowd in New York was that table partners were twice as animated as anywhere else, and always so seriously focused on each other. All meetings seemed crucial; courses devoured in a rush; faces evincing infatuation, if not with one's partner, then certainly with the evening's ever-quickening momentum.

Surely they saw the tall man in the outrageous violet silk take the chair opposite the smallest man in the place, a chunky little fellow in heavy clothes, but they saw it out of the corner of the eye, or with a movement of the neck swift enough to injure the spinal cord, and they did not miss a beat of their own conversations. The table was right before the front glass, but then people on the streets were even more skilled at secret observation than the people in the warm safety zone of the restaurant.

"Go ahead and say it," said Ash under his breath. "You are leaving, you are going back to England."

"You knew I would, I don't want to be over here. I always think it's going to be wonderful and then I get tired, and I have to go home. I have to go back to the glen, before those fools from the Talamasca start invading it."

"They won't do that," Ash said. "I hoped you'd stay for a little while." He marveled at the control he managed to maintain over his own voice. "That we'd talk about things . . ."

"You cried when you said goodbye to your human friends, didn't you?"

"Now, why do you ask me that?" said Ash. "You are determined that we part with cross words?"

"Why did you trust them, the two witches? Here, the waiter's talking to you. Eat something."

Ash pointed to something on the menu, the standard pasta he always ordered in such places, and waited for the man to disappear before resuming.

"If you hadn't been drunk, Samuel, if you hadn't seen everything through a tiresome haze, you would know the answer to that question."

"Mayfair witches. I know what they are. Yuri told me all about them. Yuri talked in a fever a lot of the time. Ash, don't be stupid again. Don't expect these people to love you."

"Your words don't make sense," said Ash. "They never did. They're just a sort of noise I've grown used to hearing when I'm in your presence."

The waiter set down the mineral water, the milk, the glasses.

"You're out of sorts, Ash," said Samuel, gesturing for another glass of whiskey, and it was pure whiskey, Ash could tell by the smell. "And it's not my fault." Samuel slumped back in the chair. "Look, my friend, I'm only trying to warn you. Let me put it this way, if you prefer. Don't love those two."

"You know, if you insist upon this lecture, I just may lose my temper."

The little man laughed outright. It was a low, rumbly laugh, but the folds over his eyes even showed his sudden bemusement.

"Now that might keep me in New York another hour or two," he said, "if I thought I was really going to see that."

Ash didn't respond. It was too terribly important not to say anything he didn't mean, not now, not to Samuel, not to anyone. He had believed that all his long life, but periodically he was brutally reminded of it.

After a moment, he said:

"And who should I love?" It was said with only the softest note of reproach. "I'll be glad when you're gone. I mean . . . I mean I'll be glad when this unpleasant conversation is over."

"Ash, you should never have drawn so close to them, never told them all you did. And then the gypsy, letting him just go back to the Talamasca."

"Yuri? And what did you want me to do? How could I stop Yuri from going back to the Talamasca?"

"You could have lured him to New York, put him to work for you some way. He was a man with a broken life; but you sent him home to write volumes on what happened. Hell, he could have been your companion."

"That was not right for him. He had to go home."

"Of course it was right. And he was right for you—an outcast, a gypsy, the son of a whore."

"Please don't make your speech as offensive and vulgar as you possibly can. You frighten me. Look, it was Yuri's choice. If he had not wanted to go back, he would have said so. His life was the Order. He had to go back, at least to heal all the wounds. And after that? He wouldn't have been happy here in my world. Dolls are pure magic to those who love them and understand them. To others they are less than toys. Yuri is a man of coarse spiritual distinctions, not subtle ones."

"That sounds good," said Samuel, "but it's stupid." He watched the waiter set the fresh drink before him. "Your world is full of things that Yuri might have done. You could have turned him loose to build more parks, plant more trees, all these grandiose schemes of yours. What were you telling your witches, that you were going to build parks in the sky so that everyone could see what you see from your marble chambers? You could have kept that kid busy all his life, and you would have had his companionship—"

"I wish you would stop. This didn't happen. It simply did not happen."

"But what happened is that you want the friendship of those witches, a man and woman married to each other with a great clan around them, people who are *a priori* committed to a family way of living that is intensely human—"

"What can I do to make you stop?"

"Nothing. Drink the milk. I know you want it. You're ashamed to drink it in front of me, afraid I might say something like 'Ashlar, drink your milk!' "

"Which you now have, even though I have not touched the milk, you realize."

"Ahh, this is the point. You love those two, the witches. And it is incumbent upon those two—as I see it—to forget all this, this nightmare of Taltos, and the glen, and murdering little fools who infiltrated the Talamasca. It is essential to the sanity of that man and woman that they go home and build the life the Mayfair family expects them to build. And I hate it when you love those who will only turn their backs on you, and those two have to do it."

Ash didn't answer.

"They are surrounded by hundreds of people for whom they must make this part of their lives a lie," Samuel continued to expostulate. "They will want to forget you exist; they will not want the great realm of their day-to-day life lost in the glare of your presence."

"I see."

"I don't like it when you suffer."

"Is that so?"

"Yes! I like to open magazines and newspapers and read about your little corporate triumphs, and see your smiling face above flippant little lists of the world's ten most eccentric billionaires, or New York's most eligible bachelors. And now I know you will break your heart wondering if these witches are your true friends, if you can call them when your heart aches, if you can depend on them for the knowledge of yourself that every being requires—"

"Stay, please, Samuel."

This put a silence to the lecture. The little man sighed. He drank some of the fresh drink, about half, and licked his heavy crooked lower lip with an amazingly pink tongue.

"Hell, Ash, I don't want to."

"I came when you called me, Samuel."

"You regret that now?"

"I don't think in that way. Besides, how could I regret it?"

"Forget it all, Ash. Seriously, forget it. Forget a Taltos came to the glen. Forget you know these witches. Forget you need anyone to love you for what you are. That's impossible. I'm afraid. I'm afraid of what you will do now. The pattern's all too familiar."

"What pattern is that?" asked Ash quietly.

"You'll destroy all this, the company, the corporation, the Toys Without Limit or Dolls for the Millions, whatever it's called. You'll sink into apathy. You'll just let it go. You'll walk out and far away, and the things you've built and the things you've made will just slowly fall apart without you. You've done it before. And then you'll be lost, just the way I'm lost, and some cold winter evening, and why you always choose the dead of winter I don't know, you'll come to the glen again looking for me."

"This is more important to me, Samuel," he said. "It's important for many reasons."

"Parks, trees, gardens, children," sang the little man.

Ash didn't reply.

"Think about all those who depend on you, Ash," said Samuel, continuing the same sermon for the same congregation. "Think of all these people who make and sell and buy and love the things you manufacture. That can substitute for sanity, I think, having other warm beings of intellect and feeling dependent upon us. You think I'm right?"

"It doesn't substitute for sanity, Samuel," said Ash. "It substitutes for happiness."

"All right, that's fine then. But don't wait for your witches to come to you again, and for God's sake never seek them on their own turf. You'll see fear in their eyes if they ever see you standing in their garden."

"You're so sure of all this."

"Yes, I'm sure. Ash, you told them everything. Why did you do that? Perhaps if you had not, they wouldn't fear you."

"You don't know what you're saying."

"And Yuri and the Talamasca, how they will plague you now."

"They will not."

"But those witches, they are not your friends."

"So you keep saying."

"I know they are not. I know their curiosity and awe will soon change to fear. Ash, it's an old cliché, they're only human."

Ash bowed his head and looked away, out the window at the blowing snow, at shoulders hunkered against the wind.

"Ashlar, I know," Samuel said, "because I am an outcast. And you are an outcast. And look out there at the multitudes of humans passing on the street, and think how each one condemns so many others as outcast, as 'other,' as not human. We are monsters, my friend. That's what we'll always be. It's their day. That we're alive at all is enough to worry about." He downed the rest of the drink.

"And so you go home to your friends in the glen."

"I hate them, and you know it. But the glen we won't have for long. I go back for sentimental reasons. Oh, it's not just the Talamasca, and that sixteen genteel scholars will come with tape recorders, begging me to recite all I know over lunch at the Inn. It's all those archaeologists digging up St. Ashlar's Cathedral. The modern world has found the place. And why? Because of your damned witches."

"You can't lay that on me or on them, and you know it."

"Eventually we'll have to find some more remote place, some other curse or legend to protect us. But they're not my friends, don't think they are. They don't."

Ash only nodded.

Food had come, a large salad for the little man, the pasta for Ash. The wine was being poured in the glasses. It smelled like something gone utterly wrong.

"I'm too drunk to eat," Samuel said.

"I understand if you go," Ash said softly. "That is, if you're bound to go, then perhaps you should do it."

They sat in silence for a moment. Then the little man lifted his fork and began to devour the salad, shoveling it into his mouth, as bits and pieces fell to the plate despite his most diligent efforts. Loudly he scraped up every last bit of olive, cheese, and lettuce on the plate, and then drank a big gulp of the mineral water.

"Now I can drink some more," he said.

Ash made a sound that would have been a laugh if he had not been so sad.

Samuel slid off the chair and onto his feet. He picked up the leather portmanteau. He sauntered over to Ash, and crooked his arm around Ash's neck. Ash kissed his cheek quickly, faintly repelled by the leathery texture of the skin, but determined at all costs to hide it.

"Will you come back soon?" Ash asked.

"No. But we'll see each other," said Samuel. "Take care of my dog. His feelings are hurt very easily."

"I'll remember that."

"And pitch yourself into your work!"

"Anything else?"

"I love you."

And with that Samuel pushed and swaggered his way through the press of those being seated and those rising to go, and all the backs and elbows clumped against him. He went out the front door and along the front window. The snow was already catching in his hair and on his bushy eyebrows, and making dark wet spots on his shoulders.

He lifted his hand in farewell, and then he passed out of the frame, and the crowd became the crowd again.

Ash lifted the glass of milk and slowly drank all of it. Then he put some bills beneath his plate, stared at the food as if telling it goodbye, and went out himself, walking into the wind on Seventh Avenue.

When he reached his bedroom high above the streets, Remmick was waiting for him.

"You're cold, sir, much too cold."

"Am I?" Ash murmured. Patiently he let Remmick take away the silk blazer and the outrageous scarf. He put on the flannel smoking jacket of satin-lined wool, and taking the towel Remmick gave to him, he wiped the dampness from his hair and his face.

"Sit down, sir, let me take off your wet shoes."

"If you say so." The chair felt so soft, he could not imagine climbing out of it later on to go to bed. And all the rooms are empty. Rowan and Michael are gone. We will not be walking downtown tonight, talking eagerly together.

"Your friends arrived safely in New Orleans, sir," Remmick said, peeling off the wet socks, and then quickly putting on fresh dry socks so deftly that his fingers barely grazed Ash's flesh. "The call came right after you left for dinner. The plane is on its way back. It should be landing in about twenty minutes."

Ash nodded. The leather slippers were lined with fur. He did not know whether they were old or new. He couldn't remember. Suddenly all the little details seemed to have fled. His mind was horrifyingly empty and still; and he felt the loneliness and the stillness of the rooms completely.

Remmick moved at the closet doors like a ghost.

We hire those who are unobtrusive, Ash thought, and then they can't comfort us; what we tolerate cannot save us.

"Where's the young Leslie, Remmick? Is she about?"

"Yes, sir, with a million questions, it seems. But you look so very tired."

"Send her in. I need to work. I need to have my mind on something."

He walked down the corridor, and into the first of his offices, the private office, the one where papers were stacked here and there, and a file cabinet stood open, the one no one was allowed to clean, the one that was insufferably cluttered.

Leslie appeared within seconds, face brimming with excitement, dedication, devotion, and inexhaustible energy. "Mr. Ash, there's the International Doll Expo next week, and a woman from Japan just called, said you definitely wanted to see her work, you told her so yourself last time you were in Tokyo, and there were about twenty different appointments missed while you were gone, I've got the entire list . . ."

"Sit down, then, and we'll get to it."

He took his position behind the desk, making a small note that the clock said 6:45 P.M., and that he would not look at it, not even steal a glance, until he was certain that the time would be past midnight.

"Leslie, put all that aside. Here are some ideas. I want you to number them. The order is not important. What's important is that you give me the whole list every day, without fail, with notes on the progress we've made regarding each and every idea, and a large mark of 'no progress' on those I allow to remain inactive."

"Yes, sir."

"Singing dolls. Perfect first a quartet, four dolls that sing in harmony."

"Oh, that's a wonderful idea, Mr. Ash."

"Prototypes should reflect some aim at being cost-effective; however, that is not the most important point. The dolls must sound good and sing even after they are hurled to the floor."

"Yes, sir . . . 'hurled to the floor.' "

"And a tower museum. I want a list of the top twenty-five available penthouses in midtown, purchase price, lease price, every pertinent detail. I want a museum in the sky so that people can go out and look at the view on a glass-enclosed gallery . . ."

"And what will the museum hold, sir, dolls?"

"Dolls on a certain theme. The exact same assignment is to be given to two thousand doll artists. Make your interpretation in three connected figures of the Family of Humankind. No, four figures. One can be a child. Yes, the description will be exact, I need to be reminded . . . For now, get the best building."

"Yes, sir, got it, yes," she said, engraving her pad with the fine-point pen.

"And on the singing dolls, everyone should be advised that eventually there will be an entire choir. A child or a doll collector could conceivably over the years acquire the entire choir, or chorus, or whatever name is best, you know, you follow me?"

"Yes, sir . . ."

"And I don't want to see any mechanical plans; this is electronic, computer chip, state of the art, and there should be . . . there should be some way for the voice of one doll to work some responsive change in the voice of another. But those are details. Write it up . . ."

"Materials, sir? Porcelain?"

"No, not porcelain. Never. I don't want them to break. Remember, they should not break, ever."

"Sorry, sir."

"And I'll design the faces. I need pictures, pictures from all over, I want everyone's work. If there is an old woman in a village in the Pyrenees making dolls, I want to see pictures. And India, why do we have no dolls from India? Do you know how often I have asked this question? Why don't I get answers? Write this memo to the vice-presidents, to the marketing people, post it! India. Who are the art-doll makers of India? I think I will go to India, yes, find a time for me to go. I'll find the people who are making dolls if no one else has the sense . . ."

The snow had begun to fall heavily outside, very white near the glass.

All the rest was once again blackness. Tiny random sounds came from the streets below, or was it from the pipes, or the snow falling on the roof above, or just the glass and steel of the building breathing as inevitably as wood breathes, the building, for all its dozens of stories, swaying ever so slightly in the wind, like a giant tree in the forest?

On and on he talked, watching her fierce little hand move with the fine-point pen. About the replicas of monuments, the small plastic version of Chartres Cathedral which the children could enter. The importance of scale, ratios. And what if there were a park with a great circle of stones there?

"Oh, and yes, a special assignment, something I want you to do tomorrow perhaps, or the day after. No, later. You do this. You're to go down to the Private Museum . . ."

"Yes, sir."

"The Bru, are you familiar with the Bru, the big French doll? My princess."

"*The* Bru, sir, yes sir, oh, that doll."

"Bru Jne 14; thirty-six inches in height; wig, shoes, dress, slip, et cetera, all original. Exhibit Number One."

"Yes, sir, I know exactly."

"She's to be packed by you, and no one else, with appropriate assistance, and then properly insured, and see to that yourself, and then shipped . . . shipped to . . ." But to whom? Was it presumptuous to send it directly to the unborn child? No, it should go to Rowan Mayfair, shouldn't it? Of course it should. And for Michael, some other memento, just as precious in its own way, something carefully crafted of wood, one of the very, very old toys, the knight on its horse, yes, all made of wood, that one, with the original paint clinging to it . . .

But no, that was not the right gift, not for Michael. There was one gift, one precious gift, something as fine as the Bru, and something he wanted to put in Michael's hands.

He rose from the desk, bidding the young Leslie to keep her chair, and moved across the spacious sitting area and down the hall to his bedroom.

He had placed it beneath the bed, the simple signal to Remmick that it was precious and must not be touched by the most well-meaning of servants. He dropped to his knees, felt for it, then slipped it out, the light blazing beautiful on the jeweled cover.

The moment of long ago was right there, the pain, the humiliation, Ninian laughing at him, telling him what a terrible blasphemy he had done, to put their tale into sacred style with sacred language.

For a long moment he sat, cross-legged, shoulder against the side of the bed. He held the book. Yes, for Michael. Michael, the boy who loved books. Michael. Michael would never be able to read it perhaps; it did not matter. Michael would keep it and it was rather like giving it to Rowan, too. She would understand that.

When he came back into the inner office, he had the book wrapped in a large white towel.

"This, this book, for Michael Curry, and the Bru for Rowan Mayfair."

"*The* Bru, sir, the princess?"

"Yes. That one. The packing is terribly important. I may want you to take these gifts down yourself. The fact that the Bru might break, it's unthinkable. Neither present must be lost. Now let's get on to other things. Send out for food if you're hungry. I have a memo here that the Prima Ballerina is out of stock worldwide. Tell me this is a lie."

"It isn't."

"Take dictation. This is the first of seven faxes pertaining to the Prima Ballerina . . ."

And on they went down the list, and when he did finally look at the clock again, with any serious intent, it was well past midnight. Indeed, the hour had dwindled to one. The snow still fell. Little Leslie's face had turned the color of paper. He was tired enough to sleep.

He fell into the large soft empty bed, vaguely conscious that the young Leslie was still hovering about, asking questions he could no longer hear that well. Extending her invitation.

"Goodnight, darling," he said.

Remmick opened the window just a little bit, the way he'd been instructed to, and the wind made a fierce howl that blotted out all sounds, all time, any conceivable lesser noise rising up the narrow margins between the dark and mournful buildings. A bit of icy air touched his cheek, making the warmth of the heavy covers all the more delicious.

Don't dream of witches; don't think of their red hair; don't think of Rowan in your arms. Don't think of Michael with the book in his hands, cherishing it as no one else ever did, except those evil brethren who betrayed Lightner. Don't think of the three of you sitting together at their hearth; don't go back to the glen, not now, not for a long long time; don't walk among circles of stone; don't visit caves; don't succumb to the temptation of mortal beauties who may die at your touch . . . Don't call them, don't beg to hear a coldness, estrangement, evasion in their voices.

And by the time the door was closed, he was slumbering.

The Bru. The street in Paris; the woman in the store; the doll in its box; the big paperweight eyes looking up at him. The sudden thought beneath the street lamp that a point had come in history where money could make possible all manner of miracles, that the pursuit of money even for one single individual could have great spiritual repercussions for thousands . . . That in a realm of manufacture and mass production, the acquisition of wealth could be utterly creative.

In a shop on Fifth Avenue only steps from his door, he had stopped to look at The Book of Kells, the perfect reproduction which anyone could own now, and leaf through and love, the precious book that had taken so many to create at Iona.

"For the Man Who Loves Books" is what he would write on the card to Michael. He saw Michael smiling at him, hands in his pockets, just the way Samuel shoved his hands in his pockets. Michael asleep on the floor, and Samuel standing over him, saying drunkenly, "Why didn't

God make me into this?" It had been too sad for laughing. And that strange statement Michael had made, as they stood near the fence in Washington Square, all of them so cold, why do people do these things, stand outdoors in snow, and Michael had said, "I always believed in the normal. I thought being poor was abnormal. I thought when you could choose what you wanted, that was normal." Snow, traffic, the night prowlers of the village, Michael's eyes when he looked at Rowan. And she remote, quiet, the words for her so much harder than for him.

This isn't a dream. This is worry, this is going back over it, and making it come to life again, and holding tight. What's it like when they lie together? Is her face a sculpture of ice? Is he the satyr of the wood? Witch touching witch; witch upon witch . . .

Will the Bru see these things from a marble mantel?

"Something about the way you held it." That's all he would write on the card to Rowan. And there would be the blue-eyed Bru staring up from the tissue, make the tissue the color of her eyes, remember to tell.

And it would be Rowan's decision, and Michael's decision, whether or not to keep those cherished gifts close, as he had done, decade after decade, like idols with which one prays, or to pass them on to Michael and Mona's baby. And maybe the big paperweight eyes of the gorgeous Bru Jne 14 would gaze upon that little child, and would they see the witches' blood as he might if ever, if ever he dared to journey there, some time after the baby had come into this world, as they say—if he dared, just to spy upon them all—The Family of Witch Kind—from the fabled garden where once the ghost of Lasher walked, and his remains were committed to the earth—from that garden which could hide another phantom, could it not, peering through a small, unnoticed winter window.

Thirty-three

Pᴇʀᴄᴇ had collected them from the airport, far too polite to inquire about the owner of the plane, or where they had been, and only too eager to take them to the site of the new medical center.

It was so warm as to be stifling, Michael thought. My kind of town. So glad to be back, and yet so utterly uncertain of anything—whether grass will continue to grow, whether Rowan will become warm and trusting again in his arms, whether he could stay away from the tall man in New York with whom he had known the most extraordinary friendship.

And the past; the past was not fun anymore and never would be, but something inherited with its burdens, its curses, its secrets.

Take your eyes off the bodies of the dead; forget the old man crumpling to the floor; and Aaron, where has Aaron gone? Did his spirit rise into the light, were all things clear finally, and forgiven? To forgive is such a gift to us.

They got out at the edge of the huge rectangle of churned earth. Signs read MAYFAIR MEDICAL with a dozen names and dates. And something too small for his aging eyes to read. He wondered if they'd stop being so blue when they couldn't really see anymore. Did that happen? Or would he have that last claim to fame even when he couldn't see the girls giving him a second look, or Rowan melting slightly, lips curled at the edges.

He tried to focus on the construction site, to realize what his mind told him, that the progress had been amazing, that some hundred men were working out here in these four blocks, that Mayfair Medical had truly begun.

Were those tears in Rowan's eyes? Yes, the smooth lady with the bobbed hair and the slim tailored suit of supple cloth was crying silently. He moved closer, what the hell was all this distance about, all this respecting of one another's privacy, feelings? He hugged her tight and, finding the softest part of her neck, placed his kisses there, until he felt her rustling against him, bending slightly, and a nice quiver running through her hands as she clasped his head, and said:

"You went on with it, all of you. I could never have expected such a thing." Her eyes moved to Pierce, shy Pierce, who was blushing now under these compliments.

"It's a dream you gave to us, Rowan. And now it's our dream too, and since all our dreams are coming true—since you're here and with us again—well, this one also will be realized."

"Now that's a lawyerly speech, with pacing and just enough force," Michael said. Was he jealous of this young kid? Women did tend to dote when their eyes fell upon Pierce Mayfair. If only Mona could see it, see perhaps that he was the one for her, especially now that in the wake of Gifford's death, her son had drifted away from his fiancée, Clancy. More and more Pierce came to sit some distance from Mona and stare. Yeah, maybe a little interest in Mona was brewing . . .

Michael reached for Rowan's cheek. "Kiss me."

"This is a vulgar display," she purred, "and you know it. All those workmen are staring at us."

"I hope so," he said.

"Let's go home," she whispered.

"Pierce, how's Mona, you've got an update?" Michael asked. They climbed into the car. He had forgotten what it meant to ride in normal automobiles, live in normal houses, have normal dreams. Ash's voice sang to him in his sleep. He heard the musical whisper in his ear even now. And would they ever truly see Ash again? Or would Ash vanish behind all those bronze doors, shutting them out, insulated by his company, his billions, remembering them only perhaps with occasional notes, though they might call, come to New York, press his bell in the very dead of night. "I need you!"

"Ah, Mona, yes," said Pierce. "Well, she's acting strange. When Dad talks to her, she sounds like she's high as a kite. But she's okay. She's hanging around with Mary Jane. And yesterday a team started work on Fontevrault."

"Oh, I'm so glad to hear that," Michael said. "So they're going to save that place."

"Well, it had to be done, obviously, since neither Mary Jane nor Dolly Jean will stand to see it demolished. Oh, I think Dolly Jean is with them too. Now Dolly Jean looks like a withered apple, but they say she is very quick."

"I'm glad she's there," he said. "I like old people." Rowan laughed softly, resting her head on his shoulder. "Maybe we'll ask Aunt Viv to come over," he said. "And how is Bea? What is happening with Bea?"

"Well, now," said Pierce with a little tilt of his head, "Ancient Evelyn has worked the miracle there, simply by coming home from the hospital and needing care, and guess who has dashed up to Amelia to feed her soft-boiled eggs and make her talk, and make her grip tight with both hands? Dad says it's the perfect antidote for grief. I wonder if Mother's spirit isn't there."

"All the news is good news now," Rowan said with a wan smile, her voice deep as always. "And the girls will be in the house, and the silence will have to wait, and the spirits recede into the walls."

"You think they're still there?" Pierce asked with touching innocence.

God bless the Mayfairs who have never seen, and don't really believe.

"No, son," Michael said. "It's just a big beautiful house, and it's waiting for us, and for . . . new generations to come."

"For Mayfairs yet unborn," whispered Rowan.

They had just turned onto St. Charles Avenue, the heavenly corridor of green, oaks in blinding spring leaf, sun mellow, traffic slow, flash of one lovely house after another. My town, home, everything all right, Rowan's hand in mine.

"Ah, and Amelia Street, look," he said.

How dapper the Mayfair house looked in the San Francisco style, with its fresh coat of peach with white trim and green shutters. And all the weeds gone. He almost wanted to stop, to see Evelyn and Bea, but he knew he had to see Mona first, he had to see the mother and child rolled into one. And he had to be with his wife, talking quietly in the big bedroom upstairs, about all that had happened, the tales they'd heard, the strange things they'd seen and might never tell anyone . . . except Mona.

And tomorrow he would go out to the mausoleum where Aaron was buried, and he'd do the Irish trick of just talking to Aaron, out loud, as if Aaron were answering, and if anybody didn't like it, well, they could just get out of there, couldn't they? All his family had always done that, his father going out to St. Joseph's Cemetery and talking to his grandmother and grandfather any time he felt like it. And Uncle Shamus when he was so sick, saying to his wife, "You can still talk to me after I'm gone. The only difference is I won't be answering you."

Once again the light changed, darkening, and the trees expanded, crowding out the sky and breaking it into tiny glowing fragments. The

Garden District. First Street. And wonder of wonders, the house on the corner of Chestnut, amid its spring banana trees and ferns, and azaleas in bloom, waiting for them.

"Pierce, you must come in."

"No, they're waiting me for downtown. You rest. Call us when you need us." He had already slipped out to lend a manly hand as Rowan climbed from the car. And then his key was in the gate, and he was waving goodbye to them.

A uniformed guard walked along the side fence, disappearing discreetly around the end of the house.

The silence was healed, the car slipping off in light and shadow, noiseless, removed, the dying afternoon burnished and warm and without the slightest resistance. The scent of the sweet olive hung over the whole yard. And tonight he'd smell the jasmine again.

Ash had said that fragrance was the sharpest trigger of memory, a transport into forgotten worlds. And he had been so right, and what did it do to you, to be taken away from all the fragrances you needed to breathe?

He opened the front door for his wife, and felt a sudden impulse to carry her over the threshold. Hell, why not!

She gave a little unrestrained cry of delight, clutching his neck as he scooped her up.

The thing about gestures like this was not to drop the lady in question.

"And now, my dear, we are home," he growled against her soft neck again, forcing her head back as he kissed her beneath her chin, "and the smell of the sweet olive gives way to Eugenia's ever-present wax, and the scent of the old wood, and something musty and expensive and delicious to breathe."

"Amen," she said.

As he went to put her down, she clung to him for a moment. Ah, that was nice! And his aging, battered heart had not begun to pound. She would hear it, wouldn't she, with a doctor's ear? No, he stood hale and quiet, holding her against him, smelling her clean soft hair, and gazing down the polished hall, past the great soaring white doorway, at the distant murals of the dining room, touched still by the afternoon sun. Home. Here. Now, as it has never, never been for either of us.

At last she slipped from him, landing on her feet. The tiniest frown came to her forehead. "Oh, it's nothing," she said. "Only certain memories will die hard, you know. But then I think of Ash, and that is something to contemplate rather than all the sad things."

He wanted to answer, he wanted to say something about his own love for Ash, and something else, something else that was almost torturing him. It would be better to leave it alone, that's what others would advise, if ever he asked them. But he couldn't. He looked into her eyes, opening his own very wide, perhaps wide enough to look angry when he didn't mean to at all.

"Rowan, my love," he said. "I know you could have stayed with him. I know you made a choice."

"You're my man," she said with a soft explosion of breath, "my man, Michael."

Nice to carry her up the stairs, but he'd never make it, not all twenty-nine steps, and where were the young ladies, and Granny, the resurrected one? No, they could not shut themselves away now, unless by some luck the entire tribe had gone out for an early dinner.

Closing his eyes, he kissed her again. Nobody could stop him from doing that at least a dozen times. Kiss. And when he looked up again, he saw the red-haired beauty at the end of the hall, two in fact, one very, very tall, and that mischievous Mary Jane, blond braids on top of her head again, three of the most gorgeous necks in the universe, young girls like that are swans. But who was this new beauty who stood incredibly tall, and looked, why, she looked exactly like Mona!

Rowan turned, staring back down the hall.

The Three Graces, they were, against the dining room door, and Mona's face seemed to occupy two different places. This wasn't resemblance, it was duplication, and why did they stand so still, all of them in their cotton dresses, merely staring as if from a painting?

He heard Rowan gasp. He saw Mona break into a run, and then rush toward him across the polished floor.

"No, you can't do anything. You can't. You have to listen."

"Dear God," Rowan said, her weight falling heavily against him, her body shaking.

"She's my child," Mona said. "My child and Michael's, and you won't hurt her."

Suddenly it struck him, as things often do, in a rush of different stages, all clattering together to take his breath away. The baby is this young woman. The giant helix produced this. This is a Taltos as surely as Ash is a Taltos, as surely as those two under the tree are Taltos. Rowan is going to faint, she is going to go down, and the pain in my chest is killing me.

He clutched for the newel post.

"Tell me now, neither of you will hurt her."

"Hurt her? How could I do that?" Michael said.

And then Rowan began to cry, blubbering hopelessly against her clasped hands. "Oh God."

The tall girl had taken a shaky step and then another. And now would that helpless voice come out, the child voice he'd heard from the other before the shot was fired? He felt dizzy. The sun was dying as if on cue, the house returning to its natural darkness.

"Michael, sit down, sit down there on the step," said Mona.

"Dear God, he's sick," said Mary Jane.

And Rowan, snapping to, wrapped her long wet fingers around his neck.

And the tall one said:

"Well, I know this is a dreadful shock for you both, and Mother and Mary Jane have worried for days, but I myself am relieved to see you at last, and force a decision as to whether I can remain beneath this roof, as they say, your child as well as Mona's child. As you can see here, she has placed the emerald around my neck, but I bow to your decision."

Rowan was speechless. So was he. It would have been Mona's voice except it sounded older, and a little less strong, as though chastened already by the world.

He looked up to see her standing there, big spill of vivid red locks, woman's breasts and long curved legs, and her eyes, her eyes like green fire.

"Father," she whispered, dropping to her knees. Her long fingers shot out and clasped his face.

He closed his eyes.

"Rowan," she said. "Love me, please, and then maybe he will."

Rowan cried, her fingers tightening on his neck. His heart was thudding in his ears, thudding as if it were growing bigger and bigger.

"Morrigan is my name," she said.

"She's mine, my child," Mona said, "and yours, Michael."

"And I think it's time that you let me speak," said Morrigan, "that I take the burden of decision from both of you."

"Honey, slow down," he said. He blinked his eyes slowly, trying to clear his vision.

But something had disturbed this long nymph. Something had made her draw back her hands and then sniff at her fingers. Her eyes flashed to Rowan and then to him. She rose, rushing close to Rowan, before Rowan could possibly move away, sniffing at Rowan's cheeks, and then standing back.

"What is that scent?" she said. "What is it! I know that scent!"

"Listen to me," Rowan said. "We'll talk. That's what you said. Now come." She moved forward, releasing him to die of a heart attack entirely by himself, and she put her arms around the girl's waist, the girl staring down at her with comically frightened eyes.

"The scent's all over you."

"What do you think it is?" Mona asked. "What could it be?"

"A male," the girl whispered. "They've been with him, these two."

"No, he's dead," said Mona, "you're picking it up again from the floorboards, from the walls."

"Oh no," she whispered. "This is a living male." Suddenly she grabbed Rowan by the shoulders. Mona and Mary Jane sped to her side, gently tugging her arms away. Michael was on his feet. God, the creature was the same height as he was. Mona's face, but not Mona, no, not Mona at all.

"The smell is driving me mad," she whispered. "You keep this secret from me? Why?"

"Give them time to explain," Mona pleaded. "Morrigan, stop it, listen to me." And then she had the girl's hands in hers, holding them tight. And Mary Jane was standing on tiptoe.

"Now just you simmer down, long tall Sally, and let them tell us the scoop."

"You don't understand," Morrigan said, voice suddenly thick and tears gathering in her huge green eyes, as she looked again to Michael, to Rowan. "There's a male, don't you see? There's a male of me! Mother, you can smell the scent. Mother, tell the truth!" It was a scream. "Mother, please, I can't stand it!" And her sobs came like something tumbling downstairs, her face clenched in pain, her tall angular body wobbling, and bending gently as she let the other two embrace her and keep her from falling.

"Let us take her now," said Mary Jane.

"Just don't do anything, you have to swear," Mona pleaded.

"And we'll meet and we'll talk, and we'll . . ."

"Tell me," the stricken girl whispered. "Tell me, *where is he?*"

Rowan pushed Michael towards the elevator, pulling open the old wooden door. "Get in."

And the last thing he saw, as he leaned against the back wall of the elevator, was those pretty cotton dresses, as the three of them fled up the stairs together.

. . .

He lay on the bed.

"Now, don't think of it now. Don't think," Rowan said.

The wet rag felt exactly like a wet rag. He didn't like it.

"I'm not going to die," he said quietly. And what an effort, the words. Was it defeat again, was it a great ghastly defeat, and the scaffolding of the normal world buckling beneath its weight, and the future forecast once more in the colors of death and Lent, or was it something that they could embrace and contain, something that they could somehow accept without the mind shattering?

"What do we do?" she whispered.

"You are asking me this, you? What do we do?" He rolled over on his side. The pain was a little less. He was sweating all over and despised it, the feel of it, the inevitable smell. And where were they, the three beauties? "I don't know what we do," he answered.

She sat still on the side of the bed, her shoulders slightly hunched, her hair falling down against her cheek, her eyes gazing off.

"Will *he* know what to do?" Michael asked.

Her head turned as if pulled sharply by a string.

"*Him?* You can't tell him. You can't expect him to learn something like that and not . . . not go as crazy as she's gone. Do you want that to happen? Do you want him to come? Nobody and nothing will stand between them."

"And what happens then?" he asked, trying to make his voice sound strong, firm, when the firmest thing he knew to do was to ask questions.

"What happens! I don't know. I don't know any more than you do! Dear God, there are two of them and they are alive and they're not . . . they're not . . ."

"What?"

"Not some evil that stole its way in, some lying, deceiving thing that nourished alienation, madness. They're not that."

"Keep talking," he said. "Keep saying those things. Not evil."

"No, not evil, only another form of natural." She stared off, her voice dropping low, her hand resting warmly on his arm.

If only he wasn't so tired. And Mona, Mona for how long had she been alone with this creature, this firstborn thing, this long-necked heron of a girl with Mona's features stamped on her face. And Mary Jane, the two witches together.

And all the time they had been so dedicated to their tasks, to save Yuri, to weed out the traitors, to comfort Ash, the tall being who was no one's enemy and never had been and never would be.

"What can we do?" she whispered. "What right have we to do anything?"

He turned his head, trying to see her clearly. He sat up, slowly, feeling the bite beneath his ribs, small now, unimportant. He wondered vaguely how long one could hang on with a heart that winced so quickly, so easily. Hell, not easily. It had taken Morrigan, hadn't it? His daughter, Morrigan. His daughter crying somewhere in the house with her childmother, Mona.

"Rowan," he said. "Rowan, what if this *is* Lasher's triumph? What if this was the plan all along?"

"How can we know that?" she whispered. Her fingers had gone to her lips, the sure sign that she was in mental pain and trying to think her way through it. "I can't kill again!" she said, so soft it was like a sigh.

"No, no . . . not that, no, I don't mean that. I can't do that! I . . ."

"I know. You didn't kill Emaleth. I did."

"That's not what we have to think about now. What we have to think about is—do we handle this alone? Do we try? Do we bring together others?"

"As if she were an invading organism," Rowan murmured, eyes wide, "and the other cells came to surround her, contain her."

"They can do that without hurting her." He was so tired, and almost sick. In a minute he was going to throw up. But he couldn't leave her now, he refused to be ignominiously sick. "Rowan, the family, the family first, all the family."

"Frightened people. No. Not Pierce and Ryan and Bea and Lauren . . ."

"Not alone, Rowan. We can't make the right choices alone, and the girls, the girls are swept off their feet, the girls are walking the dark paths of magic and transformation, she belongs to the girls."

"I know," Rowan sighed. "The way that he once belonged to me, the spirit who came to me, full of lies. Oh, I wish in some horrible, cowardly way . . ."

"What?"

She shook her head.

There was a sound at the door. It popped a few inches, then rode back. Mona stood there, her face faintly streaked from crying too, her eyes full of weariness.

"You won't hurt her."

"No," he said. "When did it happen?"

"Just a few days ago. Listen, you've got to come. We've got to talk.

She can't run away. She can't survive out there on her own. She thinks she can, but she can't. I'm not asking you to tell her if there's really a male somewhere, just come, accept my child, listen."

"We will," said Rowan.

Mona nodded.

"You're not well, you need to rest," said Rowan.

"It was the birth, but I'm all right. She needs the milk all the time."

"Then she won't run away," said Rowan.

"Perhaps not," said Mona. "Do you see, both of you?"

"That you love her? Yes," said Rowan. "I see."

Mona slowly nodded her head. "Come down. In an hour. I think by then she'll be all right. We bought her lots of pretty dresses. She likes those. She insists we dress up too. Maybe I'll brush her hair back and put a ribbon in it the way I used to do in mine. She's smart. She's very smart and she sees . . ."

"Sees what?"

Mona hesitated. And then her answer came, small and without conviction. "She sees the future."

The door closed.

He realized he was looking at the pale rectangular panes of the window. The light was waning fast, the twilight of spring so quick. The cicadas had begun outside. Did she hear all that? Did it comfort her? Where was she now, this, his daughter?

He groped for the lamp.

"No, don't," Rowan said. She was a silhouette now, a line of gleaming light defining her profile. The room closed and then grew vast in the darkness. "I want to think. I want to think out loud in the darkness."

"Yes, I understand," he said.

She turned, and very slowly, with highly effective movements, she slipped the pillows behind him so that he could lean back, and hating himself, he let her do it. He rested, he pulled a deep breath of air into his lungs. The window was glazed and white. And when the trees moved, it was like the darkness outside trying to peer in. It was like the trees listening.

Rowan talked:

"I tell myself we all run the risk of horror; any child can be a monster, a bringer of death. What would you do if it were a baby, a tiny pink thing like they ought to be, and a witch came and laid her hands on it and said, 'It will grow up to wage war, it will grow up to make bombs, it will grow up to sacrifice the lives of thousands, millions.'

Would you choke it? I mean if you really believed? Or would you say 'No'?"

"I'm thinking," he said. "I'm thinking of things that make a kind of sense, that she's newborn, that she must listen, that those who surround her have to be teachers, and as the years pass, as she grows older, then . . ."

"And what if Ash were to die without ever knowing?" Rowan asked. "Do you remember his words? What was it, Michael? 'The dance, the circle, and the song . . .' Or do you believe the prediction in the cave? If you do believe it, and I don't know that I do, but if you do, what then? We spend our lives keeping them apart?"

The room was completely dark. Pale white streaks of light fell tentatively across the ceiling. The furnishings, the fireplace, the walls themselves had disappeared. And the trees outside still held their color, their detail, because the streetlights were shining up at them.

The sky was the leftover sky—and the color of rosy flesh, as sometimes happens.

"We'll go down," he said. "And then we'll listen. And then perhaps, perhaps, we'll call the entire family! Tell them all to come, come as they did when you were lying in this bed, when we thought you were going to die—all of them. We need them. Lauren and Paige and Ryan, yes, Ryan, and Pierce and Ancient Evelyn."

"Perhaps," she said. "Know what will happen? They will look at her, in her undeniable innocence and youth, and then they'll look to us, wondering, 'Is it true, is it so?' and begging for us to choose some path."

He slid gently off the bed, fearing nausea, making his way through the dark easily from bedpost to bedpost and then into the narrow white marble bathroom. A memory came back—the first time they had come into this part of the house, he and the Rowan he meant to marry. And there had been small bits of a broken statue lying here, on the white tiles that now appeared in the soft, colorless drench of the light. The Virgin's veiled head, snapped unevenly at the neck; one small plaster hand. What had it been, an omen?

Dear God, if Ash found her, and she found him! Dear God, but that is their decision, is it not?

"It's out of our hands," Rowan whispered from the dark.

He leaned over the basin, turned on the tap, washed his face with the cold water. For a while it ran almost warm through the pipes, and then it came from the deep earth and it was really cold. At last he dried off, patting his skin with a little mercy for once, and then he laid aside the towel. He slipped out of his jacket, stiff crumpled shirt with the stench of sweat all over it now. He wiped himself dry, and took the recommended spray can from the shelf to kill his scent. He wondered if Ash could have done that, killed the scent cold so that they wouldn't have picked it up from farewell kisses he'd given them both.

And in ancient times, could the human female pick up the scent of the human male coming through the forest? Why have we lost that gift? Because the scent is no longer the predictor of danger. The scent is no longer a reliable indicator of any threat. For Aaron, the hired killer and the stranger were one and the same. What had scent to do with two tons of metal crushing Aaron against the wall?

He pulled on a fresh shirt, and a light sweatshirt over that. Cover it all up.

"Shall we go down now?" He snapped off the light, and searched the darkness. He thought he saw the outline of her bowed head. He thought he saw a glimmer of the deep burgundy of her coat, and then he did see the white blaze of her blouse as she turned, so Southern the way she was dressed, so finished.

"Let's go," she said, in the deep, commanding voice that made him think of butterscotch and sleeping with her. "I want to talk to her."

The library. They were gathered already.

As he came in the door, he saw that Morrigan herself sat at the desk, regal in white Victorian lace with high neck and fancy cuffs and a cameo at her throat, a flood of taffeta skirt showing behind the mahogany. Mona's twin. And Mona, in softer, more careless lace, curled in the big chair, the way she'd been that day when he had appealed to Ryan and Pierce to help him find Rowan. Mona, needing a mother herself and certainly a father.

Mary Jane held down the other corner, picture perfect in pink. Our witches come in pastels, he thought. And Granny. He had not realized she was there, at the corner of the sofa, until he saw her tiny wrinkled face, her playful little black eyes, and a crinkled smile on her lips.

"There they are!" she said with great flair, stretching out her arms to him. "And you a Mayfair too, out of Julien, think of it. I would have known." He bent to be kissed, to smell the sweet powder rising from her quilted robe, the prerogative of the very old, to go about clothed for bed perpetually. "Come here to me, Rowan Mayfair," she said. "Let me tell you about your mother. Your mother cried when she gave you up. Everyone knew. She cried and turned her head away when they took you from her arms, and never was the same again, ever."

Rowan clasped the small dry hands, and she too bent to receive the kiss. "Dolly Jean," she said. "You were there when Morrigan was born?" She cast her eye on Morrigan. She had not had the nerve yet to take a good look at her.

"Sure, I was," said Dolly Jean. "I knew she was a walking baby before she ever stuck her foot out of the womb. I knew! And remember, whatever you say, whatever you think, this is a Mayfair, this girl. If we've the stomach for Julien and his murdering ways, we've the stomach for a wild thing with a long neck and an Alice-in-Wonderland face! You listen now. Maybe this is a voice you've never heard before."

He smiled. Well, it was damned good that she was there, that she had taken it so in her stride, and it made him want to reach for the phone now, and begin the calls that would bring all Mayfairs together. Instead he merely sat facing the desk. And Rowan took the chair beside him.

All looked at the ravishing red-haired thing that suddenly laid her head against the high back of her chair, and curled her long white hands around its arms, breasts pushing through her stiff starched lace, waist so frail he wanted to put his hands around it.

"I'm your daughter, Michael."

"Tell me more, Morrigan. Tell me what the future holds. Tell me what you want from us, and what we should expect from you."

"Oh, I'm so glad to hear you say those words. Do you hear that?" She looked back and forth at the others and then at Rowan. "Because I've been telling them that is what was bound to happen. I have to forecast. I have to speak. I have to declare."

"Then go ahead, my dear," he said. And quite suddenly he couldn't see her as monstrous at all; he could only see her as alive, as human, as tender and fragile as all of those in this room, even himself, the one who could kill the others with his bare hands if he wanted to. And Rowan, who could kill any human with her mind. But not this creature.

"I want teachers," she said, "not the confines of a school, but tutors, with Mother and with Mary Jane, I want to be educated, to learn everything in the world, I want the solitude and protection in which to do this, with assurances that I will not be cast out, that I am one of you, that someday . . ." Here she stopped as if a switch had been thrown. "Someday I shall be the heiress as my mother has planned for me, and after me, another from her line who is human perhaps . . . if you . . . if the male . . . if the scent . . ."

"Play it off, Morrigan," said Mary Jane.

"Just keep talking," said the little mother.

"I want those things which a special child would ask, of searing intelligence and insatiable hungers, but one which is reasonable and lovable, yes, surely, one whom it is possible to love and educate and thereby control."

"This is what you want?" Michael asked. "You want parents."

"Yes, the old ones to tell their tales to me, the way it was once for us."

"Yes," said Rowan firmly. "And then you will accept our protection, which means our authority and our guidance, that you're our newborn girl."

"Yes."

"And that we will care for you."

"Yes!" She rose slightly in the chair, and then stopped, clutching both sides of the big desk, her arms like long, slender bones that should have supported wings. "Yes. I am a Mayfair. Say this with me. I am one of you. And one day, one day perhaps, by a human man, I'll conceive, and others like me will be born, from witches' blood as I was born, that I have this right to exist, to be happy, to know, to flourish. . . . God, you still have that scent. I can't bear the scent. You have to tell me the truth."

"And what if we do?" asked Rowan. "And what if we say that you must stay here, that you are far too young and innocent to meet this male, that we will set the time for a meeting . . ."

"What if we promise," said Michael, "that we will tell him? And that you can know where he is, but only if you promise . . ."

"I swear," she cried. "I'll swear anything."

"Is it that strong?" Mona whispered.

"Mother, they're frightening me."

"You have them in the palm of your hand," said the diminutive Mona nestled in the leather chair, cheeks wasted, skin pale. "They cannot harm anything that explains itself so well. You're as human as they are, don't you see? They see. Play it off. Continue."

"Give me my place," she said, her eyes growing wide and seeming to catch fire as they had when she'd cried. "Let me be what I am. Let me couple if I will. Let me be one of you."

"You can't go to him. You can't couple," said Rowan. "Not yet, not until your mind is capable of making that decision."

"You make me mad!" she cried, drawing back.

"Morrigan, knock it off," said Mona.

"You just simmer down," said Mary Jane, climbing to her feet and moving cautiously behind the desk until she could put her hands on Morrigan's shoulders.

"Tell them about the memories," said Mona. "How we taped them all. And the things you want to see."

She was trying to pick up the thread again, to prevent a flood of tears or screams, he didn't know which.

"To go to Donnelaith," Morrigan said in a shaky voice, "to find the plain."

"You remember those things?"

"Yes, and all of us together in the circle. I remember. I remember. I reach out for their hands. Help me!" Her voice rose again. But she had clapped her hand over her mouth, and when she cried now it was muffled.

Michael stood up and came round, gently nudging Mary Jane out of the way.

"You have my love," he said in her ear. "You hear me? You have it. You have my love and the authority that goes along with it."

"Oh, thank God." She leant her head against him, just the way Rowan did it now and then, and she cried.

He stroked her soft hair, softer, silkier than Mona's. He thought of the brief union on the sofa, on the library floor, and this, this frail and unpredictable thing.

"I know you," she whispered, rubbing her forehead against his chest. "I know your scent too, and the things you've seen, I know the smell of the wind on Liberty Street, and the way the house looked when you first walked in, and how you changed it. I know different kinds of wood, and different tools, and what it's like to rub tung oil into the grain for a long, long time, the sound of the cloth on the wood. And I know when you drowned, when you were so cold, you got warm, you saw witches' ghosts. Those are the worst kind, the strongest kind, except maybe for the ghost of a Taltos. Witches and Taltos, you must have some of us inside you, waiting to come out, to be reborn, to make a race again. Oh, the dead know everything. I don't know why they don't talk. Why doesn't he come to me, or any of them? They just dance in my memories and say those things that mattered to them then. Father, Father, I love you."

"I love you too," he whispered, his hand closing tightly on her head. He felt himself tremble.

"And you know," she said, looking up at him, tears draining from her eyes in stains down her white cheeks. "You know, Father, that one day I shall take over completely."

"And why is that?" he asked calmly, with a tight grip on his voice, on his face.

"Because it has to be," she said in the same sincere, heated whisper. "I learn so quickly, I'm so strong, I know so much already. And when they come from my womb, and they will come, like I came from Mother and from you, they will have this strength, this knowledge, memories of both ways, the human, the Taltos. We have learned the ambition from you. And the humans will flee from us when they know. They will flee, and the world will . . . the world will *crumble*. Don't you think, Father?"

He was shivering inside. He heard Ash's voice. He looked at Rowan, whose face remained still, impassive.

"To live together, that was our vow," he said. He bent, his lips just touching Morrigan's forehead. Smell of baby skin, fresh and sweet. "Those are the dreams of the young, to rule, to dominate all. And the tyrants of history were those who never grew up," he said. "But you will grow. You will have all the knowledge that all of us can give you."

"Boy, this sure is going to be something," Mary Jane said, folding her arms.

He stared at her, shocked rudely by her words, and the little laugh that came out of her as she shook her head. He looked at Rowan, whose eyes were once again reddened and sad as she turned her head slightly to the side, gazing at the strange daughter, and then at Mona. And only in Mona's face did he see not wonder and shock, but fear, a calculated, controlled fear.

"The Mayfairs are my kind now, too," Morrigan whispered. "A family of walking babies, don't you see? And the powerful ones should be brought together. Computer files must be scanned; all those with the double helix made to couple at once; until the numerical score has been evened, at least, at least, and then we will be side by side . . . Mother, I must work now. I must get into the Mayfair computer again."

"Simmer down," said Mary Jane.

"What do you think and feel?" Morrigan demanded, staring directly at Rowan.

"You have to learn our ways, and maybe you'll discover someday that they are your ways too. No one is made to couple in our world. Numerical scores are not our forte. But you'll see. We'll teach you, and you will teach us."

"And you won't hurt me."

"We can't. We wouldn't," Rowan said. "We don't want to."

"And the male. This male who left his scent all over you. Is he alone too?"

Rowan hesitated, then nodded.

Morrigan looked up into Michael's eyes.

"All alone like me?"

"More alone," Michael said. "You have us, your family."

She rose to her feet, hair flying out, making several quick pirouettes as she crossed the room, the taffeta skirts rustling, reflecting the light in fluid racing flashes.

"I can wait. I can wait for him. I can wait. Only tell him, please. I leave it to you, I leave it to the tribe. Come, Dolly Jean, come, Mona, it's time to dance. Mary Jane, do you want to? Rowan and Michael, I want to dance."

She lifted her arms, turning round and round, head falling back, hair hanging long and low. She hummed a song, something soft, something Michael knew he had heard before, something perhaps that Tessa had sung, Tessa, closeted away to die without ever seeing this child? Or Ash, had he hummed this song, Ash, who would never never forgive them if they kept this secret from him, the world-weary wanderer.

She dropped to her knees beside Rowan. The two young women stiffened, but Mona motioned that Mary Jane was to wait.

Rowan did nothing. She was hugging her knees with her clasped hands. She did not move as the lithe, silent figure drew very close, as Morrigan sniffed at her cheeks, her neck, her hair. Then slowly Rowan turned, staring into her face.

Not human, no, dear God, not at all. What is she?

Calm and collected, Rowan gave no sign that she might be thinking the very same thing. But surely she sensed something like danger.

"I can wait," Morrigan said softly. "Write it in stone, his name, where he is. Carve it in the trunk of the funeral oak. Write it somewhere. Keep it from me, but keep it, keep it until a time comes. I can wait."

Then she drew back and, making those same pirouettes, left the room, humming to herself, the humming higher and higher until it became like a whistle.

They sat in silence. Suddenly Dolly Jean said, "Oh!" She had fallen asleep, and now she was awake. "Well, what happened?" she asked.

"I don't know," Rowan said.

She looked at Mona, and Mona looked at her, and something silent passed between them.

"Well, I better go watch her," said Mary Jane, hurrying out of the room. "Before she goes and jumps in the swimming pool again with all her clothes, or lies down on the grass back there, trying to smell those two dead bodies."

Mona sighed.

"So what does the mother have to say to the father?" Michael asked.

Mona thought for a long moment. "Watch. Watch and wait." She looked at Rowan. "I know now why you did what you did."

"You do?" Rowan whispered.

"Yeah," Mona said. "Yeah, I know." Slowly she climbed to her feet. She was leaving the room, when suddenly she turned. "I didn't mean . . . I didn't mean it was all right to hurt her."

"We know that it's not all right," said Michael. "And she's my child too, remember."

Mona looked up at him, torn, helpless, as if there were a thousand things she wanted to say, to ask, to explain. And then she only shook her head and, turning her back on them, moved towards the door quietly. At the very last, she looked back, her face a radiant burst of light, of feeling. The little girl with the woman's body beneath her fussy dress. And my sin has done this, my sin has unleashed this thing, as if from the heart and mind of Mona herself, he thought.

"I smell it too, the scent," said Mona. "A living male. Can't you wash it off? Scrub it off with soap. Then maybe, maybe she'll calm down, she'll stop thinking about it and talking about it, she'll be all right. In the night, she may come into your room, you may wake up with her bending over you. She won't hurt you. In a way you've got the upper hand."

"How so?" Michael asked.

"If she doesn't do everything we say, you'll never tell her about the male. It's simple."

"Yes, it's a means of control," said Rowan.

"There are other means. She suffers so."

"You're tired, honey," said Michael. "You should rest."

"Oh, we will, in each other's arms. It's only when you wake and you see her sniffing at the clothes, don't be frightened. It can look kind of terrible."

"Yes," said Rowan. "We will all be prepared."

"But who is he?" Mona asked.

Rowan turned, as if to make sure she had heard this question right.

Dolly Jean, her head bowed, gave a sudden startling snore.

"Who is the male?" asked Mona, insistent, her eyes suddenly half-mast with exhaustion and slightly haunted.

"And if I tell you," said Rowan, "then you must keep it from her. Let us be the strong ones on that score. Trust us."

"Mother!" Morrigan called. A waltz had begun, Richard Strauss, strings, one of those lovely bland records that you can listen to for the rest of your life. He wanted to see them dancing, but in a way he didn't.

"Do the guards know she's not to go out?" Michael asked.

"Well, not really," Mona said. "You know, it would be easier if you told them to go away. She . . . she upsets them. I can control her more easily if they're gone. She won't run away, not from her mother."

"Yes," Rowan said. "We'll dismiss them."

Michael was unsure.

But then he nodded. "We are in this . . . together."

The voice of Morrigan called out again. The music surged. Mona slowly turned and left them.

LATE in the night, he could hear them laughing still, and the music now and then, or was it a dream of Stuart Gordon's tower? Then the keys of the computer tapping away, and that laughter, and the soft rumble of their running feet on the stairs. And the sound of mingled voices, young and high and very sweet, singing that song.

Why try to sleep, but then he was gone, too tired, too needy of rest and of escape, too hungry for the simplicity of cotton sheets, and Rowan's warm body against his. Pray, pray for her. Pray for Mona. Pray for them . . .

"Our Father, Who art in Heaven, hallowed be Thy name, Thy kingdom come—"

His eyes opened wide. "Thy kingdom come. No." The feeling of sudden distress was too vast, yet elusive. He was too tired. "Thy kingdom come." He couldn't think it out. He turned over and buried his face in the crook of Rowan's warm neck and shoulder.

"Love you," she whispered, a murmured prayer out of the depths of sleep, perhaps, more comforting than his prayer had been.

Thirty-four

THE CLEAN monotony of snow, of meetings without end, of phone
calls, of the sheets of faxes full of statistics, summaries, of the
business of life which he himself had made, reaching for the gold and
dreams.

At midday he put his head down on the desk. It had been a full five
days since Michael and Rowan had gone home, and they had not called
him, or written even a note. And now he wondered if his gifts had
somehow made them sad or been the wrong thing, or if they were
blotting him out the way he tried to blot out the memory of Tessa, of
Gordon dead on the floor, of Yuri stammering and wringing his hands,
of cold winter in the glen, and the jeers of Aiken Drumm.

What do we seek? What do we need? How can we know what will
make us happy? It was a simple thing to pick up the phone, to call
Rowan or Michael, to ask if they were all right, if they had recovered
from their journey.

And what if their voices were brittle and indifferent, and he was left
with the instrument in his hand, and the wire gone dead after careless
farewells? No, that would have been worse than nothing.

Or more truly, it was not what he wanted.

Just go there. Just see them. Without lifting his head, he pressed the
button. Prepare the plane. Fly away from the city of bitter cold, to the
lost land of love. Just look at them, see their house with its warm lights,
see through the windows they so lovingly described, and go away
without a sound, without begging for their eyes to meet yours. Just
look at them.

There will be a comfort in that.

Once all dwellings were small and shut up, windowless, fortified.
And you couldn't see the beings within. But now it was different. One

could gaze upon a perfect life as if peering at a painting. Sheer glass was enough to shut one out, and demarcate the secret turf of each one's love. But the gods were kind, and you could peep inside. You could see those you missed.

It will be enough. Do it. And they'd never know. He wouldn't frighten them.

The car was ready. Remmick had sent the bags down. "Must be good to be going south, sir," he said.

"Yes, to summerland," he replied.

"That's what Somerset means, sir, in England."

"Yes, I know," he said. "I'll see you soon. Keep my rooms warm. Call me at once if . . . Well, don't hesitate if there is anything."

A SPEAKING twilight, a city so wooded still that the creatures of the air sang the songs of dusk. He slipped out of the car blocks from the house. He knew the way. He had checked his map, and now he walked past the iron picket fences, and vines of florid pink trumpet flower. Windows were already full of light, yet the sky stretched radiant and warm in all directions. Listen to the cicadas' song, and are those starlings who swoop down as if to plant a kiss, when it is simply to devour?

He walked faster and faster, marveling at the uneven sidewalks, the buckling flags, the moss-covered bricks, so many many beautiful things to touch and to see. And at last he came to their corner.

There stood the house where a Taltos had been born. Grand for these times, with its stucco walls made to look like stone, and chimneys rising high into the clouds.

His heart beat too fast. His witches.

Not to disturb. Not to beg. Merely to see. Forgive me that I walk along the fence, under the bending boughs of these flowered trees, that here suddenly in this deserted street, I climb the fence and slip down into the moist shrubbery.

No guards around this place. Does that mean you trust me, that I would never come, in stealth, unbidden, unexpected? I don't come to steal. I come only to take what anyone can have. A look from afar, we take nothing from those who are watched.

Take care. Keep to the hedges and the tall shiny leafed trees swaying in the wind. Ah, the sky is like the moist soft sky of England, so near, so full of color!

And this, was it the crape myrtle tree, beneath which their Lasher had stood, frightening a small boy, beckoning Michael to the gate,

463

Michael a witch child whom a ghost could spot, passing in the real world through zones of enchantment.

He let his fingers touch the waxy bark. The grass was deep beneath his feet. The fragrance of flowers and green things, of living things and breathing soil, was everywhere. A heavenly place.

Slowly he turned and looked at the house. At the iron lace porches stacked one upon the other. And that had been Julien's room up there, where the vines groped with helpless tendrils in the empty air. And there, beyond that screen, the living room.

Where are you? Dare I come just a little closer? But to be discovered now would be so tragic, when the evening is descending in this raiment of violet, and the flowers glow in their beds, and once again the cicadas sing.

Lights went on in the house. Behind lace curtains. Illuminating paintings on the walls. Was it so simple that, veiled in the dark, he could draw near to those windows?

The murals of Riverbend, wasn't that what Michael had described, and might they be gathering this soon for their meal? He walked as lightly as he could across the grass. Did he look like a thief? Rosebushes shielded him from those behind the glass.

So many. Women old and young, and men in suits, and voices raised in controversy. This was not my dream. This was not my hope. But, eyes fastened to the portal, he couldn't step away. Just give me one glimpse of my witches.

And there Michael was, like the direct answer to his prayer, gesticulating in a little fury it seemed, with others who pointed their fingers and talked, and then all on cue sat down, and the servants glided through the room. He could smell the soup, the meat. Alien food.

Ah, his Rowan, coming into the room, and insisting upon something as she looked at the others, as she argued, as she made the men again take their seats. A white napkin had dropped to the floor. The murals blazed with perfect summer skies. If only he could have moved closer.

But he could see her clearly and him too, and hear the noises of spoons against plates. Scent of meat, of humans, scent of . . . ?

That had to be his error! But the scent was so sharp and old and tyrannical that it took hold and the moment slipped right out of his hands. *Scent of the female!*

And just when he was telling himself again, It cannot be, when he was searching for the little red-haired witch, there came into the room the Taltos.

He closed his eyes. He listened to his heart. He breathed her scent as it emanated through brick walls, out of seams and cracks around glass, seeping from God knows where, to stir the organ between his legs, to make him stand back, breathless, wanting to flee, and absolutely immovable.

Female. Taltos. There. And her red hair all aflame beneath the chandelier and the arms out as she spoke, rapid, anxious. He could hear the bare high notes of her voice. And, oh, the look on her face, her newborn face, her arms so delicate in her sheer dress of Point d'Esprit and her sex, deep underneath, pulsing with the scent, a flower opening in darkness and alone, the scent penetrating to his brain.

My God, and they have kept this from him! Rowan! Michael!

She is there, and they have not told him, and would that he never knew. His friends, you *witches*!

Coldly, shivering, maddened by the scent and drugged, he watched them through the glass. Humankind, not his kind, shutting him out, and the lovely princess standing there, and was she crying out, was she ranting, were those tears in her eyes? Oh, splendid, beautiful creature.

He moved out from behind the shrubbery, not by will but by simple allowance. Behind the slim wooden post he stood, and now he could hear her plaintive cries.

"It was on the doll, the same scent! You threw away the wrapping, but I smelled it on the doll. I smell it in this house!" Bitterly she wailed.

Oh, newborn baby.

And who was this august council that would not answer her plea? Michael gestured for calm. Rowan bowed her head. One of the other men had risen to his feet.

"I'll break the doll if you don't tell me!" she screamed.

"No, you won't do that," Rowan cried out, and now it was she who rushed to the girl. "You won't, you won't, Michael, get the Bru, stop her!"

"Morrigan, Morrigan . . ."

And she, crying so softly and the scent gathering and moving on the air.

And I loved you, thought Ash, and I thought for a little while I would be one of you. Anguish. He wept. Samuel had been so right. And there, behind these thin panes . . . "Do I weep, do I go?" he whispered. "Do I smash the glass? Do I confront you with your own deceptive silence, that you did not tell me this! That you did not! That you did not!

"Oh, we weep like children!"

And he wept as she wept. Didn't they understand? She had picked up his scent from those gifts, dear God, what agony for her, poor newborn!

She lifted her head. The men gathering around her could not make her sit down. What had caught her eye? What made her look to the window? She couldn't see him beyond the self-contained glare of the light.

He stepped backwards into the grass. The scent, yes, catch the scent, my dear, my darling newborn woman, and closing his eyes, he staggered backwards.

She had pressed herself to the very glass. Her hands spread out on the panes. She knew he was there! She'd caught it.

What were prophecies, what were plans, what was reason, when for eternity he had seen her ilk only in his dreams, or old and withered and mindless as Tessa had been, when she was hot and young, and searching for him.

He heard the glass break. He heard her cry, and watched in stunned, overwhelmed silence as she ran towards him.

"Ashlar!" she cried in that thin high voice, and then her words came in the rush that only he could hear, singing of the circle, the memories, singing of him.

Rowan had come to the edge of the porch. Michael was there.

But that was gone, and with it all its obligations.

Across the wet grass she came.

She flew into his arms, her red hair wrapping round him. Bits and pieces of shining glass fell from her. He held her against him, her breasts, her warm beating breasts, his hand slipping up beneath her skirts to touch the warmth of her sex, the living fold, wet and heated for him, as she moaned and licked at his tears.

"Ashlar, Ashlar!"

"You know my name!" he whispered, kissing her roughly. How could he not tear loose her clothes here and now?

She was no one that he had ever known or remembered. She was not Janet who had died in the flames. She did not need to be. She was herself, his kind, his pleading, begging love.

And look how still they stood, watching him, his witches. Others had come to the porch, witches all! Look at them! Not lifting a finger to come between them, to part him from the precious female that had fled to his arms, Michael's face wondering, and Rowan's, what was it, what did he see in the light, was it resignation?

He wanted to say, I am sorry. I must take her. You know this. I am sorry. I did not come to take her away. I did not come to judge and then steal. I did not come to discover and then withhold my love.

She was eating him with her kisses, and her breasts, her tender full breasts. But who had come now, rushing out across the flags, was it the red-haired witch, Mona?

"Morrigan!"

"I am gone now, Mother, I am gone." She sang the words so fast, how could they understand? But it was enough for him. He lifted her, and just as he began to run, he saw Michael's hand raised in farewell, the sharp simple gesture which gives permission to go, and all good speed, and he saw his beautiful Rowan nod her head. The little witch Mona only screamed!

He hurried with his beauty through the darkness, her long light limbs nothing to him as he ran, across the dark stretch of grass, along stone paths, through yet another dark and fragrant garden. Moist and thick as the ancient forests.

"It's you, it's you. Oh, and the scent on the gifts, it drove me mad."

On the top of the wall he placed her, vaulting it and gathering her up again in the dark, empty street. He could scarcely bear this. Catching her hair in a great handful, he tugged her head back, lips moving down her throat.

"Ashlar, not here!" she cried, though she was soft and submissive in his arms. "In the glen, Ashlar, in the glen, in the circle at Donnelaith. It stands still, I know it, I see it."

Yes, yes, he didn't know how, in the long hours of the transatlantic flight, bundled with her in the dark, he would endure. But he musn't hurt her tender nipples, he mustn't break her fragile glowing skin.

Clasping her hand, he ran, bringing her with great youthful strides alongside him.

Yes, the glen.

"My darling," he whispered. He took one glance back at the house, rising so darkly and solidly there, as if full of secrets, of witches, of magic. Where the Bru watches all. Where the book resides. "My bride," he said, crushing her to his chest. "My baby bride."

Her feet rang out on the stones, and then he swept her up again, running faster than they could run together.

Janet's voice came to him from the cave. Old poetry, mixed with fear and remorse, skulls gleaming in the dark.

And memory is no longer the goad, no longer the thought, no longer the mind making order of all that ponderous weight of our lives, failures, blunders, moments of exquisite loss, humiliation—our long lives.

No, memory was something as soft and natural as the dark trees rising over their heads, as the purple sky in its last valiant light, in the woodland purr of the evening all around them.

Inside the car, he took her in his lap, tore open her dress, grabbed her hair, and rubbed it to his lips, his eyes. She hummed, she cried.

"The glen," she whispered, her face reddened, eyes glistening.

"Before morning comes here, it will be morning there, and we will be in those stones," he said. "We will lie in that grass, and the sun will rise on us, inseparable."

"I knew it, I knew . . ." she whispered in his ear. His mouth closed on her nipple, sucking the sweet nectar of flesh alone, moaning as he burrowed against her.

And the dark car sped out of the multi-shaded gloom, leaving behind the somber corner and its regal house, the great leafy branches holding darkness like ripe fruit beneath the violet sky, the car a projectile destined for the green heart of the world, carrying them inside it, the two, male and female, together.

2:30 a.m. July 10, 1993

A NOTE ON THE TYPE

This book was set in a digitized version of Janson, thought to
have been designed by the Dutchman Anton Janson, who was
a practicing type founder in Leipzig during the years 1668–1687.
However, it has been conclusively demonstrated that it is actually the work of Nicholas Kis (1650–1702), a Hungarian, who
most probably learned his trade from the master Dutch type
founder Dirk Voskens. The type is an excellent example of the
influential and sturdy Dutch types that prevailed in England
up to the time William Caslon (1692–1766) developed his own
incomparable designs from them.

Composed by ComCom, a division of
Haddon Craftsmen, Inc., Allentown, Pennsylvania
Printed and bound by Fairfield Graphics,
Fairfield, Pennsylvania
Designed by Virginia Tan